DEAD LETTERS

I was about to put the scrapbook away when I saw a white paper corner sticking out of one of the last pages. I heaved the book open to that spot to see the blank back of a small white envelope. Even before I turned it over, I sensed that I'd hit pay dirt.

Heart pounding, I sat on a carton, lit a cigar, then withdrew the wad of notebook paper from the envelope and unfolded it.

June 8
Dear Ben,

By the time you get this, I'll be gone. I know it's a shock, and I'm sorry it has to be this way, but there's no choice. If you only knew—in my place, believe me, you'd do the same thing.

I've thought it over and it's the only way out. I'm going to a better place. My only regret is that I can't take along the friends I love, like you.

Good-bye,
Sara F. Gerbstadt

It was there. It was *there* all the time, damn it, and I just didn't have the brains to see it. *In my place you'd do the same thing.* Suicide? She knew me better than that.

ALSO BY ROB KANTNER

THE BACK-DOOR MAN
DIRTY WORK
THE HARDER THEY HIT
HELL'S ONLY HALF-FULL
MADE IN DETROIT

THE THOUSAND YARD STARE

by
Rob Kantner

BANTAM BOOKS
NEW YORK • TORONTO • LONDON • SYDNEY • AUCKLAND

This book is a work of fiction. Names, characters, places and incidents either are the product of the author's imagination or are used fictitiously. Any resemblance to actual persons, living or dead, events, or locales is entirely coincidental.

THE THOUSAND YARD STARE
A Bantam Crime Line Book / August 1991

ISBN 0-553-28928-4

Published simultaneously in the United States and Canada

Bantam Books are published by Bantam Books, a division of Bantam Doubleday Dell Publishing Group, Inc. Its trademark, consisting of the words "Bantam Books" and the portrayal of a rooster, is Registered in U.S. Patent and Trademark Office and in other countries. Marca Registrada. Bantam Books, 666 Fifth Avenue, New York, New York 10103.

PRINTED IN THE UNITED STATES OF AMERICA

RAD 0 9 8 7 6 5 4 3 2 1

To
Agnes and Irvin Conrad,
Clayton and Bertha Kantner:
Friends, teachers, grandparents;

Valerie, my unindicted co-conspirator;

and to the memory of D.,
Rockbridge Road 1971,
forever seventeen.

ACKNOWLEDGMENTS

Thanks to Richard Guindon for permission to use a line from "Guindon's Michigan."

Thanks also to Marcia Johnson for sharing her memories.

Once you turn 30,
don't we all play hurt?

—Richard Guindon

CHAPTER 1

I grabbed the phone on the second ring. "Not in the market. Gave at the office. Nobody here by that name. He's not in right now, may I take a message?"

Long silence. "Is this Ben Perkins?"

"No, this is."

"Ben Perkins," she said, "private detective?"

I finished kicking off my shoes and snapped open a beer. "Guilty. Who's this?"

"I can't divulge that just yet."

"Where you calling from?"

"I can't tell you that either."

"Okay then." If I was being unusually patient, it was because I was enjoying the picture my imagination was drawing of her. "What do you want?"

"I may or may not have an assignment for you."

The voice was young, accent-free, slightly husky, and unfamiliar. If she'd been put up to this by those booze hounds at Under New Management, they'd chosen well. I untwisted the phone cord as best I could, shoved the remains of the day's *Detroit Free Press* off the easy chair, slouched into it, and decided to play along. "Assignment, huh? Better warn you, I'm pretty picky."

"Oh, dear. An inhibited man."

"Damn right. I only take jobs that pay money or other valuable consideration."

"You sound hard up. I like that. Hard up men are so much more eager to please."

That smelled of put-on. Or nutcase. But it could also have been the luckiest thing to happen to me all week. Month, even. Things had been slow, gang. "What's the assignment?"

"Don't rush," she said. "I prefer to be brought along gradually."

I drank the top off my beer and fired up a short cork-tipped cigar. It was the end of a long Tuesday, not even halfway through what was turning into a long week. I'd felt whipped when I hit my apartment door, but I felt pretty good now. "Okay," I said. "You're calling the shots."

"You'll find that it's more enjoyable for both of us that way," she said briskly. "Now. You were born in Detroit in nineteen—"

"Right." I blew a smoke ring toward the poster of the scantily clad lady, leaning on a Rolls-Royce, over the caption that said POVERTY SUCKS.

"Attended Redford High School. Went to—"

"Graduated," I butted in.

"Well, of course. Went to work for the Ford Motor Company and carried out a number of diversified assignments in the manufacturing sector—"

"Hung doors on Fairlanes and Galaxies." I nodded.

"After which you took a post with the union in human relations."

I snorted. "Human relations? Sort of. 'Aggressive therapy' is a better way to put it. I counseled people one on one, utilizing powers of persuasion, you might say."

"That employment was terminated rather abruptly, evidently," she noted.

"It's a volatile business." The voice was setting off just the faintest bells. But I couldn't narrow it down to a person. Hell, I couldn't narrow it down to a *decade.*

"At which point you became a maintenance and security supervisor at an apartment complex. As well as a private detective. . . . Interesting career mix."

"Puts food on the table." I took another hit of beer. "Now, listen up. This is fun and all, but—"

"Almost done now," she said. "Physical description: Six feet even, one ninety-five, black hair, dark blue eyes."

"Close enough."

"Heavy shoulders. Strong arms. Assorted scars. And the mole."

"Beg pardon?"

"Three inches below the navel."

I froze, staring, then straightened involuntarily in my chair.

"I know a lot about you, you see," she said, a smile in her voice.

Well, that narrowed it down. Some. "Reckon so," I managed.

"Be in the Commodore Club at Metro Airport at six o'clock," she said. "Good phone isn't all I give."

Click.

Fifteen minutes later I'd showered, shaved for an unprecedented second time that day, jumped into khaki twill pants and blue twill shirt, and was bopping out of my apartment building headed for you know where.

The phone call had transformed everything. No longer was this just another throwaway Tuesday evening; now it was a sensual summer night pregnant with promise. No longer was my '71 Mustang a four-wheeled relic in dire need of a wash and a tune-up; now it was a rakish, rumbling, high performance sex ship. No longer was Interstate 94 six lanes of oily, chuckholed, high-speed death; now it was the road to mystery and excitement with Metropolitan Airport, the gateway to the world, at the other end.

For once my prospective client wasn't a buddy on the next barstool, or a friend of a friend, or a big shot hogging one side of a large mahogany desk. It was a sultry, mysterious female, complete with double entendres, just like in the books and the movies.

About time.

The Commodore Club is located on the upper level of the south terminal. The plaque next to the door says MEMBERS ONLY. The door itself is navy blue with a single gold star in the center and an elaborate brass lock beneath it. You get a key to that lock by becoming a dues-paying member. Usually.

I'm not a dues-paying member, but I have a key. It was a gift from a thoughtful client. She felt I should have access to a drinking place with a little more class than, say, Under New Management, Jugg Poltiss's in New Boston, or Tattoos, Boots & Motorcycle Parts in Willow Run. I'd never used the key before and was relieved when it threw the latch with a precision click, causing the door to sigh open on invisible hinges.

The foyer was small, tastefully dim, and free of the plant menace that has overrun so many perfectly good saloons of late. The paneling and the small desk were fake walnut trimmed with black leatherette; the cash register was tucked discreetly into the corner; the carpet was new and blue and springy underfoot; a rack to the right offered such exciting reading as *Barron's, Forbes* and *The Wall Street Journal,* and a TV screen on the wall played the current video by Dow Jones & the Industrials.

Right then I sensed that I'd find no Foosball machine in the place.

"Good evening, sir," beamed the black-tuxed host from behind the desk. He spun a book to face me and offered me a pen. "Sign in, would you, please?"

"Why for?" I growled.

"We like to know who our guests are," he answered graciously.

"Swell." I scrawled. He spun the book back around and squinted at the scribble. He was still squinting as I strolled through an arch into the main room.

As saloons go, the place was pretty tame. The room was a longish rectangle with a bar running down the right side and a series of large windows, looking out onto the apron, ramp, and runways, on the left. Invisible strings filled the air with a sound so soothing it gave me the jitters. The booths were large and plush, all in that fake leather fake wood format, with small individual lights. About half the booths were occupied, the average occupant being a forty-five-year-old man with graying, receding hair, wearing a gray suit, poring over a thick three-ring notebook with a calculator by one hand and a cup of coffee by the other.

Like I said: exciting place. And I was right. No Foosball.

I took a booth by one of the windows, about halfway down. A server marched over, a woman who looked like

Idi Amin in a tux and was about as bright and bouncy. They had any beer I wanted as long as it was Anheuser-Busch. I ordered a Busch and sat back to wait for my date.

She appeared before the beer. I'd lighted a cigar and was absently contemplating the middle distance, when I noticed a woman sitting in the opposite row of booths, about five up from me. She was olive-complected, well dressed and elegant, closing in on middle age with a lot of her snap and tone intact, and she was smiling in my direction.

After a moment I looked over my shoulder to see if it was someone behind me she was eyeing. Not this time. When I looked at her again, she winked. I was trying to match her image with a long series of mental mug shots, as she rose and walked over to me.

"You really don't remember me, do you?"

The eyes. Something about the eyes, and the voice. Yeah, right, it could be, but everything else was wrong. "Janet?" I ventured.

Her smile broadened, showing her trademark dimples. "Very good. My ego is saved. Barely." She held out a long smooth hand and I shook it. "Hi, Ben."

"Hey there, yourself."

For an awkward moment we watched each other, awed by the gulf of years. At times like that what you mostly see are the contrasts. Her hair, previously short and wavy and the rich brown of ground coffee, was collie-colored and long and straight now, but tugged tight and woven flat against the back of her head. Her teeth, once an everyday set, were precision straight and the bright white of high beams. Her build, formerly plentiful, was now svelte. Her attire, which I remembered as favoring shirts and jumpers and pleated skirts, had transformed to the easygoing all-business look: a khaki-and-black checked jacket over a black jacquard-patterned blouse and a dark khaki wrap-style skirt. And the nose? Well, it was just a nose now.

"It was the first thing I had fixed," Jan said, "with the very first money I made." She smiled at my expression.

"Don't be embarrassed. It's the first thing you noticed, and why not? People called me 'Beak' for a reason."

"People didn't. Fast Eddie did. He had a nickname for everyone, some not as nice as that."

"Everybody but you. May I join you?"

"Please do." As she slid into the booth, I began to notice the things that even time could not entirely erase. The olive skin, the full sensuous lips, the slender arms with the hands that danced as she talked. It had been a long, long time, but the essence of Janet was still there.

Idi Amin arrived at the table with my beer. "Would you care for another drink, Ms. Vento?"

"Yes, please, Arlene, thank you."

I poured beer from the bottle into the frosted mug as Idi lumbered away. "You a regular in this dump, Miss Vento?"

"I pass through here about six times a year."

"But till tonight you never saw fit to pull a prank on your old buddy Ben," I noted, drinking. "Right, Miss Vento?"

"I didn't know where you were. And it isn't entirely a prank, though I must admit I enjoyed it hugely. I'm pleased to find I can still stir your hormones." Idi Arlene delivered Janet's drink, a brandy glass with just enough amber fluid to drown a fly. Janet palmed it, swirled it, took a sip. "As for the 'Miss Vento' bit, I use my birth name in business."

She paused, perhaps expecting me to inquire as to her line of work. Perversely, I didn't. I wouldn't give her the pleasure. Funny how the rancor returned undimmed after all these years.

"As it happens," she said finally, "I'm divorced." She eyed me. "I hear you've stayed single."

"Had to. You went away to college."

Her smile was tolerant. "You'd never have married me, Ben, and you know it. More to the point, I'd never have married you."

"Stayed away, too."

She shrugged. "I love Atlanta. And you obviously

didn't exactly cling to the old neighborhood yourself. How far is Belleville from Detroit? Fifty miles?"

"More like twenty." I was half a drink and almost a whole cigar into this thing and I still hadn't learned much. "How'd you find me? And, aside from a yen for a cheap laugh, why?"

" 'How' is Fast Eddie. 'Why' is—well, do you remember Stacie Hallthorn?"

"Sure. The 'Porcelain Princess,' Fast Eddie called her."

"She and I are organizing our class's twenty-fifth reunion this year—"

"Twenty-five? It's been that many, huh?"

"—and your name headed the list of the missing. I was chatting with Fast Eddie last week, and your name came up. He told me where to find you, and what you do. When I learned you were a private detective, that's when I decided to hire you—even though time is very short."

"So," I said, pressing my cigar dead, "the assignment's for real, huh?"

"For real, all right." She leaned forward intently. "Thirteen of our classmates are unaccounted for. I want you to find them, or at least find out what happened to them. Stacie will give you the list when she gets here."

I did not want to be rude. But anniversaries, reunions, stirring around in the past, have always seemed like a first-class waste of time to me. "You don't need a detective for that. Just—"

"Jan!" came a female voice from the entrance.

She glanced over her shoulder, then leaned even closer to me. Her scent was enticing and the press of her warm hand on mine was the most familiar sensation of all. "There's something else too. About Sara. I don't think she really killed herself. I want you to—"

I blinked. "What're you talking about?"

"Ssh!" she whispered urgently. "Here comes Stacie. We'll talk about it after she leaves." With that, Janet Vento, my senior year steady, turned to welcome the Redford High homecoming queen of a quarter century before.

CHAPTER 2

I never knew her. At least not in the sense that I knew Jan. Stacie Hallthorn was Redford High royalty, a consort of jocks, an untouchable. I was a jock myself, but of the wrong persuasion; baseball in those days wasn't considered as weenie as tennis, but ranked lower on the chicks' scale than football.

I never knew Stacie Hallthorn, but I'd thought about her. Plenty.

She'd always been vivid, and the years hadn't changed that. Stacie Hallthorn was short and robustly built, especially up top. Her hair was an elaborately constructed explosion of auburn that spilled up, around and down in a feathery mound to her shoulders. Her light blue come-hither eyes occupied a face that was sweet yet sophisticated, very tanned today, and expertly made-up. Her attire was outlandishly informal: a sleeveless blue chambray outfit whacked off at the thighs, filled to capacity. Several varieties of long gold chains, a couple grand worth at least, dangled around her neck, and she also wore elaborately interwoven gold bracelets on her left wrist and right ankle. Her bare arms and legs were as tan as her face, which smiled at the sight of us as she approached carrying a manila envelope.

Jan and I stood. The women hugged, bubbling gushy greetings. Then Stacie turned to me. "Ben, Ben, *Ben*!" she cooed, then flung herself against me and kissed me on the cheek. Her large breasts pressed against me from behind the thin fabric of her outfit, a warm hand caressed the back of my neck, and her breath was honey with the sweetness of Certs. She pulled back, eyes dancing, fully aware of the effect she was causing. "It's so nice to see you again!"

"Hey, Stacie," I said awkwardly.

"You remember Stacie, Ben?" Jan asked, expertly veiling her sarcasm.

"Oh, sure." Jan slid back into the booth, Stacie followed, and I resumed my seat facing them. "You live around here, I take it?"

"Bloomfield," she answered, tossing her head.

Which could have meant Bloomfield Hills, Bloomfield Township or West Bloomfield: varying levels of very serious bucks. "Nice country," I said.

She produced a pack of Merit Light 100s from her shorts pocket and lighted one expertly with a pinky-shaped solid gold butane lighter. "Oh, I just love it up there, it's *so* nice. You live in Belleville?" she asked politely, exhaling smoke upward.

I fired up a cigar of my own. "Yeah, good old Belleville."

"That's a nice little place. I don't know too much about it." As Idi Amin paid an encore visit to our table, I felt something brush my ankle, something that felt suspiciously like a bare foot. Jan was dealing with Idi. Stacie was smiling at me. You figure it out.

We all ordered drinks. Stacie ordered a double Absolut vodka, straight up. Explosive stuff, fuel for Stealth fighters, Indy cars, and women like Stacie. I moved my ankle away. "So, what's the deal, ladies? I don't remember that you knew each other at all back then."

"We didn't, really," Jan said as Stacie nodded. She moistened her mouth with the remnants of her first brandy. "We went to the same church, is all. But then we got together to organize our tenth reunion." She squinted at me. "We couldn't find you. *Nobody* knew where you were."

I calculated. "Oh, I wasn't around. Drifting out west." That was after the feds shut down the union regime I was involved in, and before I began my current apartment maintenance and private detective gig. An eon ago. "Nice party?"

"Oh, it was marvelous!" Stacie bubbled. "We had it at the Pontch, and tons of people came. Everybody said it didn't last long enough and we should have another one soon."

Jan gave Stacie an affectionate elbow and grinned. "So what do we do? We let fifteen years go by."

Our drinks came. Stacie socked hers away with a flick of her braceleted wrist and flipped the reorder finger at Idi, who nodded darkly as she walked away. Over the rim of my beer mug I looked from Stacie's face to Jan's. "The Pontch? Why didn't you have it at the school?"

They both winced. "Are you out of your *mind*?" Stacie asked. "Nobody wants to go down there. It's like a war zone. Oh God, no. We're having this one at the Novi Hilton."

I felt my brow furrow. "At least the Pontch is in the city of Detroit. Novi isn't even in Wayne County."

"Ben. Listen." Jan leaned forward slightly, her hands cradling her brandy glass. Way back in her dark eyes I detected just the slightest spark of anger, reminiscent of that fierce temper I remembered so well. "I haven't lived here in years, and even I know better than to schedule an occasion like this in Detroit. I mean, we want people to *come* to this thing."

Stacie was gnawing absently on her left thumb, eyes partly on Jan but mostly on me, as her cigarette smoldered in her other hand. I wondered if the gesture was deliberate and decided that it was. "It's real ugly back there these days, Ben."

"It's our old neighborhood," I answered.

"Not any more it isn't," Stacie said. "Just drive on over there sometime and see for yourself."

Jan's face was somber and intent. "Non-concur all you want, Ben, but it's a done deal."

I thought, knock it off, dummy. "Yep. You're right. And I don't really care anyway. You mentioned a list of the missing. Who's got it?"

Stacie pulled a piece of paper from the envelope. I unfolded it and scanned the dozen or so typed names as Stacie disposed of her Absolut reprise, stubbed out her smoke and lighted a fresh one. "Not bad," she said, puffing. "Out of two hundred some-odd graduates, only thirteen unaccounted for. Thirteen!" she laughed. "There's a lucky number for you."

I tapped the sheet. "This guy, Al Hooker? Dead. Died three, four years ago. This one here, Margie Smarr, she's a major in the Air Force, stationed in Germany somewhere. Only reason I know that is she came back and did a 'Say No to Drugs' speech at one of the high schools; it was in the paper. And Richard Satterfield?" I looked at Jan. "You mean to tell me you don't know what Richie's up to these days?"

"I barely remember him," she retorted. "Talk about a nonentity. What was it Fast Eddie called him?"

" 'Spaz.' But that was then. These days he's a full-fledged entity."

"You're still friends?" Jan asked politely.

"Haven't seen him in years. But I know he's some kind of computer honcho or something. Lives in Ann Arbor. Doin' pretty good, evidently. He was written up in *Crain's Detroit Business.*"

Stacie, left out of the conversation temporarily, was giving me the foot again. This time I didn't move. "How marvelous," Jan said coolly. "Such a surprise. I'm even more surprised to hear that you actually read a business magazine."

"Happened to see it on a client's desk," I shrugged. "No problem finding him, hopefully." One other name had seemed familiar. I looked back at the list, thought for a moment, and made it. "Triplett. Don Triplett. You remember *him,* Jan."

" 'The Sponge'," she said, frowning. "Probably the most accurate nickname Fast ever bestowed. Far as I'm concerned, Ben, he can *stay* missing, after all the shit things he did."

I knew what Jan was talking about. Since Stacie didn't, she changed the subject. "What about the others, Ben? There's not much time. The reunion's the twenty-ninth. Ten days."

"I'll do my best." The all-purpose unarguable promise. "Can you tell me anything else that might help?"

Stacie slid the manila envelope over. "Here's a list of

the classmates that I've found, with their current addresses and phone numbers. I don't know how useful it is."

"Neither do I, but thanks anyhow," I said, grinning.

"What do you charge?" Jan asked.

I thought for a moment. "Tell you what. This kind of thing is ninety-nine percent phone work. For you, for this, no charge." Evidently they didn't know how unprecedented this generosity was, because their only response was to nod and smile. "Which one of you is my contact?" I asked, hoping.

"Stacie," Jan said. Bingo. "I'll be coming in the morning of the reunion, but in the meantime I'll be off-site, hard to get hold of." She went into her handbag and gave me a textured gray business card that said something like VICE PRESIDENT / FINANCE after her name. "Better give him your number, Stacie," she said.

"Well, I'm in the middle of moving," Stacie said. "Let me have yours, Ben." I rattled them off. She wrote them down inside a gum wrapper, then read it, folded it, tucked it away. "I'll be in touch," she said, smiling.

"Any time," I said, smiling back.

Jan cleared her throat. "Well, that about wraps up the reunion end of things. Stacie, I have an unrelated matter to discuss with Ben. Would you mind?"

"Oh, hell no," she said. "I've got plenty of time. Go right ahead."

Jan missed a beat. "Um, it's really pretty personal. Would you excuse us?"

Stacie took a drag of smoke. "Listen, kid. Do I look like someone who's easy to embarrass?" She grinned at me. "Fire away."

Jan's dark eyes went wide and round. She sighed and spoke to the table top. "I need to speak with Ben alone, Stacie."

"Oh, really? Well hey, color me gone." My heart sank as Jan slid out of the booth and Stacie did likewise. They brushed cheeks, Stacie gave me a small wave and a private smile and walked out.

"Sorry if I messed up your quickie little courtship there, Ben," Jan said, resuming her seat.

The whole thing felt odd. I mean, on the one hand, Jan knew me very well, well enough to make such personal comments. On the other hand, given the passage of time, she did not know me at all. In one sense we were intimates; in another we were total strangers. Hard to tell the difference between pertinent and impertinent in a situation like that. I kept it light. "Them's the breaks."

She smiled ruefully. "It's silly of me to be resentful. I mean, after all these years! It's my competitiveness again. I've never quite gotten control of it."

"Competitiveness? Is that what that is? I thought it was the thing Mrs. Bush says rhymes with rich."

Her dark eyes danced. "That too." She looked around the room. "Do you think we can persuade our Third World tyrant to bring us another round?"

"If we look helpless enough." I dumped down the last of my beer, set down my mug, and glanced at Jan's folded hands. Yep, I thought, no question. The mouth may lie, but the hands can't, generally. "So," I asked, "what's this goofy thing about Sara?"

She took a deep breath and examined her fingers as they intertwined nervously. "It's the real reason I'm here. I mean, the reunion thing, I could have just told Stacie how to get in touch with you and let—and let nature take its course. *If* that's what nature is going to do."

"Nature will out," I said pleasantly. "But enough about the bimbette. What's this about Sara?"

She straightened as Idi came to parade rest, took our orders and stomped sturdily away. "I never believed that she committed suicide. I don't believe it now. I want you to find out what really happened to her."

My thoughts went back, back through the years, diving into the murk at the bottom of the memory bin, and found Sara Gerbstadt alive there, alive still: slender, spooky Sara with the translucent skin, the quirky sense of humor, the awesome intellect and the array of passions that made us good time Charlies feel cheap. I've never bought the old saw that says any person's death diminishes you. A few do. Some do the opposite. Most don't mean a goddamned thing. Sara's death, I realized now, had dimmed the world a notch. At the time, during that halcyon period when life was fair and death was something that happened to others, I wasn't smart enough to notice.

"If it wasn't suicide, then what was it?"

"Well, murder," Jan answered.

CHAPTER 3

Our drinks arrived, along with an updated bill. Jan busied herself retrieving a platinum credit card from her purse. I lighted a fresh cigar. "Who do you think killed her?"

"That's what I'm hiring you to find out."

"Why now, after all these years?"

"Because I *can*, now," she said.

"You lost me."

As she spoke, her hands gestured expressively. "I never believed that Sara killed herself. Not from day one. But who'd listen to me? I was a dumb little seventeen-year-old. Knock-kneed dago with the big schnoz. Plus, I was a girl," she said sourly. "I knew none of the men, none of the grown-ups, would listen to me. I didn't even try."

The flame of an old anger was back in her dark eyes. I watched and waited and let her roll. "But what I thought then is what I think now. The investigation of her death was just a no-brain quickie. The cops grabbed the handiest theory and ran with it and buried Sara and washed their hands of the whole thing. That was then.

"This," she went on, tapping the credit card on the table top, "is now. Today, I'm one of the grown-ups. I have money, plenty of money. And I'm going to spend what's needed to find out who killed Sara and to see to it that he pays the penalty."

"Or she," I said, unable to resist.

Jan blinked. "Or she. Of course." She sat back in the booth as Idi collected the credit card and the check. "How about it, Ben?"

I fiddled with my smoldering cigar. "Number one,

let's make sure you and I remember this thing the same way. Sara died the night of the senior party—"

"—the night before graduation—"

"—at the Bubbas's house. I remember that. Must have been a hundred kids there."

"The Bubbas," Jan echoed, smiling. "Joe and Frank, right?"

"Szewczklieuski," I nodded. Identical twins, I recalled. My daddy had, like most everyone else, been unable to tell them apart. He didn't like guessing at the first name, and his mouth seized up whenever he tried to pronounce Szewczklieuski, so one day, in frustration, he called them Bubba, and it stuck.

"Sara was there," I recalled. "She went home and her folks found her the next morning."

"Dead in the garage. Carbon monoxide," Jan said softly.

"Yeah, yeah. That's right." My memories of that evening were, to say the least, murky. It had been a rowdy party. Lot of beer. Lot of brain cells died since then. I recalled something about a Tigers game. I remembered Sara, Fast Eddie, some other kids. Something about Jan being angry with me, not that that was unusual. And a fistfight, and cops, and Al Hooker puking in the mulberry bushes. I didn't remember much else. Not what the weather was like, what I'd worn, who I'd talked to or danced with.

"I remember one other thing," I said. "She sent notes to all of us. Suicide notes. Saying goodbye. Mine came a couple days after she died. Spooky as hell."

Jan looked stony. "Everyone just assumed those were suicide notes. They could have been forgeries. Or they might not have meant what we thought they meant."

"Do you still have yours?"

"You must be joking. Why? Do you?"

"You know, I just might." I drank some beer. "A minute ago I asked a question, and you ducked it. Let's try it again. Assuming Sara was murdered, who do you think did it?"

"I don't know."

I looked beyond her. "No theories? Okay. You realize all this happened twenty-five years ago? You know what that means?" She watched me wordlessly. "What it basically means is, whoever offed Sara, if in fact she *was* offed, has gotten clean away with it. For all practical purposes."

"I thought there was no statute of limitations on murder."

I waved a hand, making a Z in cigar smoke. "I'm not talking statutes. I'm talkin' real world. It's been twenty-five years, Jan. The trail, even if there was one to begin with, isn't just cold; it's covered over and tromped down. I'll betcha half the people who were at that party don't even live in Detroit anymore. Another thirty percent don't have the foggiest recollection of Sara or the party. A few remember but don't want to tell, and the rest are dead. Like Al Hooker, who resides in a white granite house over to Elmwood Cemetery. And like the Bubbas, pushing up daisies in Grand Lawn. Hell, they bought it in Nam, what, *twenty* years ago, something like that almost already! What f'rinstance if *they* killed Sara? How would I ever prove that?"

She smiled tolerantly. "The Bubbas? Kill Sara? Get real."

"Look. You be the client and let me be the detective."

"Meaning you'll take the case?"

Idi came back with Jan's paperwork. "Case?" I asked. "What case? This isn't a case. This, with all due respect, is some kind of hangover adolescent wet dream kind of thing."

She paused in her signature, looked at me, and resumed scribbling. "How perceptive of you," she said quietly. "Blunt, as usual, but perceptive." She finished her paperwork, picked up her brandy and studied its shallows. "I don't know what's happened to you in the past twenty-five years, Ben. You're scarred and weathered, suggesting that you've been through a lot. I get the feeling you've had the shit kicked out of you—"

"You should see the other guy."

She ignored that. "My path has been different, but the end result is about the same. At eighteen I had a lot of questions, and now most of those questions have been answered."

"Lucky you."

She ignored me. "At eighteen I also had many passions. I wanted to sing professionally. I wanted to be valedictorian, to beat Sara in the grades department, to get into a top college. I wanted to marry well, have six kids, and become rich. Now the passions are gone. Burned away. Passion is not a renewable resource. Once it's gone there's nothing left but to take care of business as best you can."

She flat out lost me with that one. I was surprised to hear such garbage from her. Sara had always been the philosopher of the bunch, not Jan. But then, at eighteen, everyone was a half-assed matchbook philosopher. Everyone but me.

She looked at me and now, even in the dimness of the airport bar, I saw evidence of her years in her face. I also saw the tough shell of the survivor. "But I do have one question left," she said. "That is, 'Who killed Sara?' And the one passion I have left is to find out. Will you help me?"

In this work, that decision is usually black and white. This time it fell into a gray zone. I dumped back the last of the beer and squashed out my cigar. "Give me a day to think about it."

"What is there to think about?" she retorted.

"Whether, in my professional judgment, there's any reason to help you pour your money down a rat hole. I don't work cheap."

"How much?"

I told her. She didn't seem fazed. She slid out of the booth and stood. "It's my money. It's your profession. There's no reason why we can't do business."

I joined her and we started for the door. "Let me think about it," I said patiently, "and I'll call you."

Her silence smoldered as we walked through the foyer, out the big blue door, and along the balcony to the escalator. The longer I was with her, the more familiar it all seemed: her long easy stride, the way her whole body talked, her willfulness—and the rancor between us. It had,

I saw now, never really ended; just gone on hold for twenty-five years.

"Well," she said archly as we rode down the escalator, "even if you don't help me with Sara, I'll see you at the reunion, right?"

"Quite frankly, I doubt it." She stared at me. "I've never seen any sense in rooting around in the past," I said. "It's all I can do to handle the here and now."

She shook her head. "So godamned bullheaded," she breathed. "No wonder things didn't work out for us."

I shook my head. "So godamned controlling," I breathed. "No wonder things didn't work out for us."

She looked at me, startled, and as we stepped off the escalator we both laughed. But it was the laughter of polite, wary disengagement, not amusement.

My route was right, past the Delta ticket counters and across the beltway to the parking deck. Jan was bound for the concourse to our left. By unspoken agreement we stopped and faced each other, a small island in the steady stream of airport bustle swirling past us. Tone and expression rigorously civil, she asked, "You'll call me?"

"Count on it."

I turned and walked away without looking back, joining a horde of weary business suits bound for the big sets of automatic doors. My thoughts were unkind. *You perverse son of a bitch! You stiff-armed her just to pay her back for going all uptown on you all those years ago. Grow up, already. Do the work. Take the money. What's the big deal?*

That was my head talking. My heart was another matter. The whole thing made me feel uneasy. It was all very old business, finished, put away, as dead as poor out-of-luck Sara. I seldom thought about those days. I never wanted to relive even a moment of them. This case would take me back, and I realized, as I emerged onto the terminal sidewalk, that I had no desire to go—

"Ben! Wait up!"

I turned to see Stacie Hallthorn coming at me at a half trot through the automatic doors, face alight, necklaces singing like wind chimes, breasts bouncing beneath the skimpy blue chambray outfit. She'd have stopped traffic on the airport beltway, if it hadn't been gridlocked already. The fantasy that had rushed me to the airport pounced on me again like a cat from a tree limb. "Well, now," I said as she reached me, "a dream come true."

Stacie smiled, took my arm and started us toward the crosswalk. "I was watching for you. I almost missed you in that mob. Can you give me a lift home?"

"I'd be delighted. Care for a drink on the way?"

"Thanks awfully, but I'm in a terrible rush."

"Okay. What's your address?"

"What's yours?"

"Oh."

Finally . . . at long last . . . Stacie's breathing evened out and deepened. I eased her off me, tucked the dampish sheet over her, got off the bed and began pulling my pants on in the dark. A long scratch sang on my back. I ached in a thousand places. My every movable part felt used to death. The man who walked out of my bedroom was, for the moment, a decade older than the one who had walked in.

As I suspected, we hadn't locked up the place or turned off any lights. I took care of all that, lurching about like an automaton, noticing with indifference that the clock by the stereo said 3:15 A.M.

It was hard to believe, but it had indeed happened. Me and the cheerleader captain, the homecoming queen, the president of the pep club: Stacie Hallthorn, the untouchable one, the Porcelain Princess. She was the stuff of legends and the topic of much locker room speculation, all of it unverified "my-brother's-buddy-heard-someone-say" stuff, heavily flavored with wishful thinking. It was said she insisted on tying her hair back first. (Right.) It was said that she talked all the way through it. (Wrong.) It was said she liked mirrors. (Unconfirmed.) Each discussion generally ended with someone admitting "I wouldn't mind fucking that." The rest of us would nod in agreement, as if our only concern was how to work Stacie into our busy sexual schedules.

I can't deny feeling a certain sense of satisfaction. But at the same time I was troubled. Once, she'd been about as available to me as Annette Funicello. Now, from out of nowhere, she was in my bed. Fine for now, but come morning she'd still be there, and I didn't know what the hell we'd do then.

Best to get some sleep, then deal with it. I was about to shut off the last living room light when another impulse struck, powerful enough to overcome, if only temporarily, my intense need for horizontal oblivion. I opened the bottom door of the entertainment center and rooted through a stack of old magazines and junk till I found it: my senior year Redford High School yearbook.

Sitting cross-legged on the floor, I leafed through the thick pages to the stiffly formal black and white senior pictures. Paged past the faded forgotten faces, following the alphabetical trail by Fitzgerald, Ford, Francis, Gagliano, and Gatling—to Gerbstadt, Sara Faith:

Chorus 1–4 * *Band* 1–4
Beta Club 1–4 *President:* 3,4
Debate 3,4 *Captain:* 4
Student Council 2,3 *President:* 3

Nothing about Star Student or Valedictorian. Those honors had not been bestowed at the time the yearbook was printed. Nothing about "found asphyxiated in garage." That had not happened yet either.

I looked at the picture. Sara's round face with its high cheekbones and chin dimple looked precious and fragile. Her light hair was longer than was stylish, smooth to the shoulders. The smile was posed and unfamiliar. She looked older than she was, older than she ever lived to be.

The eyes were what grabbed me. They were Sara's eyes, earnest and passionate. And now, from my outpost twenty-five years in the future, I sensed that they were something more.

Murdered eyes.

CHAPTER 4

The beers were gone, it was getting cold; time to go. We hiked up the long steep slope from the Dynamite Park picnic area by the Rouge River: Fast Eddie Anger, Gibson acoustic slung over his back, holding Sara's hand; Jan Vento and me, arm in arm and pleasantly buzzed; and the beefy, bespectacled Richie Satterfield, trudging hunched against the cold in his Redford High band letter jacket.

"Shotgun," Fast Eddie called as we neared Richie's dad's practically new Ford Country Squire station wagon. "You wheeling it, Benjy?"

"Guess so, if it's all right with Richie."

"Who cares what Spaz thinks?" Fast snorted.

"You can drive, Ben," Richie said. "I'll ride in back."

"Where shall we mere girls sit?" Jan asked sarcastically.

"Benjy's wheeling, I'm riding shotgun," Fast answered, breath showing in the cold. "Means the rest of you are sittin' nigger."

Sara dropped Fast's hand and marched away from him across the deserted Spinoza Street toward the old cannon that stood guard on the intersection island. "Oh, Eddie, for God's sake!"

"What the hell's with you, Squeak?" he retorted, as he opened the passenger door of the wagon and lay his guitar carefully in the cargo area.

"I hate that kind of talk, and you know it. It's bigoted and disgusting."

He rolled his eyes. "Come on, get in the car."

I had the driver's side door open. Jan and Richie had already piled into the back. Sara Gerbstadt stood illuminated by a street light, her shoulder length blond hair restless in the cold breeze as pinpoints of hard snow danced in the darkening air. "You know, Benjy's folks were *born* in the South, and they don't even use words like that."

"That's right," I answered. "They say 'nigras.' "

"Get in the car, Squeak," Fast Eddie commanded, dropping into the front seat and closing his door. Sara shook her head, then crossed the street, got into the back next to Richie, and pulled her door shut. "Let's roll!" Eddie said.

I fired up the big V-8 motor and looped the boatlike station wagon around the cannon and north on Spinoza. The fields and copses of Dynamite Park spread out on both sides of us, frigid and grim and still dead-looking despite the official arrival of spring a week before. To the left, a chain of trees marked the winding course of the Rouge River. To the right, in the furthest distance, a smear of misty lights indicated the backsides of bungalow homes in the West Evergreen section of Detroit. Up ahead, flecks of airborne snow twinkled in the beams of the Ford headlights. A cold grim Saturday night, but inside the wagon, bundled in coats and glowing from a hearty dose of Stroh's tall boys, we were warm and getting warmer.

I turned on the radio. The Shirelles were asking, for the nine millionth time, if we'd love them tomorrow. I spun the dial to CK and lucked into Del Shannon's "Runaway," which I could have listened to all night. Fast Eddie passed out Pall Malls and we all lit up except for Sara and Richie. "So, where we headed, gang?" I asked as I swung the Ford west on Joy Road, which bisected the park at its midriff.

"I don't care," Jan said from behind me. "Too early to go home."

"Got to be something to do on a Saturday night," Richie observed. "Anybody having a party, that we know of?"

"None that would let you in, Spaz," Fast Eddie answered.

"I just wish you would consider my feelings, Eddie," Sara said. "I'm going down to Alabama after graduation to help the civil rights groups. I care about these things. When you talk the way you do, it upsets me."

Oh, boy. Sara had had two beers and she was flying. Jan stirred in the seat behind me as I grabbed Telegraph northbound and took the big car up to fifty. "Better apologize, Fast," she said, "or she'll never let it go."

Fast sighed. "You're right, Beak." He turned on the seat, facing his steady, thin hands folded imploringly. "Please, Squeak. Please forgive me for calling 'em niggers."

"Oh, turn around and shut up," she answered, a smile in her voice despite herself.

Laughing, Fast Eddie turned and sprawled in the spacious front seat. Richie asked, "You're really serious about going south, Sara?"

"Absolutely," she answered.

"Total bullshit," Fast put in. "She'll end up hanging around here, swimming and sunbathing, before heading off for college. Gonna be a big college girl, like her uptown buddy Beak over there."

"I'm going to college too," Richie said.

Eddie strummed an imaginary guitar, cigarette glowing in the dimness of the car. "Me and Benjy, we got our heads on straight. He's got his burgeoning career in the automotive industry—"

"Yeah, right," I shot back as I grabbed a yellow and swung northwest on Grand River. "Hangin' doors on Fairlanes and Galaxies is the road to the top, all right." I was, of course, not so secretly proud of my job at Ford's, which most boys my age would have killed for.

"And I'll be touring," Fast Eddie went on. "I've already got gigs lined up for the rest of the school year. Mumford next week, then Cooley, then U of D at month end. Come June, I'm *through* with the stinkin' textbooks. I'll be workin', unlike some lazy slobs I could mention."

"So," I said, as we ran out of Detroit at Base Line Road, "what do you folks want to do?"

"Lazy!" Jan stormed. "Listen, mister. School is work, and I study my *butt* off to get my grades. I have to. I'm not a natural like Sara."

"And I study my butt off," Sara put in, "because I have to win the National Achievement Scholarship or I won't be able to go to college at all. My father can't afford it."

"That's what you'd *like* us to believe," Jan answered. "The truth is, you're feeling the cold breath of competition on the back of your neck. I was only two grade points behind you last marking period."

"Eat my dust," Sara answered cheerfully.

Fast sighed theatrically. "Such burdens you children have. Still sweating the schoolbooks while I'm trying to decide what color T-Bird to order."

"Mark my words," Sara said. "Some day you'll wish you'd gone, sweetheart."

"You could be right, Squeak," Fast said judiciously. "I'll say one thing about college—not that this'll interest you at all, Spaz—it's a damn good place to shop for puss-ah."

"You're disgusting," Jan said.

"Moreover, dear Eddie," Sara said, "you don't *care* about other girls. Remember?"

I felt uncomfortable, knowing things about Fast that Sara only suspected. "How 'bout it, people? We got any particular activities in mind for this evening?"

"You're the only one for me, Squeak," Eddie said.

"Too bad Don's not with us tonight," Jan observed. "He never had trouble coming up with things to do."

"Just had trouble paying his way," I answered grimly.

"I heard it took old Sponge all night to walk home that time," Fast said, laughing.

"From South Lyon to Detroit, that's a haul, especially in the middle of the night," I said.

"I still wish you hadn't done that, Ben," Richie said.

"Yeah, mean old Benjy," Fast jibed, angrily mimicking Richie's voice. "Put Spaz's best buddy out of the car on a cold, cold night."

"He could have gotten lost. Or hurt," Sara said quietly.

"Oh, stop it," Jan said. "I think Ben was right. Don is always mooching off us. He got what he deserved."

"A dollar for gas!" I put in. "That's all I wanted. Everybody else kicked in. But when Sponge came in with that tired old 'Why should I pay? You're going there anyway' line, I just saw red."

"He's real mad," Richie said. "Says he won't ever ride with us again."

"That a promise?" Fast asked acidly.

In the brief silence, the big Ford motor rumbled throatily. Then Richie said, "How about an April Fool's gag? Heck, the day's almost over and we haven't pulled any April Fool's jokes."

"Don't have to," Fast said. "We're riding with the biggest fool of all, Spaz my boy."

Jan said, "Too bad April Fool's fell on a Saturday this year. Couldn't do anything at school. Remember when we turned Mr. Watford's VW upside down?"

"We all got fertile minds here," Fast Eddie said. "Maybe we can come up with something."

"Oh, God," Jan moaned. "Don't you dare suggest mooning, Fast Eddie, or I'm jumping out of this car."

"And we all know," I said darkly, "that from there he'll be wanting to light farts."

"I'm a man of many talents," Eddie said pleasantly.

"A child with no inhibitions," Sara said.

"About which you have never complained, at the most critical moments," Fast Eddie observed, "unless, of course, you've been faking it."

I expected a shocked, embarrassed silence. Instead Sara said quietly, "No. I never fake it."

"Come on, gang," I said as I swerved the car left onto the Grand River Cutoff, "let's have some ideas here. One thing I do know, we're gonna need to gas this crate before too long."

In silence, the car plunged across the dark Oakland County countryside. The lights of the town of Farmington twinkled off to our right. Jan said suddenly, "Hey, did you hear about those two kids killed in a train wreck the other night?"

"Yeah," Richie said. "Car crashed into a train at a crossing, something like that."

"Downriver someplace," I said.

"Willow. The boy was eighteen and the girl was fifteen. They said the brakes failed," Jan said with a shudder.

"It was probably a love pact," Sara said.

"What do you mean?" Richie asked.

"Love pact," Fast Eddie said sarcastically, "as in suicide?"

"Exactly." Sara's voice was soft. "That's probably what it was. They loved each other but couldn't be together, so they—"

"Oh, God," Fast groaned, "here we go again!"

"It's just so *creepy,* thinking about being dead at that age," Jan said.

We'd just rejoined U.S. 16 in the farmland west of Farmington when it happened. Don't ask me why. Somehow April Fool's, the dead young people, and our need for gas brewed in my mind and BING! The idea hit me, just like that.

I stood on the brakes, swerved the car onto the gravel, and turned down the volume on the Marcels. "Oo, this is good, this is *good*! I've got the idea, folks, if you dare."

"Spill it," Fast Eddie said. I did so. In the long silence that followed, I lighted another Pall Mall. Then Eddie really floored me. "That's great, Benjy. That's a real winner. You guys like it?"

"I'm in," Richie said. "I guess. I sure hope we don't get in trouble."

"What trouble?" I asked disdainfully. "This is just for laughs, Richie. C'mon."

"Oh, all right. I think there's some ketchup packs in the glove box. . . . I sure hope we don't get nailed."

Jan was laughing. "I've got plenty of makeup. God, Ben, you have a real devious mind. Warped, too. The big question is, who's going to actually do it?"

"I will," Sara said.

Fast laughed. "I doubt it, Squeak. I don't think you could do it without puddling up the place."

"Certainly I can," she answered coolly. "And I will, too."

I flipped on the dome light. The faces of my four friends showed yellow in the smoky car. "It's all in the eyes, Sara," I told her. "It'll stand or fall on how you handle the eyes."

She nodded, smiling. "I know."

"Okay, then," I said. "Let's do it."

The Pure station appeared on the right, at the intersection of U.S. 16 and Haggerty Highway. I slowed the station wagon, flipped my cigarette out the open vent, and said, "This is it. Straight faces, people. You ready, Sara?"

"Ready," she called from behind me.

I rolled the car into the station, tires crunching on gravel. It was an old single-island place with a wide apron for semi-trucks, a pair of outhouses leaning out back, and a white ramshackle clapboard building with a sign that said JULIAN'S PURE hanging crooked on the front. Big lights beamed down from rusted stanchions, lighting up the place like a space station in the pitch-black Michigan night. A cream-on-tan '56 Chevy sedan was just pulling out, leaving the place to us.

The silence in the car was total as I shut off the motor and rolled my window halfway down. The attendant, a heavyset middle-aged man in a maroon hunting jacket and ball cap, moseyed around the car to me, wiping his hands on a rag. "Evenin'," I said. "Wash the windshield, check the oil, dollar gas, please sir?"

"Coming right up." He hoofed to the regular pump, cranked the handle, then flipped open the gas lid on the left rear of the wagon, took off the cap, thrust in the nozzle and began to pump. I could see his face plainly in the driving mirror, and I saw the change in his expression when he saw what was inside.

Sara Gerbstadt lay on her back, motionless on the hard steel deck of the cargo area. A gray army blanket covered her from neck to feet, revealing only one pasty, clenched hand. Her head was wedged against the tailgate at an odd angle, the hair matted and soaked red around her left ear. The skin of her face was an unnatural pasty white, a trickle of red leaked out the corner of her mouth, and her eyes were open, wide open and staring and absolutely still.

The attendant bent forward, as if to see better. At that moment I said, "Sir? Can I ask you a question?"

He flinched, gave me a look, and spoke through pinched lips. "What do you want?"

"You got any picks and shovels we can borrow?"

He shut off the pump and hung the nozzle, resolutely ignoring the back of the wagon. "Nope."

"Oh jeez," I said. He hoofed forward to me and I held out a dollar, at which he stared blankly. "Listen, we're from Detroit, we don't know these parts. There any lakes or ponds around here?"

He blinked and took the buck. His blocky honest face seemed pale to me, but it could have been from the cold. "Well, yeah," he said. "Walled Lake's north a couple miles, and Meadowbrook Lake's back—"

"Great," I said, smiling. "You got any ropes around here? Cinder blocks or anything heavy like that? A couple old truck wheels, maybe?"

He cleared his throat and edged away from the car. "Uh, no. Sorry, we don't. Wish I could oblige, but—" He gave the back of the wagon one darting, unwilling look. "You, uh . . . You have a nice evening!" He waved. "Drive carefully now! Bye!"

We were still laughing, ten minutes later, as we crossed Base Line Road—to find Grand River blockaded by six Detroit police cruisers, waiting expressly for us.

Jan reclined in the crook of my arm, nestled deep in the softness of her sofa. The small Thatcher Avenue living room was dim and musty and packed to oppressiveness with heavy old wood furniture, no doubt inherited from grandparents. Across the coffee table, on which our stockinged feet were propped all atangle, her Dumont TV softly murmured Channel 7, WXYZ"ing" News with Leon McNew. I, for one, was not paying attention. My right hand was casually exploring the mound of her right breast through her blouse, and I was nuzzling her neck and ear.

"Let's go down to the park," I said softly.

"I can't," she said patiently, removing my hand. "It's almost eleven-thirty. My folks will be home any time."

"That's the whole point. Once they're here, we can't leave. So we better go now. You know you want to."

"I think I've had enough excitement for one night." She once again detached my hand, which seemed to have a mind of its own. "So has my poor tired tit, so please leave it be."

"Oh, baby, you ain't seen excitement yet tonight and you know it."

"Really? What do you call that police dragnet that scooped us up?"

"A minor inconvenience."

"Yeah, right, just one of those things!"

"That's right. Must have been a slow night in law enforcement. I think it's terrible how the cops harass innocent citizens instead of going after real crime—"

"They thought we had a dead body in the car! What did you expect?"

"A sense of humor, for starters. They didn't have to threaten to strip-search us and lock us up and impound the car and call our parents and stuff. That was totally uncalled for."

"They meant to put the fear of God in us," she observed. "It worked, too."

"Not with me," I said grimly. "My daddy's got more pure hell than them guys can ever even dream of."

"Tough guy, right," she jeered. She slapped my hand. "Well, Richie doesn't have your dad, and he was plenty scared. I've never seen anyone so scared. I don't think he'll ever go cruising with us again."

"Richie's—what's the word?—passive."

"So different from you and Fast Eddie. A loner, a bookworm, a really nice, decent kid—"

"Thanks a whole lot, babe!"

"—it's strange that you've been friends for so long."

"Richie's from our block, we've been taking care of him since we were six. Sort of a reflex."

"But Eddie's so mean to him."

"Fast's like that with everybody."

"He can be so awful," Jan said. "I finally got up the nerve to ask him if I could try out for his band. He said . . .

he told me, if I ever fixed 'that big awning that sucks up your voice,' he'd think about it. What a creep."

"He don't mean nothing by that kind of stuff. . . . Come on, babe, let's go to the park, I wanna go to the paaaaark."

"No."

"Please?"

"Look at me." I did so. She kissed me full on the mouth, grabbed the thick hair at the back of my head in both of her hands and intensified the kiss, adding tongue, taking my breath away and damn near my lips too. When we broke, her dark eyes were alight. "Let me get my coat," she whispered.

"Yes, *ma'am*!" I got into my leather flying jacket, she put on her car coat, and we had just reached the door when the phone rang. "Be quick," I said.

She smiled, kissed me, and skipped into the kitchen. Thirty seconds turned into two, three, five eternal minutes which I endured by pacing and stewing. Finally she came back, coatless and serious. "You'd better go on home, Ben," she said tonelessly.

"What's wrong? What happened? God, we were all set to—"

"I can't talk about it now."

"Well, okay." I fumbled for words. "But first tell me what I did."

"It wasn't anything you did," she answered quietly. "It was your friend Fast Eddie. The one who 'don't mean nothing' by the nasty things he does?" She was pacing the entryway with coiled, caged energy, her face darkening with unfocused anger. "That was Sara on the phone. Fast Eddie broke up with her tonight."

"Oh, jeez. That's a real—"

She overrode me forcefully, slashing the air with a hand. "He took her down to the park, after we split up tonight, and he made love to her, and then the son of a bitch told her it was all over, it was fun, time to move on. Ciao, baby!" she snarled.

"You got no call to shout at me. I ain't Fast Eddie and I ain't responsible for him."

She folded her arms and leaned against the wall, suddenly tired. "She adores him, you know," she said quietly. "I don't understand it. I think he's a snake. A clever, funny, charming snake. A fun guy to be with, but a snake all the same. But Sara—" She rolled her eyes. "All Sara talks about is how creative he is. She's got all these complicated, pie-in-the-sky ideas about everything. She's wrapped so much of herself up in him, and now he's . . ." Her voice thickened and she swiped at her eyes with the back of her hand. I stepped toward her and she gestured me back. "No," she said in a knotted voice. "I don't want you. Go home. See you in study hall or sometime."

"I'll go. But first I'll tell you what I think, whether you want to hear it or not." She did not reply. "Number one, I like Sara a lot, and I feel sorry for her. Number two, Fast Eddie does shit things sometimes. Sara's ain't the first heart he's broke and it won't be the last."

"Yeah, fine," she said brusquely, stepping away from the wall, turning her back on me.

"You dumping me over this?" I demanded.

"No." She looked back at me. "I don't want you now. I won't want you for awhile. But I'll want you again. There's not much doubt about that."

CHAPTER 5

Brentwood Court is a cul-de-sac—what we in Detroit call a dead end—in a rather prosperous Ann Arbor subdivision, if you'll pardon the redundancies. 3449 is the last house on the right, a two-story salt box in powder puff blue with weathered cedar shakes. I parked in the wide empty driveway, hoofed to the double front door, knocked and waited in the August mid-day heat, hoping to hell I hadn't made the drive for nothing.

The door squeaked back and Libby Gillespie stood there behind a sullen frown. The on-again, off-again twenty extra pounds was on again with a vengeance, held in place with frayed denim shorts and a white halter top, both snug out of necessity. Her black hair hung in a straight page boy around the face that was said to have gotten all the looks in the family. If true, and no one ever asked my opinion, it was clear that the inheritance had been expended on late nights, cigarettes, sweets, heavy meals, liquor, and indolence. In short, the woman's looks did not attract me in the least. Which was a good thing, because Libby Gillespie is my sweet baby sister.

"What the hell do you want?" she asked.

" 'Well, hello there, big brother,' " I said in falsetto. " 'Long time. Don't just stand there, come on in out of the heat.' "

"Oh, all right. Come on in. But it's not much better inside. The A.C. is busted again." Libby led me into the front room, an agglomeration of chrome, glass, and leather that looked like a fetishist's wet dream. She did not sit, and she did not invite me to. "All right," she said, cross-armed, "you're in. Now: What do you want?"

"Back when Ma died, you got all her stuff," I said.

Libby blinked. "Well, Bill got the furniture, and I took the, uh—you mean, all those boxes and scrapbooks?"

"Exactly. All that junk Ma squirreled away over the years. What did you do with it?"

She looked at me suspiciously, certain I was up to something and worried because she couldn't put a finger on what. "Well, it's in storage."

"Like, in your attic, or—"

"No. A public locker facility over in Ypsi. For God's sake, Ben, Mama's been dead twenty years, and you're just now asking about her stuff?"

"Well, I've been busy."

"I'll say. Too busy to call, too busy to write, too busy to touch base with your own kin folk. There's hardly any of us left any more, you should make an effort to—"

So it was self-pitying Libby today. Well, that dog would not hunt. "Phone system works both ways, kiddo."

"Bill said you cancelled your Fourth of July fishing on Stapfer Lake. First time since Uncle Dan died that—"

"I had work to do and, frankly, I never much liked fishing anyway."

"No need to be defensive," she said with an innocent smile. "Just commenting." She tipped her head and studied me. "What exactly are you looking for in Mama's stuff?"

"Nothing specific, just want to go through it."

"I see." She brightened. "Well, sure. Be my guest. I mean, it's not like the stuff is my sole property. She was your mother too. Wait a minute, I'll get you the key."

As I waited, I ambled to the big front window and stared blankly across the street. The good news was, Libby was being cooperative for once. The bad news was, Libby was being cooperative for once. I smelled a setup, but saw no course of action other than to play the thing out.

"Here you go," she said, returning. She handed me a key and a piece of notepaper that said JOHNSON SPACE CENTER with an address on Michigan Avenue. "Enjoy," she said. "And no rush getting the key back to me. Heck, I haven't been over there in years."

"Uh-huh," I said, looking at her closely, trying to figure out what she was up to. Which was useless: I'd never been able to read her, and she knew it.

The Johnson Space Center sprawls over a couple of flat acres at the corner of Michigan Avenue and Platt Road in Pittsfield Township, an area that's having trouble deciding whether to be Ann Arbor or Ypsilanti. Despite the advance of the Ann Arbor yuppies from the west and the Ypsilanti yppies from the east, it's still a pretty determinedly hard-bitten area, what with the 23 freeway hard by, the Ypsi State psychiatric hospital to the south, the constant heavy truck traffic, and the big municipal landfill kitty-corner at the same intersection.

The Johnson Space Center, which is really just a different sort of landfill, consists of twenty-four long cinderblock buildings with steel roofs. Each building is divided into little square rooms; each room has its own garage door. The whole thing is fronted by a small clapboard office—shed, more like—and surrounded by a twelve-foot chain link fence topped with lethal coils of shimmering razor wire. Just looking at it hurts.

I parked the Mustang in front of the office building and walked in. The occupant, obviously a student, sat at a gray metal desk with one bare leg crossed over the other. A small radio was playing WIQB, a fan was blowing flies around, and the woman was engrossed in a copy of *Born Burning.* I had to clear my throat twice before she looked up at me abruptly through granny glasses. "Yes? May I help you?" she asked breathlessly.

I dangled the key. "Need to peek into Number 806. Which way?"

She squinted, lay the book down spine up, and consulted a list that was taped under clear plastic on the desk top. "Eight oh six . . ." she murmured. "Ah! Yes!" She looked at me. "Are you Mr. Gillespie?"

"Well, I'm Mrs. Gillespie's brother," I admitted.

"You owe us three hundred and twelve dollars with the tax," she announced.

"What in the hell are you talking about?"

"Arrears on rent. We can't allow access to the locker till—"

"Now, just hold it one damn minute. I'm not paying you any three hundred bucks." So *that's* what Libby was smirking about, damn her anyhow.

"Well, then, we can't allow access to the locker. Sorry."

I felt my heart pound and my fists clench, then I took a deep breath. "Look. None of this is your fault. And none of it is mine. I've got an asshole for a sister, all right?"

The woman studied me steadily. "I can relate to that," she said guardedly.

"She set me up, is what she did. Now: I'm not responsible for that locker and I'm not going to pay my sister's bills. At least, not until I see what's in the locker. If you let me go through the stuff, and it seems like something I'd want to take on, why, I'll pay the bill myself. How about that?"

She gnawed a thumbnail. "I just work here. We have rules. I don't know if I can—"

" 'Cause here's the thing," I pressed. "My sister is a deadbeat, we're talking legendary here. Hell, she still owes me two hundred dollars from when she was fifteen years old. You're never going to see any money from her. Your only chance is to let me look at the stuff, and—"

"If this bill isn't taken care of pretty soon, we're going to auction the contents off."

"Fine. Let me go through the stuff. If I want to keep it, I'll pay the back rent. Otherwise you can ship it straight to that landfill over yonder. Deal?"

She sighed. "All right. Go ahead. But don't tell anybody I did this. I could get fired." She gave me directions to the locker and added with a small smile, "In *my* case, it's an asshole brother."

I slammed out of there and wheeled the Mustang down a sundrenched lane between two of the buildings. The air was choked with sandy dust and the buildings bottled up the heat, making me soak beneath my Detroit Pistons T-shirt. I counted down the lockers, parked the Mustang in front of the garage door that said 806, unlocked the door, and rolled it up on squeaky wheels.

The locker was ten feet in each dimension, less than half full, and thickly dusty. In the right-hand corner, two his-and-hers ten-speed bicycles sat on flats. Must be Libby's, I reflected; Ma never owned such things. Daddy, either. Devil's work, she'd say. Tom Fool, he'd say. Neither had said anything for quite a few years now. Emphysema took Daddy in '63 and the Detroit riot took Ma in '67. Besides the stone over at Grand Lawn, the stuff in this locker was all that was left of them.

There were maybe a dozen cartons of various sizes and shapes stacked along the rear wall. One had fallen over and upchucked its contents: Ma's collection of worn old Baptist hymnals. The sight of them brought to mind, unbidden, the strains of "Will the Circle Be Unbroken." It was Ma's favorite hymn, and whenever Fast Eddie, who was never without his guitar, came by the place, he always sang it for her. I could see her sitting there in the kitchen, eyes closed, nodding and smiling, as Fast played and sang.

Well, I wasn't here for hymnals, or to moon around playing memory lane. I began opening the cartons one by one, checking the contents, and restacking them against the opposite wall. It was hot, dusty, and tedious work. There were a couple boxes of cookbooks. A box of junk on genealogy, fruit of my mother's lifelong and futile effort to prove that our family was important once. Several boxes of letters, all neatly tucked into their envelopes bearing two- and three-cent stamps as well as long-forgotten return addresses in places like Satolah, Clayton, and Pick Ax, Georgia. And there were the scrapbooks: great big thick things stuffed with neatly clipped and pasted articles on a bewildering range of topics, from agriculture to the Henry Ford family to religion.

One of them, in a box of its own, bore the simple label "Children." I opened it. It was obviously the last of a series, commencing the summer after my junior year in high school, when Bill was twenty-six and Libby was fourteen. The contents were, what's the word, eclectic. My mother was a magnet for paper, even paper that was none of her business. She clipped things from the newspapers, saved school papers, retrieved scraps that we'd thrown in the trash, and confiscated others left lying around our rooms. And every Saturday afternoon she'd sit at her little desk in the front room and glue everything into her scrapbooks.

Hence, as I leafed through the heavy black pages, hoping against hope, I encountered items like my first pay stub from Ford's. The *Detroit News* announcement of my brother Bill's betrothal to "Miss Marybeth Rose O'Halloran of Taylor Township" ("Watch out for them black Irish," my daddy grumbled). Redford High grade cards, mine bad and Libby's worse. A note to my mother from someone named Mrs. Evans, talking about what a nice young man I was (?) and how happy she was that I was "escorting" her daughter Elaine (??). And my high school diploma.

After that, the pages were blank. Bill was gone, I'd left home, and Libby was never around. Disappointed at having come up empty, I was about to put the scrapbook back in its box when I saw a white paper corner sticking out of one of the last pages. I heaved the book open to that spot to see the blank back of a small white envelope. Even before I turned it over, I sensed that I'd hit pay dirt.

There was no return address. On the face was written, in a faded blue scrawl:

Ben Perkins
21432 Bennett St.
Detroit 19, Mich.

The postmark fit. Heart pounding, I sat on a carton, lighted a cigar, then withdrew the wad of notebook paper from the envelope and unfolded it. The blue ballpoint scrawl covered a third of the page:

June 8
Dear Ben,

By the time you get this, I'll be gone. I know it's a shock, and I'm sorry that it has to be this way, but there's no choice. If you only knew—in my place, believe me, you'd do the same thing.

I've thought it over and it's the only way out. I'm

going to a better place. My only regret is that I can't take along the friends I love, like you.
Goodbye,
Sara F. Gerbstadt

I set the note down, stood, paced to the garage door and back, arms folded tight, cigar clenched in my teeth. I read the thing a second time and walked back out, leaned against the door frame, watched a Beechcraft Baron make a wobbly-winged approach to Ann Arbor Airport, inhaled cigar smoke past the knot in my throat.

It was there. It was *there* all the time, damn it, and I just didn't have the brains to see it. *In my place you'd do the same thing.* Suicide? She knew me better than that.

Nah. Sara had been up to something else. But someone had gotten to her, first.

I closed the garage door and locked it. Got into the Mustang and threw gravel leaving. Beat gears east on Michigan Avenue bound for Interstate 94, my cigar glowing in my teeth, my thoughts a litany of questions atop questions. *If you only knew.* Knew what? *You'd do the same thing.* Which was? *Going to a better place.* Where?

CHAPTER 6

Norwegian Wood is a large apartment complex plunked down on the shore of Ford Lake in Belleville. Within its security fence is all the good living a wretched excess of money can buy. We've got your swimming pool, golf course, sauna, whirlpool, and Nautilus room. We've got easy access to Detroit on the east and Ann Arbor on the west. We've got obscenely high rental rates and incredibly low vacancy rates. We've got struggling young people, struggling old people, and a handful of bona fide yups and dinks strategizing their way to better living through sex, oat bran, drugs, spreadsheets, and rock and roll. Best of all, we've got a full time maintenance and security staff, headed up by good old yours truly.

I fell into the gig purely by accident way back when the place first opened. It was a stopgap job, to put food on my table while I made other plans. Fifteen years later, I'm still there. The reasons are simple. The work is easy; when you've unplugged one toilet you've unplugged them all—and the security part is more a matter of protecting tenants from each other than protecting them from outsiders. I've got a staff of people—kids, really—who do most of the grunt work, leaving me time for the detective work that comes along. And the pay is decent and includes a free two-bedroom apartment with a deck that does not face the lake but will someday, I promise.

It was past three when I rolled the Mustang up to the Norwegian Wood security gate. Glenda Lay, the day guard, leaned out of her booth, glowering. "What the *hell* you want, you ugly white person?"

"Just the usual," I answered. "Rape and pillage." The

gate hummed up. We both laughed. "How's things, Glenda?"

"Not bad, Mr. Perkins." I don't like being called that by people I know. Which is why she does it. Glenda, who wears a big Angela Davis afro and listens to Al Green records, marches to her own drummer. "Haven't had to break no legs today."

"Good. Listen, I got a name to add to my personal list."

She flipped open the three-ring notebook on her desk and licked the tip of a pencil. "Yeah, I saw that one on y'all's way out this morning. Pretty hot stuff, Mr. Perkins."

"Takes one to know one," I answered. "With a name like Lay, you must be pretty hot stuff yourself."

"I get by."

"Probably get more than that, would be my guess."

"I could go screamin' sexual harassment to somebody," she said thoughtfully, "but this is such a sorry example, I'd probably get laughed out of court."

"Crayon ready, Glenda?"

"Just give it to me real slow," she said, winking.

"You trying to unduly influence the boss here?"

She smiled. "Dream on. Ain't done it with no white boy yet. Why bother, when there's so many other options, like bowling and suicide?"

"The name to add is Stacie Hallthorn. Got it?"

"Yassuh," she drawled. She wrote the name down in block letters and then surveyed the page, smiling. "My *my*, but this is a busy page! I declare, it's the busiest page in Norwegian Wood."

"Later, Glenda," I said, and rumbled the Mustang down the drive into the complex. Now that Stacie's name was on my authorized visitor's list, she'd be able to come into the complex without calling ahead first. Not that I expected her anytime soon. I'd taken her to the airport this morning to retrieve her car, and we'd promised to get together in a few days to go over my progress in locating the missing graduates; but the sexual intensity had been alleviated. At least for the moment.

Smiling at the memories, I half-jogged up the walk,

into Building One, and down to the maintenance office in the basement. All was quiet. The day's assignments were done, the job tickets and time cards filled out, the supply requisitions ready for my initials. My head day guy, Randy, had left a note saying that Doug, my afternoon kid, had called in; he'd evidently dropped his car key in the toilet and flushed it away and, therefore, had not been able to make it into work that day.

Shaking my head, I signed off on the paperwork, then slammed out of the place, sauntered up the walk to my building and up the stairs to my apartment. Fifteen minutes later I had shoes off, cigar lit, Stroh's cracked open, and blank notepad poised and ready on the kitchen table in front of me.

Now to detect!

For a few minutes I doodled. I wrote Sara's name. I wrote some dates. I wrote the word "party" about six times, and the word "suicide" twice. That got me to wondering. I called downtown and caught Elvin Dance, my Detroit police contact, at his desk. In return for a peek at the police file on Sara's death, all I had to promise him was lunch at Pasco's the next day.

Well, that was progress, of sorts. What about Sara's family? They'd lived on Santa Clara, a block over from us. But I couldn't remember the parents' names. I did recall that the father was a voice teacher, taught singing and stuff to private students in his home. Real jovial type, liked kids, was always involved in community activities with young people. The mother was a pleasant nonentity who, unlike mine, seemed content to hover in the background.

I reached for my set of Detroit area phone books. There were eight Gerbstadts listed, none at the old address. I called each in turn, and came up empty. None had ever heard of the Gerbstadts of Santa Clara Street.

Okay, so this wasn't going to be easy. What else is new? I decided to try a different tack. I flipped open the Ann Arbor yellow pages to *Computers* and buzzed down the list of names. One name jumped out at me from the article in *Crain's Detroit Business.* I picked up the phone and dialed. "Retail Computers," the female voice answered.

"Uh, hi. Is this the company that Richard Satterfield owns?"

"One moment." I rolled my eyes as static and electronic gnattering filled my ear. Then another voice: "Executive offices."

"Uh, hi. Is this the company that Richard Satterfield owns?"

"One moment." Again the gnattering. For a computer company, this outfit was awfully stingy with information. Yet a third female voice came on. "Office of the central executive, Ms. Dotson speaking. May I help you?"

"Christ, I hope so. I was calling to find out if this is the company that Richard Satterfield owns."

"Mr. Satterfield is unavailable at the moment," she answered.

At last, an answer to my question. "How do you know he's unavailable if you don't know who's calling?"

"I suggest you try again in the morning."

"I suggest you take a message for me, if it ain't too much trouble."

"Very well."

"Ben Perkins." Bitchily, I spelled it. "In case he draws a blank, tell him Bennett Street, Detroit. Redford High School. Dynamite Park, Donny Wilkins with a black eye, and the mooning of the nuns." I gave her my number. "Got all that?"

"Your message is being electronically transcribed," she said icily. "Of course I've 'got all that'."

"Peachy. Just make sure he gets the damn message, okay?"

"Fine!" The connection broke abruptly. God, people are testy these days. But only in situations where they can get away with it. Such as on the phone and on freeways and from behind government-owned desks.

Well, it would be good to talk to Richie again. To find out how the shy, soft-spoken, bespectacled bookworm of Bennett Street had turned into a hard-charging, wealthy computer mogul. To find out what he remembered about

Sara's death and the events leading up to it. To find out how the kid was, after all these years.

Meanwhile, I had other business. While jousting with the formidable Ms. Dotson, I'd come up with an idea on tracking down the missing graduates. I retrieved my senior yearbook from the living room and opened it to the senior section; sure enough, most of the graduates had activities of various kinds listed by their names.

I opened the list of missing graduates. Of the thirteen, three were already accounted for: Hooker, who was dead; Smarr, the Air Force major; and Richie Satterfield. I listed the ten survivors in alphabetical order on a piece of paper. Then I went through the yearbook and compiled information on their activities. As I'd hoped, they fell into groups. Three were in the Glee Club. Two were in Future Homemakers of America. Two more were in the Pep Club. Three listed no activities at all.

Next, I read through the graduates' activity listings in the yearbook and located the presidents of those clubs. These in turn I looked up on the list Stacie had given me. The president of the Glee Club, Colleen Gray, now lived in California. The president of Future Homemakers was not on the list; must have died. But the vice president, listed in the yearbook as Linda Sue Atwater but now, according to Stacie's list, known as Linda Sue Atwater Collinsworth Yerkey Smith, still lived in metro Detroit. Ditto for Lew Ferguson, president of the Pep Club.

It was pushing five o'clock now. My stomach was growling and my ass was going numb as it always does when I spend too much time on paperwork and not enough doing things. I was tempted to blow it off for today, hit Under New Management for the usual microwaved ground rounds, tall dark Stroh's, and serious scholarly conversation with Jimmy Joe, Norris, Darryl, and the others. But I realized that it was only two o'clock out in la-la land. Might as well give Colleen Gray a try, first.

Her number, in the 408 area code, rang about twenty times before it was answered. "Santa Cruz Okayness Center, this is Colleen," answered the breathless voice.

The sounds of screaming children in the background

suggested that the okayness business wasn't terrific at the moment. "Colleen Gray?" I ventured.

"Yes?"

"Ben Perkins in Detroit. We never knew each other, but we were in the same class way back when. Redford High—"

"I remember you," she said coolly. "You were the one who set off the stink bomb in Coach Cain's math class."

I blinked as the long buried memory came back with blinding clarity. "That wasn't a stink bomb. Just a handful of calcium carbide in a Dixie cup of water."

"They had to evacuate the whole floor, as I recall. You were also the one who smeared Limburger cheese on the manifolds of my boyfriend's car. Made the car unbearable to ride in, so I quit going out with him, which was just as well, since he went to prison subsequently. I guess that means I owe you a debt of gratitude, doesn't it?" She cupped the receiver and called, "Agnes, will you please *feed* them or *sing* to them or *dialogue* with them or something? *Christ!*" Back to me she said, "How can I help you?"

I had one foot out my apartment door when the phone rang. I stomped back in, hoping the call would be brief; my ear was numb from the talk with Colleen.

Who actually had been quite helpful. Of the three in the Glee Club, Joe Stitt had become her husband. Debbie Barr had married a Judnik and now lived in Upper Sandusky, Ohio. Nicki Micklos had, however, faded into the void.

Encouraged, I'd asked her about the three no-activities names. Carl Hickson and Don Triplett she'd never heard of. But Willard Nolan she remembered. To the best of her knowledge, he joined the Merchant Marine right after graduation.

Now, of Stacie's missing thirteen, I'd found five. Eight to go. That was the good news. The bad news was, Colleen did not attend the Bubbas's party the night before graduation. She never knew Sara Gerbstadt and could shed no light on what had happened to her.

But I felt good. Things were cooking. I'd have felt

even better if I wasn't faint from hunger. And now the damn phone was keeping me from dinner just a tad longer.

"Perkins's Starvation Diet Clinic, Ben speaking," I growled.

A man's voice chuckled. "Wrestling with that middle-aged spread, Benjy?"

"Hell no," I retorted. "Not me." The voice set off faraway echoes in the back of my mind. "Richie? Is that you?"

"Actually, these days it's Richard or Rich, typically." I could hear the years in his voice. It was huskier, more resonant, definitely more assured. "But the 'Satterfield' hasn't changed. How are you?"

"Just great." Since the hunger pangs would not go away on their own, I stretched the phone cord to the fridge and rescued myself a fresh Stroh's. Fight fire with fire, I always say. "How about you?" I asked, sitting down at the kitchen table.

"Splendid. Are you sure you're all right? I heard you were dead. Gunned down in an Ypsi bar a few years ago. It was in the papers."

"Oh, that. Just a misunderstanding. Happens a lot in this line of work."

"What work is that?"

I snapped a match to flame and lit a short cork-tipped cigar. "Private detective," I answered, waving the match dead.

"That's fascinating. Sounds exciting, too."

"Nah. Right now I'm mostly doing background investigations for Psytech over in Plymouth. Good bread but a dead snore. Far cry from the big computer tycoon I hear you are these days."

"It's a living. My God, it's good to hear your voice. So many years. How did you find me?"

Which was his way of asking *why*. I mentioned the *Crain's Detroit Business* article. "My client's the reunion committee of our graduating class," I added. "Hired me to track down the missing, of which you were one, oddly enough."

"Nothing odd about it. I keep a pretty low profile. I've lost all touch with the old neighborhood."

For a few moments, we compared notes and played catch-up. His parents were dead. His sister lived in Canada. He started Retail Computers in the late sixties and it had grown, as he put it, "very nicely." He lived in the Barton Hills section of Ann Arbor. Upscale, but not ostentatious. Kid's got a nickel or two to rub together, I thought. Kid's doing all right.

Just on the off-chance, I read him the names of the other missing grads. Several of the names were familiar, but he could tell me nothing specific. None of the rest were familiar—except Don Triplett.

"Sure," Rich said casually. "Don works for me. Started out with me back in the sixties, in fact."

"Well, that's good," I said, surprised. I'd never understood Richie's friendship with Sponge back then, and I found it even harder to understand now. Sponge had had his decent moments, but on the whole he'd always been a nasty little quick-fisted prick with a bad swagger and a worse attitude. It just figures, I thought: Sara dies, Sponge survives and prospers.

"I know you and Jan and Fast didn't like him," Rich said. "But he's turned out okay. Absolutely."

"Glad to hear it." I put a check mark by Triplett's name. Six down, seven to go. Not bad for twenty-four hours. "But finding the grads is only part of my action. There's something else I'm working on."

"Yes?"

"Sara."

CHAPTER 7

A pause the space of a heartbeat. "What about her?"

"Well," I said, "Jan thinks it wasn't suicide. She thinks Sara was murdered. Asked me to look into it. I got nothing to go on but gut feel, and that says she's right."

"Murdered," Rich said softly. His voice sounded younger now, less practiced, more familiar. "Oh my God. Why? Who would want to kill Sara?"

"Don't know, Rich," I answered, puffing smoke.

"What about the police? If she was murdered, why—"

"No answer to that one, either. I'll know more on that tomorrow." I stood and stretched, enjoying the glow of beer in an empty stomach, a glow that would shortly turn to pain if I didn't tamp it down with some food. "But maybe you can help me. I want you to think about the party at the Bubbas's house the night before graduation."

"Yes," he said tightly. "I was there."

"I know you were. We were all there. You, Sara, Jan, Fast Eddie, and a zillion others." I grinned. "In fact, old Sponge showed up too, didn't he?"

"Yes. That's right. And you got into a brawl with him. Remember?"

Vague shapes floated in the gray below the surface. "Yeah. He wasn't invited. He tried to crash the party, and I—"

"You told him to leave and he wouldn't, so you hit him. No, that's not right," Rich said with animation. "You let him hit you first."

"I did? Sporting of me."

"Yes. I really admired that."

"Well, I was younger then."

Richie was chuckling. "He hit you, and then you

decked him. Oh, was he mad. We don't talk about old times much, but I don't think he's ever forgotten that."

"Well, good. Glad I set him on the path of righteousness. You know what I remember most about you that night? Your first solo beer run."

"And my last," Richie answered.

"Jail'll do that to you. I got nailed myself like that, with a case of tall boys in the trunk, the year before."

"Jail is not pleasant," Richie agreed. "Being in court, being humiliated by the judge in front of your parents, is not pleasant either." Pause. "You know, I'm still embarrassed about that episode. I've never told anyone about it."

"What's to be embarrassed about? You went out to buy more beer and the cops caught you. Big deal."

"I've never even had a traffic ticket since then."

"So that was your walk on the wild side." I drank some beer. "Anyway, this is serious stuff here. That party was the last place where Sara was seen alive. Next morning she was found dead in her garage. So I'm trying to piece together what happened that night. Looking for clues. It's tough. Twenty-five years. What do you remember?"

"Not much," he admitted. "Nothing very specific. Music and dancing and a ton of people everywhere, coming and going. It's just so hard. It was so long ago."

"I know what you mean. I've been banging my brain against it since yesterday and I've dredged up a little. There was a Tigers game we were listening to on the radio. Jan was mad at me for some reason. Other things. But none of that has to do with Sara. What do you remember about Sara being there?"

"Oh, boy," Rich sighed. "I don't know. I'm pretty sure I didn't see her much that night. I do remember she was bombed out of her mind. You remember, she couldn't hold her beer at all. One or two and she was gone."

"Yeah."

"Other than that . . . You know something, I can't buy it, somebody killing her. No reason to, you know? No reason in the world."

"Can you buy her killing herself?"

"Makes more sense to me than murder." I sensed that

Rich was struggling for words, caught up in the emotion of a long-ago tragedy. "Sara was . . . different. A beautiful person. The only one, aside from you and Don, who never called me names and made fun of me. I felt like I lost half my friends when she went. But she was spacey, too. Had a lot of deep dark thoughts. I can see her starting that car and closing the garage door and just drifting away. I don't like it, but I can see it."

"Not me, pal. I'm gonna push on it awhile. You remember anything else about Sara or the party or whatever, give me a holler, hear?"

"Sure." His voice brightened. "Listen, we should get together. Why don't you come out here sometime? Love to show you around the place."

"Sounds good." We set Saturday afternoon at his office in Ann Arbor. "You be thinking about Sara and the party meanwhile, hear?"

"Believe me," he answered. "I won't be thinking of much else."

We signed off. I stood and hosed my cigar dead in the sink. It was six o'clock. My stomach was sending up flares. Time to get going before someone else called me. I went to the door, opened it, and nearly collided with Stacie Hallthorn.

She'd changed since that morning into snug black shorts and a scoop neck top that was a black-and-white riot of dots, stripes, and paisley. She wore a gold herringbone chain around her neck, thin hoop gold earrings, and matching gold bangles on left wrist and right ankle. Her tanned face was puffy, her light blue eyes moist, and when she saw me she stumbled into my arms, sobbing. "Oh, Ben. I just don't know what to do!"

I held her against me loosely, smothered in her sweet scent, and stared past her explosion of auburn hair, at a total loss. "What's wrong, Stace? What happened?"

"There's a gas leak in my house. The whole place smelled of it when I got there. I could have been blown up—"

"Easy now. Take it easy. Did you call somebody?"

She shuddered a long breath, regaining control.

"They told me the whole system needs work. They said I should stay somewhere else for a few days. You're the only one I could think of, and—"

"So what's the big deal?" I held her back from me and looked down into her large, moist eyes, smiling. "I'd love for you to stay here."

She blinked rapidly and said in a small voice, "I won't be any trouble, I promise."

"No trouble at all. Glad to have you." I rushed past the double entendre. "Bring your stuff?"

She tiptoed up and kissed me. "You're a *doll*! Come on. My things are in the car." She took my hand and we strolled down the stairs, out into the hot evening, across the parking lot. I got nods, waves, and a double take or two from tenants, as Stacie bounced at my side, beaming for all the world to see, now suddenly without a care in the world.

Don't get me wrong. I knew the gas leak story was pretty fishy. And I did notice the intensity of her moods and their abrupt swing from despair to ebullience. But I didn't give it much thought. I was glad to see her. Sue me.

Her car was a beige early 80s vintage Chevy sedan with mismatched tires, a snapped-off antenna, and a bumper sticker that said I'M DATING YOUR HUSBAND. "Do anything special today?" she asked as she opened the trunk.

I reached out a pair of worn suitcases. She grabbed a couple of stuffed-to-popping string bags, latched the trunk lid on the third slam, and walked with me back toward my building. I told her about my progress toward finding the missing graduates. When I mentioned Sara Gerbstadt, I found that Stacie knew nothing about Jan's suspicions, about my investigation, or about Sara herself. But the Gerbstadt name meant something, all right.

"I took voice lessons from a Gerbstadt," she said as we reentered my apartment. "Herman Gerbstadt."

"Must have been her father," I answered, slamming the door behind me. Could be a break here, I thought. "Did you know him well?"

"He was my teacher," she replied, preceding me down the hall toward the bedroom. "And there *was* a daughter. Never knew her, though. She committed suicide?"

I followed her into the bedroom and set the suitcases down as Stacie tossed her string bags on the floor by the dresser. "That was the official story. Jan doesn't think so, and I don't either. I'm looking into it."

Stacie posed before the full-length mirror and stretched this way and that, examining herself, primping her hair. "Leave the brown suitcase here," she said, preoccupied. "The other one can go in the closet."

I carried the case into the walk-in and began to clear space for it among my tumble of shoes in the corner. "Any idea where the Gerbstadts are these days?" I called through the door.

"The mother died," came Stacie's voice. "That much I know. No idea about Mr. Gerbstadt. But I hope you find him. I'd really love to see him again."

I was going to ask why, but the question died on my lips when I emerged from the closet to find Stacie undressing.

Pasco's is on Evergreen just north of Ford Road, where Dearborn and Dearborn Heights meet the city of Detroit. Over there it's Ford wherever you look: The Ford Proving Grounds, the Ford Glass House, Ford's Rouge complex, the Ford-owned Fairlane Shopping Center, and Fair Lane, the founder's estate, are all within a stone's throw of Pasco's gaunt portico. My late uncle told me that Pasco's was once a speakeasy, frequented by Ford Motor honchos up to and including Harry Bennett, Mr. Ford's right-hand thug.

I don't know if that's true, but it looks sinister enough. Pasco's is dark fieldstone on the outside and dim leather and walnut on the inside, with heavy velvet drapes, stained glass, and roomy booths with high walls that discourage eavesdropping and encourage the pursuit of furtive business. As I sat across from Elvin Dance the next day, warmish and uncomfortable in my navy blue suit, I could almost picture Bennett, that dapper little dandy, sitting there with his cronies in May 1937, deciding how to handle Reuther and Frankensteen and the rest of those union troublemakers. . . .

"Perkins! Wake up!" Elvin said, rapping the white-clothed table.

"I'm awake," I said. "Just daydreaming a minute."

"Well, let's get on with it," Elvin said as a busperson began clearing away our dirty dishes. "I do like dining at Pasco's on someone else's nickel, but the city of 'Troit's expecting me to fight some crime this afternoon too."

Elvin slapped a big catalog-sized envelope on the desk and busied himself Zippoing a Kool as the busperson finished his work. The Detroit police captain was as snazzy as ever in an expertly tailored oyster suit with faint gray stripes atop a cream colored shirt and a gray-on-peach medallion paisley tie. Gold winked from several teeth and several rings, in startling contrast to the rich leathery blackness of his skin. Elvin Dance is the toughest of the tough, a bull-like man who went on the force back in segregated days and worked his way up over the years to command rank—no patsy, for sure.

Then why, you ask, does he help a white private detective from way out in Belleville? If you think it's because we're friends, you're partly right. If you think it's because I've got something on him—well, you're partly right about that, too.

The busperson left. Our waiter brought some more coffee. When we were alone, Elvin opened the envelope and shunted out a thick tan file folder as some aimless piano music started up from somewhere. "Must say, Perkins, this is a far cry from your other gigs lately. Your dope dealers and neo-Nazis and so forth. What's the matter? Business so bad you got to go back twenty-five years to find work?"

"It's personal. The victim was a friend of mine, back in high school."

"Meanin' you was screwing her."

"Nope," I said steadily. "Just friends."

"Huh," Elvin grunted, bored. "Well, there had to be *one.* Come on, let's see what we got here." I lighted a cigar as he flipped open the file and began to leaf through the papers with surprisingly deft fingers. "Here's the summary report. Ready?"

"Ready," I said, getting out my little pad.

" 'Sara Faith Gerbstadt. Race: White.' No shit?" Elvin muttered. "Age 17. Discovered on the floor of the garage at her residence, 21419 Santa Clara, at 8:30 A.M. on Saturday, June 10, by her father and mother, Herman and Lucille Gerbstadt. Pronounced dead at the scene. Cause of death: acute carbon monoxide poisoning. Ruled a suicide. Case closed.' " He looked at me. "There you go, Perkins. Suicide. Satisfied now?"

"Come on."

"I know, I know. Let's see here." He tapped ash off his cigarette and leafed through some more pages. "Here we go. Field notes by Detective Billy Hammond. Honky flatfoot."

"You know him?"

"Hell no. It's a honky name, though. Gotta be."

"I don't see why—"

"They was all honkies in those days, the detectives," Elvin said patiently. "Hell, didn't even integrate the patrol cars till what, '59 or so?" He returned to the report. "Lemme see, lemme see . . . Okay. 'Parents were away for the night, driven by the victim's uncle to a concert in Toledo, where they spent the night. Confirmed by Toledo police. Victim attended a party at the'—how the *hell* do you pronounce this?"

"Szewczklieuski," I replied. "They were twins. We just called 'em the Bubbas."

"Why am I not surprised? '. . . at the, er, Bubba residence on Bentler Street. Witnesses state victim was despondent. Witnesses observed victim drink large quantity of Stroh's Bohemian Style Beer.' Illicitly, I might add," Elvin added darkly.

"Yeah," I said sourly, "we were all dirty through and through, 'specially when you compare us with today's kids."

Elvin took a big hit off his smoke. " 'Witnesses state victim left party approximately 11:30 P.M., driving a 1957 Ford Del Rio station wagon. Which vehicle, registered to

Lucille Gerbstadt, was found in the garage—" He turned the page—"with the victim. Also in the garage was a 1959 Ford Fairlane 500, registered to Herman Gerbstadt. Vehicle had key in ignition, ignition turned to ON, gas tank dry.' Oh," he broke off. "Looky here, the detective made a drawing of the scene."

Elvin turned the folder sideways on the white tablecloth so I could squint at the smudged pencil drawing. It was a floor plan of the Gerbstadt garage. Noted were the positions of the Ford wagon, plus the Fairlane 500. Between them was a rough sketch of a female form: the position of Sara's body. A single word was written at the back end of the Fairlane: "Soot." I pointed it out to Elvin. "What the hell does that mean?"

"Dunno. Let me read on here, maybe we can figure it out." He took the file back and read on in monotone. " 'No confirmation as to time victim returned to home. Cross-street neighbor, Mrs. Agnes Ratchford, saw an unknown car parked in front of Gerbstadt house at 11:00 P.M., but did not see victim return home.' "

Unknown car. The words gave me a chill. I wrote Agnes Ratchford's name down in my notebook, worrying the end of my cigar.

" 'Officers interviewed friends, family, acquaintances of deceased. Informants advised that deceased was despondent during interval prior to subject event. Deceased made amends in some cases and gave away valued personal possessions. Such actions confirm suicide scenario.' "

He looked at me, eyebrows arched. "Come on, Elvin," I prodded. "What else is there?"

"Not much." Elvin turned pages. "List of contents of victim's purse. Want to hear?"

"Shoot."

He crushed out his smoke. " 'One opened pack Juicy Fruit gum. One pale pink lipstick. One pack tissues. One dollar bill, twenty-two cents in change. Key ring containing key to residence and keys to station wagon and Fairlane. Cartridge pen, three spare ink cartridges. Clumps of lint and hair of assorted sizes. Driver's license, Beta Club membership card, shoe horn, comb and brush, packet of ketchup from the Wigwam.' That's it." Elvin snorted. "Well, I see something real suspicious right there. You spot that?"

I'd spotted something all right, but I played dumb. "Like what, Elvin?"

"No Kotex!" he boomed. "When was the last time you saw a broad's purse with no fuckin' Kotex in it? Is that suspicious or what?"

Without answering, I took a last hit off my cigar, crushed it out, slapped back the last of my cold coffee, and skimmed my notes. I almost didn't need to; the words were etched on the front of my mind like the carvings on Mount Rushmore. No smoking guns—nothing to take to court—but the thing was dirty, all right. Dirty, dirty, dirty.

"How about an autopsy?" I asked tonelessly as our server refilled our coffees. "Any kind of report in there?"

"Due to be in the back," Elvin said. He riffled pages. "Bingo. Okay. Identifying information and so forth . . ." He looked at me. "It was definitely her, positive ID. So forget the theory that she snuck another stiff in there and flitted off footloose and fancy free to fornicate in France or somewhere, Mr. Private Dee-tective."

"Oh well, okay," I answered, drawing a big line on my pad.

"As to the cause of death. Let's see." He cleared his throat. " 'Indications of CO poisoning. Pink fingernails, cherry red blood and musculature, necroses in the corpus pallidus and corpus striatum.' "

"Run that by one more time?"

"Cysts in the brain," Elvin answered.

"What's the fingernail bit?"

"Pink indicates carbon monoxide poisoning. Otherwise the fingernails would be purple from livor mortis." Elvin studied the report for a moment. "It was carbon monoxide poisoning, Ben. Ain't no doubt about that. No marks of violence. No sign of sexual intercourse, voluntary or otherwise. CO blood saturation was only thirty percent, but her blood alcohol was point one seven. That combination'll kill you dead."

One seven. Same as her age. And a pretty high count.

Especially for Sara, a girl who couldn't drink two without going weak in the knees. She really *had* been slapping it back at the party, as Rich had remembered.

"Something else here that may or may not interest you," Elvin commented.

"What's that?"

"At the time of the victim's death, she was pregnant."

CHAPTER 8

"Pregnant?" I asked, after a moment. "You sure about that?"

"Eight to twelve weeks, says right here on the autopsy report."

"Pregnant. Jesus."

Elvin's dark eyes flashed, his lips drew back from his teeth in a snarl, and he pounded the table once with a massive fist. "So you *was* screwin' her!"

"Cut it out, of course not."

Our waiter came at a fast glide. "Is there some problem, sirs?" he asked nervously.

Elvin glowered at him. "The problem is this white boy over here, can't keep his *thang* in his pants."

"I see," the waiter answered politely, giving me a beady little look.

I leaned back in the booth and lighted myself a fresh cigar. Elvin was, as my mother would have said, "taking on," and when he's like that all you can do is hang tight and wait him out. Besides, I needed time to think, time to adjust my notions about Sara to this new reality, time to try to figure out what it all meant.

"Did you know," Elvin asked the waiter, "that this white boy knocked up his lawyer lady friend, and he ain't even gonna *marry* her?"

"No, sir, I didn't." Beady look.

"Elvin," I said, "Carole doesn't want to get married, and she's going to have the kid, and we understand each other perfectly."

"Oh, I'm sure she understands you," Elvin grunted. "But when it comes to you understanding her, you do not in fact know dick."

"Plus which," I went on patiently, "I did not 'knock up' Sara Gerbstadt. She was someone else's girlfriend." Fast Eddie's, I thought. Jesus Christ, Eddie got her pregnant. "You can leave," I told the waiter.

"Yes sir," he said. "Thank you sir."

He glided away. The piano music tinkled on, playing something like "Variations on Chaos" or "Old Ladies in Love." Lunch hour was over and Pasco's was emptying out except for the career drinkers and deal makers like Elvin and me.

"You sure you didn't do the dirty deed?" Elvin grumbled.

"I'm very sure. But thanks for making sure."

Elvin brightened. "At least this explains the missing Kotex. I *toldja* that was a clue of some kind."

"Uh-huh." I got out my Visa card with the nearly flat numerals and flipped it onto the check. Our waiter slunk in, ducking as if he expected live rounds to be fired over his head, snatched the card and the check, and darted away. "Lemme ask you something, Elvin. As a man whose investigative experience rivals even my own—"

"Ha!"

"—what you think of this thing? Having looked over the file and so forth. Did Sara kill herself? Or was she done in?"

Elvin took a long, noisy breath through his nose, eyes reflective. "I don't know," he said vaguely. "I mean, you look at it, at the setup and so forth, and hey. People said she was despondent. Them high school girls, their hormones get to cookin' and God knows what can happen." His shoulders rose in one massive shrug. "I can see where it listens that way, tempts you to close the file."

"Yeah."

He lighted a cigarette. We looked at each other in silence. Then we both started shaking our heads. "But I don't think so," Elvin said quietly.

"*Hell,* no," I agreed.

Elvin tapped the file with an oversized knuckle, leaning forward. "It's the keys that turns it for me. Did you see that?"

"I saw that. But what about the cars? Why would she do it that way?"

"Whaddya mean?"

"Look at the cars. It ties into what you're saying, Elvin. She drove the Del Rio wagon to the party, right? Witnesses attest. But the car used for the suicide was the other car, the Fairlane. Said so in the report."

"That's right."

A bulb popped on in my head. "That's what the soot's about! Right there!"

"Hold it. Hold on, slow down."

"Get that sketch out, Elvin." He did so, smoothing back the pages of the file. I pointed to the area at the rear of the Fairlane 500. "One of the investigators noticed soot at the back of the Fairlane. Didn't think it through, I guess. But soot means the car sat there, running, for some period of time, with the garage door shut."

"Uh-huh."

I leaned back again. "Now: Let's pretend Sara wants to kill herself. She drives home in the Del Rio wagon. Pulls into the garage. Why in the hell does she start up the *Fairlane* to do it with? Why not stay in the Del Rio?"

Elvin's eyes were narrow and shrewd and he was nodding. "Then there's the keys."

"Right. She had keys to both cars on her ring. A second Fairlane key was found in the Fairlane's ignition. Where did that second Fairlane key come from? Did she go inside to get it? Why would she do that, when she's got a Fairlane key on her ring already?"

"Then there's the concrete floor," Elvin noted.

"What do you mean?"

"Okay. Here's what s'posedly went down. Gal came home. Put the car in the garage, closed the door. Found herself another Fairlane key, ignoring the one she's got on her ring already, which is horseshit right there but it gets worse. Started up the Fairlane, then lay down on the *garage floor* to die. No way, man. Girls like to be comfortable. Girls don't like to lie down on no cold greasy old *ce*ment floor. She coulda just sat there in the Del Rio with the motor running and went out all comfy-like."

On the one hand, I felt chilled again, the feeling of having brushed up against an old evil. On the other, I felt a sense of savage satisfaction. I asked, "So, how 'bout it, Elvin? You going to reopen the case?"

Elvin stared at me. Then he laughed. The waiter darted over with my credit card slip and the check. Elvin laughed some more as I entered the tip, totaled the bill, and accepted my copies. By the time the clerical work was done, Elvin was back to what passed, for him, as normal. "I don't think so, Ben."

"Hey. There's no statute of limitations on murder."

"Officially, no. But come on, man." Elvin's demeanor was conversational, casual, at the necessary emotional distance from the reality of what he was discussing. "We're headed for five hundred homicides again this year. We don't have enough people. We don't have enough money. We're sitting on a powder keg, givin' off sparks—and you expect me to go back and look at the death of some West Side white chick twenty-five years ago? No, man. No way." He put the file back into the envelope.

I eyed the file. "Any chance this Billy Hammond, the flatfoot who worked the case, is still around?"

"I can find out," Elvin said carefully.

"And, uh, if so, could he possibly be made amenable to an interview with good old yours truly?"

"I could mention it."

We sat in silence for a long moment. "So," I said finally, "you don't mind if I work on it?"

His eyes flashed. "When has my 'minding' ever stopped you?"

I considered. "Approximately never."

He glowered, thinking, and then, gradually, his face spread in a grin. "Well, my boy. Here's something I never thought I'd ever say to you. Go ahead. Investigate. Do the case. Be my guest."

As I rumbled the Mustang up to the Norwegian Wood gate, Glenda waved me to a stop. I turned down the volume on Don Henley's "End of the Innocence" and said,

"What's the problem, kid? Got a knotty security problem to straighten out?"

Glenda leaned out the booth window. She was smiling, but her eyes were serious. "Not exactly a problem, Mr. Perkins. More like a public nuisance. Can we talk?"

"Go ahead, but hurry up. Some of us have work to do yet today."

She didn't respond to the sally. "It's about your young friend—Ms. Hallthorn?"

Since Stacie and I had about twenty years on Glenda, to hear Stacie referred to as my "young friend" was a borderline riot. But something was really bothering Glenda; her speech was nearly devoid of the singsong black dialect she liked to affect with me. She sounded almost like she'd been to college. I wondered if she had. "What about her?" I asked.

"Well, she spent most of today out of doors, sir. Used the pool. Roamed the grounds. And so forth."

"What's wrong with that?"

Glenda took a deep breath. "The problem is that her attire was not, how shall I put this, entirely appropriate."

"Meaning?"

She looked at me. "She was wearing a tank top and a bikini bottom that was about as substantial as a spider's web."

"That's all?"

"First thing she did was dive into the pool without changing. Then she wandered around the grounds, soaking wet. Your friend has considerable boobs, sir. You can imagine—"

"Considerable boobs?"

"You can imagine," she said sternly, "how she looked, soaking wet, dressed like that."

I cast my eyes upward for a moment, being indeed able to imagine it. "Caused a problem for you, huh?"

"For me? Nossir. I told you I don't go for white people. But it surely did cause a problem for one of your maintenance fellers. You know the one I mean? With the hard-on out to here all the time?"

"Randy?"

"The darker one. Yeah. I can't tell 'em apart. Yeah, ole Randy was following her around and, uh, chatting her up? Is that the expression?"

"Uh-huh." I was thinking about Randy, about how horny he is for anything on feet. I figured once he discovered who Stacie was staying with, he let her be. Hopefully. "Anybody complain?"

"Mrs. J, of course. She was on the phone ten seconds after your friend appeared. Must have been glued to her window."

She was referring to Mrs. Janusevicius, our day-shift busybody. "Okay," I said, "I'll talk to Stacie, get her to knock it off." I wanted to bite my tongue at the unfortunate word choice, which was not lost on Glenda. "We don't want the little old ladies all in an uproar," I added lamely.

"Just don't let it happen again," Glenda commanded, then hit the button to raise the gate.

Three minutes later I sauntered into my apartment to find Stacie sitting on the sofa, hunched over the coffee table, slipping a new battery into her tiny wristwatch. She wore a snug blue camisole that came just to the navel, plus the skimpiest bikini bottom allowed by law. The vision of her was acres of well-toned, well-tanned skin, an explosion of loosely permed auburn hair, and considerable boobs. "Hi there," she said with her secretive smile as she snapped the back onto her watch.

"Hey," I said, shutting the door. "What've you been up to?"

"Waiting for you." She pressed the remote to shut off the TV, which had been playing one of those "reality" crime shows in which actors perform dramatized re-creations. Then she stretched her arms up to clenched brown fists, arching her back and stretching the camisole to the bursting point. "I did a little shopping, a little swimming," she said lazily, "a little TV—you know, the usual."

The coffee table bore an ashtray jammed with lipsticked cigarette butts, as well as a half bottle of Gallo burgundy, a couple of empty Cokes, a huge bag of chips, and an empty doughnut box. That explained the shopping.

"Heard you met one of my maintenance guys," I said, kicking off my shoes.

"One of those *animals* you employ, you mean," she said as she began tinkering with the wristwatch buttons. Setting the date and time, evidently. "Yeah, I went out for a stroll, and he came trotting after me dragging his tongue. Just a baby."

I was more interested in her brisk work with the watch. "You mean you know how to do that?" I asked admiringly. "Those digitals are a mystery to me. Like hanging wallpaper."

She rose, smiling, and purred, "I don't want to hear about what you're not good at." She came to me, slid her arms around me, kissed me primly through my shirt, and looked up at me with her light-blue come-hither eyes. "Let's talk about what you *are* good at."

We kissed and it got serious quick, instant ignition and swift liftoff, the kind of thing where the thirty-foot distance to the bedroom is too far to travel. So we eased to the thick carpet, kissing and whispering and breathing when absolutely necessary. I had worked Stacie's camisole up over her breasts and was wrestling with my pants. Stacie had scissor-kicked her bikini off and was tying back her hair with a rubber band when the pounding came at the door, the drumbeat of a hundred fists. "Open up, Perkins!" barked an angry male voice.

We froze. "Just ignore him," Stacie breathed.

"Police officer!" shouted the voice. "Search warrant! Open it or we'll kick it!"

Holy shit. "Get dressed," I whispered to Stacie. I fought with my pants, unjamming the zipper, then got to my feet and trotted to the door. "Just a minute," I said. Checked on Stacie, who had gotten her camisole down and bikini up and was sitting at the end of the sofa now, legs crossed, face flushed, jaw set in annoyance. She nodded at me and I opened the door.

"Hellooo," Dick Dennehy said.

I released a relieved breath. "You son of a bitch."

"What have we here," Dick asked, "a guilty conscience?"

"What do you want, Dick?"

"A moment of your time. Official business." He walked past me into the apartment. After a moment's hesitation I shut the door. "Afternoon, ma'am!" Dick said, appreciative eyes roaming over Stacie.

"Are you really a cop?" she asked, voice light, eyes watchful.

"But of course," Dick answered grandly. "Richard Dennehy, Inspector, Office of Special Investigations, Michigan State Police. Care to see my ID?"

"I'd rather see your exit," she replied.

"Which you will, I promise, as soon as I've had a moment to beat on friend Ben here." He nodded me toward the window wall. "Shall we step into your office?"

I gave Stacie a helpless shrug as I followed Dick out onto the deck. In the gathering evening the sun was a scarlet ball, roaming among puff clouds in the western horizon, and its reddish light made Dick's traditional cheap gray suit look pinkish. He's a large man whose square corners are blurring from age and the years of hours spent sitting in stakeouts and courtrooms and saloons and cafés: the cop's life, which in a drunken moment he described sardonically as "long stretches of monotony interrupted by intense bursts of boredom." His grayish blond hair was cropped close, his gray eyes looked icily through aviator glasses, and his demeanor projected the utter confidence of one who has killed and figures on killing again before it's all over.

"So what's the bit, Dick?" I asked.

His gray eyes were wide. "Wow," he said reverently. "Who the hell is that?"

"Stacie Hallthorn. Old high school classmate."

He grinned. "What're you doing? Going back and doing 'em all a second time?"

"We didn't know each other back then. This is—well, it's a long story. Forget it."

He held up hands. "Okay. Right. It's none of my business. I do have just one question, though, if you'll indulge me."

"What's that?"

"Why is she in the living room, instead of back in the Romp-Her Room where she belongs?"

"Not everybody's a slave to lust, Dick."

"Yeah yeah, Mr. Chastity Personified over here."

"Moreover," I said, "she's really a pretty nice kid—"

"Kid!" he snorted. "She's got more miles on her than a bald-headed tire. Held up well, but—"

"What are you talking about?" I asked darkly. "You just met her."

"That's true," he answered. "But I know her well. I've probably run across her a thousand, fifteen hundred times in the past thirty years. Be careful, buddy."

He was really getting on my nerves. "You know who you remind me of?" I asked. "Cassandra."

"Who the hell's that?"

"Some old myth fable person Carole told me about."

Dick brightened. "Ah yes, Carole. Now there's a *real* woman. A woman of accomplishment, judgment, and even good taste, mostly. I don't think you give Carole enough credit, you know? Not only is she an ace lawyer, not only is she carrying your child—but she also equips you with little sniglets of information to zing your old pals with."

"Damn straight. Zung you good that time, too."

He smiled. "My powers of prophecy come from the street. Cassandra's were a gift from Apollo. But the end result is the same. No one believes till it's too late."

At that moment the sliding door opened and Stacie came out, carrying two icy bottles of Stroh's. "Something to drink, Inspector?" she asked, handing me one.

He helped himself. "Much obliged." We clinked bottles and I took a swig. Dick's eyes were on Stacie. "So. Stacie. As a peace officer in the State of Michigan, I have a duty to ask if you are living with this man without benefit—as debatable as that term is—of matrimony."

She eyed him, smiling. "Staying over for a few days. Got a utilities problem at my place up in West Bloomfield."

"Well," Dick observed, "if it's your plumbing on the fritz, then Ben's the man to see."

I was really starting to get ticked. "If you've got some business here, Dick, let's get on with it, okay?"

He turned on me briskly. "Right. Trial's on for September second. Judge Hathaway's courtroom. But you probably knew that."

"Carole got notified through the court. What else is new?"

Dick shot Stacie a glance. "The other key witness has let it be known that she won't testify voluntarily. I was asked, informally, to inquire of you, informally, if you could possibly provide a little motivation in that department."

"Nope. Lynne'll either testify or she won't, and nothing I can do will change it. If I lean, I'll probably just make it worse. She ain't my biggest fan these days. Cussed me out at Jerry's funeral."

"Oh. Well, do what you can, huh? I gotta run." He raised the bottle, got under it, sucked the beer down with three hearty gulps, then handed Stacie the bottle, eyeing her keenly. "So long, lovebirds," he said, heading for the sliding door.

"What was he asking you about, Ben?" Stacie asked as we followed him into the living room.

"Murder case I'm testifying in." I had a brainstorm. "Listen, old buddy, can you run some sheets for me?"

Dick opened the apartment door and turned to face me, expression weary. "I suppose, but it'll take a few days." He reached a pad and pen out of his jacket. "Who?"

I gave him Satterfield, Vento, Anger, and Triplett. I wanted to give him Stacie, but couldn't with her standing right there. "Fast as you can. Investigation's clipping right along," I said bravely.

Dick looked at me with his seen-it-all eyes and put his pad away. "Right."

"Will I see you again, Inspector?" Stacie asked politely.

He grinned. "I consider it inevitable. Later, people." He left.

I closed the door behind him, threw the deadbolt,

then turned to find Stacie naked, waiting, and more than ready.

I entered the kitchen, turned on the light, rescued myself a Stroh's, and escorted it to the dinette table. There waited all the paperwork on my dual case: notes on the Gerbstadt "suicide" as well as notes on the missing graduates. I sat down, yawned, stretched, and made myself start studying. Thursday evening had, what with one thing and then another, turned into 9:00 P.M. Thursday night and the reunion was a week from Friday—no time to waste.

The most pressing thing was to find the missing. No problem: Phone calls and patience would do the trick there. The most important thing was Sara, and that was more than just a problem: It was looking like a big fat loser. After reading her long-lost note, I'd known in my heart she had not committed suicide—that there must have been foul play. The old police file seemed to support this idea. Even Elvin Dance, whose opinion of my role, my abilities, my very existence, is not wholeheartedly positive—even Elvin agreed with me for once.

But what now? Whoever killed Sara had planned it well, caught a run of luck, benefited from a strangely lackadaisical police investigation, and gone uncaught for twenty-five years. How in the hell would good old smokin' jokin' Ben, ex-third baseman, ex-union enforcer, flush out the guilty?

I had no idea if I'd get anywhere. No point in fretting. I'd just fall back on my tried and true formula: a little of this, a little of that; push here, pull there, punch that one's lights out—whatever it takes; stir well, sit back, and watch what happens very, very carefully. . . .

I had a couple of moves planned for tomorrow. For tonight I decided to see if I could run a few more of the disappeared to ground. I had found a name on the alumni list and was about to dial when Stacie padded barefoot into the kitchen, yawning.

She had not put the camisole and bikini back on. Instead she wore a simple silk slip that clung to her sleek tanned skin, white with tiny little black dots, the kind you see after you've been whomped up side the head, except these didn't swim around. Since it was a sexual intermission, her heavy permed auburn hair was loose around her face and spilling over her bare shoulders; plus she'd put some hardware back on: a hair-thin gold chain around her neck, a cluster of gold bangles on her left wrist. "What are you doing?" she asked, yawning again as she padded my way.

"Trying to find some more of these missing alumni people," I said. "No time to waste."

"Pretty late for that, isn't it?" She sat down across the small dinette from me.

"Good time to catch people at home. 'Nother thing is, I'm hoping somebody on the alumni list can give me a lead on old man Gerbstadt. I need to see him if he's still around, find out what he can tell me about Sara and the suicide."

"Yes," Stacie said. "Mr. Gerbstadt," she said, eyes far away. "He taught me to sing."

"Uh-huh." When she didn't elaborate, I said, "I'll be here awhile. You can go back to bed if you want."

"That's all right. I've had enough bed, at least for the moment." Her light blue eyes found me. "Can I ask a question?"

"Shoot."

"Do you have a gun?"

CHAPTER 9

"Well, sure I do," I answered, surprised. "Why?"

"Can I see it?"

"How come, Stace?"

She gnawed her lip, her pose at the table curiously childlike and vulnerable. "I don't know, I've just always wanted to—I mean, you're a private detective and all, I figured you'd have one. So could I?"

I wasn't crazy about the idea, but on the other hand I saw no harm. I went back to the bedroom and retrieved my Colt .45 automatic from the shelf in the walk-in closet. Back in the kitchen I kicked out the clip, worked the action once to eject the round under the hammer, snapped the action shut, then handed the weapon to Stacie butt-first. "Both hands now. It's heavy."

"Oh," she breathed, hefting the ugly old monster in both tanned, soft, feminine hands. "Is it loaded?"

"No."

"Mm." Two-handed, she aimed the weapon toward the oven, made a gunshot noise, then held the piece in both hands, cradling it like a precious specimen. As she touched each oily bluish surface, the color rose in her cheeks and her light eyes brightened. It made me uneasy, but then, that's the way some people are; they get off on guns, think of them as pets or relics or something. To each his own. To me, guns are about as romantic as a crescent wrench.

While she entertained herself, I dialed the number listed for Linda Sue Atwater, now known, according to Stacie's alumni list, as Linda Sue Atwater Collinsworth Yerkey Smith, in River Rouge. The phone was answered after one ring by a loud female voice: "Yeah!"

"Mrs. Smith?"

"Well, I was," she barked, "but I threw the son of a bitch out of here last week. So I think I'll go back to Yerkey. I've got nine kids, but my youngest boy is a Yerkey."

"What's his first name?" I asked, unable to resist. "Beef?"

"Now, that really is pretty goddamn funny. Whoore you?"

"Perkins. Ben Perkins. I was in the same class as—"

"I remember you," she broke in, voice a hoarse bray. "You were the one stole the statue from Big Boy's and hung it from the tree in front of the school. Tell me sumpin. How'd you get that big heavy old bastard up there?"

Funny, the odds and ends that stick in people's memories. "Trade secret," I answered. "Listen, you know about the reunion next weekend, and I'm trying to find two girls who were in FHA with you. Norma Fay Dick and Paula Johnson. Can you—"

"Oh hell yes," she said. "They both live in Lincoln Park now, we're in the same bowling league." She gave me their phone numbers. "How's that?"

"Outstanding." Four down, six to go. "Listen, long as I've got you. Did you know Nicki Micklos?"

"Nicki? Nicki . . . I don't know, but I could swear I heard once she's dead. Don't ask me where or how, but that's what sticks in my memory."

I scribbled. "Willard Nolan? Somebody told me he joined the Merchant Marine. Did you—"

"Oh sure," she answered. "Willard was in Home Ec too, d'ya believe it? He went on to the Culinary Institute. Some kinda big-shot cooking school in New York somewhere. I'm positive about that."

"Hm." Big jump from Merchant Marine to the Culinary Institute. "How about Carl Hickson? So far I'm getting zero on him—"

"I dunno," she answered, "but he used to pal around with Kathy Lentz. You know her?"

I leafed through pages. "No, but I've got her number.

I'll check. Now. One more question. I need to pick your brains about Sara Gerbstadt."

"Oh yeah," Yerkey drawled, her raspy voice darkening with dislike. "Miss Hoity-Toity Tight-Ass, you should pardon my French."

"You knew her, huh?"

"Me? Know *her*? She was too hot-snot for a factory rat like *me*. But I knew who she was. Paradin' around the school with those snot-ass straight As and awards and shit, you should pardon my French."

I leaned back in my chair and kept my voice neutral. "There was a party the night before graduation—"

"At the Szewczklieuskis!" Yerkey said excitedly. "I was there! Were you there? I don't remember you there."

"I was there. Was Sara—"

"Come to think of it, weren't you the one punched out Don Triplett when he tried to crash the party?"

"We reasoned together. About Sara, I—"

"What a rat-bastard that Triplett was. Or is. Whatever."

"Do you remember Sara at all?"

"Eddie Anger was there," Yerkey went on, voice softening for the first time. "What a nice ass that boy had on him, you should pardon my French. Still does, too. He was on *Entertainment Tonight* a few—"

"It's Sara I'm interested in," I interrupted.

"I hope he's at the reunion. I hope he's got a thing for big fat girls. The things I could—"

"Please, Linda Sue. Sara Gerbstadt."

"Her?" Yerkey snorted. "She was pig-drunk that night, that much I know. All them brains and them good grades didn't help her hold her booze none. Morosin' around, hunching her bony little shoulders, playing Little Miss Poormouth."

I was a little depressed. Yerkey's memory was like everyone else's: selective. I hear there are people with total recall, but I haven't run into one yet. Ever. "That's all you remember?"

"They announced her makin' valedictorian that

night," Yerkey said disdainfully. "As if that cut any fuckin' mustard, you should pardon my French."

"Uh-huh. Anything else?"

"About the party? Not much. I got pretty bombed myself and I let this boy take—we went—he took me home." She cleared her throat noisily. "There is one other thing I remember, come to think of it. A couple of kids were upstairs fucking like rabbits."

"Huh?"

"Rabbits! Rabbits! They were fucking like rabbits," she insisted. "You should pardon my French! In the upstairs bathroom. I don't know who it was, but man, you could hear 'em ruttin' away, oo-AH, oo-AH, you know?"

"Well, that's real interesting," I said. "Thanks for all the—"

"Well, you're welcome!" she shouted. "See you at the reunion, huh?"

I hung up the phone, ears ringing from the hammering of Yerkey's voice. Stacie had left midway through my conversation, leaving just the faintest trace of scent in the air and my .45 automatic on the table. I picked it up aimlessly, reassured by the feel of its lethal weight filling my hand. Reloaded it, jacked a round into the chamber, carefully released the hammer. Then I set it down, looked up Kathy Lentz's number on Stacie's alumni list, and called.

She wasn't there, but her husband was. Almost incoherently drunk, he mistook me for one of Kathy's lovers and treated me to a lengthy and detailed preview of my hideous, gruesome, and very slow death. When I finally got through to him, he told me Kathy spent most nights at Whisperz lounge in Southfield, "third stool from the left."

When I called Whisperz, the duty bartender told me Kathy had "stepped out" and to try later. That finished it for the night. I locked up, shut down the lights, and walked down the hall toward the bedroom. Oddly enough, I found myself hoping that Stacie would be asleep. She wasn't.

At Norwegian Wood, Fridays are either a madhouse or a cakewalk. This one was cake. The assignment load had been light all week; the guys and I had squeezed them off as they'd come in; the chore list was up to date, and I was through for the day by ten o'clock. Yowsa.

My apartment was dead silent when I got back there. I strolled back to the bedroom to find Stacie still sacked out, twisted up in the sheets, snoring. Ah, romance. I went back out to the kitchen, sat down at the dinette, and began looking at my notes.

But my mind was not on the case. It was on Stacie. We'd been together three days now and I realized that I still knew very little about her. She could talk endlessly about movies, music, and junk novels, but she was very close-mouthed about herself. Any question about her job, her history, her relationships, she expertly blew off with a retort that was determinedly off-hand and usually off-color.

All I knew was what I observed. I knew she had tremendous appetites for food, tobacco, alcohol, clothes, sleep, and—most of all—sex. I knew that she spent her time shopping, reading, or watching TV. She seemed breezy and light-hearted most of the time, but every now and then I caught a whiff of the frantic too. Much of the time I felt I was an audience of one, witness to a never-ending series of moods that she marched across stage. I felt there was no halfway with her. Either she was exactly what she seemed—the ultimate party person—or she was the most total phony I'd ever met.

Well, all I can say is, for everyone else it may have been the dog days of summer. But for me it had become the summer of a fantasy fulfilled. Let's face it: Serious relationships are very nurturing and enriching and all that jazz. But sometimes you just want to play.

Okay. Down to it. Elvin had left a message on my box with the address of Billy Hammond, the detective who had closed the Gerbstadt suicide. I looked up the address and found it in the Fullerton-Livernois section on the near west side. This encouraged me, because it meant that Billy Hammond had been an honest cop, at least too honest to take a lot of money. If he'd been dirty, he'd be living out in Birmingham or West Bloomfield now.

After seeing him, I figured on hitting the old neighborhood. I planned to pound pavement and pull doorknobs. I needed to find someone who remembered the old days, who knew what had happened to Sara's family. While at it, I might as well try to get a lead on Agnes Ratchford, the cross-street neighbor who'd seen an unknown car parked in Sara's driveway shortly before she got home. Just for the record, I flopped the phone book open, buzzed through the pages, and—bingo: Ratchford, J. M., 21414 Santa Clara, Detroit.

Had to be the same. Still there, after all these years.

I threw together my notes hastily. Flatfoot first, I figured; then the old broad. Don't call first. Just drop in and zap 'em. Could be something to this. Could definitely be something.

I had my hand on the doorknob when the phone beckoned me back. I grabbed it. "Perkins On the Fly, Ben speaking."

"Yes," came the smooth voice, "good morning, Mr. Perkins. Sam Altman from Psytech. How are you?"

"Pretty good, doc." Since Psytech, a Plymouth shrink tank, was my only regular client, I carefully concealed my impatience.

"You sound rushed," Dr. Altman observed. "I'm sorry to inconvenience you, but there's an urgent investigation I need you to undertake at once. Are you free?"

"Not exactly, no."

"Dr. Spudd, our president, routed this in here," Dr. Altman said vaguely. "The object of the inquiry is a consultant prospect in Boston. Urgent. You'd have to go over there right away and get it done by—"

"Go over there? Since when do I go anywhere? Most of those things I do by phone."

"It is unprecedented, I agree. But Dr. Spudd's note is very specific," Dr. Altman said. "You must go to Boston and be back with a full report on this individual by the end of next week."

"Can't do it. Not if it's travel. I'm up to my ears."

"There might be a bonus in it for you."

"Still can't. I'm jammed."

"I see." His voice was guarded and distant. "Let me

confer with Dr. Spudd. I too am curious about the travel requirement. I'll get back to you, Mr. Perkins. Have a nice day."

Billy Hammond lived on Stoepel just west of Livernois, within a shout of the Jeffries Freeway to the north and the C&O tracks to the south. Like most 'hoods this far in, Hammond's was old: heaved sidewalks, cracked streets, skinny little driveways, and scrubby little thirty-foot plots of grass fronting high gaunt homes, houses, and burned-out hulks. Things weren't sleepy this August Friday: By the time I found Hammond's house I'd passed up chances to own some rock, a color TV, and a black girl who couldn't have been more than thirteen.

Hammond's house was a two-and-a-half story red brick job with a gray mansard roof and bright red shutters. I parked the Mustang on the driveway as close to the house as I could get and hoofed up to the door, wondering what it was like to be a white retired cop living in a neighborhood like this.

The storm door was protected by a grid of heavy steel bars. So, I noticed, were all the ground floor windows. In response to my knock, a male voice rasped through a tinny speaker mounted in the brick: "Yes, what is it?"

"Ben Perkins," I answered to the thin air. "Captain Dance at Homicide sent me. Said you might can help me with an old case."

"Just a moment."

I loitered for five full minutes. Two black men, young toughs about eighteen with Afro flat-tops and a slow, swaggering, menacing gait, appeared on the sidewalk, watching me closely as they drifted by. They did not respond to my smile and wave. Even my charm has its limitations. Finally I heard the clattering and clonking of bolts being worked and I turned to the door as it opened. "Come on in," the man said.

I did so. The man pushed the door shut behind me and worked the multiplicity of deadbolts and burglar bars again as I found myself standing in a very Victorian entryway, bright and clean and smelling of furniture polish.

Music sounded from somewhere, violins and stuff dancing merrily around each other. The man turned to me and stuck out his hand. "Billy Hammond."

"Ben Perkins." I glanced around. "Great place. Can't say as much for the neighborhood."

"There's worse," Hammond answered. "At least around here bullets generally go where they're aimed. Come on in."

I followed him through an archway into a small parlor. It faced the street and drew light from the high barred windows. The ceiling was very high, giving the impression that the room was as tall as it was wide. Everything looked Victorian in here, too: heavy wood furniture upholstered in green velvet, carpeting that looked like it was patterned with multicolored mating snakes, matching heavy drapes gathered back with gold ropes, mirrors, books and bric-a-brac on built-in shelves that hugged each corner of the parlor and surrounded the slate-faced fireplace. The music was louder in here, violins going berserk, bringing to mind cavorting elves or something like that. It gave me the shivers. "Mind if I smoke?" I asked.

"Not at all." Hammond stood by the fireplace and watched me. He looked to be in his mid-seventies, a short guy who probably just made the department minimum, but built like a bull with heavy shoulders, thick short arms, massive legs. He wore his straight silvery gray hair like a Roman emperor, as if cut from beneath the rim of a bowl. His eyes were lost beneath bundles of eyebrows in a flat leathery face that had been lots of places and had, even so, remained curiously untouched by them. He wore khaki trousers and a maroon sport shirt that stretched tight against his bowling-ball belly. "Cap'n Dance described you as a pain in the ass private dick," Hammond said in his husky tenor.

"Well, I'm private, anyhow." I flared my cigar. "You know Elvin?"

"No. Called him just now to check you out." He grinned, a spark of interest deep in those old watchful eyes. "So you've bumped into one of my old cases? How can I help?"

I gave him the essential details of the Sara Gerbstadt suicide: names, places, dates. Hammond listened politely, rocking on the balls of his feet, then took a seat in a brocade club chair and gestured me to its mate opposite a small end table from him. "I know it's been a lot of years," I concluded. "Remember anything about this one?"

Heavy brows furrowed, Hammond gnawed on a knuckle. "Well, ye-e-es. But why do I remember it? I worked thousands of cases, and that one—"

He looked away from me for a long moment as the violin music echoed off the plaster walls. When he looked back, his jaw was set, his eyes flashing. "The bitch! The loudmouth *bitch*!"

CHAPTER 10

"Bitch?" I asked, startled. "Who?"

"That bitch across the street," he said, gesturing crudely with blunt fingers. "That fuckin' eyewitness."

"Ratchford? Agnes Ratchford?"

"That withered old cunt! She damn near cost me a promotion!" Hammond was on his feet again, pacing the carpet to the archway and back, his harsh words an odd contrast to the prim music that filled the air. "Took a year to get her ass off my back!"

"Wait a minute, now. Hold it," I said, wishing I had a nickel for every time I've said that. "Let's start at the beginning."

He had his arms folded, gripping himself as if straitjacketed. "It was a suicide, right? Nice middle-class high school girl sucks gas and croaks. Open and shut. I bought into it. My lieutenant bought into it. The medical examiner bought into it. Even the girl's *parents* bought into it. But this woman, this *Ratchford,* could she let it go? No-o-o!"

I had my pad out, pen in one hand and smoldering cigar in the other. "What happened?"

Hammond stopped walking and did a mincing little dance. "There was another car there that night!" he said in falsetto.

"Right," I said. "According to the report, Ratchford said another car was parked in front a half hour before the victim got home."

The old detective spread his arms wide and cocked his head. "And that's all she had!" he said in a wondering voice. "This mysterious other car. No description. No plate number. No ID of any kind. Just this other car. From it this

Ratchford gash inferred all kinds of dreadful conspiracies. She kept trying to make a great big deal out of this nobody little tramp who just plain got herself knocked up, was stiffed by the daddy, and knocked herself off 'cause she was just like all the rest of 'em: She could dance to the music, but she couldn't pay the piper."

His description of Sara gave me a slow burn, but I kept a lid on it. He didn't know I had a personal interest in the case and he did not need to know. "No doubt in your mind, huh?"

He shook his head, shuffled to his chair, and dropped into it. At his age, you're capable of bursts of energy, but the years catch up with you quick. "But she wouldn't let it go," he said quietly. "Kept calling me. I told her the thing was closed. So she started calling my lieutenant, complaining about me, calling me incompetent. Complained to the newspapers, to the City Council, to Jerry Cavanagh even. Nobody really took her seriously, but it hurt my record, hurt my chances for promotion. Goddamn bitch."

And here you sit in this old house, I thought, stewing in the juices of the past. What a waste. "Let me ask you something," I said, careful to keep my voice neutral. "According to the report, the victim drove one car into the garage that night, but then used the other to gas herself. Does it really make sense to you that she'd do that?"

His eyes were glassy, plainly not remembering. "Does anything women do make sense?" he mused. "I knew a woman once who had two little kids, toddlers. During the swine flu epidemic she went out and nursed some sick neighbors. Caught it herself and died, leaving her little kids motherless. Does that make sense?"

"Well, I don't know," I said uncomfortably. "It's a tragedy, all right." I punctuated with a furious toke of cigar smoke. "Another thing about Sara is, she didn't use her own key to start the car that gassed the garage. Another key was used. That doesn't make much sense either."

Hammond was slouched in the club chair, head propped on fist, watching me. "Nothing women do makes much sense," he said. "I knew a woman who went partying at a bar on the Boulevard on V-E Day. Place caught fire.

Front doors were wide open, most of the people escaped that way. But seven, all women, ran to the back for some reason. Firemen found 'em in a charred pile up against a nailed-shut door. This woman I knew was at the bottom of the pile. She led them all there. Tell me what sense *that* makes."

"People panic," I answered. "It's hard to keep a level head in situations like that. Could we talk about the Gerbstadt case, please?" I went right on without waiting for an answer. "The file also theorizes that she lay down on the garage floor. Why would she do that, when she could have sat comfortably in the car? Makes no sense at all."

"One thing I learned on the street," Hammond said, "is that it all gets easier when you quit trying to make sense out of everything. Especially when women are involved." His eyes looked past me. "I knew a woman who was in college, smart as hell, honor roll student, whole world at her feet. Got herself tangled up with a motorcycle gang and ended up down in Tennessee, smeared all over U. S. 25 West in a rainstorm. That make any sense to you whatsoever?"

"Billy." He did not respond. "Billy!" He blinked and looked at me, complexion pasty. I understood how he felt. I could have matched him, story for story. But there was work to be done. I spoke very slowly. "Why would Sara lie down on the garage floor instead of staying in the car?"

To my surprise, he answered immediately. "We figured she started out sitting in the car but changed her mind at the last minute. Suicides often do that, you know. She tried to escape but was too far gone."

"But they had an automatic garage door opener. If Sara wanted out, why didn't she just mash the remote button to open the door?"

"It was broken." Hammond's face brightened, as if he was astonished that he remembered that so readily. "It was broken," he repeated. "The techs had to disassemble part of the motor so they could get the door open. I remember that. It held up the detectives, the medics, the lab people, everybody."

I jotted down some words, mentally playing with the

thing, turning it this way and that. Ooh, yes. I was beginning to see it now. "Suicide?" I asked quietly. "No doubt in your mind?"

He heaved a deep sigh. "Whatever the file says. . . . Look, I know I'm not much help. And I'm sorry. But Christ, man, it's been all kinds of years. You know how many squeals I handled after that? How many dumb dead girls I—"

I got to my feet. "Yep. Well, I appreciate your help. All right if I get back to you if—"

He stood too, weary, stooped. "Sure. Fine," he said listlessly. "I'm always here. Where you headed now?"

"Out to Old Redford," I answered as we headed for the door. "Going to visit your friend Ms. Agnes Ratchford. Still lives in the same house, believe it or not." Hell of a break, I thought; but on a case this old I'll take all the breaks I can get.

The sound of Ratchford's name darkened and soured Hammond's face. "That bitch!" he said poisonously. "Well, be sure not to give her my best. And listen, Perkins," he added as he began the unlocking ceremony.

"Yeah?"

"Good luck with her," he jibed, eyes grimly amused. "She was a fruitcake back then. Something tells me time hasn't improved her any."

Lunch was the usual fare—a Burger Barn double cheeseburger with everything, onion rings, an icy Stroh's—consumed in the usual place: behind the wheel of the Mustang. I found a shady spot on a residential street just north of Grand River at Outer Drive, cranked down the windows, cranked up Bobby Bland on the cassette deck, and scanned my notes as I ate.

Hammond had been more help than I had any right to expect. The key was the automatic garage door opener. Broken, he'd said firmly. Well, okay. But it had obviously been working just fine when Sara arrived at the house that night. Otherwise she wouldn't have been able to drive the station wagon in.

Then, once she was inside and the door was closed, the

opener had, like magic, sort of quit working all of a sudden. Coincidence?

Could have been. But maybe not. Maybe someone, such as the driver of the "mysterious car" reported by Agnes Ratchford, had gimmicked the garage door opener. Started up the father's car and left it to fill the garage with carbon monoxide. Sara had rolled her mother's car inside and the door had closed behind her, shutting her in a pitch black lethal gas chamber.

Aside from the minor detail of having no solid evidence whatsoever, the theory felt pretty good. And if I was anywhere close to right, then this had been no impulse killing. The job had taken premeditation. Ruthlessness. Fury. I thought through the people I knew, flipping by their mental file cards one by one, looking for a match or anything even close. No one but Don Triplett felt even remotely like a possible, and that I was honest enough with myself to admit was because I'd never liked him.

Oh well, I thought, as I disposed of the lunch leavings. I ought to be used to this by now. It's detective work: uncertainty wrapped up in ambivalence, supposition buttressed by good solid guesswork. Tough business. Add to that the fact that twenty-five years had passed, knocking off witnesses and clouding memories that were not all that reliable to begin with. This case, I thought as I fired up the Mustang, is impossible to solve. Face it.

But I wouldn't let a detail like that slow me down. I may have started the hunt twenty-five years late, but I was in it to stay.

Old Redford is a section of extreme northwest Detroit which was part of Redford Township till it was annexed by the city back in the 1920s. It is, and always has been, pretty much a bedroom community, innumerable blocks of bungalow style homes interrupted at uniform intervals by the commercial strips of Seven Mile, McNichols, Telegraph, and Lahser, with Grand River slashing through from northwest to southeast.

I hadn't been back there in years, except to pass through, and I wasn't shocked at the changes. It's what you find when you get past the high tech, chrome, and glass PR palaces to the "real" Detroit, which is an insidious blend of more and less: more crime, exploitation, litter, despair; less work, money, maintenance, ambition; no hope.

Santa Clara runs east off Lahser about a block north of Grand River. The former Gerbstadt house, an overgrown two-story white clapboard bungalow, sat on the south side of Santa Clara a few doors up from Bentler. I parked at the curb in front of it and gave it the quick once-over as I got out of the Mustang; I especially eyed the garage door, closed now, innocent looking. But I did not approach. No point.

Agnes Ratchford's house, across the street, was a big Georgian built of multicolored brick with a gray-shingled, side-gabled roof, white shutters, and a chimney at the east end. A single large tree hogged one corner of the small lot; a detached brick garage occupied another, and a chain link gate guarded the single car driveway which ran in two concrete strips from the street to the garage.

I mounted the steps to the front door and knocked. The neighborhood was quiet around me, simmering in the August heat. It had that familiar feel of school starting soon. For an instant I felt the pull of a long-gone home, and I pushed it away. No time for that. Never time for that.

To my surprise, the door swung open all the way without any security preliminaries. The woman was a tiny little birdlike person, very old but sturdy looking. Her hair was light blue and all hers—a wig would have been thicker and fuller. She wore a dark blue house dress that looked new. Her deeply lined face was a composite of angles: prominent cheekbones, sharp eyes, nose, and chin. "Yes? Good afternoon," she said brusquely, voice a rasping chirp. "What is it?"

"Mrs. Ratchford? I'm Ben Perkins. I used to live—"

"On Bennett Street," she said immediately, with a long appraising look. "I remember you. You have a sister named Libby and a brother named Bill and your Uncle Dan died a couple years ago, I saw it in the papers."

I whistled. Maybe at last I'd found that elusive person with total recall. If so, I'd never tell anyone, especially the other detectives around town. "Amazing memory, ma'am. Especially since I don't recall that we were ever introduced—"

"We weren't," she retorted. "But that doesn't matter. I knew everyone and about everything that went on in this neighborhood. Made it my business to. Still do." She smiled. "You were the one having a love affair with Annie Wilder."

While trying to regain the use of my tongue, I concealed my astonishment by blinking and clearing my throat. "Wow. You're kidding. Nobody ever knew about that. Not even my friends."

"That's right," she said, matter-of-fact. "Even her husband didn't know. But I knew. Didn't approve, mind you. Heavens! Seventeen-year-old boy and a woman near forty!"

Thirty-four, I said to myself. Annie was thirty-four. She told me so. So today she'd be—oh, Christ! "Long time ago," I murmured.

"Well!" Mrs. Ratchford said. "What do you want? I don't imagine you're here to reminisce about the 'good old days,' back when we weren't the only white people left for blocks around."

"That's sort of why I'm here. If you've got time, I'd—"

"I've got all sorts of time. Then again," she corrected herself, "I'm eighty-five, so I probably have hardly any." She beckoned with a clawlike hand. "Come in, come in."

I followed her as she walked slowly but purposefully through the parlor and the kitchen and out the back door onto a screened porch that ran the width of the house. It overlooked the back yard, which was in fact a meticulously landscaped flower garden surrounded by high hedges on three sides. The drone of bees was audible in the porch and the heat was so oppressive I began to sweat under my sport shirt. Mrs. Ratchford didn't seem to notice it, but then people her age have a higher tolerance for heat than I do. "Beautiful place, ma'am."

"Thank you. May I serve you something to drink?"

"A cold beer'd be just about perfect right now, thanks."

"You may have either iced tea or fruit juice."

"On second thought, make it tea. Much obliged."

"Have a seat. I'll be right back." She left. I toured the porch, then took a seat on a white ornate wicker chair that had been painted so many times there was hardly any pattern left and no give to it at all. Mrs. Ratchford came back with a wood tray bearing a large tumbler of iced tea. "Beer isn't good for you," she told me. "My husband Junius stopped drinking beer in 1950 and look at him now, hale and hearty."

"Good for him. Where is he now?"

"Napping." She eased herself into the wicker chair at an angle to mine, facing away from the afternoon sun. "You smoke, don't you?"

"Cigars. How did you know?"

"You reek of it, of course. Reminds me of the old Goodyear plant. Please don't smoke here. Now: What do you want?"

I drank some tea. It was very strong and unsweetened, sort of like its maker. "I'm a private detective by trade, and I've been asked to investigate the Sara Gerbstadt suicide," I answered. "You no doubt remember all about that."

She nodded. "I thought you were probably engaged in some sort of enforcement. You have that look about you, hardened and wary. And of course I remember the matter. But it was no suicide, of course. It was murder."

CHAPTER 11

Her tone was offhand and certain, the voice of one unaccustomed to being disputed. I wondered how Junius had handled her all those years. My guess was that he took a lot of naps. "Why do you say that?"

"The other car, of course." Annoyance crept into her voice. "Haven't you talked to the police or researched the matter or anything?"

"Yes on all counts. But I want to hear about it from you, in your own words."

"It's a terrible waste of your time. I'll just be repeating everything I told them back then."

"I'll bear up under it somehow," I said, getting out my pad.

She overlooked my irony, if that's what it was. "Very well. Mr. and Mrs. Gerbstadt had gone away for the night. Out of town, I believe. They—"

"Did you know them well?"

"Didn't know them at all," she shot back. "They had a dog, you see. A small mongrel with dirty habits. It violated my flower beds, so I had it collected by the pound. The Gerbstadts took offense and snubbed me after that. A small price to pay. Anyway," she said, waving a hand, "all that is irrelevant. Please don't interrupt me again."

"Sorry."

Mrs. Ratchford got that faraway look in her eyes, the thousand yard stare that I was getting used to seeing on the faces of people traveling back twenty-five years. "Sara went out, of course. I learned later that she'd gone to a party. At eleven o'clock I saw a car stop in front of the Gerbstadt house. It was definitely not one of their cars. So, naturally, I watched."

"Pardon me, ma'am. What kind of car was it?"

"I have no idea. I don't concern myself with such things."

"I see. How do you know it was eleven? Could it have been later or earlier?"

"I am very precise about time. Time is our only real resource, did you know that?"

I looked up from my pad and into her sharp eyes. "What grade did you teach?"

She blinked. "Third. How did you know?"

"Lucky guess."

She rushed on. "There's no doubt about the time. I remember vividly. *The Law and Mr. Jones* had just ended, and the news had come on with Dick Westerkamp."

"I'll take your word for it."

"Of course. If I may continue?" Her silence forced me to nod. "Thank you. I saw someone walk from the car to the Gerbstadt garage and go in the side door. A few moments later, the person came back out. Got into the car and drove away."

"How long after that did Sara return?"

"About half an hour. I know that," she added, stopping me with a look, "because the *Hollywood Movie* had just come on Channel 7. Dana Andrews in *Canyon Passage.* Junius enjoys his Westerns on Friday nights."

"Sure it wasn't *The High Rocks*?" I murmured.

"I'm sure," she said tartly. "For one thing, there's no such movie."

The cubes had melted in my tea. I took a big hit and tipped my head back, watching the bees frolic among the flowers outside. I did not for a moment believe that her memory was this good, but I decided to humor her. "You remember everything so clearly. With such detail. Yet you're unable to describe the visitor."

"Of course not. It was night time. The car drove under a street light on its way out. But there were no lights near the Gerbstadt driveway. All I saw of the visitor was a shape, a blurry shape."

"What about the car?"

"I told you, I—"

"Not the make. Just some other details. Had you ever seen it before?"

"No."

"Was it from around the neighborhood here?"

"Asked and answered, Mr. Perkins."

"Just trying to jog your memory, ma'am."

"My memory is just fine. It needs no jogging, thank you, so don't waste time practicing your interrogator's tricks on me."

"Okay. As best you can, describe the car for me."

"It was light-colored. Long and low and very wide."

"Fins?"

"No. Absolutely not."

"Means it was pretty new. Fins were dying out at that time. Tell me more."

She twisted her gnarled fingers and said in a rare plaintive tone, "Oh, how I wish I could draw! I can see it in my mind so perfectly. The headlights, the grille. But describing it—"

I had a brainstorm. "Can you take a little ride with me?"

She eyed me archly. "Where?" I told her. "Certainly. We could *walk* there, you know. Walking is very good for you. Don't you believe in exercise, big strong young man like you?"

"I'm like Neil Armstrong," I said, grinning. "Said God only gave him so many heartbeats and he wasn't going to waste any of them by huffing and puffing and running around."

"I find it highly unlikely that a hero like Neil Armstrong ever said any such thing," she said as she stood up slowly. "Let's go."

I followed her into the kitchen. "What about Junius?"

"Mr. Ratchford always naps till *Sally Jessy.* He won't even know we've been gone."

The Old Redford branch of the Detroit Public Library sits next door to Redford High on the southwest corner of the angle intersection of McNichols and Grand River. It's a two-story fieldstone building with a steep-pitched slate roof, high narrow windows, red ivy growing up the west side, and 1925 engraved above the door: one of the few libraries left that still looks like one.

Mrs. Ratchford was shaking her head as I helped her out of the Mustang. "Such a noisy car! Don't the police arrest you for driving without a muffler, Mr. Perkins?"

"They're glass-packs, ma'am. Important in a high performance engine like mine. Reduces back-pressure and—"

"Thank you for sharing that with me, Mr. Perkins."

Holding my arm with one hand and her purse with the other, the old woman led me at her slow, sturdy pace into the library. It was dim inside, dim and cool, redolent of the thousands of books which lined rows of shelves on the ground and mezzanine level. All was quiet except for the occasional rustling footstep or echoing whisper; airborne dust glowed in the refracted sunlight beamed through the tall narrow windows.

The librarian's counter, a long polished wooden beauty, ran along the left. At our appearance a very young man with short dark hair, Buddy Holly glasses, a bow tie, and translucent white skin rose from a desk and came over to us. "Yes?" he asked, eyes flickering back and forth. "May I help you?"

"Yeah, we're looking for cars," I began.

"This is a library," he pointed out.

"Books about cars, okay? With pictures. Late fifties to early sixties. Do you have anything like that?"

"Of course. This is a library. Any particular make?"

"Ford, for sure. GM and Chrysler, too."

He pointed past us. "Second row on the left, very bottom shelf with the oversized books. It's all there. If you have any problems, feel free to inquire of me."

Mrs. Ratchford had seated herself at one of the large oak study tables. I retrieved several books, lugged them to the table, flopped the first one open, and leafed through the heavy glossy pages of General Motors products. "No fins?" I whispered.

"Well, just little tiny ones," she answered.

I found 1959. "Start here."

She studied the pages, leafing from one to the next

with her gnarled old hand. When she reached 1962, I stopped her. "Forget it. Nothing there?"

"Nothing even close."

I pushed that book aside and opened the Ford book. She started with 1959 again and squinted at the pages of black-and-white photos. When she reached 1962, I stopped her again. "Nothing, huh?" I asked. "I was hoping for Ford, but—"

"Oh, I found it," she answered. "I just decided to look for the car that Junius bought me later that year. Such a nice cream color it was."

"You found it? The car you saw that night? Where?"

"SHHHHH," came the librarian's voice.

"Where?" I whispered to the woman.

She turned back four pages and pointed to a picture in the lower left-hand corner. It was a publicity shot of a 1961 Ford Thunderbird convertible with the top down and a blond woman seated behind the wheel. "Convertible? You didn't mention that before," I said.

"It had the top up," she said.

"Then how can you be sure it—"

She pointed to a photo on the next page of a T-Bird hardtop. "The roof line looks a little different. Straighter."

"You're sure about this?" I asked, tempted to duck.

She eyed me coldly. "I'm sure. Now, if I may, I want to find the car my Junius bought me."

As she turned pages, I took a deep breath and let it out slowly. Could she have gotten the model wrong? Unlikely. Nothing else looked much like a T-Bird. Odds were she'd gotten the year right, too; the '61 was an almost completely different style from its predecessors.

I found myself hoping she was wrong. Because I knew that car, or one virtually identical to it. I may not remember a face for long, but I never forget a car. . . .

On our way out, the librarian asked, "Find what you wanted?"

"Yes, thanks." I stopped. "Something else you might be able to help me with. Or maybe not."

"This is a library," he said. "If it's on paper, I can help you."

"Automatic garage door openers," I said. "Got anything technical on 'em?"

He was scribbling. "Not here. But I'll put out an inquiry through the system. I'm sure there's something available somewhere in the city, and when it comes in I'll call you. Name?"

I gave him the information and escorted Mrs. Ratchford out. "What was that about, Mr. Perkins?" she asked as we drew near the Mustang.

"Oh, the cops found the garage door opener broken that night. Maybe it did just break all by itself. Or maybe it was tampered with. Gimmicked. Maybe with some technical literature I can figure out how it was done."

I opened the door and helped her into the passenger seat. Her eyes were on me all the while. "Then you believe me?" she asked abruptly. "You believe that someone murdered her?"

I got in the driver side and fired up the motor, being careful not to gun it. "I think so," I said finally. "I've got a notion of how it could have been done. The main thing is, I knew the girl, see. I just don't think she'd kill herself."

Mrs. Ratchford was nodding. "Which means someone robbed her, and those who loved her, of all those years. A wicked, wicked thing. You must find out who did it. You must see that justice is done."

I pulled out of the library lot, shot across McNichols and north on Bentler. "I'm trying, ma'am. It'd help if I could talk to other people who knew the Gerbstadts. Any ideas?"

"None. Everyone's gone. We're the last ones left on the street. For blocks around, in fact."

"How about the parents? Any idea where I can find them?"

"Mrs. Gerbstadt passed away in 1969," the old woman answered promptly. "I don't know what became of Mr. Gerbstadt. One day his house was for sale and the next day, or so it seemed, he was gone. I never bothered to find out more; I hardly knew them. Mr. Perkins," she said, bearing down on me with her old eyes, "I want that girl's killer found and I'll do anything I can to help."

"Okay. Best thing you can do is to think real hard about that stranger you saw. See if you can remember any details about what he looked like. Any details at all."

" 'He'?" she retorted. "When did I ever say it was male?"

I sighed. "Never."

"It could just as easily have been female. The light was bad, I told you that."

You'd have needed an ax to punch holes in the cigarette smoke. It hung in the living room as thick as a winter coat, undisturbed by any cross-breeze of the June evening air from outside. People were dancing to the driving beat of Del Shannon, but there was a skip in the record and it kept blasting "RUN-RUN-RUN-RUN-RUN, RUNAWAY" over and over.

I was drunk, bleary, agitated. I wanted to look for Eddie. But I couldn't get free of Al Hooker. He was right in my face yammering something about George Thomas. "Why'd Scheffing put Thomas in to run for Maxwell? What an idiot. He lost the game for us. Do you believe it, Benjy? Do you believe it?"

I squinted at him. "You're dead, Al."

Al did not react. "If Thomas had just stayed put, maybe somebody would've driven him in. Now we'll never know."

"I'm standing here talking to a dead person. You died of cancer in '81, Al. What are you doing here?"

"Of course," Al said, "if Foytack hadn't given up that home run, then we'd have—"

"Ben," came Sara's voice. I turned. I could not tell what she was wearing. The noise of the music and the dancers seemed to overwhelm everything. She was pale, anxious, unsteady on her feet. Her hand felt clammy as she gripped my arm. "Ben, I want you to take me home. Can you take me home?"

"Where's Fast Eddie?" I asked her. I saw Janet coming down the stairs, smiling; she gave me a wave with her fingers to signify that she wasn't mad at me anymore. "Where'd Fast go, Sara?"

"Please take me home," she answered, weaving. "I feel awful."

"Sara, you got a car here, right? It's just a couple of blocks—"

"Please, Ben."

"Foytack," Al told me. "Scheffing, Osborne, Boros. WWJ 950, the world's first radio station, total radio in Detroit."

"Sara—"

"I want to go home . . . please take me home . . ."

Then abruptly I hurtled through a membrane into a different world, the world of my bedroom in the dim morning light: clothes scattered, sheets tangled, Stacie a snoring, damp naked mound next to me. I rolled off the bed and wobbled upright, blinking grainy eyes, wincing at the pounding beginning of a gigantic and well-deserved hangover headache: Symphony in Agony for Timpani and Bass Drum. Saturday morning. 10:12, the orange clock numerals told me. The room wobbled and then righted. You did it again, idiot, I thought. Messed up Saturday by getting totally shitfaced Friday night.

But, I thought as I stumbled into the bathroom, it had been fun, anyway. I introduced Stacie to Under New Management, the saloon where every night is Friday night and every Friday night is New Year's Eve. We danced to the juke and sucked down pitchers, played some Foosball, heckled old friends, closed the place down, and then came back here for a session of the horizontal bop. My buddies had been impressed with Stacie. I could see it in their faces. What they didn't know was that if this affair kept up for much longer, it was going to kill me. I'd probably get planted with a big smile on my face, but I'd be dead anyway. O death, as W. C. Fields asked: Where is thy sting?

As I stepped out of the shower, the dream came back to me in one intense moment, then drained away rapidly, leaving only the memory of Sara's pale, anxious face and the sound of her voice and the names of some old Detroit

Tigers players running over and over again in my mind. "Please take me home." Had that really happened? Had she asked me to take her home? If so, I must have blown her off. This is just dandy, I thought. Now I can feel guilty, in addition to frustrated, over Sara's death.

I shaved and dressed in black denim pants, red pullover shirt, and navy blue sneakers. I'd just finished when I heard Stacie call from the bed.

I went in there. She was lying on her chest, uncovered. She'd have been the very vision of a Playboy centerfold if she hadn't had such an agonized look on her face. She called again, unintelligibly, somewhere between a shout and a long groan. Her legs spasmed, her fists clenched and unclenched, her head twisted to and fro under its mop of auburn hair. A nightmare, and not the first one, either; she'd woken me up at least twice each night.

I went to the bed and put both hands gently on her shoulders. "Stacie," I murmured. "Come on, darlin', it's all right."

She froze, then spun herself out of my grip, eyes open and wild. "Don't touch me!" she said hoarsely.

"You all right?"

I saw her throat working as she came up on her elbows and edged away from me on the bed, her expression calculating. "Don't hurt me," she said.

"Stacie!" I said sharply. "Wake up!"

Her eyes seemed to roll in their sockets, then steadied with a fresh awareness. She sagged down on the bed, her face suddenly much older. "Oh God," she moaned. "What time is it?"

"Pushing eleven. You okay?"

"Don't look at me," she said, face averted. "I feel like shit and I look worse. Go away."

"Can I get you anything?"

"No! Leave me alone! Go away, Goddamn it!"

I reached out and felt her pillow. Soaking wet, no doubt from tears. "Okay," I answered. "Coffee's on when you're ready."

I walked up the hall, mind troubled by dark thoughts that always seem to accompany a first-class hangover. Who the hell are you, Stacie? Where have you been? What's happened to you? And, behind the glib chatter, what are you really thinking?

Chapter 12

Out in the kitchen, I built myself a mug of timer-triggered joe, rescued the newspaper from the front door, and sat down to read. A pot of coffee and a couple of cigars put me in the right frame of mind for the day—what was left of it. It was almost lunchtime already.

Stacie bustled into the kitchen just as I started looking over the list of missing alumni. "Good morning," she sang, then swarmed me for a long, slow kiss. Her thick auburn hair was perfection once again; she smelled fragrantly clean, and she wore yet another outfit designed to drop off at a mere touch: a blue chambray part-shirt, part-dress; it buttoned up the front and its hem, which looked like shirttails, brushed the tops of her brown knees. Its three buttons along her sternum strained under the pressure of her breasts; to provide additional support she wore a supple brown belt snugly against her belly. Her light blue eyes were luminous and dancing as she smiled at me. "Lover," she said in an appreciative tone. "We about wrecked the place last night, didn't we?"

"No damage that a couple gallons of coffee won't cure," I said, studying her. "Help yourself."

"No thanks." She walked a slow, idle circle, stretching herself in what looked like isometric dance exercises. "So what are you up to today?"

"Got to try to track down a few more of our vanished classmates," I said, firing up a fresh cigar. "Reunion's Friday, you know."

"I know," she said indifferently. "Are you getting anywhere?"

"Six to go."

"Not them," she said, pulling a face. "The Gerbstadt thing."

"Oh. Well, I've got a little of this and a little of that. I need to talk to people who were at that party. I need to track down her father if I can."

"Mr. Gerbstadt," she said, for no reason I could think of. "Well," she said brightly, "sounds like you've got your hands full. I'm going to go crawl the mall for awhile."

"Be back soon?"

"I don't know," she said, and smiled craftily. "Why?"

"This afternoon I'm going to Ann Arbor to see Rich Satterfield. Classmate of ours, remember him?"

She gnawed her lip. "Chubby little kid with glasses? Always wore a slide rule on a holster from his belt?"

"That's him. He's a big-shot computer man now. If you're back by three or so, we can go see him together, get some supper afterward."

Her face fell. "I'll try," she said vaguely.

"Okay. Enjoy." Something occurred to me. "What about your house? You check up on that gas leak or whatever?"

She cocked her head and walked toward me slowly. "What is this?" she asked huskily. "You trying to run me out?"

"Hell, no. Just nosy."

She bent and kissed me again, fingertips gently tracing the line of my jaw. "See you later," she whispered.

"Oh yeah." She waved, walked out, and a moment later I heard the apartment door click shut behind her.

I sat there and smoked my cigar and stared at the alumni list with its hen scratches and doodles. But I was not studying or planning or even thinking about the task at hand. Instead, I was engaged in a mental conflict between ethics and curiosity. And, as usual, curiosity won.

Back in the bedroom I began going through Stacie's things. First I searched the dresser drawers she'd taken over. They were packed full of summer clothes, all of them colorful and borderline scanty and very new looking. Several even had store tags still on them. Odd that she had not packed any of her older things, but I had no idea what that meant or if, in fact, it meant anything at all.

In the back of one of the drawers I found a heavy, highly polished wood box stuffed to popping with jewelry. I'm no expert, but it all looked real enough to me. If so, it had to be thousands and thousands of dollars worth. I wondered, and not for the first time, about her money. She'd always been blithely elusive about its source. Did she inherit it, marry it, work for it, or what?

Next I checked her toiletries. It was a truckload of stuff that occupied damn near half of the bathroom vanity: several kinds of shampoo, conditioner, and mousse; lipsticks, eye shadow, mascara, eyeliner, blush, pancake, several shades of fingernail polish; cold cream, shaving cream, baby powder, deodorant, mouthwash, toothpaste, douches; tools and implements such as tweezers, scissors, emery boards, compacts, disposable razors, six combs, and four brushes; and appliances, including a warm-air comb, curling iron, curling brush, and blow dryer. Add to all that a profusion of hair clips, rollers, pins, barrettes, and miscellaneous junk, and what I had was a hell of a big mess—but what I *didn't* have was anything even remotely suspicious, at least so far as I could determine after examining each object carefully.

That left only her luggage. It was all in the walk-in closet. The two string bags lay empty on the floor; the suitcases were stacked against the wall. I popped open the first suitcase; empty. Tried the second one: locked. Hefted it and shook it and heard objects rattling around inside.

Hm.

I could have taken my .45 off the closet shelf and shot the lock open. But I didn't want to tip Stacie off. I also didn't want to waste a perfectly good bullet. I found a bobby pin in the bathroom, bent it straight, and used it to worry the el-cheapo lock till it gave up and popped open. Then I threw the latches, opened the suitcase, and examined the contents without touching anything for several minutes.

I was not surprised, at least not very.

There were hundreds of them, a real assortment. Pills,

capsules, and tablets; green ones, red ones, yellow and blue ones; some in bottles, some in baggies, many floating around loose in the suitcase. I scanned the prescription labels. Three listed Stacie as the patient. The others were for names which I did not recognize. The prescriptions were filled at various pharmacies, mainly big, anonymous chain operations like Perry, Arbor, and K mart, from all over metropolitan Detroit—as far west as Ann Arbor, as far east as Mount Clemens. I did not recognize any of the drug names but I got the general idea of their purpose from the words used to describe them: "For pain." "For tension." "For anxiety." "For nervousness." Fer sher.

I retrieved my pad from the kitchen and made note of the drug names. I took a sample of each of the unidentified medications, put them in a conveniently empty baggie, and stuffed it in my pocket. Then I locked up the suitcase, put it back where I found it, and went out to the phone.

Eric Chwalik was in a meeting and could not return my call till late afternoon. I left my apartment and car phone numbers with his secretary. Then I sat there for a few minutes, feeling the hard beating of my heart. Who am I to judge? I thought. Everybody has his or her shit and I have mine. I was suffering its aftereffects at that very moment. I was even thinking about grabbing the hair of the dog by means of the quart of Stroh's dark waiting in the fridge.

But this was just one more thing, one more unanswered question to add to the mix, one more element of what was, I could see, becoming less of a thrill and more of a problem. Eventually I'd have to deal with it.

Not now, though. I had a lot to do before going out to see Rich Satterfield. I picked up the phone, consulted Stacie's alumni list, and dialed a number in Harper Woods. It answered with an almost inaudible grunt: "Yes."

"Lew Ferguson, please."

"This is."

"Ben Perkins, Lew. Don't know if you remember me or not." I paused. "You and I were in the same class at Redford High together."

After a long wait he said, "Ben Perkins? I don't remember you from Adam, bud. What do you want?"

"Well, you've heard about the reunion next week. I'm—"

"I'm not going. I told that bimbo that when she called."

"That's not what this is about, exactly—"

"Thirty bucks a head to go all the way out to Novi for watered-down beer and warmed-over wieners swimming in hot ketchup! Pretty damn steep," he spat. "I'm in the concrete pipe business and the concrete pipe business, in case you haven't been keeping up, is lousy."

"Look," I pressed. "I've been hired to find some missing classmates, and I heard you know some of them."

"Oh yeah?" he asked suspiciously.

"They were in the Pep Club with you."

"I was the president."

"I know you were. That's why I'm—"

"That club wasn't nothing till I took it over. Mr. Richman told me it was the best pep club ever, while I ran it."

"I'm sure it was. Now, there were two people—"

"Said I was a natural born leader. That's what he called me, a natural born leader."

"A lot of people still remember that," I said, rolling my eyes. "These two people were in the club with you, and now we can't—"

"That's what I've brought to the concrete pipe business, natural born leadership. But natural born leadership doesn't help an absolutely lousy business like the goddamn concrete pipe business, which pretty much sucks these days."

"Kendall Gray," I said loudly. "June Jones. Any idea where they are?"

"Ken?" he said, surprised. "Ken works for me in the concrete pipe business here. The two of us bought my father out. Paid too much for it, I might add. Way too much. The old son of a bitch still cackles about it in his condo down in Port St. Lucie. Because the concrete pipe business is so goddamn bad, you see."

"I've heard that," I said, writing "Ferguson" next to

Gray's name. How about that, another one accounted for. "What about June Jones?"

"Her I don't remember any better than I remember you. Ben Perkins, you said your name is? What activities were you in?"

"The B's."

"Whassat? I don't remember anything like that."

"Beers, broads, and baseball. Now c'mon, Lew. June Jones. Think hard."

"I toldja, no idea!" he flared.

"All right," I said through gritted teeth. "Couple more names. Willard Nolan."

"Owns a beer distributorship in eastern Kentucky. Based in Ashland, I believe."

"You sure?" This hardly seemed related to the Culinary Institute and the Merchant Marine. Either we weren't all talking about the same guy, or the man's career was nearly as checkered as mine. "I've heard different."

"Sure I'm sure," he shot back. "You through yet? I got to get back to the pain-in-the-ass concrete pipe business."

"Two more names. Nicki Micklos."

"Nicki? Yeah, I know about Nicki," he snickered.

"What about her? Where is she?"

"Dead."

This confirmed what Yerkey had told me. "I see."

"She worked at the Parris Restaurant's main food processing plant in Rochester," he said. "Fell into a giant vat of gravy and drowned."

"Oh," I said. I shut my eyes very tightly, gave myself a long moment, then went on. "Last name. Carl Hickson."

"Carl? You mean you don't know about Carl?"

"No," I said sharply. "Care to share it with me?"

He laughed. "I think I'll just let you find out for yourself."

"Come on, Lew," I said, at the very edge of my patience. "I'm not into games. Just tell me."

"Nah, I don't think so," he said, and hung up.

Muttering, I got up from the table, grabbed the quart of Stroh's dark from the fridge, stretched, drank, and sat back down. More paperwork. Jesus, I'd never seen a case with such paperwork. I updated my notes on the missing alumni; ten down now, three to go. Only six days left. I had a feeling I'd never track them down. The word on Nolan was conflicting and unreliable; too much information is like none at all. As for Jones, no one knew anything about her. I flipped open the yearbook again. Their youthful faces looked forlorn to me, as if prefiguring their quiet disappearance. God knows, God knows what can happen to people in twenty-five years.

That left Carl Hickson. Ferguson knew about Hickson, but would not tell. I'd left word with Kathy Lentz, ostensibly a pal of Hickson's, and had never heard back. I tried her house again and got no answer. Called Whisperz in Southfield and left word for her there again. Best I could do, by phone, anyway.

I lighted a cigar. My notes were arrayed on the table in front of me. I scooped them up, shuffled them, and dealt them out again. No inspiration struck. The party, that damned party at the Bubbas's house—that had to be a key. That was Sara's last stop before she went home. Whoever murdered her had to have known about the party, had incorporated the party into the planning, had probably even *been* at the party.

Whoever it was had sat there and watched us, had used us as unwitting accomplices. In fact, whoever it was could have been *one* of us.

Nasty thought.

CHAPTER 13

I remembered more about the party now than I had a few days before. At least I thought I did. But I needed to find out more. I took a fresh sheet of paper and began listing the names of everyone I could remember who was there. Fast Eddie Anger, Janet Vento, Richie Satterfield, and Sara, of course. Don Triplett, briefly. Al Hooker and the Bubbas, since deceased. No more names. Plenty of faces—fleeting black-and-white shadows, half-glimpsed and gone, with no handles to them, no names at all. Except for one. One more. I got my hands around the squirming shape and pulled it out of the murk to where I could see it. Muhleman. Gary Muhleman. Old Gary had been there, sure enough. And I actually knew where he was. I'd done business with him, down through the years.

I found the number in the phone book and dialed. "WorldWide Auto Parts, West Detroit office."

"Hey, Gary, Perkins here, how's tricks?"

"If you'll hold, I'll connect you with Mr. Muhleman's office," Gary said. I sat back in my chair, puffing at my cigar, till Gary came back on. "This is Gary Muhleman. May I help you?"

"Perkins here," I repeated. "Who're you trying to kid?"

"What are you talking about?"

"Your little phone games. And what's with the 'West Detroit office' bullshit?"

"My house is east of here," he said defensively. "That makes this my West Detroit office. What do you want, Benjy, I'm drowning here."

I'd been to his place many times. It's a glorified auto junkyard that, even on Saturdays, is seldom confused with a beehive of activity. But Gary's an okay guy. We'd played varsity baseball together, Gary the nervous first baseman, yours truly the hot corner commando. I'd bought numerous auto parts from him. He'd crossed paths with a case of mine earlier in the summer. We got along.

I mentioned the reunion and my efforts to track down the missing alumni. He confirmed Nicki Micklos's demise in the gravy vat and had the good taste not to laugh about it. He knew nothing about the three still missing. But he recognized Sara Gerbstadt's name at once.

"Yeah," he said slowly. "Sure. She's the one who went down on a tailpipe just before graduation, right?"

"There's some question about that," I answered. "I'm asking around. It all revolves around the party the night before. At the Bubbas's house. You remember that?"

"Remember it? Hell," he said, voice full of pleasure, "it was only one of the greatest nights of my life."

"Really? In what way?"

"That was the night I copped my first nooky. Who could forget it?"

"That's fine, Gare," I said, taking a pull on my cigar. "Now, about the party—"

"Big fat girl it was. The hell was her name? Mindy? Linda? Wendy? Took her down to Dynamite Park and put it to her. God, she loved it, she couldn't get enough of it."

"That was after you left," I said patiently. "I'm interested in the party itself, whatever you can remember."

"Oh, all right," he said reluctantly. "The big Tigers game. Remember that?"

"Real vaguely."

"Vaguely? Shit man, that was one of the great games. Us against Cleveland. We blew it, right there at the end."

"It was on the radio," I said, realization dawning.

"Tigers and Cleveland were tied for first place in the American League. Cliffhanger game, we lost when a base runner got picked off trying to steal second."

"That's right!" I said, whacking the table with my fist. "George Thomas was the runner."

"Romano was the Cleveland catcher, picked Thomas off," Gary chimed in.

"That was a hell of a game," I said. "Except for we lost." I remembered the group of us huddled around the radio in the Bubbas's kitchen, drinking beer, smoking cigarettes, listening to WWJ's broadcast. I remembered how annoyed Janet had been that I paid more attention to the ball game than to her. For one brief instant the smell, taste, sound, and feel of that long-ago night came back; for one brief instant I was eighteen again.

"I remember the cops, too," Gary was saying.

"What cops?"

"Came to the front door," Gary said. "That little shithead Triplett, remember him? He tried to crash and you ran him off. So he called the cops on us. You met 'em at the front door and finessed 'em real good."

I had no recollection of that at all. I had a feeling Gary was confusing me with someone else, maybe one of the Bubbas. But his mention of Don Triplett was interesting; old Sponge had been increasingly on my mind. "Did you know Don?"

"Knew of him," Gary said heavily. "Slippery little son of a bitch. Heard he got tangled up with the law later on."

"Behind what?"

"I don't know, man."

"Could be important. Think hard."

"Don't push me, Benjy. I already told you what I know. It's just something got caught edgewise in my memory, that's all."

"Okay, all right." I consoled myself with the reminder that Dick Dennehy would dig up whatever criminal record Triplett had earned. I couldn't wait to hear. "What else do you remember about the party?"

"Well, Baloney Tony Marroni was dealing blackjack in one of the bedrooms."

"Jesus. I don't remember that at all."

"And there was that little private party in the upstairs bathroom. I mean, they weren't too shy about it, you could hear 'em going at it all the way down the hall—"

"Yeah, someone else mentioned that. Who was that, anyway?"

"I dunno, man. Sounded like they was having a great

time, though. But we all did, that night. Couldn't hardly help it."

"Everybody but Sara," I commented. "What do you remember about her being there?"

Gary sighed. "Oh, I remember she was fuckin' blotto. Zonked. Celebratin' making valedictorian or whatever. Stumbling around the place giving everybody the thousand yard stare. I wasn't surprised when she offed herself. Them bookish ones, they tend not to be wrapped all that tight."

"Do you remember her being with anyone in particular?"

"She was with you. I remember that."

"Well, I've ruled myself out as a suspect. Who else?"

"I dunno. Couple others. One I don't know the name of, some friend of hers. The other one—Fast Eddie. Eddie Anger, the singer? She spent time with him, I remember that."

"You sure?"

"Positive."

Interesting. That was two months after Fast dumped her. "What were they doing?"

"What everybody else was doing. Drinking and talking. Only reason I remember is, Fast was the kinda guy you couldn't help but watch. No wonder he's such a big hit on the radio and in records and stuff."

Sheet lightning ripped the western skyline as I barreled up Interstate 94 bound for Ann Arbor. The clouds, long rolls of alternating black and gray, spat down a smorgasbord of precipitation; I'd already motored through drizzle and a brief period of hail, and was now squinting through the whap-whap of high-speed wipers, doing their best to keep off the steady downpour. The Mustang cockpit was hot, stuffy, cigar-choked, and filled with the full-bodied sound of Pink Floyd doing "Comfortably Numb."

My environment, in other words, was about as cheerful as my mood. Stacie had not returned. Hadn't called, either. I'd really wanted her to go see Richie (excuse me—Rich) Satterfield with me. I'd planned on taking her to dinner and then gently steering her around to a discussion of her collection of pharmaceuticals. And there were a few other issues I thought we should take up, while we were at it. But she hadn't come back.

Ugly mood aside, I looked forward to seeing Rich again. I especially looked forward to hearing him tell me everything he remembered about that party. I'd do the same with Janet. Then I'd track down Fast Eddie Anger and get his version. Hopefully, among the three versions, some kind of pattern or lead would emerge. Then, if I could find Sara's father, maybe I'd get some more from him. Maybe I'd patchwork this mess together into some kind of logical or reasonable (if not provable) explanation of what had happened to Sara.

Or, I thought grimly, maybe I'll just keep banging around, flinging myself against one brick wall after another—

My car phone whistled. I answered, "Perkins's Ark, Ben speaking."

"Eric Chwalik, Ben," came his high, excited voice. "God, this is a lousy connection. Where are you, the Space Shuttle?"

"Close. Headed for Ann Arbor and we've got a storm out here. Listen, I've got a situation." I fetched my notes and the sample pills out of my shirt pocket, read the names to Eric, described the unidentified pills as best I could. "I've never heard of this stuff before, I'm more into the street drug scene."

"You just been dealing with a different socio-economic level, that's all," Eric answered. "What you've got there, that's the upscale, nice-white-folks type of shit. Clean, wholesome all-American shit. But it's still shit. Nasty shit."

"Educate me."

"Bigger'n crack, crank, and smack combined. More socially acceptable, that's all. Like booze: People think of it as the wonder drug that works wonders, but it—"

"Okay," I said patiently. "What about this particular variety I've got here?"

"Pretty typical," he answered. "Some of 'em are different brands of basically the same thing, like Tofranil and

Presamine, those are a specific type of antidepressant. Triavil and Etrafon, those are a type of tranquilizer—"

"Jesus, Doc."

"That's not the worst of it. For the average abuser, those are kind of just maintenance items. You just float along, see? She's got some heavy artillery there. Those red tablets you described, with the code number? Those sound like Parnate to me. Powerful antidepressant and psychostimulant. Heavy shit. Usually you only see that used in hospitals, rarely outpatient."

"Where does she *get* this stuff?"

"There's doctors around, their sole business is writing 'scrips. You walk in, pay fifty or sixty bucks, and out you come with a 'scrip, no questions asked."

"Christ."

"Did I call 'em doctors? Make that animals. Should be taken out and shot."

I bore right on the interstate to exit onto U.S. 23 north. The rain had quit, the freeway glistened, and the air being sucked into the Mustang felt cool and fresh. "So she's an addict?"

"Most of those things aren't addictive, per se," Eric answered. "At least not physically. Psychologically, that's another thing. I get people in here all the time who can't shake a weenie like Sinequan. Hell, I've had people addicted to Aquachloral, and that's a fuckin' suppository."

"Oh, pleasant."

"On the other hand, two of the names you gave me there were Deprol and Luminal, and those *are* habit-forming. So yeah, I'd say your friend is addicted. For starters."

"You mean there's more?" I asked grimly.

"Let me give you the usual profile," Eric said. "She has severe psychological problems that go back to childhood. She's probably been institutionalized off and on through the years. That's how she got started on the pill parade. She's a person who manages her moods with drugs. You've probably never seen her clean and sober and you probably never will. She's developed her sources of supply and she spends a significant amount of time maintaining that supply. Whatever you may think, Ben—and no matter what she says—you have no idea what's going on in her head. No idea what she's thinking or planning. She's totally unpredictable."

"Just your standard government-issue female, in other words."

"Ha ha. Very funny. If you're comfortable with that, God bless you. If it was me, I'd run like hell."

"I'm surprised to hear that, considering your line of work."

"Yeah. We talk big here about no one being too far gone. Which is bullshit. There's people that are just plain hopeless. Plenty of them, and I see more all the time. Judging from the variety of goodies your friend carries, I'd say she's one of 'em. Good luck, pal."

Retail Computer Co. occupies a long, low single-story brick building on North Main Street along the Huron River. Darkly tinted windows run around the entire building; lushly landscaped islands dot the black asphalt parking lot, and the entryway is built entirely of glass panels, sort of like those Big Boy No Smoking sections they're putting up now.

The parking lot was nearly empty. I grabbed a space by the sidewalk and strolled into the chrome/glass/leather foyer. No one was there except for a middle-aged man lounging on one of the guest chairs, reading an issue of *Investor's Daily.* He looked up at me and smiled. "Benjy! I'll be damned!"

"Richie. Ya fuckin' twerp, ya." He threw down the paper, bounded to his feet, and shook my hand as we laughed together, studying each other's faces. His was obscured by a thick full beard, but what I could see of it looked youthful, ten years behind our age at least. "Great place you've got here," I said. "Far cry from Old Redford, huh?"

"It's great out here," he agreed. "Come on, I'll show you around."

We toured the facility. What he had there seemed to be an extended disassembly/assembly operation. Old computers went in one end, were stripped down, rebuilt, warehoused, and shipped out the other end. Beyond that, I didn't understand much of what he told me. I gathered that he started the business in his garage after leaving IBM. I gathered that he did all the reconditioning himself for the first year or so as he built the business. I gathered that the used computer business was a constant battle, a perpetual race against time and, in a sense, a matter of guessing right more often than guessing wrong. To hear him talk, becoming a multimillionaire at it had been more a matter of luck than skill. I had the feeling that brains also had something to do with it. Hard work, too.

Physically, he wasn't much like the old Richie. As a kid he'd been slow and chunky, with short hair and a thin anonymous face hiding behind heavy glasses. Now he seemed amiably large to me, a little paunchy now, and stooped, as if he had back trouble. His wavy brown hair was windblown, thinning on top, and showing gray highlights. His voice had acquired a resonance and assurance that was not there when he was a kid, and he'd learned how to use his eyes on you, how to bear in on you as he talked.

Like many rich men, particularly in high-tech, egghead environments like Ann Arbor, Rich's attire was elaborately casual. He wore an open-necked short-sleeve sport shirt in a riot of small, dull, multicolored checks, over pale blue pleated twill pants and navy blue heavy duty sneakers. He wore no rings, no chains, and no watch; he blinked a lot, betraying the contacts that had replaced his Coke bottles, and his teeth were whiter and straighter than I remembered.

Overall, I was impressed and pretty damned pleased, too. In twenty-five years Richie had shucked off the shy, earnest, yet ineffectual persona and reinvented himself as a poised, assured businessman—while keeping the sincerity and kindness that had made him likable in the first place. He hadn't changed as much as Janet. He seemed younger, less hard-bitten, at heart still an innocent.

He walked me around the entire facility: reconditioning line, paint shed, warehouse, the "burn-in room" where a dozen of the big blinking monsters hummed. He showed me the office wing, which was pretty dull—face it: When you've seen one accounting department, you've seen them all. Finally he led me to his office. Throughout the tour I noticed perhaps two dozen people working busily. "Don't you ever close?" I asked as Rich held his office door for me.

"Not really," he answered. "We keep a pretty lean staff here. One and a half jobs per person instead of the other way around. Sit down."

His office was anything but flossy. Since it sat in the center of the office wing, it was windowless. The large blond wood desk occupied the middle of the room and was neatly arrayed with squared piles of papers. Along the back and two side walls were a pair of credenzas, two work tables, and a tilted drafting table, with an impressive and expensive array of electronic toys: a NeXT personal computer, MICROPUB phototypesetter, and a HP laser printer; plus a photocopier, fax machine, and multiline telephone, all no-name but not cheap. There were no decorations, plants, mementoes; nothing to distract the occupant from the business at hand.

Rich eased himself into a large high-backed executive chair and I took a wooden guest chair facing him across the desk. "Kind of expected an El Presidente type like you to have the standard big corner office," I commented.

"Well, that's the point," he said. "I'm not the president. I don't believe in a hierarchal structure in companies. And this isn't an office, it's a work space. Would you like me to bore you with about an hour's worth of business philosophy?"

"Thanks anyhow."

His grin flashed briefly within his beard. "Suffice to say that my title is 'Central Executive.' To reinforce my philosophy I positioned my work space in the geographic center of the facility." He shrugged. "It works. Care for a beer?"

"Why, sure." Rich opened a small refrigerator beneath his work table, handed an icy bottle of Christian Moerlein dark across the desk to me, and opened one for himself. We clinked bottles in a toast. "Here's to swimmin' with fat-bottomed women," I said.

He grinned. "To early times," he said.

We drank. Rich slid a heavy glass coaster across to me and I put my beer bottle down on it. How Ann Arbor can you get? I thought. Expensive designer beer, fancy coaster, no glass. "Mind if I smoke?" I asked.

"Not at all," Rich said. "Wish I could. Had to quit." He tapped his chest. "Ticker."

"Holy shit. You? Smoking? And heart trouble? Never would have figured."

"It's the business I'm in," he answered. "Lot of travel. Sales calls. Long negotiations. Big meals. Tension. Once my youth was used up, I cleaned up my act and started trying to save what's left." He gestured with the beer bottle. "This is my one remaining indulgence and I intend to keep it, thank you."

"Long as it's union-made, I'm with you. And don't give me that old-fart routine. You look ten years younger than your age, honest to God."

"It's the beard. Underneath it I'm worn and wrinkled, believe me." He was studying me. "Whereas you," he said quietly. "Tan, fit, not an extra ounce, all your hair—you've obviously made a point of living healthy."

"That's a vicious lie," I answered after getting my cigar going. "What do you think I am, un-American? I eat burgers and pizza and drink beer and coffee, and I smoke and stay up late, okay? It's just that when I'm not detecting, I'm doing apartment maintenance work, which keeps me lifting and carrying, active and outside a lot, and working hard all the time. Without that I'd be a blob in an armchair someplace."

"You always were more physical than me," he said. "So were Fast Eddie and Janet and Gary. Even Sara got more exercise than me."

"Hey, somebody had to be the brains. You got elected."

He fiddled with his beer bottle. "Sara was the brains," he said quietly. After a deep breath he said, "Since you told me your theory about Sara, I haven't thought about much else. Tell me what you've learned. Tell me everything."

CHAPTER 14

It was hard to read his expression behind that beard, but I sensed a sadness and hesitancy, as if he did not want to discuss the subject but felt obligated. Sara's death really had gotten to him, I realized. And it was obviously still something he carried around with him. Well, he always was a more emotional, feeling person. It did not surprise me to learn that he'd been unable to put the thing completely behind him, alien though that was to me.

I drew on my cigar, arranging my thoughts. "Well, I looked at the police record. Spoke with the investigating officer. Interviewed the woman who lived across the street from Sara's house, as well as a couple of kids who were at the party. What I've got out of all that ain't much, and it raises more questions still."

"I see," he said.

"For example, at the time of her death Sara was pregnant."

Rich's reaction was to raise his head and look at me intently for one brief moment. "Pregnant!" he whispered. "Oh boy. Ohhh boy."

"Got any thoughts on that, Richie?"

"Wow," he said, shaking his head slowly. "That's—that takes some getting used to. Sara pregnant." His eyes found me. "Fast Eddie?"

"Any other candidates occur to you?"

"None, offhand." He swirled his beer absently and took a short swig. "What about the woman across the street?"

"She didn't know much. All she saw was a car come and go."

"I see." He seemed to make up his mind. "When we

talked on the phone you said you felt she was murdered. Do you still think that?"

"Absolutely. Now, somebody was clever and put a lot of thought into it. Went to some trouble to make it look like suicide. But some of the physical aspects of the scene just don't make sense. And I really don't think Sara would kill herself."

Rich swiveled his chair, showing me his profile, and propped his dark running shoes on the corner of his desk. "She was depressed, you know," he said quietly.

"How do you know, Richie?" I asked, getting out my pad.

He glanced at me. "You asked me to think back. Well, that's what I've been doing. Painful stuff, Benjy. High school was not the best period of my life. Not by a long shot. Anyway, I spent some time with her there for awhile, after Fast Eddie dumped her. She was getting ready for some sort of scholarship exam competition in Washington. The National Achievement Scholarships, or something? She asked me to help her study. So I spent quite a few hours with her."

I didn't remember a thing about any of this. "When was this?"

"Before graduation, a few weeks before, I think."

"What makes you think she was depressed?"

He tipped his head back and swiveled it, exercising the neck muscles. "When we were studying, she was fine. She had tremendous concentration, incredible intensity, and she drove herself fiercely," he said, smiling at the memory. "God, I admired that. But when she wasn't studying, she moped around. Listened to sad songs on the radio. Talked about depressing things. I think it depressed her that high school was almost over. I think the state of the world depressed her, too; she was that type." He arched his brows. "Another thing that had her down was her menstruation. She had really rough periods. Had one just before going to D.C. that kept her in bed for a couple of days, we couldn't do any studying."

I looked at him. "You were closer to her than I thought. For her to tell you about her periods—"

"It's not what you're thinking," he cut in. "She thought of me as a pal, you know? Said that a bunch of times. 'You're my very special pal.'" He smiled at the memory. "I just listened to her. I may have been the only one who really listened to her in those days."

"I see."

He examined his fingers. "You look at all those things. Emotional problems, physical problems, so damn depressed—teenage stuff, but that can be potent. Lethal, even."

"Uh-huh," I answered. I scribbled a word or two. "How about around the house? Was there trouble at home there, far as you know?"

He squinted. "I don't think so. Her parents were nice people. Mr. Gerbstadt especially. He absolutely loved kids. He was constantly running youth groups at the Community Center. I know he doted on Sara, her being the only child and so forth."

"What about the mom? Mothers and daughters don't always get along all that great."

"That's true," he reflected. "Sara didn't seem to have much use for her mother. Maybe that was part of the problem." He glanced at me over the lip of his beer bottle. "Another part of the problem was Fast Eddie. I don't think Sara ever got over him dumping her. She really, really loved him. It was one of the things I never understood about her."

I drained my beer. Rich followed suit and drew replacements from his little fridge. Handy little thing, have to think about getting me one for out on my deck. I disposed of my old cigar and lighted a new one. "I know this feels like an interrogation, and I'm sorry about that," I told him, gesturing with my pad. "I wish we could have gotten together again under different circumstances."

He smiled. "So do I. But I'm happy to help and I respect what you're doing, and I know you mean well, even if your efforts are misguided."

I leaned back in my chair. "Hey, if you've got a better notion, pal, I'm all ears."

He waved a hand. "Don't take offense. I'm—"

"I'm not offended, Richie, for Chrissake." The opening I'd been waiting for was there and I took it. "What about Triplett?"

He looked away deliberately, decisively, and then back, eyes hard. "You think Don killed Sara?"

"I'm asking a question."

"Forget it, Benjy, Jesus H. Christ."

"I been remembering things. I been asking around. His rep was never all that good, and from what I've been hearing he—"

He was showing me both palms. "Don had a rough childhood. Divorced parents. Not much money. The loner sort. He got himself into jams. He did some bad things. But he didn't kill Sara."

"I may want to talk to him," I said stubbornly.

Rich shrugged. "See him here, or call him at home, he lives over in Ypsi."

I took a hit of weed. God, the bonhomie had disappeared fast. But I realized that Rich and Don had been friends all their lives and business colleagues for most of them. I could hardly expect Rich to roll over on Don, no matter how much I liked old Sponge as a suspect. "Any other thoughts?" I asked.

He shook his head. "I just don't think Sara was murdered. I think she killed herself. Sad and tragic but it does happen, Ben. It happens a lot. It happens a lot now, and I think it happened back then a lot more than people let on; it was just covered up more."

"Good point."

He smiled in a way that told me he was about to deliver a hard truth. "You know, in some ways you've changed. I think you're less impulsive than you were back then. More patient, perhaps. More open-minded. But in other ways the essential Benjy lives on. Touchy, physical, tough, jaundiced, and totally bullheaded. This thing with Sara is a prime example. The facts are all against you. An eon has intervened. Yet you plow on undeterred."

To the unasked question I responded, "I liked Sara. She was sweet, she had a good heart, and she was my friend. Someone slipped past me and killed her. I can't sit still for that. You say the facts are against me. I don't agree. I don't have much, but I'm going to work what's there till it runs out. I won't quit as long as there's a glimmer of hope of nailing the son of a bitch who did this. Okay?"

The door opened behind me and a man's voice said, "Come on, Richie, let's call it a day. Jesus."

Richie smiled and beckoned. "Don! Come on in. We were just talking about you." The man came in as I got to my feet. "Don Triplett," Richie said, "you remember Ben Perkins, don't you?"

By mutual unspoken agreement, we did not shake hands. Sponge was taller than I remembered, six two at least. His blond flat-top had given way to a gray-blond Pete Rose-style pageboy, the acne had given way to severe scars, and much good living had bulged him some; but he was still the gray-eyed, dead-faced person I remembered, watching me now through slitty eyes. He was dressed for a casual summer Saturday in a pleated white-on-white sport-shirt over brand-new baggy-thighed jeans—both, I sensed, custom-tailored just for him.

"Perkins," he said softly.

The mutual dislike stood like a separate person between us. "Heard you work here," I said.

"Don's my director of operations," Richie said proudly.

"You and your screwy titles," Triplett jibed. He fixed his gray stone-like eyes on me. "What kind of trouble you stirring up, Perkins?"

"No trouble."

"Better not." We eyed each other silently. Then Triplett said, "I'm gone, Rich. Try not to forget to lock up, okay?"

"No problem, Don," Richie said heartily. "Good night."

I sat back down as the door clicked shut. "Honest to God, Richie, that guy ain't changed a bit since we were kids, and you know it."

"You just have to get to know him. What he did was—"

"What he did was egg my car. That much I know. Sara got two flats during school one day; that was him, too, I'm sure of it. And remember the condom? Jan ain't never gonna forgive him for that one."

"If Don did those things—" Richie said slowly—"it was because he was very upset and hurt because you marooned him out in the middle of nowhere that night. He's very sorry about it all now."

"I'll just bet." I checked the time; it was past five. "Jeez, it's getting pretty late," I said, relighting my neglected cigar. "You probably have to be getting home."

"I'm in no hurry," he said matter-of-factly. "I've got no one to go home to." He made a welcoming gesture. "What else would you like to know?"

"Let's talk about the party at the Bubbas's house the night Sara died. Have you thought about that some more?"

He scratched his head. "Oh yes," he said absently. "Like I said, I don't remember a whole lot. It was real rowdy there, I remember. *Smoky,* too. Seemed like everybody was smoking. Music and dancing." He glanced at me. "I remember you were in the kitchen a lot of the time, listening to a ball game. Till Don tried to crash and you, uh, dissuaded him."

"What did you do during the party? You weren't into the ball game."

"Honest to God," he confessed, "I don't remember exactly. Talked to people and drifted around, I guess, like usual. I was never much of a party person."

"Then the beer ran out, and you went out for more," I observed.

He tipped his bottle back and drank. "Yes. I volunteered. I don't know what got into me. I was always afraid of the police, afraid of getting in trouble. That night we pulled the April Fool's dead-body prank, that made me jumpy. But I volunteered anyway. I just—" He sighed and stared at the ceiling—"I wanted to be one of the guys."

"And you got caught. Where was that? The old In & Out?"

"Sure. That was the safe place, supposedly. But the police were waiting. I spent the night in jail." His eyes were round. "Was my father *furious.*"

"Hardened criminal," I jibed. "Let's go back to Sara.

Do you remember anything else about her that night? Who she talked with, what she did?"

Slowly he brought his feet down, turned and faced me, arms flat on the desk, head cocked. "She was very drunk. That's what I remember most. But that doesn't mean she drank a lot. She never could hold it."

"Autopsy pegged her at point one seven. Which means at the time she died she had to've been at least point two oh. Pretty stinko, Richie."

He shrugged. "I don't know who she was with. I hardly saw her at all that night. I congratulated her on making valedictorian. She just—she just mumbled thanks. After awhile I took off for the beer, and obviously I never came back, so—"

I drank some beer. "What about Jan? Did you see her?"

"I remember her dancing," he said. "She danced with everyone. I wanted to ask her, but I didn't have the guts."

"Fast Eddie? Did you spend time with him?"

His eyes narrowed. "You're joking."

"Come on. Fast wasn't such a bad guy, mostly."

"Fast Eddie despised me," Rich said. "I remember him being there that night, but I'm sure he never even greeted me. I remember he played a couple of songs on his guitar. He did some dancing, and—" He slowly drew himself straight in the chair, expression, to the extent I could read it, quizzical. "He was gone for awhile."

"Gone? Where'd he go?"

"I don't know. But he was definitely gone for awhile," Rich said quietly. "People were asking about him. This, er, overweight girl in particular, asked several times where she could find Eddie, as if I had anything to do with him."

I made some notes, then squinted and stared at them, thinking hard. "Was this before Sara left?" I ventured.

"I guess so," he answered. "Had to've been. I was just leaving on the beer run."

"Right."

Rich finished his beer and began to peel at the label as he talked. "I know how this is going to sound," he said.

"But in light of the fact that Sara was pregnant, is it possible that Fast Eddie killed her?"

My first impulse was to shut him down on the spot. Instead I said, "Explain."

He looked at me and his face and tones were icy and clinical, the experienced and successful businessman putting the ducks in a row. "He and Sara were lovers. At least till April, when he dumped her. Let's say she finds out she's going to have a baby and she starts pressuring him. What does a guy like Fast Eddie do?"

"You tell me."

"Very well. Fast Eddie's band is getting hot. He has more dates than he can handle. The money is suddenly getting bigger, people are flocking to him, making all kinds of promises. Tours, record albums, movies even. Keep in mind that this isn't now; it's back then, when abortions and out-of-wedlock births were relatively rare. You remember Sara, she wouldn't ever have considered either one. Plus, she loved Fast Eddie. She wanted him to marry her, is what she wanted. Given Fast Eddie's suddenly faster track, do you really think he'd want to drag that ball and chain around with him?"

"Probably not, given a choice."

"And he was gone from the party awhile," Rich added. "Maybe he went to her house, met her there, did her in, then came back to the party, hoping in the confusion nobody'd realize he'd gone."

I knew it could not possibly have happened that way. But Rich's notion had a strong element of possibility in it nevertheless, for reasons he could not possibly have known. It was a very disturbing idea. For all of his faults, Fast Eddie was as much an old friend as Rich and Jan. It had occurred to me that the perp could be one of us, but this was getting uncomfortably close.

"It's something to consider," I conceded.

He went back to peeling at the beer bottle label. "I know what you're thinking. Fast was always nasty to me and I've got it in for him. Well, I'm talking facts here, not emotions. And I don't bear him any animosity. After all these years, that would be silly."

"Sure would," I answered, flipping my pad shut.

"I accept him for what he is," Rich went on. "A minor figure in a business that is all glitter and no consequence. He's welcome to his concert tours and MTV appearances and blurbs in rags like *People* magazine. He's even welcome to all that money. In a country where athletes are multi-millionaires while children sleep in cardboard boxes, Eddie's quite trivial."

I rose. "Well, you've given me a lot to think about, Richie. Thanks for all the help."

He stood too, looking concerned. "You have to go? I thought we could get some dinner together."

"Appreciate the thought, but I'm expecting someone at home." At least I thought I was. "I enjoyed this, Richie, let's get together again sometime."

"I'd like that," he answered, coming around his desk. "I'd better walk you out. We've got all kinds of security gizmos here." He led me across a large desk-filled room toward the hallway. "Who're you expecting at home?" he asked. "Wife?"

"Nope. Not married. Just a friend, that's all."

"Any kids, Ben?"

"No. Well, yes. Sort of." At his curious expression I went on, "A lady friend of mine, we've been real close off and on. Well, right now it's off, but she's expecting, okay?"

We entered a long hallway that opened out down at the end into the glass foyer. "Congratulations," Rich said.

"Thanks. It wasn't planned or anything. Carole's a lawyer, her practice is really picking up. Having a kid certainly wasn't on her agenda. Mine either. I assumed she'd abort, but she decided to keep it."

"Good for her," Rich murmured. "When you have a choice, do life."

"That's how she looked at it. Her choice. As for me, I—well, me, a dad? Never figured on that."

He looked at me. "You know, I do a lot of legal work and I'm always looking for a good hired gun. Maybe you could introduce me to your friend. Carole, you said?"

We entered the foyer, glowing red from the early evening light outside. "Carole Somers," I answered as we walked past the empty couches and chairs of the reception area. "Somers & Levin, Berkley. She does mostly domestic work, spouse abuse, custody matters, probate. She's the best, in my humble opinion."

"I'll remember that." He unlocked the glass double doors, put his keys away and held out his hand hesitantly. "Thanks for coming out, Benjy. It was terrific, seeing you again."

"Hey, you helped me out," I answered. "Much obliged."

Then, to my surprise, he grabbed me in a rough clumsy bear hug for a moment. I gave his back a few tentative pats and he released me. The look in his eyes was intense. "I haven't forgotten what you did for me, way back then," he said. "Billy Orr was harassing me—I always seemed to attract that kind of thing—and you took him aside one day and spoke to him and he never bothered me again."

Well, good for me. If it had happened. "Glad I could help," I said.

He smiled. "Just a word of advice, Benjy. Remember the good things you do. No one else will. They'll remember the bad you do, but never the good. Believe me."

"Thanks," I said uncomfortably. "Later, pal." I pushed through the glass doors and strode down the sidewalk toward the Mustang, sitting forlornly in the large asphalt parking lot. I felt eyes on me and turned to see Richie standing there, holding the door open, watching me. "Take care," I called.

"How about dinner?" he called back. "Thursday night at seven, Gandy Dancer."

"Sounds good," I called back.

"Bring Carole." He waved again and disappeared into the building. I boarded the Mustang, wheeled her around the lot and then out. The only remaining car was an early eighties Honda Accord that looked worse for wear. Pretty modest car for a man of Richie's means. As I motored north on Main Street toward Route 23, it occurred to me that such self-effacement was a little much, even for the new, improved Ann Arbor version of Rich Satterfield.

By the time I got back to Norwegian Wood, I'd rehearsed how I was going to handle Stacie. I was primed and ready. But she wasn't there. She had not been back in the meantime. The red light on the answering machine was flashing, and as I hit the rewind button I hoped that one of the messages was from her.

Chapter 15

"Mr. Perkins," came the heavy female voice. Her enunciation was so careful that I figured she was better than half drunk. "This is Kathy Lentz. I'm calling you back but you're not there. . . . Or maybe you are. Some people hide behind those fu—— those fri—— those darn machines. I don't know you. Do I? You're not that space rep, are you? His name was Ben. No, Dan. . . . You're Ben. You called me coupla ti—— a couple of times, here at Whisperz. I don't know you. . . . What do—"

BEEP. "Ben? Jan. Just calling to see how you're doing on the case. There's only a week to go. I'm at the Hobby Airport Holiday Inn in Houston and I'll be here all night." She gave the number. I wrote it down, glad that she'd called; I'd planned to call her anyway.

BEEP. "Mr. Perkins?" A nasal male voice, unfamiliar. "This is Dwight at the Detroit Public Library, Old Redford branch? You requested information on automatic garage door openers. That information is now available here at the library. You may call for it at the main desk. Thank you."

That was it. Nothing from Stacie. I hit rewind on the tape, wandered to the TV, and snapped it on. Frank Tanana completed his windup and hurled a junk floater that nicked the outside corner and caught Lloyd Moseby looking. The ump shot out his right fist, Moseby turned to argue, and the score graphic said Detroit Tigers 1, Toronto 0. Hoo boy, I thought. By current Tiger standards, a runaway lead.

I found some cold pizza in the fridge, nuked it in the microwave, and chased it down with a pair of Stroh's as the

Tigers went down 1-2-3 in their half of the fourth. No Stacie.

I called Whisperz and asked for Kathy Lentz. She had, once again, "stepped out." I had the feeling I'd never reach her, never get an answer on Carl Hickson. At that point I didn't care too much. I'd found all but three of the missing grads and that would have to do. I had more important things to do, like figure out what to do next in the Gerbstadt investigation. Stacie did not return or call during the top of the fourth, during which Frank Tanana gamely held Toronto to a walk and one meaningless hit.

Dinner done, I repaired to the kitchen, set fire to a cigar, and punched out the Houston number that Janet had left. She answered by briskly reciting her name.

"Perkins here," I responded. "You screamed?"

"Well, hi there," she answered pleasantly enough. "Where are you?"

"Home, where else?"

"Alone?"

"Yep."

"Isn't it awful," she mused. "The two of us, alone on a Saturday night, twelve hundred miles apart."

"Well, I'm expecting company here any minute now."

"Let me guess," she said after a moment. "Stacie Hallthorn."

"Bingo. How'd you guess?"

"I called her house and there was no answer. In fact, her phone was disconnected. Must be getting serious, the two of you."

"Not hardly." Phone disconnected, I thought. Now, what's *this* all about?

After a moment of silence Jan said briskly, "Well, I won't keep you. I was just wondering how the investigation is going."

"Found all but three of the grads. Still working."

"And Sara?" she asked quietly.

"Lot of questions. I'm moving on it. Talking to a lot of people." I took a long pull on my cigar. "I need to talk to Fast Eddie. Any idea where I can reach him?"

"I've got his number in Vegas. Just a minute." She

found it and read it to me. "What do you need to talk to him about?"

"The party the night before Sara died. I need to ask you about it, too."

"Well, go ahead," she said guardedly.

"Not now. Face to face, Jan."

"That's quite impossible. I'm in Houston through tomorrow, and Monday I have to be in Minneapolis. No way can I get to Detroit till late next week."

"Minneapolis, huh? I might be heading west, depends on what Fast is up to. I'll get back to you."

"I'll be here. Goodbye."

"Listen, Jan?"

"Yes?"

"What do you know about Stacie?"

Her voice was brittle. "What do I know? I know what I've seen and heard. She is a very attractive and vivid woman. She wears expensive clothes that always look like they'll fall off at a touch. She spends more time on her hair and makeup than I do in bed, and more time in bed than I spend anywhere. She has a lot of money, lives in a very ritzy suburb, and is a magnet for men. Doesn't that pretty much sum it up?"

"Ever been to her house?"

"No. I've talked to her on the phone and I've met her at the airport. Ben, why are you asking me all these things? I'm no friend of hers. It's business. We work together on the reunion and that's all. What's going on?"

"Nothing much. I can handle it."

"Of that I have no doubt. Goodbye."

I hung up. The baseball game beckoned from the living room. I hoofed in there and watched for a moment, cigar hanging from my teeth. The Tigers had the bases loaded with none out. Time to cash in. Instead, two went down on a double play and Stieb got Nokes to look at three consecutive strikes. End of threat.

I went back to the phone. The sky was darkening outside, Stacie wasn't back yet, and I felt like I was nowhere on this investigation, spinning my wheels in deep soft sand. Everyone remembered something but none of it fit. Theories burned hot and then died of neglect. I had a theory as to the mechanics of the thing, but it was all head movies. I didn't know enough, was the problem. What I did know bothered me. And the way I felt bothered me even more. I kept thinking about the girl with the murdered eyes. I kept imagining how it must have been for her, to come to her own house to die, set up with ruthless precision. I wanted the perp badly. Too badly.

I smothered my smoke, punched a Las Vegas number on the phone, and negotiated for a few minutes. Called Janet back and negotiated some more. Called my travel agency and negotiated yet again. Given a credit card number, there was nothing they could not do, and gladly. I hung up again, done with the damn phone for the day, and hoofed into the living room to finish the ball game and wait for Stacie, and wait for Stacie, and wait for Stacie.

She did not come back. And the Detroit Tigers, despite the most valiant of efforts by Frank Tanana, lost to Toronto 2-1.

The next morning was brilliant and cool, the sun standing high in the pristine sky, the low-humidity air smooth and just barely moving. It was pushing noon as I sat out on my deck, lounging in the sunshine, finishing the Sunday newspaper and a pot of coffee and my second cigar of the day. I looked relaxed, but I was not. I had a big day ahead of me, starting with a frank conversation with Ms. Stacie Hallthorn, who, judging from the noises inside, would appear any moment now.

The screen door slid and her voice sang, "Oh, *here* you are! Good morning!"

" 'Mornin'," I answered as she strode out, bright and breezy. She wore white skin-tight jeans below a blue-and-white striped surplice top. It just barely covered her prominent breasts, leaving her shoulder tops and tanned midriff entirely bare. A diamond-studded gold bracelet twinkled on her left wrist. Her hair, her eyes, her complexion were all perfection, as if she'd just stepped out of the pages of a high-class fashion catalog. Despite myself, I was impressed at the restoration job. "Sleep well?" I asked.

She faced me, leaning her rear against the deck rail with the sun lighting her profile, and smiled. "Like death. And speaking of death, that's what you were like last night, lover. Too bad, 'cause I was in the *mood.*"

I laid down the section of newspaper, puffed on my cigar, and said, "Cut the bullshit, Stacie."

She pushed her heavy auburn mop of hair behind her shoulders and angled her face to catch the sun. "What are you talking about?" she asked, eyes closed.

"I don't know what kind of game you're playing, babe, but I ain't playing it, see?"

She glanced at me and frowned. "Aren't *we* nasty this morning!"

I frowned back. "You came stumbling in at two thirty A.M., bombed out of your mind. You fell across me on the bed, passed out, and commenced to snoring like a damn ripsaw. I spent the rest of the night out on the couch."

She studied me intently as she nodded. "Well, I'm sorry I had too much to drink. I was with some girlfriends, and we—but I never snore."

"You snored all right," I said grimly. "And what's this about girlfriends? You left here at this time yesterday, come back fourteen hours later, and tell me you were with *girlfriends*?"

"Well, yes," she said earnestly. "I met Janie and Karen for lunch at the Lark. Then we went to Oakland Mall and Northland, and—we went to Janie's house and played cards and had dinner, and—Ben," she said, eyes pained, hands gesturing, "you said you were going out with a friend last night. The girls and I were having fun, and—and I didn't think you'd miss me."

I scooched up in the lounge chair. "I wish you'd called or something. I was worried."

Her smile had a dark, triumphant side to it. "Worried? Or suspicious?"

"Maybe."

"You thought I was with another man. Is that it?" she asked, walking toward me very slowly.

"The thought occurred to me."

Lithely, she dropped to her knees on the deck, folded

her arms on my calf, and looked up at me with her luminous light blue eyes. "I'm a one-man woman, Ben."

"Okay."

She slipped a rubber band off her wrist, rose on her knees, gathered her hair back with both hands, and began to bundle it. "And guess what, Ben?" she asked softly. "You're it."

I glanced around. "Stacie, I don't know—"

She smiled and put both hands lightly on my crotch. "And right now I'm going to give you a reminder of how lucky you are."

Torn, I swallowed hard and felt my heart pounding. "Not out here, for Chrissake!"

She caressed me. "We're on the second floor," she whispered. "No one can look down at us. If you'll open that newspaper and hold it a certain way, that'll—"

"Stacie—"

"From appearances," she said, "it won't take long."

It didn't.

Six hours later, as I stood in line at the O'Hare rental car counter, I was still thinking about it. No surprise. I'd never had sex on the deck before. Not even at night. I'm not opposed to novelty. And I've always enjoyed Sunday morning funnies. But that particular episode left me feeling vaguely uneasy.

I fully realized that it was not spontaneous sex, but sex with a purpose. Stacie did not wish to engage in any discussions that were uncomfortably honest, and she expertly headed me off. Afterward, as I got ready to go to the airport, I could not make myself bring up the subject of the pills. Save it for later, I decided guiltily. Besides, there was something else on Stacie's mind anyway.

"When will you be home?" she asked, primping herself in the full-length bedroom mirror.

I was stuffing a change of clothes in a small carry-on bag. "Tomorrow evening sometime."

She turned to face me. "Can you leave me some walking-around money?"

I stuffed my shaving kit. "Little short?" I asked casually.

"A lot short. Just a few dollars till next week, okay?"

I caught a glimpse of her gold bracelet and had an unworthy thought: Why don't you hock that? Nasty. "Sure," I answered.

"I'll be okay next week," she went on hastily. "I'll pay you back."

"It's fine, don't worry about it." I hoisted the bag and left the bedroom.

Stacie trailed me. "Somebody screwed up the paperwork on my disability," she said. "They've been holding up my checks. But it should kick back in this week and I'll pay you back."

I wondered about the specifics of this "disability." I'd been with her six days and she seemed pretty damned able to me. But I was uncomfortable with her now, off-balance, and I had a plane to catch. I slipped my ATM card out of my wallet and gave it to her. "PIN's the last four digits of my phone number," I told her.

"Okay," she said, examining it. "I won't take out too much."

Not much danger of that. "See you," I said, kissed her and left.

Now, as I negotiated the car rental, I uncomfortably recalled the third-hand assessment of Eric Chwalik: "Whatever you may think, Ben, you have no idea what's going on in her head. No idea what she's thinking or planning. She's totally unpredictable."

Part of me felt sorry for her. Part of me was coldly wary. Another part of me—the part that gets me in trouble—enjoyed the risk, loved playing with the fire, was pumped and excited, anxious to see what would happen next and how I would deal with it.

Dump her, I told myself. Do the work here, go home, and usher her out of your life. Politely, firmly, finally.

But, as I walked out of the terminal into the furnace blast of August Chicago heat, that trouble-loving side of me asked: When was the last time a woman flung herself at you like this? And how do you know it isn't the last time?

CHAPTER 16

When Fast Eddie's Las Vegas publicist had told me that the "American Born" tour was playing the Kos Arena in Chicago, I'd pictured a big domed stadium-type of place. Or a large, flossy concert hall. Or some sort of upscale outdoor venue.

Wrong. Kos Arena was a gaunt, ramshackle yellow brick sports "palace," decorated with rusted fire escapes and soot and dating from the turn of the century. According to the posters outside, the previous attraction had been WBC featherweight boxing and the subsequent one was roller derby—making Fast Eddie the cultural event of the week. And the arena wasn't actually in Chicago. It was in the suburb of North Chicago, on 22nd Street, a block from the gate of the huge U.S. Naval Training Center.

I bought a ticket and went inside, pressing flesh with sailors in whites, their noisy girlfriends, and a mass of others, mostly middle-aged. The arena was dim and icily air-conditioned, but no amount of air circulation could do away with the smell of sweat and disinfectant and mold that was excreted by the old terra-cotta pillars and walls. The usher directed me to my seat, on the ground floor about halfway down. I gave him a twenty and whispered something in his ear; he nodded and went away as I sat down on the sticky hard wood chair to watch the show.

The opening act was a new wave group called Head Crash. By the time the MC introduced Eddie Anger & the Engineers—Fast Eddie's latest rock and roll incarnation—Kos Arena held maybe three thousand people, making it about half full. What followed was a pretty standard rock and roll event: an aging star playing two dozen aging tunes for the aging faithful who knew all the words by heart.

There were pyrotechnics, gymnastics, theatrics; smashed instruments, articles of clothing hurled into the crowd, kisses for screaming fans crowding the lip of the stage; the obligatory show of lighted matches, the even more obligatory standing ovations, and three encores.

In other words, the concert met minimal expectations, and that was about all. But then, I realized as I watched and listened, that was all anybody had gotten from Fast Eddie, at least once he hit the big time. Before that, back when we were kids, he'd been driven. Carried his guitar everywhere he went and practiced it till his fingers bled. Wrote and performed gritty blues songs full of fire and passion, songs that sold records and SRO venues, songs that made him a star—not because he sincerely believed in what he was doing, but because he was adept at making audiences think he did.

That was his real skill. Since hitting it big, he'd relied on that to see him through; otherwise he'd played it safe by observing the trend of the moment. With various bands and under various names he underwent various incarnations: cute moptop, radical protester, angry poet, flower child, acid rocker, balladeer, prince of darkness, disco warbler, social critic.

These days the trend was America and being American. Old Glory was everywhere. Advertisers who couldn't afford Ed McMahon waved the red, white, and blue; nothing was sacred, not even the Statue of Liberty, the star of a deodorant commercial. So it did not surprise me that Eddie, always alert to what sells, named his tour, his new album, and its title track "American Born." Gary Graff in the *Free Press* had renamed the album "American Borin' " and, judging from what I heard that night in Kos Arena, Graff was right on the money, as usual.

As instructed, I waited at my seat while the revved-up crowd trooped out of the arena. My usher, a squat man with stick legs who probably started there when George Burns played the place in 1922, came for me as the last diehard fans were singing their way out. "This way," he said hoarsely. "He's waiting for you."

He led me down to the stage, through a locked fire

door, and into a sequence of dimly lighted tunnels and hallways that smelled like dust and dead mice. We emerged in a room whose walls were lined with dusty old theatrical junk: lights, cables, sections of scenery. In the center was a table loaded with food and drinks, and around the table stood members of the band, getting acquainted with young women of all flavors whom, I had a sneaking suspicion, they had not brought on the tour with them.

No one paid attention to us. The usher led me to the other side of the room and tapped softly on a closed door. After five seconds he opened it, gestured me in, and closed the door softly behind me.

It was a two-desk office with nothing notable about it, an office in an old building like a million other offices in a million other old buildings. The rearmost desk had been cleared off and Fast Eddie Anger sat atop it, cross-legged, arms folded, bent over with his forehead nearly touching his ankles. He did not acknowledge my arrival.

After a moment I said, "When'd you go Muslim, Fast?"

His only answer was to gesture rudely with his left hand.

"Besides," I said, "Mecca is over yonder a ways. You're prostrating in the direction of approximately Joliet, Illinois, I believe."

He exhaled a long breath, sat up straight, shook his long dark hair back from his long thin face, and scowled. "I haven't gone Muslim. This is a meditative exercise designed to reunite the inner and outer me, in order to bring myself down from the performing experience. When you give your all onstage, like I do, you can't just switch it on and off, you know."

"Yeah," I nodded, "getting older's a bitch, all right."

"This has nothing to do with aging. It has to do with art." He swung his feet off the desk and sat there, sneakers dangling, smiling. "You're looking good, Benjy."

"So are you." Fast Eddie was slim and a bit shorter than me, about five ten. He was fine-boned and had a liquid, catlike way of moving which, I suspect, was a key to his sex appeal, though I've never gotten a woman to own up to it. His brownish-black hair was parted in the middle and layered around his thin, wolflike face to his shoulders. In keeping with the cultivated slob look pioneered by that trend setter Yasser Arafat, Fast's tanned face sported stubble that was blond flecked with gold. He wore a tight black T-shirt with the Cancer "69" symbol on front and back, over even tighter black jeans. He was a man of narrow angles and quick movements and a sense of presence, of magnetism, that had not dimmed in the four years since I'd seen him.

"What brings you to Chicago?" he asked.

"Talk to you."

"Could have called."

"Tried that. Said you were on tour, couldn't be bothered."

His eyes flashed. "Damn publicists! That's the thing about success, Benjy. People think you got it made, got all these gofers to do for you. What you really got is more people to fuck things up."

"Uh-huh."

He gestured around. "Like this place. We weren't supposed to play this dump. We were supposed to be in the Civic Center. Nice house, right? Down on the Loop, right? Classy!" He pounded the desk with his fist. "My kind of room! So what happens? Somebody fucks up and forgets to mail the deposit. And here we are. Jesus!" He tapped a Pall Mall cigarette out of a pack on the desk, lighted it with a tiny butane, and exhaled. "Been a long time, Benjy. You still mad about Carole?"

"Water under the bridge," I answered.

"Just one of those things, man."

"I know, Fast."

"I'm not a total asshole, you know. I don't make a habit of bouncing my friends' girls. I get more puss-ah than I can possibly use, I'm don't need to cop someone else's. It was just that—"

"Drop it, Fast," I said tightly.

He watched me light a cigar. "Still with her?" he asked.

"It's been off and on. At the moment, off."

"How is she?"

"Pregnant."

He smiled. "Really? You do the dirty deed?"

"I did."

"Welcome to the club. I got three of 'em scattered around. L.A., Cincinnati, Norfolk Virginia. Newport, I mean. Newport News. Fatherhood ain't all peaches and cream, take it from me, bro." He dropped to the floor. "Tell you what, Benjy. Let's go out to my truck. We can whip up some drinks and talk about—what did you want to talk about, anyway?"

"Old times."

"Sounds good." He started for the door.

"Graduation," I added, following him.

"Great days," he replied, opening the door.

"Sara," I said quietly.

He glanced over his shoulder at me. "Sure, Benjy. Whatever you say. Come on."

The "truck" was a 20-foot Winnebago RV, one of those lane-and-a-half gas-hogging boxes on wheels, parked in an alley behind the arena. It was dirty white with gold trim and bore California plates and the red-and-white logo of the Davis Hendry Band on both sides. "Dave let me borrow this," Eddie explained as we climbed in the side door. "Mine's in the shop, the U-joints went. It's a hell of a lot nicer than this one." He pulled the door shut. "What're you drinking these days, Benjy?"

"Beer's fine, whatever you've got."

"Coming right up."

The RV's interior was compact and utilitarian. Behind the two captain's chairs up front was a booth that enclosed a shower stall, plus a tiny dinette and two sofas that faced each other at the back. The windows were tinted so no one could see in, but there was still plenty of light. Not much room, though, for more than two people. "Must be pretty crowded for you," I observed.

"What do you mean?" Eddie asked as he fetched a bottle out of the small refrigerator.

"Your band, crowding 'em all in here."

Fast handed me the Heileman's Old Style and we sat

in opposing sofas at the back of the RV. Pressing himself catlike in a corner of the sofa, Fast stuck a cigarette in his mouth and laughed around it as he got it going. "Band? I don't have a band."

"But those guys on stage? The 'Engineers'?"

"Club men out of L.A. and Vegas. And they ride in a chartered bus. The RV is just for me and my driver. And sometimes a guest," he added slyly.

"Oh," I said, unconvinced.

"Nobody has bands anymore, Benjy," Fast said patiently. "Bands went out with LPs. Computers are where it's at now. In the studio we can do everything, make any sound we want, with computers. We don't need musicians for that. Just me and the recording engineers."

"So your band name's a sort of inside joke."

"Exactly. When I'm going on tour, I take along cheap backup help, wanna-bes and has-beens mostly. Otherwise I work alone. Makes life a lot simpler." He squinted at me. "What's the matter? I ruin an illusion for you?"

"I guess you could say that."

"Sorry," he replied, looking anything but. "So what's this about graduation and Sara and stuff? I know Beak's organizing some sort of class reunion, right?"

"Yeah, it's on for Saturday night. You coming?"

"Probably stop by. We're playing Lansing the night before. You?"

"Don't know. Anyway," I went on, "Jan asked me to track down missing grads. She also asked me to investigate Sara's suicide. She's always been convinced it was murder, and after looking into it some I agree with her."

Fast Eddie very slowly pushed himself up, unhooked his feet from the table, and crossed one ankle over the other. "Son of a bitch," he commented, looking away from me through his cigarette smoke.

I drank some beer, letting the silence drag out. When Fast offered nothing more, I said, "Sara was pregnant at the time she died."

Fast Eddie blinked and cocked his head, half-smiling. "You sure?" he asked. "What makes you think that?"

"Autopsy report."

"Wow." He got to his feet and paced the narrow space toward the front of the RV, then turned on his heel to face me. Now his expression was dark and distant. "So what are you saying?" he asked, voice a low rattle. "I knocked her up, she put the arm on me so I zotzed her. Is that what you're saying?"

I spread my hands. "I don't recall saying anything at all. You're doing the talking, Fast."

"Well, fuck you, man!" he spat. "Me and Squeak were tight there for awhile, sure. But we broke up months and months before graduation. Whatever bun she had in the oven could not have been mine."

"You dumped her on April Fool's Day," I corrected. "Eight or nine weeks before she died. Timing's just fine."

"You accusing me, Benjy?"

"Just making observations. That's all."

He snapped his cigarette toward the front of the RV, jammed his hands in his pockets, and scowled. "Son of a bitch. I don't believe this. You think I killed her. Well, let me tell you something. Let's get something straight here, bro." He poked his chest with his thumb. "I banged her, all right. I banged her plenty, while we had it going there. But I don't think I was the only one banging her. And I sure as hell wasn't her first."

"Oh, I see," I shot back. "You're in trouble, so Sara was a slut. Sorry, pal. There's a lot of things I don't remember from back then, but I remember better than that."

"Honest to God, Benjy." He was pleading, an almost unheard of thing from Fast Eddie Anger. "I did not cop her cherry. She was well broken in before I ever got to her." He put his palm on his upper chest. "I swear on my mother's soul. On *your* mother's soul, even."

Chapter 17

I lighted a cigar, taking my time about it. "You can swear all you want," I answered. "It's just your word, and that's all."

"All right." He dropped his hand, strolled back to his couch, and sat on it cross-legged. "You think I've got a motive. What makes you think I'm the only one?"

"Here's where you make a case for Caryl Chessman, I suppose," I sneered.

"I'm talking about old Sponge," Eddie said. "He had it in for us, after you marooned him that time. Maybe he went off the deep end, and—"

"Hey," I said grimly, "I'd bury him with this in a second, if I could. But there's flat-out nothing on him."

"Well," Fast said slowly, "let's look at your old true love, Miss Janet Vento, ay kay ay The Beak."

I laughed. "Jan? Get out of town."

"Not so fast." His smile was crafty and dangerous and not especially pleasant. "Her and Squeak were like the Bobbsey Twins academic-wise, am I right? Always Number One and Two, switching positions from quarter to quarter. Well, I happen to know that Beak wanted to be valedictorian in the worst possible way. 'Cause her uncle promised her if she made valedictorian that he'd pay her way to any college she wanted. Otherwise she'd have to work her way through."

An unwilling thought popped into my mind: *Sara made valedictorian. It was announced the night of the party.* "So what you're saying is," I said slowly, "Jan killed Sara so that she'd make valedictorian and get the scholarship?"

"Hey! It's a possibility!"

I was laughing. "That's the dumbest idea I ever heard. If, for no other reason: Jan's the one hired me to investigate. If she's the perp, why the hell would she hire me?"

Fast Eddie shrugged. "Women do all kinds of goofy things. Take it from me. And there's a lot about your friend Jan that you never knew. You can take that from me, too."

"Do me a favor," I snapped. "Spare me your voice of experience. And forget Jan. She's not on the suspect list. You'll have to do better than that."

"How about Spaz?" Eddie shot back. "He always had goo-goo eyes for Squeak. But she treated him like a little brother. Maybe he went into some sort of rage, and—"

"Jesus Christ, Fast!" I exploded. "Richie was the class act of the bunch, remember? A nice kid. And so passive that—remember when we had to go with him to help him get his *driver's* license? Besides, he was in jail when Sara died, got nailed making a beer run." I set my beer down hard and stormed to my feet, fed up with Eddie's bobbing and weaving. In my heart I wasn't sure he'd done Sara, but he'd always had his selfish, deceitful side; had always been up to something. "Leave Jan and Richie out of it. What we're talkin' about here is you, pal."

"Trouble with you, Benjy, is you think you know everything. Always been that way. Real pain in the ass." He was nodding, eyes narrow, jaw set. "A lot went on around you that you were just plain fuckin' oblivious to. Like me and Libby."

The sound of my sister's name made me gape. "Libby? You and—nah."

He was nodding. "For about six months there, right up to graduation. Used to take her down to the park after school, when she told your mama she was at a friend's house studying. Which she was, in a way."

Great, I thought. Great to find that out after all these years. "Don't change the subject," I retorted. "I just got one real important question. If you're so friggin' innocent, where did you disappear to during the party?"

"I didn't disappear nowhere."

"Fuck you didn't. Folks remember. That's what you

get for being so visible; people remember things about you."

"I didn't go anywhere! Where would I go? Tell me where I went."

I grabbed his shirt front and yanked him to his feet till we were nearly chin to chin. "Maybe you went to Sara's house and did something in that garage," I whispered.

He was pale and unresisting. "Prove it."

"Oh, I'll do my best. You can count on that."

"Better bring lunch."

I shook him. "Maybe beforehand, just for sport, I'll put your head through the wall of this-here RV because you fuckin' piss me off so bad."

"I'm sorry you feel that way," he said, staring at me defiantly. "I'd never want to hurt you. Because you're my oldest friend, and I love you."

Involuntarily I let go of his shirt. He absently tugged it down smooth. "I loved Sara, too," he said abruptly. "We were through, but I still loved her and I'd never hurt her, Benjy."

He looked at me, eyes vulnerable. I looked right back, not buying it for an instant. "Where did you disappear to that night, Fast?" I asked.

"Nowhere in particular," he answered.

Which was where this conversation was headed, unless—unless I threw the car bit at him. It was mighty tempting, but I decided to save it; playing your whole hand too early is a rookie move. "Fine," I retorted. My cigar had fallen to the floor; I retrieved it and started for the RV door. "See you in Detroit."

"Back home in Detroit," he echoed. "Safe trip, Benjy."

From there things got no better. I spent the night imitating sleep in an overpriced Des Plaines motel room; the air conditioning didn't work, the toilet bowl leaked, and a party in the next room did not end till I'd made very vivid and specific threats of bodily harm to the person unlucky enough to answer the door.

My rental car broke down, forcing me to walk the final

mile to O'Hare. The rental agent cancelled the $100 "pickup" charge only after I'd repeated the very vivid and specific threats of bodily harm from the night before. Once in O'Hare, I thought my troubles were over.

Wrong again. Jan's flight from Houston was cancelled; she missed the next one, and the third was delayed during a Kansas City stopover due to technical difficulties. So it was past noon before I finally laid eyes on her, walking up the Continental Airlines jetway. I waved, she nodded and marched to me crossly. "Let's get this over with."

She led me to one of those little snack bar places where you stand at sternum-high round tables placed so close together that you brush butts with your neighbors. "Something to eat?" I asked as she set her attache case down and checked her watch.

"No," she answered. "My flight to Minneapolis leaves in exactly fourteen minutes. So you're going to have to talk fast."

"Plenty of time," I answered, grinning. "Lighten up, okay? The day hasn't turned totally to shit. You're with Perkins now."

She smiled despite herself. "You're right, you're right. Oh, God." She sighed. "Are we *ever* going to get a chance to just get together and talk without all the pressure?"

She was dressed once again for business in a long open midnight-blue jacket over a high-waisted skirt of the same color, along with a collarless white-on-white blouse and three strands of pearls. What startled me was the complete transformation of her hair. A trim and a perm had converted her tied-back, tight-ass bean counter look to a softer, more feminine, and definitely more inviting look. She'd obviously applied fresh makeup just before arriving, and she smelled of something sweet and sensual. If it were not for the tight worried lines around her eyes and mouth and the black tortoise-shell reading glasses absently shoved up into her collie brown hair, I'd have sworn she'd readied herself for a date instead of a hurried airport conference.

"Someday maybe," I answered vaguely. "Let's get

down to it, okay? Number one, tell me about Sara's sex life."

Her eyebrows arched. "What does that have to do with—"

I held up a hand. "No time for explanations. Spill."

She shrugged. "Well, it was—there was Fast Eddie, of course."

"Of course. Who else?"

"Nobody."

"That you know of."

"Nobody at all. I was her best friend. She would have told me."

"I saw Fast Eddie yesterday in town here. He says Sara was not a virgin when they first got involved."

"Oh, what does he know?" she said scornfully. "Sexists like Eddie think they're experts on women's bodies. And what does Sara's sex life have to do with any of this?"

"Plenty. She was pregnant at the time she died. But, of course, since you were her best friend, you knew all about that already."

She took a deep breath, swallowed, looked at me and then away. "Of course I didn't know that," she said, voice small. "I'd have told you. Are you sure?"

"It was in the autopsy report."

Her hands, which had gestured in accompaniment to her words, were now still. "It must have been Fast Eddie's," she said after a moment of silence. "There wasn't anybody else. I mean, all she did between the time Eddie dumped her and—and the night she died, was study for that scholarship exam in Washington and get ready for final exams here. At home," she corrected herself. "In Detroit."

"All right," I said. "So Sara's pregnant, and Eddie's the father, and Sara turns up dead. What does that suggest to you?"

She squinted at me. "Eddie? No. No," she said, shaking her head, "you're barking up the wrong tree there."

"That so? Then tell me: Where did Fast Eddie disappear to the night of the party?"

"I'm sure I don't know. Did he disappear?"

"I've got people who claim he was missing for quite awhile during the party."

"I have no idea. Next question?"

Having completed that feint, I came at her from the blind side. "Okay. You went to Emory University in Atlanta, right? Pricey. Where would you have gone if Sara had lived?"

Her eyes went round, she looked past me and then at me, lips pursed. "You lost me, Ben."

"Really? Isn't it a fact that your uncle promised you a full scholarship to the school of your choice if you made valedictorian?"

"Any *domestic* school. He wasn't funding the Sorbonne."

"Fine. And I know it's a fact you and Sara fought tooth and nail for grades. I remember the hysterical fit you threw when you got an A minus on a history final and Sara got an A."

"We always competed. But it was never nasty. We were friends, Ben."

"Sara would have been valedictorian," I said deliberately. "But she died, so you became valedictorian, and got your scholarship, and went to Emory, and lived happily ever after."

Her eyes went glacial, her knuckles whitened, her full lips went to that straight hard line I remembered so well. Had we not been in an airport snack bar, I think she would have thrown something. As it was, I think she was tempted to hurl the table to the floor. "You dirty, twisted son of a bitch—"

"Wait a minute."

"What kind of detective are you? I hire you to find Sara's killer, and the best you can do is accuse *me* of doing it?"

"Actually, it wasn't my idea," I said. "Fast Eddie is the one who made the suggestion."

"Yeah?" she retorted, mouth ugly. "What's your opinion?"

"Oh, I think you're clean."

Color was returning to her face. "Then why hit me like that?"

I shrugged. "You're hiding something, Jan. Hard-nosed business person like you, it takes more than 'pretty please' to get you to come clean. I figured if I shook you up—"

"Great," she said bitterly. Eyes blurry with tears, she picked up her attache case. "You hurt me, Ben. You really, really hurt me, you bastard."

"It's just business," I explained. "Line of work you're in, you ought to understand that." Plus, I realized suddenly, I was still angry with her. Almost as angry as she was with me.

Jan tossed her head and stormed out of the snack bar. I caught up with her on the crowded concourse and matched her furious pace. "Now that you know what Eddie thinks," I said, "maybe you'd like to revise your opinion as to whether he could have done it or not."

"No. My previous statement stands. I have nothing more to say to you. No—wait a minute—yes I do, too." She stopped and faced me, back to a display case full of brake shoes. Her tears were gone, her olive skin was flushed, her voice was strong and certain. "It's true that I became valedictorian after Sara died. And it's true that my uncle gave a scholarship as a result. But he didn't give it to me. He gave it to Darcy Washington."

"Who?"

"You probably never knew Darcy," she charged on, "but of all the black kids in our class she was the one with the best grade average. My uncle gave the scholarship to her because I made him do it. And I made him do it partly as a tribute to Sara, and partly because I refused to benefit by her death, and partly because it would have pleased her."

"Oh. I didn't— I was just trying to—"

"Darcy graduated cum laude from Howard University. Last I heard she'd been appointed a justice of the Mississippi State Court of Appeals. As for me, I went to Emory all right. But I worked my way through, waiting tables, typing, tutoring."

"That's—that's right fine, Jan. I'm—"

She stepped back. "I'll call you when I get to Detroit. Maybe then you'll be kind enough to share what *you've* done for anybody lately. Or ever."

I unlocked my apartment door and pushed. Something was blocking it inside. I pushed harder and the door opened, revealing a disaster of epic proportions, even by my housekeeping standards.

The living room looked as though Stacie had lived in it full time from the moment I left. The coffee table was piled with dishes, utensils, glasses, and ashtrays. Three dead wine bottles lay on the floor amid scattered sections of newspaper. A couple of blankets were wadded up on the couch. The TV was on with the volume turned off, John Tesh doing the *Insider's Notebook*. The patio door stood open, allowing freshly conditioned air to flow out in an arctic rush. The phone lay off the hook next to the answering machine, every light in the place was on, and one of the kitchen chairs lay on its side, blocking the path of the apartment door.

I picked the chair up and carried it into the kitchen. Dropped my overnight bag and bleakly surveyed the mess in there. More dirty dishes, a splash of mail, scattered newspapers, half-cleaned spills. A forgotten Merit Light 100 cigarette had burned a nice groove in the counter top. Jesus. No sound in the apartment. She must have gone out. Good thing. By the time she got back—*if* she came back—maybe I'd have the mess picked up some. Maybe I'd be calmed down a little. Calm enough to give her the handshaker without blowing my stack.

I hung up the phone. The answering box contained no messages, for once. Equipped with a cold Stroh's and a smoldering cigar, I went to work cleaning. I won't call my efforts exhaustive. It was Monday evening and I was tired from the trip, disheartened by the case, and entering what was becoming a ritual depression over the state of my love life. I planned only to hit the high spots here, crash for the night, and take a fresh look at everything in the morning.

I almost didn't hear the phone over the roar of the

vacuum cleaner. I shut it off and grabbed the receiver. "Perkins's Disaster Relief, Ben speaking."

"Good evening," Carole said. "My, that was a long phone call you were on."

"Hey, kid," I said. As I gratefully dropped into my easy chair, I noticed that the room looked a lot better already. Maybe this was a blessing in disguise, I thought. Thanks to Stacie, I wouldn't have to clean again till spring. "Phone was off the hook, inadvertently. How's things?"

"I had my appointment this morning," she said. "Everything's fine. Good strong heartbeat, development's on track, the doctor's pleased I haven't porked out. Now that I'm past twenty weeks she feels the chances of problems are, as she put it, 'statistically somewhat less worrisome.' "

I fired up a cigar. "Don't you love doctors? Constantly reassuring."

"Nothing's ever certain," she observed. "I am thirty-six, after all. And my being a lawyer makes my doctor somewhat wary, I think. I feel great, though. Really wonderful, for a tired old fat pregnant working hag. However, I don't feel wonderful enough to be taking any trips to Hawaii. It's sweet of you, but no thanks."

That stopped me cold for a minute. "Hawaii? What's this about Hawaii?"

She laughed. "The brochure and tickets came on Saturday. For a moment I was really excited; I've never been to Hawaii. But I have court all this week, and Mrs. Miracle can't—"

"Hold it!" I cut in. "What brochure and tickets?"

"The ones you had sent to me!" she said, sounding nettled. "I dropped them back off at your apartment last night. I wanted to thank you in person, but you were out of town."

"Hang on." I went into the kitchen, pawed through the mail, found a brown six-by-nine envelope addressed to Carole. Inside was a slick glossy color brochure headlined HEAVENLY HAWAII, a black-and-white brochure announcing YOUR FREE HAWAII VACATION and a pair of United Airlines tickets. One was in Carole's name, the other in mine.

I went back to the phone but I did not sit down. "Where'd this come from?"

"Well, didn't you send it?"

"Hell, no. I had nothing to do with it." Silence. "When did you get this?"

"It was in Saturday's mail. I just assumed it was from you, your name is on one of the tickets."

"Hey, I'm stumped here, kid. I really am."

"Are they phonies? They looked real enough."

"They're real, all right," I said, examining the tickets page by page. No indication of who paid for them and arranged all of this. Weird. "So these are—for leaving Tuesday. Tomorrow. Returning a week from Wednesday."

"And I just can't do it," she answered. "I've got hearings all day tomorrow and Wednesday. Monday's Labor Day and I'm due up at my mother's, as usual. It's too bad the tickets are nonrefundable and nontransferable. It'd be nice to go to Hawaii later in the fall."

I tossed the tickets on the end table. "Has to be some kind of gag, Carole. That's all I can figure."

She sighed. "Oh, well. And for a second there I was having all sorts of warm thoughts about you. Too bad." Silence. "I met your friend when I dropped the tickets off there last night. Ms. Hawthorne, I believe?"

"Hallthorn. So you met her, huh?" That must have been interesting. "What'd you think?" I asked gratuitously.

"I think you've finally found the perfect blend of form and function. How long has this been going on?"

"Not long. More or less fell into my lap."

"Fell, or jumped?"

"Do I sense displeasure in your voice?"

"Nothing of the sort. I have no hold on you."

"Just checking."

"I'm curious, Ben. What semantics should we be using?"

"What difference does it make? You're as pregnant as you can get. And you and me are splitsville, anyhow."

After a moment she said, "No. Semantics has to do with words, the meaning and usage of words."

"Oh, is *that* what semantics means? I guess I'm a little lost here."

"Evidently," she replied. "Let me explain. We're not married and have never been. And we're no longer involved. Yet I'm pregnant with your child. How do you describe me to others? How should I describe you? What's the word for our relationship? I checked my Miss Manners and she's silent on the subject."

"We're friends, you and I," I said doggedly. "What happens aside from that doesn't matter."

"How kind of you to sort it all out for me."

I suddenly remembered something. "Listen. I'm having dinner Thursday night with an old friend in Ann Arbor. Richard Satterfield, the computer guy, you heard of him?"

"Sure, I've read about him. I didn't know you knew him."

"Well, it goes back a long ways. Anyhow, he'd like to meet you, there might be some work in it for you. Interested?"

"I'm afraid I have plans."

"It's at the Gandy Dancer, only your favorite—"

"Sorry. But it was nice of you to think of me. I'm sure Mr. Satterfield will be sufficiently impressed with Ms. Hawthorne. God knows *I* was. 'Bye, Ben."

I hung up and paced a slow path to the window wall and back. All kinds of lines occurred to me, starting with *being apart was YOUR idea, kiddo.* Too late, as usual. The living room silently begged me to continue cleaning, but I decided to call it quits. Let Stacie finish it up when she came back. If she came back.

I picked up my overnight bag and carried it down the hall to the bedroom. The drawn shades made the room so dark I couldn't tell how badly trashed the place was. I groped for the nightstand lamp and switched it on. Nothing seemed out of place. Nothing except—

A smudge of auburn hair darkened the far pillow. The tousled covers were actually a mound from which protruded a bare brown arm. "Stacie?" No answer. The mound had a stillness to it that, coupled with the room's utter silence, locked my chest in midbreath. I went around the bed, kicking an errant whiskey bottle in the process, and shook her shoulder. "Stacie." Her eyes were closed, her hair bundled back, her lips blue, the skin of her shoulder cool and rubbery. "Stacie! Wake up! Stacie!"

The phone rang just as I got to it. "Yeah!" I barked.

"Mr. Perkins, this is Dwight at the Detroit Public Library, Old Redford—"

"Can't talk now, Dwight, I'm busy."

"A thousand pardons, but this will only take—"

"Dwight! Hang up now! I need this line. I think I've got a dead person in my bed."

CHAPTER 18

I swerved my '51 Ford Deluxe two-door over to the curb, honked the horn once, shut off the engine, and got out. Sara Gerbstadt, who sat crosslegged on the broad stone porch balustrade, looked up from her newspaper and waved. Richie Satterfield slouched on the wide porch steps, soaking up the mid-May sun; he still wore school slacks and shirt as well as his plastic pen pack and slide rule holster, and he did not stir at my approach. "Yo, bro," I greeted him, "your mama's hollerin'."

"Huh?" he asked, sitting up abruptly.

"Said if I saw you to tell you supper's on in a half hour. Hey, Sara."

"Hi, Ben," she answered, smiling. "Headed to work?"

"Yep. Mister Ford needs another eight out of me."

Sara swiveled on the balustrade and dangled her pale bare legs in the sunshine. She wore a sleeveless black top over vertically striped green and white shorts, sandals, and a black headband in the light blond hair that ran smooth to her shoulders. "I don't know how you do it, Ben. School all day and then a full shift at Ford's."

"Man does what he has to do," I answered. Translation: Man does what gets him the dough.

"Besides," Richie said, "there's only three weeks of school left. We're just about there."

"Piece of cake," I agreed.

"Except for the silly little incidental called final exams," Sara said.

"I'll pass," I said, "and that's all that matters."

"Not to me," Sara said. "I've got to ace them all. I know Jan will, and I've only got a two-point lead on her."

I fired up a Lucky Strike. "Well, darlin', if you're in

such desperate grade trouble, why're you out here loafing instead of inside pounding the books?"

"I'm trying to cheer Richie up," she said, smiling down at him. "He's in a very crabby mood today."

I kicked the bottom of his foot. "Cheer up, clown. Just three weeks of school left. Memorial Day in the meantime, then par-TEE at the Bubbas's, then graduation and summertime. Life is good, man."

"Bug off, Benjy," he said sourly.

"I was going to study," Sara said, "but I got sidetracked when the paper came. Interesting obit on Gary Cooper, and a big article about the Freedom Riders." She dropped the newspaper on the porch floor behind her, extended her arms, and yawned. At that moment, to my eyes which had been wandering of late, she looked extraordinarily pretty. "It's too nice a day to be inside studying," she said dreamily.

"Let's go down to Dynamite Park," Richie said suddenly. "Just the three of us, what do you say?"

"Ain't no way," I answered, exhaling smoke. "Your mama wants you home. And the push-boss is expecting me down to the Rouge."

"And I really do have to get some studying done pretty soon," Sara said. "*Alfred Hitchcock*'s on later and I want to—"

Richie had straightened and was staring beyond me. "What the heck is he doing?" he asked, voice suddenly sharp.

I looked over my shoulder to see Fast Eddie's brand-new white Thunderbird convertible weaving toward us up Santa Clara. The top was down, the radio was blasting "Walk Right Back" by the Everly Brothers, and Fast nearly sideswiped my Ford before he reined the T-Bird in to a clumsy bumpy stop, inboard wheels half-slanchways over the curb.

"Good way to mess up your suspension, Fast," I called. He climbed out and started toward us silently. "And thanks for not hitting my car, pal," I added.

Fast Eddie, who wore dark slacks and a blue Dobie Gillis shirt, was anything but catlike that day. He lurched up the lawn toward us, wolflike face dark and distant, and I smelled trouble even before I smelled the booze on his breath. "So what the hell are you up to, Squeak?" he growled, without acknowledging either me or Richie.

Sara had come around to the porch steps and stood next to Richie, who'd gotten to his feet and was openly staring at Fast. I spoke first: "Holy shit, Fast, you smell like old man Mealer on payday."

"Fuck you, Benjy," he rasped. Sara blanched, not because she'd never heard such rough talk but because she was afraid her mother would hear. Fast leaned toward her unsteadily. "I want an explanation, Squeak."

She stared at him evenly. "Of what, Eddie?"

Fast indicated Richie and me with his thumbs. "These two bozos sniffing around you."

"Now, hold everything," I began.

Richie came down the steps toward Fast. "You shouldn't talk to Sara that way," he said, no doubt with more bravado than he felt.

Fast grinned. "Oh, big man, huh?" He reached out with a lightning-fast hand and deftly flicked Richie's glasses off, high-arcing them into the low hedge that fronted the Gerbstadt porch.

With a cry, Richie flung himself at Eddie. I got there in time to bump Richie back roughly, then spun and bulldozed Fast away from the porch steps onto the grass. Every time he tried to dodge me I rammed him back harder. "Calm down, Ed."

"Let me at the little homo," he panted.

"Cool it," I commanded. "I don't want to hurt you, son." Eddie, giving up, raised his hands and nodded. I turned to see Richie on his hands and knees searching in the hedge for his glasses. Sara had not moved except to put her hands on her hips. "I think maybe Eddie ought to go home," I told her.

Sara's pale face was stormy. "I think you ought to let me handle this. I'm not the least bit afraid and I don't need your protection, Ben."

"Suit yourself, sweetie," I answered. I took a last hit off my weed, crushed it out in the grass, and stepped back.

Richie had found his glasses and was wiping the lenses on his shirt tail, breathing hard and glowering at Fast. Sara came down the steps, walked toward the singer, and stopped a couple of feet away. Fast Eddie, who'd jammed his hands in his pockets, was pale, unsteady, and did not seem to want to look Sara in the eye. She asked, "What's this about, Ed?"

"I hate it when you see other guys," he said petulantly.

"I'm not *seeing* these boys. They're pals, that's all. You know that. Besides," she went on calmly, "remember April Fools'? You said we had to go our separate ways. And that's what I've done. Haven't you?"

The drunken Eddie had evidently run clean out of glib. His hawklike face ran a quick inventory of glum expressions and then he said, "Hey, I get plenty of puss-ah, don't you worry about that."

"Then why are you here, making a scene and embarrassing me on my street? Why have you been so nasty to me in school, giving me the cold shoulder, looking at me like I'm not there?" He did not answer. Sara's face went gentle. "I know why," she said quietly. "You're ashamed of the way you treated me. Well, let me tell you something." She put a hand on his shoulder. "I forgive you, Eddie. I forgive you for everything."

"Aw, knock it off," he said uncomfortably.

She smiled, leaned up, and kissed his cheek. He jerked away. Sara turned. "Would you mind driving Eddie home, Ben? I don't think he should be on the streets in his condition."

So I'd be a little late to work. Big deal. "Sure, kid. Come on, Fast, let's go."

He looked at Sara. For a second I thought he was going to say something, but he just gave an awkward wave, then joined me walking across the lawn. "Can I come over to your place for awhile? Till I'm sober enough to go home, I mean."

"You kidding? Ma smells that booze on you, she'll snatch you baldheaded, and me, too. Where's your keys?"

He patted his pockets. "Shit if I know," he mumbled.

"Oh, there they are. You left 'em in the ignition." I

opened the passenger door of the gorgeous white T-Bird, let Fast in, then walked around the boatlike car and leaped nimbly over the driver's side gunwale behind the wheel. A white-over-blue '57 Fairlane hardtop pulled into the Gerbstadt driveway and idled there. As I keyed the T-Bird to purring life, I looked back at the house. Sara was back seated crosslegged on the balustrade, reading her paper. Richie had sat back down on the porch steps and was staring owlishly at his glasses as he cleaned them again.

At that moment the front door opened and two people came out: a girl I recognized from school, followed by Sara's tall, robust father.

"Check that out," I told Fast.

"Oo, the Porcelain Princess," he answered. "Yum, yum."

She wore a dark pleated skirt, light blouse, and loafers, and she carried what looked like a sheaf of sheet music. "Goodbye, Mr. Gerbstadt," she said as she walked down the steps, acting as though Richie wasn't even there.

"See you next week, Stacia," Mr. Gerbstadt replied.

"Reckon she needs a ride?" I murmured.

"I think she needs a ride real bad."

"Nah. That's prob'ly her mama there in the Fairlane."

"That's not the kind of ride I was talking about, Benjy."

But I was right. Stacie Hallthorn, very aware of her audience, walked haughtily to the Fairlane and climbed into the passenger seat. It backed down the driveway and tore away up Santa Clara. As I put the T-Bird in gear I said, "I wouldn't mind fucking that."

"In your dreams, bro," Fast answered.

CHAPTER 19

"Boss."

I was far away, down a steep hill in a dark valley, and I wanted to stay.

"Hey, boss! Wake up!"

A rough hand shook me. I blinked and looked up through grainy eyes into Randy's dark concerned face. We were in the Norwegian Wood maintenance office. I was sitting in my chair, had been sprawled across the desk. My left foot had gone numb. "What do you want?" I mumbled as the events of the past twelve hours popped into my mind like a disjointed and not especially pleasant slide show.

"Got to talk to you."

I straightened in the chair and stretched. "What about? What the hell time is it?"

"Noon. Brian's on lunch." Randy paced the floor pensively. He's a thin wiry guy who just turned thirty, a swarthy kid with long dark hair held down by a Detroit Tigers cap. He wore jeans, work boots, a tiny mustache, and a T-shirt that said FIGHT CRIME, SHOOT FIRST. As he paced, his eyes looked everywhere but at me. Like the time he accidentally dosed the swimming pool with fertilizer instead of powdered chlorine. "Heard your lady friend had an accident," he said.

I was out of fresh smokes. I fished the biggest cigar butt out of the ashtray and began to straighten it gently. "No accident. She washed down a fistful of pills with a half quart of Rebel Yell. She was sayin' the big goodbye, Randy."

"Oh, wow, man," he said quietly. "She all right?"

"They pulled her back just in time. Miracle of modern

technology." Which wasn't the strictest truth. Eric Chwalik told me at 4:00 A.M. that if I hadn't given her mouth-to-mouth, she would have died before the ambulance ever got her to Beyer's. "Doc's not sure about permanent damage. Gonna watch her and see." I flared a match, lighted the cigar stub, inhaled deeply. Ah yes. "Long night. Sorry I dozed off here."

"No problem," he said absently, still pacing his route. "Is she . . . what is she, do you think, goofy or something?"

"Don't ask me," I said roughly. "She's a pill head, that much I know. Who knows what the deal is? She takes pills because she's goofy, or she's goofy because she takes pills. There's no figuring it." The note I'd found under her body said YOU DIDN'T TELL ME SHE WAS PREGNANT. I didn't recall having told Stacie anything about Carole. Was Carole bitchy enough to have mentioned it to Stacie when she stopped by? Hard to believe but who could tell?

I stared blearily at Randy. "Sit down, willya? There's something on your mind, now tell me, boy."

He did not sit. Instead, he folded his arms and looked up at the ceiling and said, in a small anguished voice, "I was with her, man. We were together Saturday night."

I froze in mid-breath, then exhaled smoke and leaned back in my chair. I'd wondered why her hair had been bundled back when I found her. Now I understood. I kept my eyes off the kid and consciously worked on keeping myself loose. "Sit down, Randy. Tell me about it."

He commenced pacing again. "I called your place to find out about putting in some overtime, and—"

"Overtime? That what you call it?"

"Aw, Jesus Christ, boss," he shot back, facing me, "I'm sorry. I'm really sorry. I just got—when it comes to poontang, I'm—but you been *good* to me, man, and I go and— Then when Mrs. J told me this morning about what—oh, Christ, I knew it was wrong, just *being* in your place felt wrong, but she was—"

"I know, kid," I answered.

He ran out of gas then and fell more than sat in one of

the chairs, expression dull under the bill of his ball cap. "You gonna fire me?"

I leaned forward in my chair, toying with my cigar. "No."

He blinked. "Well, that's—I really appreciate it."

I studied him. " 'Cause I know how she is, see. And because at your age, under the same circumstances, I'd probably have done the same."

"You're not mad at me?" he asked guardedly.

I took a pull of cigar, absently observing my hands, how marvelously steady they were. "I think you'd better go find something to do for the rest of the day, okay?"

He hopped to his feet. "Okay. Thanks, Ben."

"Go on."

"I'm really sorry."

"Get going," I said. He left. I studied my cigar for another moment, then pressed it out in the ashtray. Rose, walked around the desk, went to the industrial-sized coffee percolator, and shut it off. Then I took each of the half dozen coffee mugs, smashed them on the floor one after the other, and left.

There was one message on my answering box. "Ben? Eric. Stacie's going to be okay. I want to keep her till tomorrow afternoon, though, just to make sure. You can visit her any time you want. It'd be good if you'd come out tonight. I've recommended that she go into rehab, but she isn't too receptive to the idea. Maybe you can help."

I rewound the tape. Sure, Eric, I thought. I'm going to take Stacie under my wing. Make her my life's mission. Forget it, man. At that point I didn't want to see Stacie. I didn't want to talk to her, have anything more to do with her, even think about her. "The problem is," Elvin Dance had said, "this white boy can't keep his *thang* in his pants." He was right, he was so right. When will I learn? When will I ever learn?

I went back to the bedroom, stripped the sheets off the bed, and threw them in the garbage. Took as hot a shower as I could stand, then debated whether to take a nap or go get drunk. No contest. I dressed in jeans, boots, and a sport shirt, loaded up with wallet, keys, and cigars, and headed for the door, bound for Under New Management. Before I could escape, the phone rang. I grabbed it. "Monastery of St. Benjamin, Perkins here."

After a moment of silence a woman's voice said, "I, uh —I have a message to call someone named Ben?"

"Speaking. Who's this?"

"Kathy Lentz. You've left messages for me here at Whisperz?"

"Oh. Oh, yeah." She sounded reasonably straight. Strike while the iron's hot. "You and I graduated high school together."

"We did?"

"And the twenty-fifth reunion is this Friday, and—"

"It is?"

"And I'm trying to track down some of our classmates who've gone missing—"

"You are?"

"And one of them is Carl Hickson. I understand you know him or about him. What can you tell me?"

"Plenty."

"Uh-huh." I waited. "Care to share with me, Kathy?"

"Just a—just a minute." The receiver was set down on something hard. A soft female voice said something unintelligible, a chorus of voices burst into laughter, and presently Kathy was back. "Mr. Perkins? During business hours Hickson is available at this phone number."

She recited seven digits and I wrote them down in my little pad. "This is where I can reach him, huh?"

"Sort of."

"Well, can I or can't I?"

"Why don't you call and find out for yourself?" She laughed with the unseen chorus at Whisperz, and hung up. I did likewise, nettled. People and their damn games. I was going to leave it for later, but my interest was aroused now, so I punched out the number.

"DSS," the female voice answered, "Carol speaking."

"Carl Hickson, please."

"This is she."

"Pardon me?"

"This is Carol Hickson. How may I help you?"

I stared unseeing toward the living room wall. Now, belatedly, I understood Lew Ferguson's smirky reaction to Hickson's name, as well as Kathy Lentz's amusement at Whisperz. A lot of fun had been had with me on this one. The silence had dragged on entirely too long when I managed, "I'm, uh—I'm Ben Perkins. We graduated high school together?"

"How did you get my number?" she asked.

"Kathy Lentz gave it to me. Anyway, I'm helping the reunion committee. You know about the reunion?"

"Kathy told me," she said warily. "I haven't decided whether to go or not."

The temptation was just to hang up then, escape the uncomfortable situation as gracefully as possible. But I found myself asking Hickson the question I'd asked of all the other alumni. "Do you remember Sara Gerbstadt?"

"Of course," she answered. "She died, didn't she? Just before graduation."

"That's right. She was at a party the night before—"

"I never went to parties," Hickson broke in. "But I know her father."

"You do?" I blurted. "Really?"

"I'm his case worker, in fact."

"You're kidding."

"We never kid at the Department of Social Services," Hickson informed me.

"I've been looking for him. Where is he?"

"If you'll hold a moment, I'll get you Mr. Gerbstadt's address."

You'd think the discovery about Carl "Carol" Hickson would be surprise enough for one day. Nope. Herman Gerbstadt's address, I realized immediately, was in Old Redford, at the corner of Lahser and Curtis. Unbeknownst to me, while sitting in Mrs. Ratchford's house, I'd only been three blocks away from the old man.

It was pushing three o'clock by the time I got there. The day was another insufferable scorcher, August in all of its hot and humid glory; even the asphalt of the streets felt soft under the wheels of my Mustang. It was a day for the pool or the beach or a nice cool saloon, a day to be sailing or a thousand feet up in my ultralight, a day to be sprawled in the shade of a massive oak tree, nuzzling the neck of a half-naked lovely.

It was not a day to be gumshoeing the streets of the city of Detroit, tracking down the elderly and elusive father of a long-dead friend. But what the hell, I thought as I parked in front of the house. You go where the thing takes you. And anything was better than sitting around Norwegian Wood, wondering what to do about Stacie, figuring out how to get up the nerve to push her off the pier.

The house was narrow, tall Victorian, roofed in curling green shingles and sided in chipped baby blue, with an L-shaped porch sweeping around the front, three stacked bay windows, and steep gables pointing in several directions as if standing watch. The lawn was a scrubby patch of matted dead weeds, a busted tire swing hung from a tree like a noose, and a gleaming white Cadillac Seville stood, with a disapproving look on its grille, on the heaved blocks that functioned as the driveway. I had a vague childhood recollection that the property belonged to a doctor or a lawyer or someone important like that. No doubt it had changed hands since then. Probably more than once.

Nothing happened when I pressed the doorbell, so I beat on the rattletrap screen door with my fist till a female voice called from inside, "It's open! Come on in, nice and slow."

The last three words bothered me. I opened the screen door and stepped directly into the metallic stare of the barrel of a gleaming old Ithaca Model 37 pump. It was held in the confident hands of a very enormous and very young black woman—sixteen, tops—dressed in a huge formless colorless smock, seated in an armchair that was giving way at the sides under her relentless weight. She wore cornrows and bright red lipstick and a scowl that meant business. "Whatchoo want?" she growled.

I raised my hands halfway. "No trouble," I said. "I'm here to see Mr. Herman Gerbstadt. I understand he's in foster care here?"

She studied me and then gave one abrupt nod. The bottomless black barrel of the shotgun lowered a bit. "Whatchoo want him for?"

"I used to know him, way back," I said. "I just want to chat a little about old times, okay?"

She snorted. "You want to waste your time talking at him, that's *your* bidness, Jack. You won't get back much that makes sense."

"What do you mean?"

She clumsily lay the shotgun down on the floor. "He's had three strokes," she said, twirling a finger around her temple. "His brains be *all* scrambled up sometime. But go on ahead, I don't mind. And mister?"

"Yes?"

She indicated a plastic juice pitcher sitting on the end table at her elbow. "Fill that up in the sink and fetch it on up to him, will you? He been screaming for it since one o'clock and I don't go up there but oncet in the morning early and oncet in the afternoon late. I have trouble making those stairs," she confided.

No kidding; she was three hundred pounds if an ounce. I picked up the pitcher. "Isn't there anybody here to help you?" I asked.

"Not till momma come home from work by and by. Go on, now. Up those stairs yonder till they quit, then open the door with all the hollering from behind it. Can't miss it; he's our only guest right now."

I carried the pitcher into the kitchen and filled it at the sink. The appliances were old but spotless; the cupboards were freshly painted and the warm summer air held the not unpleasant scent—at least to me—of turnip greens. Pitcher in hand, I crossed the clean, orderly living room toward the stair landing, glancing at the young woman as I did so. She'd turned on *Donahue* and was staring intently at the screen, feeding herself chips with one hand and Coke with the other. I shook my head as I mounted the stairs. You'd be better off dead than in the care of someone like that. . . .

The stairs were wide to the second floor and narrow to the third. As I climbed, the condition of the house deteriorated markedly. The upper floors were dirty and smelled bad; rotted plaster had been inexpertly pasted over, the carpet was worn to the nap, and I could tell the two visible light fixtures were broken without even trying them.

Give me a fiery plane crash, a Colombian necktie, a tight barbwire necklace—anything to avoid being sentenced to a place like this.

At the top landing I waited for the "hollering." Nothing. It was hot up there in the airless hallway and the heat intensified the feeling of claustrophobia and the unclean smells of the old walls. "Mr. Gerbstadt!" I called. No response. There were three doors off the hall. I tried the first knob and it opened.

The room was small, low-ceilinged, and hot despite the breeze blowing through the two open windows. The pale green walls were bare, the hardwood floors ditto except for a tattered area rug in the center. A single-size iron framed bed, more like a cot really, sat along the far wall, attended by a battered wood nightstand. A vinegar stench pierced the air: Urine, of recent as well as remote vintage, permeated the mattress on which lay the wreckage of what had once been Sara Gerbstadt's father.

He lay atop the bed's single sheet, wearing an old green surgical smock and nothing else. The hearty, robust man I remembered from my youth had wasted utterly away into the essential *homo sapiens;* Herman Gerbstadt was a living study of the skeletal system only vaguely obscured by a glaze of whiter-than-white skin. His sticklike arms and legs were bare of hair; so was his head. He lay there rigid and could easily have been dead except for the brilliant blue of his eyes staring at me from his expressionless face.

I did my best to look reassuring; save the rage for the perpetrator, I told myself. "I brought you some water, Mr. Gerbstadt."

He blinked. "Where's Julie?" he piped. At that instant I saw what his inertness had concealed before: The left side of his face was immobile, dead. The strokes had killed half of him. "What happened to Julie?" he asked, a fretful tone coloring the slurred words.

"She's downstairs. Asked me to bring this up. Let me pour some for you." The side table was a clutter of dirty utensils. I poured water into a plastic tumbler and held it out to him. He took it with his good right hand and drank, dribbling fully half of it down the front of his green smock. "Get enough?" I asked as I took the tumbler back.

"I need a straw," he said through his half-ruined mouth. "I've asked and asked but she won't bring me one. Can you get me a straw, son?"

"You got it," I promised. I stepped back from him and gave the room another once-over. No TV, no books, no magazines. Nothing for the poor old man to do but lie there and long for a straw to suck through. The anger welled up in me again and I forced it back. Not now, I thought. Not here. You've got a job to do. Do it.

"I'm Ben Perkins," I told him. "I was a friend of Sara's back in high school. I don't know if you remember me or not."

His eyes seemed to glaze for a moment. "Friend," he muttered. "Sara."

"Your daughter," I added. I didn't know how much to tell him, how much prompting I'd have to do. "She passed away—"

"I know who Sara was," he cut in. The half of his face that worked was smiling fondly. "Sweet baby Sara," he mused. Then he looked at me with half a smile and half a dead droop. "Ben Perkins," he announced.

"Yes, sir."

"How many times did you fuck my daughter?"

CHAPTER 20

Though he said it distinctly enough, I felt sure I'd misunderstood. "Pardon me?"

"Fuck my daughter," he repeated. "How many times? Answer me."

"I never did any such thing," I said as evenly as I could.

With his right hand he managed to inch himself up into a half-seated position against the bare bars of the bed's iron headboard. "Oh, yes you did too," he insisted. "Everybody fucked her. Everybody."

I resisted the almost overwhelming urge to argue with him. He's a sick old man, I thought; a burnout with stripped gears. He doesn't know what he's saying. He is not responsible. The best I could hope for was to prod some information, some facts about Sara's last days, out of him.

"I don't think Sara killed herself," I said.

"Fucked to death," he said conspiratorially.

"I think she was murdered, Mr. Gerbstadt," I went on determinedly, "and I want you to help me."

"Billy helped me," he said.

"What?"

"Billy," he repeated, blinking, licking his lips.

"Billy Hammond? The detective?"

"All of them down there at the precinct. My friends." He laughed. "They knew me. I was always a good citizen. I belonged to all their clubs. I taught their girls to sing!"

"How did the detectives help you?" I pressed, sensing I was rushing but unable to resist. "Did they cover something up?"

"With me, now," he said in a commanding voice, and

then began to sing in a quavering voice: "Coo fa-fa, coo fa-fa, coo fa-fa, coo—"

It seemed to be some sort of voice exercise. "Please, Mr. Gerbstadt—"

"That's not right!" he said imperiously. "Try again!"

"Listen to me," I said. "Listen." He was looking around the room at everything but me, his eyes going in and out of focus, a glob of spittle oozing unchecked down his chin. When he caught sight of me I leaned closer to him and said, "Whatever happened, Mr. Gerbstadt, it can't stay buried. I won't let it. It's going to come out. It's got to be told and you have to tell it."

"Dead," he answered, evidently unimpressed by my brave talk. He let himself slide down flat on the mattress again and turned his head toward the window. "Maybe I'll show you what's in the box," he said weakly.

"What box?"

"Fuck," he replied, and his eyes fluttered and closed.

"Mr. Gerbstadt," I said. He did not move. Great, I thought, so now he's gone and died on me here. I felt the papery skin under his jaw and got a slow, steady heartbeat. Gone to sleep, was all. The smell of urine, to which I'd more or less adjusted, grew suddenly stronger, fresher. I've seen and been through a lot, but that nauseated me. I walked out, closed the door quietly, and pounded down the stairs to the living room.

Julie was still parked in her grotesque Buddha-like posture in the wrecked recliner in front of the TV. She'd switched from chips to Ho-Hos, from Coke to Pepsi, and from *Donahue* to *Geraldo*, but otherwise nothing had changed. My instinct was to break a few things, starting with her neck. Instead I said, "He's wet his bed up there."

Her eyes barely shifted. "So what? He wet his bed every day. I'll clean him up at five."

I stepped toward her. "No, you'll do it now."

This time she went to the trouble to look at me. "You don't tell me what to do."

"You get your fat ass *out* of that chair and *up* those stairs and take care of that old man *forthwith.*"

Without changing expression, she reached toward the

floor for her shotgun. I got there first and kicked it away. Julie straightened in her chair and scowled at me, unmoved. "You get out of my house, motherfucker."

"You do what I told you to do. Now."

"Or *what*?" she retorted. "What'll you do to me, you no-dick honky bastard?" Her grin was hard, much older, humorless. "There ain't a thing in the world you can even dream of that ain't already been done to me."

Her voice had the hard ring of truth, but that didn't lessen my anger any. "It's a disgrace," I snarled, gesturing around. "You ought to be ashamed, calling yourselves 'foster care' and treating that poor old man this way. He's a human being, he deserves at least—"

She was laughing. "Oh, my," she mused. "A human being, eh? Poor old man? My big black *ass*, mister. He ain't no human being. And as for foster care, hey. We're not as good as a few, maybe, but one *hell* of a lot better than a lot of 'em. That sorry old bastard is lucky, *lucky* to be treated as good as we treat him."

Her armor of indifference seemed impenetrable. I tried another tack. "He was always a good man, Julie. He was a music teacher years ago, and he ran all kinds of youth programs in the neighborhood, for black kids and white kids both. He doesn't deserve to end up this way. Think about it, Julie, all I'm asking you to do is think about it."

She tossed her head. "You may have *thought* he was a good man. I doubt it. All the mess he talks at me, the grabbin' and the pokin' and that look on his face, like all he wants to do is crawl up between my thighs and die there—I'll tell you, mister," she said, nodding, "he's bad, that one is. My mama and my auntie think so too. And I'll tell you something else: He can't die soon enough to suit me. I know how that sounds, but I'm the one stuck here seeing after him, not you. If you're so kindly disposed towards him, why don't you bundle him up and carry him to *your* house? Huh?"

"I'll tell you what I will do," I said. "I'm going to get me a social worker and come back here tomorrow, and then we'll see about this. I promise you that."

"Bring 'em on, white boy," she jibed as I stomped to the door. "Bring 'em all on."

"So," Dick Dennehy said, "what'd the social workers tell you when you called? 'Yes sir, Mr. Perkins, we'll go swooping in there with you, to the sound of the mighty trump.' That what they said?"

I looked at him sourly. "From your tone of voice, I gather you know better."

He nodded. "Don't tell me, let me guess. 'We'll put it on the list.' Right?"

"Nothing that definite."

Dick sat across from me in one of the hard wood booths of Under New Management. It was Wednesday noon and a busy time at the saloon; the lunchtime drinkers from Detroit Diesel, Hydramatic, and Michigan Truck jammed the place and maintained a steady male din over the almost feminine crooning of Roy Orbison on the juke. Dick had called me that morning in the Norwegian Wood maintenance office. He was on his way to Lansing from Toledo and asked to meet me. Something important, he'd said. I assumed it had to do with the upcoming murder trial. I hoped it was no big deal. I had trouble enough as it was.

In his gray suit and aviator glasses, Dick was out of place here among all the roughnecks. But he looked as tough as any two of them, and if looks weren't enough, the artillery he packed under his coat would be. "So what are you going to do?" he asked, lighting a fresh Lucky.

"Well, I'm going back there today, like I said I would. Try to put the fear of God in the fat bitch."

Dick leaned back in the booth, cradling his cigarette in one hand and absently swirling his rum-and-coke with the other. "You can try," he answered, "but don't count on it working."

"Oh, I won't. But I got to try." I drank some Stroh's, enjoying the hard kick of the cold beer, badly needed on this hot and depressing day. "I've been in nursing homes and I thought most of them were bad. But this place—

Dick, if he fell off the bed and broke his arm, he'd lay there on it for hours till she waddled up there."

"Sure doesn't sound like the Taj Mahal," Dick observed. "But look, Ben, that's the way it is today when you're very old and have no money. And for people our age, it'll be ten times worse. Which is why I stay in police work."

"State pension?"

"Nah. Short life expectancy."

"Amen, brother." I felt a little better as I took another swig of Stroh's. Leave it to Dick to furnish a good reality adjustment. "Anyway, I need to talk to the old man some more. He said something about showing me the inside of a box. Could be something there, I don't know."

Dick snorted. "I think your case has gone down the toilet, if the best thing you've got going is this half-brain-dead old character."

"It's not looking good," I admitted. "Here it is, Wednesday. The reunion's Friday. Time's running out."

Dick held up his empty glass and rattled the cubes. "How do you get refills in this place?"

"Just like that." I fired up a cigar. "Okay, Dick, you're so fat with something you're about to bust at the seams."

He smiled. "The sheets you asked me to run."

"Pay dirt?"

My good buddy Bill, who tends bar at Under New Management when he isn't overseeing his Romulus bump-and-paint shop, rushed our table with refills for both of us. Dick sampled his new drink with utter indifference and said, "Scored on two of them, actually. Big noise is this Triplett character, Triplett Donald M.? Bad actor, man. Real bad actor."

My pulse picked up. "Tell all."

Dick extracted a sheet of newsprint from his coat pocket. "Ran 'em all through Fat Bob, our neato-keeno state computer. Fat Bob went off like a Roman candle at the mention of old Donny-boy." He squinted at the paper. "1963: convicted of armed robbery, sentenced to ten, served two. In '66 he went down for murdering his wife, pleaded to manslaughter, served five. Arrested in the strangling of his second wife in '74; two trials, two hung juries, case still open in the hope that additional evidence will turn up but, let's face it," he eyeballed me, "if it was going to it would've already."

I handled my cigar, studying its smoldering end. "So," I said, trying to keep the satisfaction out of my voice, "he likes to hurt women, huh?"

"Would appear so. It also appears that he's learned from experience, being a little sneakier about it. First one he did he broke her neck with a stranglehold in a bar full of people."

I sat back in the booth. "Okay. You've made my day already. Who's the other one you found dirty?"

He folded the paper. "Your little playmate out there, Ms. Hallthorn."

Some playmate. Dick should have been with me the previous evening when I visited her in the ward at Beyer Hospital. No makeup, hair dirty and matted, eyes half dead, face showing every long hard mile. She lay on the bed in a formless hospital gown and spoke fluent Um & Er to me as she watched a rerun of *Who's the Boss.* "I didn't ask you to check her," I said, giving away nothing.

"Tough tit. I ran her anyhow. Woulda hit pay dirt sooner, but I thought it was Hawthorne, and Fat Bob said no file. Well, I knew that couldn't be true, so I ran a Soundex and guess what? Fat Bob's got more than a passing acquaintance with her. But then, I suspect, so do most men—"

"You can consider all that said, okay?"

His gray eyes were flinty. "Touchy, are we? Too bad. What you got there is trouble on the hoof, just like I thought."

"What'd she do? Help whack Jerry Buckley back in '30?"

"Nothing that grand. What we got on her is mostly civil. Unpaid judgments and a stack of repos and garnishments; evidently she prefers not to pay bills. A little spotty about filing tax returns, too; there's some people over in Treasury who'd like a word with her. Long, long stretches of no withholding, suggesting no visible means of support."

I sat stolidly as he took a drink and went on. "Lot of traffic stuff, too. Driving without a license, driving while uninsured, driving while buxom in Birmingham—"

"Cut it out, Dick."

"Just kidding about that last one. Wanted to make sure you were still listening. And we've got some nickel-and-dime criminal stuff, too. Drunk and disorderlies from here to Port Huron and back. Loitering, failure to move, obstructing a police officer—"

I could read between the lines. "So she's a hooker, is what you're saying."

"No," Dick shot back. "I don't think so. I think she likes to party, but I don't think she peddles it. At least not in the most traditional sense."

"What the hell does that mean?"

"I'm not sure. You tell me." He took a long invigorating toke on his weed and leaked smoke as he continued. "It seems that there's an interesting little restraining order in the file up in Oakland County. It bars her from the premises and person of a certain Pontiac attorney-at-law. All very cryptic, but I checked with my spies and the story is she was being kept by this rather prominent lawyer—"

"Married?"

"What else? Anyway, in a truly amazing coincidence, he simultaneously came in line for a judgeship and decided he didn't love Stacie anymore. Evidently she threatened to embarrass him. So he got a restraining order and the assistance of the Oakland County Sheriff's Department—"

"Did he also get the judgeship?"

"But of course."

Grim, but not surprising, I thought as I worried my cigar. "But she's got no heavy criminal action, huh?"

Dick shrugged. "Nothing to interest *America's Most Wanted.* Single count of OUIL for which she took a year's license suspension which is still in effect, one theft within a building reduced to retail fraud suspended, and two counts of simple possession of controlled substances, dismissed."

"I see."

Dick whacked ash off his cigarette. "Not a pretty picture."

"No. But it ties in." I told him about the pills and the suicide attempt. "The doc wants her in rehab for at least twenty-eight days. She says she won't go, but I'm going to try to make her."

Dick was staring at me. "Why?"

"Why what?"

"Why bother?" He took a heavy final hit off his weed and crushed it. "The chick is bad news, Ben. A whacko. A drug addict and a nickel-and-dime crook. Unless I miss my guess, she's spent most of her life working the street. Not in spike heels and fishnet stockings and hot pants, necessarily, but a more upscale version of the same thing. Latches onto guys and milks them, and shoplifts and maybe peddles pills in between times to fund her three squares a day, a roof somewhere, and most importantly that gorilla on her back. She may be the greatest piece of ass since Helen of Troy, but take it from me, pal: She's unreconstructed trash."

I stared at him. "She's a very troubled person, is what she is."

"Troubled is right. Deluded, too. If she's anything like the others I've come across over the years, she probably prays to Jesus every night and tells herself that she really and truly is a very good girl, despite it all."

"I'm going to help her," I said stubbornly.

He closed his eyes, shook his head. "Why in God's name would you do a dumb thing like that?"

"Because of the old man."

He blinked open. "Gerbstadt? The drooler? What does he have to do with this?"

"Because him I can't do anything about."

"Yeah? What can you do about her?"

"Well, I can try."

"Oh, God," Dick said wearily. "Every now and then you do this. You take leave of your senses and go all altruistic and save-the-world on me. I know what'll happen. Could take weeks, maybe even months, but I predict you'll be sitting there across from me, getting loaded and moaning about what a dumb shit you were for not stiff-arming her off a cliff."

"Gotta try, Dick." I got to my feet and dealt some worn old bills out onto the table. "Thanks for the poop."

"Vaya con Dios," Dick answered glumly over the rim of his drink.

I threaded my way across the barroom, down the narrow hall past the bathrooms, around a stack of dented empty beer kegs, and through the back door. For once, I wished Dick hadn't been so helpful. For once I wished I did not know everything. Because now I was not so confident about the prospects of helping Stacie, certainly not as confident as I'd made myself sound.

I revisited all the easy excuses and dirty dodges, and what it came back to—even though Dick was right, it was nuts—was that I had to try. It had nothing to do with fulfilling old high school fantasies, and nothing to do with sex. It was exactly like being the first on the scene of a rollover accident. The driver may be dead already, but you stop and do your best anyhow.

I trotted down the short flight of cement steps and hoofed across the gravel lot past an irregular rank of vehicles, mostly pickups, vans, and Jeeps. I'd parked the Mustang in the back, in the shade of a massive oak that spearheaded an acre of virgin woods that ran between Under New Management all the way to I-275. As I hiked, my mind was on Stacie; how I was going to pick her up at Beyer's, deliver her to rehab, then go visit old man Gerbstadt again. . . .

What I did not think about, at least till afterward, was how I'd been to Under New Management thousands of times, parked back here hundreds of times. It gets familiar and comfortable, you get overconfident and careless, you don't expect trouble, you don't even think about it—not until you feel the cool muzzle of a handgun against your neck.

CHAPTER 21

"Freeze, mister."

"Your agenda, my friend," I answered, going stock-still, hands held harmlessly halfway up. "What'll it be?"

He sounded young, nervous, almost excited. He'd hidden himself between a couple of vans and come at me from behind; I'd never seen him. My first thought that it was a punk strung out on crack or maybe even ice, looking for a fast few bucks to feed the monkey. But that seemed unlikely. Your run-of-the-mill addicts are gutless wonders. They'll knock cripples off crutches, sneak into vacationers' homes in the dead of night, do smash-and-grabs, and peddle their asses. They won't hit on a hardcase hangout like Under New Management.

He prodded me with his gun. "G'wan, in there now, between them two vans."

I slowly and carefully walked on the gravel to the red-and-chrome rear of Elmer Kent's big Ford van and stepped between it and an anonymous gray Chrysler mini-whatever. Dick Dennehy was crouched behind the nose of the Chrysler, aiming a truly enormous automatic pistol at us. "Hey, Benjy," he said. "Who's your friend? G.I. Joe?"

My assailant threw a mottled-green arm around my neck and jammed the barrel of his weapon into the skin beneath my left ear. "Make a move," he hissed to Dick, "and he's history."

"Maybe," Dick said lazily. "Maybe not. What I'm getting ready to do here, in case you were wondering, is put a .41 Magnum round through your left eye. Unless you let my friend go forthwith, in which case you'll just take a slug through the knee resisting arrest or something creative like that."

The pistol barrel jammed harder into me, making me wince. "Get out of here," my assailant said tensely, "or I'll blow his brains all over this parking lot!"

Dick's eyebrows shot up. "Did I mention that I'm a police officer? Sorry. State police, and you're under arrest."

"I'm not telling you again!" the man warned.

Dick stretched his arms, squinted behind the sights of the massive automatic, and grinned. "Bet you've never seen a gun like this before. It's the latest thing: a .41 caliber Desert Eagle semiautomatic. Made in Israel. Chambered for revolver cartridges. Muzzle velocity better than 1300 feet per second. Care to see for yourself?"

We all froze in position for about thirty seconds, thirty seconds of silence broken only by the sound of my assailant's breathing, the heavy drone of the saloon's air conditioner compressor, and the almost achingly hard pounding of my heart. Then the man let out a long breath, said "Oh God," and turned me loose.

I came around fast and elbowed him hard alongside the head. His weapon flew, he started down, I caught him and bounced him off the wall of the big van, then rather peevishly threw him there again, causing his fatigue cap to go flying, and braced him. He was in his early twenties with close-shaved blond hair, freckles, large front teeth, and a prominent Adam's apple, dressed head-to-toe in a mottled green-and-black camouflage jumpsuit, complete with black high-topped boots. He was a kid, just a kid who'd watched too many Saturday morning cartoons. I leaned into his face and growled, "What's the story, asshole?"

"I just wanted to talk to you," he squealed.

Dick was beside me now, holding his massive handgun at his side. "Then why didn't you come up to us in the bar, instead of skulking around in there?"

I glanced at him. "He was inside before?"

"Could hardly miss him, in that kiddie soldier outfit. Had a feeling he was keeping an eye on us. Then I saw him follow you out. That's why I came scooting out here to run interference, you didn't look like you were paying much attention. Let's shoot him now."

The kid was sweaty-faced and scared, looking back and forth between us, obviously in much deeper than he'd ever intended to get. "In a minute, Dick," I answered. "I got some questions first." I put my hand on the kid's shoulder and leaned toward him confidentially. "You heard what Dick said. He's serious, you know. He is a cop, but he's a certified crazy. I can control him to a point, but you've got to work with me."

He nodded anxiously, glancing warily at Dick.

"Okay," I said. "Now. What's the story, kid? What d'you want with me?"

"I'm a mercenary," he croaked.

I gaped. "A mercenary? Really and for true? Hey, Dick, we're dealing with a dangerous person here."

He hefted his automatic grimly. "Yeah, if I'd known how dangerous he was I'd have shot him before instead of waiting till later."

"Really!" the kid whined. "I really am a mercenary. I run an ad in *Private Soldier,* see? Looking for assignments? I got a call the other day, man wanting me to kill somebody for him. Somebody named Ben Perkins." His eyes found me. "That's you, right?"

I let the kid go and stepped back, watching him thoughtfully as he wiped sweat from his forehead. "That's me," I admitted. "But if this is your idea of an assassination attempt, I suggest you hang onto your day job."

"This wasn't an attempt," the kid said. "All I wanted to do was warn you. I figured, as long as I was at it, I'd practice my intercept tactics. I practice my tactics all the time, everywhere. Have to, to keep my skill level high."

"Must make you a real hit at parties," I observed.

"Church, too," Dick said. "Turn around, kid. Assume the position."

"I'm on *your* side, men!" the kid protested. Dick raised his weapon. "Okay, all right!" the kid said hastily and turned, putting his palms up on the wall of the van.

As Dick frisked him, I bent and picked up his weapon,

a Charter Arms .32. "So. Someone hired you to kill me. Spill it."

"I didn't take the job," the kid retorted. "I don't do that kind of thing. I'm a counter-insurgency specialist. I work the world's trouble spots. Africa, Central America, places like that. But I'm always willing to put my skills at the disposal of law enforcement, and—"

"And law enforcement is indeed grateful," Dick growled, straightening. "He's clean, Ben."

The kid turned around and took a deep, relieved breath. "I thought, maybe if I could get this guy to agree to meet me, I could set up a sting with the cops and catch him. So I pretended I would help him, talked to him, tried to set up a meet. But something made him suspicious. He said he'd call me back. That was three days ago and he never did."

I popped the cylinder out of his weapon, ejected the rounds into my palm, and gave them a long high toss back into the trees. "How'd he identify himself?"

"He didn't. Said just to call him Sir."

"Why'd he want Ben dead?" Dick asked.

"Dunno. All he said was, it had to be done quick, real real quick. Told me where you live. I was just up there and they sent me down here." The kid's eyes were on me. "He said he'd pay me ten grand, half up front."

"Whoa!" Dick laughed. "For that kind of dough, I'd consider doing the job myself."

"Very funny," I growled, snapping the cylinder shut. I stared grimly at the kid's horsey face. "Anything else you can tell me?"

"Nossir. I did the best I could. Figured I had a duty to warn you if I could—somebody's gunning for you."

I held out his pistol butt first. "G'wan. Scram."

He took it and stowed it in one of the deep hip pockets. "Yessir. Thank you, sir."

"Excuse me," Dick said, tapping my shoulder. "Does this mean I can't shoot him now?"

" 'Fraid so."

"Oh, shit," he sighed. "Well, guess I'll have to arrest him then."

"Come on, Dick, let it slide."

"Hey!" Dick retorted. "I was here, remember? Weapons were pointed. Threats were made. Crimes were committed, and as a police officer I have to—"

"I was only trying to help," the kid whined. "Honest to God, sir, I'm real sorry I got carried away with the gun and stuff."

"Next time, use the phone," I advised him. "Now take off."

He did so, moving at a fast walk toward the saloon with nary a look back. I faced Dick, who was scowling at me. "I rescue your ass," he grumbled, "and you won't let me have my fun."

"You have my heartfelt gratitude, if that helps," I said.

"It doesn't." He stuck a Lucky between his lips and lit up, inhaling his first drag down to his knees. "So who's after you, do you think?"

"Dunno," I said. "It's not like I'm into anything heavy these days. Nothing that calls for something like this."

Dick studied me. "How about your good friend Triplett Donald M.? His sheet makes him sound more'n capable of something like this. Maybe you should inquire of him."

"Maybe I will."

He studied me. "I take it you're not carrying."

"Nope. I leave it at home, most of the time."

"Well, a word of advice for you. Start."

By the time I found Triplett, I was frustrated, hot, and most of all thirsty. So it's probably good that I found him in a bar: the venerable Tattoos, Boots & Motorcycle Parts saloon in Willow Run, tangled up between U.S. 12, the wrong side of Ypsilanti, and the old bomber plant.

The joint was nearly deserted. A couple of bikers in colors were engaged in a quiet conversation in a corner booth. A whale-sized bald-headed bartender was refilling a long row of grungy looking ketchup bottles from an industrial-sized canister of Heinz. The sound system had 'ABX on, and when I came in they were finishing up The Smithereens' "Wall of Sleep." For a place where chains and brass knuckles are considered tools of communication, old Tattoos was pretty peaceful that day. But it was Wednesday.

Triplett sat at the bar, beer glass in one hand, cigarette in the other, poring over the current *Sporting News*. Not for him the casual yupster look I'd seen him in at Retail Computers; today he was shirtless, wearing a worn sleeveless denim jacket over black leather pants and jack boots. His blond pageboy haircut looked silly, but I had the feeling that few jokes were made about it, even in here. Triplett had that air of unfocused meanness that some guys carry around; the permanent shoulder chip, the clenched fists, the attitude of having been done wrong and someone was gonna by-God pay. I've found that such men can be dealt with no problem, if you're toting a piece of pipe.

He heard me coming, squinted at me, and straightened, waiting, light eyes wary, acne-scarred face set in a sneer. "What the hell you doing here, Perkins?"

"I drink here." I gestured to the massive bartender. "Cold one, Billy."

"Coming right up, Ben."

I looked at Triplett and grinned. "See?"

He was unimpressed. "How'd you find me?"

"You weren't at work. You weren't at home. Your wife said I might find you here."

"She did, huh?"

Billy delivered my beer. I drank the lid off. "She did. She seemed reluctant. She gave me the impression you might treat her unkindly if you knew how I found you. I told her I'd check on her later, and that if she happened to've gotten hurt, say, falling down the stairs or running into a door or something, why, I'd made some phone calls."

He let a long moment go by as he took a final hit off his cigarette, flicked it to the floor, and crushed the hot sparks with a jackboot. "I think you ought to mind your own fuckin' business."

I let that go, turning myself to face forward on the stool as if I didn't care what he thought, which was true; and as if I wasn't in the least nervous, which was untrue.

I was about to change tactics when a woman came strolling into view from the game area around the corner.

She was a young/old dark-haired chunky one in cutoff jeans and a snug T-shirt that said GOOD GIRLS GO TO HEAVEN/BAD GIRLS GO EVERYWHERE. Triplett, who was lighting a fresh cigarette, said without looking at her, "Hi there, Marcie."

She ducked her head and steered a course that gave us wide berth. Triplett, chuckling, stepped off his stool and reeled her in by one fleshy arm. "I said, hi there, Marcie."

She did not fight and she did not run. She just stood there glumly as he put his hands on her shoulders and beamed down at her. "I gotta go, Don," she whined.

"You forget your manners, little girl?"

She blinked. "Hi, Don," she said, swallowing the words.

"That's better." He steered her to his stool, seated himself, and pulled her between his legs, snuggling her plentiful ass against his crotch with a bare arm around her midriff. She stood, stiff and unresisting, as he kissed her neck and caressed her arm. "You were looking for me, now weren't you?" he said, voice velvety.

"Come on, Don, please. *Please.*"

From her chopped, washed-to-death black hair to the red-polished nails on the dirty toes that stuck out the front of her sandals, this was one tough, street-smart kick-ass truck-stop mama—yet Don clearly scared her. "Come on," I put in.

His hand was working its way under her shirt. "Come on what, Benjy?" he asked gently.

"Let her go, man. We got business."

"We can do business just fine," he answered, pulling her tighter to him. "She likes me. Don't you, Marcie?"

There was no defiance in her. Just glum resignation and the eyes of a cornered jackrabbit. I said, harder, "Turn her loose."

He grinned. "But that would disappoint her, Benjy!"

I edged off the stool and stood, loose and balanced on the balls of my feet, my awareness going to that higher place in which the physical takes over. "Remember the Bubbas's party? I let you hit me first. I won't be that charitable this time. Let her go."

He put his mouth to Marcie's ear. "Tell him to leave you be," he said. "*Tell* him."

"Leave me be, mister," she said tonelessly.

"Tell him you like it."

"I like it."

"Tell him you're Don's girl, any time he wants."

"I'm Don's girl, any time—"

"All right!" I snapped, sitting back down. Belatedly, I understood it was a lost cause. I understood that no one—not the bikers, not the bartender—cared what Triplett did to Marcie. I understood that Triplett was baiting me and that, perhaps, if I refused to bite, maybe he'd let her go. I even understood, having been around, that there are lots and lots of Marcies in the world. What I did not understand, and still don't, is why so many of them keep coming back for more.

Triplett, laughing, wrapped both arms around Marcie's waist and hoisted her up and back till she straddled his thigh, dandling there like an oversized infant, a great big flesh-and-blood sex doll. For a moment I wanted to abandon my feeble rationalizations and say to hell with the investigation. I wanted to detach Marcie from him, and then coil that pageboy blond hair of his in my hands and double-dribble his face the length of the bar: THOMPa THOMPa THOMPa THOMPa—

The only catch to this heroic scenario was that Marcie would be left behind to take the consequences. So I abandoned my fantasies and pressed on with the questioning. "Your wife know about her predecessors?"

He nuzzled the unresisting Marcie's neck. "Not unless you told her. Did you tell her I killed them?"

The woman did not react. I asked, "Oh, you *did* kill them?"

His hand worked its way under Marcie's shirt. "Maybe. Jury said I did the first one."

I waved a hand. "But did you really? Just between us old classmates."

"Could be, Benjy. Could entirely be." One hand was entirely out of sight now, up high, cupping and squeezing.

With the other he spun his empty beer glass on the bar. Ambidextrous. "Cold one, Billy."

"Coming right up, Don."

I lighted a cigar, being very slow and deliberate about it. "Working half days?"

"What's it to you?"

Marcie's eyes were on me. " 'Cause I might sign on with Richie myself, if he gives his men afternoons off to go to the bars."

"I don't give a shit what Richie does or thinks. I do my own thing at all times. Thanks, Billy." He drank.

"But he called you director of operations. Doesn't that mean you have to actually be there and do work and things like that?"

He snorted. "Him and his fuckin' titles."

I looked at him. "I mean, what do you do there? Do you fix computers or what?"

"I don't go anywhere near 'em." He laughed humorlessly. "Man could get electrocuted, playing with tools. There's much better things to play with, right, Marcie?"

Her only answer was one blink of her dead eyes. I sighed, more frustrated than angry. "Do you boss the people who do the work, then?"

"Man, that's the worst work of all. Fuck that noise." He tongued Marcie's ear. "Speaking of which," he murmured.

She flinched. "Please," she said dully.

"What do you *do* at Richie's place, then?" I pressed.

"This and that." Whatever he did to Marcie under her shirt, it made her wince. "Be nice to me," he said. It was an order, not a request.

"Please, Don. Let me go."

He extracted his hand. "Sure thing, doll. All you had to do was ask." She slid off his knee, straightened her shirt, started away. "Out in the van," he added.

She turned and asked faintly, "What?"

"You heard me."

She trudged out the front door without a look back.

Don Triplett's acne-scarred face was not triumphant,

just satisfied. He took a hearty pull of beer and lighted a fresh cigarette from his dying one. "Any other questions, Benjy? I got a date."

Slowly, carefully I took a big swallow of beer and knocked excess ash off my cigar. "You know why I'm here."

"Do I give a shit?"

"I'm here because I'm trying to find out who killed Sara Gerbstadt, way back then. Did Richie tell you?"

"He mentioned it. You and him want to whack your porcupines behind all that old shit, be my guest. Just include me out."

"You were at the party," I said. "You tried to crash it, remember? You and I had an argument and you left. Where'd you go after that?"

"I don't remember."

"Come on. It was the night before graduation." He didn't answer. "Did you go anywhere near Sara's house?"

"Maybe."

"Well, did you or didn't you?"

"It's possible."

Oh, *Christ* was he enjoying himself. I let my mind dart around the perimeter of the problem and could find no lever, no fresh angle of attack. I mean, kicking his head in was always an option, but for that to happen he'd have to make the first move. More fun that way. "Answer me one question," I said.

He drank. "Ask away."

"Did you kill Sara?"

He looked at me. "To be honest with you, I've killed so many smart-mouthed roundheels, I quite frankly cannot recall."

That nearly tore it. But I kept the lid on. The look on his face was knowing and speculative as I dismounted the stool. "I'm not through with you," I said, throwing a couple of singles onto the bar.

He laughed. "Took the words right out of my mouth, Benjy."

Outside, I spotted Marcie sitting in the front seat of a big red-and-chrome Dodge van. For a minute I was tempted to head over there, have a word with her. But nothing I could say would change a damned thing, so I left.

I unlocked the apartment door and pushed it back, allowing Stacie to enter. I followed and closed it behind me, bracing myself. The moment of truth, I thought. It had been a silent drive home from Beyer's. She seemed to be waiting for the other shoe to drop. I was deliberately letting the suspense build, figuring the edgier I made her, the more receptive and agreeable she'd be.

First I feinted her with an irrelevancy. "I found Mr. Gerbstadt yesterday," I told her as she sat listlessly on the sofa.

She looked at me. Her light blue eyes were glassy, her face wan, her auburn hair limp and dull as if it had been washed to death. She wore the most modest garment I'd been able to find for her: a snug one-piece knee-length knit dress, striped horizontally in green and white. No jewelry. No makeup. No animation. The drug-free Stacie acted as old as I felt. "How is he?" she asked.

"Pretty bad. I'm going back to see him this afternoon."

She licked her lips. "Can I come along?"

"No. I'm taking you home."

She bowed her head and studied her hands, particularly the dull chipped red polish on her nails. "I want to stay here with you," she murmured.

"That's not possible, Stacie. It's time for you to go home."

She looked at me anxiously. "Don't do this to me."

I shrugged. "Everything ends, Stace. You got to go home sometime."

A tear sprang to life in her left eye, welled, and rolled. She ignored it. "I don't have a home," she said to the empty air. "I was evicted, and . . . they put my things out on the street, and . . ." I did not move, just stood there and watched her. Slowly, she covered her face with her trembling hands. "I don't have anywhere to go."

I'd guessed as much, and should have been prepared, but the serious pain made me hurt too, made me want to take her and hold her and promise her protection from the world. Instead, I took a very, very deep breath and said evenly, "Okay. I'll take you to a homeless shelter, then."

She dropped her hands and looked at me with an expression of disbelief almost instantly replaced by dull jailhouse resistance. "I hate those places."

"There's not much choice."

"Let me stay here. Please."

"No. You're bad news, kid."

She brushed away the single tear. "I'll do anything."

"I know about the drugs, about your judge friend."

"You can have me any time you want. Any way you want."

"I know about your police record and everything."

"You want other girls, you want threesomes, I know people, I can bring them here—"

"I know about your little episode with Randy, too."

She broke down then, buried her face in her hands, and rolled down onto the sofa, trembling and writhing as she wailed. "PLEASE don't leave me. PLEASE don't send me away. PLEASE, Ben. PLEASE."

I stood there motionless, arms folded across my chest, looking down at her. I didn't think she'd hit bottom yet, but I'd pushed her as far as I could. I let her cry till I could stand it no more, then said, "There is one other option."

She coughed and snuffled. "What?"

"That rehab place Dr. Chwalik told you about."

"I don't—I can't—"

"It's quite simple," I cut in, voice even, neutral. "You go there. You put in the twenty-eight days and you work the program. You do all that and I'll come back for you."

"I can't—"

"There's no choice, Stacie. It's either that or I'll take you to a shelter. Or I'll put you out on the street. That's a promise."

Slowly she raised herself to a sitting position. Her eyes were bloodshot and ringed in red; her complexion was sallow. She looked thoroughly and absolutely beaten. "You'll take me there?" she asked.

"Right now, today."

"And you'll come back for me?"

"When it's over."

"You promise?"

"Promise."

She took a slow look around the room. "All right," she whispered.

I felt no sense of triumph. All I'd done was bully the helpless Stacie into taking the only real choice available. This would be no reclamation project for me; I'd never felt there was any future for us and I felt no differently now. All I wanted to do was set her upright on the road to recovery. How far she took it was up to her. "Good," I said blandly. "Go on, get your stuff together."

She stood. "Could I—could we go see Mr. Gerbstadt first?" she asked shyly.

"Oh, I don't think so."

She blinked and swallowed. "Please. It would do me good to see him again."

I didn't like it. I didn't want to lose any time getting her into rehab. And seeing that creepy old man might really upset her. But I couldn't stand her whipped submissiveness. Let her have something, I told myself. Let her have this. "Okay."

Her smile was tentative, half-formed, but there. "Thank you," she whispered. She came to me and gave me a prim cold kiss on the lips. "Let me have a few minutes," she said. "I've got a lot of packing to do."

CHAPTER 22

The western sky was knotting up into a threatening mess of grays and blacks as we rolled into the Old Redford section of Detroit. As I'd done the day before, I parked at the curb in front of the big Victorian house on Lahser, then led Stacie up onto the porch and tapped on the screen door. "You can put away the artillery," I called into the darkness. "It's just little old me."

"Sheeit," came Julie's voice. "Who that with you? Don't look like no social worker to me. I thought you was gon' bring a social worker to straighten my fat black ass out."

"It's just a friend. We want to see Mr. Gerbstadt again."

"Come in, then."

We entered to find Julie in her usual position, slowly wrecking the recliner chair with her massive, inert bulk. Today the food was brownies, the drink was Vernor's, and the TV was *Sonya;* otherwise, everything was as it had been the day before, including Julie's sparkling mood. "Don't be too long up there," she growled as we walked by. "You got him so worked up yesterday, I like to've never got him calmed down."

"What'd he do? Piss his bed?" I asked sarcastically.

"Just do what you came to do," she said poisonously, "and then get the *hail* out of here."

Stacie gave me a long wide-eyed look as we started up the stairs. She looked noticeably better. She'd made herself up, primped up her hair, inserted a tiny diamond earring into each lobe, and sprayed on some kind of pleasant subtle scent. She wasn't the bombshell she could be, but she was no longer a burned-out husk either. Resilient "Remember what I told you," I said quietly as we walked up the stairs. "The old man's pretty goofy. It's hard to understand him and he's got one ugly mouth."

"I'm sure I've heard it all before," she replied.

The first thunder rumbled in the distance. As we reached the top landing I heard the staccato report of raindrops on the roof over our heads. I opened Gerbstadt's door and peered in at him. He lay on his side in his green surgical smock, facing away from me. "Mr. Gerbstadt?"

He twitched as if pinched and looked at me. "Oh," he rasped, "you. Come in. Come in."

We entered. The room was dark from the gathering gloom outside. Gusts of cool wind sent the thin white drapes dancing and made the room smell cleaner and fresher than it was. Gerbstadt's head, as shiny and hairless as a skull on display, was propped on a pillow. The rest of him, what was left of him, lay supine and half dead. He dragged himself up till he was half leaning against the bars of the headboard. "Who's that with you?" he asked in a hoarse cackle.

"It's me, Mr. Gerbstadt." Stacie's mouth was white and flat, her hands fidgeted, and she stayed resolutely by my side. "Stacie Hallthorn. Remember me?"

The thunder spoke again, closer. "Come closer," the old man said, holding out his clawlike right hand. "I can't see you."

She stayed put. "You taught me to sing," she said, voice tight.

"Come over here!" he rasped.

She faced me, pasty and old looking. "I have to find a bathroom," she managed, and slipped out of the room at a fast totter. I wasn't surprised. I was, in fact, relieved. I hoped she'd wait for me downstairs, or outside in the car.

"Where'd she go?" Gerbstadt demanded suddenly.

"Out," I answered. "Remember yesterday, when we were talking? You said you'd show me what was in the box. I'd like to see it."

"No," he said darkly. "I'm not ready."

"Where is the box?" I asked kindly. He pointed downward. "Under the bed?" He nodded. "Let me see it."

"No. Not yet," he puffed.

"Fine," I answered, resolving to take it before leaving whether he liked it or not. "Sir, do you remember yesterday when we talked about Sara?"

"I remember Sara," he answered. "Nice pussy."

I blinked at that, but let it go. All those short circuits inside that polished skull—I could almost see the sparks, smell the smoldering insulation. "Tell me about Sara's friends. All the people who knew her best."

The thunder banged in earnest now, punctuated by jagged streaks of lightning out the west window. Gerbstadt rambled on, barely intelligible under the steady din of rain on the roof. The best I could figure was that he was talking about boys. He said Eddie Anger's name several times, a twisted snarl on his face. He mentioned me and Richie Satterfield and names I'd never heard. As the thunder front passed by, receding to the east, he said, "—thought she was yours, dint you? Betcha didn't know she was thinking about Daddy whenever she did it. Daddy was her first. Daddy was her *best.*"

I stared at him. Suddenly a lot of things made sense. Maybe even her death; maybe it *was* suicide. I believed him, believed he was telling the truth. As sometimes happens, the truth did not cleanse; it made me angry and sick. "Daddy," I echoed when I could manage it. "You?"

"Who the hell else?" he cackled.

"Did you kill Sara?"

"Kill Sara," he sang. "I could have. Oh yes. After Marty I could have. After Marty took her from me."

"Who's Marty?"

"I could have, yes. She's back."

"What?"

"Pussy," he said dreamily, eyes looking past me.

Instinctively I turned. Got just a glimpse of a human shape—female—*Stacie* and then I was hit, a solid blow to the side of the head. I went to my knees as the world did a slow jerky counterclockwise spin. She swung at me again, two-handed, both hands around the barrel of—my gun, that's my gun, she's got my *gun*—

Then everything was gone, gone as if it had never been.

"—just the two of us."

"You hit him. You knocked him down real good."

"—the two of us now, Mr. Gerbstadt."

My vision returned then. The wall, green wall, the green wall of Gerbstadt's room. Floor level, dirty shoe molding, chipped paint. I lay on my stomach. My hands were bound behind me, very tightly. Felt like some kind of tape. My feet seemed free but weighed about twelve tons each. My mouth was full of the thick taste of blood. My head felt like it was being held down by an elephant's foot, and it was pounding, each impact shooting a spear of pain to the center of my skull and making my vision shiver.

Springs squeaked. "Can we talk, Mr. Gerbstadt?" Stacie asked.

"I'm not much of one for chitchat, honey," he wheezed.

"I know. I remember."

One, two, three, *now.* Straining against the elephant's foot I lifted my head, turned it, lowered it to the floor again overly hard. When the burst of pain had subsided, I found that I could see the bed fairly well. Gerbstadt had not moved. Stacie stood over him, leaning on the bed. My .45 automatic lay on the sheet down by the footboard, within her easy reach. But it didn't look like she planned to use it anytime soon; for, in her left hand, out of Gerbstadt's sight, she held a short, shiny boning knife.

At that moment, for the first time since she hit me, I wondered if I was going to get out of there alive. I strained at my wrists; no give at all. Stacie had done the job well and, besides, I was as weak as a kitten. Every time I strained, my vision went flickery and the throbbing in my head threatened to send me under. You stupid bastard, you stupid, ignorant son of a bitch—

"—can't *believe* it," she was saying. "How could you forget? I lived on Pickford just this side of Evergreen. Stacie Hallthorn. My parents were Bob and Sylvia. Mother used to bring me for my voice lesson on Tuesday afternoons, four forty-five. You really don't remember?"

"Did I fuck you?" he asked guardedly.

She held out her free hand to him. "What do you think?" she asked gently.

His smile was half a grimace as he raised his hand to hers. Instead of clasping with him, she grabbed his wrist, bent his hand down to the wood side table, came over hard and fast and speared him to the table with the boning knife.

Gerbstadt's good eye bugged wide and then wider, as if about to explode. His back arched, his good arm flopped against the pain of the knife, and his mouth strained to scream. But he never made a sound, because Stacie produced a large fluffy wash cloth from under her arm and stuffed it into the old man's mouth, twisting it and tamping it, working it in till his cheeks bulged. Then she stood and watched him as he twitched and strained, making faraway sounds down deep in his wasted chest. I did not see her expression till she turned and caught me watching.

She looked satisfied.

"I'm not going to hurt you, Ben," she told me.

She turned, picked up my .45 automatic and, with a languid movement, slid herself onto the bed near the foot, facing the struggling Gerbstadt. She arranged herself crosslegged, the hem of her dress hiking well up her thighs, showing miles of tanned skin. She put the .45 in her lap, unsnapped a rubber band from her wrist, and began to bundle her hair back as she addressed the old man.

"When I was eight," she began, "you touched me for the first time. You also made me touch you. That went on for awhile. The next year you made me jerk you off . . ."

I worked my wrists back and forth, back and forth, trying to produce some give, any give at all. The throbbing in my head was a little better and my legs felt like they might support me again sometime this month. If I could just buy some time . . .

"—in the ass," she said matter-of-factly. "Became a regular thing along with the blow jobs. It never stopped hurting. There wasn't a time you put it in me that it didn't hurt. Every Tuesday, the last fifteen minutes of the lesson, you really—you really made me sing." Her composure began to go then, her hands handling the .45 automatic, stroking it spasmodically. "You ruined me, Mr. Gerbstadt. You made me weak, I never had the chance to get strong, there's never been anything for me. Men, jobs, children, nothing—no peace—nothing for me anywhere . . ."

Gerbstadt's struggles were weaker. I wasn't sure, but it looked in the dim thunderstorm light from outside like his face was darkening, his mouth a jagged slant of rictus. I struggled harder at my wrists and felt my skin rip.

"I wanted to tell," Stacie said, "but those pictures . . . you were always so sweet to me beforehand, and then called me slut and whore afterward. What could I do? I was just a little girl. I was weak and you were strong. You had no right, no right to do that to me. Why did you do those things to me? I've always wanted to know, Mr. Gerbstadt. Tell me . . . Mr. Gerbstadt? Where are you?"

He had not changed position. He still half-slouched against the bars of the headboard. But he no longer moved.

"Oh," she said in a small voice. "Did you go and die on me?"

No reply. My guess was that he inhaled the wash cloth and strangled on it. But maybe it was nothing that gruesome. Maybe his heart just gave out.

"You cheated me," she observed softly. "You got away. You weren't supposed to get away." She hefted the .45. "Let's see," she murmured. Being careful of her long thumbnail, she pulled back the hammer with a double click. Then she delicately arranged her hands around the handle of the weapon, held it against her belly aimed at the old man, and fired.

The close-range slug ripped into Gerbstadt's chest and tossed him around like a rag doll. He came to a blood-soaked rest with his head near the table where his hand was speared, his eyes staring lifelessly up toward the ceiling. Stacie was whimpering and holding the .45 gingerly: "Oh, *shit,* that hurts! Jesus!"

A second wave of thunderstorms was marching on the city of Detroit, heralded by the booming of what sounded like naval guns outside. A gust of wind lunged through the western window, making the drapes dance again. Stacie did not notice. She was examining the .45. "Oh, I see," I heard her say. "It cocks itself."

Against my better judgment I made a protesting sound. She ignored me. Turned the weapon muzzle up, sniffed the snout, kissed it, licked it. Slid it into her mouth and then out; her mouth was barely big enough to accommodate it. When she looked down at me, her expression was blank. "You were right, Ben. Everything ends."

My heart was racing wildly. I managed to force words through my dry mouth. "Don't. Don't."

"I'm sorry about hurting you," she answered. "But it's all your fault. Don't you see that? Your fault, Ben. Your fault." Her eyes filled with tears. "You shouldn't have saved me before. You should have just let me go."

"Stacie, no," I said hoarsely, thrashing at the tape which had become slippery with my own blood.

She held the weapon in both hands, muzzle up, and inserted one thumb through the trigger guard. Opened her mouth and slid the barrel in like a popsicle, deep and then deeper. After a long moment she pulled it out. "Something's wrong," she murmured. "What's wrong with this thing?"

It's the grip safety, I thought. The .45 automatic is designed not to fire unless you're holding the grip properly. Safety for all. Stacie rearranged her hands. Inserted both thumbs through the trigger guard and slid the barrel into her mouth again.

That time it worked just fine.

CHAPTER 23

BEEP "Ben? Brian over at the maintenance office. Hey, it's eight-thirty and you're not here yet. Just wondered what's up, if you're out of town or on a case or whatever. Don't worry about us over here, we're fine. We'll be a little shorthanded with you out, since Doug called in already, he got two flats on Dixie Highway down in Monroe and has to wait around for spares. Randy'n me split up the jobs and we'll get her done. So let us know, okay?"

BEEP "Mr. Perkins? Alice Chalmers at the Wayne County Morgue. We have the remains of one Hallthorn, S., white female, in our possession, which you formally identified last evening? The homicide squad and the medical examiner have released the remains for disposition. I'd appreciate your advising us as to the next of kin or the responsible party. If you are in fact the next of kin or responsible party, I'd appreciate your advising us as to arrangements for funeral and interment. Thank you."

BEEP "Hey, boss-man, this is Glenda, your duty Negro out at the front gate. Just thought you should know you're suddenly popular with the press. I done sent away two print guys and a Channel 4 team already. Broke my heart to chase that last one; guy was Kevin Bacon all over again, looked right tasty for a white individual. May I say in conclusion that it is indeed an honor to be in the employ of a person as prominent as you, sir. 'Bye now."

BEEP "Ben, it's Carole. Pick up the phone . . . I know you're there, now pick up the phone! . . . Have it your way, damn it. I just now got a call from Captain Dance of the Detroit police. He told me, informally, about the incident you were involved in last night. I am very distressed, Ben, *very* distressed to learn that you underwent six hours of questioning at the Sixteenth Precinct without availing yourself of counsel. May I remind you that I am your lawyer, and Shaughnessy Levin is your lawyer, and either or both of us would have been available to assist you. From what Dance says, you're in the clear, but call me ay-sap, if not sooner."

BEEP "Elvin Dance, homicide. Checked up on your weapon and it'll be out of impound by first of the week, meaning Tuesday, since Monday's Labor Day. Check with the property desk down here at 1300 and be sure to bring your permit. Weapon'll prob'ly need a good cleaning before you can use it again. With those type of suicides you usually get blood and tissue and other matter sucked up into the barrel, something to do with negative pressure in the barrel after discharge. Have a nice day."

BEEP "Good morning, Mr. Perkins. This is Sally calling from the office of the Central Executive at Retail Computers. Mr. Satterfield wishes me to remind you about your dinner engagement with him this evening? Gandy Dancer, Depot at State Streets, Ann Arbor, seven peeyem. Mr. Satterfield wears a sport coat and tie, typically. Please call me if you wish to discuss this."

BEEP "This is Dwight calling from the Detroit Public Library, Old Redford branch. It is Thursday, August 28, half past eleven. Once again I'm constrained to remind you that we are holding the literature you requested on automatic garage door openers. Since valuable library resources have already been expended locating this information for you, it would be *very much appreciated* if you would stop by and pick it up."

Don't hold your breath, Dwight, I thought as I mashed the rewind button. I didn't plan to go anywhere any time soon. I'd been holed up here in my apartment since the cops turned me loose at the dark grim hour of 2:00 A.M. When I got home I showered, bandaged my head and wrists, pounded down a fistful of aspirin, and slept fitfully for several hours. Then I showered again in a fruitless attempt to get the slaughterhouse smell out of my nostrils, rebandaged, reaspirined, and slept some more.

Now it was noon. I'd showered yet a third time, taped

myself up, dressed in cutoff jeans and a Detroit Tigers T-shirt, and equipped myself with a cigar and a Stroh's dark. It was time for heavy thinking and drinking, more of one than the other, guess which.

Afterward I'd break the box open and see what was inside.

But first, booze. Booze to dull the memory of a ceiling speckled with auburn hair and brains, the rest of Stacie inert on the bloodslick bed with one eye open, the other gone, face collapsed beyond recognition . . . as well as Julie downstairs, sporting a second red smile between her third and fourth chins, no doubt inflicted by the boning knife as Stacie came back in from the car with my automatic in her hand. . . .

Gerbstadt. He was the father of it all. He'd destroyed Stacie just as surely as if it had been his thumbs on the trigger instead of hers. I felt she was just one of a long list of victims. A list which may have been headed up by his own daughter.

I didn't think he killed Sara. His alibi had been verified, according to the police report—some concert down in Toledo. But if he was sexually abusing her—if he was in fact the father of her unborn child—perhaps he sent her on the road to suicide. Knowing she was pregnant by her own father would have been pure torture for her. It could have pushed her over the edge. And in light of this new information, even the physical aspects of her death could support suicide. Elvin and I had wondered why Sara would drive the Del Rio wagon home from the party and then inexplicably use the Fairlane 500 to fill the garage with lethal carbon monoxide. Switching cars might have been Sara's way of fingering the ultimate villain. For the Del Rio belonged to her mother, while the Fairlane, the instrument of Sara's death, was her father's. . . .

I drained the beer and began another. What about the car Mrs. Ratchford saw? a quiet voice asked. (An old woman's addled memory. Maybe.) And what about this "Marty" person the old man mentioned? (An old man's sick ravings. Maybe.) What about your stubborn conviction that Sara was too smart, too strong, too *brave* to kill herself? (Wishful thinking, maybe.) What about that little red sign that blinked SETUP SETUP SETUP on my mental console? (Overheated imagination, maybe.)

Forget the perps. In this business, it's the maybes that kill you.

Suddenly the second beer was gone. I felt a little lightheaded, a little removed. Perfect. Let's go do it.

I went into the kitchen. The gray gunmetal lock box sat almost ceremonially in the center of the dinette table. It was eighteen inches square, battered and old, dull and somehow evil looking. Aside from its location, it was exactly as I'd found it under Gerbstadt's bed shortly before the cops arrived the night before.

I took a screwdriver from the utensil drawer and commenced prying at the old riveted latch. Probably nothing in here but old bills, I thought. Vacation pictures, a diploma or two, maybe an old bank book.

Innocent stuff like that.

At first I resolved to ignore the knocking at the door. But there was something familiar about the sound, so I peered through the peephole to see Carole standing there. I opened the door. "Sorry," I said, "we're closed."

"You threatened dinner," she replied. "Gandy Dancer, as I recall."

"You turned me down."

"I changed my mind. Woman's prerogative."

"Wait a minute. We're all equal now, women aren't supposed to have prerogatives."

"We do when it suits our purpose, buddy boy. May I come in?"

"Sure, of course, sorry." I stepped back, she entered, I closed the door behind her. "Frankly, food's about the last thing on my mind right now."

"You've got to eat." She sniffed, and her eyes narrowed. "You can't live on beer, you know."

"I'm giving it the old college try."

"Come on, Ben. I've had a long week, I'm getting hungry, and I'm all dressed for the occasion."

She was, too. She wore a tan business suit, generously

tailored in front to allow for the gentle bulge of pregnancy, over a white silk blouse with a long strand of pearls. She'd allowed her heavy wavy blond hair to grow out some, making her look softer, more feminine, more radiant. As usual she'd been sparing with the makeup around her dark Mediterranean eyes and full mouth. For what she described as a "tired old fat pregnant working hag," she looked great: five foot nine of beauty, brains, and vitality.

"We can always just stay in and visit," I replied. "If food's what you want, that's easy too. Times like this is why the good Lord invented Little Caesar's."

She grimaced. "I can't eat that stuff. I'm a pregnant lady, remember? We are the parents of a future young American person."

I forced a smile. "Well, if Junior down there picked up any of my genes, he'll welcome a big greasy slab of pepperoni double-cheese right about now."

"On the other hand, she might have a taste for the finer things."

"Hey, steak's good too, no problem."

"Come on, Ben, I really want to meet Richard Satterfield."

I raised my hands in surrender. "Okay, all right, we'll go."

She came to me then, shook her head with a worried half-smile, and surprised me with a gentle hug and a sisterly kiss. "Are you all right?" she asked, holding my hands tightly.

"I'll live. Something to drink?"

"Please."

I led her into the kitchen. As we passed the dinette, she gave the opened lock box and the scattered piles of papers and other items a curious look. I found a diet Vernor's in the fridge, equipped Carole with it, and escorted her into the living room. She took the sofa, crossing one long elegant leg over the other, and I resumed the position in the easy chair with a cold Stroh's in one hand and a smoldering cigar in the other, propping my big bare feet up on the coffee table.

"Are you really all right?"

"Well, I got a big gash on the side of my head here," I said, gesturing. "She socked me with the butt of my gun, the lip of the magazine carved a nice slice, I guess. My wrists are ripped up from where I tried to tear myself loose. Other than that, I—"

"I mean emotionally, Ben. The woman—Stacie—she's the one I met here last weekend, right?"

"Uh-huh."

"She was pretty special?" Carole asked, voice neutral.

"Not the way you mean. Nothing long-term."

She looked away toward the window wall. "Captain Dance said it was an ugly scene, pretty gruesome even by Detroit standards. Two murdered, one suicide. He also said it's a miracle she didn't kill you too."

"Who can figure a fuckin' whacko?" I asked roughly. "Maybe she left off me because I never hurt her, tried to help her. I was going to put her in rehab, then help her get back on her feet. Daddy Ben here, the big know-it-all fixer."

"You tried," she said gently. "You went up against tough odds and you did your best."

"It just ain't right, what happened to her."

"But inevitable, probably," she observed. "I can't speak to the justice of it. But one thing I do know: If she'd taken you with her, that would have been the ultimate injustice. Think about that."

"Would've ruined *my* day, that's for sure."

"Mine too."

I smiled and looked away, breathing evenly for a moment. Times like that you're scraped raw, the slightest little thing can get to you. I adjusted myself in the chair and asked, "Want to hear about the case? Chapter and verse?"

"Sure, if you want to tell me," she answered coolly. "I know you tend to be close-mouthed about—"

"Let me bounce it off you, see what you think." I gave it all to her. Sara, Fast Eddie, Richie, Janet, and me; the graduation party, the suicide that felt like murder and then like suicide again; the police report, Sara's pregnancy, Agnes Ratchford and the mysterious car, Billy

Hammond and the suspicious investigation; old man Gerbstadt and his appetite for very young girls.

And Don Triplett, with the blood of two women on his hands.

And my appropriation of Gerbstadt's lock box.

Her expression said, *When will you ever learn?* "That's illegal, you know. Theft, obstruction of justice, concealing evidence."

"Guilty on the theft," I said wearily. "But forget the rest. There's no justice to obstruct, for one thing. Stacie done took care of that. And as to the evidence—well, I suppose you could call it evidence, but it don't matter any more, least not to anyone but me."

"What is it?"

"Come on in the kitchen. I'll buy you another drink and show you."

CHAPTER 24

I found her another Vernor's and armed myself with a fresh Stroh's. At the dinette I had a last minute attack of cold feet. "This is pretty rough stuff," I said. "Sure you want to look?"

"Show me," she answered tightly.

I dug into one of the big manila envelopes, extracted a handful of snapshots, and handed them over. At the first one, Carole blanched. "Oh, my God in heaven!" She leafed quickly through them, punctuating each glance with a pained sound. "Is the man Gerbstadt, do you think?"

"I presume so. Timed camera shots or whatever."

"Oh, God, the expression on this poor child's face." She tossed the snaps face down on the table and hugged herself hard, expression icy. "I don't want to see any more."

"Don't blame you."

Her lips were parted, complexion flushed, eyes burning. "You know what I think? I think that Gerbstadt has gone to a special place in hell."

"If there is such a thing."

"Even if there isn't, from what you say, he died very slowly and very painfully, and this is very good."

She swept into the living room. I picked up something else from the table and followed her. She'd shucked her jacket, kicked off her pumps, and resumed her place on the couch. She looked like I felt now, more weary than angry. "How many are there?" she asked me after a moment.

"Pix? Couple hundred. Best I can tell, a couple dozen girls. Stacie's in there. Sara too."

"So you were right. He was molesting her."

I sat down and lighted a fresh cigar. "He was obsessed with her. There's a diary in there, he started it when she was born. All he wrote about was Sara. What she did, what she said, her vital statistics, her grades as she grew up, her activities, friends, favorite TV shows and books and movies. And then, when she was nine, he started—"

She held up a hand and looked away. "Please spare me."

"He wrote about that, too," I said. "I didn't read much of it. After I got the general drift I skipped to the end, to see if there were any clues about her death."

"And?"

"Zip. In fact, he stopped writing just after she got back from the National Achievement Scholarship exams in April."

She pondered for several moments. "So the case is over? It was suicide after all. Right?"

"That's what I thought. Till I found this." I handed the letter to her. At her doubtful look I said, "It's okay. Go ahead."

She examined the envelope. "Metairie, Louisiana. Suburb of New Orleans?"

"Right." I watched her extract the single sheet of paper, unfold it, and read. Mentally I read along with her.

June 30

Beloved Sara,

Please, *please* call me or write to me and tell me what's going on! Why haven't you answered my letters? Why do they hang up on me when I call for you? I've been in agony since that day at the train station when you didn't show up. What about our plans? What about our *baby*? Please, *please* call me—write to me—*come* to me! Everything is ready and waiting for you. I'll meet the train every morning till I hear from you or—please God—till I see your pretty face smiling at me!

All my love,

Marty

"Oh," Carole said, rereading quickly. "Oh my." She looked at me, squinting. "June 30. How long was that after—"

"Three weeks, she'd been dead three weeks."

"But he didn't know," Carole murmured. "What's the story, do you think? Any way to track this Marty down?"

I snorted. "I doubt it. We got no last name in a city of two hundred thousand, going back twenty-five years."

She tapped the note. "So what do you *think* happened?"

I gnawed my lip. "I've been thinking about that and I've got it to where it listens. See what you think." I drained my beer, promising myself it was the last one. "This guy's from Metairie, right? Now where is she going to meet somebody from a place like that? Prob'ly the scholarship exam thing in D.C. that she went to in April."

"If you say so," Carole answered. "Seems flimsy to me."

"Couple things support it. The old man told me Sara cut him off 'after Marty.' And that diary of his, he quit writing in it after she got back from the exam thing in D.C."

"You'd be laughed out of court. But okay."

"They met," I continued, "and I guess it was the big big story. She's rebounding from Fast Eddie, for one thing. She's the romantic sort, got her head in the clouds all the time. And we know now, her dad made her life a hell on earth; she was looking for an out. Comes now this Southern boy and it's like a thunderbolt for both of them. They trip the light fantastic there in D.C. They make all kinds of promises and stuff. When she gets home, she cuts off her old man once and for all. Tells him she belongs to someone named Marty now."

"That must have been quite a scene," Carole observed.

"Then she finds out she's pregnant."

"Here's a disgusting thought," Carole said quietly. "It could have been her father's."

"I don't think so. Richie told me she had a real bad menstrual period just before the D.C. trip. He was helping her study, he was in a position to know. So she went out there in the middle of April, did the big bounce with Marty—"

She was counting weeks. "Fits," she confirmed.

"After she finds out, she gets in touch with Marty. They make plans. She's going to run away to him," I went on in monotone. "But she's scared to death of her old man. She doesn't want him finding out where she's going. So she keeps it secret from everyone, including her friends. She puts these cryptic letters in the mail to let us know she's all right—must have been planning to get her diploma and then scram—"

"But she died first," Carole said.

"Yeah."

We sat there for a long moment. Carole's expression, as she stared off into space, was unreadable. "Do you suppose," she asked finally, "Marty ever found out what happened to her?"

"Don't know."

"Do you suppose he still wonders about her?"

"Don't know that, either."

She looked at me. "One thing's for sure. It wasn't suicide."

"Right. Why would she kill herself? She was about to start a new life. Everything was going her way. No way would she have killed herself."

"So we're back to murder?"

"Right. Back to murder."

By every standard, it should have been a great evening. Great restaurant, great food, great company, great conversation. But I was barely there for it.

The Gandy Dancer, one of Ann Arbor's top eating

spots, is housed in an old Gothic-style building that was once the city's train station. Despite the modern-day intrusion of kitchen, hostess stand, tables, chairs, oyster and liquor bars, you can see how it was once: a train station that actually looked like one. Soaring ceilings, stained glass windows, plenty of dark aged wood, gleaming brass fixtures, fieldstone and Pewabic tile. As a restaurant the place is run with dignified informality; the menu is expansive, the food well prepared, the service not overly intrusive, and every time a train comes rumbling into the Amtrak station next door, patrons and workers alike give it a round of applause.

The four of us ate at a table in a sort of anteroom off the main restaurant floor. Richie was all rumpled, tweedy elegance: dark plaid shirt, no tie, well-cut jacket, khaki pants. He bestowed twinkling and bemused attention upon his date, a woman introduced to us as Ann, a self-described computer software engineer. She was about Carole's age but darker, shorter, more intense. She was pleasant enough, and always right there with eye contact, quick friendly smiles, and proper casual touches. But I sensed all that was a disguise for an utter absence of warmth.

The talk through drinks, soup, salad, and dinner rolled right along with little help from me, fueled by the mutual fascination between Carole and Richie. She was interested in his philanthropies and managed to badger him into telling us, modestly enough, about the Episcopalian youth camp he endowed in northern Michigan, the land he bought in downtown Detroit for a park, the college scholarships he funded every year, the medical research he sponsored, and the executive he kept on the road in a full-time search for smaller, equally worthy causes. He was interested in her law practice and got her to tell about her pioneering use of wife-battering as a murder defense, her successful campaign to pressure state governments into tracking down and prosecuting child-support deadbeats, her seminar work, and the book she planned to write.

The food, what little of it I ate, was good. The booze was much better and I made the rounds from beer to start, red wine with the meal, brandy afterward. As I listened to the conversation and nodded at all the right places, the world went bleary around me. People seemed different. I couldn't feel my feet.

The coffee came, along with the check. Carole poured coffee for everyone; Rich grabbed the check before I could say a word, scribbled something on it, and handed it back to the server to the tune of "Thank you, Mr. Satterfield, so good to see you again." The women doctored their coffee, I pushed mine to one side, Richie put his pen away and looked at me. "So, Benjy," he said, smile faint behind his beard, "what's new on the case?"

I set my coffee cup down, lighted a cigar with tremendous concentration, and glanced at Ann. She looked not in the least puzzled, so I assumed Richie had filled her in. "You mean Sara?" I asked, the words feeling alien in my mouth.

Richie nodded.

"Well," I said, "I'm absolutely positive she was murdered."

Ann's eyes glinted, Richie's narrowed. "You've learned something new?"

"Yep." I told them about the man she'd evidently met at the D.C. scholarship exams. About the letter I'd found in old man Gerbstadt's lock box. About the child abuse. About Gerbstadt's death and Stacie's suicide.

When I was done, Ann was sitting back in her chair as far as she could get, pale and grim, gazing into space. Richie looked faraway and Carole was staring into her coffee cup. "My God," Richie murmured at last. "How dreadful."

"All in a day's work," I answered jauntily.

"Ben," Carole said.

Richie cut in diplomatically, "But what about evidence? If it was murder, who do you think did it?"

"Got two candidates," I said. "The first is your erstwhile friend and colleague, Triplett Donald M."

Rich nodded gravely. "I knew you'd learn about his record."

"Why didn't you tell me up front, Richie?"

He spread his hands and bore down on me. "Don's

been a project of mine. He came to me after his second brush with the law—"

"Brush! Supposedly he used his car to run his wife through the garage door without opening it first. Said his brakes failed."

"—and," Rich went on, "I gave him a job, I gave him emotional and financial support, I helped him put his affairs in order, and he's been a productive citizen ever since."

My lips had started not to work so well. "You ought to take a real hard closer look at him, Richie, swearda God," I mumbled.

"And," Rich said reasonably, "I'm sure you have no evidence connecting him with Sara's death."

"He was around that night," I answered. "He had it in for us, remember? After that time I kicked him out of the car. He's got a mean streak wider'n the Detroit River."

Rich smiled, humoring the passionate drunk. "If and when you have evidence, of course I'll support you, Ben. Sara was my friend too."

"Who's your other suspect, Ben?" Carole asked.

"Fast Eddie," I said remotely. "He'd dumped Sara but he was still possessive. He was always possessive of girls. And I loved him like a brother, but he could be one nasty little prick. Not much I'd put past him. I can see him in this, I really can."

"You don't really believe that," Carole said.

"Oh yeah I do." I took a deep drag of cigar and addressed Richie. "Fast was at the party that night but he disappeared for awhile. No accounting for where he went. Well, I know where he coulda went. And I'll tellya where he coulda went. Sara's house. He went into the garage and he gimmicked the automatic garage door opener. Then he started up her daddy's car and left it running in there, left it to fill the garage up with carbon monoxide while he came scooting back to the party before anybody missed him."

No one said anything.

"She came home," I went on. "One-eyed drunk. Hit the garage door opener and rolled into the garage. But the garage door was gimmicked and it came right back down again instead of staying open. He probably fixed it so the light didn't come on, too. So there she is, Sara. So drunk she can hardly stand . . . tired . . . scared to death in the pitch black, and she's overcome by the carbon monoxide and she falls on the floor and after awhile she dies there."

Carole took my hand and squeezed it hard. "That's all supposition," she said quietly. "You shouldn't smear Eddie this way, Ben."

I turned on her. "Why don't it surprise me all to hell that you're sticking up for him? Huh?" She didn't answer. "Besides, I do have something," I went on. "The neighbor lady across the street? She saw a car stop at the Gerbstadt house awhile before Sara got there. It was Fast Eddie's car."

"How do you know?" Richie asked.

"He had a brand-new 1961 Ford Thunderbird. Remember? He was just starting to get some big bucks doing concerts, and he bought the T-Bird with it. I'll never forget that car, long as I live. Mrs. Ratchford, the neighbor lady, I took her to the library and she picked the car out of a book, just like a mug shot. Tellya something, friends and neighbors: That makes Fast a *better* suspect than Sponge, in my book."

Carole let go of my hand. "You really trust an old woman's memory, twenty-five years down the line?"

"She remembers what TV shows were on that night," I retorted, thinking: At least she *says* she does.

"Fast Eddie, huh?" Richie murmured. He poured some more coffee for Ann and himself from the chrome carafe the server had left. "So. What are you going to do next?"

I held up a finger. "Keep on sleuthin'," I said dramatically, "till I bring the perpetrator to justice!"

Chapter 25

Forty minutes later Carole handed my keys back to me. I unlocked my apartment door and let us in. She locked the door behind us, shucked her jacket, and helped me out of mine without being asked. "Let's get you to bed," she said.

"Took the words right out of my mouth, babe," I answered.

She put an arm around me and we walked slowly into the kitchen toward the hall. I felt dull and drained, not especially drunk anymore, just played out. "I really screwed up tonight, didn't I."

"Let's just say you were extra colorful."

"Damn. Richie's probably pissed as hell."

"I wouldn't worry about Rich. But I have a feeling you won't be seeing Ann anymore."

"She did look sort of pasty there toward the end, didn't she."

"She was doing fine till you described Stacie's suicide. I think that finally tore it."

"Sure hope I didn't mess up Richie's act with her."

"Not to worry. They aren't close. In fact, it wouldn't surprise me to learn that she's a paid escort."

"Really?"

"Really."

"Huh. Who'd of guessed it." I hit the hall light. "Don't you have to go home?" I asked.

"Mrs. Miracle is with Will, remember?"

"Oh, yeah." My thoughts were a swirl, a formless jumble; words reached my lips with no prior planning. "I'm quitting, you know."

"The case?" she asked, surprised.

"Yep. It's a stone loser, kid. Was from the beginning."

She gave me a brief squeeze. "I never thought I'd hear you say that."

"Cut your losses," I mumbled, "and get out."

"Eminently realistic, yet utterly uncharacteristic."

"Save your strength for the wars you can win."

She pushed the bedroom door open and led me in. "Lie down now."

"Oh, yeah." I more or less dropped onto the bed and lay inert on my side, watching her. Carole turned on the bedside lamp, closed the door, and briskly stripped me to my skivvies. Then she kicked off her pumps, unslung her pearls, and laid them on the dresser. Turning her back to me, she unself-consciously shimmied off her dress, blouse, and nylons. Now she was naked except for a lacy low-cut brassiere and lacy panties. She turned to me, in the lamplight all shapely legs and arms, curves and plains, firmness, softness and private places; a glowing, creamy-skinned knockout, no less sensual for the lush swelling of her pregnancy.

She sat down on the edge of the bed and ran her hand through my hair. I touched the satin skin of her belly and she put her other hand on mine. "Not tonight," she said. "I never take advantage of a man who's had too much to drink."

"Damn," I said thickly. "An ethical broad. And here I've spent the better part of the evening angling for a sympathy screw."

She bent and kissed me on the temple. "You know," she said, "for the first time since I've known you, I think you could honest to God use one. But I don't think it's a good idea. For either of us."

"Actually," I said after a moment, "to be totally honest, I don't think I could do it. Fact is, I'm not sure I'll ever do it again."

Carole rose and started to rearrange the cover sheet. "Give it time," she answered as she settled the sheet over me. Then she slid herself beneath it, snuggled up against my back warmly, and snaked her arms around me. She felt very warm and very good. "Sex isn't everything, Ben," she whispered. "It's okay to need to be held every now and then."

"Uh-huh," I murmured.

"It's even okay to need to cry."

Instead, I fell asleep.

Friday morning dawned hot, humid, and glum. The gray sky hid the sun and bottled up the moist air close to the ground, causing instant perspiration and a feeling of low-grade anxiety, as if all hell was about to break loose. And the northbound traffic on I-275 was even heavier than usual; this was the Friday before Labor Day weekend and a lot of people were evidently playing hooky, judging from the number of slowpoke RVs, pop-ups, and boat trailers that clogged the road.

But I felt good. In fact, I felt great. I'd slept soundlessly and dreamlessly. I'd bounced out of bed at the first honk of the alarm. No hangover, which was a miracle, and I felt almost unconscionably cheerful. I helped Carole hit the road and then prepared to invade the Norwegian Wood maintenance office and get my boys back on track. This plan was derailed by Jan Vento, who called to tell me she was back in town for the reunion, had taken up residence in the Novi Hilton, and wanted to buy me breakfast. So now I was on my way up there, fighting traffic to the accompaniment of the dynamite Brian Lee blues band on the tape deck.

Still and all, I was in a superb mood. Sure, I had to make an appearance at the class reunion that night. And, sure, I had to square the books with Jan. And, sure, there were Stacie's loose ends to resolve—her possessions and her remains.

And—sure, I have to admit it—I'd failed to solve the case.

But there's no law that says every case must, or can, be solved. Any cop'll tell you that criminal detection is an either-or thing; ninety-five percent of the time you nail it down really quick or not at all. To have a fighting chance, you have to hop on it within twenty-four hours. Each day that passes lessens your chances of success. By that standard, twenty-five years puts you into a pretty deep hole.

Lesson One, then, was: Get on it quick or forget it. Lesson Two was equally important: Never investigate your own friends.

Then there was Lesson Three: Leave the past alone. Live the life you've got today, and let the rest go.

Once this reunion business ended tonight, so would my brief and painful trip down memory lane. No more reminiscences. No more talking to yesterday's faces. No more reliving murky old episodes. No more time wasted on pawing through dead papers and forlorn mementoes at the Johnson Space Center. No more. It was all Tom Fool, as my daddy would have said.

The Novi Hilton is one of those new-style hotels that is instantly anonymous, resembling as it does so many other hotels and office complexes along the I-275 corridor. Its seven stories of gray and glass and maroon trim sits on the northwest corner of the Eight Mile Road interchange, safely over the line in Oakland County, and stares south down the freeway, advertising itself with big red letters that can be seen a mile away.

The dining area was called Orchard Cafe, for no special reason. I spotted Jan at a corner table which was wedged between a brass railing and the zigzag wood partition that separated the eating area from the walkway that ran between the lobby and the ballrooms. As I approached her, I recalled the harshness with which we had parted in Chicago, and I wondered what kind of reception to expect. My worries were put to rest when she saw me, smiled with a flash of dimples, and rose. "Good morning," she said warmly, extending both hands.

I tossed the big envelope I was carrying on the table, took her hands in mine. "Hey, kid, welcome home."

She glanced around, smiling. "Not much like home, actually. Wrong county, as you pointed out. But this is probably as close as I'll get."

"We can always take a run over there later, if you want."

"I'll get back to you on that," she answered, releasing my hands after a brief squeeze.

I sensed she expected a kiss, but I hung back. "Sleep well?"

She sat. "Like a lamb." I took the wicker-backed chair opposite her and turned my coffee cup business side up. As a server scurried over and filled it, I gave Jan the once-over. Her severe businesslady look was gone this morning; she was on holiday and it showed. She wore a snug white cotton tunic over a short skirt in soft white leather, with very sheer white stockings and open-toed, open-heeled pumps. Her permed collie-brown hair was immaculate, her olive face lightly made up, her brown eyes progressing from warm to serious. "Where's Stacie?" she asked without preamble. "You were awfully cryptic on the phone this morning."

I took my coffee cup in both hands and looked her in the eye. "This envelope here, this is the reunion stuff," I began uncomfortably. "Notes, receipts, the class list, and so on. You're going to have to take it over, make sure everything is squared away for tonight. Stacie died Wednesday, Jan."

Jan froze. "She's dead?"

I nodded.

Jan pursed her lips and stared at me, registering surprise, denial, then acceptance as she abruptly set her coffee cup back down. "What happened?"

I gave her the *Reader's Digest* version: the drugs, the suicide attempt, the episode with old man Gerbstadt, the porno pictures, the diary entries about Sara, the never-delivered letter from Sara's lover in Louisiana.

Jan sat silent through all of it, motionless except for her eyes, which looked alternately at me, past me, and at me again. At the end she raised her coffee cup, then set it down without drinking. "Poor Stacie. I knew she was—well, *flighty,* I guess you'd say. Moody, too. But I had no idea. . . . And poor Sara! Her father was—I just don't believe it. I *knew* her father. I was in his house hundreds of times. He never so much as touched me. Never."

I didn't answer. The server brought more coffee and

asked to take our orders. Jan ordered a continental breakfast. I stood pat with coffee, and lighted a cigar. "Maybe," I ventured, "because you were Sara's best friend, her dad felt you were off limits, in some sense."

"Maybe," she said through clenched jaw, "he felt that I'd kick his balls up around his ears if he so much as looked at me funny. Which I most assuredly would have."

I made a lame attempt at levity. "Pretty harsh talk for an Aunt Pittypat-type Southern lady."

"I'm still a Detroit girl," she answered without smiling, looking away. She cleared her throat and said, "You know what else bothers me? I always thought I was Sara's best friend, but now I really wonder. There was so much about her I didn't know. I never knew her father molested her. I never knew she was pregnant. I didn't know about this Marty person from Louisiana—I didn't know anything about any of that."

"Sara wanted no chance of a leak," I guessed. "She planned real careful and real well, except for one thing. It never occurred to her that someone would set her up and kill her."

Jan listened, considered, then nodded grimly. "Had to've been. Certainly wasn't suicide. How do you think it happened?"

I explained my theory about the gimmicked garage door opener, the dead inside light, the Fairlane left running, filling the garage with poison gas. I described what it must have been like for Sara when she pulled into the garage and the door came back down, locking her in darkness. "She was bombed out of her mind," I added. "Disoriented, in the dark. Doesn't take much CO to put you under, especially in that concentration. She never had a chance."

Her expression was steely, her eyes alight. "You've been busy," she said. "You've found out a lot. I'm very impressed. What's your next move?"

"Well, there isn't one." I whacked ash off my cigar without looking at her. "The case is over, it's done. There's nothing left to pursue. I'm walking."

"You can't quit. Not now. You're just about all the way there."

"There's nowhere to take it. Forget it, Jan, it's over."

Flecks of red appeared in her cheeks, signaling the rise of her famous Italian temper. "You can't quit now. You have to press on. *Find* the person who killed Sara. I want that person *found,* Ben. I won't take no for an answer."

"It's done," I retorted. "I got nothing left to work with."

Her full mouth was hard and unforgiving. "But surely you have your suspects. Who are they?"

Unwillingly I said, "There's Don Triplett, for one. And I want it to be him. And he was around that night and won't account for his activities. But there's no motive. He had no reason to kill Sara."

"He was mad at all of us," Jan pointed out, scowling. "He egged our cars and flattened our tires and—"

"Sure, but that's a long ways from murder, Jan."

"All right. We'll come back to that. Who's the other suspect?"

"Fast Eddie."

She frowned. "What makes you think that?"

I poured us both more coffee. I was sick of this subject. Annoyed at Jan's stubbornness, so familiar from years ago. And surprised anew at the resurgence of the old rancor between us. "He disappeared during the party, for one thing. I got witnesses to that. And I got another witness who saw his car, that brand-new T-Bird of his, at Sara's house shortly before she got there."

Jan was shaking her head. "But he had even less motive than Sponge, for God's sake. The whole idea is ridiculous."

"Who knows why people do things?" I shot back. "Maybe he found out she was pregnant, maybe he changed his mind about dumping her—who the hell knows?"

She was pensive, locked tightly inside, thoughts far far away. Finally, slowly: "Whoever did this had some mechanical aptitude, right? I mean, to booby-trap that garage door opener took some skill. Fast was always a total klutz with tools, you know that."

That rang true, but I blew it off. "Eddie's smart, God damn him. He could have learned," I said darkly.

Jan's breakfast came. "Take it away," she told the server, "I'm not hungry." She looked at me determinedly. "You're off base about Eddie. And I think I know why. You have a love-hate relationship with him. Everyone does. Right now you're really furious with him and it's clouding your judgment."

She had me there, and I didn't deny it. "That son of a bitch, the number of times I've wanted to step on his smirking, stinking face—*always* up to something, *always* sneaking around. It's like he was determined to live up to that nickname 'Fast,' which his daddy hung on him when he was six years old, did you know that?"

"His father understood Eddie early," Jan said, smiling.

I gestured with my fist. "And when I saw Fast in Chicago the other day, what does he tell me? What does he let slip, just to stick a needle in my ribs? He tells me he was making it with my little sister. Libby was just barely sixteen, and already pretty much the mess she's never gotten over being, and he's doing it to her. All these years later I find out this."

Janet, distracted by thought again, said nothing.

"And as if that's not enough," I ruminated in the silence, "there was my friend Carole, way back when, our first time around—we were having a rough time there. And who should come along but Fast Eddie, and he does the job on her, too, while I have my back turned."

She started to say something, held back.

"Why don't I break his fucking neck for him?" I wondered aloud.

Janet's face was flushed, her eyes staring down at her locked hands. The sight brought me up short. "What is it?" I asked abruptly. "What'd I say? What's the matter?"

She looked at me, expression unreadable. "There's another reason Eddie couldn't have killed Sara," she said tonelessly. "I was saving it in case—please don't be angry with me—"

I forced myself to relax. "Just tell me, for God's sake."

"That interval when he disappeared from the party?" she said with difficulty. "I know where he was. And he wasn't at Sara's, Ben. He was with me."

I slowly eased myself back in the booth, watching the flush fade from Jan's face, and did not answer.

"You were involved in that stinking baseball game. I was mad at you, *so* mad at you for ignoring me—and Fast was, I mean, I never liked him, but he was so *on* that night, so vivid, so *alive*—"

I did not get angry. It all happened a long time ago, no point in getting riled now. And it was typical. Damn typical. So damn typical it was borderline *hilarious.*

"Where'd you two lovebirds go?" I asked grimly. "Upstairs bathroom?"

"Yes," she answered, startled. "How did you know?"

"Lucky guess."

"We were going to use his car," she added. "But it was gone."

So the T-Bird had taken a little trip—*without* Fast Eddie at the wheel. Somehow, I doubted he'd lent it out. Fast Eddie wasn't known to be generous. But he was known for leaving his keys in the ignition.

I was homeward bound, motoring south on I-275. The traffic was much lighter now, which was a good thing. I wasn't thinking about driving. I wasn't listening to Brian Lee, who was playing his heart out. Quite effortlessly I'd picked the case up again and was handling it, turning it over and over, feeling it, studying it, looking for soft spots, clues, answers.

Let's assume that it was, in fact, Fast Eddie's Thunderbird that Mrs. Ratchford saw in front of Sara's house that night. Let's assume further that it was Sara's killer who "borrowed" the car and drove it to Sara's house intending to gimmick the garage. Why would the killer do this?

Obviously, it was a contingency move. The killer went to some trouble to make Sara's death look like suicide. But in case that didn't work—in case the cops were more vigilant in their investigation than they'd been—and in case, further, someone spotted the perpetrator in front of Sara's house, as Mrs. Ratchford had—said perpetrator wanted suspicion to fall on Fast Eddie.

Why Fast Eddie? Easy. He was a handy and logical suspect. For all of his talent, he was not well liked. He already had a reputation for ruthless womanizing. And he'd been extraordinarily cruel to Sara.

(But that wasn't common knowledge. . . . Only Sara's close friends knew about that . . .)

I damn near missed the exit to I-94, but caught it at the last instant and roared west toward Belleville. The Brian Lee tape kicked over but I barely noticed.

As I'd felt all along, this had been anything but an impulse killing. There had been planning on top of planning, shrewdness, and ruthlessness. And there was another aspect, one Jan had mentioned.

Mechanical aptitude.

I was surprised I hadn't thought of it before. But then, I'm more or less a tool fool myself, and I tend to take such skill for granted. It always amazes me to encounter people who don't have so much as a screwdriver in their houses.

Okay, so the perp knew tools. Of the people I'd encountered on the case, who fit the bill? Fast Eddie was certainly out. Even Sponge, much as I liked him for this bit, had never messed around with tools, as far as I knew. Ditto for Jan, Richie, old man Gerbstadt, the Bubbas—

(Can't range too far afield. Perp was close. Real close. Close enough to know the parents were gone. Maybe even close enough to know about Sara's poor capacity for booze.)

—there wasn't anyone else who exhibited any sort of mechanical skill back then.

But how about *since*?

From out of the locked closet came the memory of Stacie, alive again in her camisole and bikini and considerable boobs, effortlessly changing the battery and resetting the time on her digital watch. . . .

But could that be? What about motive? Stacie never really knew Sara. At least that's what she said.

I backed off from it and took another run, in my

mind's eye pacing the row of suspects like a general conducting a full dress inspection.

And then: Oh. Oh, yeah, yeah.

I found myself smoking a cigar. I could not remember having lighted it. This can't be, I thought. Too many reasons why not.

But then, a more devious voice responded, maybe you should take a look at those reasons. Wiggle them, poke them, see how much stress they take. They look real enough, but maybe they aren't. Maybe they're illusions.

Maybe you been had, sucka.

The ways, the means, the possibilities came to me faster than I could digest them. Pretty soon the chain of what-ifs had led me off into uncharted territory. The Hawaii tickets? The silly-assed mercenary? Maybe even the goddamn *Psytech assignment in Boston*? I'd never discerned a pattern to those events, and there wasn't one unless you considered that each could have derailed the investigation.

Oh, if this was how it went, then it was *beautiful.*

How to try to prove it. A tall order, but hell, I had nothing more interesting to do today.

As I approached the Norwegian Wood gate, I honked the Mustang horn furiously. Glenda obligingly raised the arm so I was able to charge through without stopping. I rounded the curve, descended the slope, and screeched to a halt in front of Building 1, then trotted up the walk toward the service entrance. I'd decided to pop into the maintenance office for ten seconds. Brian was the only kid on the job today and I wanted to make sure he wasn't snowed under.

I blew through the door into the building. Staircase to the right, fire door to the left; carpeted foyer cool, dark, and silent. I'd just reached the stairs when I caught just the tiniest flicker in my extreme peripheral vision. I ducked and dodged, but not nearly fast enough to avoid the wire garrote as it dropped in front of my face and around my neck.

CHAPTER 26

In a purely instinctive gesture, I'd gotten my hand in between the garrote and my neck. Had I not done so, I'd have been a goner.

Even so, the garrote bit into my wrist, slamming it against my throat, and squeezing. The man behind it knew his business. He leaned against me, tightening the strangle-wire, trying to force me to my knees. Our breathing was the only sound in the dim foyer: his hard, mine harder, developing a rasp as the pressure from my wrist began to constrict my throat. I tried to quell my panic and to ignore the sharp pain from the wire's bite, jockeying my feet for balance and position, countering his every move in a sort of slow, hideous dance.

Abruptly I drove him backward as hard as I could. The wire loosened for an instant but not long enough to free me. He hit the wall but that didn't seem to bother him. In fact, he turned it to his advantage. Retightening the wire with fierce strength, he turned me and squeezed me toward the corner, pinning me to the wall. I wasn't getting enough air. One more shot, I thought, back toward the stairs, I'll take us both down—

I heard the door open. A voice said, almost contemptuously, "Oh, shit." Noise and commotion and suddenly the wire was gone and I found myself down on one knee, wheezing, shaking my head, trying to clear my vision as my ripped-up wrist streamed blood down my fingers. I turned to see Glenda Lay off her feet, up on the man's back, snarling and cursing, a hard forearm across his throat as if to rip his head off as she pounded at his face with her fist.

Though big and strong, she was no match for him. He

tucked his head down, rotated her, and bashed her against the cinderblock wall. She stayed stuck to him. He bashed her again and she gasped with pain. He'd just upended her to the floor when I got there. I was pretty peeved by then and in no mood to play fair. Before he even saw me I stomped his kneecap and, as he screamed and buckled, I caught him and frog-marched him and then threw him down the stairs.

He screamed once when he landed the first time, but by the time he reached the bottom he'd shut up.

Glenda, back on her feet, grabbed me and we held each other, as if needing our mutual strength to stay upright, panting for air. "Oh God, Mr. Perkins, you're bleeding everywhere. You all right?"

"I'm all right. You all right?"

"I'm all right, I'm all right. You sure you're all right?"

"I'm all right."

"Leggo of me, then. You're messin' all over me." She stepped back and fussed nervously with her big Afro, then kicked at the garrote with her sneaker. "He meant bidness, didn't he. Friend of yours?"

"I didn't even see his face, tell you the truth. Good thing you showed up, Glenda. Thanks."

"Any time, suh."

"Too bad I have to write you up for leaving your post."

"It was just for a minute! I came up here to ask for a raise."

"Well, too bad there's no money in the budget. And I don't give raises to people who've been wrote up." She glared at me and we both laughed. I extended a hand and she shook it. "Come on. Let's go figure out who that clown is."

We ran down the stairs. The man lay face down, one leg bent oddly, blood staining the floor around his head. I grabbed his hair and turned his face.

Glenda said, "He came rolling in about ten minutes before you. New tenant applicant, he said. I pointed him toward Marge. You know him, Mr. Perkins?"

"Nope," I answered, letting his head go. "Never saw him before in my whole entire life." I patted him down, found his wallet, took it, and stuffed it into my back pocket I straightened and told Glenda, "It's a John Doe, is what this is."

"Uh-huh."

"So call it in, Glenda. You know what to say."

"Maybe you better coach me a little, my bein' a slow African sort of person, you know."

"You came into the building and you found this poor bastard lying here. That's what you tell 'em."

"That's right, I remember now. I'll take care of it Reason for this, Mr. Perkins?"

"Yes."

The Hawaii brochures and tickets were right where I'd left them, under a pile of junk on the living room end table. The old yearbook was a little more elusive, but I finally found it beneath the sofa. As I dragged it out, something glittery came along with it. It was one of Stacie's dangling earrings. I stared at it for a long moment—*yeah there's still all that to do*—then put it gently on the coffee table, went to the phone, and dialed.

Elvin Dance came on after an interminable wait "What do you want?" he growled. "I'm busy."

"Detroit Homicide? Busy? Say it ain't so, Elvin."

"It's the Friday before Labor Day," he said darkly "We're having our pre-holiday clearance sale."

"All I'm after is some teensy-weensy paperwork," I answered, and explained.

"Sheeit," Elvin answered after a long moment. "I thought you done quit that old case."

"I never quit, Elvin, you know that."

"Yeah? Well, you're prob'ly out of luck on this one anyhow."

"How come?"

"I doubt there's a report or a file to find. Most of those type of things are never formally adjudicated. They're handled informally by the precinct and the record expunged if the perp stays clean."

"This one went to trial. Has to be a file somewhere."

"You sure?"

"Positive."

"Oh," he said unhappily. "Well, I'll put somebody on it. Can't say for sure if—"

"It's the report I want," I overrode him. "Court records I don't care about. The report is what I want to see."

"We'll try," he said doubtfully. "But what's in it for me?"

"How about a nice juicy collar, handed to you on a platter?"

"Fat chance, white boy. But come on down after awhile, I'll give you what we can find, gratis. It's pret' near the weekend, I'm feeling easy today."

"I'll be there in a couple of hours. First I'm seeing a guy in Ann Arbor, then another guy on the west side."

"What for?"

"Nothing much, just a couple more long shots."

"What do you want me to tell you?" Curt Goldflower asked. "Looks like a typical direct mail package to me. That's all."

"You're an ad whiz," I said. "Study the thing. Give me your impressions or whatever. Anything that comes to mind."

Goldflower adjusted his rimless glasses, leaned back in his chair, and examined the Hawaii brochures, the tickets, and the envelope. He was a scholarly looking, curly haired man in his mid-thirties, dressed informally as usual in a darkish plaid shirt, loose thin black tie, corduroys, and loafers. You'd never make him for a honcho, but that's what he was: co-owner of TGB Advertising in Ann Arbor, sole occupant of a corner office decked out with computer, massive oak drafting table, a cluttered desk, and a phone console with endlessly blinking lights. I'd encountered him on a case earlier in the year. I'd never expected to need his peculiar brand of expertise. But this wasn't the first thing about the Gerbstadt case to surprise me.

Goldflower flipped the color brochure onto his desk. "This is a nice job, here," he said. "Four-color process with a fifth added, full bleed, nice coated stock, spot varnish, and embossed and that die cut there, that must have—"

"Whoa, whoa, whoa," I cut in. "Easy, now. English, please."

He sighed. "What I'm saying is, this brochure wasn't done by whoever did the other brochure. The style, the quality standards, totally different."

"Gotcha."

He picked up the black-and-white brochure. "In fact, I'll bet you—Hold on a minute." He pawed through the mess on his desk, found a jeweler's loupe, slid his specs down his nose, and screwed the loupe into his right eye socket. Through it he examined the brochure. "Yeah, I was right," he reported. "This isn't an offset printed piece, like the other."

"What is it, then?" I asked, feeling a tad helpless.

"Well," he said, extracting the loupe and sliding his specs back up, "I think this brochure was probably done on some kind of desktop publishing system with a color inkjet printer."

"But it's got illustrations and everything," I argued.

Goldflower shrugged and grinned. "Amazing what you can do with ten thousand bucks of computer and a half-hour of training."

I squinted. "What, you don't think it's well done?"

"Rookie city." Goldflower snapped the brochure with his finger; it skated along his desk toward me. "Too many type styles, point sizes, weights. Inappropriate leading and kerning. Either the right just function was screwy or the operator just threw in extra spaces willy-nilly. Those illustrations are clip art, available at Itty Bitty Software City and just about anyplace else. And the layout is—well, the politest term I can think of to describe it is workmanlike. Shall I continue?"

"No. I've heard enough." I got to my feet. "Thanks, Curt. You're a pal."

"Any time, Ben."

At the door I turned back to him. "One more thing. These desktop publishing systems. What kind of brand names we talking about?"

"Hardware or software?"
"Both."
He told me.

From there I headed east, bound ultimately for downtown with an intermediate stop at WorldWide Auto Parts, Gary Muhleman's glorified junkyard in the Jeffries-Evergreen area on the west side of Detroit.

The look, sound, and feel of the place never changes. There's mountains of scrap and rows of junker cars; the stink of gas and grease and rubber; the deep-throated roar of diesels as trucks haul cars in, double-bottoms haul scrap out, and tractors rearrange inventory; and, most vividly, the sound of the huge industrial-strength crusher rendering someone's former pride and joy into a flat crumpled mat of rusted steel and busted glass.

I found Gary Muhleman alone at the counter in WorldWide's small, dark cinderblock office building, staring grimly at a greasy copy of *Tradin' Times*. He's my age exactly but looks older (at least I hope to God he does), with tufty brown hair giving way to an expanding bald spot, jug ears, a wasted face anchored by a large nose, and a chronically venomous expression. He wore a baggy blue twill jumpsuit with "WorldWide" embroidered in white on one breast and "Stupidvisor" on the other. When he saw me his venomous expression, which in and of itself means nothing, broke into a crooked grin. "Hey, Benjy, what's happening?"

"Not much. Looks like you're all set for the reunion tonight, Gare."

"Well, I plan to shower first," he laughed. "What can I sell you today?"

"Nothing, thanks. I'm in sort of a hurry here." I tossed the yearbook onto the counter. "Want you to play the mug shot game for me."

He squinted at the yearbook and back at me. "With that? What for?"

"I was talking to you about the party the night before graduation. About Sara Gerbstadt, remember?"

"The one who sucked the tailpipe. Right."

"You said you saw her with Fast Eddie at the party. And with someone else. I want to know who that 'someone else' was."

"Damned if I know, Benjy. Christ, that was—"

I flipped the yearbook open. "Look through the pictures. See if anybody jumps out. Take your time, Gare, but hurry."

I rolled out of there feeling grim but unsurprised. Fought the early noon hour traffic downtown to police headquarters and parked in a police-only zone by the Wayne County Jail. I'd have been surprised to find Elvin seated peacefully at his desk; despite his rank he insists on working the streets himself, and sure enough he was out on a squeal.

But he'd left the paperwork I requested with a desk officer. I carried it back out to my Mustang and ripped the envelope open to find two thin pages photocopied onto old-fashioned Slimox paper. The printing smeared at a touch, and the handwriting was barely legible, but the thing was readable enough. Two words, in particular, jumped at me like a poke in the eye with a sharp stick.

Phone tip.

Right.

Several times were noted. I wondered if they jibed with my theory, or killed it. Only one way to find out. I fired up the Mustang and made the long drive out to Old Redford.

The Bubbas's old house was gone, leaving an empty lot occupied by weeds and saplings as well as parallel strips of cement that must have been the driveway. I looked up and down Bentler Street, trying to match my memories with reality. Impossible.

Well, at least the streets were still here. The streets would not have changed in the past twenty-five years.

I checked my watch and then drove south several blocks and west on Santa Clara, stopping in front of the former Gerbstadt residence.

Five minutes. That's all it took—even if you drove nice and easy, so as not to be noticed.

I checked the time again and drove on, west on Santa Clara to Lahser and then south. Patiently endured the heavy traffic past Grand River and McNichols, all the way down to Fenkell and the site of the old In & Out. That was gone, too, of course. In fact, the whole corner on which it sat had been leveled and bulldozed over. A sign bravely announced the impending construction of a strip mall, but it had been there long enough to acquire considerable weathering and a couple of bullet holes.

As the Mustang rumbled in eager idle, I made note of the time, turned the police report over, and sketched out a rough itinerary. Plenty of time, I realized. All kinds of time. Obvious, almost blatant, once you sat down and looked at it. Trouble was, no one had ever sat down and looked at it. Till now, anyhow. And the story hadn't ended with Sara's death. It had continued on its merry way, till I barged in. . . .

Lunchtime had come and gone, and I was getting hungry. But I was on a roll. The plump little fluffy ducks, once scattered all over the pond, were getting lined up in a row now. I was afraid that if I stopped, even to eat, they'd go off on their own again, quacking and honking and jerking their empty little heads to and fro.

So I jammed the Mustang into first and, for the sheer joy of it, spun a hot smoking doughnut in the Lahser-Fenkell intersection and roared north again, headed back to the old neighborhood.

The door swung open, revealing the sturdy birdlike old woman, wearing a green house dress this time. "Good afternoon, Mr. Perkins," she said formally. "I've been expecting you."

"How come, Miz Ratchford?" I replied.

"As Junius pointed out," she said, leaning on the door with a clawlike hand, "detectives always come back at least once and ask more questions. Like Lieutenant Columbo. For the life of me, I don't understand why that young man can't organize his thoughts better. Such a *terrible* amount of time he wastes in his investigations."

"So I remind you of Columbo, huh?"

"Hardly, Mr. Perkins. Lieutenant Columbo is a sweet teddy bear of a man who outwits the culprits with brainpower. Why, he never even raises his voice. Judging from the shape of your nose, I have a feeling that your methods are considerably less elegant."

"Columbo doesn't work the streets of Dee-troit City."

"That's true. He does not." Her old eyes danced just for one fleeting instant. "How can I help you, Mr. Perkins?"

I held up the yearbook. "Got some pictures I want to show you. That person you saw across the street that night —I want to see if any of these faces jump out at you."

Her expression went steely. "I believe I told you that the light was very poor. All I saw was a shape, and a blurred one at that."

"Ma'am," I answered, "with all due respect, I'm the detective here, and it could be I know what I'm doing. Please, ma'am, it'll just take a minute of your time."

"It's not my time I'm concerned about," she retorted, "it's yours. You're too young and busy a man to be frittering away your time on hopeless ideas like this. But come on in, by all means."

I pulled the screen door and stepped inside. Mrs. Ratchford pushed the door shut behind me. "And perhaps, if you'd be so kind," she added as she led me up the hall in her slow purposeful gait, "you'd explain to me just what went on in Dr. Mink's old house the other day."

" 'Scuse me?"

She gave me a look over her shoulder. "The old Victorian place on Lahser. The double murder and suicide. The news flashes were distressingly sketchy. Perhaps you'd be kind enough to fill in the blanks for me. I'm old, Mr. Perkins, but I still like to keep up."

Ninety minutes later I sat at the corner of Bentler and Grand River, absently gunning the big Mustang motor. I wanted to turn left on Grand River, but the Friday afternoon traffic was a solid river at this point. So I waited, and watched for a hole in the traffic, and thought about my theory once again.

I was right. No question. But all I had was bits of this and pieces of that. There was no smoking gun. Without that, I'd never be able to hammer the perp.

Could I run some sort of con? Possible. But it would have to be exceedingly cute. After all, the joker had sailed through the original investigation without attracting the slightest bit of suspicion. It would take some doing to spook the hard case twenty-five years later. Given a few days, I could probably manage it. But the reunion, the only time all the players would be within arm's reach, was just a few hours away. . . .

I waited, and watched, and waited. *Still* no hole in the traffic. McNichols intersects Grand River right at that spot. The traffic signals operate by whim. I should have remembered what a bitch this intersection was—I used to *live* there, for Chrissake! Right over there, across from me, was good old Redford High, that towering structure of grim red brick; Redford High, in appearance not unlike some prisons I've seen; Redford High, from which I graduated twenty-five years before with a class that would reunite that night. Not there, at the scene of the crime; but at a slick hotel in the bucolic climes of Novi, very far away.

And, of course, next to the high school stood the fieldstone Detroit Public Library, Old Redford branch.

The library. Dwight. Automatic garage door openers. "Valuable library resources have already been expended locating this information for you."

Well, okay. I didn't really need the material on automatic garage door openers any more, but what the hell, I thought, go take a look. Get Dwight off your back. Check out the old lady's claims, while you're at it—and maybe there's some timing questions you can clear up, too.

But mostly I did it because it was a hell of a lot easier to turn right on Grand River than to turn left.

Chapter 27

The librarian, replete with his short dark hair, Buddy Holly glasses, bow tie, and translucent white skin, scurried out from the back room. "We're just about to close," he began, and then stopped short. "Oh. It's you."

"Hey, Dwight. Doin' a land-office business here, I see."

"It's Labor Day weekend," he answered. "I'm closing up in just a few minutes. Frankly, I should have closed hours ago. There hasn't been anyone here all afternoon."

"Glad I caught you," I said, smiling reassuringly. "I'd like to see that material on automatic garage door openers that you tracked down for me, please."

His eyes were resentful. "You didn't return my calls and you didn't come in," he noted. I didn't answer. "I'm not even sure the book is still here," he added. I just looked at him. "We don't keep things forever, you know."

"Perhaps you could go check," I suggested easily.

His eyes flickered. "Perhaps I could."

"I'd be much obliged."

"It'll take a few moments."

"That's fine. While I'm waiting—where do you keep the sports books?"

He was already retreating into the back. "Mezzanine," he said over his shoulder. "Third row from the stairs."

I clomped up the stairs to the mezzanine level. There were a lot more sports books than I expected. I skimmed the titles and was surprised to find a five-volume set called *Detroit Tigers Day By Day.* I lugged Vol. III to a big oak table by the mezzanine rail, flopped it open, and began leafing pages till I found the game I wanted. The detail was astounding. There was a complete play by play of the game. There was a picture of the crucial play, George Thomas trying to steal second on a pop foul by Steve Boros. There were complete player, team, and league statistics. There was even information on weather, attendance, and elapsed time. I copied some facts into my little notebook, grinning. One more nail, folks; one more nail.

Then I descended the stair to the ground level. Dwight still had not returned. The churchlike silence of the old library echoed with the sound of my shoes on the slate floor. Just the finest silvery sheen of dust hung in the cool air, illuminated by sunbeams from the tall narrow windows. A nice place to kill an afternoon, if you ever had that kind of time. Back in the corner I spotted a sign that said NEWSPAPERS. I wandered back there.

Well-thumbed current issues of the daily papers hung from bamboo rods on racks. Three big machines, which seemed to be microfilm readers, stood along the wall. Gray cabinets next to them held microfilms of Detroit newspapers going back to the 1940s. They had the *News,* the *Free Press,* even the long-defunct *Detroit Times* there, neatly sorted into drawers that were labeled by date. For the hell of it, I selected the *Detroit News* reel for the month of my graduation, loaded it on a reader, sat down, and began spinning the crank, looking for the correct date. . . .

Some time later a throat cleared and Dwight materialized beside me. He lay a thin book on the table. "Here it is," he whispered, out of habit, I guessed. "Make it fast. I need to close up pretty soon."

"Thanks," I answered absently. He disappeared. I squinted at the screen and wrote down a few more things. I was slack-jawed with admiration at what I had found. No errors. Not even one. The woman was amazing.

Finally I shut the machine off, put the microfilm away, and picked up the book Dwight had brought. It was old, worn, and bound in brown cardboard reinforced by green cloth tape. The cover bore the utilitarian title *AUTOMATIC GARAGE DOOR CONTROL: An R-L Do-It-Yourself Book.* The copyright date was 1955. Stone Age stuff, I thought; but Gerbstadt's door control unit probably resembled this one in most important respects.

I opened the book to find page after soft, yellowed page of dark grim typewritten text, illustrated with simple line drawings. Within ten minutes I'd figured out how the perp had gimmicked Gerbstadt's unit—or at least how I'd have done it.

The key was a pair of limit switches. One was the door-open switch, the other was the door-closed switch. They had the same function: Shut off the drive motor and engage the reversing relay. All the perp had to do was remove the door-closed switch completely, and replace the door-open switch with one that engaged the reversing relay without turning off the power. A five-minute job with screwdriver and pliers.

The result? Sara activated the opener and rolled the car into the garage as the door opened. When the door had opened completely, it was supposed to stop and wait for another signal. Instead it reversed itself and started right back down. When it had closed completely it was, once again, supposed to stop and wait for another signal, but the door-closed switch was gone. So the motor kept right on grinding, mindlessly, till it burned out or, more likely, tripped the circuit breaker. This explained why the cops found the door closed and the opener broken the next morning.

I flipped the book shut, stood, stretched. Good stuff to know, but certainly no smoking gun. As I picked the book up, I noticed that the back cover had a paper pocket pasted to it. Slipped into the pocket was a signout card from the days when the library lent books on a totally manual system. The card included spaces for the handwritten names of borrowers as well as rubber-stamped due dates.

I was not surprised to see that the book had been borrowed only four times under the old manual system, with dates going back thirty years. What surprised me was the name of the second borrower.

"Stunned" is probably a better word.

I looked away sightlessly, then back. The name was the same. Bingo.

I felt no joy. No pleasure, even. All I felt was grim satisfaction as I headed for the desk to negotiate with Dwight.

I certainly didn't have enough to convict. I probably didn't have enough to indict. I may not even have had enough for an arrest. Tough. What I did have was enough to smoke the perp out from undercover.

And that would do quite nicely.

The reunion was two hours old before Fast Eddie Anger finally arrived.

Up till then the occasion had been, as we once said, Dullsville. Not that the arrangements were deficient; they were just fine. The Novi Hilton ballroom was clean, roomy, well-equipped. The decorations, including banners, balloons, old movie posters, and the mandatory crêpe paper streamers, were festive enough. The wieners swimming in hot ketchup were palatable, the beer was icy cold, and the six-member rock band managed to play serviceable renditions of hits from our senior year, including "Will You Love Me Tomorrow," "Blue Moon," "Runaway," and "The Twist."

But I just wasn't in the mood. At heart I really did not want to be there, and once there I found myself thinking about the people who weren't: Sara Gerbstadt, the Bubbas, Nicki Micklos, Stacie Hallthorn. I was profoundly uncomfortable in my navy blue suit. Most of all, I was uptight because a little later I was going to make my move, and it did not promise to be pleasant. I planned to round up the suspects, get them away, drop the bomb, and see what happened. Hopefully my little con would work. Hopefully the perp would knuckle under peacefully.

Hopefully I wouldn't end up wishing I'd brought a gun.

Carole and I arrived about 8:00 P.M. Jan Vento was already there, supervising two of her cronies at the registration table. I introduced her to Carole and the two women shook hands and murmured polite things through fixed smiles. Upon seeing that Carole was pregnant, Jan shot me a look, but said nothing. Carole and I pinned on name tags—mine with a cutout of my senior face pasted to it—and went into the ballroom.

All told about a hundred grads, most of them with dates, showed up. Rich Satterfield, who came stag, arrived right after we did, looking sharp in an expertly tailored charcoal gray suit. Considering his phenomenal business success, I expected him to be gregarious. I was surprised, then, at the way he hung close to Carole and me. He seemed relaxed enough, even bemused; he smiled and nodded and chatted briefly with people who approached him but otherwise he kept mostly to himself. Funny, I thought, how the old high school personalities came back, as if we had never grown up, as if twenty-five years had not passed.

The three of us drank and talked, wandered and chatted, sat and snacked. Carole and I slow-danced once. Jan joined the group about an hour into the festivities and we sat at one of the larger tables with an ever-changing circle of visitors. Gary Muhleman, odd-looking in an ill-fitting tuxedo, sat with us till he spotted Linda Sue Atwater across the room. Beth Heinzeroth stopped by to pass out real-estate business cards. We were reintroduced to Carol (neé Carl) Hickson, who looked so sexy it was downright scary. Debbie Barr Judnik greeted us loudly, weaved over to the band, and threw up at the guitarist's feet.

"Typical Redford High bash," someone observed.

As the booze poured and the minutes marched by, the noise volume built and the inhibitions faded. There was dancing and drinking, kissing and hugging, and even some crying; there was also a yelling, screaming argument, a thrown drink, and a fistfight in the lobby. Old misunderstandings were resolved and new ones were started, rumors were revived and put to rest.

Through it all our little group sat. Carole chatted easily with the others and seemed to enjoy herself. Jan was high-spirited and vivacious whenever she wasn't glancing archly at Carole. Rich chuckled a lot, and I smoked cigars and waited for Fast Eddie. For what I planned, I needed Fast Eddie. It just wouldn't be the same without him. . . .

Finally, two hours into the reunion, I heard his name in the distance. Beyond the ballroom entrance and through the glass wall of the hotel I could see a long white shiny Cadillac stretch parked at the curb. Doors opened, a crowd flurried, and here came Fast Eddie Anger at a fast trot. He wore a snug black-on-black tuxedo and carried a black electric guitar by the neck. His wolfish face was all smiles as men and women recognized him and rushed him, calling his name, shaking his hand, patting his back, escorting him like a flying wedge into the ballroom.

Good, I thought. Finally. Let the games begin.

Rich Satterfield caught my eye and shrugged. Carole and Janet watched, entranced, as Eddie made his way toward our table. By now he had a gold pen out and was autographing papers, programs, even the back of a woman's hand. We were all standing by the time he arrived. "Wow!" he said, beaming at each of us. "What a welcome! How are you guys? Great to see ya!"

Jan embraced him. They whispered to each other for a moment, then she took him by the hand and led him to the platform where the band members stood, instruments in hand, obviously surprised. Fast shook hands with them and formed them into a huddle as Janet took the microphone from the lead singer and spoke to the audience.

"Not that any introduction is needed," she said, voice echoing in the ballroom, "but I'd like you to welcome the most famous member of our graduating class—and, probably, the most famous graduate of Redford High School ever—Mr. Eddie Anger!"

Applause and cheers. Suddenly the atmosphere was electric. Even I, who'd seen Fast perform at the Kos Arena, could feel it. Suddenly, we were part of an *event.*

"Eddie's agreed to do a few tunes for us," Jan went on. "And so . . . here he is!"

She handed Fast the mike and left the stage as he counted off for the band and broke into the hot bluesy chords of "45 Auto," one of his early hits. He sang it with all the fire and passion that had been absent from his performance in Chicago and he owned this audience, he absolutely *owned* it. I realized once again how talented the man really was. Fast Eddie was deceitful, self-serving, and obnoxious, but when he had a guitar in his hands and cared as much as he did tonight, he was brilliant.

After that the band sat down. Fast accompanied himself on the guitar and sang the slow, mournful, yet hard-edged "Downriver Blues." This was his first and, to date, biggest hit; it had reached No. 3 on the *Billboard* Top 40 behind Bobby Vinton and ahead of the Kingsmen and would probably have gone to No. 1 were it not for the intrusion of a number called "I Want To Hold Your Hand."

When that was over and the applause died down, Fast spoke to the audience for the first time. "Great to be here," he said, face shiny with perspiration. "Great to be back here with my old friends. 'Specially Jan, and Richie, and Benjy. I love you guys. I love you all."

Applause broke out and I clapped hard about three times and then dropped my hands.

"For the finale," Fast went on, "we're going to do something a little more recent. However, to get the right sound I need a girl backup singer, and we're fresh out up here." This brought a chorus of female voices and an almost hysterical waving of hands. Fast grinned and, smiling slyly, continued, "There's someone here tonight who always wanted to sing but ended up becoming an accountant instead. Tonight's her big break. Jan? Janet Vento! Come on up here, babe!"

Jan reddened, stripped for once of her career woman cool. She held up her hands and shook her head. The applause continued and she gave in, of course, and went back up onto the platform where Fast gave her a microphone, whispered some instructions, and counted off the band.

The song was Robert Palmer's "Addicted to Love," a hard-driving, percussive dance number. Fast bellowed the verses and Jan, initially nervous, harmonized with him on the chorus. By the third time around she'd loosened up consideraby. She shared Fast's mike, sang practically cheek-to-cheek with him, and improvised a dance in which they kept bumping hips on the second syllable of "ad*dic*ted." The crowd clapped one gigantic beat, the band played its heart out, Carole held my hand tight and looked on with eyes alight, and it was over all too soon, even for me.

As the audience gave a standing ovation, I cupped my hand and whispered in Carole's ear: "It's time."

She nodded. I stood and fought my way toward the platform as Fast and Jan descended arm in arm. They were flushed with exertion and smiling as I worked my way to Fast's side. "Hey, people, I was thinking," I said loudly over the din. "Let's take a run over to Dynamite Park and get outside a six-pack, just like the old days. What do you say?"

"Sounds like a winner, Benjy," Fast said exuberantly as the band cranked up Roy Orbison's "Running Scared."

"Let's do it," Jan chimed in. "But . . . is it safe?"

"Benjy's a big tough private eye," Fast informed her, grinning. "With him around, we're as safe as babes in arms."

Give me a break, I thought. "Meet us out front," I said. "I'll wheel it."

They nodded and split off from me, working their way toward the ballroom entrance. I returned to the table where Carole and Rich were on their feet. "We're going to the park, Richie, you coming along?"

"Well, sure," he said crookedly, smiling behind his beard. "I'd have been surprised if we hadn't ended up there." I took Carole's hand and the three of us started out. The noise volume was such that I almost didn't catch Rich's next comment. "Won't be the same without Sara."

"No, it won't," I answered. I expected him to mention Sponge. But he didn't. I guess Richie hadn't expected Sponge to show up at the reunion, after all. Well, I hadn't either.

We left the ballroom. The lobby was scattered with couples chatting and others smoking and gawking at Fast's limo parked outside. Carole squeezed my hand. "Give me a minute?"

"Sure. Hang tight for a second, Richie." Carole and I stepped toward the hall. "What's up, kid?"

"I think I'll just take a cab home," she told me. "I'm

tired, and they're your friends, and I have no special desire to go to a park in Detroit after dark."

"I hate to leave you on your own like this."

"I can take care of myself," she answered.

"I know, babe. Well, if it's really what you want to do."

"It's really what I want to do."

And it also turned out to be the smartest thing she could have done, in the end.

Chapter 28

We entered Dynamite Park from the north, the four of us, in my Mustang with the top down. The night was warm and humid, the air alive with the lights and sounds and smells of the metropolis all around us. We were, to all appearances, a happy crew. And we should have been. Jan was giggly-drunk, Richie chuckling-drunk, and Fast Eddie, still up from the performance and high on the applause, was brittle and gregarious and under the influence, I suspected, of a substance other than alcohol.

As for me, I was cheerful enough and talkative enough, but nowhere near drunk enough. Worse, I found myself sobering up fast as we entered the park, jumpy about what was ahead.

The merrymaking quieted somewhat as we rolled south on the wide lanes of Outer Drive into the heart of Dynamite Park. Though many of the street lights were burned out, a three-quarter moon shone brightly. In its silvery light the vast flat plains of the park, broken up by clumps of trees, looked scrubby and neglected. The play equipment, which appeared in occasional clusters, was old and uncared for. Even the sign at the park's entrance: DYNAMITE PARK/DETROIT DEPARTMENT OF RECREATION/COLEMAN A. YOUNG, MAYOR, was defaced by graffiti.

"Sure has changed," Fast said as I swung east on Tireman, headed for the small bridge over the Rouge River.

"Not much money for parks anymore," Richie said.

"I sure wouldn't want to be alone here," Jan said, voice oddly nervous. "It seems awfully spooky and scary to me."

"It was spooky and scary back then, too, Beak," Fast

Eddie answered. "We were just too damn dumb to realize it. We're pretty close now, aren't we, Benjy?"

"Yep," I said, wheeling the Mustang south on Spinoza. The road curved gently as the thick forest approached us from the west. Presently the pale lights of the bungalows of the West Evergreen section showed dimly to the east, and the intersection of Spinoza and Sawyer drew into view, with its center island and antique Dahlgren cannon guarding the park from the city of Dearborn Heights to the south.

"Well, some things haven't changed," Jan said happily as I circled the island and then parked on the shoulder. We disembarked and loaded up with supplies from the trunk: Richie and Fast Eddie carried a twelve-pack each, Jan clutched a bundle of newspapers, and I took the emergency 9-volt floodlamp.

The tall grass and weeds rustled around our ankles as we walked toward the fringe of trees. The park was silent and yet, if you listened for it, you could hear the city's resonance: low, almost subliminal. The feel of it cheered me and made me forget my nervousness for a minute, because it was the sound of our youth, of the city of Detroit, like us still alive despite everything.

Some old rusted play equipment and overgrown picnic benches stood in a jagged row by the fringe of trees. We walked past them and entered the woods on a hard-dirt path that headed steeply downhill almost at once. Leading the way, I shined the floodlamp down to the very bottom of the slope to the site of our old meeting place.

This was a heavily wooded flood plain for the Rouge River. Once upon a time there had been a low fence down there, steel bars supported by large fieldstone posts. The steel bars were long since gone, but the fieldstone posts were still there: five feet tall, marching along in a row toward the river off to our left. Gigantic oak trees towered over us; in the woods we could see the diagonal remains of fallen trees and limbs, left untended to decay into the ground. This was our "secret" place, fifty yards from the road, surrounded by the city of Detroit, yet private and remote.

There was much aimless talk as Richie and I collected some dead limbs and built a small, hungry fire. The yellow light of the flickering flames rose aromatically and we cracked beers and made ourselves comfortable in the warm woods, laughing nervously about how much harder it was to get comfortable now than it had been twenty-five years before. Fast shucked his tux jacket and sat cross-legged on a log to my left, a dark, almost inimical presence. Richie kept his gray suit jacket on, but tugged down his tie and leaned, half-sitting and half-standing, against one of the stone posts on the other side of the fire from me. Jan had taken off her pumps on the steep walk down and her pale blue gown glistened in the light of the fire as she sat, languid and svelte, on the log on the other side of Eddie.

As for me, I sat on an old flat stump and waited for the opening.

We talked, drank down our first beers, talked some more. I ran my mouth on automatic pilot and, for the life of me, I can't remember exactly what was said. There was something about the Huron River raft race. The mooning of the nuns was certainly brought up, laughed over, dispensed with. Jan recited a list of the boys she dated in high school along with ratings, in which I came out surprisingly well.

Eventually, predictably, Fast and Richie started a grab-ass. I'd clean lost the thread of the discussion when I heard my name. "Benjy," Richie said, gesturing at Fast, "you were there, weren't you? It was Boyanowski who beat me in the fifty-yard dash. Not Eddie."

"Bullshit, Spaz," Fast said, shaking his head. "I whipped your ass that time, son."

"I know who killed Sara," I said.

I'll never forget their faces: Eddie's dark and vulpine, Richie's bearded and benign, Janet's olive, dimpled, and smooth. The faces of old friends, watching me, all eyes.

Fast was first off the dime. "Oh," he laughed shortly. "So this is the part where the detective gathers the suspects together and reveals the villain. Sort of like that old broad, whatever her name is."

"Agatha Christie," Jan answered.

"Well," I admitted, "I'm no Agatha Christie. But I sorted it out, just the same."

Fast Eddie lighted a cigarette. His narrow face glistened with perspiration. "You really think she was killed?"

"Definitely. My instinct said so from the beginning. Certain physical aspects of the crime scene supported it. And there was one more thing, the clincher." I told the group about Sara's lover from Louisiana. "Sara wouldn't have killed herself. In the most fundamental respect her childhood was terrible, but at that point, at graduation, she had everything to live for."

Jan and Richie, who'd already heard the story, said nothing, but Fast was gaping at me when I finished. "Holy shit," he breathed. "So she had something going after all. I always wondered about that."

I just smiled, remembering how possessive he had been. "So Sara was murdered. But I've had the damndest time trying to figure out who. Facts were scarce and everything pointed every which way. Hell, as of this morning I'd even thrown in the towel. But then Jan said something that jump-started some thoughts. I went over everything in my mind again. I thought about what *had* to be true about the person who killed Sara."

No one said anything. I lighted a cigar. "First, the person had to know her pretty well. Knew how moody she was, despondent a lot of the time, liked to talk about death. The killer had to know she was going to that party; had to know she didn't handle booze well. The killer also had to know about her family and about that automatic garage door opener. Right?"

The only sound was a car passing by on Spinoza.

"Okay. I figured that the killer had to've been at the party at the Bubbas's. Wanted to make sure she was good and loaded. The killer set up one hell of a slick cover, and no one suspected a thing.

"What else about the killer? A coward. Couldn't knock Sara off face-to-face. Had to do it by remote control.

"Very careful. Good planner. Mechanical aptitude. And clever too. Only problem was, there was a witness.

Two witnesses, actually. But the witness the perp knew about has been cashing in ever since."

I looked around at them: Richie, Jan, Fast Eddie. "So, what do you think? Who fits the bill here?"

"Sponge," Jan said.

" 'Fraid not." I turned my head. "You were the one, Richie. You killed Sara."

Rich straightened. In the yellowish flickering half-light his bearded face seemed devoid of expression. He cleared his throat. "This is a joke, right?"

"No joke," I answered. "I got you, man."

Jan and Eddie were imitating cardboard cutouts as Richie shook his head slowly. "But I wouldn't do that. I loved her."

"There was more to it than that, wasn't there?"

"What are you talking about?" he retorted.

I sighed. "You aren't going to make this easy, are you?"

"I'm not going to make this anything." He was assertive yet patient. "This is your fantasy, Benjy. Jesus God, I don't believe this."

"You loved her, all right," I said, exhaling smoke. "In fact, unless I'm very wrong, you were head-over-heels, crazy-in-love fuckin' *nuts* about her. Something along those lines. Am I close?"

"Were you banging her, too, Spaz?" Fast jeered.

"Be still," Jan hissed.

"You're totally off base," Rich answered me.

"I don't think so," I answered. "No one knew how you felt at the time. No one but Sara, probably. You told her and she shrugged you off. You couldn't stand it. It snapped something inside you."

"The whole notion is crazy," Rich said, "that I'd kill someone I loved."

"It's not crazy at all," I said. "Happens all the time. All extreme emotions are alike. All of them can lead to violence. A person as blindly, single-mindedly obsessed with Sara as you were is very capable of murder—if he doesn't get his way."

Richie was expressionless as he examined his beer can. Then he set it down on the stone post and straightened.

"Well," he said heavily, "I've heard quite enough." He started around the fire toward me, bound for the footpath. "And I warn each of you: This slanderous talk had better not go any further. I—"

I stood, tossed my dying cigar into the fire, and stepped in Rich's way. "Where you goin', boy?"

"Out of my way."

"Get *back* by that post over yonder and shut your yap."

"Ten bucks on Benjy in the first round," Fast said cheerily.

Rich glanced at him. "Shut your fuckin' mouth, you weasel."

I leaned into him. "Get *back* where you were, son. I won't tell you again."

"Please," Jan said to no one in particular.

Rich eased back away from me. "Okay! All right!" he said, gesturing both hands into the air as he returned to his fence post. "It's your party, Benjy."

"Hey. I'm not any crazier about this than you are, pal." I scooped out four fresh beers and threw the empty twelve-pack carton into the fire. "I don't go in for dramatic confrontation scenes. Normally what I do is bring in the cops and walk away. But this one is different. This one is part of us, all four of us. It's only right that we sort it all out amongst ourselves before we get anybody official involved."

Rich's chuckle seemed forced, not as warm and mellow as before. " 'Official'? You really, seriously think the police would be interested in this half-baked theory of yours?"

"Sure, why not?" I handed fresh brewskis to Fast and Jan. "Drink up, guys. This is a party, remember?" Fast grinned crookedly; Jan looked sick. I tossed one in Rich's direction. He allowed it to fall to the ground. Shrugging, I opened my own beer and took up a new position by another stone post, leaning negligently against it. Now Jan and Fast were to my right, and Rich's route to the path was clear. This was deliberate. I was telling him I could easily run him down if he made a break for it. And part of me wanted to. That cold fury was beginning to churn inside me as I thought about what Richie had done.

"You know who I am," he said. "I do have some prominence. I have friends, contacts, a reputation; you can't—"

"Oh, cut it out," I said as I fired up another cigar. "You killed her, Richie. I've got all kinds of stuff. Part of it is assumptions, the rest is facts. Let's take care of the assumption part first.

"The main assumption is that you were nutso about her. So crazy you couldn't see straight. You took every opportunity to be with her. You were helping her study for that exam. You were at her house a lot, knew all about the garage door opener and so forth. Okay so far?"

He said nothing.

"She didn't want you romantically," I continued. "But I have a feeling she confided in you. Big things were happening for her right in there. She couldn't keep all that totally to herself; she had to confide in someone. It wasn't Jan. It sure as hell wasn't Fast and it wasn't me. So I think she probably told you about this guy in D.C. that she met. I think she told you about being pregnant and about her plan to run away. She told you because she had to tell someone, and you were the only one she could totally trust."

"Is that true?" Jan asked, voice tight. "Did you know?"

He was shaking his head. "I didn't—"

"How about let's talk mechanical aptitude," I cut in. "It took skill to gimmick that garage door opener. You had the aptitude, all right, but it just didn't blossom till a few years later, when you spent the first year of your business repairing computers yourself. You bragged to me about that in Ann Arbor."

He folded his arms.

"You were at the party," I went on. "You told me you hardly saw Sara at all there. In fact, you told me that twice. You were lying. Gary Muhleman says you spent a lot of time with her. Easy to see why; you wanted to get her as drunk as you could."

"That's not true," Rich whispered.

"How about the beer run?" I drove on. "We were

running low on beer and you volunteered to go get more. Nobody thought about it at the time, but that was damned uncharacteristic of you, Richie. When it came to doing anything illegal, you had a serious case of cold feet."

"Chicken-shit pansy-ass is more like it," Fast said.

"But you *had* to make that run," I went on. "It gave you a reason to leave the party. Of course you didn't go straight to In & Out. You stopped at Sara's house, gimmicked the garage door opener, started up her dad's car to fill the garage with carbon monoxide. *Then* you went to the beer store—where, surprise! The Sixteenth Precinct fuzz caught you."

"I did *not* go to Sara's," Rich flared, "and the police *did* catch me, and yes, Eddie, I *was* frightened. I've always been afraid of the police, all right?"

Fast made a clucking sound. Jan put a hand on his arm. I crumpled my empty beer can and said, "You got caught, all right, but it was no fluke. You called yourself in. The police report on the incident shows that an anonymous caller tipped the cops that an underaged kid was going to make a buy. That call was logged at 11:10. I figure that was after you'd been to Sara's and before you went to the beer store."

"Benjy," Rich said hotly, "you can't prove any of this."

"Oh yeah I can, a lot of it. What about timing? Glad you asked me that." I gestured a thumb at Fast and Jan. "Late in the party, these two decided on some slap 'n' tickle."

I looked at Fast Eddie. He stared fixedly at me, then into the fire as he took a long tug on his beer.

"They needed a nice private place," I went on, "and Fast, being Fast, suggested the roomy back seat of his '61 T-Bird. They slipped outside but, lo and behold, the car was gone."

"That always did mystify me," Fast said, "but it showed up again, so I didn't—"

"That was about three minutes to eleven," I barged on. "The reason I know that is that Jan remembers the Tigers game was just ending, and according to the record books it ended at 10:57. Okay? The car was gone because you took it, Richie. You took it to buy yourself a little extra insurance. If anybody spotted a car at Sara's, you wanted it to be Eddie's, not yours."

"You tried to set me up," Fast mused. "After all we've meant to each other, Spaz! I am profoundly shocked."

"And the car *was* seen, by the cross-street neighbor. At 11:00 or a minute after. Plenty of time for you to get there from the Bubbas's house. You did your business there, went back to the party, and switched to your own car. Called the precinct at 11:10 and tipped them. Then you went down to In & Out, bought the beer, and got nailed at 11:35, according to the report. I retraced all this and timed it and it fits just fine."

Rich said nothing. He continued to lean against the post, head at a slight slant, the gray suit jacket hanging open around his plentiful belly. The fire hissed and crackled in the silence and then Jan spoke softly. "Is it true, Richie?"

"No."

"Sure it is," I said. "You set it up slick, Rich, I'll hand you that. Covered all the bases and made it stick these twenty-five years. You did get lucky in one respect. The dad, old man Gerbstadt, had his share of dirty little secrets. He didn't want anybody looking too close. He was pals with the precinct detectives and got 'em to go easy. So your alibi never got looked at, not till now."

Rich took a deep breath and straightened. Voice strained, he said, "One part dreams, one part supposition, and two parts damned lies."

"Then why'd you try to railroad me off the investigation?"

He missed a beat. "I didn't—"

"Oh, yes, you did," I retorted. "You tried several times. First you pulled strings at Psytech to get me assigned to some job in Boston. I'd told you I do work for them, remember? Area big shot like you knows all the heavy hitters. How long have you been chummy with old Dr. Spudd over there?"

"I've never met the man in my life."

"Well, we'll never know, because they're so tight-lipped. But I think you got Spudd to do you a favor, somehow. Didn't work. Then, later, I was approached by a pain in the ass mercenary. He told me he'd been contacted by someone looking to knock me off. My guess is that was you, too. You probably figured ordering a hit was like reserving a hotel room, right?"

"You've lost it," Richie said softly. "Totally lost it."

"And," I said, holding up a finger, "you even bought a vacation trip for me and Carole. To Hawaii, for this week only. You wanted me out of town till after the reunion. Figured I'd have lost enthusiasm for the case by then."

He was staring at me. "That's insane!"

"No, it's actually pretty clever," I answered. "But I was curious about one of the brochures that came with the tickets. Ran it by a graphics guy. To him it looked like a home-grown job done by someone not too expert, produced on a Micropub system, judging from the dot pattern or something like that."

"I'm not the only one with a Micropub system!" Rich said.

"Only one I know."

The ensuing silence was broken by a long hissing gurgle as Fast drank off his beer. Jan sat hunched, arms folded, eyes on the dying fire. Richie shook his head a couple of times and finally spoke. "There've been many times over the years that I've wondered about you, Benjy. Wondered what you were doing. Thought about getting together. I figured it would be great. I never thought—it never occurred to me that you would orchestrate such a monstrous fantasy about me."

"Cue the violins," Fast said.

"Yeah, very touching," I added. "But it won't fly. You were eyeballed, Richie. The cross-street neighbor who ID'd Fast's car also eyeballed you. Picked your face out of the yearbook just this morning. She's credible as hell, kid, even knows what TV shows played that night. Jury'll love her."

Rich's face looked blank, as if he'd gone into a shell. I charged on. "Then there's witness number two. None other than Mr. Don Triplett."

"Whoa!" Fast said. "Sponge was in on this too?"

I nodded. "And he's been holding it over Richie's head ever since. Which is why Rich has given him a cushy executive job for all these years, without expecting him to work or anything."

"That's absurd," Rich said tonelessly.

I shrugged. "It's what he told me, before he died."

Now, for a moment, the whole park was utterly silent.

"He jumped me this morning," I said, taking a long hit off my cigar. "Tried to strangle me. Last-ditch effort to protect you, Rich, and to protect his gravy train. To disabuse him, I had to throw him down the stairs. Fractured his skull. He died at Wayne County a couple hours later. But not before he gave a chapter-and-verse statement about what happened to Sara that night."

"Huh," Fast snorted. "First time old Sponge ever did anything for anybody."

"Shut your fucking mouth," Rich said tightly.

"And then there's the book I found at the library," I added. "A technical manual on automatic garage door openers. It had a card listing borrowers' names pasted on the back. Care to take a guess, Richie, as to whose name I found?"

Rich gnawed his lip. Opened and closed his mouth, took a deep breath, and said, "So that's what happened to it."

CHAPTER 29

"Oh, Richie," Jan said sadly.

"I was going to throw it away," Rich said. "But it disappeared. I'll bet my mother found it and returned it to the library. I didn't dare ask. I didn't want to call attention to it."

I said nothing.

"What's the matter?" Richie asked in a hard voice, taking in all of us. "You're looking at me like I'm some sort of evil person!"

Fast Eddie snorted. "Whaddya expect?" he sneered. "A standing ovation? You killed our friend."

"*Your* friend?" Rich flared. "You were no friend to her, Eddie. None of you was the friend to her that I was. None of you knew her like I knew her. None of you."

Jan, who'd masked her face with her hands, looked at me between fingertips. "I feel sick. Let's go now, okay?"

"Not yet," I said. To Richie I added, "Go ahead. Tell us. This is your only chance. It's why we're here. Tell us everything."

Rich sighed. In the firelight he bent and picked up the full beer I'd tossed him earlier and began to clean off the top. "I loved her, all right," he said to no one in particular. "I loved her from the instant I saw her. She was all I wanted, all I thought about, all those miserable days in high school. She's why I studied hard and got good grades, so I could be in the Beta Club with her. She's why I took clarinet lessons, so I could be in the band with her. She's why I hung around with you guys, so I could be with her."

He snapped the beer top open. A spume of beer spritzed out and Rich held the can away from him for a moment till the dripping stopped. "Her going with you,

Fast, that drove me nuts," he went on. "I knew what you were doing to her. But somehow I endured it. It was part of the humiliation of being me." He glanced at the singer's sullen face as he took a pull of beer. "You were the skinny good-looking kid with the gift of gab. I was the chubby tongue-tied four-eyed one. When you wanted a girl, you'd write her a song and sing it to her, and she'd swoon into your arms. When I wanted a girl, I'd write pathetic poems in study hall. Hell, I couldn't even call a girl on the phone without scripting out my end of the conversation first. . . ."

He drank some more. In the silence we heard another car pass by out on Spinoza. Rich was staring into the fire. "Things started looking promising when Eddie dumped her. Then came my big chance: She asked me to be her study coach for that big scholarship exam in D.C. I dropped my own work, let my own stuff go to hell so I could help her. And one afternoon I told her. At her house, I—" He looked up and away, lost for a second. His expression was unreadable behind the beard, but the pain rang loud and clear in his voice. "I told her I loved her, I told her everything. She was . . . she didn't laugh. She was, uh, kind. Gentle. Her response was something on the order of, 'Not now, not yet.' There was hope in that. Till I realized, later, that she'd finessed me, worked me like a pro."

Jan put in, "Oh no, Richie, no. Sara never played games with people's feelings."

"I'm sorry, Janet," Rich answered, "but you didn't know shit about what was going on. None of you did." He drank some more. "Back she came from the scholarship competition in D.C. And she asked me to take her out. Man, I was excited. I figured my time had come. We went to Grand Lahser Hamburger. And she told me—I remember this exactly—she asked if I'd be her 'very special pal.'

"I didn't understand, at first. But it turned out she needed someone to tell some things to, and she'd elected me. Well, this wasn't as good as I hoped for, but it sure seemed better than nothing, till I heard what it was she wanted to tell me."

"Marty," I said.

He nodded. "She went on and on about him. That's when I knew I'd been dealt out again. I tried to understand. I certainly didn't give Sara a hint about how I felt, but I began to do a slow burn. First Fast Eddie, now some *nigger.*"

Jan and Eddie shot him a look. I said, "Marty was *black*?"

"What else?" Richie retorted. "You know how she felt about them, felt *sorry* for them, wanted to *help* them, planned to go south and *live* with them. . . ."

No one said anything.

"Well," Rich continued purposefully, "you can see how it went. She told me she was going to run away to be with Marty. A few weeks later she told me she was pregnant by him. She was thrilled. Thrilled! At that point I couldn't kid myself anymore. It was all unraveling, everything I'd thought about and dreamed of for a couple of years, was falling apart. All on account of some nigger from Louisiana. I did *not* want him to have her. If I couldn't have her, *no* one could have her. And it was obvious to me she wasn't headed for any kind of decent life anyway. Living down there, interracial marriage, halfbreed kid, the romance'd have worn off quick. But mainly I could not let her leave.

"I loved her, but there was no way I could let her live.

"I began to make plans."

I felt, at once, satisfied and depressed. "What about Triplett?"

Rich shrugged heavily. "He was angry at you for evicting him from the party. He followed the T-Bird, thinking it was Fast, when I drove it away. He saw me stop at Sara's, and shortly after that discovered that it was me, not Eddie. A few years later he came to me and he mousetrapped me. I had just gotten my company up and running. I couldn't afford any trouble. I put up with him as a cost of doing business, but it wasn't easy." He looked at me. "I'm not sorry he's dead."

The fire was nearly gone. I bent and mechanically added some dead sticks to it. Much of his statement fit in with what I had surmised. What I had not figured on was the intensity of the violence in him, even today. This Richie, who was probably the real Richie, had never been a friend of mine.

As the flames built hungrily, I folded my arms. "You realize I'm turning you in for this, Rich."

"Hear! Hear!" Jan murmured.

Fast stood and stretched. "I'll tellya, Benjy," he said with a weak smile, "you know how to cap a memorable class reunion, pal."

"Just a minute," Rich said tensely. "Let's talk about this."

I'd about had enough of him. "Talk about it? We've done talked the thing to death. It's jail now, Richie. Hard time and lots of it, as God is my witness."

"Hear me out. Please."

"Oh, why not?" Jan answered acidly. "Give me a fresh one there, Fast."

As Eddie cracked a beer for her, Rich said, "I don't deserve to go to prison because I am not a murderer."

Before I could respond Eddie cut in. "Oh yeah. Right," he spat. "You killed Sara but you're not a murderer. Interesting concept, Spaz."

"It was a crime of passion," Rich said. "I've spent twenty-five years thinking about it and I know what I'm talking about. I'm not like people who kill for a living, or kill to make money; who make a business of it. What I did was a one-time shot, the result of adolescent passion. Certainly the law would never judge a man like me as harshly as it would some vicious crack cocaine dealer."

"Actually, you probably got a point there," I answered. "The law ain't negotiable, but justice sure is. I can see it now: The judge takes a look at you, and what he sees is a nice white plump country-club type, just like him. And he thinks to himself, aw hell! So you waxed some cheap nooky all these years ago. You're a nice fella now, and of the moneyed class too. You talk real nice, dress good and, boy, the jails sure are crowded these days." I rapped an invisible gavel. "One to ten, suspended, and a hundred hours community service."

"You really think it could go like that?" Jan asked, wide-eyed.

"Might, could." I looked at Rich. "That's why I'm bent on making your life as uncomfortable as possible meanwhile. You'll be interested to know that the cop I'm handing you over to is a man of color. I'm sure your rationalizations will fascinate him even more than they do me."

Rich looked away, then drained his beer and dropped the can. "I understand your anger. *All* your anger. Sometimes I get angry about it myself. But it was all those *years* ago, Benjy. And you know what I've been like since then. I've been good to everyone. I've created jobs, businesses—hell, I invented an entire industry! I've earned millions of dollars. *Millions.* But I have restricted myself to a modest standard of living and funneled the profits into good causes. That never would have happened if it weren't for Sara. She'd be *proud* if she knew."

Jan made an ugly sound. "Don't you ever speak her name in my presence again," she hissed.

"What happened to Sara," Rich charged on without responding, "defused my anger and resulted in immeasurable good for many, many people. What's one trivial little life next to that?"

"Are you through yet?" I asked.

He showed us his palms in a conciliatory gesture. "What is it you want? Contrition? How much more contrite can I be? I never wanted it to happen and God knows I've paid for it. I've suffered. I've never had a relationship with a woman. Never been able to. Fact is," he said uncomfortably, "I'm stone-cold impotent." He looked at each of us, one by one. "If I deserve punishment, isn't that punishment enough?"

"I'm sure the state's got a remedy for that," Fast said lazily. "Guys in the big house have a pretty active sex life, don't they, Benjy?"

"Heard tell."

"Stop it," Jan said acidly, setting down her beer.

Rich's face became drenched in sweat. "In the name of God," he said. "In the name of our friendship, Benjy—"

"Sara was our friend, too," I cut in harshly. "You took her away from us. I don't have the brains for all these word hoops you jump through. What I do know is, you murdered a person, and that ain't right, and you are going to answer for it."

He straightened. He squinted, ran a hand through his tousled hair, grimaced. "I don't think so," he answered. He came out of his suit coat pocket and aimed a small handgun at me. "I don't agree with you at all there, Benjy."

As we locked stares, I felt my heart sink. It had occurred to me that Richie might resist. I'd even considered the notion that he might come armed. If my own gun had been available, instead of in the custody of the Detroit police, I'd have brought it, just in case. And, for sure, with any other perp—Sponge, for instance—I'd have handled the whole thing differently.

But this was Rich Satterfield, my childhood friend. A twisted character beneath it all, but still gentle, passive Richie. I'd decided I could handle this unarmed. If the backup I'd arranged didn't work out—and it wasn't looking good—no problem. I'd been sure that the whole thing would go down peaceable and I'd end it by chauffeuring Richie to the slammer, case closed.

Nice move, ace.

"What is that?" Jan asked in a curiously innocent voice.

"It's a gun, stupid," Fast said. His voice had gotten suddenly thick with tension. Fast Eddie never did have the guts for physical confrontation; I could not count on him or Jan for help here. It was me and my bare hands versus Richie and what looked like one of the Beretta semis, .22 or .25. Small caliber, but it'll kill you dead enough. Eight shots. Plenty for all.

I kept my voice as neutral as I could. "What's that thing for, Rich?"

He swallowed. "I'm going to kill you."

He was twelve feet from me, on the other side of the dying fire. The only available weapons were sticks, dirt, and fists. No match for a bullet. A head-on charge didn't appear to be a good percentage play. I couldn't wait to find out what was. "You'd have to kill all three of us," I answered.

"Obviously."

I felt the tension, the strain, from Richie and Jan. No doubt what they were thinking was, *You're the big tough private eye, you got us into this, now get us out.* "You're not going to kill anybody, Richie," I said gently.

He waggled the pistol. "Stand up!" he ordered the others.

They did so hastily, and raised their hands without being told. My mind was a blur: Talk him down, talk him down, keep him talking, take it easy now, take it *easy*. "Think it through, Rich. You kill us, and I guarantee you'll go to prison."

"Afterward I'll shoot myself in the leg," he said rapidly. "I'll say we were attacked—the attacker got you three first, and I grappled with him—"

"You won't have time."

The small pistol was rock-steady in his large hand, pointed at my chest. He sounded more confident as he said, "Now I suppose you're going to try to bluff me," he jeered.

"No bluff. I arranged for the cops to meet us here," I told him. "They should have been here by now. They'll be here any minute. You won't have time to set anything like that up. It's over, Richie, don't make it worse."

"You know something, I'm getting tired." The speaker was Fast Eddie Anger. He had lowered his hands and stood next to Jan in a pose that was curiously unafraid, almost cocky. "Let's cut to the chase, what do you say?"

"Shut up," Rich said.

"Beak," Fast said, "step back now. Step back." She backed up a couple of uncertain steps, hands halfway raised. Her eyes looked huge in the half light. Fast said to Rich, "I'm going to walk up to you and take that gun away. And you're not going to shoot me. Or anyone else tonight."

Rich shifted the pistol from me to Fast. I tensed, calculating, and Rich aimed back at me again, rapidly. The angle between me and Fast was too narrow; Rich could still cover both of us pretty well. But maybe there'd be an opening, depending on what Fast Eddie did.

Rich said, "I'll be more than happy to start with you. In fact, you *should* go first, you son of a bitch."

"Please, please," came Jan's anguished voice.

"If we're all going to die," Fast said to him, "let it be here in Detroit. That's only fitting. If we're all going to die, let it be together. That's fitting too. You see, I love you, Spaz. The three of you here, I love all of you." He started toward Rich. "You're not going to shoot me. You're going to give me the gun so we can all go home."

"Stay put or I'll shoot!" Rich said.

I braced myself. One more step—

Fast held his hand out. "Give it to me."

Rich shot him in midstride. The report was a flat metallic snap, quiet as gunshots go; did not even echo in the trees. Jan screamed. Fast stopped and half crouched and looked back at me, mouth twisted, eyes intensely curious. "Oh," he said. "Oh, that hurts." Then he dropped to his knees and toppled over onto his side on the ground.

Rich blinked rapidly. The gun swiveled toward me. I spread my arms and said, "Okay, Richie. My turn."

He did nothing. Did not move a muscle. Just watched me.

"Do it," I said softly, "or I'll knock you down and stomp you."

"Ben!" Jan gasped.

Still Rich stood there, blank-faced, empty-eyed. I took two steps toward him and he didn't even blink. I remembered what I'd said a moment before: *The killer couldn't knock Sara off face-to-face. Had to do it by remote control.*

For Fast Eddie, Rich had been able to work up enough fury. Would the same be true for me?

Only one way to find out.

"Here I come," I said tensely. Walked toward him around the fire. Up the path the bullet that would kill me could take. Neared him and reached him, pushed the gun aside, then removed it from Richie's unresisting hand as he just stared, and stared, and stared.

Only then did I realized he wasn't staring at me at all. He was looking through me and beyond me, doing the thousand yard stare at something only he could see.

Then I hit him.

CHAPTER 30

"Perkins! That you down there, boy?"

Jan and I were crouched over the unconscious Eddie. We'd stopped the bleeding with strips of cloth ripped from the hem of her evening gown, and covered him as best we could with my suit jacket. His pulse seemed okay, if a little rapid, but his entire left side was soaked with blood and his skin was pale and clammy. "Down here!" I called. "Quick, Elvin, there's a man down."

Deliberate footsteps sounded from the dark trees and then Elvin Dance emerged into the small faint pool of lamplight, dapper as ever in a dark business suit and a natty looking felt hat. He had his hands in both coat pockets and looked about as anxious as Buddha. "Oh," he observed as he strolled over to where Richie lay, "you've got two men down, not one."

Jan wiped her bloodstained hands on her dress. "For God's sake call an ambulance."

"Yes, ma'am," he answered, giving the coldcocked Richie the once-over. A couple of uniforms came down the hill, shining their chrome flashlights, and ranged about the clearing, examining it idly. Elvin came over and inspected Fast. "Wait a minute," the cop said. "Ain't this Eddie Anger? The singer?"

Fast's eyes opened. "Ah," he said hoarsely. "A fan."

Jan dropped to her knees and bent over him. "Oh, Eddie, are you all right? How do you feel?"

"Shot," he said, and coughed. "They plugged me. Gave me a slight dose of lead poisoning." He coughed again. "Mother, I've come home to die."

"For Chrissake call EMS," I told Elvin.

He ignored me. "I hated what you did to 'Ain't No Mountain High Enough,'" he told Eddie.

"Sue me," Fast rasped.

"As to EMS," Elvin said to me, "we'll call 'em, but there's gonna be a wait. It's Friday night, you know, and things is hopping around town tonight."

"What kind of attitude is that?" Jan asked angrily, getting to her feet. "This man is *shot*, he could be *dying*, and you just shrug your shoulders and—"

"What I was about to say," Elvin put in heavily, "is we'll take him in the squad car."

"Fine," I answered. "And don't forget the perp over there. He shot Eddie with that-there pistol in front of two witnesses. Which I assume is enough to lock him up."

"He'll be dealt with," Elvin said. "First we better get this boy on the road to Sinai." He waved over one of the uniforms. "Wouldn't do to have a celebrity croak on us. City's rep is bad enough as it is."

Elvin, the uniform, and I picked Eddie up as carefully as we could. Jan trailed behind us as we carried him up the dark hill through the trees and out across the moonlit grassy field toward the cars. I had hold of his right side and I could feel the sticky warmth of blood—lots and lots of it. "He's oozing pretty bad," I said. "You guys are gonna have to fly with him."

"We'll do that," the uniform said.

We'd just reached the RMP car when Eddie coughed and raised his head a little. "Huh-uh," he said. "No cop cars."

"Shut up, Fast, we're getting you to the hospital," Jan said.

"No cop cars," he said. "Benjy take me."

"You're nuts," I said angrily. "We'd have to wedge you in the back seat and there's barely room for—"

"Shotgun. I always ride shotgun. You know that."

"You're better off with the cops," I insisted.

"You won't let me die," Fast said, and coughed. "If you take me I know I won't die. You take me, Benjy."

I looked at Elvin. In the moonlight his scowl was plain to see. "You heard the man," I said.

"Okay," he grumbled, "but it's his fuckin' funeral."

We carried Fast to the Mustang. Jan opened the passenger door, climbed into the back, and adjusted the bucket seat to create the most room in front. We spread Fast out as best we could in the bucket seat, covered him with coats, and belted him in. The uniform ran back to the RMP to use the radio as Elvin shut the passenger door. The police captain clenched a fist. "Kick ass."

"You just take care of our fresh perp down there."

"Gotcha."

"They're waiting," the uniform called from the RMP. "I'll run interference for you."

"Forget it, sonny," I said, cranking the big 302 motor. "You'd just get in the way."

We blasted out of the park on Joy Road, bound for the Southfield Freeway a mile or so east. The four-lane street was dense with traffic, Friday night partiers in full cry, and I made the best time I could, running red lights and using as many lanes as I needed.

Jan ignored my heroics at the wheel. She sat on the edge of the back seat, leaning between the bucket seats, holding Fast's hand. "Now he's burning up," she said anxiously as we ran the red at Evergreen.

"We'll be there in ten minutes tops," I answered. "How 'bout it, Fast? You hanging in there, bro?"

"You're not going to let me die, are you, Benjy?" he asked in a weak voice.

"Aw, hell no," I said with heartiness I did not feel.

The singer's voice was toneless and distant. "I got something to say to you, Benjy. Two things."

"Shoot," I said, and kicked myself at the word choice.

"That was a hell of a piece of detecting you did there. Pinning whacko Spaz with the deal—finding that old lady to ID him—nice work."

"Thanks, buddy." I hurled the Mustang into a smoky, shrieking, two-wheeled controlled skid onto the northbound Southfield ramp, narrowly beating out a charging Mack truck. "But I got to straighten out something. The old lady didn't finger Richie. Just the T-Bird."

"You bluffed him?" Jan asked, climbing off the side wall.

"Yep. She never saw him."

Fast coughed. "Cute." He coughed again. "Well, at least you got Sponge to sing, may he rest in peace."

"Uh, that was a bluff, too. Wanted to shake Richie up. Looks like old Sponge'll be with us a long time yet."

"But he *did* finger Richie, didn't he?" Jan asked.

" 'Fraid not."

Fast said, with genuine admiration, "You are the sneakiest, most devious son of a bitch I've ever seen, Benjy."

"Takes one to know one, pal."

Silence in the hurtling car. Then Fast cleared his throat. " 'Bout me and Beak that night? You know, I never wanted you to find out about that. I'm sorry, man."

I kept the Mustang in the left lane and the speed needle above a hundred, flicking the solid, low-slung monster from lane to lane, leaving the slowpokes behind. "It's all over with, Fast. Forget it."

"Funny how things work," he observed. "I done lots of things I'm not all that proud of. But that one, that one I'm really ashamed of."

"Don't talk," Jan said. "Rest."

"And it's not like she was all that good, either," Fast added. "Talked all the way through it. Fuckin' motormouth."

With a hurt, indignant sound, Jan turned abruptly and sat cross-armed in the bucket seat. "I thought people on their deathbed always said profound, touching things," she said coldly.

"Hey, it's the truth and you know it. And so does Benjy. Right, bro?"

I concentrated on my driving.

Jan said, "And here I was changing my mind about you, Fast. You were so nice to me back there at the reunion, letting me sing with you. And what you said to Richie in the park, when he held the gun on us? All those things you said about loving us? I was scared to death there, but you really touched me, Fast. Now you turn around and—"

"Remind me. Next time I'm up against a man with a gun, I got to come up with a better line. That one didn't work worth shit." He coughed again. "Should have known better," he said, voice weaker. "Always knew Spaz was a wacko, always knew it. Now he's probably done killed me."

The Jeffries interchange passed in a blur. "We're almost there," I said. "Hang tough, Fast. We're almost there."

" 'Course, if I did die, it'd give the album a hell of a boost. The title track might even crack the Hot 100."

"Stop it, Eddie," Jan said.

"Seriously," he said. "Remember when Elvis died? Somebody said, 'Good career move.' " Neither of us responded. "Maybe I can teeter on the brink for a few days," Fast said thoughtfully, "and then make a courageous recovery. What do you guys think? Will it fly?"

The door to room 321 swung back at my knock and there stood Jan, resplendent in a loose gray-striped side-button top over white pants. "Good morning," she said, smiling. "Come on in."

I followed her inside and closed the door. "What time's your flight?"

"Not till noon," she said cheerily. "I've got all kinds of time. Go ahead, have a seat, I'll be right with you."

As she bustled into the bathroom, I took a chair by the big uncurtained window. Around the room were the signs of impending departure. On the small round table next to me were the remains of Jan's continental breakfast. Outside it was a warm gentle sundrenched day. A breeze waved the trees beyond Interstate 275. Traffic clogged Haggerty and Eight Mile, going about its Labor Day weekend business. A small V of birds traversed the sky from left to right.

As for me, I was whipped. Yesterday had been a madhouse: first a solid four hours of catch-up on Norwegian Wood maintenance, then a couple of hours of questions and answers at Detroit police headquarters, followed by an hour or so at the hospital. Today was looking a little easier. Only tomorrow, Labor Day, would I be able to kick back. I planned to gather up Carole and her son and sneak out of town with them, probably up to Carole's cottage on the Thumb, where we could swim and sail and lie in the sand for one precious day.

My challenge now was to get to that without thinking too much.

I had a cigar going by the time Jan came out of the bathroom. Her hair had that soft, loose look, she'd made herself up lightly, and she was giving me the full dimple treatment as she sat crosslegged on the unmade bed, her bare feet tucked neatly in her thighs. "Do you realize," she said, "that this is the first real privacy we've had since this whole thing started?"

"Well, it's been busy, me investigating and you on the run and so forth."

"Yes. We've both been running WFO."

"What's that?"

"Wide Fucking Open," she said, eyes sparkling.

"Uh-huh, yeah."

Smiling, she rocked on her rump. "Did you go see Fast after the cops were done with us?"

"Yeah. He's doing fine. A crew from *Entertainment Tonight* had just finished with him when I got there."

"Boy doesn't waste time," she said.

"Nope. The P.R. machine is cranking." I tapped ash off my cigar. "He'll be asking you to sign a release."

"For what?"

"For the story of what happened. He's planning to peddle it. First he'll get a ghost and do one of those true crime books, then he figures on a movie."

"You are joking," she said darkly. I didn't answer. "Did you sign?"

"Sure."

"What's he paying you?"

"A dollar."

"Are you out of your *mind*?"

"I also got his promise not to use my name or my face

or any other part of my anatomy. He said that was all right with him, any schmuck could be the detective."

She rolled her eyes. "You're nuts, Ben. You could have gotten five grand at least."

"Reckon I just don't have your head for business, sweetie."

"Evidently not," she said coolly. "He wants my release, he's going to pay very, very dearly for it."

"That's your call, kiddo." I finished my cigar with a hot hit and crushed it in the glass ashtray.

She studied her fingernails. "What about Richie? Do you really think it'll go the way Captain Dance said?"

I shrugged. "He's the authority, I'm not. But look at it this way. For shooting Fast, they got Richie cold on assault with intent to commit murder. That's worth life. On top of that they'll stack first degree for Sara's death, just to get a little more negotiating leverage. Being as he's wealthy and white, with a clean record, they'll probably let him cop to felonious assault. Four years is the usual tariff, but as a first offender he can draw six months in county jail, and that'll be it."

She didn't miss a trick. "Felonious assault for what he did to Fast," she noted. "What about Sara?"

"That's by far the weaker end. They'll drop it entirely in exchange for guilty on Fast Eddie."

She looked away. "After all that?"

"After all that."

"Was it worth it?" she murmured.

Not if you include Stacie, I thought. "Sure it was. We got the son of a bitch. It doesn't bring Sara back, but Richie's life'll be a tad less comfortable from here on out."

"That's what you wanted?" she asked.

I shrugged. "Not hardly. I always want it all. But I usually end up settling for what I get. How about you?"

She looked steely. "What I wanted was to avenge a certain knock-kneed dago teenage girl with a big schnoz, whose suspicions weren't taken seriously. I wanted to prove she was right all along. And you did it."

"Well, good," I said lamely. "So we both win."

She looked suddenly startled. "Oh yes, I almost forgot!" She slid off the bed, went to the dresser, and took something out of her purse. "This is for you."

The check, drawn on Citizens & Southern Bank, was made out in an amount equal to the exact number of days multiplied by my exact daily rate. Correct to the penny, as befit the trained accountant. "Thanks," I said, tucked the thing away and stood.

"You're welcome." She looked into my eyes. "There's one other piece of unfinished business." When I didn't answer, she smiled and slid into my arms and kissed me hungrily. As she melted herself against me, warm and vital and gently urgent, I felt the faintest faraway longing. At the same time I heard a cold, protective voice that said *Oh no you don't.* After a polite interval in the clutch, I eased her back from me and said, "Hoo boy."

She was smiling mischievously. "You've been ignoring my hints, Ben. Shame, shame, shame."

"Well, it's just that—"

"I mean, I don't *have* to go back to Atlanta today. Tomorrow's Labor Day, we could stay here, and . . . get it out of our systems, so to speak."

"That's a right fine idea. But it's just not on, kiddo."

She held onto me. "You found me attractive enough twenty-five years ago."

"And you're still a doll. But back then you weren't married."

She blinked and stared and released me reflexively.

"Or a mother," I added.

Her olive skin darkened as she laughed shortly. "So you've been investigating me."

"God, no. It's your ring finger there, it's obvious you wear rings on it most of the time."

She winced. "Shit! And I rubbed lotion on it every night!"

"Plus, there's just an aura you have. I don't know how to explain it, but people who are involved, people with kids, there's something different about 'em. I'm sort of a foster stepparent type of person myself, maybe that's how I can sense it, and I sensed it in you from the get-go, like vapor off ice."

She was way beyond me. "What difference does it make?"

"Pardon me?"

"Ben," she said impatiently, "what we do here—if it doesn't matter to me, why should it matter to you? Far as I'm concerned, it's not even adultery, really." She smiled. "You were my first."

I took her hands in mine. "I remember. And it was special. But that was then. I've learned something, down through the years. At least I've tried to. I've learned that doing the right thing isn't such a bad idea, even when all other systems are 'go,' like now."

She closed her eyes for a long moment and, when she opened them, they were a little shiny. "I understand." Slipping out of my hands, she wandered away, aimlessly examining the open-mouthed luggage on the dresser. "Funny," she said. "Till now I always thought Richie was the straightest of the bunch. Turns out it was you all along."

"Knock it off," I retorted. "You think passing up a free no obligation romp is easy? Hell, no. It's the hardest thing I've ever done."

She looked at me archly. "Do it a lot?"

"This makes an even once."

"How'd I ever get so lucky?" she asked, not bothering to hide her bitterness.

I think at that moment she realized I was on to her. Had I sensed any genuine warmth in her, my answer to her pass might very well have been different. But it was a hostile pass, a coldly planned attempted conquest that sprang from the anger that remained between us even after the issues that provoked it were long forgotten.

But I played out the scene on the high, if not entirely honest, ground. I walked to her, kissed her forehead, hugged her gently. "You are lucky, darlin'. You got your spouse and kids and career and health."

"It reads better than it lives."

Most things do, I thought. I stepped back from her. "Go on back to Atlanta and live well."

She trailed me to the door. "Ever get down our way?"

"Can't say that I do."

"Well." She bobbed her head and shook my hand firmly. "See you at our fiftieth, then."

"Wouldn't miss it," I said, and left.

Chapter 31

It was a crisp, sunny Tuesday morning in mid-September. I was in my favorite position—well, one of them—at the helm of my top-down Mustang, rumbling north on Telegraph Road. Occupying the back seat was a bulging black leather overnight bag plus a big old Gibson acoustic guitar. Riding shotgun was Fast Eddie Anger, fresh from the hospital and bound for the left coast—just as soon as we concluded what he cheerfully called "a sentimental journey."

Fast Eddie braced himself in the bucket seat, chain-smoked cigarettes, and observed the scenery as the wind danced his longish dark hair around his skinny face. He wore all black: snug corduroys, T-shirt, sneakers, goggle-like sunglasses. He was, if anything, thinner than before. His face was bonier and sallow with institutional pallor. He moved stiffly and awkwardly, as if in a lot of pain yet. He denied that, sort of. "If I got any pain," he confided, "it's in the balls. Haven't gotten off in two weeks. That's unhealthy, you know. Not that anybody out at St. Joe's gave a shit."

"What happened?" I jibed. "Was your charm and notoriety lost on the nursing corps out there?"

"They didn't give me nurses. They gave me *guys.* I call that ridiculous," he sputtered.

"I call it sensible."

"Go ahead, laugh. While I was in the hospital, fighting for my life, you've been out in the world, scarfing up puss-ah."

There wasn't much truth in either end of that. Fast's life was never in real danger, and I hadn't been much of a party animal. I had, in fact, devoted the interval since Labor Day to extricating myself from the past and jump-starting my life again. I'd wrapped up the loose ends of Stacie Hallthorn's sad life. Rescued my .45 automatic from the Detroit police. Testified at Richie's preliminary hearing, after which he copped, right on schedule. He did better than I expected at the back end, drawing one to three, all but thirty days suspended.

Fast Eddie, meanwhile, skillfully parlayed his injury into quite a public relations event. Local TV covered his helicopter transfer to St. Joe's in Ann Arbor. The wire services picked up the story and splashed it in newspapers nationwide. A brief item appeared on *Entertainment Tonight* in which, inevitably, what happened to Fast was linked to Detroit's reputation for violence—as if people don't get shot in Las Vegas or Los Angeles. Reporters from the tabloids kept a steady vigil, at least till it was clear he was not going to die. Casey Kasem and Rick Dees ran musical tributes to Fast on their countdown shows. Video press releases covering Fast's progress appeared regularly on MTV.

Evidently all of this was paying off. "D'ja hear about 'American Born'?" he asked as I swung east on McNichols.

"What about it?"

"The single entered the Hot 100 this week at number sixty. Album and video are getting lots of play too. And what about *The New York Times*? D'ya see that?"

I hadn't, but Carole had. In the previous Sunday's paper, some professor/shrink type wrote about Eddie's shooting. Using a lot of big words and mumbo-jumbo, the shrink turned everything into sexual symbols—the gun, the bullet—and concluded that the shooting was probably the result of homosexual rage.

"Heard about it," I answered him. "You going to sue?"

"Why do that, for Chrissake?"

"Well, how about because they suggested that you have a, uh, alternative sexual orientation?"

"Number one, there's two thousand women around the world who know better. Number two, if it was one of those slimebag tabloids, I'd sue in a second—but this is *The New York Times*, man. The *Times* wrote about me. Isn't that something?"

Just in the nick of time, we reached the old neighborhood. Feeling self-conscious and intrusive and profoundly uncomfortable, I slowly rolled the old streets while Fast Eddie sat atop the seatback like a prince in a motorcade, looking around, commenting, enjoying himself hugely. We cruised Holcomb Elementary and Redford High. Checked out the vacant lot where the Bubbas's house once stood. Stopped briefly across from my old house on Bennett, Sara's on Santa Clara and, finally, Fast Eddie's on Orchard. What was left of it was a burned-out, boarded-up husk leaning over a weedy, overgrown, debris-littered yard.

Fast stared at the place for a long, long time. Then, abruptly, he slid down in the bucket seat, ebullience gone. "Looks awful, doesn't it?" he asked softly.

"It ain't what it used to be," I agreed.

He waved a hand. "I mean the whole neighborhood. It looks . . . grungy and smaller and, I don't know, low-rent."

"It's just older," I answered. "Believe me, for a Detroit neighborhood this one's held up pretty well. Check out Little Beirut if you don't believe me." Fast was staring at his old house again and did not answer. "I'm sorry, bro," I said. "I know it must hurt real bad to see it like that."

He looked into his lap. "It's a real bitch, man."

"Yeah."

He looked at me. "I was going to shoot part of my next video here. To show the fans where I sprang from, you know? The warmth bit and all that. Well, screw that idea. Come on, Benjy, let's get on up the road and pay a visit."

I glanced at him. "Not enough time. Your flight's at—"

"We got all kinds of time. Let's go."

Fast's good cheer returned as we motored northwest on Grand River. I was amazed at how well he remembered the old landmarks. "Northrop Funeral Home? That was there back then. Methodist church, yeah, and the post office, right, Benjy? All the same."

"Uh-huh."

"What about these car lots? Those are new."

"I think that was all houses then."

"Yeah. Oh man, the Mount Vernon Motel! That's still here! D'ya believe it?"

"My memory ain't as good as yours. But something tells me they didn't advertise 'Moderate Rates' and 'Water Beds' back then." Abruptly, and with a definite lack of enthusiasm, I swerved the car left and through the wide open gate of Grand Lawn Cemetery.

We fell silent as I motored slowly past the big duck-sprinkled pond and into the heavily wooded west end of the huge cemetery. Gravel crunched under the Mustang's wheels, gray squirrels darted through the grass and up the trunks of the massive trees, and a light breeze rustled the leaves. If anything I felt even more uncomfortable here than I had back in the neighborhood. "Let's see," I muttered, "I think it's over here to the right. Section 14, yeah."

"You don't remember?" Fast asked.

"Haven't been in awhile."

"Since when?"

"Ma."

"Oh, man," he drawled. "I thought *I* was bad. I haven't been in a long time either, but I got an excuse, I don't live here."

"You handle it your way, I'll handle it mine."

"Hey, you don't have to bite my head off. Just observing, that's all."

Halfway down the flank of Section 14 I parked the Mustang half on gravel and half on grass. In the absence of the engine's rumble it seemed very silent all of a sudden, except for the wind in the trees, the gnattering of birds, and the ocean-roar of traffic on Telegraph and Grand River. Fast and I walked up the slight rise under the vast umbrella of trees, dodging gravestones and bushes as the dew dampened our shoes. He looked lynxlike and intent, walking at a half-stoop, his big Gibson clinging to his back, hanging neck down by its strap. He looked very familiar, and I suddenly realized that Fast, though older, hadn't really changed at all, and was the only one of us who had not.

Most of the plots in this section were six- or eight-person jobs, with one large upright family marker and small flat stones for the individuals. Fast's parents had not gone in for that sort of extravagance. They were marked by a single sandy brown stone with just the names and dates, in the center row at the top of the slope. Fast and I stood there and looked at it for a moment. Then without comment we walked two plots to the right, where the simple grayish-black headstone said:

LEWIS BENJAMIN PERKINS
1898–1963

ELIZABETH RACHEL PERKINS
1909–1967

The dates struck me, the difference in their ages, and all kinds of incoherent thoughts played bumper car: how Daddy had been but a teenager when he came up here, alone, to go to work at Mr. Ford's; how he'd already reached middle age by the time my brother Bill was born; how there hadn't been a marker here at all till I arranged it after Ma's death—Daddy didn't believe in such things, or Ma either: "Vanity," they called it, "a seeking after wind"—

And in the midst of all that the last thing I expected to hear was a guitar, but there it was: Sprightly chords at a cheerful pace and then Fast Eddie began to sing "Will the Circle Be Unbroken."

He stood spread-legged, eyes on the gravestone, half-smiling as he strummed and sang, nice and easy in his clear tenor, just like in the old days in our kitchen on Bennett Street. And it all fell in on me then. My chest seized and a powerful ache took my throat and my eyes welled up. I turned away from Fast, swallowed and breathed and blinked, taking *hold* of it, getting on *top* of it. Doing my best, anyhow. The past, the past, the son-of-a-bitching past. It's not dead at all; it lives as long as you do. Stacie Hallthorn, for one, had proved that. She also proved that what you are is all the things that ever happened to you—and that "too late" comes too soon, for each of us.

At that moment I resolved to go pay the storage fee on

Ma's stuff at the Johnson Space Center, and maybe try to get together with my brother and sister a little more often —nothing mushy, mind you, just check up once in awhile—

The guitar had stopped. "Oo," Fast murmured. "Nice piece."

I cleared my throat. "It was Ma's favorite," I managed.

"Not that, idiot. Babe alert. Down the hill there."

She stood twenty yards away, halfway between us and the lane, a svelte blond woman in an elegant dark business suit. Evidently she'd arrived in the bottle-green Audi 90 that sat behind the Mustang now. She waved at us hesitantly, and before I could say anything Fast was headed toward her, slinging his guitar back over his shoulder. I trailed along.

"I'm sorry to intrude," she said as Fast neared her. "You're Eddie Anger, aren't you?"

"Sure am," he said, smile bold. "And a lovely lady like you is never an intrusion, sweetheart."

I placed her then, which was incredible, considering how long it had been. "Debbie Miller," I said.

She looked at me and her eyes narrowed and then brightened. "Ben? Ben Perkins?"

"She lived behind us," I told Fast. "On Thatcher."

"Kitty-corner," she chimed in. "I was two years behind you guys in school. But I remember you." Though she made a pretense of addressing this to both of us, she already had eyes only for Fast.

Which he knew full well. "Well, isn't this pleasant?" he said. "We were just here to pay respects to our late parents."

"Me too," she answered. "I get out here once a year or so. What a treat to run into you here! Do you have some time? Can I buy you lunch?"

"We'll work something out. Won't we, Benjy?"

"Whatever you say, Fast," I replied, lighting a cigar, having been through this many times before.

Fast took Debbie's elbow and started strolling her toward the cars. "What line of work are you in, Debbie?"

"I teach English at the U of M."

"Really? That's interesting. Maybe you can help me with a lyric I'm working on. It's really tough . . . maybe the two of us can figure out a fresh angle . . ."

I drove home alone, but not as alone as I'd been.

"Virtually impossible to put aside until the final horrifying showdown." -- *People*

Edgar Award winner Jonathan Kellerman once more explores the corruption of California's golden dream and produces a novel of complex characterization and non-stop suspense.

TIME BOMB
by Jonathan Kellerman
author of **Silent Partner**

By the time psychologist Dr. Alex Delaware reached the school the damage was done: A sniper had opened fire on a crowded playground, but was gunned down before any children were hurt.

While the TV news crews feasted on the scene and Alex began his therapy sessions with the traumatized children, he couldn't escape the image of a slight teenager clutching an oversized rifle. What was the identity behind the name and face: a would-be assassin, or just another victim beneath an indifferent California sky?

Intrigued by a request from the sniper's father to conduct a "psychological autopsy" of his child, Alex begins to uncover a strange pattern of innocence, neglect, and loss. Then suddenly it is more than a pattern -- it is a trail of blood. In the dead sniper's past was a dark and vicious plot. And in Alex Delaware's future is the stuff of grown-up nightmares: the face of real human evil.

TIME BOMB. On sale wherever Bantam Books are sold.

AN300 -- 8/91

Morfydd was thinki[illegible] [illegible]ad told her when she f[illegible] [illegible]ot heard him come, but now he was there directly across the stream, and her first impression was one of many flowing fringes, a blanket of fringes everywhere like the edges of a tasseled bedcover. Then she looked squarely at his face.

Her heart thumped wildly, but not from the surprise alone. She was not easily surprised. And she had seen many of these tribesmen come to trade or beg for food. But she knew as she looked at him that this one was not the same. This one held a lance fully ten feet long and his face was painted white and black and even from this distance she could see the darkly piercing eyes watching her.

Almost on the instant of seeing him, she felt the wind spring up, coming in a hard gust from the high plains to the west, chilling and distant and foreign, and forever thereafter in her mind she identified this one on the pony with that wind. A Comanche wind, for she knew he was Comanche.

Then she heard the first scream from behind her, and then a high-pitched yammering of voices sounding as nothing she had ever heard, and knew then, too, why the birds had stopped singing.

She dropped the buckets and ran for the stockade.

Douglas C. Jones

SEASON OF YELLOW LEAF

A TOM DOHERTY ASSOCIATES BOOK

SEASON OF YELLOW LEAF

Reprinted by arrangement with Holt, Rinehart and Winston

First Tor printing: July 1987

A TOR Book

Published by Tom Doherty Associates, Inc.
49 West 24 Street
New York, N.Y. 10010

Illustrations by the author
Map by Anita Karl and James Kemp

ISBN: 0-812-58450-3
CAN. ED.: 0-812-58451-1

Library of Congress Catalog Card Number: 83-117

Printed in the United States of America

0 9 8 7 6 5 4 3 2 1

It was a time when they did what they had always done. Earth Mother was good, Sun Father was powerful, Moon Mother was loving. Their young people begat, their children grew. Their arrows flew straight, their blood lances flowed with courage. But they were in the Season of Yellow Leaf.

AUTHOR'S NOTE

THROUGHOUT the following, all principal characters are fictional. Place names are given in familiar form to avoid confusion and to allow the reader to place the action in known locations.

And although many languages are spoken in dialogue, only English is used, with an apology for having to identify the tongue.

A note of appreciation: To Ernest Wallace, E. Adamson Hoebel, and T. R. Fehrenbach, whose published studies of Comanches were essential. And most especially to Fred Brown, friend, devoted consumer of chili, and himself Comanche, who has been a valued consultant and critic for this work.

In fact, the story is hereby dedicated to the memory of Fred Brown's maternal grandmother, who, were she still living, would understand all the secrets of the high plains warriors and their women only scarce touched on here.

COMANCHERÍA
N
Bent's Fort
Arrowpoint R.
(Arkansas R.)
Medicine Cr.
SANGRE DE CRISTO MTS.
Salt Fork
GLASS HILLS
Cimarron R.
Santa Fe
ANTELOPE HILLS
INDIAN
WICHITA MTS.
Washita R.
Canadian R.
PALO DURO CANYON
Pintada Cr.
LLANO ESTACADO (STAKED PLAINS)
Prairie Dog Town Fork
TERRITORY
NEW MEXICO
Peace R.
Red R.
Fort Worth
Double Mt. Fork
TEXAS
El Paso del Norte
Concho R.
KETCHUM MTN.
Pecos R.
San Saba
Madoc's Fort
Devil's R.
Colorado R.
Brazos R.
Trinity R.
San Antonio de Bexar
miles
0 50 100
SIERRA MADRE
Rio Grande
MEXICO
Salado R.
SIERRA DE LOS ALAMITOS
COAHUILA
DURANGO
Gulf of Mexico

ONE

It is the way our fathers showed us.
We need no other.
We want no other.
It is the Nermernuh road!

1

THE SINGLE HORSEMAN WAS motionless at the crown of a small hill under a moon coming full. There was a strong westerly breeze, stirring the pony's mane but not the tail, for that was clubbed for war, a neat, tight bun with a number of feathers sprouting from it like the gently waving petals of some dark flower.

The wind touched the man's long hair also, fanning it out beside his face where the eyes showed a glint of moonlight. Across his naked left shoulder was a shield with the painted hourglass-like design that was symbolic of a buffalo hide, and feathers hanging there, too. In his right hand was a lance that thrust skyward, hide-wrapped and streaming fringes, and across his back the lumpy quiver for the short bow, and the arrows vaned with owl feathers and tipped with tin warheads obtained last winter in trade from a New Mexican. One buffalo hide in exchange for two packs of arrowheads, twenty to the pack.

The pony stood without movement, for this was a well-trained war stallion and the pressure of the rider's knees was all that was needed to instruct the horse on behavior. And now it was time to be still and silent and so the pony was, the long buckskin fringes of the rider's leggings and moccasins reaching below the horse's belly, almost touching the sparse clumps of bunch grass that grew on the sandy knoll. Hanging from the pony's lower lip was a willow hoop no more than three inches across, and stretched on that a drumhead of human skin, scalp hair streaming down from it, silken soft, a show of defiance attached like this to the pony's mouth, a show of defiance to chill the blood of enemies.

It was late May. Time for the new grass to have come and the war ponies to have fattened on it. This pony was not fat but rather tough and hard from travel, for they had come a long way. The rider was not a central-Texas Indian, not from this hill country east of the Edwards Plateau. This was a high plains predator, come down from the edges of the Staked Plains, avoiding the villages of peoples more or less on friendly terms with the white man.

He had been here before, this man with the lance flowing rawhide tassels and squirrel tails. He had been here only a season ago, in the last time of new green grass and full moons. But then he had come trading horses stolen in Mexico. And below, in the valley of the tributary of the Colorado River, was the group of white men who had taken the horses and promised weapons in return—percussion muskets—but had given only two ancient flintlocks that never worked.

Now he had returned, to collect something even more valuable than weapons in revenge for those flintlocks: female children to grow to womanhood among his own people and someday give the dwindling band new babies. Or male children to ransom among the Mexicans or to sell along Red River, where one might sometimes find other tribes from the north willing to buy. All provided the children taken were tough enough to survive a war party's travel. A great many were not. But some were. He knew this because all of it he had done many times before.

The feathers in his pony's tail and on the shield—and even one hanging from the haft of the blood lance—marked him as a respected warrior in his band. For his people did not take feathers lightly, and those they wore had all been earned against one or more of many adversaries. And there were always adversaries enough to go around, for when his people began to run low on enemies, they rode out looking for new ones.

Below, in the sloping valley and near the river, were the black square forms of buildings. As the rider watched, the last light went out in the window of a house, the last orange rectangle gone now, leaving everything in the night's greenish blue moonglow.

Somewhere from among the buildings he could hear a

screech owl calling and, far to the west where the high plains rose, the distant yammer of a coyote. Brother Coyote, the clown and semi-god whose flesh he had never tasted, for one did not eat any of the gods, even the semi-gods, unless one was starving. Then one ate anything he could kill.

Coming on the breeze too was the faint odor of sage, although he had seen little of it during the past two nights' travel. For he had traveled at night, denning during the daylight hours like a wolf hiding from the hunter.

He had noted everything he needed. The fields of corn and cotton planted outside the stockade walls of the small fort. The houses inside the walls, and the sheds and barns outside, and a few houses there as well. Some good horses in the corrals and a few mules on the far slopes of the valley, where there were other dark forms he knew to be cattle.

Enough seen for his purpose, so with the pressure of his knees he turned the pony and the moon struck light squarely across his flat, high-cheekboned face where a stripe of white paint ran across his eyes and below that the whole face was painted black. He was bred and born of a great warrior society, where the men for generations—since coming down from the mountains and into the high plains—had hunted to live and had lived to fight; in their lexicon no words were more hallowed than audacity and courage. He was a Comanche and now he rode toward a far stream marked by the low, dark outline of mesquite. Where the others waited!

When the white man rose from his bed the moon was gone and it was pitch dark. The sounds of the night were gone as well, even the wind's whisper stilled, as though suspended in some vacuum of silence during those minutes just before the sun announced its coming with a stripe of gray-blue light across the flat eastern horizon. The old night seemed to hold its breath in terrible anticipation of its approaching death.

He moved with the jerky, hesitant motions of old age, although he was not really old in time but only in muscle and bone, these having paid heavy dues over long years of hard work, minimum sustenance, and little sleep.

His wife made no movement in the four-poster as he slipped from beneath the thick comforter and dressed in the dark, knowing where each item of apparel was located on the chair and dresser beside the bed. First, before the homespun shirt or duck trousers or high-laced shoes came the hat, which he pulled down hard onto his mat of uncombed hair. For his hat was always the first thing on each morning, last thing off at night. Only on two occasions was he bareheaded: when he was holding religious services, either privately or for his entire flock, and when he blew out the lamp and slipped beneath the covers each night.

In the second room of the house—which was half adobe, half clapboard lumber hauled in by oxdrawn, high-wheeled Mexican carts from San Antonio de Bexar, one hundred twenty-five miles to the south—he lit a coal-oil lamp. This room was his kitchen, parlor, and countinghouse, and also served as a bedroom for his two children, who slept in small bunks at the far side of the room, away from his desk and the lamp. He could hear their breathing and it gave him a great sense of accomplishment as well as an overwhelming weight of responsibility.

Each morning for sixteen years he had gone through this ritual, rising before his family, before the rest of his followers, to read from the Book—only a few passages, to start him on the day, for later there would be more reading from it—then to lament that it was a long way to Glamorgan, all the green ocean between; then to scribble the notes he needed to assure himself that on this day all would be done that needed doing, not only by himself for his own family but by the others who had come here with him and who clustered around his leadership like ewes around a ram in a country infested with wolves.

He mused on that a moment. It was not a dangerous country. In spite of all those stories his Mexican friends told, there had been peace and tranquility since the founding of this community. For so long in fact that peacefulness was taken for granted. It had been years since they had closed the gates to the small stockade at night. Only a few still carried firearms to the fields when they worked the crops or the cattle.

When he glanced back through the ledger book of events, he frowned. It was true and now he knew it. Crops were hard to grow in this high, dry land. Only enough could be scratched out each year for a little cotton and that sent to the markets in the towns to the east. Only a little subsistence of okra and tomatoes and Irish potatoes. Only a little corn for the animals. But at the thought of animals, his face brightened. It was good country for animals. There was the river and adequate graze, and perhaps soon the settlement would realize his fondest dream: to bring in sheep.

His was a face hardened by wind and rain, the wrinkles running like eroded gullies from the corners of his eyes. The lower half of his face was covered with a thick growth of beard, white like his hair, all of it having once been dark and showing a glint of copper in the proper light, but long since gone to gray. It was a face stubborn and determined, for all its changing show of emotion as he read previous notes. Hardest of all were the lips, uncompromising and perhaps mean, but at least almost lost in the foliage of the whiskers. His eyes were blue, very nearly transparent, but with a metallic shine when he had made up his mind or was in the excitement of a sermon.

Taking the quill and dipping it in the tin of pokeberry ink, he noted the date on his ledger. He had done this for a long time, since before leaving Wales, making his own calendar as the days went past and only one mistake in all that period. In 1823, his first year in Texas, and that corrected on the next trip to Houston. With labored concentration he wrote, the quill making little scratching sounds on the ledger page.

"Saturday, May 26, 1838. Fifty-five years old this day."

After a few more notations he blew out the lamp and sat for a moment in the darkness, listening to the breathing of his children. Then he rose and made his way to the door and out into the compound of the stockade.

There for some time he stood beside the house, smelling the land. It was a dry smell, yet it bore the once-a-year lushness that always came in the spring. Much more delicate than the odors of his native Welsh valleys, but certainly noteworthy to one with a nose trained to the soil. He was thinking also of the date. Fifty-five years old. And as he did with each passing birthday, he recalled the procession of the years, not with nostalgia but rather with a sense of accomplishment, a thing of which to be proud. At other times he held close rein on his pride because it was his belief that pride went before a fall and was not a joyous thing in the Lord's sight. But on each of his birthdays for a long time he had allowed himself this small transgression.

His name was Madoc Parry and his origin was a sheep farm near Aberdare, county of Glamorgan, Wales. He had grown to manhood there, in the time of early Methodism, learning almost from infancy the emotional verses and haunting harmonies of the Welsh hymns written by William Williams.

The call to ministry had come early to him, but had been thwarted for a number of years by the financial burden of higher education, which was generally required for ordination. When the new Methodist church became a denomination apart from the Church of England, and then the Primitive Methodists broke off from that in 1811, he became a lay preacher, an exhorter.

But Madoc Parry was restive in that time of beginning rationalism, and uncomfortable with the idea that salvation came only as a result of humble supplication. He was soon looked upon as something of a Presbyterian, enjoying as he did discussions and arguments on theology and the benefits of the Sacrament. Sir Isaac Newton and his like had had their impact on Madoc Parry, a logical and rational man.

When old Moses Austin began his drive for a colony of Anglos in Spanish Texas, Madoc responded. Perhaps it was predestined, he thought. After all, his first name came from that old Welsh prince-explorer who had discovered America in the twelfth century as legend had it. The basis for this story was that someone had found a tribe of American aborigines who spoke Welsh. It didn't matter that after this first discovery, the Celtic-inclined red men had never been found again.

As he was collecting his followers for the great venture,

two things happened that would have their effect on the rest of Madoc Parry's life: he married, being thirty-nine himself, and his bride twenty years his junior; and Mexico gained her independence, meaning there was no longer any such thing as Spanish Texas. But Stephen Austin, Moses' son, continued with the old ideal, working hard with the infant government in Mexico City, and by the time Madoc Parry arrived in 1822, grants were there for the asking. They found their plot of ground isolated from all neighbors around them, prayed over it, began to cultivate it, and called it Madoc's Fort.

On a tributary of the Colorado River of Texas it was, and selected not only for its isolation but for the beauty of the sycamores and hornbeam along the streambed and, farther up the slope—where they put the buildings—a stand of chinkapin oaks.

It had been hard work, but gratifying. Best of all was the birth of his daughter, Morfydd Annon Parry, whom everyone called Morfanna and who was the greatest pride of all his prides. Though smallish from the start—and still small for her ten years—she was a beauty, with the bottomless blue eyes of her Da, and dark hair that glinted copper in the sun. And she was intelligent, beyond all Parry's dreams of intelligence.

Then little Dafydd was born, only four years ago. But something wrong there, slack lips and almost no hair at all, even now, and a deep, vacant glaze to his eyes. Madoc seemed not to notice. Or perhaps he willed himself not to.

They had a school at Madoc's Fort where more than the forms of their religion were taught. There were numbers and figures, and because Madoc and all the others could see that this was a multilingual land, there was English grammar as well as Welsh and even Spanish, for by then there were hired people in the settlement who were Mexicans. Already Morfydd could speak not only the language of the Anglicans, as Madoc called it, but her own native Welsh, although she was a born Texan, and some Spanish and even a smattering of Indian words from the various casual visiting tribesmen. She was one of those gifted with an ear and a tongue for words, no matter what their origin.

Leaning against the wall of his house, Madoc Parry

thought of all this and was only vaguely aware that some of the horses in the far corral seemed to be making an ungodly fuss about something. As though a black bear might be near, although nobody had seen a black bear this far off the Edwards Plateau since the second year of their coming.

Just a snake, he thought, and went on with his recall, frowning now. Only two years ago had ended the war for Texas independence. He had been with the troops at San Jacinto when they captured Santa Anna. But a bitter war, for Madoc's younger brother, Estyn, had been at Goliad when the Mexicans captured it and took the Texas defenders out, lined them up against a wall, and shot them all dead. It left a bitter taste in Madoc Parry's mouth each time he thought of it.

Yet there was no rancor in his heart against his own Mexicans, as he called them. For each of the menfolk among them had fought for Texas independence beside the Anglos.

Nor, despite the stories they had heard of horrible deeds, was there any rancor against the Indians. His people had traded with all manner of them: the Caddo tribes and the Tonkawas—who everyone said were cannibals, but who were a tall and handsome people—and even some of the wandering Comanche bands.

Comanches had never impressed him favorably. They were generally a squat, awkward group of men. Except on horseback. Then, Madoc had to admit, they were quite splendid. But, being no horseman himself, he counted this small in his mind's ledger. He saw them only as childlike heathen, easily taken advantage of in trading.

Sometimes it made him uneasy that he was capable of swindling. But after all, he explained to himself, if the Lord placed opportunities before a Christian man, then they could not be ignored. It was not a part of his creed except in the secret sections of his soul, where nobody else could read it. Except perhaps the Comanches.

"Good morning, Grandfer." The voice came from one of the many Owen men who were part of this settlement, and Madoc Parry recognized the sound of it as the dark form passed near him on the way to the barns, although it was not yet light enough to see clearly.

"Good morning, Bangor Owen," he said, voice rough with the first words spoken on this day. And there was in the tone of it acceptance of his place here as grandfather to them all, though since Estyn's murder against that Goliad wall none of them were his kin except his wife and the children Morfydd Annon and Dafydd.

Behind him in the house he could hear his wife rousing the children from their sleep, and soon a light appeared in the one window. He heard the stove grate opening and the soft murmuring of his Morfydd speaking with her mother.

Fifty-five years old, he mused, and me here woolgathering is it, yet many's the blessings on us all.

He took a pail from its peg against the outside wall and followed Bangor Owen toward the milking barn. Around him he could hear the settlement rising, going to its early work, preparing for the new day that was now showing its advance in the east. A clear day, no cloud yet seen to catch the sun's rays, and the dome of the sky toward the west still purple with the night.

MORFYDD ANNON PARRY sat on the edge of Dafydd's bunk, helping him pull on the smock shirt he wore in warm weather. She wore one like it, only slightly larger, and under it trousers of the same material. Homespun. Her hair was tied back behind her ears with a red ribbon, a little faded now from her having worn it almost constantly since her Da brought it to her from Houston on one of those once-every-three-years trips he made to the town that stood near the coast and was more than two hundred miles away. A journey that, had he made it in the old country, would have carried him across Wales, across England, and into the channel beyond.

Well, she thought, soon it will be better, when they have Austin properly laid out as the new capital and it only eighty miles south along the Colorado. Then Da would go to town once very two years, perhaps. More ribbons then and even factory-made shoes and not the home-stitched ones made here by Uncle Bangor Owen.

Of course, Bangor Owen was not her uncle and she knew this. But to the children of Madoc's Fort, every man was uncle, every woman aunt.

"I didn't hear my mockingbird so far this day," Morfydd said, and her mother turned from the stove where she was stoking a reluctant fire from the small dead branches of brush gathered by the children on the prairie.

"Birds, is it?" Her mother spoke in Welsh as Morfydd had. "Water pails empty, and birds, is it? Your bird, no less. As though it were God's own creature no longer, but yours only."

"He sings each daybreak," Morfydd said sullenly. "But not this day."

"So repast for the red fox he was, this barren, savage land. Now talk of birds no longer, and off you, the water."

Morfydd yanked Dafydd's smock down viciously and his head popped through, the round face with dead eyes not blinking. And she thought, This one too is God's creature and crazy as a rock lizard and maybe that's the reason she speaks harsh and clamps her lips tight.

"Stay here, sit still, Dafydd, until the morning food." Otherwise he might follow her like a puppy.

She went quickly to her morning's work, which was the fetching of a pair of two-gallon buckets of water from the stream. There was water already for the cornmeal-mush breakfast, of course, because each household here had four water buckets. This was required because sometimes—usually—water taken from the river had to set for a day to allow the silt to settle. So two buckets of fresh, two of day-old water for cooking and what little bathing was done beyond the banks of the stream.

As she moved out through the open stockade gate and down toward the line of hornbeam and sycamore, she skipped a little, liking the feel of the gritty sand beneath her bare feet. This was the best of times for her, out of the house and away from the older ones. She loved them and they her, she was sure, yet somehow all were hard and brittle about it, with never the tender touch. There was in her some desperate yearning for the tender touch, but it seldom came except when Uncle Bangor Owen, who was her favorite of all the uncles, came to discuss settlement plans with her Da.

Best time because of the calm freshness, the wind laid and resting. Now the sun was almost ready to burst through the horizon and bathe everything in soft orange light that would turn brassy hard later. Each day she went like this, skipping, when there were still cool gray and blue shadows under every scrub bush and the air was sharp-tasting on the tongue. Each day, to draw her water from the stream and then back up the hill, coming into the compound just as the sun appeared.

There were the other children going for water, too, as they always were. She avoided them as she always did, lingering along the slope until they were well back from the river, carrying their sloshing buckets to the settlement.

She looked along the far western ridges, whence the birds usually called to her. There was only silence now. Not even the horned larks that were always in a twitter with the coming sun. Not even the crows that were always in flocks along the edges of the plateau. She wondered why the silence, the unusual quiet that made a small shiver pass up her back. But then thought no more of it.

At the river's bank she squatted, settling the buckets gently so as not to disturb any more silt than necessary. As the buckets filled she looked along the bank, noting whether the watermark showed a lowering of the water. For she knew that Da would ask her at the breakfast table immediately after grace was said.

"More water or less this day, Morfanna?" he would ask.

Perhaps the river had risen in the night, for she saw in places farther along the bank that there was no dark mark above the surface. Da would like that.

She watched minnows playing in the small pool nearby, where in summer when the water was down, she had dug out the little glinting salamanders and kept them in a bucket until her mother realized only three of the pails were sitting on the water stand where there should be four.

Her gaze went to the far bank. There under the hornbeam on one such morning she had seen an armadillo and her young come to drink and caught with the night run out on her. Morfydd knew about armadillos. She knew that these strange little creatures had young in litters all of one sex, either boys or girls, never mixed. She knew this from her Mexican friends, the workers at the settlement. She liked her Mexican friends, because there seemed more happiness there than among her own people. They had fed her what they called chili con carne made from the armadillo, hot to the tongue and making tears come to her eyes with its harshness, but somehow possessing a certain quality that pleased her.

Her Mexican friends had told her many things. She had learned much about this wild country and it made her feel native here, although her Da insisted she was native to Glamorgan, a place she had never seen and could visualize in her mind only from what he told her of it.

She was thinking of that when she saw the horseman. She had not heard him come, but now he was there directly across the stream, and her first impression was one of many flowing fringes, a blanket of fringes everywhere like the edges of a tasseled bedcover. Then she looked squarely at his face.

Her heart thumped wildly, but not from the surprise alone. She was not easily surprised. And she had seen many of these tribesmen come to trade or to beg for food. But she knew as she looked at him that this one was not the same. This one held a lance fully ten feet long and his face was painted white and black and even from this distance she could see the darkly piercing eyes watching her.

Almost on the instant of seeing him, she felt the wind spring up, coming in a hard gust from the high plains to the west, chilling and distant and foreign, and forever thereafter in her mind she identified this one on the pony with that wind. A Comanche wind, for she knew he was Comanche.

Then she heard the first scream from behind her, where the buildings stood, and then a high-pitched yammering of voices, sounding as nothing she had ever heard, and knew then, too, why the birds had stopped singing.

She dropped the buckets and ran for the stockade.

THE FIRST GROUP came from the east, riding slowly out of the sun. There were nine of them, all carrying lances. They seemed in no hurry.

As was usual at sunrise, Madoc Parry was in the fields, looking at the new plants and making an assessment of the crops before breakfast. As though he could tell from day to day how much they had grown overnight. And there were those in the settlement who claimed that if anyone could do such a thing, Grandfer was that one.

Madoc Parry did not hear them until they were quite close. They were coming across cultivated ground and there were no metal bit chains to clink their warning, no squeak of cured leather. For they rode high plains saddles made of rawhide and bone, with wooden stirrups, copies handed down through the generations since the time their forefathers had first seen the Spanish horses and had copied the designs of the Spanish accouterments, but using wood and bone and rawhide instead of iron and cured leather. Or else no saddle at all, but bareback, with only woven horsehair ropes tied in three places around the ponies' bodies for handholds. Except for breechclouts, knee-length moccasins, and a few bone necklaces, they were naked, their hair flowing loosely.

As he rose from the inspection of his plants, Madoc Parry became aware of their presence. He was looking directly into the new sun, and even after he raised his hand to shade his eyes, he had trouble making out the details of the riders. Then they were close around him and he saw that they were Indians, come to trade, he supposed, or to ask for a cow or two. Madoc Parry, one hand still raised, opened his mouth to shout them off his plowed ground. He still had no inkling of what they were or why they were here because he failed to read the meaning of the lances and the black paint on their faces.

Three of them brought down their lances and touched Madoc Parry with the iron warheads, almost gently it seemed to Bangor Owen, who was running out from the stockade. But quickly too, and Madoc was on the ground without a sound, writhing there, and Bangor Owen saw two more of them leap down from their ponies and saw the flash of sunlight on the blades of their knives as they bent to the Grandfer and began their work.

The others were kicking their horses into a gallop, coming directly toward the stockade, and at the same time two other parties broke from the trees along the river, shouting now, hair streaming back. Bangor Owen got as far as the near gate to the stockade when the arrow struck him high in the back, and going down he saw yet another group of the wild horsemen already inside the compound walls from the other side, and heard the screaming and saw the whirl of ponies and men and the billowing skirts of running women, heard one gunshot and no more, and went into a murky blackness.

As in a dream, he felt the earth tremble when the ponies swept past him, then others coming back and toward the far corral, and he was vaguely aware that they were taking all the horses. From the buildings he heard the screaming still, and the high yammering of the other voices. He tried to struggle upward, to raise his head to see, but could not. He began to feel the dull pain in his back, where the tin arrowhead was pressed hard against his shoulder blade, and he knew even in his half-consciousness that the shoulder blade had probably saved his life and lucky the arrow had not been shot from closer range or perhaps it would have penetrated even that.

He lay facedown, and after a while, the turmoil in his mind and in the stockade making it all a bramble bush of impressions, he felt his head being jerked up by the hair, a sharp, white-hot pain along the top of his head and blood suddenly running down across his face and into his staring eyes. Then his face dropped back in the sand. He knew he had been scalped, a small portion taken from the head where the hair was thickest and longest. He wondered when they would come back once more and do to him what they had done to the Grandfer, with the knives playing along his body. But they did not come.

He slipped into total darkness but could, for a short time, still hear the ghastly sounds from the stockade. Then that was gone too and there was only the terrible heat of the rising sun and his blood caking in the sand under his face. Finally, even that sensation was gone.

By the time evening came, and with it the men who had managed to escape in the mesquite, his face was stuck to the ground in his own dried blood and when they lifted him gently and turned him over, the mat of black soil clung to his face like a stove lid.

"He's alive," he heard someone say. "They passed him up with their knives."

Bangor Owen began to gasp, trying to cry but with no water left for tears and the thirst a stabbing pain under his ribs. He could hear a pair of coyotes on the far western ridges starting their sundown wailing and he knew he had been lying there all day.

"How many?" he whispered, and they knew what he meant.

"Seven men dead, Bangor Owen, and one woman. And two women carried off with them and two children as well."

They were washing the caked blood from his face with a lifted canteen, and he held his mouth open to catch some of it.

"The children?" he asked, and once more they knew what he meant.

"Your woman and the three children safe in the river bottom."

Then the tears did come, hot and salty to the taste.

And to the west, far out on the plateau, still moving hard and already fifty miles from Madoc's Fort, the war party moved intently, silently, driving the ponies on. Behind them on captured horses rode the captives, naked and blistered in the sun, Morfydd Annon Parry among them.

2

FOR MORFYDD THERE WAS LITtle recollection of the first day. Initially there was the terror of being swept up and onto the pony and held there, the humiliation of being stripped naked—except for the hair ribbons—and then the sunburn that became more excruciatingly painful as the day wore on, then the soreness in her stomach and along her thighs, her feet tied with rope beneath the belly of the horse they put her on—one of her father's mares.

She saw little of what happened at the stockade, only once someone running and run down from behind and lanced. Through her tears and screaming she could not tell if it was man or woman, much less recognize a face. She heard the frightful noises from the buildings and they seemed to melt into all the rest of the coming red day, unbelievable and horrible and beyond any chance of reasoned thought.

Once the war party began to move, she tried to make them untie little Dafydd, his crying and unintelligible babbling a piercing throb in her ears. She shouted at them in Welsh and English and finally a few words in Spanish, but they moved on, ignoring her and pushing their ponies hard. She saw then, but was only consciously aware of it later, that they all had more than one pony, some having as many as four, in addition to the horses taken from the fort corral, so they constantly changed mounts. But they left the captives on the same horses all day, Morfydd and Dafydd and the two naked women who had been struck across the faces with bows until they were bloody and almost unrecognizable. She may have made one terrible mental effort that day: not to recognize them in their shame and humiliation.

The captives were kept close behind the main body, their horses pulled along with lead ropes. Often, one of the men swung away from the party to watch for pursuit, holding his shield above his head to shade his eyes from the sun as he looked along the backtrail. Riding to catch up, he would come in close among the captives, striking them across the back with the haft of his lance. Morfydd expected relief to come riding up from behind at any moment.

By noon she had lost all ability to see anything about her, to hear any cries from the other captives, to note anything of the country. After her own early outbursts of anger, she had remained silent, and when the rear guard men came past her they looked at her with a fierce interest.

The country was rising to flat plains and there were fewer trees by midafternoon. Some cacti, and in the sky a few vultures wheeled high behind them now and again and then disappeared. The war party kicked up a number of roadrunners, that strange ground cuckoo with the long, rushing stride.

By sundown, Morfydd had begun hallucinating. In the sun's red dying she could see the swarms of ruby-throated hummingbirds that came down from the Edwards Plateau each summer to feed on her mother's hollyhocks; Dafydd's whining had taken on the sound of the bitch wolf's howling that spring when Da had found the den and killed all the seven whelps with a shotgun.

The first night they lit only a small fire of wood that was dry and almost completely smokeless when it burned, in a hole dug a foot deep into the plains soil. It was as though no fire were there at all, showing reflected light only on someone standing directly over it.

It was well past dark when Morfydd heard the two captive women screaming and crying. And she knew what was happening. She had heard the stories told at the settlement—not stories meant for her young ears but said quietly by lamplight at her father's desk when he talked with Bangor Owen and the others—about what happened to women caught in the kind of warfare the plains tribes waged, and she awake in her bunk and listening.

"They are used like mares in heat, many times over," had said her Da.

"Yes," had said another. "Like the old wars of the Greeks and Romans, with women prizes and taken many times. As with the rape of the Sabine women."

And Morfydd knew of mares in heat and of cattle and hogs as well, and although she did not know the details, she knew what was happening now.

The first really lucid thought of the day came then, the first since she had dropped the buckets and run for the fort that morning. And in the form of a question, in a mind that had always been inquisitive and inquiring. Only now it came with a sudden burst of bitterness.

If the men had known so much about plains warfare as they indicated over the low-glowing, smoking lamp, why had they all been so surprised? Why, having known these things, had they left the settlement so unprotected after years of knowing danger, even if only through hearsay?

Then it came to her anguished mind that the danger had always been there but the men at Madoc's Fort had failed to sense its depth. And coming to that, she ground her teeth and cried out in utter fury and despair, and bitterness as well that they could have been so blind. But perhaps despite that and the loneliness real as a bubble of scalding air in her chest, she called up all the toughness of her heritage.

From nearby in the darkness, she could hear Dafydd snuffling in his sleep like an old dog dreaming of bears. But now she could develop no compassion, not for anyone but herself. She wondered for an instant what had happened to Da and her mother, but closed that out quickly because she knew it would be painful to think on and would accomplish nothing but to increase her sense of hopelessness. And she willed herself hope, and defiance, with that stubborn, tight-lipped determination of her Welsh kind.

Once during the night, the warrior who had taken her came and shook her from an agonized half-sleep and gave her a drink of water from some kind of skin bag. After she had had her fill, she lay stiffly as he felt her, his hands somehow gently moving along her arms and legs and belly and everywhere, exploring her dispassionately as he might a puppy. Then he was gone and she slept, this time without dreaming.

The next morning he came to her again and untied her, for she, like the other captives, had been bound with braided horsehair ropes. He gave her water again and watched her drink with his black eyes that showed no more fleck of interest than if he were watching a lizard going through the sand. But at least she realized then that she was being selected, for what reason she knew not, for so far as she could see, none of the other captives had been given water.

He threw a bundle of clothing in her lap, her own smock and pants stripped off the day before. As soon as she pulled them on over her blistered body she was tied to a horse again, but one of the small Comanche ponies this time. As they rode out with dawn breaking, she saw what was left of the carcass of the horse she had ridden the day before and knew they had eaten it during the night and tried to recall the smell of cooking meat but could not.

The second day was much the same as the first. Even with her smock, the sun blazed hurtfully against her back, and the pain in her lower body and legs was almost unbearable, sending its stab up through her belly with each step the pony took. The warriors paid no more attention to them than they had before, perhaps even less, riding on toward the west, speaking to one another now and again in short, sharp coughing sounds, pointing out landmarks as they rose on the horizon.

Dafydd was silent now, tied to his horse as before, lying facedown on the pony's neck, the mane in his face. He made no sound; his eyes were glassy and blood was caked across his back where one of the warriors had struck him with a bow the day before.

They no longer sent riders back to watch for anyone following. And none of them fell back to taunt the captives or jab them with the blunt ends of lances. About midday, they paused long enough to cut one of the captive women loose and she fell to the hard plains soil like a pink, wet sack and lay still and naked and they rode off and left her there. Morfydd tried not to recall who this woman was, although she could not put from her mind that only two days ago, whoever she might have been, all the children at the fort had called her auntie.

They came to the Cap Rock Escarpment, a line of bluffs running off into the plains in each direction as far as she could see, in some places rising to over two hundred feet. Here, half the group split off, taking the other captive woman and Dafydd with them, and Morfydd could not find the strength to protest even weakly and even had she done so, she knew it would have taken no effect. She watched them moving away along the face of the escarpment, toward the north, growing smaller even as she watched, soon only flecks of color in the drab expanse of high plains scrub, and then gone. Her own group, with her the only prisoner now, moved up a steep defile in the bluffs and finally out onto the level ground above, where a westerly wind blew into her face with a fierceness of wind she had never known before.

That night found them well onto the high plains, table-flat and mostly treeless. Once more they tied her on the ground and ignored her. The fire was not so small this time, but still kindled in a hole. She knew they were not afraid of being followed so deep into Comanchería, a word she had heard the Mexicans use at Madoc's Fort. She heard their talking and laughter and once saw one of them hold up a streaming trophy and knew it was hair.

Morfydd was not yet asleep when the warrior who had carried her from the slope above the stream near Madoc's Fort came in the darkness and squatted beside her. Once more he gave her a drink after untying her, then thrust a piece of meat into her hand. It was stringy and tough, and even as she wolfed it down she knew it was a chunk of her own father's horse and raw. But she ate it all, and then he allowed her to drink again.

"*His-oo-Sanchess,*" he said, placing one hand on his own breast.

He spoke again, words of which she had no comprehension, and as he spoke he touched the red ribbons in her hair. Then again, softly, "*Sanchess,*" and he touched himself.

She could see the dark gleam in his eyes from the fading light of day, gone except with enough remaining skyshine to reflect. The black and white paint on his face had run down in streams, washed out by sweat, and she found herself surprised that Indians perspired. Then he spoke again for what seemed a long time and in what she thought was Spanish, although she could not understand a word of it.

He represented to her then some dark and savage shape from a nightmare, yet one somehow benign, a creature with whom, in this desolation and strangeness of land and night, she was somehow becoming familiar. And so the fear was gone, replaced by a daze of unreality, as though she would soon wake and everything would be as it was before, her walking back to the fort with two pails of sloshing water.

But her anger was real enough. Anger at the searing pain of sunburn, at the torment in her sore legs. And anger at this dark man and everything that he had brought. She felt a fierce pride as well that he had tried to communicate with her in a language he had heard her speak perhaps in those first moments the day before, when she was screaming and kicking. She couldn't remember what she'd said, her heart at that time pumping so hard it had blotted out any recognition of words.

But at least she knew his name now. Sanchess.

After he was gone, she slept, but was wakened in the night by three of the other warriors. They squatted around her, feeling her body, their hands beneath her smock and pants. She could see their outlines against the stars in the vast dome of plains sky and she lay stiffly, frozen with fear.

There was considerable talk among them. Then Sanchess appeared, towering blackly over them and his few, sharp words ended the discussion and everyone moved away from her, back to their own fire, which was still burning dimly.

And she knew. The others had argued to take her as they would a grown woman, as she had heard them take the other two the night before, as she had heard her father and Bangor Owen speak of it, and she knew that Sanchess had told them she was only a child. And with horror, yet with great relief, she knew that he was leader of this war party and that she belonged to him.

And because Sanchess claimed her as his only, not to be shared with others, and because he was powerful enough to make it so, the Comanches gave her the name Chosen.

THE ENCAMPMENT was at one of the small artesian springs that could be found along the eastern edge of the Staked Plains, near the headwaters of the Middle Concho River. It was not a war encampment but a gathering of a few families that had split off for the summer from their main group, the Nakoni Comanches, who roamed considerably farther north than this.

Here they were near the Pecos, where their fathers had destroyed the old Pecos Pueblo and from where they could send raiding parties into Mexico or into central Texas as the spirit willed. There was sweet water and a few cottonwoods and soapberry, and there were herds of buffalo only an easy ride in any direction. It was a good campsite for Comanches, and they had their lodges scattered through the sparse growth of timber, with the tipi of the band's headman at the center of it all.

There were more than a dozen tipis, not counting the menstrual lodges for the women to use at their time of isolation. In this band were a total of almost thirty fighting men and as many women, about the same number of children of all ages, as well as hordes of vicious, bony dogs with long ears and powerful jaws, and a horse and mule herd counting more than four hundred animals. And only recently more than a hundred horses had been driven off toward the west to trade with Comancheros.

It was a proud camp because they had all they needed. And they knew they would be dangerous for any enemy coming near, if indeed any enemy could find them in this isolated pinpoint of the great plains. Their young men were strong and brave and their leaders wise and knowing in war and hunting and finding water. And they were proud also because they had Iron Shirt.

On this day, Iron Shirt walked among the lodges, a blanket wrapped about his shoulders. It was warm, yet his old wounds from fighting the Utes and the Pawnees were somehow bothering him, a bad omen. He was fifty-eight summers old, born in the white man's year of 1780. Old enough to have heard the stories of his father and grandfather about the old days, when the Nermernuh had come down into the south plains and driven out the Apaches and fought the Spaniards and then the Mexicans and always the white Texans, whom they considered a separate breed from all other enemies.

Yet not so old that he might not still lead a war party. But it had been a long time since he had done so. He was the leader of his own family group, and in the council of all the family headmen he was the leader there as well. He was the biggest peace chief in the camp, which meant that they moved when he said so and camped where he said to, but of course there was usually a good deal of argument about such things among the family headmen and if anyone didn't want to follow him, he could go his own way and no hard feelings.

As he walked, the children and even the dogs avoided him, for although like all the older men in the band he was sometimes subjected to practical jokes by the young ones, in broad daylight when Iron Shirt walked, no one came near unless he beckoned, for they knew he had very large thoughts in his mind.

On this afternoon, watching the women cure the meat from the latest hunt, hanging it like long, red-black cloths on drying-pole racks, he was thinking of the war party that was out, not heard from for a number of sunsets now, and his son Sanchess leading it. Overdue it was, but how could one tell what a war party might come across, what temptations might turn it aside, what enemies it might encounter? Surely this was too far south and west for the Osages, those tall, handsome, and courageous men who came from the place of many trees to hunt the buffalo, and in whose country grew the Osage orange wood, called by the French the bois d'arc because it was the best wood known for making bows.

Iron Shirt feared none of his enemies, not even the Osages. But they were a breed to be avoided at all costs. Bravery is not the same as stupidity.

"Stop your thinking on Sanchess and his war party," Iron Shirt's oldest wife, Woman Who Runs, had said.

Maybe she ought to know. She was the boy's mother. Boy? Fully twenty-one summers he had lived and boy no longer, but a hunter of game and a leader of war parties. For three summers now he had gone out as headman against the Utes or Lippans. But not so often against the white man.

The passing seasons went by so rapidly! Only yesterday in his mind was the boy, running about the camp half naked, then later playing in the pony herd at night, slipping under the edge of the summer tipi to learn about copulation and other enjoyments with the older girls who rode the horses at night too, just for the fun of it.

And now Sanchess with two wives of his own. Wapiti Song, a good Nakoni now with child. And Sunshade, the fierce woman from the Kwahadi band, whose people lived far out on the Staked Plains where there were no trees and everyone carried a rawhide shield, even the women, to hold above their heads and shade them from the midday sun.

He knew the Staked Plains well. Llano Estacado, the Mexicans called it. Iron Shirt knew much of the Spanish language too, from his years of trading with the Comancheros. But he knew little of the Kwahadi, a band of The People, yet far distant in their ways. And now he had a daughter-in-law from among them.

But another day almost gone and Sanchess not yet returned. If it was a successful war party, they would ride into camp during daylight, even camping out on the plains near the camp through the night to come in that way, with the sun. If not successful, they would creep into camp at night, like the tiny elf owl, timid and licking their wounds. Now another night was coming on, to make Iron Shirt sleepless, wondering what had happened.

It was better to have been a war chief, when he could

rouse other young men to come along on a raid. Then there was no sitting in camp among the women with nothing to do but smoke and talk with other old men of hunts and of battles with the Navahos. One could only sleep so much of the passing day and night, and with his son out, even sleep troubled him, bringing with it dreams he could not understand.

At the far edge of the encampment he paused and allowed the high plains wind to dip into this break in the land and touch his face. It felt fine, the wind, fresh and cool and without malice. Wind was good. It brushed against his hair and made it dance.

He was not an unusual man in appearance among the Nermernuh, The People. He was rather short and squat, with legs seeming too spindly to carry his massive body. His face was broad and flat, copper-colored, with dark blotches under the eyes and flecks of pale skin across the high cheekbones. He wore his hair as most of the older Comanche men did, braided down either side of his face and the braids wrapped tightly in deerskin and a plait hanging down his back from the top of his head, unwrapped, and tied at the end so the hair would splay out like a small pony's tail. Of course, when he was on a war party, he allowed it to flow free except for the scalp lock on top. But it was a long time since he had worn it that way, and now each morning his two wives combed it and greased it and set the braids and wrappings just so, in keeping with his position as headman.

His face was smooth, wrinkled only slightly, and there was no hair there because it had all been plucked out by the roots as soon as it appeared, even the eyebrows. It gave him a moonlike expression when his face was in repose, but one of fierceness when he was angry and when he laughed. His eyes were black and, as with most of the men of his people, the sclerae were always bloodshot. His lips were a thin line, wide and not unknown to smiling.

As he stood on the edge of the encampment, away from the few trees and the tipis, he watched a group of small boys coming in from the prairie with armloads of dried buffalo dung, especially good for burning. Now and then one of the boys would throw a piece of the dried dung at one of the other boys and this would bring a return volley. He could recall when he was a boy, throwing buffalo chips at his companions, and the hint of a smile touched his lips. Then the boys saw him and stopped playing and went about their work, looking very serious and hurrying toward the camp with the stacks of chips.

Iron Shirt thought of his older son, Bear in the Willows, away in New Mexico to trade hides taken during the last season of cold moons, when the band had gone to the San Juan Mountains to hunt wapiti, the big deer with magnificent antlers. Dangerous it was, hunting there among the wintering villages of their old enemy, the Utes. Cousins, the Utes, they and the Comanches both having come originally from the Shoshone, far to the north. But sometimes cousins are the worst of enemies.

Of all the band's young men, Bear in the Willows was the most practical of them. He would rather trade horses than steal them. And perhaps this time he would return with guns from the Comancheros.

Sanchess was another matter. No trading for him if there was a chance to call together some of his friends and go on a little war party. Bear in the Willows was filled with wisdom, Sanchess with fire. It was good to have such sons because, to survive, The People needed trading as well as hunting and raiding. It was a fine business, taking horses and captives from along one edge of their territory and then trading these things for white man's goods somewhere else. But even so, Iron Shirt worried when his remaining sons were away. He had lost his eldest only two summers ago in a skirmish with the Tonkawas, those terrible people who ate the hearts of their dead enemies. At least Iron Shirt had heard this was true, but he had never seen it.

Coming out to stand beside him was Big Wolf, headman of another family in the band, who had The People's respect almost equal to Iron Shirt's. Big Wolf was naked above the waist, showing skin much darker than Iron Shirt's, and showing as well a line of fat over the drawstrings of his loincloth and leggings, the result of too much lying in the sun and eating buffalo fat and liver. For a long time the two stood silently together and the women in the camp who saw them wondered what they might be planning. They had been in this encampment for a full changing of the moon and everyone knew it was about time to move because Nakonis were always changing campsites, whether they needed to or not.

The two headmen held their arms folded across their bellies, knowing they were watched. They saw a kite, hunting, and some of the little flycatchers that nested in yucca plants, and heard a cock mockingbird calling but did not see him.

"The sun moves slowly when one waits," Big Wolf finally said.

"Yes. I had a dream last night. It was about those Kiowas with Sanchess."

"They will break off and go back home somewhere along the route."

"Yes. I dreamed of them. A strange people."

"Well, those Kiowas are strong fighters. My father told tales about when they were our enemies and we fought them."

"Yes, my father too," Iron Shirt said. "Now we are friends. But a very strange people, with their sun dance. Do you remember the time we were hunting with a party of them and our people killed a bear and ate it? The war almost started all over again right there."

"No, I do not remember. I was in Mexico, as I have told you. However, I know of it. You have told me," Big Wolf said.

"A strange people. Bears are gods to them and eating one is like eating a man, they say."

"Well, bear is not my favorite meat, either," Big Wolf said, and they both laughed as they had many times before with this small joke.

"We grow old," Iron Shirt said. "Telling the same stories over and over again."

"Ah, but each time the telling gets better!"

They were almost ready to turn back to the encampment once more when they saw the rider. He came into view at the far end of this small depression in the prairie, riding against the skyline of the plains. He circled his pony and waved a lance in the air.

"Now they come," Big Wolf said, and both of them turned and hurried back to the village, moving rather awkwardly on their short legs, the fat shaking along Big Wolf's belly.

"They come!" Iron Shirt shouted, unable to contain himself.

He ran to his own lodge, and already, having seen these headmen dashing along like overweight boys, everyone sensed the excitement. The children rushed screaming toward their own tipis. The women dropped awls and scrapers and knives, and left pieces of meat still to be sliced for the drying rake lying on the ground, each running to her own lodge to comb her hair and put on paint.

The dogs caught the excitement as well and ran yammering through the camp, snapping at one another and a few stopping to wolf down great mouthfuls of the chunk meat abandoned by the women and left lying on the ground in their haste. But nobody cared. There was plenty of meat, and besides, it was time for celebration with a war party coming in, even for the dogs.

At the pony herd, the young boys there sat stiffly on their horses and watched, and as the mules and horses began to pace and mill, they held them in check and cursed their luck, but only for a short time, knowing the celebration would last long enough for everyone.

"What is it?" Comes Behind shouted, her head in the tipi door. She was the second wife of Iron Shirt, very young and with a long face that came from her Cheyenne blood, and not yet with child. But Iron Shirt was very proud of her because of her beauty, and even though she came from a northern tribe, she docked her hair as any Comanche woman did, at shoulder length, and let it fly loose like the mane of a good pony.

"Make preparations, woman," Iron Shirt shouted. "They come. And the sun still here."

Inside the tipi, Iron Shirt threw aside his blanket, the pain of old wounds forgotten now, and found the garment that had given him and his father and grandfather their names: a smock of Spanish chain mail. Now it was little more than a covering for his shoulders over a deerskin shirt, the rest of it having rusted and fallen away through the years.

This mail shirt had been taken by his grandfather from a Spanish soldier a long time ago, when The People had fought various expeditions sent against them out of New Spain. It had been handed down from father to son over three generations in a very special way. Each time, as the wearer of it felt death coming, he changed his name so that afterward it might not be something The People could not pronounce. And so each man—grandfather, father, and son—could wear the garment and the name as well: Iron Shirt.

As he pulled it over his head to cover his shoulders and then placed the pronghorn antelope headdress tight down on his thick hair, he thought of how the shirt had given his youngest son a name already. When the boy was three summers old, he had found the mail shirt in his father's trappings and put it on and danced through the village with it. And thus his name: His-oo-Sanchess, The Little Spaniard.

Woman Who Runs was in the tipi now, and the two wives helped him complete his toilet, pulling his best leggings up his legs, brushing down the fringes with their fingers, bringing out the ocher paint for his face, finding his best moccasins, the ones that were almost knee-length and had trailing hair at heel and toe from the tails of buffalo.

"Is he coming?" Woman Who Runs asked, a little breathlessly in her old age.

"Yes, woman. What do you think this is all about? I saw the signal," Iron Shirt said. "Uncover my shield and wash your face, woman, and put on paint. Our son comes!"

3

Morfydd Annon had no notion of why they stopped on the barren plains in midafternoon to scrub off old paint and put on new and rub down the horses with grass to make the hides glisten in the sun. They pulled the tangles from their loose hair with a bone comb passed from one to the other. One had a small parfleche bag of grease and they used this on their hair, rubbing it in with their fingers. They seemed excited, talking more among themselves than they had at any time since the raid.

They had sent a scout ahead for some purpose Morfydd did not yet understand, and after he returned and completed his own toilet, they ate a few mouthfuls of dried meat. Sanchess gave her a small piece and although it was tough and stringy, she ate it greedily and it tasted good. He gave her water and when she was finished drinking he took her down from the Indian pony.

Immediately that she was free of her binding ropes and her feet firmly on the ground, she kicked him in the shins and he grunted and tried to seize her hair and she bit him on the arm. Then he laughed, showing great white teeth, and cuffed her on the side of the head with enough force to make her ears ring. He caught both of her arms in his hands and lifted her and sat her not gently on the ground. She was quiet then as he squatted beside her, all show of laughter gone from his face as suddenly as it had come.

She stared at him closely for the first time, and saw the red-rimmed eyes and the wide, flat bones under the skin of his cheeks and the corded muscles in his neck. He rubbed grease into her hair and dusted her smock and pants with the flats of his hands, roughly, muttering now and again in Comanche words that held no meaning for her but had some tone of menace. Then he placed her astride one of the Madoc's Fort mares, one with a saddle that had been taken too, and she was not tied. The seat and the saddle finder were hot to her sore thighs, but she made an effort to show no sign of it.

"*Casa,*" Sanchess said, pointing toward the west where all she could see was the uninterrupted plain. She knew the Spanish word, but it made no sense to her then.

Looking down at him as he stood for a moment beside her mount, she could see a small stream of blood running along his arm from the place where her teeth had made their impression. He seemed completely unaware of it.

As she sat on the big mare the men all squatted near their ponies, doing something she did not first comprehend. They took small willow wands from saddle pouches, and strips of rawhide thread and bone awls. She saw that they were preparing the scalps. The skin was fleshed with knives and pierced with the awls, making a ring of holes around the circular edges, these threaded with the rawhide strips and stretched on the willow wands, formed into hoops. It took only a few moments. When it was done, they applied some of the grease to the strands of hair and it shone brilliantly in the sun. All of these were attached to the lance of Sanchess, from the warhead down the shaft. There were nine of them.

With Sanchess mounted now and holding the butt of the lance on one thigh, the hair of the scalps blowing out like pennants in the constant wind, they rode forward once more. They were in a tight group, with only two of them following, keeping the captured animals close behind. At first she could see nothing that made this place different from any of the others she had seen during the past two days. Then suddenly they were dipping down into a draw cut by water, a depression invisible until they came to the lip of it. And ahead she saw the village and felt a new sensation of foreboding.

There was a line of trees, cottonwoods, the branches showing bone white through the leaves, and among them stood the conical skin lodges, the color of bread dough and smoke-blackened at the top where the tipi poles splayed out like Spanish bayonets. There were clusters of prickly pear and mesquite, more stunted here than those she had known around Madoc's Fort, and yucca, and a few dwarfed pinyon along the slopes of the draw, dark green, almost black.

Coming toward them was a long column of people, chanting and singing, led by a woman carrying a long pole with horses' tails tied to it and her face painted red. There were many women here, and most of the men were older than the members of the war party. As Sanchess drew near, all the ponies prancing with excitement, the people parted, allowing the raiders to ride between lines of shouting, leaping Indians. Behind the men and women and children were packs of dogs, more dogs than Morfydd had ever seen, barking and leaping. On the breeze she caught the smells of smoke and dust and roasting meat.

Her mare was close-held on a lead rope by Sanchess, but as they moved along the lines of people on foot, some of the women leaped in and jabbed her with pointed sticks. She felt little pain from it, the whole whirling mass of painted faces, the wailing songs and the yammering dogs mesmerizing her.

Coming near the village, the warriors kicked their ponies into a trot and left all the people running along behind, on either side of the captured horses and mules. Morfydd saw the drying racks with meat hanging from them and thought it was clothing put out to dry. She saw the piles of dried buffalo chips at each tipi and the designs painted on the lodges themselves, earth-colored drawings of animals, circles, stars, lines, bands of ocher and yellow and black.

With Sanchess pulling strongly on her lead rope, they broke into a gallop as they entered the village and rode straight through it and beyond to the horse herd. Suddenly he turned and pulled her from the mare's saddle and swung her behind him. To keep from falling off as he wheeled, she clasped her arms around his middle and felt the hard, lean muscles of his belly.

They left the captured animals with the rest of the village pony herd watched over by a number of boys, shouting and waving, and one older man who didn't appear to be a Comanche, even though he had dark hair and eyes. They turned north, galloping, Sanchess waving the scalp lance, all of them making the little piercing calls she had heard at Madoc's Fort. They rode in a tight circle around the village, going to the north, then to the east and finally south and back into the village from their original direction of entry, and all the people were waiting, setting up a clamor of singing and shouting, waving sticks, the dogs still rushing among them wildly.

When they were back with the others, the war party broke up, each man going to his own lodge, surrounded by family and always the dogs. The singing stopped but there was still the high-pitched sound of talk and laughter. Again, some of the women ran close to Morfydd and jabbed her with their sticks until Sanchess drew up and pulled her down with him beside a tipi that had black wolf heads painted on it. He pushed her to the ground on the shaded side of the lodge and left her. A number of children ran up to stand close around her, pointing, babbling.

There was a man with a pronghorn antelope headdress. Across his shoulders was a mantle of metal, like a shawl over his fringed buckskin shirt. He and the woman who had led the procession out to meet the raiders were with Sanchess, touching him, and there were three younger women there as well, laughing and talking, two of them running their fingers along his bare back.

One of the women moved to Sanchess's pony and tied the lip-rein to a foreleg, hobbling the horse beside the lodge and close enough to Morfydd for her to hear the horse breathing heavily through flared nostrils. Morfydd saw the hard, flat face of the woman, small-nosed and dark-eyed, and felt her harsh words. The watching children shouted and jumped up and down as the woman flayed Morfydd with a small whip, slender strips of cured animal skin attached to a polished cottonwood handle.

But it lasted for only a few heartbeats and the woman turned back to Sanchess, touched him again, and followed him into the wolf-head tipi with another of the young women. The children ringed about Morfydd moved closer, clamoring and trying to touch her with their switches. She cowered on the ground, covering her face with her arms.

There was a stinging blow across her bare arms and she reached out almost instinctively, her hands closing on the switch. She yanked it hard and felt it come free of the boy's hands, a boy about her own size. She rose to her knees and slashed at him with the stick, hitting him across the eyes, and he jumped back, laughing, and the other children shouted and waved their wands.

She had no idea where he came from, but suddenly he was before her, a man heavy and squat, wearing a head-dress with buffalo horns sprouting from either side as though they grew out of his ears. His eyes were bloodshot and he smelled of old fat and woodsmoke. She tried to hit him as well but he quickly snatched the switch from her hands, giving a loud grunt.

The fat man said something to her in a low, harsh voice and cupped her jaw in one hand and lifted her face. With the fingers of the other hand he pressed her lips apart and inspected her teeth, just as she had seen her father do with horses. He grunted again and released her, turning quickly for a man of his girth, and confronted the children, who had drawn back and were silent now, watching with bright eyes.

He spoke sharply, his words coming like pellets of hail against hardwood shingles. The children turned and ran, going in all directions away from the fat man, some looking back apprehensively over their shoulders.

Hanging from his waist was a buffalo robe, and he took it off as he moved to Morfydd's side once more. This time he spoke more gently as he pressed her down and covered her with the robe. Lying under it, she heard his softly shuffling steps move back toward the wolf-head tipi, and then there was silence, even the dogs having run away.

WAPITI SONG and Sunshade were washing their husband, using water from a buffalo paunch that hung from one of the lodge poles. He lay naked at the rear of the lodge on a pile of deerhides, and as the medicine man came into the tipi, he rose on one elbow. There was a small fire of buffalo dung in a circular hole at the center of the lodge and it cast a hard, yellow light across his eyes.

The women continued their work as though no one had come at all, sponging Sanchess and drying him with fresh-pulled grass. They greased his skin lightly with oil rendered from buffalo fat, kneading the muscles gently and crooning little wordless songs that sounded like a soft wind blowing through new-leafed mesquite.

"I will not stay long while you are being welcomed by your wives," the fat man said, adjusting the horn headdress on hair that was not so long and thick as it once had been. "I will not abuse your hospitality."

"You abuse nothing, Finds Something," Sanchess said. "My lodge is your lodge, always."

Finds Something grunted and sat down. He complimented Sanchess on the success of his raid. They spoke of the weather and the next buffalo hunt. Each knew, and so did the women, that all of this was polite preamble to more serious talk.

Sunshade rolled a cigarette for her husband, using the rough-cut tobacco they obtained from the Mexicans and a wrapper of dried blackjack oak leaf. She lit it with a straw wand ignited in the small fire, puffed it a few times, and passed it to Sanchess. Then she sat back against the rear wall of the tipi with Wapiti Song, both of them silent, watching.

Finally, Finds Something came to the real business at hand.

"That girl you caught. I'll buy that girl from you. She would be better than a litter of puppies to keep me warm at night."

Sanchess sat up, cross-legged, his face calm and showing no expression. But his mind was busy. This was a powerful man, Finds Something. A medicine man in things of the spirit, in the ways of Sun Father and Earth Mother. And also the best man in the tribe for healing wounds, dog bites, and broken bones. Snakebites, too.

"I do not wish to sell that girl," Sanchess said. "I will keep her a little while, until she has learned her place here. Then I will make a gift of her to my father."

Finds Something suspected that meant Iron Shirt. Like all Comanches, Sanchess used the term "father" not only for his real father but for his father's brothers as well, and there were two of those. So Finds Something needed to be sure.

"Iron Shirt."

"Yes. My father."

Now it was time for Finds Something to think about it. Iron Shirt! That wasn't so good. Iron Shirt had strong medicine too, although he did not sell it to young men as Finds Something did. And he had counted many coups on live enemies and killed many Pawnees and Utes and even a few Navahos. No white men, though. Except for Mexicans. And Iron Shirt's stories of valor were the best told around any fire. And he knew the tribal history, from the time The People had come down from the mountains, from the time they had broken off from the Shoshones and had gotten the horse. But even though it appeared hopeless, Finds Something enjoyed dickering, so he went on.

"I'll give you five horses for that girl," he said.

Sanchess grunted, staring into the fire. Everybody knew that Finds Something had many ponies. At one time he had owned over a thousand of them, more than anyone else in the band, maybe even more than anyone else in the whole tribe, maybe even more than the whole nation of Skidi Pawnee. But since he had gotten too fat to ride, his herd had diminished. Now he had only fifty, and many of those were mares to pull the travois necessary to carry him when the band moved. He was too heavy for any of his ponies to carry him astride.

"That is a good offer," Sanchess said. "Have a smoke with me."

He drew on the cigarette and passed it across the fire to the fat medicine man, and Finds Something took it, lifting it to the sky, then to the earth, then in all four directions before he puffed a few times.

"That's good tobacco," he said.

"Yes, my brother, Bear in the Willows, brings it from the Mexican trading."

"Now about that girl you caught," Finds Something said, puffing slowly, the cigarette smoke around his face like spiderwebs.

"I'll not sell her. After I give her to my father, he may sell her. But first I'll make a present to him, a nice gift from the man who gave us the bad guns that time."

"I remember. Well, it's a good moon for your revenge," Finds Something said. "I'll give you eight horses. A stallion and seven geldings, all with high spirits."

"That's a good offer," Sanchess said. Finds Something passed the cigarette back across the fire to him. "But I think I'll keep her."

"She has spirit too, like a good horse," Finds Something said, wanting to remind Sanchess of those eight ponies he had offered. Sanchess said nothing. "She fought back just now, and her only a child. She drove the others back!"

Sanchess laughed.

"Yes, I expected it. She gave me these." And he pointed to three deep scratches across his shoulder and to the toothmarks on his forearm. "So I think I'll not sell her."

"Then I'll go, and let you copulate with your wives," Finds Something said, and rose with a loud grunt and pushed his way through the tipi door flap. Outside he paused to stare at the buffalo robe, humped up with the girl under it. Sanchess's pony was nuzzling the robe, but the medicine man could see no movement from beneath. He shook his head, thinking that at least Sanchess might have offered him some of that fine tobacco to take home and smoke with his wife. He adjusted the headdress, grunted, and turned toward his own lodge, where he would make ready for the victory celebration.

IT WAS HOT under the buffalo robe and soon Morfydd was as wet as though she had been thrown into the spring. For the first time since they had taken her she cried. But only for a little while. Not from fear or desolation at being alone among these foreign people, as much as from pure rage. She wiped her nose with her hand, and the cheeks where her tears were hot and salty. She would not allow them to see her cry. Now or at any time, no matter what they did to her. Nor would she suffocate under this smelly hide with the hair still on it.

As soon as she lifted a corner of the robe, the high plains wind ran underneath and began to cool her. She had only a small view of the camp, as though looking through a tiny tipi door, but it was enough.

There was the lodge nearest them, where she saw the

man with the long-fringed deer robe and the metal shawl. He was moving about, giving instructions to the women. One of them, the old one who had led the procession and whose face still glinted red with paint, was working on a shield that was heavily hung with buffalo hair or scalps, Morfydd couldn't tell which. There were four eagle feathers on the shield as well, and the women gently brushed the vanes. In the center of the shield was a design, painted red and brown, in the shape of a turtle.

Beyond, women and children were preparing the dance ground. The lance with the scalps was standing upright there, the butt end carefully buried in the smooth prairie sand. Near that were a number of large log drums, sections of trees hollowed out, debarked, and polished, stretched with animal skins at one end. There too they were piling buffalo chips and dead branches from the cottonwoods, along with bits of mesquite. It would make a bigger fire than any Comanche fire Morfydd had seen with the war party, and kindled on the flat, without any hole to hide it.

Watching all this, she realized how safe they felt themselves to be here, far out on the plains, far out of reach of their enemies. Since her capture she had held in the rear reaches of her thinking an image of white riders coming toward her, close behind the war party. But now she knew there was small chance of any rescue. She was hidden away in the vast reaches of wilderness, in an alien land, among an alien people.

But it made small impression on her. There was no longer any dread or despair, because all of that had come and left her leaden in her thinking, even though she was perfectly well aware of what was happening around her. It was as though all of this were happening to some other little girl, some stranger, some other being, who was lost and forgotten by those among her own people who had survived the attack at Madoc's Fort.

Sometime before full dark, one of the women came from the wolf-head tipi and gave her a drink from a hollow gourd, kicked her a few times, spat on her, and returned to the lodge. Morfydd could hear laughter and talking there, the voice of Sanchess deep-sounding above the noise of the women.

Only a little later some of the other women came and dragged her from beneath the buffalo robe, washed her, and painted her face with ocher. They took her to the dancing area and tied her wrists to stakes driven into the ground. Directly before her was the Sanchess lance with the scalps blowing out from it, but she did not look at it. No one tried to switch her or jab her with sharp sticks, because they were all too busy. The children were well back, and the dogs too, all in their way understanding that very large preparations were under way and it was best to stay out from underfoot of the women. The children watched with their large black eyes, the dogs sitting on their haunches with tongues hanging from open mouths.

The great fire was lit as the tip of the full moon edged above the eastern rim of the valley. It was not kindled from one of the other fires in the village. Finds Something came out, shaking a buffalo-scrotum rattle, grunting and mumbling his medicine songs, and lit the piled wood and chips with a Mexican flint-and-steel fire starter.

Then the old men came out and sat around the drums with their switches and sticks for beating. Then the women came and behind them all the other men, faces painted, wearing their best leggings and skin shirts, except for the members of the war party, who were naked to the waist. There were beads and bracelets of Mexican silver. The men wore the distinctive Comanche moccasins with trailing tufts of hair at toe and heel. And each had a bandanna knotted about his neck or held in place by a joint of buffalo backbone. The warriors' hair was loose in the low breeze, except for a single plait down the back.

Sanchess came with his wives and a gaggle of children following him. A single eagle feather trailed down his back beside the scalp lock, and across his forehead were four tiny braids coming from the mass of loose hair like glistening black snakes to fall across his eyes. All the black had been scoured from his face and it was now painted with ocher and a single white splash beneath one eye, like a tear.

The old men began to stroke the drums and a group of singers came out to squat near them, starting the first chant, singing softly of Sun Father and Earth Mother and of other spirits that were in the rocks and on top of the buttes and in the depths of water. Then the singing grew in volume and intensity and the people swayed as the singers chanted of enemies and victories and coups counted and scalps taken.

The dances started with the women in one long line, the men in another, facing them. A fine dust rose into the firelight as the many feet shuffled across the hard, grassless surface. Some of the dancers began to sing too, and the drummers settled into a hard, surging tempo. They joined the two lines, making a circle. And now some of the women ran toward the scalp lance and slapped at Morfydd with small willow sticks. The medicine man moved closely around her, his bloodshot eyes gleaming hot in the firelight.

There was a whip holder, a brave man chosen by Sanchess for his victory dance. The whip holder used a short-handled, otter-skinned lash to strike men or women who were not dancing with the frenzied passion he felt was required for such a victory celebration with scalps to show for bravery.

The only pause in the dancing came when the whip holder called a halt to chant from the middle of the circle, singing of his power and of the enemies he had touched when they were still alive. After each recital, the dancers shouted and clapped their hands and other warriors moved into the light of the fire to sing of their own great exploits.

Among them was a warrior taller than the rest. He had slender legs and a long, narrow nose because his mother had been a Kiowa. His legs and arms were slashed with black paint and he wore a sash of many colors, one end trailing behind him like a gigantic tail. On his head, above a face smeared completely with white, was a crow headdress, the wings down either side over his ears, the eyeless head and black beak bobbing across his forehead as he danced.

They shouted at him, calling him pukutsi, a man who did unexpected things and whose name was Claw. But he ignored them, dancing backwards to the strong throb of the drums, his eyes turned to the sky. In his mouth he held two arrows, war-tipped, with the heads at right angles to the notch in the shaft base. This was to show them as war arrows, designed to enter between the horizontal ribs of human enemies. Now and again he pretended to pin himself to one spot by pushing an arrow through the tail of his sash and into the dance ground, and at these times the hoots of the people became loud and derisive.

More wood was brought and thrown onto the fire, the cottonwood making a bright flame and the mesquite burning deep red and very hot. The wind played columns of sparks into the night, sending them dashing along the stream, through the trees and the tipis. The scalps on the lance of Sanchess waved out gently, their oily texture catching and throwing back the light of the fire, and the fire seemed to dance too.

Roasted meat was brought and during each pause they ate and listened to each succeeding warrior tell of the raid on Madoc's Fort. There was liver as well, fresh from a kill only two days before and barely seared over one of the smaller fires ringing the dance ground, eaten like that, almost raw and with the liquid from a buffalo gall bladder sprinkled over it.

To Morfydd it was a night beyond any reality she had ever known. It was not the abuse she suffered, because that was slight. It was not fear, either, because she had become deadened to that. It was the noise, the sounds they made as they danced, the drumming just behind her. All of it beat against her ears with a relentless monotony that almost drove her mad, hour after hour. It was singing she could not even identify as such, having been reared on Welsh harmonies.

And yet, as the night wore on into the morning hours, and still the dancers stamped with small, delicate steps, mouths open singing, the throbbing pulse of the drums beneath it all, the rhythm began to move through her bones. As though it were a great heart beating, a single great heart for all of this. By morning she was babbling incoherently, yet in time to the drumming.

4

DURING THE DAY SOME OF THE most important things were done, things expected after a successful raid. The spoils were distributed. Sanchess made gifts of mules and horses to old women who had no sons or husbands able to make raids. Others he gave to the peace chiefs like his father, out of respect for their age and wisdom. And a nice mare—the one Chosen had ridden into camp—he gave to Finds Something, the medicine man, because Finds Something had power and his favor was not to be ignored even though not actively sought.

After each of the other warriors who had been at Madoc's Fort took his share, nothing was left for Sanchess. This was not unusual, for often after stealing animals he found himself empty-handed through generosity. Yet it was not mindless generosity. For when others led war parties, they would remember Sanchess and repay the favor. It was a hedge against broken bones or old age or anything else that might keep him from going out himself.

But he kept the girl, Chosen. It pleased him to see his father look at the girl with obvious admiration for her beauty and strength and spirit, even though she was small in stature.

And now that the frenzy of the celebration was closing its petals like a night-blooming flower in the sunlight, Iron Shirt and Big Wolf questioned him, for in their place as peace chiefs they needed to know all things that might effect The People.

"Did you see buffalo?" Big Wolf asked.

"We rode near many herds, but avoided them downwind because we didn't want any hunting parties who might be out to see us," Sanchess said. "We rode through many droppings, fresh droppings."

"Were you able to find water?"

"Not much. It is dry for this season. Later, when the hot days come, it will be difficult to travel in that country without plenty of extra horses to kill and take their blood to drink," Sanchess said.

They sat in Iron Shirt's lodge, smoking, and all were tired from dancing and lack of sleep. But this was business that had to be completed while everything was fresh in Sanchess's mind.

With them was Running Wolf, Big Wolf's son and one of Sanchess's closest friends and an important warrior on the raid. But he said nothing, only smoked and listened, for questions must be answered by the war leader. Running Wolf would speak only if spoken to, and he did not expect this to happen.

He had been born in the same season as Sanchess, and they had grown to manhood together. Each had killed his first large game at the age of fourteen summers. Each had proven himself in war in Mexico at the age of fifteen summers.

Running Wolf had one wife and two children, both sons. He was therefore considered to be a young man blessed and looked upon kindly by all the spirits associated with childbearing, for his wife had never had a miscarriage. She was Grasshopper, daughter of one of Iron Shirt's brothers, and doubly blessed because she was not only fruitful but the most beautiful woman in the band. Many times young warriors had come secretly to her lodge, begging her to go with them on war parties they were leading, promising her many horses. But she would only laugh.

"Running Wolf would cut off my nose," she always said.

Running Wolf wore distinctive face paint: two white stripes along the edges of his wide mouth to symbolize the fangs of a wolf. When he went out on hunts or raids, he painted two black marks beside those. He looked very fierce in his paint. And his ears were pierced from lobe to crown and he wore small, polished mussel shells in them, much in the manner of an Osage he had killed near the Crossed Timbers in his seventeenth summer. He was the acknowledged champion of the band at killing buffalo with the lance.

He squatted quietly now beside his war leader. For although he had counted more coups on live enemies and killed more with the bow than Sanchess had, Running Wolf was a follower, and the man he most liked to follow was his friend Sanchess.

"And the white man. Did they pursue you for long?" Big Wolf asked.

"They did not follow at all. They were taken by surprise."

Both Iron Shirt and Big Wolf grunted in approval, for taking an enemy by surprise was the very best way for Comanches to fight.

"We saw them running for the timber along the river," Sanchess continued. "They were very frightened. We rode hard only the first day."

"You didn't ride at night?"

"There was no necessity."

"And exactly where was this place?"

"Where we traded the horses last springtime, and the white man cheated us. It's four days' hard ride from here."

"Yes, I remember," Iron Shirt said. "You told me before. On the morning-sun side of the big plateau, near the Colorado River. Well, it was a fine raid. I wish your brother were here to enjoy your homecoming."

Sanchess laughed. "Bear in the Willows will come only when he has obtained guns for us."

"Yes, so he said. It would be good to have guns. But not those old ones that never work. Would you like a nice gun, Running Wolf?" Iron Shirt asked, smiling slightly.

"No!" Running Wolf said. "A bow is much faster. And I don't like the smell those guns make when one shoots them."

The old men chuckled.

"Sanchess, it is a great honor that all the warriors gave you the scalps they took to place on your lance. That doesn't happen often,'' Big Wolf said. ''And in your honor now, The People will hereafter call that place the River of Broken Guns.''

They all laughed again, and now each of them knew the questioning was finished. Woman Who Runs brought them raw liver sprinkled with gall, and after they ate they crawled to various places in the tipi of Iron Shirt where robes were waiting, and slept out the day.

IT WAS DARK when Morfydd woke. She could hear a baby crying somewhere. But the crying stopped soon and then there was only the sound of a mockingbird making his night calls from far along the little stream. On the plains a pair of coyotes were howling to each other. The camp itself was silent, even the dogs, who were sleeping or out with the pony herd.

She waited for the baby to start its crying again, but it never did. She could recall seeing any number of infants in cradle boards, carried about by the women like baskets of fruit, held in one hand at their sides. Yet until now she had heard none of them crying. At Madoc's Fort there had almost always, night and day, been the cry of a baby somewhere within the settlement.

She could remember clearly now, as though seeing it with her eyes, her mother rising in the dark of night and going to Dafydd's cradle and crooning to him as he lay whimpering. And sometimes the crying stopped only after her mother had picked him up and walked back and forth, holding him tight against her breasts and gently patting him on the back, her feet making their soft whisper on the floor, back and forth, back and forth.

Her mind was clear now, from the long sleep. She tried to recall everything that had happened during the night of dancing. There had been a few moments of blind panic when she thought they were going to roast and eat her, or else feed her to the dogs. The idea seemed funny now, absurd, but she had been hearing such stories all her life.

They had untied her at dawn and dragged her back to her robe outside the wolf-head tipi and given her water and meat. She remembered tearing at it with her teeth, kicking the snarling, snapping dogs away, finally making them retreat with her viciousness, swallowing greedily even as she lashed out with her feet. Then she had slept, but before she pulled the robe over her head, she was aware of the brightening of the land with the coming sun.

Now it was almost as if she were alone, left abandoned under her robe, even by the dogs. She lifted a corner of the robe, and once more the plains wind crept beneath with a freshness that made her catch her breath. It was dark, the moon not yet risen. But in this high, dry country the stars were dazzlingly bright, seeming to shed down on the land particles of light that gave form to objects all about her.

The great fire was no longer burning, nor were any of the smaller fires of the night before. The odors of the village were whipped away by the movement of cool air, and now she could smell the stunted pinyons and junipers that clustered along the upper rim of the little valley like black lace around the edges of a woman's funeral collar.

Morfydd's pants were wet and smelled of urine. She had no idea when this had happened and she felt no humiliation at having wet herself, although it had been many years since she had been trained to the Madoc's Fort outhouses. Unusual circumstances required unusual solutions. But now she realized that she had yet another need, one that had not been satisfied since her capture, and she moved from beneath the robe and stood for a moment, testing her legs, then walked away from the tipi, feeling rather than seeing the line of trees where they grew thickest along the watercourse. One dog trotted out to sniff at her, but immediately moved away when she kicked him. They were coming to know her scent already.

She found the water by walking into it, having no idea it was there because it made no sound in its running. She fell, wetting herself completely, and it felt cold and good. On hands and knees in the shallow pond, she drank; then, rising, she felt the silvery run of water along her limbs. She moved downstream, walking carefully along the sandy bottom until she was well away from all the lodges. This spring was a large one and the water from it ran for some distance from the source, flowing along the little valley until it disappeared into a cleft of rock outcrop and continued its flow beneath the surface of the surrounding plain.

Moving from the stream into a small stand of mesquite, she stood once more, listening. The coyotes were still barking and she could hear the horses in the pony herd nearby, softly popping bunch grass loose with their long teeth. She undressed, then rolled her clothes into a bundle, scooped out a small depression in the soil, and relieved herself, filled the hole, and returned to the water naked, carrying her clothes beneath one arm. Standing knee-deep in the center of the stream, she loosened her smock and pants and washed them, rubbing the fabric against itself beneath the surface.

All of it was done mechanically, without thought, as though it were a Madoc's Fort chore, something she had been required to do since the beginning of memory and now had become automatic. But she knew what would come next. She would walk away from this place, back toward her own kind, under cover of darkness, her mind fresh now for the first time since that morning when Sanchess had scooped her up from the prairie as he rode past.

Everything since then had been oppressively confusing, sometimes threatening, always numbing. But her position now came with clarity, the past few days overcome, a time to be forgotten, forced from the mind. Even the things that she knew now had happened at Madoc's Fort. Without even realizing it, she had come to know that sometimes terror and horror can be so overwhelming as to wash out sorrow and despair along with the effort to forget all the whirling shapes and sounds of fear and pain. Leaving only a kind of melancholy. And perhaps determination.

Now her mind was clear and she felt sharply aware of the moment. Her body was strong from the food they had given her and from the long sleep after the dancing. She was satisfied that she could do what needed doing and she bent to take a long drink of water from the stream, her face deep in the coolness.

She had no sense of distance but she knew which direction the war party had traveled. Always west, so now she must walk east to her people. She thought only of that.

Going east. It did not occur to her that during the long ride from Madoc's Fort they had not crossed a single flowing stream, had not camped at a single sweet-water spring.

And if her bare feet found a spiny cactus or a rattlesnake in the darkness? Or if she blundered into a buffalo herd or came across the path of a hunting wolf? She dismissed all such considerations even though they made her shudder. Escape was the thing, no matter the obstacles.

She moved back to the bank and shook out her clothes. As she started to step into the pants, she saw one of the surrounding mesquite trees move. She had been taught that to see anything in the dark, one must not look directly at it, so she shifted her eyes to one side. And saw that it was no mesquite tree at all, but a man, outlined dimly against the stars, yet there, and as the dark shape moved closer she saw the outrageous crow headdress she remembered from the dancing. Her hands froze on the wet clothing and she stood naked, waiting with her chest pounding as he walked toward her, close enough now for her to smell him.

His face was still smeared with the white paint of celebration, making a dull outline in the night, like a floating skull. The moon was still below the eastern plain, but starlight was enough. She tried at the last moment to run, but he had her then, speaking to her softly, soothingly. He gripped her arms with both hands, pulling her close to him, and she shuddered as she felt his nakedness. When she tried to cry out, he clasped one hand over her mouth.

He ripped the clothes from her hand and threw them aside and dragged her away from the stream, still speaking to her softly, urgently. He made no exploration of her body as the warriors had done after the raid, but the pressure of his fingers on her flesh was more terrifying than anything that had happened so far among these people. In a vivid flash of recall, she saw in her mind the body of the woman lying naked and bloody in the bunch grass on that first morning after Madoc's Fort. She was limp, beyond any power to fight back, to pull free.

The man pressed her down onto the sandy slope and in that horrifying moment she was suddenly aware of another form, not so well defined, above them both. She felt the lurch of bodies above her and the crow headdress was gone, somewhere back among the shadows of the mesquite, and another voice now, harsh and hard, spitting words.

It was over as quickly as it had begun, and she felt the blunt, hard fingers of Sanchess lifting her to her feet. Then, holding one of her hands in his, he led her back to the lodges.

WAPITI SONG was sleeping when Sanchess pushed aside the hanging hide door and moved into the low firelight of the wolf-head tipi, but Sunshade was still awake, squatting at the fire hole. She raised her eyes as Sanchess entered, drawing Chosen behind him, naked and shivering. Sanchess pushed the child to one side and made a quick gesture with his hands. She understood at once and lay down, pulling a hide robe over her body.

"What is she doing in my lodge?" Sunshade asked.

"I want her here now. Outside she is a temptation."

"You'd think she was your best war pony."

"No one would take one of my horses," Sanchess said. "But a child is different. That pukutsi, he never does what you expect a man to do. Taking a child to the bushes."

"She went there herself, we heard her go," Sunshade said. "Pukutsi did not take her. And she is not so much child as you think. She is only a runt."

"Well, someday I may have to kill that pukutsi," Sanchess said, moving to Sunshade's side and dropping to his knees to rub his hands across her back. There was a special thing between these two because she was barren, having lost three sons already by miscarriage, and Sanchess knew it was something always at the rear of her thinking.

"You'd better give that Chosen to your father right away," she said. "That Chosen is going to be a trouble to you."

"She can help you and Wapiti Song with gathering the chips and wood. Or carrying the water or tanning the hides," Sanchess said.

"I need nothing from this Chosen," Sunshade said, and spat into the fire. Sanchess laughed.

"You are worth three wives," he said, kneading her

shoulders, "and a few slaves besides. But I will keep her for a little while and teach her some of the language before I give her to my father."

"These white ones are hard to teach. Let Iron Shirt teach her. He knows Spanish and Ute and even some of the Texas white man's talk. He is a man who enjoys such things."

"I'll keep her for a little while."

"It's too bad we can't castrate the women captives as we sometimes do the men," Sunshade said. "As we did with Lost It, that man you gave to your father in the last season of raiding in Mexico, and as soon as you caught him, too, not waiting."

"He's a good slave for my father. But Chosen will be a daughter, I think, and someday my father will get many horses for her marriage."

"A good slave to your father? Lost It, a good slave?" Sunshade laughed harshly. "He is no help to your father's wives. He is always with the pony herd. But at least since his manhood was taken, he's not rutting around among the women." She raised a hand toward the girl, who was lying under the hide robe with only her eyes showing. "As this one will be rutting among the boys in the pony herd before long."

"She will give someone good Comanche children someday," Sanchess said, and he withdrew his hands from her back abruptly and there was a cold set to his jaw that told her there had been enough of this conversation. "When the sun comes again, give this child leggings and moccasins and a dress."

"I have none so small."

"Then make them," Sanchess said, rising and moving to the back of the lodge and slipping under the robe where Wapiti Song was sleeping.

Sunshade spat into the fire again and was aware that Chosen still watched. She rose and moved to stand over the child, staring down with hard eyes. She bent and pulled back the robe.

"Come out of that robe," Sunshade said. "I'm going to make you fine clothing, you little bitch fox."

She lifted Chosen to her feet and the child stood naked

in the firelight, eyes wide. Sunshade moved about the lodge, talking loudly all the while to keep her husband awake. She pulled pieces of tanned hide from various kit bags, along with her awls and thin strips of rawhide and a ball of horsehair string and a bone needle.

"Shade is going to make you a dress such as chiefs' wives wear, because the great Sanchess has said you will one day rule us all, like the wicked spirit that lives on top of Tucumcari Mountain, because you are such a fine little runt of a bitch." She spoke with harsh sarcasm that she knew the child could feel without understanding a word. "Rule with such greatness, you bitch fox, that the people will be willing to eat nothing but owl dung in your honor."

Roughly she began to hold chunks of animal skin against the child's body, marking it with her fingernails where she would cut it with one of her knives.

"Oh, yes, a fine robe with ermine skins trailing because you are such a prize in this band and because you will not run off among the ponies with all the boys each night and copulate like a coyote in heat!"

The head of Sanchess appeared above Wapiti Song's robe.

"Woman! What are you shouting about?"

"I'm only doing what you asked, husband," Sunshade said. Wapiti Song was giggling under her robe.

"Well, do it in silence! I'll set that pukutsi on *you!*"

Shade laughed abruptly, harshly.

"That pukutsi? He would be more useless than your father's castrated Mexican in the hands of a real woman!"

Sanchess grunted with disgust and defeat and yanked the robe back over his head.

MORFYDD ANNON learned over the next few days that she was in greatest jeopardy when Sunshade was near, and the first wife of Sanchess always seemed near. Once, on the day after the hide clothes had been sewn to cover her nakedness, the girl thought all the village was so occupied with preparations for a move that the chance was right for slipping away. She got as far as the last tipi before the ground lifted to the high plains beyond. There Sunshade caught her from behind, a stream of harsh words coming from her mouth.

Shade pulled her back to the wolf-head tipi and inside, holding Morfydd by the hair, and tied the girl's thumbs with rawhide to two of the lodgepoles, arms outstretched. Then came the switches, a handful of them, but Shade only waved the willow sticks before Morfydd's face and did not whip her.

She was left until nightfall, tied to the poles. When she was taken down that evening while Sanchess sat before his fire and ate, watching with little interest, the two women rubbed her thumbs with tallow, then gave her food and water, chattering all the while between themselves, as detached from their work as Morfydd had seen the women of Madoc's Fort when they were quilting and exchanging the newest gossip.

During the nights that followed, twice the girl tried to slip from the lodge and into the darkness and then away toward the east. But each time as she rolled back her robe cover to rise, she saw Shade watching from across the fire. And each time she pulled the robe back over her head and cried but was soon asleep, too tired from the day's work to stay awake even with the pain of the lingering sunburn. Too exhausted even to think for a moment of home and the smell of her mother's kitchen.

Shade herded her like a working mule during the days. Carrying wood or buffalo chips, fetching water in buffalo paunches, folding hides and tying them at Shade's sign-language direction. And the possibility of escape was growing dim in her thinking because Shade was always there. And others watched her as well, wherever she went. Not obviously but with intensity, as though she were a young mare given to straying.

At those times, seeing the others with their eyes on her, she began to think that maybe she was important to them. It left a strange feeling of triumph—almost as if they, and not she, were held hostage. Of course, she had no words in her mind to express such things but there was a growing sense in her of having a place among these strange people, no matter whether or not she wanted it.

The other women in the band made no further effort to

punish her, although from time to time as she passed a group of them, with Shade close behind, they jeered and made faces and clapped their hands. The children watched from a distance with a curiosity that soon waned until finally they paid her no mind at all. Sometimes as she went through the camp, a dog would run out growling, then silently sniff her heels, and she would kick and Shade would snort with what Morfydd supposed was a laugh.

The men ignored her completely.

And in the lodge at night, Sanchess and his wives ignored her as well. She stayed in her assigned corner, hearing their words of unknown meaning, watching them eat and laugh. They laughed a great deal, a thing Morfydd had never associated with Indians.

Thinking of Madoc's Fort, she could not remember as much laughter there, except sometimes among the men working in the fields when one of them said something the others thought funny. But there was little mirth and gladness in the home, with her father frowning over the failings of his crops and slow growth of his herds and her mother watching with deep, terrible concern as the baby sat blank-faced in his bed, staring without seeming to see. And for the first time she realized how hard this new life was for them even though it had been the only life she herself had ever known.

Now and again one of the women would throw a chunk of roasted meat in her direction. At first she thought of refusing to eat, but then decided it was a futile protest. She suspected they would let her starve as casually as they fed her.

And many times, during those nights in the tipi, she thought Wapiti Song looked toward her with some show of tenderness and compassion.

BEAR IN THE WILLOWS came into camp at night. A bad sign, like a war party returning from defeat and with casualties tied facedown on the ponies. He had no guns and far into the night he sat in his father's lodge, Sanchess immediately behind him, and told of the Mexican trader Mendoza of the Pintada branch of the Pecos River in New Mexico, who had guns but would not trade them for hides, insisting on captives so he could ransom them.

Mendoza of the Pintada was well known to them. He had eyes that bulged from his head, staring in two different directions at once. Sometimes The People called him Man Who Cannot Decide Which Way to Look. He was as short and slender as a yucca stalk, but with a melon-like belly. His black beard looked as though desert mice had made a nest there, and he always smelled of strange herbs he had eaten.

Each summer, in the late time before first autumn and during the great buffalo hunts, Mendoza came onto the plains with his two-wheeled carts drawn by oxen. He came among them as a Comanchero, but he was liked least of all the regular traders. He did not try to take their women because he had been in the business long enough to know that Comanche hospitality did not extend to providing women for white men's beds. He never overstayed his welcome, having come to know too that white men did not winter among the Comanches as they sometimes did with other tribes.

Yet he was disliked. Because of the whiskey. Whiskey was his most important trade item. Other Comancheros had whiskey too, but Mendoza seemed to have an inexhaustible supply. Some of the young men, and some of the old ones as well, were perfectly willing to trade for it because they enjoyed whiskey. But even these knew it was a bad trade, good hides in exchange for a thing that made them crazy and afterwards sick and then was gone and nothing left to show except empty stone jugs with openings so small that they were of little use to the women. Of course, usually there were not even jugs left. They were broken and the insides licked for the last drop of liquid.

Now all that Bear in the Willows could show for his travels was a burlap bag filled with jugs of Mendoza's whiskey, a few metal arrowheads, a fire starter, three long-handled spoons, and a few small hand mirrors for wearing in one's hair.

"It is a great humiliation," Bear in the Willows said. "I should have taken our hides to some other place, but the members of my party were ready to come back."

"The Pintada is a long way from here," Iron Shirt said.

"Yes. We drifted north, following antelope herds. We killed a few but we didn't have enough horses to run them down in relays as the Kwahadi do. So we had to ambush them. We killed only a few. So finally we had to trade and come back because I knew you would be waiting to move the village."

"Yes, we'll be going back the way you have come. We need lodgepoles," Iron Shirt said.

"It is a great humiliation," Bear in the Willows said.

He was much like his brother, only heavier. They wore their hair in the same way, more often loose than braided, and wrapped down the sides of their faces. But there was seldom the fierce glint of anger in Bear's eyes as in those of Sanchess. And his mouth was loose and rather full-lipped for a Comanche. He had a single wife, Owl Calling, who was a Wichita and already going to fat, though still young. They had an infant daughter, and Bear spent much of his time in camp playing with the child as she crawled about, out of her cradle board and in the shade of a mesquite-brush arbor.

Everyone said, "Someday Bear is going to want a lot of horses for that daughter!"

"Well," Iron Shirt said, trying to comfort his eldest son, "those were not such good hides anyway. Let's see some of that whiskey."

Bear slipped a jug from the burlap bag, remarking on the uselessness of such cloth, not tough enough for leggings and incapable of shedding even a few drops of rain. He uncorked the jug and handed it to Iron Shirt, who lifted it to the sky and then to the four corners of the earth and drank. Sanchess took the jug and did the same and finally Bear drank, gasping, his eyes beginning to water.

"It's hot whiskey," Iron Shirt said. "It boils in my belly. Let me have some more. Perhaps it will help me to see my medicine again. I need my best medicine for the trip to the mountains."

Sanchess stayed for only one more sip of Mendoza's whiskey and then left his father's lodge and went to the wolf-head tipi. Everyone was sleeping and the fire was very low. He looked at Chosen for a long time, thinking about what his brother had said about Mendoza wanting captives in exchange for those guns. Finally he found his own robes, stripped naked, and crawled into them. But he did not sleep. He waited for what he knew would come and his mouth twisted bitterly.

Soon he heard the first of it, a low singing that grew louder as he listened. He recognized his father's voice and then Bear's as well. From other parts of the camp came more singing and shouting and laughter, and he knew some of the jugs had been passed to other lodges. Just before dawn, someone staggered into the walls of the wolf-head tipi and he heard the incoherent babbling of a man, whoever it was, then heard a long wail from Finds Something's lodge and then someone by the watercourse, vomiting with a great gagging. The white man's whiskey always brought the same sounds with it, and he knew them well.

Yes, he remembered Mendoza of Pintada from the first time he had seen the little Mexican. The first time he could recall having seen any of the Comancheros. The band had been with a large party of Paneteka Comanches, raiding in Mexico, and on the way back had taken a long sweep up the Rio Grande through New Mexico to trade captured horses. At one point his father and his father's brother, Goes Ahead, had veered off from the main body and found the Mendoza trading post on the small stream that in summer was nothing but a dry wash. They had Sanchess and Bear in the Willows with them to tend the extra ponies.

It had been the sixth summer in the life of Sanchess, and Bear's eighth, and Mendoza of Pintada had only a small belly then but he had smelled of those strange herbs. The boys were left sitting beside the pole corrals while the men went inside the adobe house for the trading. It had been very hot, with no trees to shade them. It had taken a long time.

After a while they saw Iron Shirt and Goes Ahead come out onto the small veranda, where a latticework roof of peeled poles created a checkered pattern of shade and sunlight. They squatted there and the boys saw them passing a jug back and forth, Mendoza of Pintada moving between the other two, laughing. Soon, Goes Ahead was lying down, his knees drawn up, and then Iron Shirt lay down beside him and the boys could hear him singing.

They watched through the afternoon and once Mendoza came to them, carrying a jug of whiskey and smoking a long, thin cigar, as black as old mesquite bark. He stood before the boys, laughing and pointing toward the two men lying drunk on his veranda. He poured a little of the whiskey over Sanchess's head and laughed even harder. He thrust the cigar between Bear's lips and commanded that he smoke and breathe it into his body because it would make good medicine. Because he was afraid, Bear did it and grew sick and turned on his side and threw up.

When Mendoza tried to force the cigar into Sanchess's mouth, Sanchess clamped his jaw tight, so Mendoza poured more whiskey over his head, still laughing and smelling of the herbs and the whiskey.

After a long time of having his entertainment with them, the Mexican went back to his house. Goes Ahead was on his hands and knees, trying to crawl back inside, but the wife of Mendoza had closed and barred the door. Mendoza found it all very funny. He squatted beside the men, and as each rose from his stupor, he gave them more whiskey. The afternoon was wearing on toward evening, and now both of the men lay as though dead. Finally, with Sanchess watching, Iron Shirt struggled to his hands and knees, crawled out into the late sunlight, and was sick, vomiting, then collapsing to lie in it. Sanchess was crying.

Well into darkness, with Mendoza in his *casa* and a light burning through the window there, the men staggered back to the corral. Only two of their horses were left, and one mule, all the others having been traded for the whiskey and taken by Mendoza's wife to a corral beyond the house. They were ashamed and said nothing and Goes Ahead stopped twice to vomit. They rode away silently, the two boys on the mule following behind.

Yes, Sanchess remembered Mendoza. He had seen him with his carts many times since that summer seasons past. But it was the first time he remembered. He remembered his father limp and crazy and throwing up, and he remembered Mendoza laughing.

But it was tradition among The People to treat their Comancheros with respect and never harm them. Because next to hunting and fighting, the Comanches liked trading best. Besides, the Comancheros were their surest means of obtaining the white man's metal and cloth and many-colored blankets. It was an old tradition to regard Comancheros as friends. It was a tradition that Sanchess had been thinking about for a long time. Since that afternoon he and his brother had spent in hot humiliation beside one of Mendoza's horse corrals. It was a hard thing to forget!

5

WHEN THE DAY FOR MOVING came, the women were up early, taking down the lodges and bundling belongings in robes for packing on the travois. The young boys ran in the mares from the pony herd, and many of the tipi poles now became travois poles. Those left over were attached as drags to the smaller, weaker horses, making empty travois that might be needed if they killed a lot of game along the way.

There were a number of foals born this same spring, and they ran with great excitement through the breaking camp because they had never been here before, among the humans. But they never ran far from their mothers. The women didn't mind the foals getting in the way. They represented the future wealth of the band. The dogs, who represented nothing except cousins to Brother Coyote, stayed well back. They had learned that the women were impatient at having dogs underfoot when a move was in progress.

War shields were encased in their hide covers, but these and the weapons were placed carefully aside, not packed, because the men would go well armed. Everyone knew they would be traveling north and west and that the possibility of running into a Ute hunting party was great. Or worse, their old traditional enemy the Jicarilla Apaches, whom they had met and driven away when they first came down from the northern mountains. The new arrows made by the old men during the winter were placed in the quivers, and hunting lances were readied to tie on the top of travois bundles so they could be reached quickly when they saw buffalo.

Finds Something's wives had his riding travois ready early. He sat on the stretched hides between the poles as though it were a throne, calmly watching all the movement about him as he slowly chewed willow sticks to clean his old teeth. His wives always cut a lot of willow twigs when they had the opportunity, and kept them in a small bag for him. Everyone knew it was a part of his medicine, chewing willow twigs.

All the drying racks were cleared of meat and the meat packed in parfleche bags or simply tied in bundles, because the meat was stiff and hard like white man's shingles. The racks were left standing because everyone expected soon to be in a country where there was plenty of wood for making more.

There was a great hurry. Each group of family women was anxious to be near the head of the column. Whoever arrived at the next stopping place first would get the best campsite. The peace chiefs' wives could claim a place near the center of the village, no matter when they arrived.

The young girls and some of the boys went to the spring to fill all available bladder bags with water, Morfydd Annon among them. Sunshade had pointed toward the stream and spoken and Morfydd, seeing all the other children and remembering her own morning chore at Madoc's Fort, understood. "Water" was the first Comanche word she learned, although she responded to their name for her, Chosen, without knowing what it meant.

Her new moccasins felt heavy on her feet. She was accustomed to going barefoot in this season. But they were soft and well made, Shade's stitches strong and tight in the cured leather. Her only discomfort now that the sunburn was almost gone was in her belly, as though she were carrying a lead ball there from eating a diet so heavy in meat.

She ran to the spring and the other children paid her no more mind than they would if she had been a real Comanche. Except for one, Morning Thunder, the boy she had switched across the face on her first day in this band. He grinned at her and helped her fill her water bags and spoke a string of words she could not understand.

For the first time since Sanchess had rescued the girl

from the pukutsi, Shade was not near at hand. She thought there might be an opportunity to slip into the mesquite and hide until the band had moved on. But Morning Thunder stayed beside her, grinning widely.

After only a short pause to look around at all the activity, Morning Thunder still talking rapidly, they moved back into the camp. There was so much excitement, and she found it suddenly contagious. Perhaps reluctantly, she began looking forward to what might happen now, like coming to the end of one chapter in a book and wanting to turn the page to the next.

The men had run in their best ponies the night before, tethering them near their lodges overnight. Now they looked to saddles and bridles, and when all was in order they took up the shields and quivers and the war lances and mounted, moving slowly across the watercourse and up the slope past the rest of the pony herd. They waited in a loose group for Iron Shirt and Big Wolf, who were riding through the village, calling for the women to hurry in their work and not leave anything important behind. When the two peace chiefs were satisfied, seeing some of the women already up on travois ponies, they rode to the men and the march began.

No orders were given. Everybody knew what he was supposed to do. A few of the younger men rode out wide on either flank to keep watch and avoid surprise from any enemies, or to signal the presence of buffalo herds nearby. The war leaders with big reputations took their position just behind the peace chiefs and the others fell in behind, forming long columns, one man behind another, so that if anyone came across their trail and saw their tracks, they would find it impossible to decide how many fighting men were in the party.

Leading the men was Iron Shirt, his sons close beside him. Then Running Wolf and Claw, the pukutsi, and all the rest. Near the end of the group was Finds Something on his riding travois, still sitting as straight as his big belly would allow, looking backward toward the old campsite, seeing the women and children stringing out from the cottonwoods and soapberry and coming up onto the hard plain, the trails of the travois poles kicking up a fine dust that was whipped away immediately by the wind.

Mounted on Finds Something's travois mare was his favorite wife, Horned Lark, the only woman in this forward party of men. She carried her own quiver and bow, for she was as efficient with this weapon as some of the men. Almost as efficient as Sunshade.

As the men rode west across the high, hard ground, the rest of the band snaked out behind them, some following in single file, others fanned out to either side, each pony making its small cloud of dust, each travois marking its double-track etching on the earth.

Everybody rode. The women were up on travois horses and extra mares. Many carried cradle boards with babies lashed at their knees. Small children and all the girls rode on top of travois bundles or behind the women on the travois horses. Any boy five summers old was expected to ride alone and keep pace; most rode geldings. All the foals were here, with the mares, switching their tails and taking little bites at their mothers' flanks. And among the travois horses were the dogs, trotting with heads down, tongues out.

Finally, at the rear of it all, came what was left of the pony herd, strung out for a quarter-mile across the plain. Boys of more than ten summers moved with them, along with Lost It, the castrated Mexican, each with a long length of braided rope to whip the ponies along if they paused to graze.

The wives of Sanchess were leading the group of women and children, Chosen up on a small mare. With the feel of a horse between her legs, she felt a quick little urge to wheel about and ride as hard as she could. Toward home and her family and the others who were the same color as she, who spoke the same language, who all lay down for sleep each night in the same bed where they had slept the night before. But she knew as she thought of it that such a thing would be useless. Her mare was old and dragging a travois besides, and riding on either of her flanks were Wapiti Song and Sunshade. Shade's gelding was not pulling anything; it was free to be ridden as quickly as Shade chose.

The two women had become almost casual in their attitude toward the girl. But Chosen knew they continued to watch closely and that they had had much experience in such things. In spite of everything that had happened, Chosen found herself admiring these two women, for they knew what was expected of them and they did it all well. As well, she thought, as the women at Madoc's Fort. And the tasks set for these Comanche women perhaps in no way comparable to anything her mother and various aunts had been expected to perform. They were never required to prepare the day's food without a stove, they were never required to handle horses as well as any man, they were never required to guard captives.

For three days they traveled northwest, along the southern edges of the Llano Estacado, camping each night without tipis, making low fires in holes so their camp could only be seen at very close range. The country began to change, becoming more rolling and with juniper dotted along the slopes. They saw antelope but made no effort to hunt them. Antelope took a long time to hunt, and once a kill was made, there was not much meat.

Sanchess and Running Wolf amused themselves by betting as they went along. Betting on whether they would see a gecko lizard before they saw a roadrunner, or other such things. Next to fighting and hunting and trading, they liked gambling best. At one point, Sanchess had lost seven horses, but by the end of that day he won them back.

On the third day they saw pony tracks, unshod. There were no moccasin prints, so they were unable to decide who it might be.

"Others of The People, perhaps," Big Wolf said.

"No. Too far west. Likely Apache," Iron Shirt said.

"No," said Big Wolf. "Too far east. Likely Ute."

"Likely."

Claw, the crazy pukutsi who was the best tracker in the band, said there were about twenty ponies, going fast and toward the south. The droppings were fresh, maybe left that same morning.

"A party of Utes," he said.

Iron Shirt asked, "Why are they in such a hurry?"

Claw stared at him blankly and Iron Shirt frowned, the creases in his forehead deep, like knife scars.

"Maybe it's a war party," Big Wolf said.

"That's bad," Iron Shirt said.

"Maybe they're running," said Claw. "Somebody may be following them."

"That's even worse," Iron Shirt said.

They took no chances and doubled back on their own trail after darkness fell, moving about a mile before making camp without fires. Some of the fighting men stayed awake, ready to make an ambush in case somebody might be coming up on them from either front or rear. They knew as well as anyone that some tribes, their own included, sometimes made night raids against an enemy, even though each of them individually dreaded the thought of dying in the dark.

Travois were left packed and the women and children slept on the ground and it was cold. Shivering and miserable under her robe, Chosen knew that whatever enemies of the Comanche were out there, they were her enemies as well. And she knew, without knowing the words, that enemies might be there. She could read the seriousness in the faces of the men and the apprehension in the women, and could even feel the suddenly silent foreboding among the children, who, since the tracks were first sighted, had become quiet, no longer laughing or calling to one another.

Yet she crawled from beneath the hide covering late in the darkness, when she thought most of them would be sleeping, and started to creep away, with little conviction or hope of success, but because it was a thing she expected of herself. At first on hands and knees and finally rising and feeling her way with her toes to avoid stepping on anyone.

But then, silently and without warning, she was taken in someone's arms and it was only after being half dragged, half carried back that she knew it was the second wife of Sanchess, whose hands seemed more tender than Shade's ever had. Together they lay beneath Wapiti Song's robe, close enough to Sanchess for Chosen to hear his breathing. There was a reassuring sense of safety in the arms of

Wapiti Song and lying so near the great warrior. Soon she was sleeping, the enemies beyond forgotten.

Before dawn, the whole camp was alerted and the men stood in small depressions on their ponies, watching the horizon. But the approaching sunlight revealed nothing but the vast, rolling land, with the morning's wind kicking up little dust devils. Bear in the Willows saw a wolf far along their backtrail, and hearing that, Iron Shirt observed that if a wolf was there, a man likely was not. But still, he took no chances.

"We need a lookout on the backtrail," he said, "and a scouting party ahead. I'm uneasy about why those people were in such a hurry."

"I'll take the backtrail," Claw said.

"All right," Iron Shirt said, for although the pukutsi was a little crazy, he was a good fighter and knew how to watch backtrails. "Now we need that scouting party."

"I'll take it," Sanchess said.

"I'll go too," Running Wolf said, sliding the hide casing off his blood lance so that the two scalps hanging behind the warhead fluttered out brightly in the sun. When the women saw Running Wolf bare his lance, they muttered among themselves, knowing there could be danger close by.

"Good," Big Wolf said. "Ride hard toward those far mountains until the sun is high, then wait."

"I'll bring up extra ponies," Running Wolf said, and wheeled away, galloping his horse back to the herd.

Among the women, Chosen could feel a new kind of excitement now. They watched Running Wolf going back for extra horses and said nothing. Chosen saw the hardness of their faces as their eyes began to search the horizon constantly. Even the children were quiet, eyes large and shining black, and they watched too, an important thing because their eyes were sharper, not yet irritated by many years of sun and blowing sand.

This is a hostile land, Chosen thought. We are moving away from the places where they feel safe. And when Sunshade touched her shoulder and pointed to the horizon and spoke, Chosen knew what it meant. "Watch" was the second Comanche word she learned.

And it meant a great deal more than the word itself. It meant they were asking her to take part, to do something for the band other than slave labor, carrying water and buffalo chips and heavy bundles of hides.

She began to see the features of their faces for the first time, the broad copper and yellow and walnut-brown faces. And the blunt, powerful fingers on heavy hands, and the bodies and legs and feet and hair. Before, all she had really been aware of were black eyes, bloodshot usually, from windswept sand. But now she saw it all, the solid flesh and bone that made these beings people like herself.

Not animals. Not demons sprung from the depths of earth, but people who talked and walked, who laughed and ate and drank and raised their children to the only life they knew. Who loved and died and were mourned, and who had fears just as she herself had.

It made a chill pass down her spine, riding beside the fierce Shade, watching the horizons for mutual enemies, for dangers evil to them all. To think of them as no different from herself except in speech and custom was no longer horrifying. It was in a strange way exciting.

And it came to her in some fashion that all the harshness, all the casual indifference to her living or dying, was a test of her will, a prescribed program passed along through the generations among them, undertaken intentionally to find out whether she had the physical and mental toughness to become one of them. Otherwise, would they not already have killed her?

She knew that her acceptance of them, and theirs of her, was much more than mere acceptance. It was a matter of her living or dying. And she sensed that the patience of these people might be limited and she knew without having to think about it that when the patience ended, they could be suddenly deadly.

If there's a place for me, she thought, it has to be here. Because now there is no other. The other is in the past. How far in the past? She could not remember nor did she want to. She forced herself not to recall those images of Madoc's Fort because they were still too painful, though growing dim now. Each day it was a little easier. And she knew her futile attempts at escape were finished.

It was simple enough. It was the oldest of genetic urgings: to live, no matter what the accommodations required. But with Chosen it was more. It was pride, now that she knew, because her test had been passed, and she had been taken among them now to "watch." And as they rode side by side, she could see Shade's face somehow soften and she knew that the first wife of Sanchess somehow recognized Chosen's thinking as clearly as she would recognize her own husband's face.

THEY SAW no more sign that day. Even so, they hurried. They passed some small buffalo herds without pausing to hunt. They moved up the Pecos for two more days, avoiding all but one of the pueblos along the way. The one they did not avoid was a small one, and while the band waited on high ground nearby, some of the warriors rode in for the garden vegetables these people grew.

The place seemed deserted. They all knew why. When these people saw Comanches coming, they hid.

"Once there were soldiers at these places," Iron Shirt said.

"I remember," said Big Wolf. "In the time of our grandfathers, there were soldiers with metal hats at these places. But they're gone now."

"Yes. Because our grandfathers drove them away," said Finds Something, and they all laughed.

The young men found very little in the town. It was too early in the year. But they came back with a few hide bags of yellow squash and some dried corn, still on the cob.

"That's hard stuff," Finds Something said. "The women have to beat it with rocks to make it edible."

"We learned that from the Pueblos," Big Wolf said.

"Why anybody would eat such stuff when there are buffalo to kill is a mystery known only to certain spirits," Finds Something said, and crawled back onto his riding travois.

Late that day they crossed the divide between the Pecos and the Canadian rivers. They found many buffalo there, and after another day of slow marching they pitched lodges and made preparations for taking meat. They were in a stand of small juniper trees and the soil was very sandy and fine. Here there were many of the smallest brothers, the desert mice, and always in the sky red-tailed hawks who were there because the mice were.

On this night before the hunt, Morning Thunder came to the wolf-head tipi and ate some meat with the Sanchess women and then gave Chosen a horned lizard he had caught.

"You see?" Sunshade said to Sanchess that night in their robes. "Already they come sniffing around her. That Chosen is going to be a trouble for you."

"Now a horned lizard," he said. "But someday my father will get many horses for her."

Sanchess was pleased. He had seen that Sunshade had begun to treat the girl as though she were a younger sister. And he knew that giving Chosen to his father was not going to be easy.

THE BUFFALO were there, in massive black clots like dried blood that had been splattered across the land for as far as they could see. The herd was grazing slowly toward the north, and the shaggy backs of the humped beasts seemed to flow over the small ridges and into the sharp ravines. They were feeding on bunch grass, in those areas where the juniper did not grow so thickly. There were mesquite and chaparral here, and prickly pear. The great herd grazed over this land unafraid, and following them were thousands of crows, feeding on the droppings, and a few of the scissor-tailed flycatchers.

The women and children came out to watch the start of the hunt. Later, when the first kills were brought in, there would be no time to watch. They stood along a low ridge among the juniper, smelling its fragrance. There was sage too. They could see the herd before them and the hunters off to the east in a line and slowly riding toward the buffalo. Most had bows, but Running Wolf and a few others carried lances.

There were no orders given along the line of hunters. The People did not control their hunts as other tribes did, with policemen. Yet each man knew he must wait for the chief hunter, Running Wolf, to move in for a kill. Then they would all move. They were coming into the herd in the best possible way, the rising sun to their backs so they were hard to see, the wind at their faces so the herd could not catch their scent until it was too late.

Running Wolf moved patiently, knee-guiding his pony toward a young bull grazing at the edge of the herd. He was within an arrowshot of the bull when the bull lifted his heavy, bearded head and snorted. Running Wolf kicked his pony into a full gallop, bringing down the lance. The bull turned and took only a few lumbering steps before Running Wolf was beside his left flank and charging in. He thrust hard with the lance, arm and shoulder and the charge of his pony behind it, driving the point into the belly just behind the ribs, the shaft then ranging up into the vitals.

Running Wolf's pony veered sharply to one side to avoid the bull's fall, just as he had been trained to do with the thrust of the lance. The bull went down, heels over head and with a loud bellow, kicked a few times, and did not get up again.

Along the little ridge, the women shouted, "Hoy! Hoy!" and waved their hands. They saw the others going into the herd now, the buffalo starting to mill and then some of them breaking into a dead run away from the hunters. The men with lances did as Running Wolf had done, riding alongside the left flank of their quarry. The bowmen moved close against the right flank, bent across their ponies' necks, aiming their arrows just behind the ribs from close range. Sometimes the arrows, driven by the horn-reinforced bows, struck so deep that only the feathered vane was visible against the red-flowing hides. And sometimes even the vane was buried. They tried to kill with only two arrows, because the longer a buffalo ran, the tougher the meat.

Chosen thought she could see Sanchess, bow-hunting, two arrows between his teeth. She tried to seek him out, but the dust had begun to roil, and she was not sure. She tugged at Sunshade's skirt and pointed and spoke Sanchess's name, and Sunshade ignored her, but Wapiti Song said yes, it was Sanchess.

When the herd was finally set in motion, the sound of it rolled across the land like distant thunder and even from where the women and children watched, the earth trembled. Woman Who Runs began a soft, wailing buffalo song, shuffling her feet. A fine dustcloud was slowly cutting off their view, but above that they could see the crows, making startled calls and scudding off toward the western mountains like rainclouds before high wind.

On a farther ridge, Iron Shirt and Big Wolf and the other elders were watching too, as was Finds Something, on his riding travois. They nodded with approval because soon there would be much fresh meat and many hides, horns for cups and for stripping to strengthen bows, hooves for boiling into glue.

Each man killed only one or two buffalo, then rode back to do the skinning and quartering. The young boys, the ones who had seen ten summers, brought out extra horses to bring in the meat. The hunters worked quickly on the carcasses because it was a dangerous time, bent to the work, when enemies or charging buffalo bulls might take them by surprise. They peeled off the hides first, then separated the flank meat from the ribs, then chopped off the hindquarters and shoulders with hatchets. Finally they took the internal organs, slitting the belly, some pausing to open one of the buffalo's four stomachs to scoop out handfuls of half-digested grass to eat.

Everything was rolled into the hide or hung by ropes on the extra horses, and the boys started back with their loads of meat. That was the signal for the women to hurry back to camp, for now their part would begin.

The People were proud of how they took meat. Unlike most of their neighbors, Comanches shared the work, the men starting it on the site of their kill, the women finishing in the village. But what a frenzy of work the women did!

Chosen had watched the men at Madoc's Fort butchering cattle, but there had never been anything like this. Through all the camp the women and girls were using knives to filet the meat, racks having already been set up the night before for drying. Some of the best parts, like the liver and tongue, and some of the hump and shoulder, were chunked off and set aside for immediate roasting.

Sinew was taken from along the spine and the backs of the leg bones. It was an important material for making strong cord for bowstrings. Stomachs were set aside so the gummy contents could be eaten, then parfleche bags made from the linings.

Bent over their work, Sunshade and Wapiti Song now and again tossed a bloody chunk of meat to the ring of dogs around them, to keep them back from the butchering. As she pulled a stomach from among the intestines, Sunshade motioned Chosen to her, slit the stomach, and cupped out with her hand the mash of moist grass and gave it to the girl. Chosen tried not to think of where it had come from, but it had a sweet taste and she ate it all.

The women showed her how to drape the strips of meat on the drying racks and soon her hands were sticky crimson, the blood running off her arms like water in a heavy rainstorm. For a time the smell of the blood, the slice of knives through the red meat, the crunch of hatchets on bone had sickened her. But she became accustomed to it and soon it was no more appalling than watching her mother roll out dough at Madoc's Fort.

Sunshade could work buffalo as well as any woman in this band, and Chosen watched her, fascinated. Ribs were stripped of all meat, flank steaks and chucks and heavy neck muscles were chunked out for roasts. Livers and gall bladders came out whole. Intestines were opened and cleaned and kept from the dogs because they made good pouches for storing the stone-ground meat, the pemmican, that would keep the whole winter.

The odor of roasting meat was strong. The urgent voices of the working women were like singing, and all of it had a pulse like dancing. The mood affected each of them, perhaps Finds Something most of all. Although the lodges were scattered through the juniper, he found what he supposed was the center of the village and did his scrotum-rattle dance, his feet barely moving below his great belly as he shuffled in a circle, singing to the spirit of the buffalo. Some of the women were laughing at him, but only behind his back.

The children were laughing as well, running through the encampment holding pieces of roasted meat or raw liver or handfuls of stomach mash. The dogs were happy too, but remained quiet, expectant, staying out of range of the women's kicks but knowing this was feast day, their tongues hanging like the pukutsi's battle sash.

Meat was prepared not only for families who had men on the hunt, but for widows and for couples whose sons had been killed by the Pawnees or Utes or whatever enemies there were, and for Claw, the pukutsi, who had no wife, no mother. He was crazy and unpredictable and most of the women did not want him in their lodges, but they would never let him go hungry, even though he had been touched by a medicine they could not comprehend.

Many of them suspected his forebears were from the small Comanche band called Something Together. They were called that because they were said to accept incest within their band. It was a thing to laugh about, but a thing that could be serious as well. Those people saw different spirits from the ones seen by anyone else. As did Claw, the pukutsi.

Chosen had seen him many times since that night after the victory dance when he had pressed his nakedness against her. At first she didn't realize he was the man, but later she saw his crow headdress and knew. She viewed him now with strange compassion, for although he had frightened her that night—and was even a little frightening in broad daylight without the face paint or the headdress, with his viciously thin lips and burning eyes—he had spoken gently to her.

He has never tried to touch me since and hardly ever looks at me, she always thought when she saw him wandering among the lodges, doing his strange little dances. She felt sorry for him because the others treated him as if he had some physical deformity, even though in fact he was a handsome man despite his bitter expression. Already, Chosen sensed that being an outcast among these people was a hard thing.

And so the women prepared his meat, and Chosen was glad. She did not know that they did it with good reason. It was a fine trade. The pukutsi would kill at least three buffalo this day, and only one would be enough for him.

The other two would be shared by the women who did his butchering.

When the men came in, they squatted at the fringes of this great activity and smoked and told how they had made their kills. Some of the women went among them with raw liver sprinkled with gall, and they ate for a long time before going out for the second run into the buffalo. When it was time, they rode to the pony herd for fresh horses.

The hunting went through the day, and at sundown the men slept. But the women worked on into the night, before fires that were large and made them uneasy in this dangerous country. At the edges of the fires, in hot coals, the roasts cooked, spitting and sizzling, and above the flames were the spits of mesquite wood where the tongues hung, turning brown and dripping their juice into the fire with little explosions of heat and light.

Sunshade and some of the other women did not sleep at all that night. They worked into the morning, finally finishing the meat and then beginning on the hides, stretching them on pole frames and starting to flesh them with rib bones. Later, the brains, carefully placed out of reach of the dogs, would be rubbed into some of the better robes to give them softness.

Although Wapiti Song had long since gone to her lodge, Chosen worked through it all with Sunshade. When the sun came, her eyes were swollen and her hands blistered. She spent that day trying to stay awake, kicking the dogs away from the piles of bones drying in the sun so the marrow would be crisp and good for winter soups. The dogs were big-bellied by then, bloated with their feeding, but still they tried for more.

Why don't they kill off some of these dogs, she wondered. And then wondered again if perhaps the stories she had heard of dog-eating among all Indians was really true. She had seen no evidence of any dog in this band being eaten. She wondered yet again whether she could eat dog if the time came. Perhaps. She had eaten that stomach mash.

I have done a lot of things I never did before, she thought. I wonder if Dafydd is still alive.

And she was amazed that she had not thought of him for many days.

THEY DIDN'T stay long on that hunting ground. They knew it was the time of year for Utes to be coming out to the buffalo ranges, and some surely would take the route of the Canadian River to the plains. They moved into the fringes of the Sangre de Cristo Mountains, where they would find lodgepole timber, keeping many scouts out as they moved.

It was a beautiful country with deep canyons and heavy stands of straight-trunked pine. There were many kinds of berries, and the children gathered them to eat or to dry. They would be good, ground into the pemmican later in the summer. The water was fresh-running and cold and there were deer and squirrels and rabbits. The young boys tried their bow skills on the small game and when one of them managed to kill a rabbit, there was a little celebration.

But they were uneasy in the mountains. They could not see the far horizons or feel the plains wind in their faces. They felt trapped by the close formation of big trees. They could not feel the vastness of the night sky domed over them and speckled with stars. Iron Shirt was anxious to leave, and so were all the others. Except for Chosen. She loved the smell of the pines. She had never seen such large trees before, reaching almost to the sun at midday.

Then it rained for two days, dampening their spirits further, for they were a sun people. Tipis began to smell musty and damp because the high plains wind was not there to dry them. But the sun came again and they completed their work, cutting trees and peeling the bark. The women did this work while the men scouted for Utes or lay about in the lodges, smoking or gambling with dice they had from the Comancheros.

Sanchess won nine horses from Running Wolf, but lost them back again.

"I would hate to be caught here by the Utes," Big Wolf said each night around the fire where the headmen gathered in Iron Shirt's lodge.

"Yes, or the Jicarillas," Iron Shirt said. "They are a

bitter enemy, those Apaches. They remember how the grandfathers of The People drove them out of the buffalo plains. They have long memories."

"And sometimes they fight together, as friends, those Utes and those Jicarillas," Black Mountain said. Black Mountain was the grandfather of the boy Morning Thunder, who had given Chosen the horned lizard, and his son Gizzard was one of the best fighters and war leaders in the band. Black Mountain was respected, even though one of his hands had been crippled by a white man's bullet during a raid in Texas. "I'm glad those people don't have any more guns than we do," he said.

"This timber bothers me," Big Wolf said. "It always bothers me when we come here. There is no room to run the horses against an enemy."

"We'll have the women hurry in their work," Iron Shirt said.

"They are sometimes hard to hurry," Black Mountain said. "They sometimes seem to have minds of their own."

At about this time each evening, Finds Something loaded his pipe and said his little prayers and they all smoked. They could hear the soft wind among the pines, not the hard-driving sound of their own high plains wind. It made Big Wolf shiver.

While they were camped among the pines, Wapiti Song delivered herself of a son. It required the help of Sunshade and Woman Who Runs because it was a hard birth, but a live one. Chosen was required to stand close by to lend whatever help she could, and she was sickened by it. Then enthralled. Wapiti Song was in great pain but gave no sign of it except to grind her teeth.

Woman Who Runs had a cradle board ready for her new grandson. She showed Chosen how to use it, and it became the girl's duty to watch after the baby. She had done it before, with her brother Dafydd.

She had been a mother to Dafydd, throughout each day of his life. Dressing him and pulling him about the fort compound by the hand, keeping him clear of the stream because he seemed to have no fear of water and would have walked into it along one of the sloping banks. Often she had to feed him each mouthful of food at table because he made such a mess of it himself. Keeping him clean, from the very beginning, because her mother's time was taken up by her labors. The bread making, the house cleaning, the washing and ironing, the sewing.

There had always been a stubborn rebellion in Dafydd, resisting her at each step, silently and sullenly, making her task a difficult and irritating one. With Wapiti Song's child, it was not the same.

The baby was kept in the cradle board all day, even when he was feeding at his mother's breast. The board had a soft skin covering that laced along the front. At the back was more soft leather, padded with moss, and more moss for a diaper, which was not changed until the end of the day, when the baby came out to be wrapped in a soft hide to sleep beside his mother. It was a messy business, but Chosen did not complain, nor did the baby. He had enormous black eyes and a mop of raven hair, and Chosen soon came to love her duty with him. Especially she enjoyed the daily bath, using warm water heated in a hide bag over a low fire and applied gently with the fingers. Afterward she powdered him with a chalky substance made from ground cottonwood roots.

They named the child Getting the Lodgepoles. Sanchess painted a large black circle above the door of the wolf-head tipi to show that a new warrior had arrived. They had a modest celebration because in Ute country they could not afford a big one. Sanchess gave away four horses.

But they moved quickly after that. Iron Shirt was troubled about those Utes. Under his left arm he had an old scar from a Ute hatchet, which he claimed always ached when the enemy was near. They set out due east, and everyone knew they were going to the Llano Estacado where they would summer with the Kwahadi.

Sunshade became almost like a girl in her happiness, giggling and making little jokes and tickling Sanchess under the arms when they were in their robes together. She was glad to be going back to her own people, even if only for the summer and possibly the fall hunts.

But Wapiti Song saw a sadness in her face, too, because Shade would be returning to her people without a child of her own. And one night as they were camping without tipis once more, on the march and beginning to approach the plains, Wapiti Song suggested something to her husband that at first amazed him.

"We will allow Shade to become Getting the Lodgepoles' mother for a while, when we are among her people."

"What are you saying, woman? He is your child. Are you ashamed to call him so?"

"She has no child, and going among her own people," Wapiti Song said. For a long time they lay in the darkness, silent. Sanchess loved her more then than he ever had before.

"But she cannot feed the child," he said softly.

"I'll feed my son. But in the shadows of the lodge, where no one can see."

"They may want to watch her feed him."

"Sunshade and I can manage that little bit of trickery."

"You women. What devious beings you are," he said, and pulled her close against him and laughed gently.

After that, Sunshade was happier than ever and even smiled at Chosen from time to time. And often she looked at Wapiti Song with a soft light in her eyes. It would be an easy trick because much of the rearing of that baby would be hers to do anyway. The feeding part could be arranged with only a small bit of subterfuge. And her father would call himself Grandfather and be very proud. Out of his gladness he would probably give Sanchess a couple of ponies too, because the Kwahadi had many horses.

TWO

We have had many enemies.
We have understood them all.
Except the white man.

6

WHEN THE WHITE MEN CAME to it, they ever afterward spoke of it with awe and told of it through all the generations. When the Comanches came to it, they only assumed it had been put there for their purpose and called it the Canyon of Prairie Dog Town Branch of Red River.

Wind and water over the centuries had etched a great chasm into the high plains of what would someday be known as the Texas Panhandle. It was impossible to see in that featureless expanse of the earth's surface until one came to the very edge and then it suddenly dropped away in multicolored grandeur to a vast, meandering floor where water flowed and vegetation was abundant. When the Spaniards first blundered onto it, they were astonished that it would be there in the flat prairie that stretched to all the horizons like the sea. A huge, magnificent feature of the terrain, yet invisible until the hooves of their horses were almost on the rim.

The Spanish soldiers did no comprehensive measurements, but had they done so, their astonishment would have been even greater. At some points the massive defile was twelve hundred feet deep, five miles wide. Enclosed in it was a valley floor of about six hundred thousand acres, and it ran for thirty miles southeastward toward the central plains. They cut some of the small trees growing there for their campfires and found the wood so hard that they named the place Palo Duro.

The canyon had many tributaries, some so small that a man could hardly squeeze through them. Others were wide and long and ideal for penning horses with only a few strands of rope across the mouth of the arroyo. In the main canyon floor there was sweet water, water that was the beginning of the Red River, only a few feet wide here but flowing for hundreds of miles toward the Mississippi, where it emptied just short of the Gulf of Mexico.

Along the stream were cottonwoods and back up the slopes were clusters of prickly pear and bunch grass and pinyon, and then, running up the base of each lift of rising ground, the cedars. There were mesquite and yucca and buffalo grass and a variety of berry bushes, some thistled and the fruit bright red in the sun.

The water flowed in quiet ripples across sandstone pebbles or silt the color of blood. When one of the plains tornadoes came, with downpours of rain, it became a raging torrent. It was cold, even in summer, running as it did from the deep springs under the surface of the surrounding plain.

Within the floor of the valley were knolls and mounds and buttes, some brush- and tree-covered, some naked rock. And rising far above all these were the bluffs and the rim of the canyon proper. The rock in the cliffs had been stratified eons ago and now cut through, making layers of red and yellow and pale orange color. The walls rose straight to the plains above, without foothold and only here and there the persistent pinyon in tiny clusters or long ribbons of dark green.

The countryside around the canyon for miles in all directions was inhospitable. It was a low-vegetation tableland that thrust up in high-rising escarpments on both the Texas and New Mexico sides. When Coronado's men first came toward it, they were impressed by the lift of rock cliffs and they named it Llano Estacado, or, literally, "palisaded plains." But later, "palisades" was lost in translation, for the Anglos called it the Staked Plains.

Whatever the language, no one doubted its magnitude. It covered about thirty thousand square miles. It was hot in summer, cold in winter, and the wind had the force of a thing solid, like metal, driving before it invisible particles of sand. It was a desolate and isolated land, untouched through many years by white traders who moved up the

Arkansas to establish their posts in Colorado. It was many hard days of travel across hostile country from the nearest outpost of Spanish and, later, Anglo civilization along the Brazos or the Colorado, and equally difficult to reach from the Rio Grande. Even after the Santa Fe Trail trade was begun, the wagon traces were generally cut only across the far northwest corner of the great tableland, swallowed up by all the rest. These traders never stopped to settle. They were only passing through. They were not immigrants or soldiers there to stake claims for hearth or country.

When the Comanches came to Llano Estacado, they were already rich with Spanish horses. Riding across the great flatland, they saw its desolation. They soon learned of the isolation as well, and it pleased them. There were no trees but there were a great number of buffalo, more than they had seen on any northern range. And after they discovered its mysteries, they knew how to find sweet water there.

Best of all was the canyon. They discovered ways into Palo Duro from its head where the erosion continued, still eating into the plains. These were narrow, rugged defiles, pitching down sharply to the canyon floor. But horses could traverse many of them, and sometimes travois as well.

The canyon pleased them greatly. For it not only provided good water, wood, and a safe haven from the high plains' brutal winters; it was also a hiding place that could not be seen easily from afar, as a mountain could be seen and therefore discovered.

So they claimed it as theirs, both plains and tableland, in the manner of the Spaniards but with one exception. The Comanches did not go back whence they had come. They stayed and drove everyone else out, including the Jicarilla Apaches.

Many of the bands of The People moved farther south, into country less formidable. But the Kwahadi had found their home. They established this land as their own personal domain. During the good months they hunted across the sun-bleached plain and during the bad months they went into the canyon. Sometimes, as time passed, others of the Comanches came to visit with them, to hunt through the hot days on the Llano Estacado among the great herds and stay on for the winter in Palo Duro.

DURING THAT first winter, she lay in her robes at night snug and secure, listening to the howl of the plains wind far above, rushing across the rim, blowing snow before it like tiny white arrows shot from a powerful bow. Here on the canyon floor, there were only momentary gusts against the walls of the wolf-head tipi, and the snow fell almost vertically.

She could never recall having been so warm in cold weather. There was a lining of hide now, attached to the insides of the lodgepoles and folded toward the center of the tipi at the bottom to keep out the small, searching fingers of wind. As the cold days came on, she was amazed at how the small fires of dried buffalo dung kept the lodge heated. Usually when they came inside, it was only a few moments before they shed their winter clothes, the smocks and robes with the hair still on.

The tipi always smelled of cooked meat and cured leather. And when Sunshade closed the smoke flap at the apex of the conical lodge, there was always the thick scent of burning wood, for although mostly they used chips, Shade always had a small piece of long-burning mesquite on the fire. It was like an incense.

Chosen knew that in this winter she would have a birthday but she had no account of the days that had passed and so did not know exactly when it came. Only that she was eleven years old. But she did not think of it in that way. She thought of it now as having seen eleven summers.

Long since, she had decided that she would never see any other life, that she would never return to those times among her own people, to events and places and even faces that were already growing dim in memory. Now *these* are my people, because there are no others!

She wondered where all the horror had gone. And fear. And yes, even hatred. But it had somehow gone. Even knowing what they had done to her own people, even knowing she should hate them. But so much had happened. So much life exploding around her, so much changing, so much new, and there had never been enough time to think seriously of hatred, a thing that perhaps needed a little reflection to ripen.

All of this was unclear in her young mind. Yet it was there, in murky but powerful images, known if not understood. And as the todays became more vivid, the yesterdays grew gradually fainter, some already faded away forever.

At first, when she realized that she was growing into this band and this life, she fought it. Such a struggle seemed a duty not only to herself but to the memory of those from whom she had been taken, especially her Da. Not really because of any great affection he had ever shown her, but because he was the center of the world she had always known. The resistance took the form of those futile attempts to escape. And after she realized the futility, it became like silent prayer. Each night, before she slept, she repeated to herself her Christian name. Morfydd Annon. Morfydd Annon. Morfydd Annon.

And now, lying in her winter robes and listening to the Llano Estacado wind, she said it to herself again, out of habit. Morfydd Annon Parry. But she added, Who has seen eleven summers!

WHAT A SUMMER this last one had been, and the fall as well. Events and The People swirling around her like the clouds of yellow butterflies in a field of bluebonnets to the east where she had been born.

First, meeting the Kwahadi, Sunshade's people. They were very dark, some almost black from long and constant exposure to the open sky, and she began to know then that Comanches, like herself, turned color under the sun. For a few weeks she had sunburned all exposed skin, blistered and peeled, sunburned again, blistered and peeled again. But finally that was past and now she looked at her hands and saw that they were as dark and brown as were those of many people in the band, darker than the skin of Comes Behind, Iron Shirt's young wife.

There had been the fun of deceiving the Kwahadis about Wapiti Song's baby, making them believe it was really Shade's. Chosen began to suspect that it was not a long-lasting deception, even though none of the Kwahadi would say so out of courtesy and good manners, and they understood the good intentions behind the little trick. And Shade's father had given Sanchess two horses anyway.

There was Wolf's Road, Shade's younger brother, a handsome man with powerful arms and legs and a face with straight nose and wide mouth. He was known as the best racehorse breeder among the Kwahadis, and he took many fine hides in payment for bets he won against disgruntled Nakonis like Gizzard and Bear in the Willows, who fancied themselves pretty good horse breeders too.

Wolf's Road had offered to buy her. He had offered twenty horses, but Sanchess steadfastly refused. It gave Chosen a glow of pride because it meant she was something of value. But a little disappointment as well, because she thought Wolf's Road was the finest rider of ponies she had ever seen. And horses were beginning to be important to her now, though she came from a culture almost completely pedestrian.

And the buffalo hunts! There had been nothing like them in her memory, for the one her own band had conducted on the Canadian in the spring was small in comparison. In the mad melee of preparing meat, Chosen began to take a more active part, and by the coming of fall she was almost as good with a knife as Shade, though not nearly so strong.

They made pemmican for the winter, pounding the dried meat into mush and with it cherries or wild plums or sometimes mesquite beans. All of this they packed in small parfleches and sealed with melted tallow to make the packages airtight. It reminded Chosen of mincemeat, or perhaps a heavy black bread that could be sliced like a loaf of rye.

It was in this time that she became aware of an ability to see more clearly what was happning around her. As though everything that had gone before had been obscured by the constant variety of change in her life. She saw the boys of the band playing around the encampment and in the horse herd, going naked until they had at least eight summers. She saw it now without embarrassment. The little girls wore smocks, but the boys only moccasins.

And the kind of play! Even before they put on their first loincloths to protect their coming manhood, the boys rode the horses in the pony herd, practicing tricks like picking up comrades lying flat on the ground as they rode past at a gallop. And weapons! Every boy had a small bow and blunt arrows and shot at everything, being taught by the grandfathers how to stalk and how to kill game or enemies. Horses and weapons and eating consumed all their waking hours until they were old enough to start thinking about the girls.

And the little girls, from the time they could walk, learning how to maintain a campsite, working beside their mothers. Learning how to make fires, how to cook meat, how to flesh hides, how to rub buffalo brains into hides to make them soft, how to handle travois mares.

And the men, whose faces had at first seemed strange and vacant of expression, like flat copper coins. Now she understood that much of this was created by lack of facial hair, with whiskers and eyebrows plucked out. And Claw, the pukutsi, even plucked his eyelashes!

All of this she was seeing as if for the first time that summer and fall. And learning the language. Shade was her teacher, but not the only one. Although Chosen was still of the wolf-head-tipi family, she spent much time with Woman Who Runs during the day and with Iron Shirt at night. Sitting at the fire with her, Iron Shirt spoke sometimes in Spanish, sometimes a few words of English, always opening new roads into his own language.

Often, too, the young boys and girls would gather at Iron Shirt's fire to hear him tell over and over again the stories of The People, how they had come from the far mountains and obtained the horse, how they had fought with the Kiowas for a long time and then made peace, how a growing boy or girl found his or her own medicine.

As the autumn waned, the band gradually moved toward the eastern edge of the Llano Estacado. Soon, Chosen saw why. They were moving close to the canyon. When she first saw it, the immense, rugged rock faces of the gorge frightened her.

And the day finally came, when they still camped on the plains, that the sky clouded over with a fine white mist, the sun shining through it as though through water. The wind began to shift to the north, and at midday they saw the reflection of the sun in the high ice crystals, making it appear that there were half a dozen suns.

When they saw that, they broke camp in a frenzy of haste. The pony herd was driven ahead of them into the steep defiles of the canyon and on toward the floor. The dogs dashed about wildly, barking, hackles up, sensing the danger from the sky. The wind increased in fury so that it was hard to stand, and as the travois were loaded, the horses were led by the women, running as they pulled the reins. Some of the meat on the drying racks was left to blow away. A few hides came loose from the travois loads and sailed across the plain. But before the first snow came, slanting across the earth in sheets, they were below the rim.

And then Chosen was no longer frightened of the canyon, but recognized it as a friend.

Morfydd Annon Parry. Who has seen eleven summers.

AFTER THE FIRST storm there were good days again for a long time. But the air was sharp and in the morning Chosen could see her breath when she went for water from the stream that flowed at the base of the small cedar-covered knoll where the family of Iron Shirt was camped. It was a good time, with plenty of food and not much to do except keep the camp clean and work on hides. There were many dice and stick gambling games, among men and women both, and the children made traps for rabbits and hunted lizards.

Shade seemed to be sewing constantly, making shirts and moccasins. In his tipi, Iron Shirt was making arrows of hackberry wood. Bear in the Willows had brought him owl feathers, the best for vanes because blood did not affect their texture. He was working on a bow too, of good ironwood reinforced with horn. He had been working on that bow a long time, and when it was finished, he said, it would send an arrow completely through a bull buffalo and out the other side.

Often, Chosen rode along the valley floor with Morning Thunder, who seemed to have developed an interest in the girls at an earlier age than most boys, and who appeared almost every day at the wolf-head tipi for a handout of pemmican and to grin at Chosen. They spent a lot of time among the horses, and there every day Chosen saw the Mexican herder, Lost It. He was a strange little man whose face always seemed to be dusty and whose eyes had a cloudy vacantness. He never spoke to them, only to the horses, even though she tried to speak with him in Spanish.

Sanchess gave her a horse of her own, a little gelding spotted with brown and black on a coat mostly white.

"If you are going to ride so much, you need a pony of your own," he said, and she understood enough of what he said to realize she had just become a woman of property. Not like Sunshade, who owned six horses of her own, but a woman of property nonetheless.

On one of those crisp mornings, Chosen and Morning Thunder came onto a group of the men castrating two-year-old colts. They sat their ponies on a high outcrop of sandstone above a wide meadow along the stream where the men were working. Morning Thunder leaped down and began talking, too fast for her to understand. She dismounted as well, and they squatted together in the manner of The People. And seeing that she did not understand, he spoke more slowly, using his hands to make signs that would explain it all. She began to understand when she saw the men with knives.

"They crush cedar foliage. They mix it with mud from the riverbank," Morning Thunder said, his hands working. "They place the mudpack on the wound and it heals quickly. And Finds Something has a special medicine he puts in it, too."

To her it seemed a terrible thing to be doing, but at least she understood enough to know that this was how The People controlled the breeding of their herds. Morning

Thunder made a long speech about stallions and mares and geldings, which was mostly incomprehensible to her.

While they were there, the Mexican came up to stand beside them. And it startled her a little when he spoke in Spanish to her.

"They only keep the best colts for the mares."

She was ready to respond, to make conversation, but as soon as Lost It spoke, Morning Thunder spat out a string of harsh words she did not know and the Mexican quickly turned and walked away into the cedar.

"He is only a slave," the boy said arrogantly. "Your father did the same thing to him as they are doing to the colts down there."

"Iron Shirt did that to him?"

"Not Iron Shirt. Sanchess. When he caught the Mexican, he gave him to Iron Shirt. But first he cut him." And Morning Thunder laughed.

For a moment she was sure her command of The People's language had failed her. And Morning Thunder, seeing her confusion, made sure she would know.

"He's just a gelding," he said and laughed again. "A slave gelding."

It sickened her and she rose quickly and went to her pony and rode away with her stomach churning. Still hearing the laughter behind her.

For a long time after that, she refused to ride with Morning Thunder, even though he said they would go along the canyon and visit the Paneteka and Wichita bands who were camped downstream. And it was even longer before she could look at Sanchess without a shudder passing along her shoulders. And each day when she went to the pony herd to rub down her horse with grass she saw the Mexican and tried not to think of what had happened to him. But it was hard to do.

AS THAT winter wore itself out with blowing, and the hint of spring came with soft winds along the canyon floor, everyone started thinking about moving. For Nakoni, they had been in the same camp for a long time. Even so, twice during the winter they shifted campsites inside the canyon.

Others of The People said Nakonis were always moving and never got to where they were going.

Iron Shirt was as restless as the rest and thought it a good time to call a council of headmen. They needed to talk. It happened like that every winter, no matter where they were, and each of the headmen came to Iron Shirt's lodge where they smoked and talked for a long time about what had happened to them during the cold moons of snowfall and wind. Then finally they came to the real issue.

Because it was his lodge and because he was chief headman, Iron Shirt sat in the position of honor, facing the tipi door from across the fire. Next to him sat Big Wolf and Black Mountain, grandfather of the boy Morning Thunder. Then there was Finds Something, wearing his buffalo headdress, and Iron Shirt's older brother, Goes Ahead. These men were the established government of the band for such things as traveling and hunting and selection of camping places.

Goes Ahead was the oldest of them, and one of the elders of the entire band. He had tried to lead war parties and raids too late in life, after his senses were dulled with age. In the excitement of running some horses from a Navaho corral one night, he had fallen with his horse and broken both legs. They carried him away and splinted the breaks, and when they returned to the village, Finds Something did what he could with his medicines. But one leg came out shorter than the other and both gave him great pain. His lined face was now always set in the expression of a woman giving birth, but he did not complain except to his wives.

Behind the peace chiefs were some of the young men, some of the best war leaders. Sanchess was there, and Running Wolf and Finds Something's son, Hawk Man. Claw, the pukutsi, was there as well, looking fierce and crazy in his old crow headdress. And Iron Shirt's younger brother, Stinking Bottom.

Iron Shirt was not happy with Stinking Bottom. Although he was about the same age as Sanchess, he had never led a war party. He had started with a good name acquired from Finds Something after two days of medicine-making and gift-giving, but soon his nickname was all anyone remembered—Stinking Bottom. As a child he had been slovenly. After puberty he got worse. He seldom took a bath and after a raid south of the Rio Grande, he had developed angry looking sores on the most private parts of his body. It was the disease of the Mexicans, transmitted through their women. Of course, none of The People knew what it was or where it came from. His three wives had given him only one live birth, and that baby had been blind and had to be destroyed.

But even though he was not too clean and no leader of warriors, he was brave enough. Iron Shirt was glad of that, at least. But Stinking Bottom did not bring much pride to the family.

"Those Kiowas who were on the raid with my son," Iron Shirt said. "They said we would be welcome to their summer sun dance."

Sanchess nodded but said nothing. Because this was not a council for war, the young men were expected to keep their silence. They were there to listen, so when they became peace chiefs they would know what to do. While the elders smoked a ceremonial pipe, passing it from one to the other, the young men smoked cigarettes wrapped in cottonwood leaves.

There were no women in the lodge at all. Iron Shirt's two wives had been sent to visit the grandchildren.

"A strange people," Big Wolf said. "But good friends, those Kiowas."

"I remember when I was a young man," said Goes Ahead. "We had this raiding party to steal some Arapaho horses north of the Arrowpoint River."

"Yes, the white man calls it the Arkansas," Iron Shirt said, hoping to head off a long tale. But Goes Ahead went on anyway.

"We had a bunch of Kiowas with us. We got into a little fight with the Arapahoes and killed one of them. One of the Kiowas cut off his head and dragged it around the prairie. It frightened the others and they left. We didn't get many horses that time. Arapahoes don't have many horses to steal. Mexico is better."

"Yes, you told us that before," Iron Shirt said to his

brother, but not in a scolding way. He had great respect for this brother, who had to go through each day with that great ache in his legs. But sometimes Goes Ahead allowed his mind to wander in council and forgot what the business was about. "Those Kiowas said they would have their sun dance somewhere along the Washita this year."

"That's where it usually is," Finds Something said. "Or on the Medicine Creek."

"They call that the Timbered Hill River," Goes Ahead said. "I have hunted there with them."

"About this sun dance," Iron Shirt said impatiently.

"That country along the Washita makes me nervous," Finds Something said. "You can't see far enough."

"Those new people are moving in there too," Black Mountain said. "I talked with some of the Wichitas down the valley this winter and they told me there are a lot of those new people coming in. Moved there by the white man in the east. They told me these new people are just like white men themselves."

"I know about them. Cherokees. Or one of those other tribes," Iron Shirt said. "But most of them are still east of the Washita. East of the Crossed Timbers, far downstream along the Arrowpoint River. The Washita is still Kiowa country."

"They say these Cherokees are almost as big as the Osage," Goes Ahead said, and some of the others muttered and shook their heads. "And have a lot of guns."

"We are not worried about the Cherokees along the Washita," Iron Shirt said, more impatient still. "That is still Kiowa country."

"We could hunt with them," Big Wolf said. "Except for bear."

Everyone laughed, even the young men, because they all knew of the Kiowa taboo on killing bears.

"I don't like hunting with those Kiowas," Black Mountain said. "They want everyone to do what their chiefs say on a hunt."

"We are not talking about hunting," Iron Shirt said. "We are talking about visiting their sun dance."

"Our young ones could see it," Goes Ahead said.

"Some of them have never seen a sun dance. A strange thing to watch, that sun dance."

"It's all about their gods," Finds Something said with authority, being the expert among them on gods and spirits and such things. They all nodded.

"Every man must approach his gods in his own way," Iron Shirt said.

"That's what we say," said Black Mountain. "But the Kiowas approach the gods the way their medicine chiefs say. They call them owl doctors. It's a tradition."

"But it is interesting to watch," Goes Ahead said. "When I was young, I saw a Cheyenne sun dance. That was before we were fighting them all the time. I was very young. They cut their skin and inflict great torture on themselves. I think it was Cheyennes. It was a long time ago."

"We are talking about a Kiowa sun dance," Iron Shirt said. "They don't cut themselves or push sticks under their skins like the Sioux and others in the north. It would be a good time. There would be much feasting and we could visit old friends among them."

"They have turkeys there, along the Washita," Big Wolf said. "I have always liked those turkeys, you throw them into the fire until all the feathers are burned black, then peel off the skin and eat it. I've always liked that."

"I would rather eat lizards and frogs," Black Mountain said with disdain. Everyone laughed.

"Big Wolf will eat anything," Finds Something said.

"No," said Big Wolf. "I will not eat the white man's pig."

Everyone nodded vehemently. But now Iron Shirt's patience had gone completely. So he made the decision. If they wanted to follow, good. If they did not, good.

"I will go to the Kiowa sun dance this year," he said. "It's time for a change."

Everyone around the circle nodded and he knew they would all go.

"I have talked with Wolf's Road, the Kwahadi brother to my youngest son's wife," Iron Shirt said. "He will go with us. He has never seen a sun dance of the Kiowas. And besides, he might find a wife among them. He is very particular about wives because he has more than twenty-two summers and is not married yet.''

''The Kiowas have strong women,'' Goes Ahead said.

''Wolf's Road. Yes, that's good. He looks like a fine fighter and we may need him if we see those Cherokees,'' Black Mountain said.

''There will be no Cherokees,'' Iron Shirt said.

''Well, whoever we may meet. That Wolf's Road looks like a good war leader to me.''

''Yes,'' Iron Shirt said, glancing back along the row of young men and meeting Stinking Bottom's eye. ''All the Kwahadi young men are war leaders!''

Finds Something filled the pipe again, raised it to the sky and to the four corners of the earth, and they began to smoke. The pipe had only passed partway around the circle when there was a crackling sound at the door flap of the tipi and they heard giggling, fading into the night.

Sanchess rose quickly and moved to the door and raised the flap. There, set close against the tipi, was a small fire of brush, flaming up. Sanchess stomped it with his feet, realizing too late that the fire concealed a mound of fresh horse dung. All the others laughed, slapping their thighs, and Sanchess did too, after a moment.

''Those young boys, they will be good warriors someday,'' Black Mountain said, chuckling. ''They know how to make practical jokes.''

''Pretty good,'' Big Wolf said. ''Except for all that giggling. They'll have to learn to be quiet if they expect to steal a lot of horses when the sun is gone!''

IT WAS A good night. Cold, but good. Winter was running out. The skies showing above the canyon were deep blue, the clouds all gone to the east, and as the sun set that day on Llano Estacado, the shadows of purple and gray had already been in Palo Duro for many hours. The stars came out sharp-edged, like glass traders' beads held in the light of a white-flaming fire.

Iron Shirt came to the wolf-head tipi that night for the evening meal. His younger wife, Comes Behind, was in the small tipi behind the main family lodges. Chosen knew very little about that small tipi, except that from time to time one of the women went there for a few days. She supposed that they had made their men angry about something important and were therefore put aside as punishment until the anger cooled.

Woman Who Runs came to the wolf-head tipi as well, and she sat at the rear of the lodge with the other women but did not help serve the meat. There was a rabbit, caught in a snare Wapiti Song had set in the cedars behind the family ridge that morning. Roasted brown over the fire, it sent an aroma through the lodge that made Chosen's mouth go wet. But only the men ate it. The women shared with them bowls of marrow and crushed mesquite beans, very rich, very sweet. Woman Who Runs had brought a few persimmon cakes that she said came from a sister of hers who was with the Paneteka band down the valley. They were crisp, the seeds having been removed and the meat pulverized with stones and then laid out in last fall's sun to dry. They were a little old, but still good.

The men talked of buffalo and horses, of how certain stallions had been up on certain mares, and their expectation of a good season of foaling in the spring. And they talked of Bear in the Willows, gossiping like old women and making their own women giggle.

"He stays close to that tipi of his," Sanchess said.

"Yes, he plays with that daughter as if she were a new pony." Iron Shirt said it with a chuckle as though he might himself understand such things, maybe as if he wished he had a daughter. It was still a possibility, with Comes Behind sure to become pregnant soon.

After the men ate and smoked cigarettes, the older people left, Woman Who Runs going before. At the tipi door flap, Iron Shirt turned and looked at Chosen.

"Come, I will show you a thing."

Outside they stood for a long time silently, waiting for their eyes to become accustomed to the dark. Then Iron Shirt spoke in Spanish.

"Many stars."

Chosen saw him turn to her, and he was again silent for a long time. She thought he might scold her now for serving the rabbit wrong, in some taboo manner. But his voice was gentle when he finally spoke again.

"You have a great admirer," he said in Comanche, and she understood. "Wolf's Road. Sunshade's brother. He's a brave warrior, they say. He will go with us to visit the Kiowas. Perhaps he expects to find a wife among them. Or perhaps he wants to stay near so he can maybe buy you someday. He is a brave warrior, they say. A good husband for somebody."

Iron Shirt paused and looked up to the canyon rim above, and although there was no moon, they could see where the rim was because that was where the stars began.

"I'll tell you how he got his name." Iron Shirt raised his arm and pointed toward the sky. "Do you see that white mark? Like silver dust?"

"I see it."

"When he was born, it was a night when that mark was very bright. And so they named him for it. That is the Wolf's Road. It's the night path the wolf takes across the sky."

Chosen looked at the band of stars across the dome of black, and what he had said made a shiver go down her back. She tried to recall something from the past, and when it came to her, she had no way to express it in Comanche.

"I call it . . ." She stopped, because she did not know the word, and Iron Shirt laughed softly, an old man laughing gently at a child.

"Milky Way," he said in English. Then, in Comanche, "I have heard it called that by the white man."

"Yes, Milky Way," she said, also in English, and hearing the words from her own mouth was like the sound of distant voices, long forgotten.

"It's a good name," Iron Shirt said. "Milk is good. Sometimes when I was a young man and hunting and killed a buffalo cow with calf, I would slit the great bag above the udders and press my mouth there and drink the milk and blood. Milk and blood. A good thing to drink."

She felt no revulsion, but rather was fascinated with the mental image he placed in her mind.

"I like Wolf's Road better," she said.

"Yes, it's a good name," he said, and suddenly was gone, moving silently off toward his own lodge in the darkness.

For a time she remained outside the tipi, looking at the Milky Way, at the Wolf's Road, and thought again that it was a better name. And was somehow glad that the thought came to her in Comanche words, not in English.

When she went back inside, the others were already in their robes. She moved over to stand close to Sanchess and Wapiti Song where they lay, and between them saw the face of the baby, Getting the Lodgepoles. He was awake, the large eyes open and staring brightly from the round, dark face. In the dim light of the lodge fire she saw him smile at her.

IT WAS IN that time of fading winter when Chosen discovered the true nature of the little tipi behind the family camp where the young women went from time to time. On a night when some of the women were already beginning to pack travois bundles for the trip ahead, she had stomach cramps all night, and in the morning when she woke, she was horrified to find her robes bloody and her smock as well. Until she found the source of the bleeding, she thought some small vicious animal had crept into the lodge during the night and bit her.

Sunshade was awake, cooking morning meat in the one iron pot they had from the Mexicans. It was suspended over the lodge fire by a pole frame and already the water was boiling and Shade was dropping in dried buffalo strips. She glanced at Chosen when she heard the quick breathing. The child was standing, holding her robes at her side, and Shade saw the traces of crimson there and on the smock. She clucked her tongue against the roof of her mouth and moved quickly, taking the robes from Chosen's hands and pushing the girl from the lodge.

"You should have told me," she whispered harshly, vehemently. "Sanchess will be very angry because you have done this in his tipi, near his weapons."

"Told you what?" Chosen asked. "I only knew now."

Shade stared at her a moment, clucked again, and roughly

led her around the wolf-head tipi and toward the small lodge that stood empty now about fifty paces into the cedars.

"Get inside," Shade said roughly.

There was already a robe bed there, and a fire hole but no fire. Chosen squatted in the cold tipi and began to cry, wondering why Sanchess would be angry with her simply because something had made all her insides start running out. Her stomach ached painfully. But soon she heard Shade returning and she wiped her tears away with the backs of her hands.

Shade was carrying live coals in a turtle-shell dish, and a stack of chips and a few sticks of mesquite wood. She quickly kindled a fire and when it was going yellow and bright, she went to the bed and shook out the robes, clucking all the while as Chosen had heard Woman Who Runs do when she was perturbed.

After another trip to the wolf-head tipi, Shade was back once more with a small parfleche of mesquite beans and a bladder of water. She placed the beans beside the fire and hung the waterbag from a lodgepole. Once again she started to leave but paused at the door flap and looked at the girl.

"You must stay here until it is past," she said. "I'll bring more food and some leather so you can make moccasins. When it's over, we'll put you in a sweat lodge with water and hot stones so you can be cleansed before you come back into Sanchess's lodge."

Chosen stared at her wide-eyed, not comprehending any of it although she understood the words. Sunshade made a little gasping sound of despair and came back and squatted before the fire.

"You don't know about this?" she asked. "Those people of yours didn't tell you?"

For a long time they sat across the fire from one another, saying nothing and hearing the new morning wind slipping up the valley and whispering against the flap at the tipi door. So Shade told her.

"It is the time that comes to all girls," she said, speaking slowly and using her hands to make signs that would help the understanding. "When it comes, a girl is no longer a girl, but a woman. It is the thing that must happen before you can have children, the thing that must happen before you marry a brave man. When it starts, it will go on until you are an old woman. It happens for each woman a little differently. It is the thing that makes you a woman, different from a man. It is good and all women do it. But when it comes, you must stay away from the men because when a woman is like this, she takes away a man's power and medicine. You must never, never touch his weapons or his horses, or else they will become useless to him, without power. You must not sleep near him. After it goes, and it will heal itself, you must be cleansed so a man's power will not be taken by its memory."

She stopped abruptly, and Chosen knew it was finished. She sat stunned, unaware even that Shade was leaving. But at the door of the tipi, Shade paused and looked back and she was laughing now.

"I'll bring some of that soft moss we use in Getting the Lodgepoles' cradle board," she said. "You will have a diaper for about five sleeps. Then, to celebrate your womanhood, we'll have a little feast, after the sweat lodge."

When Shade was gone, Chosen tried to understand what had been said. It was beyond her. It was more confusing than trying to understand The People.

And then a sudden bitterness made her cry again because she had never been told. But it lasted only for a little while, only until she recalled that although the Comanches might speak of it, among her own people the custom was that precious little conversation ever touched on such things until necessity required.

During her stay in the menstrual lodge, Wapiti Song, whose milk was gone and who had weaned the baby long since, came due and joined her, bringing Getting the Lodgepoles with her. It was better after that because the loneliness was gone.

They sewed moccasins and watched the baby crawl naked across the tipi floor, played dice games and talked of many things. After the pain left her stomach, it was not so bad. Chosen learned a number of new words, Wapiti Song teaching her patiently and with great kindness. She also learned that Wapiti Song was only seventeen summers old.

Before she left the small tipi in the cedars, the wind had become gentle and warm. From the meandering stream below them, they could hear each evening the little spring frogs making their annual song. And at dawn each morning there were mockingbirds calling from the cottonwoods.

"We will move soon," Wapiti Song said.

And the girl thought, Chosen. Who has seen eleven summers. And become a woman!

7

AT FIRST, IRON SHIRT HAD been happy. They were going to visit the Kiowas, among whom he had many friends. They were going to a country where there was more timber and water. He had never said it aloud, but he liked that country better than the dry, mostly treeless high plains. He liked the band of The People who lived there, the Kutsateka. It was the place he had taken Comes Behind as a wife, buying her from another Comanche who had bought her from a Kiowa who had captured her from the Cheyenne. She had cost him twenty horses, the largest price anyone could remember ever being paid for a wife. But Iron Shirt had always considered it a bargain, for Comes Behind pleased him greatly.

And he remembered the bluecoat white men there, on the Canadian River just five summers ago.

"We had a big meeting," he said to no one in particular on the night before the move. Woman Who Runs grunted, knowing she was about to hear a story she had heard many times before.

"They came from the man they called the Great Father, in the east. They had many guns and good horses, but very heavy and with a lot of saddle on them," he said, slowly puffing his evening cigarette. He was glad to see that Comes Behind was listening attentively, although he knew she had heard the story many times too.

"Yes, I saw them," Woman Who Runs said, tying bundles of hides together with horsehair string so they would be ready for the travois the next morning. "I was there."

Iron Shirt ignored her and went on.

"Those were fine-looking men. In their blue coats, all alike and with bright metal buttons. They had men with them who spoke for this Great Father person. These men wore black coats and white shirts and tall hats, some made of beaver skins. We made a treaty with them to allow all those new people to come in from the east. Cherokees and others I can't remember. But they were fine-looking men, those bluecoats."

"Were these the Texas white man?" Comes Behind asked, already knowing the answer.

"No, no, no," Iron Shirt said, making a face of mock horror and puffing smoke violently. Comes Behind laughed as she knew he expected. "These were not Texas white men at all. The Texas white men are not our friends. They are a separate country. There is one of them, a man named Houston, who is all right. I've never seen him, but the Panetekas have, many times. I guess he is still a good man. But those Texas white men, they never do what he says. No, the bluecoats were not Texas white men. Texas white men never do what their leaders tell them."

"It sounds like your own band," Woman Who Runs said.

Iron Shirt ignored her again. He went into a long, detailed listing of the gifts given by the bluecoat white men. And finally Woman Who Runs left the tipi, shaking her head and clucking her tongue. But Comes Behind stayed. She could tell that Iron Shirt was happy to be leaving the canyon and she wanted to do nothing to spoil it for him.

But the next day Iron Shirt was not happy at all. Sanchess had decided to go on a little raid, as he called it, and would catch up with the band later, well before time for the Kiowa sun dance. There was nothing a father could do, or a peace chief either, when a young war leader wanted to go out. What disturbed Iron Shirt most was that Sanchess said he would take only Running Wolf and the Kwahadi, Wolf's Road. And Chosen, to help with the extra horses. She had become good with horses, Sanchess said.

All of this, Sanchess had told his father after waking him in the darkness well before the sun came. Sanchess said he wanted to be out of camp before the whole band began its move, and because it was always better for a raiding party to leave when it was dark. Or maybe he had waited until the last moment so his father would have little time to protest. When the camp roused itself, going about this move lazily with a number of Kwahadis there to say goodbye, Sanchess and his little party was already gone.

"I don't like it," Iron Shirt grumbled to his oldest wife.

"Don't tell me about it," she said, dragging travois bundles over to the door flap.

"It's dangerous, taking only two men. They might run into enemies."

"They took plenty of extra horses, I suspect. They don't have to stand and fight, they can get away."

"I don't like it," he said, pulling a trade blanket around his shoulders to ward off the morning chill. "And he knew I wouldn't like it and so he told me when I was still half sleeping. He knew I would rather have him on this move with the rest of us. He knew that's what I wanted."

"We are getting to be just like those Texas white men you were talking about last night," she said sarcastically. "Nobody pays any attention to you big headmen anymore."

"Woman, I am already in a bad humor. Don't try to make it worse."

"When you have a good son, you can expect him to ride out sometimes," she said. "Now get out of here and go say goodbye to those Kwahadis wandering around the camp. I'm going to take down this lodge!"

Iron Shirt stalked out of the tipi angrily, tugging at the blanket across his shoulders and muttering to himself. He thought he heard Comes Behind giggling.

THEY RODE south at first, the rising sun on their left shoulder and the escarpment to the right after they exited the canyon mouth. They rode hard and before noon found their way up the cliffs and onto the Llano Estacado. Then directly west, the new spring wind in their faces, still with the chill of winter in it and the smell of old snow.

They had seven extra horses, and at first Chosen could not keep them closed up to the three men riding ahead.

Finally, Wolf's Road fell back with her and together they got the herd bunched and ran them in close behind Sanchess and Running Wolf. After that, all the ponies seemed to understand what was expected because each of them was a well-trained hunter or warhorse, and there was no longer any trouble.

Wolf's Road led them to a small spring in a sandstone outcrop about midday, and they rested the horses and had water and dried meat. Chosen stayed mounted on her little gelding to keep the ponies from straying as they grazed after drinking, and the men squatted beside the water and talked. So far they had not put on paint, but now, passing around a hand mirror, they streaked vermilion across their cheeks. But they used no black.

That afternoon they rode harder still, the sun in their faces, and by nightfall made a fireless camp along the Running Water Draw of the Brazos. It was cold. Each of them had only one robe thrown over his saddle to use as cover, and Chosen lay shivering on the ground for a long time.

She was beyond wondering about why she was here. She knew those three could have handled the horses without her. Perhaps even better without her. So, as had now become almost second nature, she put it out of her mind and tried to sleep. There were many coyotes out, some yammering very close by, others far off to the west.

They had said nothing to her all day. Not even Wolf's Road, when he came back to help with the horses. At the spring and now, in the darkness, they spoke in low tones together. It was only a murmur of sound in Chosen's ears. Once, just before she slept, she heard Sanchess among the ponies, speaking gently to each one in turn.

He was checking hobbles. With only three men, they would all sleep, no night guards out, and he didn't want any of the horses wandering off during the night. He tested each of the tough rawhide ropes tied around the horses' forelegs.

Sanchess was thinking that maybe they were taking a big chance, posting no night guards on the herd. Here they did not have the camp dogs to alert them to intruders, nor were there young children playing in the herd. But they had seen no sign of other riders all day, and did not expect to see any tomorrow. It was too early in the year for hunting parties to be out, unless somebody was starving, and game had been so plentiful over the past season that they didn't expect this either. So they would all sleep. They might need to be rested tomorrow.

Back with the others, Sanchess took out his tobacco pouch and they all rolled cigarettes and lit them with Wolf's Road's Mexican fire starter. They smoked a long time in silence until finally Running Wolf broke it.

"There was not much preparation for this."

"It's a small thing," Sanchess said.

"I would feel better if there had been some dancing and singing and some chance to go out alone in the dark and speak with my medicine."

"You can talk with your medicine now," Sanchess said. "This is no large thing. It's for trading, not fighting."

"You didn't say that before," Wolf's Road said.

"I say it now."

"Why did you bring that girl?" Wolf's Road asked. "Are you trying to tempt me? Are you trying to run up the price?"

"No, I will have use for her. I know a man who likes to trade in captives, especially white ones."

There was a long pause, the cigarettes making three pinpoints of deep red in the darkness as they drew on them. Sanchess knew the other two were turning over in their minds what he had said.

"Are you talking about who I think you're talking about?" Running Wolf asked.

"Maybe."

"You are going to sell that girl?" Wolf's Road asked with some annoyance in his voice. "I will pay you a good price for that girl."

"We'll see what happens," Sanchess said, and he mashed out the fire at the end of his cigarette and poured the remaining tobacco back into his pouch, feeling the opening in the dark with his fingers.

"I think I know where we're going now," Running Wolf said. "I wish there had been some singing before we left."

But Sanchess was already rolling himself in his sleeping robe. Running Wolf said nothing more, and soon Wolf's Road was in his robe too. Then Running Wolf moved away from them and away from the ponies and knelt to feel all the secret things inside his medicine bag.

MENDOZA OF Pintada was up early that day. There was much to be done. In only a short time now he would be expecting the two vaqueros who came from the south each year to make the trip with him into the Comanchería for the trading. The large two-wheeled carts were behind the adobe building, the axles greased and the palings repaired. Each of them would carry many buffalo robes, and this year perhaps there would also be fox pelts and deer. And of course the Comanche boys would surely have squirrel and rabbit skins to trade for a few glassy trinkets.

The carts always went out lightly loaded with beads and arrowheads, whiskey, pots and pans, mirrors, and thin woolen blankets, all cheaply had in the south, at El Paso del Norte. But when they returned they would be heavy with hides. At the thought of his lucrative business with these red heathen children of the plains, Mendoza's uncoordinated eyes bulged and gleamed with greed.

This year he would go directly out onto Llano Estacado and, after a time there, turn south to the Colorado, where he could expect to find a few bands. Perhaps even to the western edge of the Edwards Plateau and back by way of Comanche Springs, and if he was in luck, he would cross the trail of some war party returning from Mexico with good horses and a few captives. Of course, he would not pay much for Mexican captives because their ransom was never too good. Texas white women were best. Or girls. They sometimes brought much money, in hard gold coins from families ready to spend all their life savings to get captives back.

Mendoza knew the tribes had been taking captives for a long time, for centuries maybe, as a way of life and to increase the populations of their bands. But after they found a market for these unfortunate people, the practice had grown large. The thought that he had contributed to this traffic in human beings bothered him not at all.

He was working in what he called his countinghouse, the front room of the adobe *casa*. There was a small counter that gave the room its name, behind which he stood when the red men came in to his post for trading. Now he sat on a chair in the center of the room, a tablet and pencil in his hands, carefully inventorying the half-gallon and gallon jugs of harsh whiskey he would carry with him into Indian country. He knew how important it was to keep track of the whiskey. Those Indians would steal a man's eyeteeth while he slept if great care was not taken to account for everything at all times.

The walls of the room were windowless, and shelves ran all around except at the front, where the door led out onto the porch with the lattice pole roof. At the other end of the room was the doorway into the kitchen and bedroom, hung with long strings of beads to discourage flies from entering the place where food was prepared. And never worked. There, beyond the hanging beads, he could hear his wife pounding out the cornmeal for tortillas, and from there came the smell of cooking beans and chilis. Sometimes she worked outside, where there was a clay oven, but today was too windy so she was inside.

Mendoza of Pintada worked through the morning, the sweat running from his thin face and into the uncoordinated eyes, making him curse and call on the saints to give him comfort in his labor. He wore a pair of duck trousers held up by suspenders and his only shirt was the exposed top half of dirty flannel underwear, buttonless. Shirt and pants were splotched with sweat. Mendoza was almost totally bald now, and so there was nothing to catch the drops of water that sprang to the surface of his scalp. Each one ran down his face and dripped from his chin.

In the kitchen, Mendoza's fat wife hummed as she worked. It was a good life. The Comanches never bothered them and she understood that her husband was safe because he was a trader among them, and it made her feel comfortable, even though at times through the years there had been Apache scares.

There were all the things intelligent trading had brought.

She could hear her two goats in the pen behind the house. Their milk was rich and made good cheese. And all around the *casa* she could hear her chickens clucking and scratching in the hard ground. In the hutch set tight against the back outside wall were her rabbits. A good life indeed!

At midday she boiled three eggs for her husband and took them to him in the countinghouse, on a clay platter with chilis and a few tortillas, for she knew that when he was making preparation for travel into the Comanchería, he never paused for a noontime repast.

After that, she sat at the *casa*'s only window, sipping beer she had made herself, from a large crockery mug she had also made herself. The window faced east and she looked across the sun-bleached land, seeing the shadows change as the sun reached zenith and then began to pass on toward the west. She could see far across the rolling countryside, sage and mesquite and juniper dotting it in clumps of green. It was too early now, but soon the prickly pear would begin to flower, showing splashes of bright red and purple. About a mile distant, there was a long, gentle ridge and she watched the hawks flying above it, hunting desert mice and lizards.

But then the hawks flew away and she thought that strange. For a long time she watched, and then she saw them. A small body of horsemen crossing the rise and riding directly toward the *casa*.

When she called to alert her husband, Mendoza cursed and ran to the open doorway and peered out, squinting against the brightness of the land. He saw them, and he counted three grown men and what appeared to be a lad, with a remuda of perhaps a half-dozen horses. They seemed in no hurry and Mendoza was not apprehensive, but to be on the safe side he went behind his counter and took out the percussion musket he kept there and capped it. He carried the gun back to the door to watch again.

As they came closer, he saw they were Comanche. He saw also that they were not wearing black paint and he relaxed and carried the gun back to its place behind the counter, out of sight. By the time he returned to the door again, they were near enough for him to see that the small one was a girl and the sun cast red glints from her hair. A Texas white, he thought, and licked his lips.

When they drew rein at his hitch rail before the porch, he studied their faces. He thought he could remember seeing them before, but he was not sure. It was not unusual, for when he went among them, mostly the elders and the women did the trading with him, the young bucks like these staying well back. But there was something familiar about these faces.

Mendoza smiled broadly and greeted them in Comanche. He had learned long ago that to speak with one of these people a man had to know their language, because they were usually disdainful of learning anyone else's. He knew that was why Comanche was the trade language of the south plains, and he had made a point to learn it well over the years.

"Welcome to my lodge," he said, bowing slightly. "Come down from your ponies and I will serve food."

They said nothing and dismounted, one of them motioning to the girl to come down too. They followed Mendoza into the shadows of the countinghouse and squatted against the walls, watching him with their black, fierce eyes. The girl they placed in one corner and she sat watching Mendoza also, and Mendoza saw the color of her eyes and licked his lips again, thinking, Blue eyes and red hair, surely a Texas captive.

The woman brought tortillas and a bowl of meat in red gravy. The men passed it from one to the other, eating with their fingers, all without speaking. They gave some to the girl, and Mendoza was glad to see it because it meant she was a very important captive. He continued to speak, saying nothing of consequence but knowing they needed a little time before coming to business.

The three men looked very much alike to him. They wore their hair loose except for a small plait at the tops of their heads, falling down their backs. They were naked from the waist up, except for garish bandannas held at the neck with a joint of buffalo backbone. Their leggings and moccasins were heavily fringed and each man carried about his waist various small leather pouches and sacks for their tobacco and medicine trinkets. He found nothing handsome about them.

After the food, Mendoza gave each of them a tin cup with a few drops of whiskey. Whiskey always helped trading he had found. He rolled cigarettes for them in cornhusk wrappers and they smoked silently, their eyes now moving to take in all of the room. Mendoza could hear his wife humming in the kitchen and knew she was unafraid. But something about this made him a little uneasy in his mind.

Finally he knew who the leader was when the one in the center spoke.

"I am His-oo-Sanchess. We have come to trade. You have traded with my people for a long time. But first we need to water our horses. It's been a dry journey."

"Yes, the trough is filled. I filled it this morning for my own horses." Mendoza lifted a hand and pointed. "It is there, at the corral beside the *casa*."

They rose without speaking and moved quickly and silently from the room, leaving the girl in the corner. Mendoza looked at her a long time, smiling. Slowly he moved to her and bent down, touching her cheek with his fingers. He touched her lips as she stared up at him, expressionless but not trying to pull away.

"Who are you?" he asked softly in Spanish.

But she said nothing. After a moment he shrugged and walked away, returning to his place behind the small counter and waiting. She watched him, her eyes never leaving his face. And from time to time Mendoza smiled at her, nodding his bald head.

THE CORRAL beside the adobe building was like many in this country, made of peeled mesquite poles sunk in the hard ground and standing upright side by side. There was a stone trough mortared with mud, and they led each of the horses to it in turn. They drank themselves, dipping their faces into the water as the ponies drank.

"He looked at her like a man hungry for meat," Running Wolf said.

"The way his eyes go in different directions, I don't

know where he's looking," said Wolf's Road. "I would hate to see that girl sold to a man like him."

"We'll see," Sanchess said. "When the horses are finished drinking, bring them back to the door. We'll be leaving in a hurry."

For the first time since Sanchess had mentioned selling Chosen, Wolf's Road grinned broadly.

Inside, Sanchess walked directly to the small counter, not looking toward the corner where the girl sat. He placed his hands on the wooden top of the counter and looked along the shelves behind Mendoza, and he saw that Mendoza was smiling. He was always smiling, showing long teeth in the skull-like head with no hair.

"I have come for guns," Sanchess said.

"Ah. Guns are very valuable," Mendoza said, bobbing his head and smiling. "I'll not trade those horses you have for guns."

"I'm not talking about horses," Sanchess said, and Mendoza's eyes flicked toward the girl sitting in the corner.

"Ah. Well, that girl might be worth one gun. Is she a Mexican?"

Sanchess knew that Mendoza knew that the girl was not a Mexican, but he also knew that this was part of the dickering.

"No. She's from Texas. Far to the east of here."

"Ah! What's her name?" Mendoza asked.

"I don't know. Her father was a white man named Parry," Sanchess said, and he pronounced it Pa-ree, with the accent on the second syllable. "He lives on the Colorado River. He traded with us once, but cheated us."

Now Sanchess was looking directly into Mendoza's eyes.

"It's bad to cheat in trading. I have a reputation among your people."

"Yes. You have a reputation," Sanchess said. "Do you have guns?"

"Ah," Mendoza said, and reached under his counter and brought forth a small wooden box, well polished. It had a metal clasp and he flipped it open and raised the lid and inside was a pistol lying in a velvet lining, and a number of small accessories. "Ah, here it is. A Texas

Paterson Colt pistol. A very fine weapon. It shoots five times after each loading."

"Five times?"

"Yes. A revolving pistol. I have it from a trader in Vera Cruz. Five times."

"Will it kill a buffalo?"

"Well, if you are close enough to the buffalo when you shoot it."

"We don't hunt buffalo from far ridges," Sanchess said. "But I'd rather have one of the long guns."

"I have no long guns," Mendoza said, and was glad he had placed the musket back under the counter. He lifted the revolver from its case. "But this is a fine weapon. You see, when the hammer is cocked, the trigger comes down for firing."

"Show me how it works," Sanchess said.

He was aware that Running Wolf had come in behind him and was standing beside the girl. At the door was Wolf's Road, leaning lazily against the jamb. Both were watching closely, eyes bright in their dark faces.

Mendoza loaded the pistol, first carefully removing the cylinder and tamping powder into each chamber, then pressing down a lead ball.

"It's a .36 caliber," he said, and Sanchess had no notion of what that meant.

Mendoza replaced the cylinder in the frame of the pistol and pressed a cap onto each nipple. All of these—powder, balls, and caps—came from their own containers in the velvet-lined box. It was very impressive.

"Let me see it shoot," Sanchess said.

Mendoza hesitated, his eyes casting about the room. Their eyes were on him, unwavering, even the girl's. He shrugged.

"All right. Outside."

In the latticed shade of the porch, Mendoza aimed at one of the mesquite-post roof supports and fired all five cylinders. It made a great cloud of dense white smoke and the noise caused the horses at the railing to rear and paw the hard ground. The bullets tore jagged holes in the hard wood, and after the last shot, Sanchess went over to place his fingers on the splintered wounds.

All of them had come out to watch, except the girl, and now they followed the Mexican back into the counting-house while he waved the pistol, speaking rapidly, extolling the virtues of such a weapon. Each of the men took their stations as before, Running Wolf beside the girl, Wolf's Road at the door, Sanchess and Mendoza facing each other across the small counter. The pistol was still smoking.

"Will you take the girl for that?" Sanchess asked.

Mendoza hesitated for only a moment, then nodded, laughing.

"Show me how to make it ready to shoot again," Sanchess said.

"Ah. It's easy, you see?" Mendoza went through the whole procedure again, slowly, with Sanchess watching carefully. When he was finished, Mendoza lay the pistol in its velvet-lined box, where it gleamed viciously. "Now, my friend, you should think about trading for some of those horses if you'd like a few arrowheads and nice blankets. Or maybe red ribbons for your women."

"I'm only interested in the gun," Sanchess said, watching Mendoza closely now. "And a few of those black cigarettes."

"Black cigarettes?" Mendoza looked confused, but only for an instant. "Ah. The cigars. Yes."

"Yes," Sanchess said. "And because you gave us your hospitality and have been honest in trading all these years, I will throw in one horse along with the girl, for the gun and the black cigarettes."

Mendoza relaxed visibly now, laughing loudly. He turned to his shelves and produced a box from which he scooped out a number of crooked black cigars. Sanchess motioned with his hand quickly, and the other two Comanches moved and took a handful of cigars each, then backed away to their places. They slipped the cigars into tobacco pouches at their waists. Sanchess did the same, except for one, which he placed in his mouth. Mendoza, laughing, lit it with a sulphur match, which created a lot of smoke and made Running Wolf wrinkle his nose at the smell.

"And now for me, I will throw in a little whiskey," Mendoza shouted, and he brought a half-gallon jug from the stack at the rear of the room and banged it on the counter.

"Good! Now you will smoke with me," Sanchess said, and Mendoza nodded emphatically, reaching for his box of cigars once more. But Sanchess raised his hand. "No. Smoke mine. When I was a small boy, you offered me one of yours, do you remember? Now I offer you one of mine."

Mendoza stopped smiling. His mouth gaped open and the sweat ran along his cheeks in shiny little streams. He stared intently into the face of Sanchess, first one eye and then the other focusing on features gone suddenly harsh and hard.

"I do not remember—"

Sanchess, with a quick movement of his hand, thrust his lighted cigar between Mendoza's teeth and it hung there, the smoke curling upward to the low ceiling, where it spread in a blue veil.

"And a drink of my whiskey, as you gave me a drink of yours that day," Sanchess said. "Do you remember now your hospitality?"

Sanchess's right hand lay lightly over the revolver in its velvet-lined box, and with his left he worked the cork from the jug. He lifted the jug and splashed some of the whiskey over Mendoza's head, and it ran down his face with the sweat, darkening the underwear around his neck. Mendoza gasped and stepped away, his back against the shelves along the wall. The cigar still hung loosely from his lips, and his eyes bulged.

"It was only a small joke—"

Sanchess lifted the pistol, cocking it with his thumb as he had seen Mendoza do, and shot Mendoza just below the breastbone. Mendoza jerked violently and fell forward, his head striking the rear edge of the counter. Sanchess cocked the pistol again, turned toward the door where the beads hung, waited for only an instant, and when the woman appeared with a meat cleaver in her hand, he shot her. She took one more step in the direction of her husband, who lay crumpled behind his little counter, and Sanchess shot her a second time. She fell on her face and gave a great sigh and lay still.

Sanchess carefully replaced the pistol in its velvet bed and closed the box lid and latched it. He replaced the cork in the whiskey jug.

"I'll take this whiskey of Mendoza's to my father," he said. "My father sometimes enjoys the white man's whiskey."

They moved quickly through the place, taking what they wanted, and the girl sat in the corner as though in a trance, her eyes glassy and her chest heaving with trembling breaths. They took a few blankets and some packets of tin arrowheads and some red cloth for making bandannas and the percussion musket with powder and balls and caps. They went into the kitchen and ate, scooping beans and meat from the pot with their hands, cracking eggs and drinking them raw. They took a number of tortillas to eat on the way back to The People. When they brought food to the girl, she tried but could not eat it.

Mendoza's blood was running from behind his little counter in a dark pool and they moved back and forth through it, making soft splashing sounds and leaving their moccasin prints across the floor, red and shining.

8

IT WASN'T SUCH A GOOD SUMmer as Iron Shirt had thought it would be. Sanchess came back well before the Kiowa sun dance and in time for the first hunts of the season. When he caught up with the band, they were encamped on the Cimarron in the prairie grass regions just west of where the blackjack and post oak of the Crossed Timbers began, close to the Glass Hills, knolls that sparkled in the sun because of the gypsum deposits there.

Although the small party came in with two guns, a number of horses, and other plunder, there was no victory dance. There was no paint on the faces, even the faces of the three warriors. There was only a feeling of gloom, and soon, when everyone knew what had happened on the Pintada because Running Wolf told them, the dark mood deepened as though someone had violated a powerful medicine.

Sanchess went immediately to his lodge, sent his wives away, and sat smoking with no one to see except Chosen, who squatted well back in the shadows behind him and said nothing, remembering the blood running slowly across Mendoza's clay floor.

Close by, Iron Shirt sat in his lodge as well, glowering into a small fire. His irritation with Sanchess seemed to seep out and infect the whole camp. The women went about their work silently. The children stopped playing.

"I don't like it," Iron Shirt said to his wives. "Killing that Mexican was bad. We've been trading with him for many seasons."

"There are plenty more Mexicans to trade with," Woman

Who Runs said. "Besides, our son had to have his revenge one day."

"Revenge for what?"

"For that time Mendoza insulted him, and he only a child, pouring whiskey on him. And for the whiskey Mendoza gave you all the time, to make you crazy. Every time Mendoza came among us, I could see our son's hatred growing."

"You had a little of that whiskey too, if I recall rightly."

"It didn't make me crazy as it did you."

"The dreams from it were good!"

"The dreams were from white man's whiskey. They were white man's dreams!"

Iron Shirt thought for a minute that this woman should be switched for her insolence. It had been a long time since he'd had to switch her, back in the young days when she was beautiful and all the warriors were always trying to get her to go on a war party with them. Not that she'd ever gone. But sometimes she'd needed a little switching to tame her high spirits. Maybe she needed a little now, some willow branches laid strongly across her old butt. But then again, maybe not. What she said was mostly true. In fact it was all true. Maybe she needed switching for being right all the time!

"Bring me my tobacco," he snorted.

And when she brought it he would not allow her to roll his cigarette, but rolled it himself in a wrapper he liked best, dried post-oak leaf. But she was not rebuffed. She continued to gouge at him with her sharp tongue.

"What would you have done, old man?" she asked. "If you hated a man as Sanchess hated Mendoza, and you still with hot blood?"

"Well, that depends," he said, puffing. "A man has to do what he has to do, I suppose. At least Sanchess didn't violate our hospitality by killing Mendoza when he came onto our ground."

"You've got all these people of yours unhappy with your cloudy face," she said. "Your son deserves your smile, now that he's back safe. So go out there and smile and let them all see."

Iron Shirt grumbled some more but eventually did as she

suggested. And the women began once more to talk and the children began to chase the dogs and laugh, and Finds Something came out of his tipi and lay on his back and sang one of his medicine songs.

But it was an unhappy time for Iron Shirt. Even here, where he could stand by his lodge and watch the children playing in the Cimarron, which ran very wide but only hock-deep to a pony, most of the water flowing downstream in the sand below the riverbottom. Even here, where there was more grass than sand and where he could see the beginnings of the Crossed Timbers, the oaks standing in solid rows along the stream lines and marching up the rises to the ridges in dark green formations. Even now, with so many hawks out hunting, a good sign.

There was the business of the distribution of Mendoza's plunder.

Sanchess kept the revolving pistol and all the horses, save one pony each for the two men who had been with him on the Pintada. Iron Shirt didn't like it, Sanchess keeping all those horses for himself. Horses were stolen to be given away, to show a man's generosity.

The musket Sanchess gave to Goes Ahead, and everything else to Running Wolf to give away as he saw fit. And Running Wolf gave it all. Arrowheads to the hunters, beads to the young women, hand mirrors to the war chiefs like Gizzard. He gave two blankets to old Spider, the widow whose husband and sons had all been killed or had died, and who refused to die herself and had to be cared for by the band. They would not leave her to die on the prairie, they would not throw her away. Some had suggested it, but Finds Something and Iron Shirt had always spoken eloquently against it. They and only they had any notion of the kind of power the old woman had acquired since her menopause many seasons ago, a power not to be tampered with. They never spoke of it to anyone, not even to each other, but they knew an old woman's medicine, once she had it, could bring terrible things down on The People if she was not happy and well fed and warm in winter.

So at least that part of it was good, making a large present to Spider. But even that was a mixed blessing, for the gift had come from Running Wolf's hand and therefore Sanchess could take no credit for it.

Maybe the old gnome would frighten Chosen even more because of that, more than she had already, just walking past. Iron Shirt had seen it, the girl avoiding the old woman with fear in her eyes as Spider hobbled through the camp, using one of her lost sons' blood lances for a walking stick, muttering incantations to herself, showing her old, worn-down teeth.

Then there was the business of Wolf's Road.

He was becoming a large worry in Iron Shirt's mind. The tipi of Wolf's Road was prepared and maintained by Running Wolf's wife Grasshopper, because Wolf's Road had no woman of his own. But there was more to it than that.

Running Wolf and Wolf's Road had begun to call each other brother. Not unusual among close friends. And of course, Running Wolf was sharing his wife with Wolf's Road as all brothers shared their wives, sending Grasshopper to Wolf's Road's tipi with considerable frequency.

"It's a thing brothers do," Woman Who Runs said, as though he needed such a thing explained to him. "You shared me with Goes Ahead."

"But not with Stinking Bottom," Iron Shirt said, avoiding the issue. "And he never sent any of his wives to us."

Woman Who Runs laughed. "Stinking Bottom's wives are all crazy. He never shares them with anybody. Besides, they are too young for you two old men."

"What bothers me is Sanchess," Iron Shirt said, ignoring her insult. "He is as close to this Kwahadi as Running Wolf is. What if they begin to call each other brother? And share wives?"

"You're a wicked old man," she said, seriously now. "They would never do such a thing. The young men may be wild and unpredictable, as you once were, but they would never be brothers because Sanchess would never offer Shade. She is Wolf's Road's sister, did you forget? And Wolf's Road would never take her and Shade wouldn't go. If that happened, they know you'd have to kill somebody."

Iron Shirt thought about it. He knew that a sister-brother

relationship was a strong taboo among The People. That was what worried him.

"I remember my father telling of a time when a brother and sister copulated and they killed the woman and nobody would talk to the man," Iron Shirt said. "He had to live on the edge of the camp and finally, because nobody would have anything to do with him, he left and was never seen again."

"He probably went to live with the Something Together band," she said, and laughed. "They do that all the time."

"You are full of gossip, old woman."

"Gossip is good because a lot of it is true. And I know that story because I heard your father tell it. And even if Sanchess has not heard it from your father's lips, he knows its meaning. He is too smart to do such a thing as call the Kwahadi his brother."

But despite her assurances, it troubled him. And so did the cedar flute.

Only two nights after Sanchess returned from the Pintada, Iron Shirt heard it. When he went outside the lodge he saw Wolf's Road sitting beside a small fire of chips near the wolf-head tipi, playing. The sound of the soft, mellow notes made the hackles rise along the back of Iron Shirt's neck.

"He's playing love music to that child Chosen," Iron Shirt said to his first wife. "I don't like it."

"Once you were the best cedar flute player in the tribe," she said, her words tender with the memory of it. "And my father was very proud when you played outside his lodge."

"Your father was proud when I gave five horses for you. That's when he was proud."

"It's a nice sound in the night."

"That girl is too young to have a grown man like the Kwahadi playing outside her tipi."

"She has become a woman."

"Well, maybe so. And I expected this to come. But not so soon. Maybe in a few more seasons. I don't like it."

"Come to bed, old man," she said gently. "And I'll rub your battle scars."

From her bed robes, Iron Shirt heard Comes Behind giggle. A conspiracy of wives to make light of me, he thought.

"I need a young woman to rub my wounds tonight," he said truculently, hoping to make Woman Who Runs jealous. But she only laughed again, more gently still.

"Come to my bed, old man, and I'll make you like a stallion."

He could hear Comes Behind trying to muffle her laughter.

"You're a shameless old woman," Iron Shirt said with small conviction. "Shameless as a mare in rut. And I don't need a shameless old woman to make me like a stallion."

But after he finished his cigarette and returned the unburned tobacco to the pouch, he rose and moved to the bed of his first wife and there, before too long, was like a stallion. And he thought, Tomorrow I'll have to cut some good, strong switches, just in case.

AND IN THE wolf-head tipi only a short distance away, Chosen lay awake, still hearing the sounds of the cedar flute in her mind although the playing had ceased a long time ago. She knew what it meant. Since the first night when Wolf's Road had come with the flute, Shade had been looking at her with a small smile on her face, a small light in her eyes. So Chosen knew. And it made her heart thump inside her ribs just from the thought of it.

IN THE dim memory of her early childhood, there had been a trip to San Antonio de Bexar at fiesta time. It had been a kaleidoscope of color and sound and laughing faces, of eating and drinking and dancing. The Kiowa sun dance brought back that memory with a startling clarity.

They found the Kiowas as expected, along the Washita River in what the bluecoat white man now called the Chickasaw Nation. The camp was in a bend of the river where a smaller stream flowed in, and when The People arrived the Kiowas were already preparing for what they would call their Peninsula Sun Dance. They called each one by a specific name, Iron Shirt explained to Chosen, and then painted it on their calendars. This was the pictographic representation of their history, sun dance by sun dance, done on buffalo hide.

"It's a beautiful thing," Iron Shirt said. "But The People have never had the patience for it."

All the Kiowa bands were there, with their lodges set just so in a large circular pattern, each group having its own place in the arrangement.

"There are so many of them," Chosen said.

"Yes, it appears so," Iron Shirt said, smiling. "We seem small beside them now. But that is their whole tribe. Never in memory have all the bands of The People come together at one time. The Kiowas do it every year."

"Why don't we do it?" Chosen asked, and hearing her say "we" as she did, Iron Shirt smiled broadly.

"Because our bands are spread over much territory. Some of us are almost strangers to one another."

It was the great holiday of the year for the Kiowas, the summer sun dance. A special time. The elders sat in front of their tipis and received visitors, and the old women gathered along the river to gossip and wade in the cool water. The young men and women were dressed in their best clothing and they paraded through the camp, flirting. Dogs copulated or fought between the lodges, and the children ran like flights of sparrows everywhere, chirping.

The pony herd stretched for a great distance along the stream and many of the ponies were painted or had feathers in their manes and tails. The smoke of the fires rose like blue-gray tree trunks into the upper air where the breezes caught it and spread it in a thin veil across the valley. There was the rich smell of roasting buffalo tongues. And there was gambling everywhere. In the afternoons there was horse racing with heavy bets of robes and blankets, and sometimes confident racers even wagered their wives.

Young warriors led their best ponies across the camp circle, well groomed and shining and with battle trophies hanging from the saddles. Young mothers walked proudly with cradle boards, allowing the bright sun to shine on the tiny brown faces of their babies.

At sundown the drums began. And the singing. There were dances for everyone, even the children and old women, and sometimes it lasted almost all night.

There were white captives in the Kiowa camp. Those who had been with the band for some time and survived were indistinguishable from the real Kiowas because they had browned in the sun and wore the same kinds of clothes. Some of these were wives to chiefs; some were warriors in their own right, having taken the Kiowa road; and some had been adopted by Kiowa families.

But some of the captives were still slaves and did the heavy work of the camp, carrying water and firewood. They were hardly to be seen at all because they had learned to stay out of the way, to make themselves unobtrusive.

Iron Shirt located the Comanche campsite across the Washita from the Kiowa village because he said that although the Kiowas were good friends and true and he loved them very much, he always liked some space between his own people and anybody else, even friends.

A few of the Kiowa warriors rode over and greeted them, but this was not official. It was done more from curiosity than anything else, and everybody understood that. The official part would come later, after the Comanche women had the travois unpacked and were putting up the lodgepoles.

Then a delegation of Kiowa elders, led by Dohasan, rode across the river to welcome Iron Shirt and his people, and Iron Shirt met them wearing his Spanish mail and antelope headdress. He looked very grand, waiting peacefully on foot, because everyone knew that a Comanche was warlike only when he had his best pony beneath him. His two young bodyguards, Stonefoot and Otter Tongue, were beside him, their faces painted vermilion. The People never made a big thing of bodyguards for their chiefs unless they were trying to impress someone like the Kiowas, who set great store by bodyguards.

Immediately behind Iron Shirt were the rest of the Comanche headmen, wearing their best, with faces painted for celebration. And behind them were the war leaders like

Sanchess and Gizzard, mounted, because war chiefs were always mounted when they met anyone, even friends.

Dohasan was a large man, well made and handsome in face and body. And graceful, slipping down easily from his pony and walking to Iron Shirt. They clasped one another by the arms, Dohasan speaking in Comanche as well as any Comanche could. He invited Iron Shirt's people to the celebration of the sun dance, and Iron Shirt turned to Otter Tongue and instructed him to go through the Comanche camp and spread the news of the invitation. Now it was official!

After that, Iron Shirt's band completed their campsite and then the serious visiting began. The river here was shallow and there was a constant flow of people back and forth across it. There was the sound of talk and laughter, and terrible dogfights broke out when some of the Comanche mongrels went to inspect the Kiowa camp.

Chosen watched it all from her place beside the wolf-head tipi or from the Comanche bank of the Washita.

"You don't cross that river," Sanchess had said sternly, and Wapiti Song and Shade looked at one another and giggled when he said it. Later, Shade explained to the girl.

"Those Kiowas," she said, laughing. "During their sun dance time they are very promiscuous. You'd end up in some warrior's bed robes."

It did not embarrass Chosen, for by now she had come to recognize and accept The People's way of speaking forthrightly about such things. In fact it was somehow complimentary, even a little thrilling. But the edict disappointed her as well, because she could not cross to the Kiowa camp and see them close up.

But she saw them just the same, at her own place in the Comanche camp, for many of the Kiowas came. The women did not impress her much. But some of the men were exceedingly beautiful, with women's faces almost, finely featured. They were more slender than the Comanches, and usually taller, and their noses were delicate and their lips well sculpted. They wore many tiny braids, some falling across the dark eyes that seemed to seek her out, looking for a long time at her red-glinting hair. And that was thrilling too!

When they spoke, the harshness of the sounds issuing from those fine lips astonished her. Like rattling stones in a tin bucket. She knew languages well, yet when the Kiowas spoke she could find nothing in it that was structured like any other tongue she had ever known. It was like the sounds issuing from some distant dream, completely incomprehensible.

On the first night, after Wolf's Road had played his evening recital on the cedar flute and then departed for the dancing across the river, Morning Thunder came. He lay outside the wolf-head tipi, whispering to her of the joy to be found playing in the pony herd, inviting her to crawl under the hide wall and join him. She lay silent until finally he went away. It was funny, Morning Thunder whispering as though she were heavily guarded, yet she was alone in the tipi. Sanchess and his wives were in the Kiowa camp, watching the dances.

Morning Thunder was a strange boy, she thought, so aggressive in his manner with her. She had noted that most Comanche boys became shy and bashful at that age when the girls came around. In fact she had also noted that usually it was the girl who made the advances. She knew that her two friends, Cactus Wren and Yam Eater, not much older than she, had already been in the night's dark bushes with various boys whom they had whispered out of their parents' lodges.

These two girls had come to Chosen only after a long inspection last winter in Palo Duro. They had met at the stream, and at first they had glared at Chosen as though she might be an insect. But this had changed and after a while they spoke to her and then began to help her fetch her water, for both were larger and stronger than she. Then there were visits to the wolf-head tipi, the three girls sitting in the sun, talking and giggling as they sewed moccasins.

Cactus Wren's father was a fierce warrior, Saddle Cloth, a man close to Iron Shirt's bodyguards and their teacher in such things. Surely he knew of the girl's dallying in the night, yet so far as anyone knew he had never scolded her. Yam Eater's father was Red Moccasin, one of the lesser elders of the tribe, who had taken but one wife all his life.

The People said that after his wife was killed in a high plains tornado, Red Moccasin had been dominated in his own tipi by the girl, even though at that time she had only ten summers. Now she had many more than that, and everyone said she would make someone a terrible wife because she could twist any man around her toes and fingers as she willed. And Chosen had seen how she used her bold eyes on the young men, embarrassing them with her forwardness.

Lying in the dark, thinking on these things, Chosen could hear the drums and the singing from across the river. The high chants and the low moans and the throbbing. All of it seeming to come with such strength that the hide wall of the tipi pulsated like a giant bellows.

Yet there was a gentle quality to it, the sharp edges of the sounds softened by distance. There was a warmth about it, about the voices and the drums, and she recalled the first time she had heard it, or something like it, seasons ago. Now there was no terror. Now it seemed only another part of the natural night that made sleep easy, as clean as the river, as clear as the dome of stars, as living as Earth Mother beneath her. And so she slept, with the music in her ears. An untroubled sleep.

THE FIRST three days were mostly preliminary. It was the having-fun time before the serious ceremonies began. The People took part in the dancing and horse racing. Wolf's Road won two mares, and Bear in the Willows lost a fine elkskin jacket that his wife, Owl Calling, had spent the whole winter curing. The women played shinny, and there was much feasting on tongue and buffalo-hump steaks. The Kiowas had conducted one of their great hunts only the week before, so there was meat for all, even the dogs. There were dice games and foot races, but the Comanches only watched these, preferring to be on horseback if speed was required. And always the feasting. Wild cherry mush and baked sego lilies and walnuts, and the harsh little prairie onions that left their taste for hours afterwards.

Each day Sanchess brought Chosen meat or fruit or nuts

from the Kiowa camp as she sat beside the wolf-head tipi or alongside the river, watching all that was happening.

"Don't cross that river," he said again.

And Yam Eater on the third day came back giggling and telling a tall tale of how a big Kiowa warrior had taken her to his tipi, and she provided all the details, making Chosen blush because this was frank language, even for a Comanche.

But then the sacred part began and The People stayed clear of it, watching from afar. This was a Kiowa thing, and although they were welcome to watch, they were not expected to take part. It wasn't their medicine.

Cactus Wren and Yam Eater had seen a sun dance before and they explained to Chosen what was happening, the three of them sitting on a high point of the riverbank, looking across the water. Sometimes Shade came, as though she were keeping an eye on Chosen, but usually she stayed only a little while. And sometimes Wolf's Road hung about, digging his toes into the clay bank and cutting his eyes toward them, and Yam Eater flirted with him brazenly. But when he was near and Shade came, he quickly moved away, wanting no one to see any sign of affection between him and his sister, and seeing this, Shade would smile and feel sorry for him because of his frustration.

"They've killed a bull buffalo," Cactus Wren was saying. "They'll bring the head and put it on the sun dance pole."

They watched the ritual of raising the pole and then placing on it the buffalo head, facing east, and other things like hawk and eagle feathers, then the little doll-god Tai-me, representing their most precious medicine. And then other things. The medicine men moved in exact patterns, ordering it all in proper sequence, their bodies painted red and yellow.

Around the central pole the Kiowas constructed the sun dance lodge. The rafters radiated out like the spokes of a giant wheel to uprights set in the ground. Brush of cedar was placed on the roof, and when it was done it looked like a great circular tent with the sides rolled up.

The young men who were to do the dancing moved into the lodge, painted in many ways, walking just so after entering from the east, moving in a circle to take their places. Elders and medicine men sat around the edges of the lodge, their faces bright with paint, their hands shaking gourd or buffalo-scrotum rattles. Some were blowing fierce little notes on eagle-bone whistles. From across the river, Chosen could see and hear it all. Most especially she could hear the piercing calls of the whistles.

"One of them is the head medicine man," Yam Eater said. "He tells all the others what to do or it doesn't work."

They watched the young dancers circling the central pole, looking toward the opening at the apex of the roof. They were singing now, the high, vibrant tones moving like the silver ripples in the water of the river where the sun touched them.

"They dance like that for four days and four nights," Cactus Wren said. "Looking for their power."

"It's a strange way to look for medicine," Yam Eater said, and she laughed a little nervously because it wasn't always safe to criticize the ways a man came to his power. "Finding your medicine with a bunch of people close around. That's a strange way."

Once the initial rituals were completed, but the young men still dancing, the whole thing became a little boring for the Comanches, so they moved back into their camp and built some brush arbors where the babies could play in the shade and the women could have their stick and dice games and the men could eat and sleep. Bear in the Willows had found a honey tree and they all ate a little on slices of pemmican. There were pecans too, from a grove they had found on their ride from the Glass Hills. There were even a few persimmons, but they were green and hard. Yam Eater persuaded Morning Thunder to eat one, and it made tears come to his eyes with its puckering bitterness. But he grinned at Chosen, his eyes watering, and ate all of it.

From time to time they would walk back to the river and look across. The young dancers continued around the pole, staring upward, blinded by Sun Father, and singing.

"It's a strange custom," Iron Shirt said to Chosen as the two of them stood above the Washita, watching. "But every people have to find their power in their own way."

"I like to watch it, Father," she said, and he blinked

rapidly, still with his eyes focused on the sun dance across the river. She had never called him father before.

And in his bed that night, when Woman Who Runs came to rub his back with melted bee's wax and crushed cedar leaves, he told her.

"That Chosen is all right," he said. "She has come to mean much to me."

"Yes, old man, she is like a daughter."

By the fourth day, some of the dancers had fallen and lay as though dead, in deep trances. This aroused some interest among The People, but not much. The best part for them was already past. Even now, the medicine priests continued their chants, loud and compelling.

"I think they call those men owl doctors," Shade said. "It's hard to tell what Kiowas are saying sometimes."

"I remember when we found the bones of a great cannibal owl," Woman Who Runs said. And she shivered. She went on to describe the fossilized bones of a mammoth, although she did not call them that. She held her hands far out to her sides. "They were this long and very hard. I was only a girl then. But I knew from my grandmother the story of the great cannibal owl who comes and eats people in the night. It was the only time I ever saw its bones. It was very frightening and we never camped in that place again."

It was on the fourth day that the Chickasaws came. There were only two of them and they were given all possible hospitality because they had come without weapons in their hands. Chosen stared at them, fascinated. They were small men, very dark and finely boned, and they wore turbans with blue jay feathers down the back. In their ears were highly polished mussel shells, many of them, more even than Running Wolf wore in his ears. They rode big, heavy horses with white man's saddles, high-horned and with iron stirrups.

They stayed only long enough to eat a few portions of buffalo tongue, and then rode away, never having gone across the river to the Kiowa camp. Even though the bluecoat white man said this was their country, they seemed uncomfortable in it. Or maybe it was Wolf's Road who sent them away, trying to get them to race one of their big horses against his best pony. When they pretended not to understand, Wolf's Road became very arrogant and insulted them with his bad manners. So they left quickly.

"I don't like it," Iron Shirt grumbled. "Acting like a barbarian with those men. They were nice men."

"A young warrior has to rub against somebody all the time to show he's a man," Woman Who Runs said. "It keeps his blood hot."

"I wanted those men to stay. I wanted to talk with them about the bluecoat white man. My blood is hot enough without being rude."

THERE ALONG the Washita, as she lay in her night robes and listened to the drums and the singing from across the river, it came to Chosen that the sun dance of the Kiowas was more than a social gathering. It was religious, a major part of their spiritual life, and she wondered for the first time why The People had no such organized activity of their own.

She knew a great deal about religion, having been bred and reared in a Welsh community where her own father was leader and pastor. Now it came to her with something of a shock that of all the things she still most vividly remembered—perhaps even missed—of her old life was the ordered, recurring, repeated dogma. And pondering further, she knew now that among The People there was no such thing!

Maybe this was the strangest aspect of her new life, for in all her previous experience she had seen the church as a part of life, not only among her own people, but with everyone in the white world. Especially among the Mexicans she had known at Madoc's Fort. But here there was nothing of the sort.

Sometimes at Madoc's Fort she had heard the men talking about tribal religions, and in each instance there seemed to be an effort made to place this foreign belief in the framework of their own. A kind of arrogance that supposed all people must surely see the light as it was pronounced in the white man's Bible.

But in the camp on the Washita she began to realize the

frailty of such reasoning. The People's spiritual life was distinct and separate from anything she had ever known, at such a distance from the teaching she had taken at the feet of her father as to be at first incomprehensible. But now it was coming slowly to view, like figures advancing from a dense fog.

She had supposed that Earth Mother, Sun Father, and Moon Mother were like the Trinity of her father's sermons. But now she knew that wasn't so. Now she knew she had been trying all along to force The People's beliefs into a familiar mold. She wasn't even sure that The People had a spiritual Supreme Being, a single all-powerful deity. But she had seen—or at least she supposed she had seen—that the great gods of the Comanches were considered by them to be distant and indifferent. They never prayed to them. She had often watched as the men offered their pipes to the sun and to the four directions of Earth Mother, but their serious prayers were directed to lesser, more secret forces.

No, they sought help from personal gods, spirits closer to the everyday life of camp and hunt and war and journey routes. Each man and woman of this band selected his or her own gods, who were most effective for them alone. Individually, she thought. Their church is a single person raising a single voice. Not a community of supplicants.

Not supplicants, either. They did not pray for forgiveness of sins. They simply asked for help in surviving, and if their days were marked with success, their gods were happy with them. If not? Well, maybe look for other gods.

There was a deep intensity in their association with the spirits that guided their lives. There was nothing they did that was not touched by those spirits, even dominated by them. These were a people of many priests, yet none. For each was his own. Each of them dealt from day to day with the invisible shades necessary to make things work.

And so they sought, alone, benevolent gods in the woods and crags and most especially among the animals they knew so well and with whom they shared Earth Mother. No central God who ordered all things. No parsons, no sacraments, no church as she had come to know it in her previous life.

An astonishing thought to one brought up on Calvin and Wesley: the only church is carried about within the soul of every person, and there only.

Yet there was one shared belief. The People knew there was an afterlife. To them it was not an article of faith, but a fact. It was a place just like Earth Mother, except that the weather was always good and the game plentiful. So far as she could learn from Shade's stories and Woman Who Runs' telling of departed ancestors, everyone went there. The evil with the good. Because to The People, death was the great equalizer and when it came, everyone had a new beginning.

Of course, she knew from listening to Sanchess and the other men that sometimes one did not gain entry to the place beyond the sun. It was not a matter of how one lived, but how one died. If a man passed in the night, they said, his spirit might be unable to find the road and would therefore wander forever in the darkness. Or if one was strangled, the spirit could not escape the body. Or if one was scalped or badly mutilated, his soul was condemned to live out eternity in this same land, roaming about the distant hills and woodlands in the moonlight, moaning.

And so she had come to know why warriors risked their own lives to save a fallen man from the enemy's scalping knife. Not an act of bravado, but almost a religious ceremony. Like a baptism to ensure heaven.

All of this was a way of looking at life and death that had come out of Central Asia many centuries ago, and although she knew nothing of this, the more she learned of The People's spiritual life, the more she had the impression of a soft wind blowing from some far place, vast and distant, beyond the roots of her own Christianity. Primordial it was, and increasingly it played its exotic and mystical influence on her thinking. Until now, beside the Washita, listening to the drums and the singing, she began to have some dim recognition of its meaning.

And the next morning, as Shade was preparing the first meat of the day, Chosen asked her.

"Where did The People begin?"

Shade looked at her for a long moment before she spoke.

"Many seasons ago, in the mountains."

"But how did we begin?" Chosen asked, not even aware that she had said *we*. "How did we get here?"

"What difference does it make?" Shade said impatiently. "We're here. That's all that matters!"

And so she came to know, too, that The People were not concerned with beginnings, but only with *now*.

THE KIOWA dancing was finished. They broke camp quickly, each band going its own way for the rest of the summer hunt. Iron Shirt and his band went with Dohasan's group, traveling up the Washita and then across the Canadian to the Cimarron, past the Glass Hills and still northward, fording the Salt Fork of the Arkansas and on again to Timbered Hill River, as the Kiowas called it. The Comanches called it Medicine Creek because there had been so many Kiowa sun dances held along its course over the seasons.

There, the plains were rolling and lush with deep grass, so green it was almost blue. To the west of their hunting camp was the lift of gypsum hills, and when Chosen saw the glint of the sun on the thin layers of crystal mineral, there was a flashing moment of recall as she remembered the glass her Da had hauled in from Houston one summer for windows in the house at Madoc's Fort. It made a sudden knot come into her throat, but then she was busy with the other women, putting up the camp, so the memory and the knot went away.

Yet throughout the rest of that summer as the hunters went out each day with the Kiowas, she would look across the valley and, seeing the glinting hills, think of those windows. And she found it difficult now to see the features of her own Da's face in her mind. Only the gray hair was always there. It made her melancholy for a while each day, but any anguish had long ago washed itself away, even though she had come to realize that the white hair hanging on Sanchess's blood lance was her father's!

THEY HAD finished the last of the summer hunts and were

moving south toward winter campsites in the Wichita Mountains when the bad news came. Iron Shirt was visiting one night in Dohasan's lodge, and already the wind had turned sharp and there was a sudden, chilling despair in the quivering call of the coyotes. And each day for a week now the sun was listless in a steel blue sky, shining without heat. High above were the thin clouds, heavy with ice crystals, and at night the stars were sharp-pointed with cold.

It was the worst kind of bad news. Three women and a child in one of the Kiowa bands traveling close behind them had come down with the white man's spotted sickness.

Iron Shirt was as polite as he could be under the circumstances, but he left in a hurry, riding quickly with his two bodyguards to his own camp. And even though it was late at night, he roused the elders, sending Stonefoot and Otter Tongue to cry them from their sleep. There was considerable grumbling until they heard about the spotted sickness, and then they all agreed that Iron Shirt had done the right thing, calling this council of headmen.

They were gone before the dawn came, lodges, dogs, pony herd, and all, leaving an empty prairie where the campsite had been. There was grumbling now among the women, but Iron Shirt didn't care so long as they moved fast. He knew about the festering sickness of the white man and how it seemed to leap from one person to the next, sweeping through whole tribes and leaving the children lying with great sores and hot as a stone left overnight in a large fire. He knew that Finds Something, with all his medicine, could do nothing about it. He knew of the Mandans, far to the north, whose whole tribe had vanished with the sickness. He had heard firsthand of Kiowas suffering from it. And dim in the tribal memory of The People was the attack of the disease on the Shoshone. Spotted sickness. The white man's smallpox!

He knew of only one thing to do. Run from it as fast as their horses would carry them. Run as far as possible, as quickly as possible. And so they ran.

They fled southward, away from the sickness, pushing the ponies so hard that some grew lame and had to be killed and eaten. But they did not slow their march. They camped each night on the open prairie, not taking the time to pitch lodges. They were up before the sun and they moved all day, and sometimes into the night, before stopping. Finds Something wore out seven travois horses trying to keep up. Everyone knew that if he fell behind, he would be left.

The winds were cold, and twice they traveled through flurries of snow. The horses grew tired and quarrelsome and were hard to handle. There was not time to rub them down each day, and some took distemper and had to be killed. There was no time to make a cedar-smoke vapor tent for them. The dogs grew bony and sullen and fought constantly among themselves.

Each night, Wapiti Song held her baby close in her robes beside her, because she was afraid he would die of cold. And the mother of Otter Tongue, one of Iron Shirt's bodyguards, became so sick she would not go on, refusing to move one morning after she had the travois packed. She insisted that she be left with her favorite robe and thrown away because she was ready to make her journey beyond the sun. So they left her on a windswept little hill, sitting on her robe, and they rode away, leaving her for the wolves.

That night, Otter Tongue came to the fire of Saddle Cloth with three horses and took away Cactus Wren as his wife, for, as he explained, he had no one now to tend his tipi and his meals, and besides, he had been watching her all summer and wanted her for his woman.

It was a fast way of doing things, and Saddle Cloth would have preferred the usual way of the suitor, leaving his horses outside the tipi, letting the family then have a council to decide whether to take the ponies or not. And maybe a little cedar flute playing. But these were suddenly hard times, and one could not expect the usual things. Besides, three horses were a good price and Otter Tongue was close to Iron Shirt, and Saddle Cloth wanted no hard feelings from that quarter. So Cactus Wren was married on the trek from Kiowa country.

They didn't stop until they came to Ketchum Mountain, south of the Conchos, and there they made winter camp with a band of Panetekas. From the area of their last hunt to this place they had traveled almost five hundred miles, and that as quickly as they could move the ponies without killing all of them.

At least now there were lodges up, and good fires, and visiting with the Panetekas. It was small consolation for Iron Shirt. It had been a bad summer for him, with one irritation after another. He sat in his lodge and brooded, trying to think things through. There was a great pressure on his mind, but he could not define it. It was a stone rolling downhill and he had no way of stopping it. But some things he knew.

On their way to this place they had seen a number of buffalo, killed and skinned and the meat left to rot on the ground. All of these animals had been gunshot. At first they had no understanding of it. They had never seen such a thing before. Then Big Wolf came to it.

"It's the white man. They are killing the buffalo for their hides!"

Everyone was angry that the white man would leave good food to rot on the ground. But there had been too many things to think about as they ran to the south, and soon it was forgotten. But Iron Shirt had not forgotten, and now there was time to think about it. He knew these Texas white men were not like the Mexicans. When they started something, they seemed to keep at it forever, more and more, bigger and bigger. He wondered if that was true now. He wondered if those rotting buffalo with nothing used but the hides meant something bad was coming.

And he listened to the Panetekas grumbling about the white man moving farther and farther out into the buffalo range, west of the Brazos, north from San Antonio de Bexar. Making their sod houses and cutting up the land and putting in cattle. Shooting at everyone on sight with their long guns.

And to distress him further still, during the Moon of Greatest Cold a Wichita came into camp with news that many of the Kiowas camping north of Red River had been struck by the spotted sickness. They had died like trapped otters, the Wichita said, writhing in their beds. Dohasan's band had been one of those so afflicted, and it saddened

Iron Shirt to think of those fine people, his friends, helpless in their lodges.

What made everything worse was the lack of buffalo near this winter camp. There was not enough to eat. The boys were out every day now, trying to trap jackrabbits.

One night, with the last of winter howling outside his lodge, Iron Shirt sat for a long time at his small fire, thinking. Woman Who Runs felt the strange fear in him, when there should have been at least a little happiness because they knew Comes Behind was pregnant. But there was only the fear and she could feel it. She sat close behind him, waiting in case he had need for words spoken aloud.

"I don't like it," he said finally. He spoke quietly so that Comes Behind would not be wakened, but there was a different sound to it as well, none of the old defiance. She didn't try to banter with him now, but instead moved up close beside him, as was her privilege as his first wife and the mother of a great war chief.

"You remember those nice men we saw at the Kiowa sun dance? Those Chickasaws?" he asked. "Why are they in this country? Why did they leave their own land and come into what has been ours and the Kiowas'?"

She said nothing but made him a cigarette. Only now there were no more dried post-oak leaves for wrappers so she had to use sycamore, which was not so good. She lit the cigarette and passed it to him and he offered it to earth and sky and the four directions before he smoked, but his movements were listless, as though he were daydreaming.

"I've been thinking about that," he said. "They come into our country because the white man has come into theirs, just as the white man is coming into the Paneteka country. So they had to move on, those Chickasaws."

"It is the usual thing," she said, trying to encourage him. "People moving. The Kiowas are always talking about how they were in that place called the Black Hills once, with our friends the Crow. But then the Sioux came and drove them out."

"Yes, and why did the Sioux come? Because someone else had driven them, and someone else had driven those who drove out the Sioux. Until at the end of it, you come to the white man."

"The white man did not drive us out and we came here, or our fathers did, and drove out the Apaches."

"But from the east, all these people coming, and that is where the white man is. In the east."

She made no effort to understand it. And even Iron Shirt, coming to it slowly over time, agonizingly, and coming to it correctly, had no way to validate it, no way to know if it was really true. Yet he felt it, and it made a cold little squirming in his guts.

"And now the Panetekas say the white Texas men are using Tonkawas and Lipans to scout against them, to attack their camps and their hunting parties."

"We must stay close to the Llano Estacado," she said. "Perhaps it's safe there."

"Perhaps."

"Come to bed, old man."

"Yes. I've got to stop all this worrying. These things may or may not be true. But they trouble me, like a small cloud on the far horizon. But I think it's not so small, and each season brings it closer!"

BY SPRING, THE CAMP HAD BEgun to smell. After their long flight from the sickness and then a winter when there was not enough meat, everyone had been sullen and ill-humored and undisciplined. So the sanitation had not been very good. And the odor grew as did the sun's heat. This campsite at the base of Ketchum Mountain they would later call Stinking Place, but they would remember it for something else.

Iron Shirt's traveling council had already been held. They were going back north, across the Llano Estacado and into the country of Colorado, north of the Arkansas, where there was to be a great peace meeting. North into the high plains, where the snow mountains could be seen in the western distance. A place their forefathers had traversed long ago, but a place many of them had never seen.

A white man named Bent, who had a Cheyenne wife and ran a trading post there, had been successful in getting some of the chiefs together. So there would be Comanches and Kiowas on the one hand, Cheyennes and Arapahoes on the other, to settle their differences and work out territories. It was a chance to make old enemies friends. So long as they stayed in their place, of course.

There was a joy found in Nakoni camps only at the prospect of moving again; spirits were higher than they had been since the hunts of last summer on the Timbered Hill River. There was much laughter. Chosen and Yam Eater were constant visitors to Cactus Wren's tipi, and the three of them sat in the sun and talked and giggled as they always had, even though Cactus Wren was wife to a great warrior now and already with his child.

When Otter Tongue was near, Yam Eater flirted with him brazenly, and Cactus Wren seemed to enjoy it as much as her husband disliked it. As a bodyguard to Iron Shirt, Otter Tongue had to maintain his dignity, a thing Yam Eater seemed unable to comprehend.

Running Wolf and some of the others found a small buffalo herd not far from the campsite, and he and a number of the Panetekas and some of Iron Shirt's men went out for a small hunt. There was fresh meat for the first time in many moons, and it was good, and they were making their preparations casually, in no hurry now and knowing they were moving toward a land rich in buffalo.

With the coming of spring, Shade had given Chosen a fine smock of deerskin, decorated with elk's teeth. Shade had somehow managed to hoard those elk's teeth for a long time. Now they were on Chosen's bosom. She was the envy of the other young women and girls, and some who remembered where she came from were jealous. But Cactus Wren and Yam Eater were happy for her. They seemed to have forgotten that Chosen had ever been anything but Comanche.

This was the time that Chosen saw some of the power held by women of The People. On a clear, sunny day, Shade took Sanchess's war shield to the edge of the camp and placed it on a tripod of short poles. She slipped off the cover and preened the feathers and hair that decorated it.

By then, Chosen had come to know that a warrior's shield was a very important part of his medicine, and to see Shade cleaning that shield made a great impression on her. As Shade worked in the bright sunlight, the rays cleansing the buffalo hide and the ornaments, Sanchess sat nearby, a blanket over his head, but watching. No one else came near. When the process was completed, Shade led the way back to the wolf-head tipi, carrying the shield back in its cover now, Sanchess a few paces behind and with the blanket still over his head.

"Someday I'll carry my husband's shield," Cactus Wren said.

"You're carrying enough of his already," said Yam Eater, and they all laughed.

And during that time of preparation too, Comes Behind went to Woman Who Runs and told her of the terrible morning sickness. It was made no better by the smell of the camp. Such admission of weakness was unheard of among The People, but Woman Who Runs felt compassion for the young wife and so told her to go upwind and gather spring flowers. That meant Woman Who Runs would be doing all the work for that day, but she didn't mind. Spring made her feel strong.

Comes Behind walked out of the camp in midafternoon, happy to take some fresh air for the benefit of her unborn baby. At nightfall she was still gone. Iron Shirt seemed unaware of her absence until Woman Who Runs told him, and then he became agitated and said something about cutting some willow switches and some more about young wives who wandered out across the prairie, daydreaming when there was a lot of work to be done.

But Woman Who Runs could see his concern and she went to the wolf-head tipi and told Sanchess, and Sanchess caught up a horse and rode a wide circle around the camp. But he found nothing. All of Iron Shirt's anger was gone now.

"Get Finds Something," he said, frowning. "He'll know what to do."

The news of Comes Behind went through the camp like a cold wind and they were all reminded of the hard times of the winter and many whispered that maybe the hard times were not past. They were quiet, each family staying near its own lodge and eating its evening meal in silence. They waited for news, and for Iron Shirt to do something.

When Finds Something came he brought his most powerful medicine in a small leather bag. He made a song to it, standing in front of Iron Shirt's tipi. Then he walked around the lodge four times and built a small fire at the door flap, lay on his back, and made another song. After the song was done, he rose and walked twenty paces toward the east, lay down again, and made yet another song, then did the same for the other three directions. It took a long time, but when he was finished he pushed his way into Iron Shirt's lodge and announced that Comes Behind would find her way home before the sun came.

Iron Shirt didn't sleep all night. He paced outside his tipi, and inside, Woman Who Runs kept hot soup for him in her Mexican trade pot. But he ate none of it. When the sun rose, Comes Behind had not appeared.

Everything stopped, all the preparations for the march north. With the head peace chief's young wife missing, they were concerned about what it meant, and most especially now that she was carrying his child. The old men sat in their tipis, not coming out even after the sun was high. The children were kept near their own lodges. The women prepared food but nobody ate very much. Any dog coming near them was likely to be kicked viciously for no real reason. All the young men paced about the camp like animals on a tether, looking toward the horizon, uneasy, nervous.

Sanchess and Bear in the Willows stayed close to their father, close enough for him to call. But they said nothing. They knew it was not a time for idle talk and there was no way they could reassure him.

It was Gizzard who first saw it. He came reluctantly to the wolf-head tipi where Sanchess and Bear were squatting in the sun, watching their father pace in front of his own lodge. He came reluctantly because he thought he knew what it meant, the thing he had seen.

"I think you should look at something," Gizzard said to them. They stared at him with red-rimmed eyes. "Come with me."

Gizzard led them to the edge of the camp and pointed eastward, toward the Edwards Plateau. There, low over the horizon, was a wheeling flight of vultures, some of them sweeping down close to the ground. Sanchess counted more than the fingers of his hand and knew this was not something as small as a dead rabbit.

"Go tell our father," he said to Bear. "I'll run in some horses."

THEY FOUND her in a deep dry wash. She had been stripped

naked, raped, scalped, and her belly cut open. The child would have been a girl.

Most of the young men had ridden out, all with weapons but with no paint on their faces. Now they stood along the edge of the ravine, watching as Gizzard, Sanchess, and Bear moved down to wrap the body in a saddle blanket. Their eyes were hard but they showed no other expression, because they had seen many such things in war. Only Sanchess growled like a wolf and ground his teeth as he placed the unborn baby in the blanket beside her mother.

They carried the bundle, which seemed very small and weightless, up the steep wall of the wash and placed it gently on the ground, the men then moving back to form a circle around it. They waited for Sanchess to speak, for although Bear was the eldest, it was the war leader now who must lead. For a long time Sanchess stood above the pitiful little bundle, his eyes steady on the eastern horizon, the flat country running toward the San Saba River. Above them the black scavenger birds still circled, their dihedral wings motionless in the hot updraft of plains air.

"Pukutsi, how long ago and how many?" he said finally, his eyes still looking into the distance.

"Nighttime," Claw said, for he had done his work quickly. "They likely took her from near the campsite. None of her prints coming here. Then they brought her along with them to this place."

Everyone but Sanchess looked at the small depression in the ground near the lip of the ravine. There were few mesquite here, and on the sandy earth were black splotches of dried blood and a scattering of Comes Behind's clothing.

"Five horses," Claw said, holding up his fingers. "All iron-shod except one. Prints of three different pairs of boots. One pair of moccasins."

"What tribe, the moccasin?"

"Lipan."

There was a low growl of anger around the circle.

"The boots? Texas or Mexican?"

"Can't tell for sure. Sometimes they're all the same."

"How far ahead?"

"Maybe half a day's ride," Claw said. "They didn't camp here. Maybe they camped farther on, after they did this. There, to the east. If they did, maybe they're not so far ahead. Maybe less than half a day."

Sanchess took a long breath and, for the first time since coming from the ravine, looked into the faces of the other men. They seemed to lean forward expectantly. He lifted a hand toward Running Wolf, and Running Wolf moved to his side.

"Go back to the camp and bring up extra horses, enough for five men," Sanchess said, and his words were harsh and came like hailstones. "I'll go along their trail and you follow. Take Wolf's Road to help with the ponies."

"I'm going," Bear in the Willows said.

"No," Sanchess said, looking at his brother and then moving to him and placing a hand on his shoulder. "You need to take this wife and daughter of our father back to him. You need to be with him, his eldest son. Don't let him see unless he insists. This other job, I'll do."

Bear thought about it for a moment, his jaw muscles working, and everyone there knew he wanted to go with Sanchess. But they saw the wisdom of Sanchess in this thing and when Bear agreed, there was no disgrace in it. Everyone knew his job would be the harder of the two.

"I'll go with you," Otter Tongue said to Sanchess.

"No, you need to be near my father, too. You and Stonefoot. I will take Claw and Gizzard and Wolf's Road and Running Wolf. No more."

Already Wolf's Road and Running Wolf had detached themselves from the group and were mounting their ponies, kicking them in a headlong drive toward the campsite. Running Wolf had his blood lance out of its casing, the polished ironwood shining in the sun as he dashed away, his high voice yipping.

"For the sake of my father, make a good funeral for her and the child," Sanchess said to the others, and many of them nodded. He slipped the Paterson Colt from his belt and handed it to Bear. "You keep this for now. It's a time for our own weapons."

Claw and Gizzard moved back to their horses and squatted there and took paint from their belt pouches and began to streak their faces with black.

Without speaking, the party returning to the camp lashed

the small bundle behind the saddle of Bear in the Willows. They started back, a long double file with Bear and his burden riding alone between them. Sanchess did not look after them, but began his own preparations.

He took the cover from his lance and his shield, and the feathers and scalps fanned out in the wind. From a belt pouch he took a willow-hoop scalp and tied it to the lower lip of his pony. It was a powerful part of his medicine, the first scalp he had ever taken. From a Ute, when he had fifteen summers. The pony, almost as if he understood what it meant, rolled his eyes, snorted, and pawed the ground. Then Sanchess painted his face with black.

They moved away toward the east, Claw watching the tracks of the five horses that had gone before. They went slowly, giving the two Wolfs time to catch up with the extra horses. At about midday they came on a campsite and Claw dismounted to feel the ashes of a fire. He circled the site on foot, looking closely at the ground while Gizzard and Sanchess watched from their ponies, lances up, shields high on their left arms.

"Maybe still half a day ahead," Claw said. "They didn't sleep long. Still going east."

After that, the two Wolfs came up and they began to move fast then, changing horses often. When he saw droppings, Claw stopped to dismount and feel them with his fingers.

"Close now," he said once. And later, toward sundown and well out onto the Edwards Plateau, he said, "Very close now."

At nightfall they stopped because Claw could no longer read the trail. They rubbed down the ponies with grass and waited while Wolf's Road made a wide swing toward the east in the darkness. He was back by moonrise, a late quarter moon.

"I saw their fire," Wolf's Road said, and Sanchess grunted with satisfaction. "We can be there well before the sun comes. They're beside a small river."

"San Saba," Sanchess said. "Lead on a little way. Then we'll tether the horses."

The pale moon offered enough light for them to see the terrain and they rode quickly, Wolf's Road leading. Now and then they heard the call of a long-eared owl. In a stand of mesquite, Wolf's Road drew rein.

"Very close," he whispered. "The fire may be out by now, but I know where it was."

"Everyone, pick your best pony," Sanchess said softly.

They drew the extra horses into a small coulee and hobbled them with rawhide thongs, then rode ahead once more, very cautiously, testing the wind. Sanchess led them wide to the south of where Wolf's Road had seen the fire, so that when they moved in close the horses at the camp would not smell their stallions. Each of them had a long quirt with a rawhide loop at the end. They slipped the loops over their horses' muzzles so they could twist the quirts as they rode and shut off the whinnying they knew would come as soon as their ponies became aware of strange horses.

Topping a small rise, Wolf's Road drew in and pointed ahead into a saucerlike depression where the mesquite did not grow, near the river. The wind was laid and they could see in the moonlight silvery wisps of smoke lying in the quiet air.

With a motion of his hands, but no words, Sanchess positioned them in a line, abreast. Gizzard and Claw strung their bows and Wolf's Road slipped from his saddle pouch a large Spanish trade hatchet. They sat for a while and then moved forward slowly, walking their ponies, and the hooves made little whispering sounds in the hard sand. To the east, coyotes were calling mournfully. Soon they could see the dark forms of horses near the smoldering fire and then the cocoonlike bedrolls.

Once more they stopped, motionless, waiting, watching. One of the camp horses lifted his head and snorted, looking in their direction. Sanchess whispered his instructions.

"Move quick. But I want to see their living faces before you kill them!"

IT MIGHT have been a funeral for a great warrior instead of a young woman and her daughter. While Bear in the Willows and Otter Tongue walked with Iron Shirt through the camp, back and forth, the women prepared the body.

Iron Shirt never saw it but Bear had to tell him what had happened. Iron Shirt's face twisted in agony and tears ran down his cheeks and now he was bowed, walking like a crippled man as his son and bodyguard walked beside him. Back and forth. Back and forth.

Woman Who Runs supervised the preparations. They washed Comes Behind with warm water and rubbed her skin with buffalo fat. They dressed her in a fine deerskin robe heavy with fringes and placed about her neck many strings of glass beads and one necklace of Mexican silver. They pulled the remaining hair over the ugly wound at the top of her head, sewed her belly shut with horsehair thread. They moved the body into a sitting position, placed the baby in her lap, and wrapped it all in buffalo hide, drawing rawhide lashings tight to hold everything in place.

When it was finished they formed a procession, everyone in the band strung out behind the small spotted pony that carried the body. Many were wailing and some had already slashed their arms with knives. Woman Who Runs and Bear's wife, Owl Calling, walked beside the pony, holding the bundled body upright in the saddle. Behind the pony walked Iron Shirt, a blanket over his head, and the other elders and family members, everyone looking at the ground. Shade was there and Wapiti Song with her baby in a cradle board on her back and Chosen, who was weeping.

They moved to a deep cleft in Ketchum Mountain's base and lowered the body into it, facing east. Finds Something was singing a death song. Gently they placed large stones on the body, then smaller ones, then finally shoveled in sand with their hands. The wailing increased as they marched back to camp. Iron Shirt and his family remained and when everyone else was gone, Iron Shirt killed the pony over the grave with one slash of his knife across the throat. Woman Who Runs was the last to leave. Kneeling over the grave, she made diagonal cuts across her two arms with a skinning knife, cut a large hank of her hair and threw it on the grave, and put dirt on her face.

All day, old Spider sat in the center of the camp, wailing. Finds Something lay before his lodge door, chanting. All the women and most of the children seemed to be crying out in anguish and it filled the late day and early night with sound. It went on and on, well past moonrise. It showed the respect they had for Iron Shirt and his family.

Iron Shirt sat all night in his lodge, staring into the small fire. His elder son and his bodyguards were with him, well back in the shadows. Woman Who Runs had gone to the wolf-head tipi, where she and the other women tried to sleep but mostly lay awake in their robes. When the sun came, she went back to Iron Shirt and forced him to eat some soup. But he had little stomach for it.

All day he did not move. Or smoke or talk with anyone. Around him the camp was strangely quiet, The People going about their work silently, watchful, waiting for Sanchess to return. Many times during the day one or another of the young men went to the edge of the camp and stared toward the east, but they saw nothing.

In midafternoon, Woman came into the wolf-head tipi and said to Chosen, "Go to the old man. Don't talk. Just sit with him."

When she went into Iron Shirt's lodge, Stonefoot and Otter Tongue were both there and they glared at her. It frightened her but she went to the back of the tipi and sat there in the shadows, directly behind Iron Shirt. After a few moments the two warriors rose and left silently.

He said nothing to her but she knew he was aware of her being there. She could feel his rage, silent and impotent, and it made the tears start in her eyes. She wiped at her cheeks with her hands because she did not want him to see tears in case he turned to her. But he never turned, and after the day had worn down, Woman Who Runs came into the lodge, the slashes on her arms red and ugly. She had thrown ashes onto her head and it made her hair look gray.

"You need to eat something, old man," she said.

"Leave me alone!"

Woman lifted her hands and Chosen rose and they both left the tipi. But Stonefoot and Bear in the Willows were just outside and they went in, so the chief would never be alone with his anger and his grief.

It was well after dark when Sanchess came. His party rode straight into camp, each man going to his own woman. There was no shouting of welcome. In the wolf-head tipi,

Sanchess's wives looked at him silently and he said nothing to them. He went to Chosen's robes and woke her and led her from the tipi by the hand. In his other hand was a rough bag, of the white man's burlap.

"Come," he said, and they went to Iron Shirt's lodge, where Sanchess called out softly.

Woman Who Runs appeared at the door flap and quickly came out into the dim moonlight that was just beginning. She looked into Sanchess's face and he into hers and then she put her hands on his shoulders.

"Did you find them?" she asked.

"Yes," he said.

"Then go in. Your father waits. I'll go to your lodge until you're finished." She seemed not at all surprised that Sanchess had brought Chosen with him.

Iron Shirt was at the fire still, and when Sanchess came in he looked up, his eyes weak from lack of sleep. Chosen, knowing her place, pulled away from Sanchess's hand and went to the rear of the lodge. She sat watching as Sanchess stood for a long time before his father, the burlap bag in his hand.

"You found them." Iron Shirt stated it as a fact, not a question.

Sanchess squatted and opened the burlap bag, quickly, as though this was a thing to be finished. Onto the floor of the tipi he dumped a pile of scalps, a heaping bundle of hair. They were not cured in the Comanche way and they looked terrible. Chosen stared at them in horror. Gently, then, from his belt Sanchess took another scalp and handed it across the fire. Iron Shirt took it and stared at it for a long heartbeat.

"Yes. It's hers," Iron Shirt said. The words came with great difficulty. "I will have Finds Something put it in the grave with her. Maybe she can gain entry to the land beyond the sun now. Maybe not."

"It's the best we can do," Sanchess said.

Chosen watched as Iron Shirt placed Comes Behind's hair gently on the tipi floor beside him. Then he looked into his son's face once more.

Now Sanchess took from the scalps four others, each fresh, one with the hair very long and black. He laid them aside.

"These are for the lance of my father," he said. "The others I will burn. They are not for us to keep."

"Yes, burn them," Iron Shirt said bitterly. "I had heard of these kinds of men. But I had never believed it until now."

"Yes, Father, they were hunters of scalps."

"I have heard that certain Mexican and sometimes even a few Texas people offered the white man's hard money for scalps, but I didn't believe it until now." Iron Shirt's voice broke and he swallowed a number of times and then went on, explaining it all to himself as much as to the others.

"How can it be, to pay for such a thing? The People have always taken scalps to show battle honors. To show bravery. And of course, to scalp an enemy is to keep him from the land beyond the sun so we don't have to worry about him when we get there. But paying money for scalps? I didn't really believe it until now."

Sanchess said nothing, letting his father's grief run out through his mouth, knowing there could be some relief in that. But now Iron Shirt was silent and tears once more ran down his cheeks. When he spoke again, there was great trembling in his voice.

"A girl child for my old age. And now gone. I wouldn't have believed it until now."

"Father, I've brought you this girl child," Sanchess said. Iron Shirt made no sign that he had heard. "Father, I've brought you this girl child, the gift of a daughter to you."

Slowly now, Iron Shirt turned his head and looked at Chosen and she could see the redness of his eyes. He nodded ever so slightly and spoke in a whisper.

"Yes. She means much to me."

Sanchess rose to go, but Iron Shirt looked into his face once more and spoke with words that had the authority of a chief.

"Who were these men?"

"Three white men and a Lipan who was their scout."

"Yes!" Iron Shirt said savagely. "I've heard there are white men who go around hunting scalps for bounty, as though we were all wolves."

"Yes."

"I didn't believe it until now."

"It's true!"

"Sanchess? How did you treat them?"

Sanchess and his father looked into each other's eyes for a long moment and then Sanchess spoke slowly, shaking his head, the black paint on his face glistening in the dim firelight.

"The Lipan had to be killed quickly," he said, and added something that made Iron Shirt's eyes blaze with a deep, hot fire.

And then Sanchess was gone.

No one ever learned anything more of what had happened on the banks of the San Saba. None of the men who were there told of it. They did not sing of it in their coup and victory dances. They did not brag of it to their wives. They did not explain to anyone the details of how the four new scalps came to hang in the lodge of Iron Shirt. It was as though all of it had been a bad dream, a powerful and destructive medicine never to be mentioned. All that The People ever learned was what Sanchess had said to his father:

"The white men took a long time to die!"

THREE

The years are like the willow-hoop wheels
our children roll about our camps. Each
season flowing into the next until
it comes back to the start again.

10

THOSE WERE GOOD TIMES FOR Chosen. Good seasons and good years. They all ran together and into one another, with only an occasional harsh memory to mark them. There was a special tenderness toward her in Iron Shirt's lodge because perhaps she had replaced the unborn daughter lost near the San Saba. And it was good, too, because although she had developed a deep respect for Sanchess, he frightened her a little and being of another lodge was better. Now he was her brother and his attitude toward her became one of almost complete detachment, as though she did not exist.

And with Shade and Wapiti Song there came a subtle change as well. Now they were no longer competing with her as a prospective wife of their husband. Now she was a younger sister, to be protected and made even more Comanche than she already felt herself to be.

When she made mistakes in language, which happened less frequently now, Woman Who Runs would look at her and smile and shake her head and say, "Aw, daughter! What a stupid thing you are!" But with affection, perhaps a reflection of Iron Shirt's, perhaps her own.

Until now, Chosen had been treated kindly. At least after those first few days so long ago. But she had been an outsider nonetheless. A blue-eye. But when she moved into Iron Shirt's lodge, she became in all respects a member of that family, with the attendant privileges and responsibilities.

Wolf's Road played his cedar flute now before the tipi

of the head peace chief. Everyone laughed about it. "At least he's persistent," they said.

The flute-playing came to a climax when the band was camped along the Arkansas for the great Cheyenne peace treaty. One night Iron Shirt walked into the evening and asked Wolf's Road to stop his playing.

"Does it annoy you, Father?" Wolf's Road asked.

"It's a good sound. But I would like it better if you came back to play your little songs in a few seasons. You might have a better chance then of getting what you want."

"I want that little woman. Above all others."

"Well, you might get her," Iron Shirt said. "But it's going to take a lot of horses. Now, for a while, let me enjoy having a daughter in the lodge. So there's someone who will listen to my stories."

After that, Wolf's Road stopped playing. But he could usually be seen nearby when Chosen moved outside the camp, riding with Morning Thunder in the pony herd. And Morning Thunder was aware of it.

"That's a big hatchet he's got," Morning Thunder said, and Chosen laughed because of the double meaning but also because she enjoyed the attention.

It was on the way to the great treaty that Shade pierced Chosen's ears so she might decorate herself suitably as Iron Shirt's daughter and a prospective bride to some brave man.

"It's been too late coming," Shade said. "It should have been done a long time ago, but I couldn't waste my time on the ears of a nobody, a captive."

Shade took a number of long prickly-pear spines, heated them, and, holding Chosen's earlobes between her fingers, thrust the needle-sharp barbs through the flesh. Three in each earlobe. It hurt like fire, but Chosen managed not to cry. After the bleeding had mostly stopped, Shade replaced the spines with lengths of horsehair, knotted at one-inch intervals. The next day she pulled one of the knots through each hole, and the next day another, then another. By the time the end of the strings were reached, the job was complete, each of the openings in Chosen's ears clean, scab-free, and uninfected.

Woman Who Runs gave the girl river-mussel shells and small glass beads, all strung together with horsehair and held in place by hoof glue. After that, on special occasions, Chosen hung her ears with the little flashing objects, which rattled heavily beneath her hair, making a small jingling sound.

Woman instructed her in face paint as well, explaining that black was never worn by women except in mourning and that the bright yellows and reds could be patterned across the cheeks and lips in any way Chosen desired. She began to use ocher each day in the part of her hair, which hung loose and unbraided to her shoulders. She was past the time for little-girl plaits and not yet far enough along for an old woman's braids.

She was opening to the world, and it to her. On the Arkansas that summer she saw more lodges than she had ever thought possible to exist. The chiefs had gone ahead at first to talk and smoke and agree that raiding between the two factions would be no more. Then the bands moved up for the visiting and gift-giving. When she first saw it, she caught her breath in awe. The conical tipis seemed to stretch along the river in both directions, all the way to the sky.

But the most noticeable stir of the meeting came when the Comanches and Kiowas drove in their ponies. As the great herd came down to the river, the Cheyennes and Arapahoes on the far bank exclaimed and pointed. Their excitement continued through the next day as they were given horses, one for each of them, women and children included, and the war chiefs and headmen got as many as five each. In return they offered white man's trade blankets, guns and powder, and metal pots.

"Those Cut Fingers have never seen so many horses," Iron Shirt chuckled.

"Cut Fingers?" Chosen asked.

"Yes," he said, and held up the index finger of his left hand. "Sometimes the Cheyennes like to take a finger from a slain enemy who was brave and dry it and make a pendant of it. One of the chiefs we talked with had such a pendant necklace with nine fingers. A great warrior in his day."

Chosen noted that there were not so many dogs in the Cheyenne camps as were generally found among The People's lodges. And after they left the Arkansas and moved south to the Llano Estacado for the summer hunts, she thought there were not so many of the mongrels in the Comanche camp. Iron Shirt, in an expansive mood because of the success of the treaty, laughed about it.

"Those Cut Fingers, they eat dog all the time," he said. "I think maybe some of their young boys slipped into our camp and stole a few."

"It doesn't matter," Woman said. "We had too many anyway. We always have too many. But I don't understand anybody who would eat Coyote's cousin, Wolf's little brother."

"Every man to his own gods and his own way of doing things," Iron Shirt explained. "And those Cheyennes are all right. Look at the guns they gave us. Good gifts from a tribe we don't have to worry about anymore, coming at us from the north."

And with that, Chosen began to understand something about protecting boundaries and securing territories.

That summer Iron Shirt's happiness was boundless. There had been the great treaty, of course, but more importantly, Wasp returned. Wasp was Iron Shirt's grandson, a man now of seventeen summers, who had gone with his mother to the Paneteka when only a babe, after Iron Shirt's eldest son was killed. Now he had returned to the camp of his fathers, without a wife but already proven as a warrior, with trophies to show for it.

Wasp was very much like Sanchess, with the same dark, fierce eyes but not so heavy yet. Iron Shirt had a separate tipi erected for him so he would not be tempted as he lay in the same lodge with his new aunt, Chosen. But Wasp showed her little interest.

In that entire summer, Iron Shirt was distressed only once, when he heard that another peace council had not been so successful as the one along the Arrowpoint River. He heard it from the Panetekas. Some of them had gone into San Antonio de Bexar in good faith to negotiate, and many of their leaders had been shot and killed in the white man's council house. Afterward the Comanches had mounted a raid that swept down across Texas all the way to the salt waters of the gulf, where they drove some of the whites out into the water in boats. But on the way home they were ambushed and many killed, a great defeat inflicted by the Texas long guns and the pistols, like the one Sanchess had from the Pintada, that fired many times with one loading.

"I wish I had been there, though," Iron Shirt said grimly. "I would have liked to see those white men going out in their boats to escape our hatchets."

But taken all together, it was a good summer. Fall and winter too, as they camped in Palo Duro and let the winter winds pass harmlessly overhead. Iron Shirt spent many happy hours in his lodge, speaking with the headmen of the Kwahadi band, telling them what a good peace had been made in Colorado. They had not been there, the Kwahadis. They never attended peace councils but sometimes they were willing to hear about them.

But even though there was much good, Iron Shirt often lay in his robes at night pondering those Panetekas who were killed when they went in to talk peace with the white man. Then he put it from his mind. San Antonio de Bexar was a long way off and was the Panetekas' problem.

And he thought of the buffalo they had found along the Canadian, like the ones they had seen in the south, killed only for the hides. But there had only been a few. Maybe they'd be the last, he thought, and the white man would have enough of buffalo robes and would go away to the east whence he had come.

IT WAS the time when Morning Thunder started his search for power. He was coming strongly into manhood and Chosen was aware of it. He meant much to her, having been the first person in this band to accept her as one of The People, even though on their first meeting she had switched him across the face.

And Morning Thunder made sure that she was aware of his urges.

On one of their rides in the pony herd during the spring following the year of the great treaty, they stayed on the prairie until well after dark. The band was encamped along the Double Mountain Fork of the Brazos, and there was the smell of sage in the air, and night-singing mockingbirds.

They were rubbing down their ponies with grass when Morning Thunder came to her from behind, quickly, and put his arms around her, under her smock. She was startled and a little frightened, and as he pulled her to the ground she became physically ill. Not because of what she knew he was trying to do and what was surely about to happen, but because she had long thought of him as a brother.

She did not fight at first but allowed him his clumsy explorations. But then suddenly he was over her and she felt a sharp pain. She drew up her knees and scratched at his face and he gasped in surprise and drew back. She rolled from beneath him and was up and on her pony in one quick movement, leaving him on his hands and knees in the grass, humiliated and angry.

For a long time after that he avoided her. She made no overtures to him, either, as some of the girls would have done. But after a while he began to come near Iron Shirt's lodge before sunset, when the women were usually sitting outside exchanging the day's gossip. Still she ignored him, and to increase his frustration, Wolf's Road was always there then as well, frowning fiercely and fingering the Spanish trade hatchet at his belt, as though he were protecting private property.

So Morning Thunder decided it was time to find his power.

Gizzard was glad that his son was coming to the time of life when he thought of hunting and raiding and not of prowling around the pony herd at night with the girls. He set Morning Thunder off in the right direction, giving Finds Something two horses for the appropriate services. Finds Something did a little ceremony for the boy, all very secret, and sent him out to a nearby hill. Morning Thunder took his pouch of tobacco, a blanket, and a parfleche of water and marched off to take his vigil, singing the songs that Finds Something had taught him and fingering the sacred objects Finds Something had given him: a hawk's claw, the dried tip of an otter's tail, a number of brightly colored stones. He found a place at the top of the hill, among the rocks and facing east, and sat down and waited for a vision.

He sang and waited for four days and four nights. But no vision came. Once he thought he dreamed of a wolf, but he had to reject that. He couldn't take the same medicine as his archrival, Wolf's Road. Such power would do him more evil than good.

He was ready to give up and go back to camp, embarrassed at his failure. Then on the last day, he saw a roadrunner kill and eat a sidewinder rattlesnake. He went back to camp elated, and ran directly to the tipi of Finds Something, and Finds Something listened attentively to all of it and then put together a roadrunner medicine kit, although he later admitted to his wife that he had never known a man with roadrunner power and didn't completely understand it.

With his leather pouch of roadrunner medicine hanging at his groin, Morning Thunder went through the camp proclaiming that he was no longer Morning Thunder, but Roadrunner. Everyone immediately shortened it to Runner, of course.

He painted himself as Finds Something had instructed and danced for two days and nights before his father's lodge, then went out to circle the camp for another day, singing his new songs. Gizzard gave his son two stallions, and Runner's grandfather, Black Mountain, gave him a bow reinforced with horn and a quiver of arrows vaned with vulture feathers, next best to owl. Big Wolf, who was no relation to him, gave him a war club made of leather-wrapped willow with a large stone attached to the end, a stone the size of an Osage orange.

So now Runner was ready for his first hunt and war party. With this new status, he tried to pretend that Chosen was something not to his liking, avoiding her haughtily. But anytime she was near, his eyes went to her and he thought of those rides in the pony herd.

The hunting for this new man was immediately at hand and within a few days he had killed his first buffalo with the horn-reinforced bow and some of the vulture-vaned arrows. Black Mountain had a small celebration for him and there was dancing and feasting. Chosen was there, but she did not dance. And Black Mountain gave Finds Something another horse in appreciation for his work.

"What's he going to do with all those horses?" Wapiti Song asked, giggling. "He's got more now than anyone except Sanchess, and can't ride a single one."

The war party for Runner wasn't long in coming, either. The elders had met and decided it was time to go to Mexico, and then the whole band would become a war party. They were going with a group of Panetekas, and this was good because the Panetekas knew Mexico as well as anyone. They were always raiding there.

It was in that time too when Stonefoot eloped with Yam Eater, leaving her father, Red Moccasin, distraught because he had lost his daughter and had no horses to show for it. Everyone sympathized with him. Eloping was not the way to do things, they said. And too bad the man had been one of Iron Shirt's bodyguards and camp criers.

"I wish she hadn't gone," Chosen said. Now she had only one close friend left, Cactus Wren, and Cactus Wren was busy now caring for her baby boy.

"That girl was a terrible nuisance," Woman said. "She was bound to cause trouble among the young men, the way she flirted with them all."

"She was always laughing," Chosen said weakly.

"There will be no laughing when they get back," Iron Shirt said. "There will have to be an accounting. Red Moccasin deserves to be paid for his daughter. But maybe they'll never come back."

The next day Sanchess went to smoke with old Red Moccasin, and gave him two horses. But it wasn't enough to make anyone happy.

THE HUNTS that year were daily affairs, because they wanted to lay in enough pemmican to last a long time. The Panetekas came to join them a full moon before the trip was planned and they hunted together, moving gradually toward the south and going more and more onto a war footing because they were nearing Lipan country. Before anyone saw the first of the south-migrating snow geese going to winter prairies in Mexico, they were on the march, still hunting along the route.

It was on one of these small, fringe-of-the-march hunts

where Bear in the Willows fell. The men were hunting in sight of the camp and some of the women had come out to watch. The move for that day was ended and all the lodges were up. Woman Who Runs was shouting her little buffalo-hunt cry, "Hoy, hoy, hoy," when she suddenly stopped with a gasp and Chosen, standing beside her, saw Bear's horse go down, a complete somersault, Bear flying over the pony's head.

He was in the midst of a small bunch of cows with calves, very dangerous anyway and one of them wounded. This cow turned on Bear and gored him, lifting his body up and flinging it backwards over the shaggy hump. They couldn't see him strike the ground because of the dust. Woman Who Runs tried to rush out to him, even though the buffalo were still milling around, but Shade held her back.

Running Wolf was there almost at once, lifting Bear with one arm as he ran his pony past, just in time to avoid another rush by the enraged and bloody cow. Gizzard was there as well, and between them they galloped out of the herd and on toward the camp, still at a dead run and Bear hanging between them.

They charged past the women without pause, going straight into the campsite, Gizzard shouting for Finds Something, who was having his evening medicine smoke in his tipi. By the time he came out, the two hunters had Bear lying on the ground on his back. His intestines were running out of a huge gash in his left side, and his ribs above the wound were pressed against the skin and there was blood coming from his mouth.

Finds Something began shouting orders. They lifted Bear and carried him into Finds Something's lodge and lay him gently on a buffalo robe. Finds Something tried to get the intestines back inside Bear's body, but it was a hard task. His hands were as bloody as though he had been butchering when he sewed the wound shut with horsehair string and a bone needle. Bear lay on his back without making any sound, eyes glassy, red bubbles forming at the corners of his mouth.

By then Iron Shirt and Sanchess were in the tipi, but they stood well back with Gizzard and Running Wolf, giving Finds Something and his wife, Horned Lark, space to work. They made a mash of certain grasses that Finds Something took from one of his medicine bags, and pressed it against the wound. Horned Lark held it in place while her husband prepared the prickly-pear dressing. He always carried prickly pear with the spines burned off, and now he took a number of large ones and split them in half and placed the exposed, milky interior of the cactus leaves against the wound.

"Hold it tight," Finds Something said.

Outside, the women had gathered in a tight group and they were keening. Woman Who Runs' voice was pitched high above the others, wailing.

Finds Something bound the prickly-pear dressing against the wound with wide rawhide straps wrapped around Bear's body. Bear still had made no sound except for the moist breathing. After that, Finds Something went outside and danced around the lodge where Bear lay, singing his healing songs. But inside the tipi, the men looked at Bear and knew none of it was going to work. They had seen enough wounds to know.

Bear died before moonrise, silently and without ever closing his eyes. Most of the band's women were sitting in a semicircle at the door of the tipi, singing. Woman Who Runs slashed her arms with a knife and was bleeding on Chosen, who tried to comfort her.

"Your brother is gone," she wailed, handing the knife to the girl, and Chosen made a small, tentative cut across her left forearm and the blood ran down and dripped from her fingertips.

They buried him with the coming sun, the Panetekas joining in their grief but staying back along the fringes of Iron Shirt's band. They buried him in the usual way, in a sitting position and facing east, heavy stones laid across the grave and on top of that his favorite horse, throat-cut.

Iron Shirt walked in the pony herd, weeping, and his brother Goes Ahead was with him but could offer no comfort. Stinking Bottom trailed close behind them, head down. Through the camp they could hear the keening of the women, and some of the dogs were howling.

Iron Shirt thought of his son Bear in the Willows, gone now to the land beyond the sun. That was a happy thing, but sad as well. Only one son left, and that one a son who often did things to irritate him. Bear had never irritated him. But Bear had never been a war chief, either. And Iron Shirt thought, Most of my irritations have compensations. But there is no compensation for losing a son.

It was expected that Sanchess would take Bear's widow as his own wife now. That night he went to her tipi, stopped her wailing, and brought her to the wolf-head tipi along with her child. Now Sanchess had three wives and two children and two lodges. And on the tipi of his dead brother, where Owl Calling and her daughter would live after that first night, Sanchess painted the head of a wolf, in black, to honor his brother's dying.

With the following morning, they moved on again toward the south, Iron Shirt's family trying to leave their grief behind.

Within three days Sanchess had yet another tipi in his family circle. Shade and Wapiti Song had long expected it, and the poles and hide covering were ready. A man of Sanchess's growing responsibilities needed a lodge to himself where he could talk and smoke with friends or sit at his fire and think. So the wolf-head tipi became three, and each evening the women laid a rawhide rope between Sanchess's lodge and their own, so that if he needed them in the night he could tug his end of a rope and at the other end it would rattle a gourd in Shade's and Wapiti Song's tipi or in Owl Calling's, and they would come.

It made Iron Shirt proud that his son would have three tipis. Yet it gave him pause too, for even as the number of lodges increased, the number of young fighting men seemed to dwindle. Bear in the Willows gone now, and Stonefoot run off with that flirting girl. And the boys not growing fast enough to take their places. Even Wasp, his grandson, seemed to lack any interest in taking a woman and producing his own share of sons for the times ahead. Iron Shirt began to have the uneasy feeling that soon they would need all the young fighting men they could get.

11

WHEN THE SPANIARDS FIRST came to the New World, they were looking mostly for precious metals. They found very little. At least not enough to fulfill their expectations. But they continued to look, marching always farther to the north along the coastal lowlands and then up the great central plateau and across the Rio Grande.

In the process they destroyed all the tribal peoples of Mexico and in their place established missions where the priests could convert the heathen to the Cross and at the same time use them for slave labor.

Over the years of the conquest, many such missions were built and around them small towns grew. But only small towns usually, especially along the Mesa del Norte, for the land was so harsh that there was little to sustain large settlements.

Gradually it became apparent to the Spaniards that there was no El Dorado, no city of gold, and so they lost interest. There were some serious ranching enterprises along certain rivers, but little else, and as the turbulent later times came, there was no incentive to spend much effort on what was mostly desert and scab rock. The unfortunate peoples who lived there were left to their own devices.

The wild tribes north of the Rio Grande soon discovered these helpless settlements. The raiding began a long time ago, almost a century before the American Revolution. And after Mexico threw off the Spanish rule, conditions got no better. Mostly they got worse. Few efforts were seriously made to protect the northern peoples.

And the raids increased. Each year the wild tribes came. Sometimes many, sometimes only a few, but all of the raiders were generally unmolested in their savage attacks. They struck deep into the northern tier of Mexico, spreading destruction like the seeds thrown from a planter's hand, taking thousands of horses and no one knows how many human captives. Northern Mexico was ravaged as few other places on earth have ever been. And one of the principal marauders was The People.

At first no one knew who they were or where they came from. They only knew that these newest horsemen were pushing Apache tribes before them. Finally, from the Utes, they got a name for the invaders: People Who Want to Fight All the Time. Or, as the Utes themselves said it, *Komanchia!*

WITH THE entire band moving, and the Panetekas as well, they were strung out over a long distance. The pony herd was large and it took much work by Lost It and the Paneteka herders and the young boys to keep the ponies bunched and moving in the right direction. The warriors were carrying lances now, their faces painted black so that if any Lipan scouting parties saw them they might be frightened away.

Water was a constant problem, but at least there was plenty in the Rio Grande where the Devil's River ran into it. They crossed into Coahuila there and paused for a few days, allowing the horses to graze. They were following a well-marked route now, a trail beaten down by many horses and travois over the seasons, a trail the Mexicans and Texans called the Great Comanche War Trail.

There was much discussion in the elders' council about the lack of water in the mountains where they would make their raiding camp. A few said they had too many horses for the water available and some should be turned loose on the prairie and left behind. But such logic was overcome by their affection for horses, so none were left behind.

"Later," Iron Shirt said, "we can kill off horses as we need to, when water is scarce. And dry their meat."

"That's good," said Long Knife, the Paneteka headman. "You won't find any buffalo where we're going. Meat might become as scarce as water."

They moved directly south, maintaining wide-ranging scouts day and night. They had little worry from Mexican soldiers because the central government didn't have the time, the money, or the inclination to worry much about raiding parties in the northern provinces. The People knew this from experience. But there were always local tribes or raiding Apaches who might do them a little harm if they went unprepared. So they went prepared.

There was an excitement in it, this being a new and dangerous land. It was a kind of excitement The People enjoyed.

They crossed the fringes of the Donkey Hills and went on to the Salado River, where they camped for a few days, watering the herd. Then almost due west across the Sierra de los Alamitos and into Durango. There they located in a high mountain valley where there was spring water and enough vegetation to graze the herd. And easy access out into the Mesa del Norte, the great central plateau between the eastern and western Sierra Madres.

On those first evenings, Iron Shirt told the tales of other raids into Mexico, and many of the young children of the band came to listen, lying in a circle around his lodge fire on their stomachs, Chosen and Woman sitting well back in the shadows.

"Our fathers and grandfathers came here many times," Iron Shirt said. "And our friends the Kiowas. I have heard that one band of Kiowas came raiding into Mexico and went far to the south. Many days' ride. More than three seasons' ride. There they found great trees lifting to the Sun Father, with vines like ropes hanging from them, and birds of many colors like young men painted for a war party. And in these trees, the Kiowas say, were little men, little hairy men with tails longer than the armadillo, but when they tried to talk to these little men, even in sign language, the little men said nothing and ran away through the branches."

CHOSEN COULD stand at the western edge of the camp and look out through a break in the mountains and see the flat, high plain of the central plateau of Mexico. It was all such a terribly inhospitable country, worse than any she had ever seen. Harsh sun alternated with deep, raging clouds that swept in with driving rains, the last of the summer storms and the only rainfall of any account this area would receive all year.

The ground under her feet was hard and white with limestone, and the vegetation ran mostly to cactus and agave, with its cluster of knife-blade leaves at the base and sprouting a long stem with hard, round blossoms at the top, like pincushions. There were cassava and mesquite, but juniper only in scattered places. There were a few vermilion flycatchers and mockingbirds, but little else she could recognize except the hawks and vultures.

Lizards were everywhere, some of them vicious-looking and large. And rattlesnakes and hairy tarantulas. If she turned a rock, she was sure to find at least one scorpion, translucent pink and with little shining eyes.

And for her and the other women, it was boredom. They went about the daily routine of household chores and tending the babies. Owl Calling's daughter had eight summers and already they were teaching her the things a woman does. Getting the Lodgepoles was at the worst age, old enough to run through the camp naked but not big enough to defend himself from the dogs.

Iron Shirt's family women built a brush arbor and spent a lot of time there, in the shade. Even though the nights had turned chilly, the days were hot still. They played dice and stick games, and sometimes shinny in the cool of evening, using a ball of wrapped horsehair. But mostly it was waiting and watching the men prepare for raiding.

It was a long time before any parties went out. Shade explained that they were establishing their plans, the scouts coming in each day with information of surrounding terrain and settlements and movements on the few roads, warning of any dangers they might encounter once they left the mountain meadow. Within a short time everyone knew that there was a town nearby, a small one, that would have to be eliminated before they expanded operations into the Mesa del Norte.

Each night the elders and the war chiefs held their own

separate councils. The elders were coming to terms with scarce water and grazing for the herd, the war chiefs planning their first foray. All the men were preoccupied with planning, and at night Sanchess pulled on the ropes leading to his wives' tipis infrequently.

But finally the days of preparation were over. The warriors brought in their horses and gave them extra time to water at the spring. The ponies were carefully groomed and designs were painted on their flanks in red and black, and feathers were attached to their manes and tails.

Shields were taken from their covers, and lances as well. They counted the arrows in their quivers and applied fresh sinew and glue to the bending parts of their bows. Finally they spent a long time squatting before their lodges with hand mirrors, painting their faces in black designs.

On this first strike, Sanchess would lead, for his reputation had spread even to the Panetekas. When she first heard of it, Chosen felt a burst of pride at knowing that the man so honored had taken her into his lodge a long time ago. And better still, in the last night before the raiders rode out, Wolf's Road played on his flute again, close by Iron Shirt's lodge, no matter what the old peace chief thought. The camp was mostly silent that last night, except for the flute, and everybody heard it and said it was good. There was hunting and fighting and trading, but one should have a few love songs thrown in now and again, they said.

There was not the singing and dancing that was usual before a war party went out. Perhaps there would be for later sorties, but this first one had been planned carefully and everything was very serious. Before he left, Sanchess came to Iron Shirt's lodge and they touched one another without speaking, Sanchess's face glistening black with paint. And before he pushed aside the tipi door flap to go, he searched once in the dim light at the rear of the lodge and for a brief moment his fierce eyes looked into Chosen's, and it made a chill pass down her spine. But made her proud as well. It was the first time he had looked directly on her since she had come to Iron Shirt's lodge.

THERE WAS a new moon. They'd waited for it to make their

first raid because they needed the light to move in unfamiliar country. They dropped down out of the mountain meadow and through the pass onto the sloping plains where the Sierra Madre gave way to the central plateau. The landscape looked as though it had a silver crust, and the mesquite, black in the moonlight, was like clusters of dark mushrooms breaking through.

They moved at a set pace, for they knew how much distance had to be covered before dawn. Gizzard and Wolf's Road had scouted this town and the route to it, so they moved with confidence.

"It's not a large town," Wolf's Road had said. "It sits on the plain and hard to come close to in daylight. But we came close enough to see that there are some horses."

"How many people?" Sanchess had asked.

"I don't know. Not many."

The countryside was bare and desolate around them, and the growth they passed seldom came above their ponies' heads. Somewhere back toward the mountains a pack of wolves was yammering and sometimes when they rode past areas dense with cactus, they could hear the bark of an elf owl.

"I hope that bird is good luck," Running Wolf muttered to the rider beside him. "I'd feel better about this if there'd been a little dancing before we left."

Sanchess rode in the lead with Wolf's Road and Gizzard, showing the way. Immediately behind him rode Shade. There were a few other women in the party as well, because on these raids in Mexico nobody knew what was likely to happen and when women might be useful. Shade was leading two extra horses, both war stallions, but she rode a gelding herself. Mares were seldom taken on war parties. On her saddle hung a bow and quiver, but before they left the campsite Sanchess had told her, "Catch up all the children you can. Let the men do the rest of it and stay out of their way."

They came to a small intermittent stream and rode along it as the moon moved two fingers' width across the sky. Then they turned south and left the river and were in level, flat country covered with mesquite and prickly pear. Well before dawn they halted downwind from the town and everyone changed horses while Wolf's Road and Gizzard rode ahead for a look at the final ground.

It was only a short time before Wolf's Road was back, running his pony. In the moonlight his eyes were shining with excitement.

"Something you need to see," he said, and led Sanchess away from the group and toward the town.

It was a scattering of adobe buildings, set in no particular pattern. The shine of the moon made the buildings look as though they had been whitened with limestone paint. They heard cattle lowing and as they came near, where Gizzard sat his pony behind a clump of mesquite, they could see a corral on the near side of town.

They did not speak but moved their horses slowly forward, the three of them riding abreast. Coming closer still, Sanchess could see the high posts of the corral set in the ground and, inside the pole fencing, the dark shapes of horses and oxen. Holding quirt loops on their own ponies' muzzles to keep them quiet, they rode close enough to see the shine of the horses' eyes.

Then Sanchess saw it. Tied to the tops of five of the corral posts were human heads, partly mummified in this dry air, but looking like skulls with long hair blowing out from each of them in the gentle predawn breeze. They reined in and stood for a moment, then with a movement of his hand to keep the others in place, Sanchess rode ahead once more.

He moved to the corral and along the edge farthest from the town, looking up at the drawn and partially decomposed faces shining in the light of the dipping moon. The empty sockets of the eyes seemed to stare down at him as he rode past, and he felt a cold chill pass along his back. He made only a short inspection and then walked his pony back to the others.

"What does it mean?" Wolf's Road asked.

"I told you before," Gizzard whispered. "They were of The People."

"I can't tell who they were," Sanchess said. "Maybe Apaches. But whoever they were, they were caught by these Mexicans and their heads placed as a warning to us."

"To us?" Wolf's Road asked.

"To anyone coming for their horses and children," Sanchess said. "How long ago would you say it was?"

"I can't tell," Gizzard said. "I've never seen heads left unburied in country like this. Maybe last spring."

"If that long, the buzzards and crows would have eaten them by now," Wolf's Road said.

"They've eaten the eyes. The rest is hard to eat. And maybe these Mexicans kept the birds away," Sanchess said.

"What will we do?" Gizzard asked.

"As we had planned. Take all the horses. Kill the cattle. They're too slow-moving to suit me in getting away from here."

"And the people?"

"Kill them! Except for the children. But we've got to be quick and sure. These are dangerous Mexicans. The heads show they have courage."

They brought the raiding party up close before the dawn, and entered the town with first light, walking their horses. Only one dog barked. It seemed to be the only dog in this place. An old man came from his house to urinate beside his door, unaware of anything but his need. One of Wolf's Road's arrows struck him in the ribcage and he fell without a sound, the water still running from his body.

As much as they disliked fighting on foot, this was a special case and they dismounted and entered the buildings, four and five men quickly through each door with hand weapons held ready. They made no sound until the first Mexican scream, and then they started their own battle shouts. It lasted for only a few heartbeats.

Before the sun was up, everything that could burn was burning, sending up an oily black cloud of smoke to be caught in the predawn breeze. They methodically killed the oxen with hatchets, not wanting to waste arrows. Sanchess had the heads removed from the corral posts and buried. As they rode away, the sun still not up, a number of the people of the town who had managed to hide could be seen running in frantic little groups toward the south along an ill-defined road.

"There are some more," Running Wolf said, his lance ready, anxious to do some of this work on horseback.

"Let them go," Sanchess said. "It's enough for today."

And his power as a war leader was such that Running Wolf reluctantly turned away from further slaughter.

They took away seventeen horses, some of them hardly worth the effort, and four children. Two boys and two girls ranging in age from five to eight summers. By midmorning they were well back toward the mountain pass to their meadow.

CHOSEN HEARD of it all from Shade and from the idle talk of the warriors, then more of it still when they had a victory dance and each man sang of his deeds. It was only a small celebration because this had not been a fight against traditional enemies with weapons in their hands. This had been a raid to clear the way for further operations, with little honor attached, and not a single scalp was displayed, although a few had been taken.

It stunned her, even after all this time. From her almost forgotten memories she recalled her Da reading of the fall of Jericho, the sack of Troy, the destruction of Carthage. Those had been empty words then, because she had been incapable of understanding any of it in human terms. But now she could see that war as The People and their enemies waged it was of a kind with the wars of the ancients that her Da had read about.

She listened and knew. She looked at the forlorn, dirty, terrified captive children, their eyes glazed with shock and fear, and finally she knew what those long-forgotten readings meant. Even though she had gone through the same experience herself, it was only now that it all came to her.

She watched, as the days passed, the captives fighting with the dogs for scraps of food, and was glad when the Panetekas took them away. The Panetekas had discovered certain towns close by, where such captives could be ransomed for horses and silver, and after nine suns they were back with ten good ponies and a sack of beads and silver trinkets. Plunder and trade! Chosen wondered if perhaps that had been part of it at Jericho and Troy and Carthage as well.

And she heard Iron Shirt grumble, "We should have kept those girl children. Someday they would have given us sons for the band."

Then this, like all things, faded from her mind in its harsh details. But she continued to hope that once this was behind her, she would never see Mexico again.

12

MEXICO HAD GIVEN IRON Shirt a false sense of security. There were many dangers there, all of which he understood. In his own country once more, he found incomprehensible peril.

When the Mexico camp broke up, the Panetekas returned the same way they had come. But Iron Shirt led his band due north, crossing into Texas where the Pecos emptied into the Rio Grande, then up the Pecos all the way to New Mexico. They camped near the great cave where the bats flying out at evening looked like a foaming raincloud.

They found traders there with their high-wheeled carts ready to move out into Comanche country to the north and east. Most of the children The People had taken captive were ransomed for metal goods and horses, the band becoming rich in ponies once more, replacing those they had eaten in Mexico, plus many more.

"Now some of these girl prisoners must be kept," Iron Shirt said. "For our generations."

And so some were, in Gizzard's family and in the lodge of Red Moccasin, because he had lost his daughter to elopement.

For the summer hunt, they moved east and finally to Sulphur Springs Draw and then, as fall came, on north to Palo Duro once more, where Shade and Wolf's Road could visit their Kwahadi family for the first time in many seasons, and where so many crows wintered in the canyon with them that later they would call it the Cold Season of the Crows.

Iron Shirt talked with many Wichitas and Kutsateka

Comanches and some of his own Nakoni people who had news of the white man. The Texans wanted peace now, but only on their terms. During this time, before Texas became a part of the great eastern chief's country, many councils were held. Mostly with the Panetekas.

At each of these meetings, Iron Shirt heard, The People complained about whites moving into the buffalo country. But the Texas white men—even Houston—were unable to stop it, even had they wanted to, for if one of their number wanted to move west, he did it. No matter what was written on a flimsy piece of paper in Austin. And Houston knew, too, that he stood almost alone among his people in a pacific policy toward the "Comanch'."

The Texans agreed to establish trading houses in Comanche land so The People could have what they needed. Of course, what The People really needed and what the white traders offered might not be the same. And even though some of these places were built, sometimes once the council broke up the whole plan was forgotten and The People waited for the trading posts in vain.

Increasingly the white Texans moved westward and always the young Comanches raided their herds because the Texas government could not protect the settlers, and always then the white Texans mounted raids against the camps of The People. Iron Shirt could see no end to it.

Often the young warriors were becoming irresponsible, going out on raids that jeopardized The People because they brought little gain, but only attacks in retaliation. This was true even among bands like Iron Shirt's, which had been relatively untouched so far by the white encroachment.

Through all this talk, Iron Shirt looked at his family and longed for past days, the days of his youth, when all they had to worry about were Utes or Pawnees. He knew it was a sign of age, thinking of old times as the best. And his wounds hurt him terribly and sometimes in the mornings he had to lie for a long while in his bed robes, flexing his muscles until they were alive enough to support his growing weight.

Iron Shirt looked often at Chosen during that winter and saw that she was becoming a woman in every way. He knew that soon she would be leaving his lodge fire forever, and it saddened him.

But Sanchess made him happy. More and more now, and Sanchess still a young and vigorous man, he was becoming a peace chief. He had begun to sit with all the councils of the elders. No one invited him. But no one objected, either, since his power as a war chief had by that time become so great. He came and sat at the rear of the tipi while the older men talked. Later he moved to sit in the select circle, opposite his father.

But Wasp and Roadrunner were becoming a problem. Often during that spring as the winter slipped away, they disappeared for days, going out with other young men on war parties and attacking anything that came in their path, viciously and without regard for consequences. Sometimes Wasp returned with scalps and there was much celebration and many victory dances. But Iron Shirt and the other headmen were uneasy about it, looking for the white man to come for revenge.

One night while the mockingbirds were singing of spring's coming, Iron Shirt sat smoking with Big Wolf and Sanchess and he complained about the reckless young men and how hard it was to control them.

"It's the way of young men," Big Wolf said.

"I don't mind the horses and scalps they bring in," Iron Shirt said. "I don't mind the raiding. But there must be some consideration now of what will happen as a result of it. Some consideration of where they steal these horses and kill these men."

"A young man's blood is hot," Sanchess said. "It is a part of being a young man. They must show their power."

"You should speak to Wasp. He worries me. He's wilder than any young man I've ever known. Why doesn't he take a few wives and start getting us some new babies? It's impossible to talk with him."

"There's only one way to stop a man like that," Big Wolf said. "And that's to kill him."

"I could not kill my own son," Sanchess said, referring to his brother's son as his own. "And if anyone else did it, I'd take vengeance on him."

"No one is serious about killing anybody," Big Wolf

said. "I mention it only to illustrate that there's nothing you can do to stop a young man going to war."

"My old life has become a burden on me," Iron Shirt complained, shaking his head. "All the things that were once good have now turned bad and against us."

"I think you worry too much," Big Wolf said.

And Iron Shirt thought maybe it was true.

That summer they hunted the Medicine River range once more, but they saw only a few Kiowas. Then in the winter, they camped in the Wichita Mountains and a number of their old friends were nearby. There was much visiting back and forth until the snows came.

It seemed to snow each day and night. No one could remember such snow. They called it the Winter of the Great Snowfall, and before long the drifts were so deep that the ponies had trouble moving, even among the sheltering timber where the horses ate the bark from trees.

The weather turned very cold and gradually they began to forget the danger of white men and other enemies and thought only of staying warm. Meat became scarce and the young men went into the surrounding valleys to hunt for deer or bear. But they didn't find very many. During the Moon of Deepest Cold, some of the band were eating bark along with the horses. Then they started to eat the horses.

It was in this very worst of times that Spider, the old medicine woman, came to Iron Shirt's lodge.

He was sitting bundled in robes before a low fire in midmorning when he heard her outside the lodge, making one of her medicine chants. He went to the door flap and pushed it aside and saw her, trampling a small circle in the snow as she shuffled about, her dead son's blood lance in one hand. Her head was back and the high, keening noises came from her old mouth like the call of distant wolves.

Looking back into the tipi, Iron Shirt saw Chosen, wide-eyed and frightened at the singing.

"Don't be afraid, daughter," he said. "The old woman will not harm you."

Iron Shirt went out and stood watching the old woman dance, a trade blanket over his shoulders. Spider danced a long time, and when she stopped, her breathing made a great cloud of white vapor before her wrinkled face. She glared at Iron Shirt from her little, red-rimmed eyes, and to him they were like hot coals in a dying fire.

"I have a little pemmican," he said. "Would you like to eat, Grandmother?"

She pointed a bony finger at the sky and then at Iron Shirt's face and her voice was a hard, cackling sound when she spoke.

"They will come for her," she shouted. "They will come for that blue-eye and kill The People and scalp them all so that none will go to the land beyond the sun."

"Come in and eat, Grandmother." Iron Shirt felt a shiver of cold run down his back.

"You must throw her away. Or they will surely come and murder The People!"

Her arm was still up, the bony finger pointed toward his face. He knew his own hands were shaking a little, but his anger was coming up in his throat like hot vomit.

"Go back to your own lodge and do your singing," he said sternly. "Your visions are not for my family."

"They will come," Spider shrieked. "They will come and take her. It has been in my dreams since that thoughtless son of yours brought her here. She is a curse on The People! Brought on us by that man Sanchess, who is alive now when my own sons are dead."

Iron Shirt remembered the time Sanchess had come in with stolen horses but had given none of them to this old gnome. The thought of it made him speechless. He felt a sudden movement behind him and then knew Woman Who Runs was there. In her hand was her largest skinning knife.

"If you don't kill her, I will," Woman said softly. "She is a witch and a sorceress. Everyone in the band knows it."

But before Iron Shirt could answer, Spider whirled and began her dance again, kicking up fleecy little clouds of snow. She sang words they could not understand, and Iron Shirt had to restrain his wife. Spider stopped her singing abruptly, glared at them, pointed her finger once more, turned, and walked through the snow toward the edge of the camp, where the timber came down close and dark. They watched her struggling through the deep snow, using her son's lance as a walking stick. She walked past the last of the lodges, still going toward the trees, a stooped figure growing smaller and smaller and finally disappearing into the woods. Iron Shirt heaved a great sigh.

"You should have killed her," Woman said savagely.

"No," he said softly. "I'm afraid of her medicine!"

At nightfall, Spider was still gone. No one had the courage to go looking for her. Iron Shirt sat at his fire, trying to forget all of it. But the memory would not leave his thinking.

That spring, one of the boys hunting rabbits in the woods found what the wolves and coyotes had left of old Spider. They had eaten all of her except the right hand, and it was still clenched, with the finger pointing. It frightened Iron Shirt as nothing had ever frightened him before, and Finds Something, the only other man who understood Spider's power, lay on his back before his tipi and sang medicine songs for four days and four nights. But it helped Iron Shirt's misery not at all. He would believe for all the rest of his days that it was the curse of old Spider that brought the Osages to them.

CHOSEN HAD never seen any of the tall warriors from the Ozark Plateau until that spring.

They were breaking camp; Iron Shirt was anxious to be away from the mountains where he knew Spider's spirit moved among the trees. Maybe he was too anxious. He and the men had already moved from the little valley before the camp was completely broken up.

Woman Who Runs had Iron Shirt's lodge down and on the travois and was moving out of the western edge of the old campsite, picking her way between the naked lodgepoles where other women still worked. The wolf-head tipi was down as well, and loaded, and Wapiti Song and Lodgepoles were already out of camp, following along the trail of the men who had gone before. The second of Sanchess's lodges was loaded, but the pony was still standing as Chosen and Shade helped Owl Calling to take down her tipi. Chosen's little calico gelding was rein-tied to Shade's travois horse, waiting patiently.

Of the warriors, only Claw the pukutsi remained, doing the last of his little crazy dances here where The People had gone through the worst winter since Ketchum Mountain.

Chosen was working near a small stand of jack oak, her back to the timber, when she heard a sharp little cry from the far edge of the camp. She rose from her work and looked and saw women running. She thought it was perhaps a wolf or a bear, and was aware of Shade moving quickly to the travois horse where her bow and quiver were hanging.

Then Chosen saw them. There were about a dozen of them, big men with their hair roached along the tops of their glistening heads, their faces painted yellow and black. They were running into the clearing of the old campsite, waving weapons and giving a hard, coughing war cry. Chosen saw one of the men swing a hatchet, striking down a running Comanche woman.

She stood rooted to the ground in horror and watched Claw rush forward and station himself between the other women and the intruders, shouting his own war cry now and striking an arrow through his long sash and into the ground. He stood before them defiantly, waving a buffalo-scrotum rattle in one hand, a hatchet in the other.

Shade was screaming at Chosen to move, and instinctively she turned back toward the woods, close behind her. There, leaping directly toward her, was another of these strange men, and he was so close she could see the black paint gleaming across his eyes and the snakeskin woven into his high roach of hair. He was almost on her, holding a knifeblade hatchet up to strike.

He was so close she went rigid with terror, awaiting the blow to her skull. There was the strong twang of a bowstring and the big warrior jerked to a halt, an arrow suddenly embedded in his belly with only the vane showing. He took another faltering step and pitched forward.

"Run, you little fool!" Shade was screaming, and when Chosen turned, she saw Shade crouched, threading another shaft to the bow in her hands, snarling, "Osage! Osage! Osage!"

Chosen was on the little gelding then, leaping to his back, kicking him free of the travois horse. Owl Calling was frantically trying to pull a skinning knife from among her belongings and beside her was her daughter, Sage Girl, standing slack-jawed and immobile with fear. Chosen swung her pony past the girl and reached down to take her by the smock; then, holding Sage Girl in one hand, Chosen kicked her pony toward the trail, dragging the girl with her.

Behind her she could hear the Osages shouting, and she thought she heard Shade's bowstring again.

At the western edge of the campsite she met the first warriors coming back. Wasp and Roadrunner rode in full cry, like wolves, and with weapons up, and not far behind came the older men, Gizzard and Running Wolf. As he passed Chosen, Running Wolf was stripping the cover from his battle lance and laughing. And dragged along beside Chosen, Sage Girl was trying now to mount the gelding, but Chosen did not pause, instead kicking the pony with both heels.

Chosen continued to ride wildly until she came to the elders. They were coming back too, grim-faced. She pulled in beside Iron Shirt and he reached out and touched her and only then did she release Sage Girl, who fell to the ground beneath the gelding's belly, gasping for breath.

"Osages," Chosen panted, and Iron Shirt nodded and rode on.

Afterward, Chosen recalled how Iron Shirt looked at that moment, riding back toward a fight gray-faced, his lips harsh, eyes flashing. It was the only time she had ever seen him with weapons in his hands.

Now she waited, her pony prancing with excitement and racing in small circles among the women on travois horses who had come out of the camp early, and Finds Something on his travois and Horned Lark, his wife, with her bow ready. From the direction of the camp they could hear the shouting and there was one gunshot, like the pop of a cork from some Comanchero's trade-whiskey jug. Soon other travois ponies were coming, hurrying, the women looking back over their shoulders. Chosen saw Owl Calling and rode to her.

"They have run away," Owl Calling panted. She still held her skinning knife in one hand, but it was not colored red. "Those Osages, they ran away when our men came."

"Shade?" Chosen asked, afraid of what she would hear.

"She's coming," Owl Calling said. "But they killed the pukutsi!"

When the men came, they looked grim. Wasp was leading Claw's pony, and draped across the saddle like a bloody blanket was the pukutsi, throat-cut. There were two women dead as well: one of the wives of Stinking Bottom and one of the two wives of Cloud, Black Mountain's youngest son. And Roadrunner had a deep gash along his ribs where a bullet had passed and he wore it proudly, grinning at Chosen as he rode past.

When Shade came, riding her travois pony, she held the scalp of the Osage who had made his run at Chosen, her hands still bloody from taking it. Then Iron Shirt was there, calling for them to move quickly toward the Red River and the south. It was the second time Chosen could recall their running out of this Wichita Mountain country, once from the smallpox, now from the Osage.

There was great difficulty in getting the young men to move. They wanted to go back and follow the Osages, who had disappeared into the timber as quickly as they had come.

"We will run them down like wolves," Wasp shouted in his grandfather's face.

"Osages are not wolves," Iron Shirt said calmly. "This was likely only a small group from a very large party. The Osage do not come into this country unless in strength."

"I will hunt them down alone," Wasp said.

At that moment Sanchess rode in from his advance scout along the route to Red River. He came directly to his father and sat staring at the confusion all around him.

"What are you shouting about?" he asked, glaring at Wasp with his fierce eyes.

"The Osages have killed three of our people," Wasp said, and Iron Shirt quickly gave Sanchess the details.

"We are moving the band south, and fast," Iron Shirt said. "We don't know how many more of them there might be."

Wasp started to shout something else, but Sanchess cut him off with harsh words, like hatchet strokes.

"Yes, we are moving," he said, staring at Wasp. "Each of you has duties to perform for The People now. Start performing them."

For a moment the people in the band watched breathlessly, thinking maybe Wasp would still protest. But under Sanchess's hot glare he finally wheeled his pony away and rode toward the head of the band.

They didn't stop until they were well past Red River. It was high where they crossed, and some of the travois were lost in the stream. They buried their dead, but the ceremonies were short. Many of the young men still rode the backtrail, hoping some of the Osages would follow.

"It's been a long time since we fought the Osages," said Iron Shirt. "Perhaps some of their young men are as wild as our own, killing anything they find in their path. Driven crazy by the white man. They have had to put up with the white man longer than we have."

"That pukutsi," Woman said. "He was a strange man. But very brave!"

And Chosen remembered the night near the headwaters of the Concho, so long ago, when Claw had come to her naked and Sanchess had intervened. She was sorry for the pukutsi, yet somehow proud as well that he would take his stand to protect the women until they could get away.

She wondered if perhaps the mark of Claw's hatchet might be on some of those Osages now. Maybe he had even killed one or two. She hoped so. But it would do The People no good, of course, if Osages had been killed and dragged away by their companions before they could be scalped. With their strange roach of hair intact, they would enter the land beyond the sun and wait there to cause more trouble later.

It didn't occur to her how dramatically her thinking had changed since that night of her first terror, since the time she had come to The People. By now she had almost forgotten how she had come, then only ten summers old. And now sixteen and a Comanche!

IRON SHIRT'S worries increased with the seasons. During the summer after the Winter of Great Snowfall, he kept hearing the stories. A group of Delawares, who were friends with the whites and often scouted for them against The People, murdered a number of Kutsateka along the West Fork of the Trinity. A war party went out to avenge the dead and struck a white farm settlement. Then the Texans sent a revenge raid because of that. It was the usual thing now. But this one Iron Shirt could not forget, for the Texans had struck the Paneteka band that had been in Mexico with Iron Shirt's people and one of the people killed was Long Knife, a close and old friend whose people had had nothing to do with the raid on the white farmers.

What troubled him most was that others could not seem to see this thing and how it could destroy them. Yet maybe a few had some small knot of worry in their souls, unable to understand it but knowing that things were not turning out right anymore. Maybe they were all going a little crazy with something they could no longer control. Maybe they would all turn into pukutsi, standing brave but hopeless before the onslaught.

"We have not fought the white man in a long time," he grumbled. "Yet they are our enemies."

"Some of your young men have fought them," Woman said, and Iron Shirt made no response because it was true.

NOW IT WAS time to take meat again and stop worrying. For the first time in his memory, Iron Shirt was glad to be out of the country north of Red River, where Spider's spirit stalked across the dark ridges. He moved the band to the White Fork of the Brazos for the summer hunts, and it was a good time because they found many buffalo there. Here they were visited by a small hunting party of Kickapoos.

"More of these people with guns the white man has made come into our country," Iron Shirt said.

The Kickapoos were fed and treated with great hospitality, but it was an uneasy time until they left, for everyone knew what good fighters these men were. None of The People except Iron Shirt seemed to realize that here was yet another group of people come into their country, and that each buffalo they killed was one less for the Comanches.

But old fears were forgotten now. It was a good summer. The fighting sap of the young men had run back down in their veins, and now all their energies were taken up with killing buffalo. The children were growing. Running Wolf's two sons and Getting the Lodgepoles were already riding in the pony herd, although none were old enough yet to wear loincloths. There were only a few summer storms bad enough to blow down any of the tipis. Yet there was enough rain to keep the prairie flowers blooming, blue and red and yellow under the bright sun. There were many sage grouse, and the young girls searched out their nests and found the little speckled eggs. There were many new foals in the herd, and the dogs were more numerous than ever before.

It was in this time, toward the fall, when the white peace party came. It was the time when Iron Shirt made his last great oration and came to the peak of his power.

It was Running Wolf who saw them first. He was skinning a kill, down off his hunter and bent over the carcass when the pony snorted in alarm. The horse had been trained to do that, to alert Running Wolf when he was on the ground and defenseless.

Running Wolf left the dead buffalo and went up on the pony immediately and saw them coming, maybe two miles away, a party of three men and two extra pack mules. He reined toward the camp, going straight out at a gallop.

The hunt that morning was forgotten and the buffalo already killed were left on the ground unskinned. All the men came into camp riding fast, and uncovered their shields and lances and put black paint on their faces.

"There are only three of them," Iron Shirt said. "They are coming openly. Let them ride in and we'll feed them."

The young men were in no mood to be friendly, and as the small party approached they went out yipping, kicking their ponies. They circled the party and then formed two lines an arrowshot away on either side. They could see now that there were two whites and a Tonkawa. Making threatening gestures with their lances, they escorted the three and their mules into Iron Shirt's camp, showing their black faces.

Iron Shirt greeted them and offered them food and said it was good that they came with their guns in saddle scabbards and not in their hands. The two white men spoke through the Tonkawa, who relayed their words in fluent Comanche and, unlike The People, came directly to the point.

"We are a peace commission from Austin," the Tonk said. "We have come to speak of a treaty between us."

It was rude to speak so abruptly, and there was a mutter of anger among the young men. But Iron Shirt ignored this and once more invited the men to dismount and have food. There was fresh buffalo-hump steak and tongue, he said.

They sat in the shade of Iron Shirt's brush arbor and ate and smoked. The People ringed close around them and stared at the long hair on the faces of the white men. Some had never before seen a white man so close. A few of the women giggled behind their hands, pointing to the bushy eyebrows and the tangled whiskers. The young men grumbled that these white men had a great nerve, bringing into a Comanche camp this Tonkawa, whose tribe was The People's deadly enemy.

The elders gathered with Iron Shirt and sat facing the white men and their interpreter, all very grave. Black Mountain and Big Wolf and Finds Something were there, and Sanchess as well. After they had eaten and smoked and eaten and smoked again, talking all the while about the weather and the plentiful buffalo on this range, the white men turned once more to the business at hand.

"We have come from Austin," the Tonk said. "We have come to invite you to a treaty meeting where we can make peace with one another."

"Where is this meeting place?" Iron Shirt asked. "I would hate to go all the way to someplace like San Antonio de Bexar. It is a hard trip. And once before when you asked our people there, you killed them in the council house."

"That was a long time ago," the Tonk said. "There will be no killing now. The meeting place will be along the Colorado at a place called Owen's Springs."

"I have never heard of it," Iron Shirt said. "But we could find it. Is this to be a peace with the white man or with the Tonkawas?"

"With the white man and all the white man's friends," the Tonk said, and Iron Shirt wondered if that last part had actually been said by the white men. "This is Mr. Goodwin and Mr. Toole. They represent the Great Father in Austin."

"I would like to have a peace with the Texas white man. I would like to agree that the Texas white man stay in his place and we stay in ours."

"That is a detail to be worked out later, at the council. Mr. Goodwin and Mr. Toole say that you should come in and there will be many gifts, and for that you will free all your white captives."

"We have no white captives," Iron Shirt said with a straight face, and he saw the hint of a smile on the Tonk's long, handsome face.

"There will be many gifts, anyway. We are going to all the bands of your people to have them come in."

"All the bands? The Kwahadis?"

"We have not found them yet."

"They are hard to find, unless they want to be found," Iron Shirt said, and all his headmen nodded.

"Let us talk of your band now," the Tonk said. "We extend an invitation to accept the white man's hospitality and make peace. We will meet in the fall, when the leaves turn red."

"I don't know much about the white man's hospitality. And going down the Colorado just before the cold comes isn't so good. It makes a long trip back to winter camps."

Iron Shirt rubbed his chin and thought about it for a long time. Then he spoke softly to each of his headmen in turn and they nodded. He could see them looking at the Tonkawa with ill-concealed hatred in their eyes.

"All right, let me go to my lodge and discuss this thing with my chiefs," Iron Shirt said. "You are welcome to stay here in the shade where it's cool and eat some more meat."

The elders marched off to Iron Shirt's tipi, very dignified and with blankets over their shoulders, waddling a little because they were no longer slender like warriors. Sanchess did not accompany them. He stayed near the brush arbor, arms folded, and everyone knew he was there to keep anyone from insulting these visitors, at least until after a decision was made. When someone drew near, he looked at them with his fierce black eyes, and that was enough to keep everyone well back.

In his lodge, Iron Shirt listened to all of the elders. Each made his speech, standing before the others. They smoked after each talk, Finds Something providing the pipe, Iron Shirt the tobacco. Each of them was an echo of the last.

"These white men come among us with a Tonkawa. These white men we know to be liars about treaties with The People. These men should all be staked out on the prairie and left to die."

"Kill them," Black Mountain said.

"Kill them," Big Wolf said.

"Kill them," Finds Something said.

Finally it was Iron Shirt's turn. He sat staring into the fire, saying nothing. The others waited silently. It took a long time. Once, as he was thinking, Iron Shirt asked for the pipe again and they all smoked without speaking. The sun ran across the sky and Iron Shirt was still thinking. It was almost sundown when he rose, groaning with pain from his stiffness after sitting so long in one position. Bent forward, the others watched his face closely.

"Our people are a proud people," he began. "Part of the pride is our courage. Part of it is our kindness to strangers who come without weapons against us. Except, of course, for certain enemies. But even, sometimes, them too. There has been compassion. Like this Tonkawa. He has come unarmed to help the white man and our own people to converse. He is not our enemy now. He is only the voice of the white man.

"Our young men have always been brave in war. Now we are asking that they be brave in peace. We may not take this road, because the white man has often deceived The People. But we should not, because of past wrongs, kill the men who sit among our lodges.

"We are the Nermernuh, The People. We are not barbarians. I say we should send these men away and tell them we will wait and see about this peace. Maybe we will go to their council, maybe not.

"I say with all the wisdom my forefathers have been

kind enough to give me that now is the season for killing buffalo, not for killing men who come to us in peace."

Iron Shirt sat down and everyone stared into the fire, each with his own thinking. After a long time, Finds Something lifted his face toward the smoke hole at the top of the tipi, where the sky showed purple in the setting sun.

"Hoy!" he said, and all the others nodded and Iron Shirt knew he had won.

The elders did not return to the arbor. Instead, Iron Shirt directed Otter Tongue, who had stood at the lodge door through all the deliberations, to tell the visitors that there would be more talk with the morning sun.

The People watched silently as the three men moved their horses and mules a short distance along the river to make camp. Sanchess and Running Wolf stayed awake all night near the white men's tents to keep any of the young men from slipping in and killing the Tonkawa in his sleep.

"That Tonk knows," Running Wolf laughed. "I suspect he will not spend much of this night sleeping."

THERE WAS no sun the next day. The sky was covered with low clouds, dark and foreboding. The wind had freshened, and with it came the scent of rain, and all the women moved around their lodges, pegging down the hide covers and tightening horsehair ropes on the smoke-flap pole.

But even though they needed no shade, the elders sat under the brush arbor once more as they had the day before, all of Iron Shirt's headmen behind him and the white men and the Tonkawa in front as he made his oration.

"Our hearts are glad that you have come," he said. "We will always remember it and think on you with kindness.

"You say the Texas white man wants peace. We want peace as well, so we can hunt and feed our women and children in the wintertime when it's cold and bellies cry for hot meat. We do not want to spend our lives looking behind to see if a white man's party with guns is after us.

"Our people have been in this land for a long time, since our forefathers came. It was before the living memory of any of us, and you as well. It is beyond your memory because you were not here then. Your forefathers were not here then. But ours were!

"In this country we made the road we wanted to travel forever. There was much game and timber and sweet water and grass for the horses. It has been this way until only a few seasons ago.

"Now the white man comes and has not said he will allow us to keep any of this for ourselves. To live as we want to live. To hunt as we want to hunt. To make war on our traditional enemies as we want to make war."

Iron Shirt paused and looked for a long moment at the Tonkawa. And the Tonkawa avoided his eyes even as he translated the words for the white men.

"We ask now only the same thing we asked of those people who have been our enemies but who were not white. When we made a treaty with those people, like the Cheyenne and the Arapaho, we gave them certain country and they gave us certain country. And we said to those people, if you do not come into our country and destroy the buffalo, we will not come into yours. That's what we ask now.

"Many times you have broken your word when there was supposed to be peace. Our own young men, too, have been warlike when there was supposed to be peace, for they are afraid when they see your people coming onto our land. Because soon they know it will no longer be theirs.

"I have heard it said that you will give us trade houses. But you want us to take the metal tools you white men use to scratch at the earth and plant seeds. We are not seed planters. We have never been seed planters, even our forefathers who came from the far northern mountains before there was the horse. We will never be seed planters. We are hunters, and we will always be hunters.

"So go back to your chief white man and tell him. We want no trade houses. We want only our land where we can travel the road of our fathers. And when your white chief agrees, then come to us again and we will share meat with you and talk of a treaty.

"Goodbye!"

Pulling the blanket over his head, Iron Shirt turned from

the brush arbor and walked slowly to his lodge, Otter Tongue close behind him. The people stood well back, silently, their faces calm now before these white men and the Tonkawa, proud of the words their headman had spoken. The white men rose and doffed their wide-brimmed hats and turned to their horses and rode away.

THE RAIN began to fall before they were far from Iron Shirt's camp. It came in a hard, driving downpour before the wind. Behind them, everyone had disappeared into the lodges except for Lost It and the young boys watching the herd to keep the ponies from running away if the hail came.

Bent into the rain, the peace party men rode, a blanket covering the Tonkawa's head, the wide-brimmed hats protecting the faces of the white men.

"Well," shouted Mr. Goodwin, "I'm glad to be out of that place and even in bad weather let's put some distance between us."

"A hard-looking lot, those young men," Mr. Toole said.

"Well, what do you think our chances are of ever seeing that bunch again?" Mr. Goodwin asked.

Mr. Toole laughed sharply, the water running from his whiskers and bushy eyebrows.

"Not a jot in hell, unless we come with a company of Rangers!"

And Mr. Toole was right. For although Iron Shirt and his people waited well into winter for the white peace commissioners to return, they never did.

13

NEVER-CHANGING PALO DURO! They were there again for the winter, and this a mild one, the young men going out onto the Llano Estacado well into the cold months to hunt, to bring in fresh meat. There were many feasts that winter, of tongue and hump steak and raw liver sprinkled with gall. The children were happy, their bellies full, and they played with much laughter, exploring the canyon and each other.

The lift of the red and gray walls around them seemed to shut out all the bad things that had happened on the plains to the east, all of the troubles that multiplied there with each season. The water ran clear and fresh along Prairie Dog Town Branch of the Red, and the mesquite beans were sweet. And the rabbits fat and easy to catch.

There was dancing for many occasions, just to celebrate living. There were dances just for the joy of dancing, for no special purpose. But always they created a special purpose to please one or another of the spirits that guided their destiny.

And there was the warbonnet!

It came from the white man Bent, the white man who had arranged the great treaty between The People and the Cheyenne. It was delivered by a special Cheyenne emissary and presented to Iron Shirt as token of esteem.

"It's a magnificence," Iron Shirt said, and could speak no more because of his great emotion.

It fit down tight on his still ample hair, a rainbow of feathers fanning out behind his head in all directions. And that was only part of it. It trailed feathers in a double row down the back so that the last of them brushed the ground when he walked. All eagle feathers too, and tipped with black and tiny red fluffs of down. All along the base of the feathers was a soft hedge of porcupine quills. The People had never seen anything like it.

The first time he wore it there was feasting and dancing all night, with the Cheyenne messenger as an honored guest. Then, at dawn, Iron Shirt sat in his lodge, looking at it, feeling with his fingers the texture of the vanes on each feather.

"I wonder if Bent made this," he said. "Or if it was our friends the Cheyenne."

"What's the difference?" Woman Who Runs asked. "That white man Bent's got a Cheyenne wife."

"It would take a lot of courage to earn this many eagle feathers."

"You had enough," Woman said, and laughed. "Only it's been so long ago, you've forgotten. I'm here to remind you of how brave you were when you gave my father those horses for me and rode out all the time with a lance in your hand and the turtle shield on your back."

"Yes," he said, his eyes dimming. "That was a long time ago."

After that, Iron Shirt wore it when there was a big meeting of the elders or when the band wanted to impress visitors to their camp. When he did, all the people in the band were as proud of it as was Iron Shirt himself.

When the Kwahadis saw it, they said it was a wonderment. Iron Shirt told them that was what came from going to peace treaties and doing the right thing. So they said maybe it wasn't all that wonderful. The next treaty meeting, they would stay at home as they always had, they said.

It was a time for tranquility. There were only a few domestic problems, such as when Stonefoot and Yam Eater came back with two young children, both boys.

They came without making a big fuss about it, pitching their tipi on the edge of the encampment one evening so that the next morning the people saw them there. It became a little tense. Everyone knew that some kind of arrangement had to be made with Red Moccasin for his daughter, gone now these many seasons, even though she had returned at last and with two fine sons.

"Eloping is almost as bad as adultery," Woman said. "We need to ignore them both until Stonefoot makes some kind of settlement with that old man."

But on the second day, Chosen went with Cactus Wren to visit Yam Eater at Stonefoot's lodge. And Yam Eater seemed no less young and flirtatious than she had been before. They giggled together and the two married women talked of babies and lovemaking and caring for a husband while Chosen listened, hoping to learn something.

Toward the end of the visit, Yam Eater said that Stonefoot beat her a lot, sometimes for no reason she could comprehend, and it saddened Chosen. But she supposed that was part of being a wife.

The People gave Stonefoot a guarded friendliness, for he was a great warrior who had counted many coups and killed a number of enemies at close hand. As the days went by and Red Moccasin did not confront him about this business of eloping with Yam Eater, the People began to whisper about Red Moccasin's courage. He was afraid to face Stonefoot directly, they said, because of Stonefoot's reputation for anger.

But the afternoon came when Red Moccasin went to the tipi behind Running Wolf's lodge and found Wolf's Road sitting before his fire, thinking. It was a balmy day and the sun had been strong since morning. There was the sound of jays calling from the cedars and of woodpeckers hammering the cottonwoods, as though it were summer.

Wolf's Road welcomed Red Moccasin to his lodge and offered food and tobacco. He knew why Red Moccasin was there. They sat together for a long time, smoking and talking of castrating horses. Finally, Red Moccasin came to the point of his visit.

"I'm going to Stonefoot," he said, "to ask for what is mine."

"Yes," Wolf's Road said. "He owes you something for your daughter."

"It's a matter of honor. Surely she is worth something. She has given me two grandsons and I am very proud. But I cannot visit in that lodge and play with them and tell them stories until honor has been satisfied."

"I understand that," Wolf's Road said. But nothing

more. He had sympathy for this old man, but Red Moccasin would have to say outright what he had come for, even though Wolf's Road knew what it was.

"I am an old man," Red Moccasin said. "Stonefoot is a great warrior and in all his youthful strength. I need a champion."

"Did you have someone in mind?"

"Yes. I wouldn't feel right, asking one of Iron Shirt's family. It would be taking unfair advantage because Stonefoot was once Iron Shirt's bodyguard and crier. So I cannot ask one of Iron Shirt's family."

Wolf's Road knew the old man could only mean Sanchess, who would make the best possible champion. But there was wisdom in the words, and Wolf's Road remained silent, waiting for the old man to go on. It took some moments because Red Moccasin was having difficulty saying these things.

"I would ask one of the young warriors of my own band, the Nakonis," he said finally. "But it would be better to have someone like you, a Kwahadi, and then there would be no special interest to be served. It could all be done with fairness."

"Then you want me for your champion?"

"Yes. I would like you to be my champion."

Wolf's Road puffed slowly on his cigarette, watching the smoke curl toward the top of the tipi, where the smoke flap was open to the sky. He thought about it, even knowing that a warrior of his own stature could never refuse such a request. And knowing that Red Moccasin knew this as well.

"As you say, I am not a Nakoni," Wolf's Road said. "And I will not speak for you. But I will go and see that there is fairness. But only that."

"It's all an old man can ask."

"When will we go?"

"With the sun's coming," Red Moccasin said with great relief.

The next morning, when Stonefoot came from his lodge to urinate, he found Red Moccasin and Wolf's Road sitting in front of the tipi, wrapped in their blankets. Red Moccasin was in front, Wolf's Road behind and to one side.

Stonefoot noted that Wolf's Road had fresh paint on his face, ocher and white.

Without saying anything to them, for courtesy was not involved in such things, Stonefoot walked behind his lodge to relieve himself. When he returned, he squatted before them and offered tobacco. They accepted and he called Yam Eater and she appeared, bringing a pipe and a tobacco pouch. As soon as she had handed these things to her husband, she went back quickly into the lodge, head down, never once looking at her father.

Stonefoot loaded the pipe and offered it to the sky and the four directions, and they smoked. Stonefoot and Red Moccasin spoke of the mildness of the winter, but Wolf's Road said nothing.

"Would you have some meat with me?" Stonefoot asked.

"No. I have already eaten. I have come for something else."

Stonefoot grunted and smoked the last of the tobacco in the pipe bowl. Then he spoke, looking at Wolf's Road.

"What business is that?"

"I have come for what you owe me for my daughter," Red Moccasin said.

"I have given you two grandsons."

"That was after you owed me."

Stonefoot grunted again and rose, his face cloudy and hard. The other two remained seated, their blankets around their shoulders. Wolf's Road's eyes were hooded and there was no expression on his face at all. It was like a rock in a stream, gleaming with the paint, eyebrows cleanly plucked.

"What do you think she's worth?"

"I have plenty of horses and a captive Mexican girl besides," Red Moccasin said, drawing himself up straight under the blanket. "But you brought back with you a fine percussion gun. I would take that. It's a good bargain, a gun for my daughter."

Stonefoot's jaw muscles worked into hard knots and his lips were set in a straight line.

"That's a good rifle," he said. "I bought it from a Wichita for many horses."

"I don't want horses. I'll take the gun for my daughter,

I don't care how many horses you gave for it. I think it's fair."

Stonefoot looked at Wolf's Road, but Wolf's Road sat with his eyes half closed, looking into the cedars behind the tipi.

"I'll think about it," Stonefoot said.

The old man rose slowly, groaning with the effort, pulling his blanket up around him.

"I'll wait in my lodge for you to bring the gun," he said. "For my humiliation, you can pay me a trip to my own lodge with it. I'll not take it now. I think that's fair."

Red Moccasin turned then and walked away, and Stonefoot watched him until he was gone among the lodges of the camp. Then Stonefoot turned his dark face to Wolf's Road, and now his teeth were bared like those of a snarling dog.

"Did you come to listen, or can you talk as well?"

Wolf's Road continued to stare at the trees behind the tipi. But after a few moments he rose and looked directly into Stonefoot's face.

"It's a good bargain," he said. "He could have asked for more."

"I like that rifle."

"It's something of value then, something you should be willing to give for your wife," Wolf's Road said. "Bring it to the old man before the sun sets this day. It's a good bargain. And a thing expected of you by all The People."

Stonefoot thought about it. Wolf's Road was like a brother to Running Wolf. And a brother to the favorite wife of Sanchess. Running Wolf, Sanchess, and Wolf's Road, three men who could make very bad trouble for anyone, even for a man like Stonefoot, who knew his own power. Maybe even Wolf's Road alone was bad enough. These Kwahadi were very serious sometimes.

But an effort had to be made to save that rifle.

"What will happen if I don't bring it?"

Wolf's Road looked at him for a long time, unblinking, his eyes as hard and black as chips of obsidian. When he spoke, it was slowly and without any show of anger or impatience.

"Then I'll kill all your horses."

Wolf's Road turned and walked away, holding the blanket about his shoulders, his oiled scalp lock trailing down behind his head.

By sunset, Red Moccasin had his percussion rifle and everyone relaxed and was happy again. Except for Stonefoot. But he knew it was better to lose one rifle than all his horses!

So Wolf's Road was accepted completely into this band. He had been with them a long time, but now he had championed an old man wronged, and against one of their big warriors. His prestige was limitless. He had already proven himself a fine hunter and brave fighter and, of course, the best rider of racing ponies any of them had ever seen.

Nobody knew what he'd said to Stonefoot, because Stonefoot told no one, least of all Yam Eater. But The People saw the results. That was what mattered.

"He's all of those other things," they said. "And a good diplomat as well!"

They were glad that such a man had left the band of his fathers and come to them. And they all knew it was more than his friendship for Running Wolf and Sanchess. It was that blue-eye!

With his added stature, Wolf's Road began to play the cedar flute before Iron Shirt's lodge once more, as he had done long ago and once in Mexico. And even a headman as powerful as Iron Shirt could not ask him to stop. It would wound the dignity of a chief to humiliate a man like Wolf's Road. Besides, it was now obvious to all that Chosen was ready in every way for a husband.

Yet they could understand Iron Shirt's reluctance to have the girl leave his lodge. He seemed proud when the flute-playing first began, but then Chosen had been of the wolf-head tipi. After she came to Iron Shirt as his daughter, the picture changed, for then she became his to keep or allow to leave. And they understood that sometimes an old man with a daughter was very protective of her.

So at night they listened to the flute of Wolf's Road, and during the day watched Iron Shirt's lodge, expecting something to happen. There was much gossip among the women, and some said Roadrunner would take that blue-eye himself if Wolf's Road didn't hurry with his courtship. Roadrunner was becoming a very fine young man, a good hunter and raider. His father, Gizzard, was a respected warrior. His grandfather, Black Mountain, was one of the big headmen in the band. Roadrunner already had a number of horses, and his own tipi always stood close by his father's. He'd make a good husband, they said.

But they also knew that Iron Shirt would never force his daughter to marry anyone she didn't want, although it was his right to do with her as he pleased. They said that Chosen didn't look at Roadrunner in the same way that she looked at Wolf's Road. And that made a big difference.

In the Moon of Fading Winter, Wolf's Road disappeared from the camp. He was gone a long time, and everyone thought they could see Roadrunner edging closer to Iron Shirt's lodge every day. Each time he went to the pony herd, they expected him to return with a horse or two for Chosen's father. But it didn't happen.

Woman Who Runs had already built a brush arbor beside Iron Shirt's tipi so he could get fresh air each day after the sun had warmed the earth. He was there alone on the day they would remember, bundled in his blanket and robes, watching Woman and Shade and Chosen crushing mesquite beans in front of the wolf-head tipi.

There was the sound of children playing near the stream. Iron Shirt could not see them because of a stand of pinyon, but he could hear their laughter. Somewhere farther along the canyon, dogs were barking excitedly, as though they had denned a rabbit. In the high arch of the blue sky, captured between the two rims of the canyon above, hawks were wheeling.

It was midmorning when Running Wolf came up from one of the small valleys within the canyon floor, leading four horses. Across the withers of one of them were tied two freshly killed pronghorn antelope.

Chosen saw Running Wolf at once and stopped pounding the mesquite beans on the large stone before her. The other two women noted her expression and the direction of her eyes and stopped talking and looked as well. All of them knew what was happening. Those four horses belonged to Wolf's Road!

"It's Running Wolf," Woman said needlessly.

"Yes," Shade said, and laughed. "With horses!"

Chosen was unable to speak, even had she wanted to, because her throat had suddenly gone dry and tight.

They saw Running Wolf go directly to the brush arbor where Iron Shirt sat, tether the horses to one of the arbor posts, and then squat facing the headman. They could see him talking, and in a minute Iron Shirt took out a pipe and tobacco and they smoked, first offering it to the spirits. The two men seemed to talk forever as Chosen watched, feeling as though she were breathing through cactus spines.

They saw Running Wolf turn and lift his hand toward the four horses and the two antelope. They watched the two men smoke again, then talk some more. It was unendurable!

Finally, Running Wolf rose and walked back the way he had come, quickly now, and Iron Shirt, without looking at the horses again, threw off his blanket and robes and walked to his lodge, head down.

"Come," Woman said, and, taking her mesquite beans, started for her husband's lodge. She took only a few steps, then turned to glare at Chosen. "You too, girl. Don't you know who this is all about?"

Iron Shirt was already at his place before the tipi fire when they got there. Chosen thought he looked angry, and that frightened her. Then she decided it was only his expression for deep thinking.

"Do you want the whole family?" Woman asked, and Iron Shirt grunted.

It took some time to gather them all, and Iron Shirt sat without a word. At last they were there, Sanchess and Iron Shirt at the fire, Woman sitting close behind her husband, Shade and Wapiti Song and Owl Calling and Chosen and the two children well back against the lodge wall, in the shadows.

There was no need to waste time now with polite openings. Everyone had seen the horses tethered at the arbor.

"Wolf's Road has sent a warrior to speak for him," Iron Shirt said. "That's a good sign. It shows he is not as brash as some young men are. It shows his respect for his elders.''

''Yes,'' Sanchess said. ''Those are good horses!''

''He sends the message that he will bring antelope from time to time, for me and my woman to eat.''

''They are fat young antelope.''

''I suppose so,'' Iron Shirt said. ''I have never liked antelope as well as buffalo. But antelope is all right sometimes, if you don't eat too much of it.''

They were silent then, and everyone knew what they were thinking, except for Chosen. She sat as though one of the horses had kicked her in the belly.

''Well, this is a family matter,'' Iron Shirt said. ''We are all involved because this daughter of mine is a special case.''

Everyone knew what he meant, and Sanchess nodded.

''Would you have this man Wolf's Road as a brother-in-law?'' Iron Shirt asked, looking directly at Sanchess for the first time.

''Yes,'' Sanchess said. ''He's a good man. I would be honored to have him as a brother-in-law.''

Iron Shirt sat frowning, staring down at the meager fire. They could hear the children laughing in the streambed below, and jays calling in the cedars on the ridge behind them. Chosen was sure they could all hear the thumping of her heart as well.

''It presents a serious problem,'' Iron Shirt said. ''This Wolf's Road may be a good man, but he is already the brother of one of your wives, Sanchess.''

A small smile moved across the mouth of Sanchess before he spoke.

''A brother and a brother-in-law are two different things. You can stop worrying about that. I've seen you worry about that for a long time, without putting it in words for me. Now it's time for you to stop that worry.''

''Hoy,'' Woman said softly.

''Be silent, woman,'' Iron Shirt said irritably. ''I'll get to you after I'm finished talking to my son.''

''Father,'' Sanchess said, his smile broad now, ''a brother and a brother-in-law are two different things. They are not the same. Wolf's Road will remain as he is now in this band, in the circle of Big Wolf's family, not of ours. His tipi will stay where it is now, near that of Running Wolf, who calls him brother."

Iron Shirt grunted, but before he could speak, Sanchess raised his hand, and his power as a war chief was so great that even Iron Shirt held back his words.

"I will not send any of my wives to him," Sanchess said. "He is not my brother."

"Hoy," Shade said, and tried to suppress a giggle.

Slowly, Iron Shirt twisted his body until his eyes were on Woman.

"And you?'

"Yes," she said.

Then Iron Shirt turned his eyes to Shade, and without his speaking, she said, "Yes!"

Wapiti Song and Owl Calling, not accustomed to being asked about such matters, nodded quickly, and Iron Shirt looked at Chosen.

"Daughter, I will not force you to a man you do not want," he said. "If you want this one, then go with the other women and dress out those antelope. All this talking has made me very hungry."

Everyone in that part of the canyon had moved to vantage points from which to watch Iron Shirt's lodge, because this was a marriage they had all anticipated. They saw the women of Iron Shirt and Sanchess lift the two antelope from the horses and hang them from drying racks and start the butchering. They saw Sanchess come from the lodge and untie the horses and lead them into the nearby gulch where Iron Shirt's herd was corraled. And while they watched they heard a loud shout, like a war cry, and the beating of a pony's hooves, and looking along the course of Prairie Dog Town Branch, they saw Roadrunner on his best horse, running down the canyon. And some of them felt sorry for him.

After the meat was dressed they hung it on tripod poles, and Getting the Lodgepoles was stationed there with a long club to keep the dogs away. While Owl Calling stretched the hides on frames, the other women built a sweat lodge of willow bows covered with hides. A large fire of cottonwood and mesquite branches was kindled beside the sweat lodge and stones were placed in it. Water was brought from the stream.

Seeing all of this, the people watching knew this was going to be a large wedding, and they went to their own tipis to bathe and put paint on their faces.

The women of Iron Shirt and Sanchess attended Chosen closely in the sweat lodge. They poured water on the hot stones and scrubbed her with cedar, wrapped her in a blanket and marched her back to her father's lodge, and there placed across her shoulders the smock with elks' teeth that Shade had made many seasons ago. They painted her face vermilion and rubbed ocher into the part of her hair. All of her possessions were tied together, the little calico gelding brought up from the herd, and the bundle lashed to his withers.

When Wolf's Road came, he came on foot, carrying his cedar flute and dressed in his best buckskins, long-fringed and decorated with Ute scalp hair. Under his left eye was a white smear of paint, like a teardrop, done in honor of his bride's brother Sanchess, who often wore paint in that manner. Across his shoulders was a new trade blanket, red-and-gray striped.

Woman was watching from the tipi door flap, and when she saw Wolf's Road coming, she pushed Chosen out. The girl stood with her eyes on the ground as Wolf's Road came to her and placed the blanket over her shoulders and then led her and the horse away. They went down the slope of the hill where Iron Shirt's family lodges were, crossed the stream, walked past Running Wolf's tipi, where he and his wife, Grasshopper, stood grinning, and on to his own lodge.

It was as fine a wedding as anyone had ever seen. And it wasn't over yet.

Iron Shirt sent Otter Tongue through the camp, and to the Kwahadi's as well, announcing a marriage feast for that night, with dancing. The old men brought out their drums. The two antelope were cut into roasting chunks. Mesquite beans and dried wild cherries were mashed together to make a sweet mush.

As twilight came, the drums began. The People, all in their finest leggings and moccasins, ate and laughed and danced. The dogs ran in circles around them, barking wildly. The parents of the bride sat proudly before their tipi in the light of a great fire, receiving visitors. Iron Shirt was wearing his Cheyenne feather bonnet.

Sanchess gave Running Wolf a fine pony. There was more dancing. When the antelope were eaten, more meat was brought, and pemmican and honey. The sound of the drums echoed against the high-rising walls of Palo Duro. And the children played in the pony herd.

AT FIRST there was only complete and utter terror. She knew he was saying words to her, gentle words, and holding her close under the heavy buffalo robe covering. But she could comprehend little except the pounding beat of drums from across Prairie Dog Town Branch. She knew his hands were on her and his face against hers. She heard his breathing and felt its hot warmth against her mouth.

And then the terror was gone and there was only the warmth and the close, dark interior of the lodge, where there was the smell of sage and burning mesquite and the body of her husband.

FOUR

There are not so many buffalo anymore!

14

MORE AND MORE, IRON SHIRT spent his time seeking out the conversation of those who could tell him about the white man. His Paneteka friends were most helpful because they had always been in closest contact with the Texans. But there were other sources of information as well: the Comancheros who came onto the plains each year with their high-wheeled carts; the Wichitas and Wacos and others who moved back and forth between Comanchería and the white man's country; some of the Kiowas who had contact with traffic along the Santa Fe Trail; and some tribesmen who went to Taos each year for the trading there.

Much of it was most confusing. Much of it was only vaguely understood. But one thing was clear. Now Texas was a part of the bluecoat white man's country, with a great headman in the east. It presented difficulties. At any time, the bluecoat white man might send soldiers to help the Texas white man. This was most disturbing because Iron Shirt had long considered the bluecoats to be his friends. The Texans could never be. There was too much blood and bitterness there.

When Texas came into the Union, The People had to deal with two white fathers. A part of the annexation agreement was that Texas, having been an independent country, still held claim to all the land within its borders. North of the Red River, in a territory or a state, the unclaimed public domain was the property of the Great Father in the east, and therefore he could make promises as to its availability for future hunting and living space. But in Texas no such thing was possible because public domain there was Texan, administered by the white headman in Austin.

And Texas was selling unclaimed land to immigrants, encouraging them to move west. Into Comanche country. And they arrived, with their cattle and plows and women and children. The only pause came with the war between the bluecoats and Mexico. Then, for a while, there was peace between The People and the whites, for all kinds of reasons Iron Shirt could not understand. But he knew it wouldn't last long.

So he worried. Except for the bright moments in this sunset of his life. As with the arrival of a new grandson.

CHOSEN WAS strangely complacent about the whole business. Her confidence may have sprung from the activity of the older women who assisted her, took her in hand. They appeared to know what they were doing.

Horned Lark, the wife of Finds Something and a medicine woman in her own right, supervised the preparations well in advance. Woman Who Runs helped, but Shade was made to stay away. She had a bad record for issuing stillborn babies and one didn't tempt the bad spirits that seemed to hover around her at birthing time.

They were encamped that fall on the Canadian River where it curled its way along the northern fringe of the Antelope Hills. They came in late summer from Timbered Hill River, where they'd watched another Kiowa summer celebration. This one was called the Dakota Sun Dance because a number of Sioux had come south to visit.

Iron Shirt had done a lot of talking with the Dakota men, who knew a great deal about the bluecoat white man. Of course, they knew nothing about Texans. Iron Shirt was astonished to learn that the Sioux didn't raid very much, by Comanche standards. They had no Mexico. They had no Comancheros. They had no Llano Estacado. And also, by Comanche standards, they didn't have a very large pony herd.

After the Kiowa festival, in which many Kiowa and Comanche horses were given to the Sioux as gifts, Iron Shirt moved the band south for the last of the summer hunts before going back into Palo Duro for the cold season. And it was here that Chosen would have Wolf's Road's child.

It was a good camp with much grass and sweet water and stands of shin-oak timber. There were many cardinals in the cedars, and often in the gray mist of dawn they saw little blue herons in the stream and it excited the children very much because it was a bird they did not often see.

They found no sage growing here, and sage would be necessary when Chosen's time came. But Horned Lark always carried a small supply in a parfleche for just such an occasion.

The birthing lodge was erected by the women well away from the other tipis, for no men would be allowed near. Unless there was trouble, and then Finds Something might be called in to take over the procedure. No one expected that to happen. Chosen had been free of morning sickness, and with her advancing pregnancy she seemed to grow stronger, with the glow of life in her eyes and cheeks.

"All that's a good sign," Horned Lark said. "That baby in her is going to be a good one!"

Because it was still warm weather, the birthing lodge was not a hide-covered tipi but a brush arbor with brush walls, so the wind could circulate through. Inside, they built a box-frame of logs and filled it with cedar boughs and covered them with trade blankets to make a bed. They drove stakes into the ground on either side, for Chosen to hold with both hands when the pains came. They dug two holes and lined one with clay, the other with rawhide. The clay pit was for water and the other for the placenta, which afterward would be carried to the river and thrown away.

Then they waited.

The days passed and Iron Shirt was irritable because all he could do was sit and wait. It didn't help that Wasp and Roadrunner were out on a raid with some Kiowas. And Woman was getting so old she couldn't move as quickly as she once had to satisfy his needs. And while they were waiting, a party of Wacos came through with the news of a great sickness among the Paneteka, the disease that caused diarrhea, muscle cramps, intense thirst, a deep faint, and death. The white man's cholera.

Many of the Paneteka died, the Wacos said, leaving the band only a shell of its former self. Iron Shirt knew he had lost a lot of old friends once more.

"Those Paneteka are unlucky," he said to Woman. "Something bad is always happening to them."

"They live too close to the white man," she said. "Something bad always happens to people who live too close to the white man!"

But then the Panetekas were forgotten because Chosen's time had come. It was the middle of the night, and before Horned Lark arrived, Woman already had the girl in the birthing lodge and the pains were coming hard.

They undressed her and made a fire and heated stones. They filled the water pit, and when the stones were hot they added those. Sage was rubbed on Chosen's belly and some of it burned in the lodge fire to make a thick, musty smell. All this while, the two old women were keening softly, as though at someone's funeral.

They rubbed Chosen's back with warm water and made her drink soup that was very hot. Horned Lark pushed down on her belly with both hands, gently at first, but then with considerable force. Chosen lay on the cedar-bough bed, gripping the stakes on either side. Once she rose and they helped her walk around the lodge, bent almost double and grinding her teeth to keep from crying out.

Then, quickly, it was done and Horned Lark cut the cord with a skinning knife and the singing turned to the high-pitched, happy sounds of celebration.

They named the boy Kwahadi because he came so fast, like a running antelope. Not fast after the marriage, for that had been more than a year ago. But fast in issuing from his mother.

"That Chosen's a small one," Woman said proudly. "But with the wide hips for making babies."

The sun was hardly up when they brought the baby and the new mother back to Wolf's Road's lodge and he painted a large black circle above the tipi door and started giving away horses. He gave away so many horses he was left with only a few, maybe fifteen.

Iron Shirt gave away horses as well. Before it was finished, Horned Lark went back to her tipi leading seven good ponies. Finds Something lay on his back all day before his lodge, singing his best songs, and Woman Who Runs, sitting in the lodge of her son-in-law and holding the baby, said, "This one will be a great chief someday!"

"I told you," Iron Shirt said. "That's a good daughter!"

"Yes," Sanchess said. "I should have married her instead of giving her to you." And they both laughed because it was a good thing.

At first Kwahadi's eyes had the same smoky blackness of all babies of The People, but by the time he had seen seven moons, they had turned dark gray and sometimes, when the sunlight struck his head just so, there was the glint of copper in his hair. But there were still the high cheekbones of his father's kind, as well as the finely formed lips and the solid body with short legs, and the hands with powerful fingers that gripped his mother's hair when she nursed him, seeming never satisfied to let go.

Sometimes Chosen sat in the sun with her son in her arms, singing soft songs. They were the ones she had heard Wapiti Song sing to Getting the Lodgepoles. But now and again she hummed an old Welsh lullaby, the memory of its notes and cadences strong in her mind, even though the words were long forgotten.

"Well, I'm not sure I like her singing those white man's songs," Iron Shirt confided in Woman, but she only laughed.

"They are only sounds. And you watch how you talk about him, old man. He's going to be a great chief someday!"

"Good! He means much to me!"

CHOSEN HAD learned by now that Comanche babies didn't cry much. They learned from the start that it did little good. They would be held by their elders when the elders felt it was time to hold them, and not before. Kwahadi cried the least of any she had known. He would watch from his cradle board, his wide eyes darting after any movement around him. She was convinced that they were the brightest eyes she had ever seen and that the newborn haze had left them within moments of his arrival.

The boy grew as did all Comanche boys. First were the

days when he was carried by his mother or one of the aunts, his moss diaper changed each evening, his bath given each day and afterward the rubdown with cottonwood-root powder. Chosen found it especially satisfying to watch Wapiti Song do those chores, because it brought memories of when little Getting the Lodgepoles was an infant. He was not so little now, already riding like a man and helping Lost It handle the pony herd.

Then, with the seasons passing—and in peace, because Iron Shirt moved the band always to places where he thought there would be the least chance of friction with the white man—the boy grew and was soon running through the camp naked, chasing the dogs with switches and then with a small bow and blunt arrows that Iron Shirt had made him. And after that, the time going so swiftly that Chosen could hardly keep track of it, Kwahadi in the pony herd, riding at first only his mother's little gelding pinto, a horse growing old and gentle now.

By the time he had four summers, Kwahadi could stand on the gelding's rump or withers, upright and without any handhold, while the horse moved through the herd. Sanchess had made him a small quirt with willow wood and antelope hide, and for many hours he would lie along the gelding's back, dreaming of things a boy dreams of, flicking flies from the horse's neck with the whip end of the quirt.

He became adept at trapping rabbits, at hitting grasshoppers with arrows, at rolling the willow hoop, at chief-of-the-hill, a rough-and-tumble game in which he seldom seemed to lose among boys his own age. Wolf's Road gave him a young stallion, already broken, and Shade made him a small smock of deerhide decorated with tails of buffalo, each one larger than either of his hands. When Chosen groomed her husband's shield, Kwahadi sat beside Wolf's Road, watching, and listening to his father explain power and how to get it.

Chosen taught him as much of the language of the Spaniards as she knew. He came by his mother tongue as all Comanche boys did. But she taught him none of her own original language because she could remember little of it now and besides, he was Comanche. No matter the glint of gray in his eyes and of copper in his hair when the sun struck just so.

THE UNEASY peace was finally finished. The war between the whites and the Mexicans was long past and now there were forts across the spine of Texas—Chadburne and Belknap and Phantom Hill, among others—and sometimes there were many bluecoat soldiers there, warning by their presence that marauders would be punished. And when this was true, the wild tribes were relatively quiet.

But more often than not, inside the forts were only a few infantrymen or dragoons, and The People disdained them, for they did not allow themselves to be caught in a stand-up fight with men who had long guns and fought on foot. Iron Shirt explained often what he had heard of these bluecoat soldiers from the Sioux at the Kiowa's Dakota Sun Dance.

"These men who have no horses except those big ones that eat only corn, they are not to be feared. They cannot pursue. They move like hoof glue, slow and unchangeable in their course. But never come near them. The Dakotas of the north and the Cheyennes and Arapahoes have told me. They are a killing kind. They can kill your horses from far off, and when there are many of them together, they shoot their guns together and it's like a hailstorm.

"But they are easily avoided. The ones you must fear are the ones with better horses; they are not bluecoat soldiers at all. They are the ones the Texas white man calls Rangers, and they all have these vicious little guns they can hold in one hand that will shoot many times with one loading. Those are the ones you must fear. They are worse than the Osage. And nobody needs the Dakotas or Cheyennes to tell us this."

Even as he told them, he knew he was encouraging the young men to go on the blood trail under certain conditions rather than others. Yet he could not avoid in his heart whatever advice he might give that could save the lives of The People's young men.

The country was being cut by the wagon wheels of many whites now. Some going to New Mexico. Some going to the far west where the sun slept, looking for the yellow metal in a place called California. Some driving freight from Kansas to Santa Fe. And some just coming, to build their sod houses and cut the grass with their plows and plant their seeds and grow their corn and children.

For a long time now, Iron Shirt had avoided the Trinity, where the band could once have gone to hunt and live out any summer. Even some of the headwater rivers of the Brazos were becoming dangerous and the buffalo less plentiful. More and more, he tried to move his camps so that the young men who lusted for the war trail would have to go a long way to strike the white man. But even then, they would sometimes go and be gone for many sleeps.

And going to Mexico, where the warriors could burn out their energies, was even more dangerous. Not after crossing the Rio Grande, but before. For there were many settlements in south Texas now, and whites who shot at anything. Worse still, the settlements were a great temptation to the young men to take horses and scalps along the route. The world was drawing in, like the circumference of a circle of white man's trade cloth shrinking in the rain.

"But they will go anyway," he muttered to himself. "They will make war somehow, no matter how far they must ride. It has been so for generations. And now they will not listen to reason. They grow crazy with all these things they do not understand."

Woman Who Runs heard him talking to himself and said nothing. She was becoming a little tired of such talk. It was about all she heard from him anymore.

THEY WERE encamped on Coldwater Creek at the northern edge of Llano Estacado, close enough to Palo Duro so that with the changing of season they could go quickly into the canyon. It was a night of moonlight with silver over the land almost as bright as day. There were a few coyotes howling close by, but then they were silent with the coming of another sound. Sanchess was almost asleep in the wolf-head tipi when he heard it.

Wasp was dancing through the camp, announcing his intention of making a war party. He danced and sang for only a little while and then a few of the band's young girls were out, dancing among the lodges, singing for Wasp and his intention. Sanchess listened and knew what it meant.

Wasp stayed in his lodge the next day. Many of the men were out hunting, but Wasp never appeared. Sanchess stayed in camp as well, thinking that he might speak with his brother's son about this raid. It was a bad time, because a war party now might bring retaliation from the white man, and Sanchess knew the worst time to be struck by the white man was in winter camp.

Then he remembered how it had been in his younger days, and he could not bring himself to confront Wasp with his misgivings.

That night Wasp sang again, going through the camp. Otter Tongue, still Iron Shirt's bodyguard, danced with him. And later the girls sang in their high voices under the moon. Sanchess lay in his robes and listened, knowing what it all meant.

And again on the next day, Wasp stayed inside his tipi. But Sanchess went to Otter Tongue and held council with him.

"It's a bad time to be going out," he said. "It's time now to go into winter camps."

"You've grown old and forgotten what this all means," Otter Tongue said.

"Listen to me, I know what it means," Sanchess said, his black eyes gleaming with anger and his lips growing hard. "If you leave my father now, with the move of the band coming soon, I will take it as a great humiliation to him. And to me as well!"

Otter Tongue looked into the eyes of Sanchess and shrugged and turned to his hunting pony. But that night he did not sing with Wasp and the young girls, and before dawn on the coming day, when Wasp left on his blood trail, only two others went with him. Otter Tongue was not one of them.

When he knew they were gone, Sanchess lay for a long time in his robes, past sunrise, thinking about it. He knew his father was right, yet his blood tingled to be with them, his lance in one hand, his shield in the other, challenging any enemies they might find. But the words of his father kept coming to him, and they were stronger than his need for war. It was a terrible thing in his mind because it meant that for him everything had changed, forever.

THE THREE riders moved slowly along the high ground cut by Carrizo Creek, far west of Palo Duro, where they knew that by now the rest of the band was moving into winter camp. They had been out for fifteen sleeps and had seen nothing but a Ute hunting party moving back toward the mountains from the buffalo ranges. It was too large to think of fighting, with perhaps twenty warriors and a number of women, who could be as dangerous as the men.

"Besides," Wasp said, "we're looking for revenge on the white man."

"We could steal some of their horses tonight," Roadrunner said.

"No, it's best we don't go near such a large party," said Cloud, youngest son of Black Mountain, and Roadrunner's uncle.

"All right, it's best," Roadrunner said, nodding, the hand mirror that hung in his hair swinging back and forth like a small skillet.

"We're looking for revenge on the white man," Wasp repeated.

So they watched from hiding as the Ute party passed, far enough away to keep their own horses from making a fuss over strange ponies.

Their purpose was not completely clear to any of them, even to Wasp. It was just a revenge raid because of the treaties the white men had broken. It didn't matter that their own band had never entered into any such treaty. It was simply Wasp's medicine that told him this was the moon for revenge.

"Besides," Wasp said, "any white man who comes into our country must be punished so that others will not follow."

After the Ute party had passed, they rode on toward the north, despondently, for it appeared that in this country west of Llano Estacado they would find no white man in this season. Maybe not in any season. They didn't know because they had never ridden the war trail in this area, being young men. Twice they saw tracks but made no attempt to follow because the horses were not shod and because in either case there were too many ponies, indicating a large party.

"We should have ridden down the Brazos," Cloud said. "We have come in the wrong direction for white men."

"We should have more warriors," Wasp complained. "But there has been so much talk by the elders against war parties that the other young men grow afraid, I think."

The other two knew he was talking about Iron Shirt, and they also knew Wasp would not mention his name out of respect for the old headman.

The air was crisp with autumn, and the few hardwoods they saw were turning yellow and scarlet. They saw many black-masked butcher birds, the loggerhead shrikes.

"Maybe that's a good sign," Cloud said. "Those birds painted for war."

They rode two more days, making fireless camps each night and eating dried buffalo meat. The sky was clear and chill. It helped take the enthusiasm out of everything because it was always cold before morning. They were ready to turn back to the east, toward Palo Duro. And then they saw him.

It was in the afternoon. He was riding a large bay horse and leading a string of pack mules, picking his way among the scrubby water birch near the river. They watched him until sunset, keeping just below their own skyline.

"Tomorrow we'll play a joke on this white man," Wasp said. "Tonight we'll wash the black paint off our faces."

They were close enough to see the white man's fire after dark. They lay on their bellies along a razorback ridge above his camp, their horses hobbled behind them in a stand of pinyon.

"He's got that fire in a hole," Roadrunner said. "Just like one of The People."

"Maybe this is a white man who's learned much," Wasp said. "Maybe he's been out here a long time, trading. Like a Comanchero."

"He doesn't look like any Comanchero I ever saw," Cloud said.

"His fire's too big or we wouldn't be able to see it from here."

"Maybe he's not afraid of being seen," Cloud said.

"Then he's a fool!"

"Maybe we ought to go in there and kill him while he sleeps and take that horse and those mules," Roadrunner said.

"We'll wait," said Wasp. "Tomorrow, once he starts along his trail again, we'll play a little joke on him."

Then they slipped back down the ridge and slept under the bellies of their horses until first light.

HE WAS an old man with long, white whiskers and a tangle of uncombed hair that hung like mattress batting from beneath the fur cap he wore. The cap was made from a skunk pelt, the white stripes running back to the tail that still hung down from the rear. He was dressed in buckskin with long fringes, and on his feet were Crow moccasins decorated with quill beads. He had done a lot of trading with the Crow in past years, and with the Shoshone as well, and wintered many times with both tribes. He had trapped beaver in the clear mountain streams of that northern country.

He was going to Taos with a summer's kill of buffalo hides. He didn't like trading in buffalo hides, but now the beaver trade had gone. And buffalo were easy to come by.

This was to be his last year of such a life. Now he would sell these hides in Taos and return east. And maybe hire out to the army as a scout after a long drunk in St. Louis or wherever. He'd heard the army was looking for scouts, particularly for men like himself who knew a lot about Indians and tracking and other such wilderness things. He was proud of his ability to deal with Indians.

Those who knew him called him a mountain man. But he called himself a trapper. Of course, these past few seasons he had taken hides with his Hawken rifle and not with traps. But he still called himself a trapper.

He had never been this far south before. But he had wanted for many years to come, to see the old Spanish settlements in New Mexico. He could have sold his hides at Bent's Fort on the Arkansas, but he wanted to see New Mexico and maybe some of these southwestern tribesmen. He had seen a lot of tribesmen in his time. Even the Blackfoot, who were very touchy sometimes, and dangerous. But he had seen enough of those northern Indians to know them well. Now it was time to see some more, here in the southern plains. He enjoyed seeing new Indians.

They came at him from the west that morning, with the sun in their faces, and he could see no black paint. All good signs, three men coming with the sun in their faces and making no attempt to keep their stallions quiet and no black on their faces. And none of them had firearms. That was good too. Looking for trade, or for whiskey, most likely. A lot of these people were looking for whiskey now, more than ever before. He had a little jug hanging behind his saddle.

He didn't know what they were, but he assumed they were Comanche. He'd never had any business with Comanches, but he'd heard about them. They'd traded horses to every tribe all the way to Canada. These were young men, he observed, and carried lances. Well, Comanches always carried lances, he'd heard.

One of them raised his hand in greeting as the three rode closer, another good sign. He raised his own hand but kept the other on the Hawken that lay across the saddlehorn. He didn't know any Comanche, but he expected that Shoshone would do and he knew a lot of that.

"It's a good day," he shouted. He could see they understood. They were smiling. One of them angled off to one side and looked at the mules. The other two came straight on.

"Yes, a good day," one said, smiling. "You've got some hides there."

"Yes, a few hides," he said. "Going to Taos to trade. You know Taos? Taos?"

The young man nearest him raised his face toward the sky and cawed like a crow, loudly, making the mules fidget nervously on their lead ropes.

"That's his medicine," the leader said. "He makes a sound like crows when he's happy. He's a little crazy."

The rider who had moved out to the side wore a hand

mirror in his hair, just above the right ear. As he moved his head, the sun reflected in it, shining in the mules' eyes. They began to move back against the lead rope he held in his hand, pulling strongly. One of them brayed and started to kick.

"We've got some ponies back in that draw," the leader said, turning and pointing. "Good ponies. We'd trade for some whiskey. I see you've got some whiskey on your saddle."

"It's not very much," he said, trying to hold the lead rope steady. The mules were prancing, pulling away from the reflected sun in the mirror.

"We're out hunting."

"I saw a small herd back up the river yesterday. You should ride there," he said.

The crazy one threw back his head and cawed again, a number of times. Some of the mules began to kick, pulling hard on the lead rope, the mirrored sun in their eyes. The mountain man was yanked back in his saddle, trying to hold the lead rope. He was half turned, hanging on to the rope, when he realized that the man on his flank was lunging his pony forward, like a cat jumping, his lance coming down. And he knew in the last second that it was too late to get the Hawken turned to fire.

The point of the lance struck him just below the ribs, and as he went off the bay, he saw the others in a red haze, jumping their horses toward him, their own lances out before them.

AFTER THE scalp dance in Palo Duro Canyon, Iron Shirt sat furiously before his fire. Woman stayed away from him. He was like a wounded grizzly in this mood, and lately it seemed to come on him as regularly as the moon's change.

"Witless," he said. "Killing an old man with white hair for a bunch of worthless hides and a few mules. The bay's not bad. But it's all witless. It's the kind of thing that makes the white man very angry!"

Woman said nothing, working on a hide smock at the rear of the tipi. Iron Shirt waited for her to rebut him, but she remained silent.

"In the old days, all the warriors went out, after the Utes or Apaches or other honorable enemies. Then they came home. And everybody knew what it was about. I remember one time with the Tonkawas."

"I've heard that story," Woman could not resist saying. "I am not a child, listening to you tell how it was when you were young."

Iron Shirt grunted. "Well, it's no good now, these young men going out with three or four. What kind of way is that? And maybe the white man coming behind!"

"They've never gotten here yet. They always stop."

"Someday they won't stop. They are so close now that even their big horses that eat only corn can come to us. A war party of three men! Who ever heard of a war party of only three men?"

And Sanchess was equally upset. After the celebration was finished and Wasp had given the mules to the girls who had helped him sing of his war party, Sanchess went to Wasp's lodge, which was set well back from Iron Shirt's. His face was clouded with anger and his black eyes were gleaming.

He found Wasp alone at his fire, smoking.

"Yes, Father," Wasp said, calling Sanchess father because he was brother to his real father. "Smoke with me."

"There's no time now and nothing in my heart for small talk," Sanchess said. "You've become as wild as a pukutsi. Nobody knows what you'll do next."

But Wasp only laughed, stroking the Hawken rifle that lay across his lap.

15

THE PEOPLE WERE FAMILIAR with the harsh nature of high plains weather. Sometimes the spirits who controlled such things became very upset with whatever normally upsets spirits and visited the land with violence to show their displeasure.

There were the twisting winds, powerful enough to lift a horse off the ground. They were always accompanied by fierce lightning and thunder, and often rain was driven so hard before the gale that it could almost drown a standing buffalo.

And there was the cold. It swept down from the north country, spreading ice and snow across the land, freezing ponies' hooves to the ground, turning all water solid so that sometimes game died of thirst. Most troublesome of all was the cold's unpredictability. Many of The People could recall in stories to their children the years when spring's buds were already coloring the landscape red and yellow and suddenly the sky would go leaden, the winds would come, and the ice and snow and cold death.

One of those sudden and violent chills fell across the land in the year that Wasp was accused of adultery with Stonefoot's wife. Some of The People were sure there was a connection.

It was a relationship that had been progressing for some time, and many of them knew of it. A great many of the women sympathized with Yam Eater because Stonefoot had turned grouchy and sometimes he beat her. Wasp, on the other hand, was a handsome and successful warrior and had no wife of his own, even though he was well past the time for taking one.

At first they had met at wooded water holes along the streams and well away from camp, or on some secluded hill covered with deep grass and sage. But then they grew bolder, and often Yam Eater could be seen leaving Wasp's lodge in the middle of the day when Stonefoot was out hunting or grooming his horses in the pony herd. It was a secret well kept from Iron Shirt, but Sanchess knew. He made no move to stop it because he could not bring himself to interfere with a young man, even his own brother's son, who was feeling his stallion blood and gaining prestige for himself by taking another man's wife. It was not the accepted way for gaining prestige, but neither was it unheard of.

In that year of the quick spring chill, Stonefoot had returned from the pony herd one afternoon well before he was expected. Some said maybe his medicine had whispered to him that he should watch the lodge of Wasp and he might find a surprise. For whatever reason, Stonefoot watched. And saw.

That night, many of The People could hear the shouts from Stonefoot's lodge, and even though Yam Eater made no sound, they knew he was applying a switch to her. And the next morning, with many of The People watching covertly, Stonefoot appeared at Iron Shirt's tipi door flap, wrapped in his best robe and carrying his pipe.

Iron Shirt came out for the first breath of new air, completely unaware of why his former bodyguard had come to visit and was now sitting outside the lodge. But everyone else knew. This was going to be a claim for damages.

"Why does he go to the old chief and worry him with it?" Grasshopper asked her husband.

Running Wolf laughed. "He would rather press his case through the old man than to Sanchess alone," he said. "Stonefoot is not stupid."

After smoking a full bowl of Mexican trade tobacco, the two of them sitting cross-legged in their robes, Stonefoot came to the point.

"Father, I have been wronged by a member of your family!"

Iron Shirt's eyes widened, but he quickly controlled his

expression and waited, sitting in his robe with his hair loose and blowing out across his face in the morning wind.

Knowing that Iron Shirt would say nothing at this time, Stonefoot continued, "I have found my wife committing adultery with Wasp."

There was no flicker of interest in Iron Shirt's eyes, and he held his face immobile.

"Why do you come to me?" he asked. "Why don't you speak with Sanchess?"

"Because," Stonefoot said, "Wasp is the son of your eldest son, gone long ago to the place beyond the sun. But even so, you are a great man and you know I love you and you will be fair."

"Are you sure of this thing?"

"Yes. I saw her come from his lodge yesterday. And last night she admitted to me that she has been with him often."

Iron Shirt's face was blank, blanker than the moon, and his eyes seemed to see nothing.

"Then the boy and Sanchess, who is his father now, should be here to listen to your accusation. That's fair."

Otter Tongue had come by that time, and was standing close beside Iron Shirt's tipi and watching to see that no harm came to his chief. Iron Shirt knew he was there and, without turning, beckoned to him and sent him for Wasp and Sanchess.

"We will smoke again while we wait," he said.

Sanchess came, looking much as his father did, robe-wrapped and expressionless, his hair not yet done in braids for this new day. He sat just behind his father, and Stonefoot showed his nervousness now by almost dropping the pipe when Iron Shirt passed it to him.

When Wasp came, he came with hair fanning across his painted face and naked to the waist except for the bandanna around his neck. Hanging from his legging belt was a stone war club, and his eyes were bold and arrogant. Stonefoot became more nervous still.

"Now you can make your accusation to his face," Iron Shirt said.

Stonefoot swallowed a number of times. He smoked the last of the tobacco in the bowl and returned the pipe to some hidden place under his robe. Then he looked at Wasp squarely.

"You have known my wife, Brother," he said, calling Wasp brother because now they had shared a woman as a wife. "I'm here to ask damages for that."

Wasp drew himself up straight and folded his arms across his bare chest. Iron Shirt could not avoid thinking how much he looked as Sanchess had looked in younger days.

"I have many horses," Wasp bragged, and Iron Shirt ground his teeth together. "I will buy her if you no longer want her."

"Would you buy my children too, like slaves?" Stonefoot said, a note of bitterness in his voice. And Iron Shirt began to feel sorry for this former bodyguard of his.

"It's fair that you have something for this insult," Iron Shirt said. "What would you have?"

"I want two good horses. Stallions," said Stonefoot. And then, with boldness, he looked squarely at Sanchess. "And that pistol taken from the Mexican on the Pintada. I have lost one good gun because of this woman. It's fair that I have another."

"I cannot speak for the small pistol," Iron Shirt said. "I can only speak for the horses."

"I'll give the pistol," Sanchess said, not raising his eyes from the ground. "And one stallion. But nothing more. That's all this is worth."

Stonefoot started to protest, when Sanchess raised his face and looked directly into Stonefoot's eyes. There was a long silence and then, abruptly, Stonefoot nodded.

"That's fair," he said.

"I'll give the horse," Iron Shirt said.

"No, Father, I came for nothing from you," Stonefoot said.

"He's right," Sanchess said. "It's my place to give the horse and the gun too. And from now on, Brother, try to control your woman."

So Otter Tongue went to the herd and led the stallion back and took the pistol from Sanchess's hand and delivered both to the lodge of Stonefoot. There he saw that Stonefoot had slashed Yam Eater's nose a little with a skinning knife. At least, Otter Tongue thought, he had not cut the nose off as everyone had supposed he would do. Sometimes that was done by jealous husbands when there was infidelity in the lodge.

It was a good horse, a trained hunter. But Stonefoot was not completely happy with the arrangement, even though he knew there was little he could do about it. He was most unhappy about Sanchess calling him brother. What had that meant? Had he been in Yam Eater's robes too?

Then Stonefoot laughed at such a notion, thinking that Sanchess had said it only to make him nervous, to make him think. And he did think. He couldn't stop thinking about Sanchess calling him brother. Maybe he should confront Sanchess again and ask for some more horses. Then he decided that wasn't a very good idea.

WASP CAME to the wolf-head tipi in the night, still with his hair loose and paint on his face. And still arrogant. He and Sanchess smoked cigarettes, and after a while he offered Sanchess one of his best ponies to repay Sanchess for the hunter now grazing in Stonefoot's herd.

"I don't want your horse," Sanchess said. "I want you to remember that I've done this thing for you. And stay away from that woman."

"Stonefoot grows old," Wasp laughed. "He cannot make that woman happy."

"He's not that old. He's the kind of man who might go crazy the next time and kill you. It has been known to happen when a man finds his wife copulating with another man who is not his brother, without an invitation to do it."

"And what would you do if such a thing happened?" Wasp laughed, and Sanchess knew that this young man did not believe anyone was brave enough to try to kill him.

"If he did that, then because I am your father I would take revenge on him. I don't want to kill one of your grandfather's old bodyguards. He was once one of the bravest warriors in this band, braver than you'll ever be. So stay away from that woman!"

Wasp's face went cloudy and his lips set in a hard line.

He rose abruptly and left without another word, rudely. Sanchess had expected it to happen that way.

Later, when most of the camp was sleeping, Wasp rode through the lodges with all his horses, making little barking noises. Roadrunner was riding with him. Sanchess had expected that as well, and he knew before he slept that Wasp was going out again to find the blood trail and that he might not be back here for a long time.

THEY WERE camped on Wolf Creek in what the white man was calling the Cherokee Outlet. They had only just begun to get their first spring hunting camp established, having moved here from Palo Duro less than a moon ago. It was rolling grassland and one could see for a long way, especially from some of the higher ground.

After the affair with Wasp and Stonefoot, Iron Shirt wanted to look a long way. He wanted to look so far he could see into his youth, when all he had to worry him was dancing and hunting and riding out to harass his enemies.

He went to the pony herd with the dawn that day and cut out his favorite horse. This was a little roan stallion with white stockings on two feet, an old horse now, long past hunting, but still Iron Shirt's favorite. He rode east of the camp, noting as he passed through the lodges that most of The People were still sleeping. He crossed a small dry wash and went on beyond to a rising crest of grassland and sat there, allowing the coming sun to warm his old bones as he stared off toward the east, toward the Crossed Timbers and the places where he had fought the Osage in times past.

It was a bright morning with only a low bank of cloud to the northwest, almost lost in the shadow of the land where the sun's light had not yet reached. The fresh breeze played along his cheeks and blew his loose hair back from his face. He raised a little song to all the good spirits of morning while the pony beneath him grazed on the lush spring grass.

In his youth, when he had been at the height of his power as a war chief, he had often been able to make time stand still. It helped him many times in forgetting the pain of wounds. Now he tried that medicine again and it came, because he willed it so strongly, wanting to forget the pains he felt now. Not only the pains of his flesh and bones, but the pain inside from everything that was happening. He didn't think specifically of Wasp or of the white man or of the diminishing herds of buffalo. He simply sat his pony after his song and made time stand still, even though the sun did not stop in its march up the sky.

Somewhere in a dark corner of his mind was a small question, but so small he was hardly aware of it. The birds were not singing. There were no hawks in the sky. As his gaze went out toward the east, the grass began to lie flat along the ground and ripple like the green waves of water he had once seen on the great gulf south of Texas. Yet he had no real sensation of the wind against his back until the pony began to fidget and snort.

A cold chill passed along his body. He supposed that was the hand of some spirit that always came when he was making time stand still. Then his hair began whipping along his cheeks and his ears began to grow cold. He shook himself from the trancelike thinking and knew at last that the wind had begun to blow, hard and cold, cutting with its fingers through the trade blanket across his shoulders, and he thought that trade blankets were not as good as buffalo robes for keeping out the wind.

The pony had been drifting before the wind, keeping his rump toward it, and when Iron Shirt tried to turn him, the horse snorted and fought the reins. Finally, Iron Shirt got him around and then saw the sweeping gray clouds coming like a thousand Utes from the northwest, the little shadow he had only partly noticed before. The sun was suddenly a copper disc, growing dim and then disappearing like a fire with water thrown on it.

It began to rain before he had gone far, and the pony resisted at each step, going into the wind. Iron Shirt felt the particles in the rain, which cut into his nose and across his cheeks and lodged ice in his nostrils and ears. He kicked the pony hard and used the quirt and now the rain was coming in sheets, slanting across the land, and in it were the hard pellets of ice that stung like tiny bullets.

He could see only a few feet in front of the pony's ears, and they came to the dry wash suddenly, without warning. Only now the water had begun to boil along its course and the pony jerked back violently and Iron Shirt went off the side of the saddle, rolling down the bank, feeling a bone in his right arm break. But he didn't hear it because the wind was now howling with such force and intensity that it wiped out all other sounds or thoughts of sound.

He struggled to his feet, waist-deep in brown, rushing water, icy cold. Twice he fell, but each time found his feet and somehow reached the far bank of the gulch, where he clawed his way up, using his one good hand. The right one had gone numb with cold and pain.

It had turned dark as night. Iron Shirt staggered on toward the campsite, his feet dragging in the deep grass where the snow and ice were choking the ground. He fell many times. The trade blanket blew from his shoulders, whipped away and gone instantly in the wind. Then he fell one last time and lay with his face in the icy grass, feeling the water hardening along the fringes of his hair.

Then the darkness came down over his eyes, and once they were closed for only a little while, the lids froze shut. He felt a strange warmth going through his body, and a deep drowsiness. And with the snow beginning to drift over him, he slept.

IT WAS painful, coming back from sleep. The first thing he saw was the interior hide wall of his lodge, the tipi fire sending flickering shadows everywhere. Then Woman Who Runs was bending over him, wiping his face with a soft deerskin cloth soaked in warm water. He knew there were others there, but he couldn't focus his eyes on any of them. There was a gentle keening, and he knew from looking at her face that it was not Woman doing the singing. And he knew there was a deep, searing pain through his chest.

"I was out doing some thinking," he whispered, and the words hurt his throat.

"You do too much thinking, old man," Woman said. "Your son-in-law found you two sleeps ago in that storm we had. What a place to lie down and sleep!"

"I was doing some thinking." He saw Chosen's face then, as she bent to ladle soup into his mouth. It was scalding hot, but he swallowed it and thought, So Wolf's Road found me. That cedar-flute player. Good! Maybe he'll amount to something yet.

Then he moved his eyes and saw Shade and Wapiti Song and Owl Calling. He tried to move his right arm because it hurt, and then felt the splint and knew that Finds Something had been there. Now and again he thought he could hear the medicine man singing, and in his mind was a picture of the fat old man lying on his back in front of the lodge. He could hear no sound of wind against the tipi walls, and when anyone went out or came in, there was a flash of bright sunlight as the door flap was lifted.

"The storm's finished?" he asked, the words painful in his swollen throat.

"Yes," Woman said. "Now be still and eat some more of this soup."

Iron Shirt's breathing was labored and harsh, like wind blowing through a hollow reed. When Woman or Chosen wiped his mouth with a deerskin cloth, he could see red on it. Between mouthfuls of soup, he could taste the blood.

"I want Sanchess and Wolf's Road and that newest grandson in here," he said. "I have a talk for them."

"You don't need to talk," Woman said, but in her tone he knew he would have it as he wished. As he always had.

So they came, and as they gathered, Sanchess held the boy Kwahadi in his arms. Sanchess sat before his father's bed, the boy on his lap, and Wolf's Road stood behind. All the women moved back into the shadows of the lodge, and Iron Shirt made his talk.

"I'm going to tell you a thing," Iron Shirt said, his voice rasping. "It's about the white man."

He coughed weakly, and Woman moved back to his side and wiped his mouth where the bloody foam collected.

"You should know these things. Some of you will be great peace chiefs someday, maybe. And these are things a peace chief needs to know.

"Sometimes the white man has made treaties with different bands of The People. And with the tribes in the north, like the Cheyenne, who became our friends at the great council meeting on the Arrowpoint River long ago. In these treaties, the white man often said that when his people come into our country, to settle there or just to move across, they must first be given permission to do so. Then the white fathers in the east or in Texas would give us a lot of presents."

Again he coughed, violently, his chest heaving and the water running from his eyes.

"Stop talking, old man," Woman said. "You are talking too much."

"I have always talked too much," he said. "I will do no differently now. And when I get to the place beyond the sun, I will likely talk too much there, as well.

"Now, these treaties. Although they tell us their people will come only if we agree, those people come anyway. In great numbers. And our young men go crazy seeing this, and they want the blood trail even when they know it's time for hunting to lay in meat for the cold times.

"When our young men go on the war trail, the bluecoat soldiers are sent to protect these white people who have come onto the land. These soldiers are sent by the black-coat white men with high hats and long strings around their necks, like I saw once many seasons ago in the country north of Red River. These black-coat white men make the treaties and then allow their own people to break them. And when our young men go crazy because of it, the black-coat white man sends the soldiers. This I have heard. This I know."

Iron Shirt stopped talking and lay with his eyes closed, but Sanchess knew he was not finished. After Woman had bathed his face again with the deerskin cloth, Iron Shirt opened his eyes and lifted his left hand and continued.

"I've always liked those bluecoats. They were our friends once. I have spoken with many headmen and they have told me that these bluecoats are reasonable men, most of them, although I suppose they have a few wild ones like we do. But they understand us. They're here, on the buffalo ranges, and can see. They're warriors, like us. There is always a trust between warriors, even when they are enemies from time to time.

"But the black-coat white men are another matter. You

cannot escape them and they make all the rules for their great fathers in the east or in Texas. You never see them because they are away from here, making their rules. And you cannot avoid the people of the black-coat white man, because they come, no matter what the rules tell them to do.

"So you must stay as far away from all of them as you can. Keep the band moving toward the west and live mostly on Llano Estacado. Of course, we have many enemies in the west, like the Utes and the Apaches. But they are better than the white man.

"Stay away from the white man. As long as you can. I don't know how long that will be. Maybe not long. They keep coming."

He coughed again, his eyes dim, and Sanchess could see that his father was growing very weak. The boy in Sanchess's arms was still, watching with large eyes as Woman wiped the blood from Iron Shirt's lips.

"I have learned many things. I have learned how to make war when I was a young man like you. I have learned how to keep the peace when I was an old man like me. I have learned how to manage arguments so everything is fair. I have learned the best hunting ranges and when to move the camp.

"But the biggest thing I have ever learned is about the white man. And that thing is you can do nothing about him!

"Once there were many buffalo. Now there are not so many. The white man kills them, and all those people he has sent out here, they kill them as well. Soon there will be none left.

"Once there were many of The People. Now there are not so many. A few have been killed by the white man's bullets. A lot more have been killed by the white man's sickness. Someday, maybe, there will be none of The People left, either."

Iron Shirt lifted his hand unsteadily and pointed to the boy in Sanchess's lap.

"Maybe someday he will be a great peace chief. If we last that long, he will have to be a peace chief. The time of war chiefs will be past. I had a dream about him. Maybe the dream will come true. Maybe he'll be a great peace chief. The time is coming when war chiefs cannot save The People."

He lay back and closed his eyes, and Sanchess knew he was finished. Sanchess rose with the boy and carried him from the lodge and waited for Wolf's Road to follow. Night had come and they stood looking at the black sky with its many stars, each a point of tiny light, and over all of it the dusty, silver trail from which Wolf's Road had his name.

Sanchess looked down into the boy's face. He could see the eyes shining in the starlight.

"Did you hear your grandfather speak?" he asked.

"Yes," the boy said.

"Good," Sanchess said. "Always remember his words."

He handed the child to Wolf's Road, knowing that Kwahadi was too young to have understood any of it. Sanchess was not sure he himself understood it all. He stood beside his father's lodge and watched as Wolf's Road took the child away, carrying him in his arms because this was a special thing.

Chosen came from the tipi and stood beside Sanchess for a long time before she spoke.

"Is he dying?"

"Yes," Sanchess said. "The chief is dying."

She moved away quickly then, following her husband, and Sanchess knew she was crying.

NORMALLY THE men prepared a man for his grave after his spirit had departed for the land beyond the sun. But now Iron Shirt asked Woman Who Runs to do it before he began his journey. She undressed him and bathed him and rubbed his skin with cottonwood-root powder, like a baby. She braided his hair carefully, and wrapped it in elkhide. She painted his face with ocher and yellow, as for a celebration. Then she dressed him in his best buckskins with long fringes, and over that placed the remains of the Spanish chain-mail smock. And she put on him his best moccasins with trailing buffalo tails, and the warbonnet of many feathers that had come from the Cheyenne.

As she worked, keening softly all the while, Iron Shirt's mind went to the days of his youth, when the buffalo herds were across the lands and were so large that a hunter could not ride around them in a day, and when there were raids into Navaho country to steal horses, and when they had been in Ute country and could see the snow mountains, and when he and two companions had killed a grizzly bear with lances.

All of it ran together in his thinking, like paint running together on the face of a warrior grown hot in the sun. Even the sounds, all together. The snort of a buffalo cow protecting her calf, the call of the wapiti and the night songs of mockingbirds and hunting owls and the daytime cries of the hawk. The distant yammer of coyotes and the barking of camp dogs when the Kiowas came to visit. The taste of liver with gall and of roasted tongue, and the wind in his loose hair when he rode with a lance in one hand, the turtle shield in the other.

Iron Shirt died in the early morning, his favorite time, and they buried him with the whole camp mourning, the women cutting themselves with knives and hacking off their hair and throwing dirt and ashes over their heads. They buried him in the usual way, in a sitting position as though he were ready to speak again, then covered him with heavy stones and killed four ponies over the grave.

And Stonefoot wept as much as any of the women, for this had been his chief, the man for whom he had been bodyguard and camp crier for many happy seasons, until the woman came into his life. And under whose leadership and teaching he had become one of the great warriors of The People.

16

THE ELDERS OF THE BAND WERE in disarray. After Iron Shirt was in the ground, there was no one of them powerful enough in council to be considered headman, no one of them whom all the band would follow. Not Goes Ahead, growing very old and more crippled with each passing sun. Not Big Wolf or Black Mountain, both old as well and very much inclined to look backward instead of toward the future.

There was disunity, and many fierce arguments broke out each time the band moved. Sanchess watched silently, seeing some of the families going away to join other bands because of the uncertainty.

The elders set up their own tipi where they would meet. Not like the days of Iron Shirt, when he called them to his own lodge. There was little respect for the elders' lodge, and even more than usual the young boys played tricks on them, setting fire to the tipi door flap when they were inside, causing them to come out coughing from the smoke, or throwing discs of buffalo dung against the walls of the meeting place to interrupt the proceedings.

For almost a year, Sanchess did not appear at the meetings of the elders. He busied himself in many ways. He oversaw the breeding of his pony herd. He led a small raid against a ranch high up the West Fork of the Trinity, an event for celebration because it had been a while since the band's greatest warrior had taken out a party. But it was disappointing to many, because it was not a blood trail. Horses and mules were stolen, but no captives taken, or scalps either.

Most of all, he spent his time with his nephew Kwahadi, teaching the boy what he knew of horsemanship, even though the boy's father was one of the best riders in the band. Teaching him the use of the bow and a small lance, and how to ride among the buffalo, how to skin out a kill. The boy was still very young, but he was strong and quick to learn.

And Wolf's Road taught his son as well. Among other things, how to make a cedar flute and play it.

"That boy can already play as well as his father," said Woman Who Runs, who now lived in the tipi of Shade and Wapiti Song, behind the wolf-head tipi.

"I had always thought that lovemaking was a thing one did not have to be taught," Sanchess said. "But maybe that Wolf's Road knows more about it than I do."

"You know enough," Shade said, laughing.

And Woman said, "Hoy! Hoy! All my sons have known these things!"

If Sanchess and Wolf's Road had the boy with the sun, when night came he belonged to his mother. Chosen would sit with Kwahadi before her tipi fire, for now she had her own lodge and slept apart from Wolf's Road, except when he called for her. She told the boy the stories she had heard from Iron Shirt's mouth. How The People had come down from the mountains of the north, saying goodbye to their Shoshone cousins. How they had come to have the Spanish horse, although that part was a little vague. How they had migrated and fought all enemies to conquer the south plains and become the greatest warriors and horsemen of all.

Wolf's Road worried a little about the boy's attachment to his mother, and equally about his attachment to Shade, Sanchess's wife and the boy's aunt, who often came to Chosen's lodge to visit in the night and tell a part of the story of The People's history. But finally he decided it was a good thing. He and Sanchess would teach the boy how to be a man. Chosen and Shade would teach him pride in being one of The People. From the four of them, Kwahadi would gain an understanding of honor and courage. Already the boy walked through the camp fully clothed and wearing moccasins with squirrel tails trailing from the heels, as though he were a man. And Wolf's Road decided that among the four of them, they would teach the boy the most important thing of all: dignity!

THEY WERE camped on the Canadian when Sanchess took his place in the circle of elders as the band's headman. He became peace chief not because he was elected, and certainly not because his father had been in that position before him, but because everyone knew his counsel was strong and his leadership powerful. They would follow him as they would follow no other.

Many of them had profited from his raiding. Many of them had followed him on the war trail. He had taken scalps, and even more importantly, on at least three occasions he had touched living enemies with his hands when they held weapons and were resisting. He and Running Wolf and Gizzard and Wolf's Road made up the most formidable group of fighters in the band, perhaps even in the tribe. And for many seasons he had listened and watched Iron Shirt, and from that knew how a peace chief was supposed to act.

He took up the robe of peace chief not because he wanted it but because he could no longer watch silently as his father's people kept moving away like thistles flying before a high wind.

It should have been named the summer of new leadership. But it was remembered rather as the time of great bitterness and frustration.

It was evening of the day when a few Wichitas had come through and visited and shared their meat. Sanchess called a meeting of the elders as his father had, sending Otter Tongue through the camp. They came to the wolf-head tipi now, for, like his father, Sanchess could see no reason to erect a special elders' lodge as some bands did.

Chosen brought the boy at the appointed time, for Sanchess had asked her to do this, and all the others were a little surprised the first time they met and there among them was a child. But they understood that Sanchess wanted to teach Kwahadi how the council worked, even at this early stage in his life, and they understood.

On this night, Running Wolf came as well, a little while

before the elders arrived, and took his place at the rear of the lodge. Sanchess was sitting at his fire, and when Running Wolf came in, he smiled.

"You are joining the elders now?" he asked.

"Only as your bodyguard. That Otter Tongue is a good bodyguard and village crier, but you need at least one of your own."

"I don't need a bodyguard," Sanchess said, the smile disappearing from his lips. "No one here will harm me."

"Yes, you do need a bodyguard," Running Wolf said. "It's for appearances, not safety. Head chiefs need bodyguards for appearances."

"There are no strangers here to impress."

"I will impress all of our own old men, including my father."

Sanchess laughed suddenly, a harsh, bursting sound, and Running Wolf knew he could stay. He was glad, even though the arrangement might irritate Otter Tongue for a while, because he never came into the meetings but stayed outside the tipi.

"Just remember your place," Sanchess said.

"I never speak in the presence of older men."

And Sanchess laughed again. It felt good, having his friend sitting directly behind him.

When the others came they seated themselves and smoked, Finds Something first offering the pipe to all the spirits. They spoke of how well the hunting progressed, and of the drying of meat by the women. Running Wolf sat silently at the rear of the lodge, the child Kwahadi beside him. Goes Ahead told many stories of the old days, which everyone had heard before.

"That was the first time I saw how those people in the north bury their dead," Goes Ahead was saying. "They don't bury them at all, but put them on scaffolds aboveground. The Crows do that. These were Crows, I think. It was long ago and I've forgotten who they were. Those Crows are fine-looking people. But they have a very strange way of burying their dead. High above Earth Mother."

"Every man to his own medicine," Finds Something said.

Then they came to the purpose of the council meeting.

"Those Wichitas we saw today," Big Wolf said. "They told us there are Pawnees north of us, killing buffalo."

"Maybe they were not Pawnees," Goes Ahead said.

"The Wichitas ought to know Pawnees," said Black Mountain. "They're cousins. Besides, once you see a Pawnee, you remember what they look like."

"Then we need to have the young men go out," Goes Ahead said. "We need them to gather some Kwahadis and go out and kill those Pawnees who are on The People's buffalo range. I remember once when I was young, we went out in a large party to fight the Pawnees. There were Kutsatekas and some of our own band. It was a good fight."

Sanchess, sitting at the position facing the tipi door, stared into the fire, and some of them recalled that Iron Shirt had always done that, listening to the others, then thinking about it before he spoke. Now they waited, even Goes Ahead keeping silent.

"There's no need to jump like a frightened colt," Sanchess said finally. "Maybe we'll need a large war party. Maybe we won't need any war party at all. The young men should be hunting now. So before we suggest that they all go off on a war party, maybe we should have a scout."

"That's a good suggestion," Goes Ahead said.

"There's something about all this that makes me nervous," said Finds Something. "Maybe we ought to let it pass."

"It's dangerous to have Pawnees around," Big Wolf said. "Especially when the young men are gone from camp so much, running in the buffalo herds."

"That's right," said Black Mountain. "We don't want them coming in here and running off some of our horses or stealing some of our children."

"We'll have a look, then, with a small party," Sanchess said. He looked up at Black Mountain. "Ask your son, my friend Gizzard, to come in and talk later. He knows how to make a scout and use good judgment."

After the meeting of the elders, it took only a short time for everyone to know that some of the young men were going out. But there was no singing or dancing. It was just a scout that the headman wanted, and maybe the singing and dancing would come later, if they had to send a war party.

Chosen watched as the four men who would make up the scouting party came from the wolf-head tipi later, under a new moon. They looked like shadows against the hide walls of the lodge. One of them was her husband. The others were Running Wolf and Gizzard and Cloud, Black Mountain's sons. They stood for a while in front of the wolf-head tipi, talking with heads close together.

She had a night fire in front of her lodge. She usually went to Wolf's Road's lodge only when he called her there at night. But now she went to prepare his weapons. She took down the shield and the quiver and the lance, but left them in their cases. She placed all of this on the floor near the tipi door, the shield on top so it didn't touch the ground. Then she waited.

Soon she heard Wolf's Road coming, talking with Running Wolf. And Running Wolf was complaining.

"I'd feel better about this if there was some singing and dancing!"

"It's only a little scout," Wolf's Road said. "We probably won't find anything. If there were any Pawnees there, they're probably gone now."

When he stepped into the tipi and saw his weapons ready, he smiled, and she thought him very handsome. She helped him gather his other gear: his medicine parfleche, his cluster of bags with face paint, his tobacco pouch. She packed a larger parfleche with meat taken from the drying racks that same day. He watched her as he undressed.

"I won't be gone that long," he said. He began to bathe himself with water from a rawhide bag hanging from a lodgepole. "There's enough meat there for the entire summer."

"What you don't need, bring back," she said. "How far will you go?"

"We'll see. Gizzard leads, and I think if we don't see anything closer, we may go all the way to the Arrowpoint River. Just to be sure there are no Pawnees around to harm you."

"I could go with you and tend the extra horses."

He laughed and drew her toward his robes at the rear of the lodge.

"Who would stay here and teach our son?" he asked, pulling her down to his bed.

"Many people teach him."

"But you best of all. Now he's saying some of those words the Mexicans use. You never taught me any of those. I can't speak with my own son anymore." But he was laughing, and she knew he was proud.

"I will teach you anything you ask me to teach you."

Then there was no more talking and they lay in the robes for a long time, until the fire in the hole at the center of the tipi had died to embers. As she lay with him, she listened to the mockingbirds in the trees along the river and the sound of distant coyotes, and she heard horses being led through the camp.

She was awake when he rose and dressed to leave and join the others. But she pretended sleep, knowing that now he would not want to talk, that now his thinking was on what lay ahead.

After he was gone, she stayed in his robes, still with the scent of her husband strong in the lodge. She wondered why sometimes when she lay with him it was good, and sometimes not so good. Then she stretched and smiled and lay ready for sleep in his bed, knowing that this night it had been especially good.

THERE WAS no apprehension in camp while Gizzard and his three companions were out. It was just a small scout, they all said, and Gizzard was an experienced warrior and knew how to avoid danger. The hunts went on each day, uninterrupted, and the butchering continued as it always did.

The women of Iron Shirt's family worked together, along with Grasshopper, the wife of Running Wolf. Woman Who Runs was getting too old for the heavy work, but was able to do the other tasks, like cleaning out the guts and stripping the sinew from backbone and legs. Shade and Wapiti Song and Chosen and Owl Calling did most of the work, with Sage Girl helping. Sage Girl was a grown woman by all standards, and Owl Calling was happy to see a lot of the young hunters shyly mooning around nearby when they returned from their run in the buffalo herds.

Getting the Lodgepoles was in and out of camp each day, old enough now to take the packhorses out to the hunters as they were skinning out a kill and then lead the ponies, meat-laden, back to camp. Sometimes he was in the pony herd as well, helping the hunters who came in for fresh horses to rope their next mounts.

Kwahadi spent a lot of time in the pony herd too, but he was often back at the wolf-head tipi, the center of family butchering. Each time he came, Chosen gave him a nice piece of liver sprinkled with gall. And with the red juice still dripping from his chin, he would go back to the horses or pause in his work long enough to play a game of chief-of-the-hill with the other children of the band.

Or else he would go alone to the river and catch turtles with a woven willow net. Turtles were good, roasted in their shells over the low embers of a fire. He learned to cook them himself, over his own fire, and eat them himself also, for most of The People would not put anything in their mouths that came from the river. But Kwahadi liked them, having tasted them during one of the winters when buffalo meat became scarce and Chosen had shown him how to eat many things other than buffalo meat.

"That Kwahadi," Shade said. "He spends a lot of time to himself when he ought to be playing with the other children."

"He looks at the river and thinks of the day when he'll grow large enough to ride beside his father," Chosen said.

"Yes," Woman said, chewing on a piece of roasted tongue. "He needs to think. He'll be a great chief someday."

Sometimes Cactus Wren or Yam Eater came to the wolf-head tipi to visit in the afternoon. After a while, Chosen would take them to her own lodge and they would watch their children growing. There was a harsh scar along Yam Eater's nose from Stonefoot's knife, but she laughed about it and said it made her very attractive to some of the young men in the band who knew what it meant. But she never mentioned Wasp, nor did the others.

They played dice games and ate fresh buffalo meat and

spoke of the times they had spent together over the past seasons. And all agreed that it was one of the best summers anyone could recall. There had been many wild plums and grapes and the harsh little prairie onions and the small black-jack-oak acorns that could be saved and in the cold months peeled and boiled to eat with bone marrow and crushed mesquite beans. A good time.

The scouting party returned after five sleeps, and came in the night. Chosen was almost asleep in her lodge when she heard a distant wailing. Then there was the sound of horses going through the camp slowly, and the howl of a wolf, which she knew was not the howl of a wolf at all, but Finds Something starting one of his medicine songs. She waited, a large knot of fear growing inside her chest.

She heard ponies just outside the tipi, and a voice calling her name softly. As she rose, she could see that the boy was awake too, his eyes above his robes, shining in the last light of the lodge fire.

Running Wolf was standing at the tipi door flap, holding the lead ropes on his horses, and she knew he had come directly here before going to the pony herd. Maybe before even going to his own lodge. The knot in her chest almost choked her.

"Tomorrow I will come," Running Wolf said. "You will move to my tipi now. He showed much bravery."

And he turned and walked away, leading his ponies, his head down. She could feel Kwahadi standing immediately behind her. She turned quickly and placed her arm around him and led him back into the lodge.

"Get in your robes," she said, her voice soft but not shaking. "Your father will not come."

The boy did as he was told, going quietly and pulling the robes over his head. Chosen stood for a long while, looking at the form of her son in his bed. She was having a hard time bringing air into her body. She took a water bag from a tipi pole and doused the fire, because now she wanted darkness here. Groping, she found her skinning knife and moved to her own bed and began to slash her arms, making diagonal cuts along each of them. She could feel the sudden, hot rush of blood from her flesh, feel it running down her arms and dripping off her fingers.

She hacked at her hair, feeling the blood from her hands wetting her face. From far away she heard new wailing now, from Gizzard's lodge and from Black Mountain's, and then a new keening from the area of the wolf-head tipi, and she knew it was Shade.

Lying on top of her bedding, she stared into the darkness. But she did not wail or cry or make a keening song as she had done when Iron Shirt died. Something inside her rose along with the hard knot that choked her. Something from long ago, something that made her clamp her teeth tightly together and remain silent in the darkness. But after a moment she rolled to her side and vomited on the tipi floor.

From the rear of the lodge came the sound of quick, heavy breathing, and she knew her son was listening to the retching. But other than his sharp swallows of breath, he made no other sound.

SANCHESS SAT before his fire in the wolf-head tipi, grinding his teeth in anguish and anger. His eyes glinted as they had when he took out the war party against the scalp hunters on the San Saba. Cloud and Running Wolf sat before him, for now the sun had come, and with it the time for telling what had happened.

"Tell me," Sanchess said, and his voice sounded like the growl of a hungry dog.

"We went to the Cimarron," Cloud began. "We searched along it and saw many herds, but no Pawnees. We rode toward the rising sun at first, then north toward the Arrowpoint River, then back toward the setting sun."

"We saw no Pawnees," Running Wolf said. "And no sign of any. But close to the Arrowpoint, we saw wagons. A line of them with white tops and pulled by mules."

"With women and children?" Sanchess asked.

"No. They were traders' wagons, going toward the place of the Comancheros."

"New Mexico."

"Yes. Gizzard said we should watch for a while," Cloud said, talking fast, as though he wanted to get it finished quickly. "So we watched for a while. Then Gizzard said he would go down and talk with these white men with the wagons."

"Why did he want to speak with them?" Sanchess asked, leaning forward.

"Gizzard said maybe they had seen some Pawnees. He would ask them to smoke with him and ask them about the Pawnees."

"They were riding good horses," Running Wolf said. "And they all had guns."

"How many?"

"Maybe fifteen. And they all had guns," Running Wolf said. "Gizzard rode down, holding up his hand like this." Running Wolf held up his right hand, palm out. "All the white men saw him and came out to meet him, and when Gizzard was close, we saw the smoke of the guns. Gizzard fell and his pony came back toward us, running and afraid of the noise."

"There was no black on my brother's face," Cloud said, and the tears had begun to run down his cheeks. "He went in peace.

"When Gizzard was lying on the ground, some of the white men came on toward him, on their horses. Wolf's Road said they were going to take Gizzard's hair, so all of us rode down there, but they didn't draw back. They started shooting at us with their guns.

"We stopped," Cloud said. "There were too many guns. Like the time we fought those Fox and Sauk people. Except Wolf's Road went on, to save my brother's hair. He caught up my brother, bending down from his pony, and took my brother's jacket in one hand as he rode past and carried him back to us."

"But one of the white men's bullets found him," Running Wolf said. "He came on to us, dragging Gizzard, and then we all went back away from the white men, Wolf's Road bleeding badly from the back and still holding Gizzard in one hand alongside his pony."

"He wasn't even wearing black paint," Cloud said, almost wailing. "He didn't hold weapons in his hands. They killed him and he wasn't even wearing black paint!"

"We found a small spring and bathed Wolf's Road in the water," Running Wolf said. "Gizzard was already dead. Wolf's Road died before the sun was gone. It was very hot, so we buried them there as best we could."

"In the darkness we went back," Cloud said. "We were very hot for revenge. They had their fires so anyone could see, as if they were so powerful they didn't care who saw. We left our horses well back and slipped into the camp, and Running Wolf killed one with a hatchet while he slept. But there were many awake, keeping guard, and the man made a lot of noise in his dying, so we slipped away."

"It was all we could do against so many," Running Wolf said. "Even with more warriors it would have been bad, because they had all those guns."

"We rode away," Cloud said, "and the next day we saw the tracks of many shod horses, going all in a line. Two lines."

"We followed awhile," Running Wolf said, "because we wanted to see who they were. They were going in the same direction as the wagons. They were bluecoat soldiers. We saw them from far off. Then we came here."

"How many bluecoat soldiers?" Sanchess asked.

"Maybe twenty. Maybe more. They were a long way off when we saw them."

"How far from here?"

"More than a day's ride when we saw them," Running Wolf said. "And going away from us then, along the line of the Cimarron."

Sanchess threw his blankets aside and rose, his face clouded with anger. He walked past the other two and out into the young sunlight. There were no children playing among the lodges. The sounds of wailing and keening were everywhere. A dog was gnawing on a bone near the lodge, and Sanchess kicked him and the dog howled and ran off toward the river, tail down.

The fire burned in his blood and his mouth was set in a hard line. He paced back and forth. Running Wolf and Cloud came from the wolf-head tipi but stood well back, keeping silent, their eyes averted. Finally, Sanchess went to them and spoke.

"My anger is not against you. It was a good scout. You found out what we needed to know. You've both lost a brother. I've lost two friends. The band has lost two of its best warriors. Maybe this will teach us all that now is not a good time to ride up to white men for talking."

"I'm going to get a war party up," Cloud said.

"I can't stop you. But before you start singing for revenge, let me think about it and we'll talk again."

Sanchess thought about it for two days, alone in his lodge. Shade brought his food each morning and each night, but he said nothing to her and she spent no time in his tipi. Once, Woman Who Runs came and sat near her son's lodge and sang a death song. The rest of the camp mourned their dead.

Sanchess thought about those white men with their guns. And he thought about that column of soldiers, close to the route of the wagons. His bones ached to be on his best war pony, leading once more against an enemy. He wanted the lance in his hand. But with such enemies, he knew how dangerous it would be. So he called Cloud and Running Wolf to his tipi finally, and no war party went out.

TRADITIONALLY, The People had allowed traders to cross certain portions of their country without interference. Good traders themselves, headmen counseled successfully against making war on such parties, because if the trails became too dangerous, no more traders would come. And some of those goods came to the Comancheros and ended up in Comanche lodges the following winter. It was good common sense not to take spoils on the short term to ensure a constant flow of goods over the longer period.

But now that had begun to change, along with everything else. The pressure of more immigrants, more traders everywhere, made any of them likely targets for attack if they were weak enough and exposed enough.

When New Mexico became a territory of the Great Father in the east, The People and the Kiowas saw a large increase in traffic along the trail to Santa Fe, because now there was no possible problem with Mexican authorities when the traders arrived at their destination. And more and more, the traders took what they called the Cimarron Cutoff, which led them across the northwestern section of the Llano Estacado buffalo range.

Usually these were large outfits, well armed and capable of defending themselves. Such groups were safe because The People and the Kiowas made war only when the odds were in their favor.

But the trade was very profitable, and occasionally a foolhardy group came without enough men or guns. And their greed was so great that they ignored safety and took the Cutoff, turning sharply toward the southwest from the Arkansas in Kansas, because it was shorter and not so difficult a journey as the one through Raton Pass. They did this even though they knew that, surely, once they came to the Cimarron it was dangerous country from there all the way into the shadow of the Sangre de Cristo Mountains.

Aware of these things, Sanchess remembered what his father had said about the white man coming on, no matter what happened. No matter what the White Father said he should do. No matter the danger. And he thought that the white man was surely crazy to place himself in such jeopardy for nothing more than a few pieces of the metal money. Further, he thought bitterly, now their fear makes them dangerous too, like a rattlesnake shedding its skin, striking with the deadly fangs at anything that moves.

And he thought, They have reason to be fearful. For he knew that these smaller parties were fair game. The mules and horses were stolen at night, and sometimes the bold warriors went in during daylight and there was killing. The white freighters had learned that along the trail to Santa Fe it was better during such attacks not to be taken alive.

For in their desperation, the Comanche and Kiowa young men were doing terrible things now to show their anger at the white man's coming. And Sanchess, even though he knew Iron Shirt had been right about avoiding the white man, could not completely fault those young men. They were fighting for their hunting ranges in the only way they knew how!

17

RUNNING WOLF WAS A GOOD husband. Because he called himself brother to Wolf's Road, it was he who disposed of Wolf's Road's property and Chosen got most of the ponies. Some of the best racers in the band were in her herd now, and she was a woman rich in horses. With Running Wolf's sons, Chases the Red Fox and He-Dog, as well as her own Kwahadi, she had plenty of help in tending them. Besides, Lost It, who was still in the pony herd of Sanchess, watched them as well because he remembered that a long time ago Chosen had been kind to him. And later, when she went to groom her little gelding, she always talked to him in Spanish. With Iron Shirt gone, she was the only link he had now to his native tongue. The boy Kwahadi never spoke to him, even though Chosen was teaching the boy some of Lost It's language.

Chosen had her own tipi once more after a few sleeps in Running Wolf's lodge. And Grasshopper treated her almost as an equal, even though there were prerogatives for a first wife. Grasshopper went to Running Wolf's lodge often without being asked, just as though she were a man coming to smoke and visit. Chosen went only when called. She learned that Running Wolf called often.

Kwahadi found himself with two older boys whom he called brother, and it was good because they could teach him and watch over his welfare at night when they played in the pony herd. Sometimes Chosen had the three of them into her tipi for a pot of soup made from marrow bone and rabbit and flavored with sage. She liked watching them as they sat like warriors in a line, very solemn and dignified, while she brought them their soup in gourd bowls.

She suspected that these three were instrumental in many of the practical jokes the boys were always playing on the elders of the band, and especially on fat old Finds Something. This could be very dangerous, playing jokes on a medicine chief, things like smearing fresh horse dung along the edges of his tipi door flap while he slept. Who knew when such a man would become angry and bring all sorts of bad medicine down on them with his power? It showed great courage, almost as much courage as running from the lodge during a thunderstorm and shaking one's fist at the lightning.

But Finds Something always laughed about the jokes. He and Black Mountain spent many warm afternoons in Black Mountain's brush arbor, talking about the days when they had been young and did the same things.

Of course, the boys were never brash enough to play their tricks on the elders when they were meeting in the wolf-head tipi. They, like everyone else in the band, were not anxious to have Sanchess look at them with his cold black eyes that seemed to carry in their gaze as much power as might be found in the medicine bags of Finds Something and Horned Lark together.

Chosen knew she was pregnant again during that summer of the bad scout. It came soon after the party returned, so she didn't know who was the father of the child in her body. It could have been Wolf's Road, from that last night before the scout went out. Or it could have been Running Wolf, from the week in his lodge after the scout returned.

It didn't matter. It brought her great happiness, not the least of which was that now, for a time, she wouldn't have to face confinement in the menstrual lodge with each passing of the full moon.

From time to time she woke in the night and felt a strange presence in the tipi. On those occasions she would rise and go outside and stand in the coolness for a while, looking at the sky where the silver path of the wolf's road marked its way across the blackness. And afterward, when she was back in her robes, the scent of her first husband's body seemed to fill every corner of the lodge. At those times she was sure that Wolf's Road was the father of this new child.

THAT FALL, when they were moving back toward Palo Duro Canyon for the winter, Wasp and Roadrunner returned. Their shields were decorated with hair and they rode proudly, bringing captured ponies with them and Wasp bringing a Kiowa wife whose name, as best anyone could understand it, was Going a Long Way for Sweet Water for Her Father. They always had trouble with Kiowa words.

Wasp called her Sweet Water, and everyone else did the same. She was a large woman, probably older than Wasp by a good many seasons, some said, and she could speak only a few words of The People's tongue. But she seemed pleasant enough and did her work well and stayed out of other people's business. All of which was important for a good wife, they said.

Roadrunner brought back with him a long, brutal scar across his left cheek, to go with the one he had on his side from the Osage bullet north of the Red. He was still unmarried and proclaimed his intention of becoming a pukutsi, a man who did unexpected things. The first night in camp, he killed one of his captured ponies and ate some of it, even though there was plenty of buffalo meat in camp from the fall hunt. Most of the children of the band stood in a wide circle around him as he ate, watching wide-eyed and astonished because even though they were children, they knew a man did not eat his horses unless there was nothing else to eat.

There was a great celebration for the return of the two warriors, as though everyone thought it made up for the two lost on the bad scout. It made everyone more comfortable, except for Sanchess and Chosen, but for different reasons.

Black Mountain held a feast in honor of his grandson's return, and many of the people in the band visited his lodge, where Roadrunner sat and spoke only now and then, saying things that were unexpected. He told about the time he had killed a white man on the trail to Santa Fe and, undressing him to take his clothes, found that the man had no skin on the end of his penis. Black Mountain said it was likely another white man's disease, and he hoped Roadrunner had not caught it. And Roadrunner reassured his grandfather, saying that he had everything on his penis that had always been there.

In the family of Sanchess there was celebration as well, with two fires built before the wolf-head tipi, where the meat was roasted and where the people of the band came to eat. Wasp danced late into the night, and his songs told of how he and Roadrunner had spent a lot of time with the Kiowas, where he had gotten his wife, and how he had been many times on the war trail with the Kiowa young men who were savaging the route to Santa Fe.

Or he sat cross-legged before one of the fires, telling of what he had seen. Sanchess was silent, listening, in his mind a growing uneasiness that this son of his older brother would be here firing the spirits of the band's young men with stories of attacks on the white men. As he heard Wasp's words, he could hear in his thinking the words of Iron Shirt.

"There's a young man among the Kiowas," Wasp was saying. "I've been on the war trail with him many times against those wagons that go along the Cimarron. He's very strange, stranger than any pukutsi I've ever heard of. He has almost no hair and what he has is the color of a desert plant, dried out. His eyes are very pale, like those of a dead white man. He was a captive a long time ago, but now he is a warrior among the Kiowa. Very young, but brave. They call him Skull because his head is round and hairless like a skull and his eyes are empty."

Then he began to describe with great relish some of the things he had seen Skull do when they had taken a white man captive. Things done with a hot hatchet, heated in the fires of burning wagons, or with a knife. And Chosen, hearing these things, rose and walked back to her own lodge and stayed there, not wanting to hear more.

She knew that with these changing times there was much ferocious action on the war trail. She even came to realize that there always had been, for it was the way war was waged on the high plains, by all parties involved. But it was a thing that now she had no intention of listening to, and she left, pulling Kwahadi with her, even though he protested.

"I want to hear him tell of how to be a brave warrior," he said.

"There are better ways to learn than from Wasp," she said. "Or from some crazy Kiowa."

"I'll go when you're sleeping," he said defiantly.

So Chosen went back to the wolf-head tipi, but only long enough to find Shade. And when Shade came into Chosen's tipi and the boy was sitting at the fire, his handsome face sullen, she stood before him as aunts are supposed to do, hands on hips, her own face clouded with anger.

"Go to your robes," Shade said harshly. "You're not so old yet that I can't tie your thumbs together and hang you from one of these lodgepoles for a few days."

Kwahadi's humiliation made his face go slack and he turned quickly to his bed and pulled the robes over his head.

"And don't try to fool me, pretending to sleep," Shade said. "I'll be here all night to see that you don't misbehave for your mother."

She went outside to join Chosen, and the two of them sat in the darkness, watching the flicker of fire from the wolf-head tipi, listening to the singing.

"He's got high spirits," Shade said. "Like my brother, his father."

"Soon he'll do what he pleases, like his father."

"Yes. But not yet."

They listened to the drums from the wolf-head tipi. The shadows of people passing between them and the fires there were dark shapes floating across the ground, faceless and nameless. Chosen shivered.

"I think that man who Wasp talks about is bad medicine for us," she said.

"That's in the mind of Sanchess as well."

"Crazy men should be avoided."

"Maybe he's holding back the white man," Shade said. "He's killed enough of them, from what Wasp says."

"Some of the women are dancing now."

"Yes. I saw your friend Yam Eater there."

"I didn't see her husband."

"Stonefoot? No. He's not there. He allows his woman to run around the camp like one of the dogs." And Shade laughed. "That Yam Eater. She's bad medicine too."

It was hard to avoid stories about Skull that winter. The Kwahadis had heard of him, and the Wichitas as well. Even the white man knew his name. He had plundered the trail to Santa Fe many times, never leading a war party himself but going with anyone that carried the blood lance there. They said he was coldly courageous, apparently without any fear at all, and sometimes even foolish in the chances he took. But mostly there were the stories of his brutal treatment of any captives who were taken.

He was not like a Comanche pukutsi. He never sang or danced, they said. He had no wife, but was taken care of by the women of the man who had captured him. He kept to himself in camp, and even the Kiowas were a little afraid of him.

THAT WINTER in Palo Duro was a hard one. There was more snow than usual, the fine mist of it sifting down from the open sky between the rims of the canyon and laying a blanket of white over the lodges. Prairie Dog Town Branch froze, and Lost It used trade cooking pots to melt snow so the horses would have water to drink.

Shade had another miscarriage, which didn't surprise anyone, considering her record in such things. Besides, she was getting too old to have babies. Wapiti Song gave Sanchess another son and they called him Winter Boy. Chosen grew big around the middle and this time she had a great deal of morning sickness and misery. Some said it was that blue-eye weakness finally showing up.

The children built tipis of snow and played at being husbands and wives, the boys trapping rabbits and the girls cooking them over small fires of cottonwood twigs. The young men gelded the colts they'd singled out as not good enough for breeding. The old men made arrows, for although there were a number of guns in the band now, most of them agreed with Running Wolf that the bow was faster than the gun, what with all that stuffing powder and ball down the muzzle, and was just as accurate.

During the Moon of Greatest Cold, Goes Ahead walked down the canyon with a robe across his shoulders. He walked painfully, his crippled legs barely able to make headway in the drifts. He never returned, and that night his family began to mourn him. And the next day the women of the wolf-head tipi and Chosen sat in Shade's lodge, sewing moccasins, and spoke of it.

"He's gone looking for those early times he's always talking about," Shade said.

"He'll find them, too," Woman Who Runs said. She had made only one slash along her arm because since Iron Shirt's funeral she could find little heart for mourning anyone else, even Iron Shirt's brother. "He'll find them. In the place beyond the sun."

"He's thrown himself away," Wapiti Song said.

Hearing that, Chosen felt a shudder pass along her belly where the new baby waited. Someday this child will do the same thing, she thought, only a long time before that, I will have done it as well. It's better for a man to die in front of his enemies, still young and no burden to his family. But what does a woman do? And Woman Who Runs, almost as if she could hear Chosen's thoughts, answered the question in a low voice.

"Soon it will be time for me to follow him, to lie on my final robe. I'm growing useless now, like one of my husband's old horses."

The fall hunts had been good, and there was meat throughout the cold season. But by the time the bunch grass began to sprout green, there was little pemmican left and everyone ate sparingly. It was a time for boiled acorns and the plants they found in the canyon whose roots could be baked, stripped of bark, and chewed like marrow bones.

It was the Moon of Fresh Winds when Chosen gave birth to a baby girl. Woman and Horned Lark attended again, with help from Grasshopper and Walks in the Morning, Running Wolf's mother. It was a breach birth, and before it was finished the two older women stood back in the shadows of the tipi, keening, and Walks in the Morning took charge. She had given birth to one of her own sons this same way.

"Those feet-first babies," Walks said. "They come out dead sometimes."

It was a small baby, and Chosen could see none of the robust, red-faced health she had seen in Kwahadi. And the child cried more than any Comanche baby anyone had ever heard of or seen.

Big Wolf gave away a few horses to celebrate his new granddaughter, and Sanchess did the same, to honor a new niece. A boy would have been better, everyone said, but a girl child was cherished too. Of course, not so many horses changed hands when a girl was born, and sometimes none at all.

Chosen named the child Snow Blossom because at that time there were many dead yuccas, with the snow caught in the brown pods. Running Wolf was proud and painted a yellow crescent on Chosen's lodge to show that Moon Mother had given the band a new daughter.

Shade spent even more time than before in Chosen's tipi. She found satisfaction in tending someone else's baby, maybe because she had never been able to care for one of her own. She said each day that this was a fine baby. But Chosen could see the tiny arms and legs, frail and colorless and cold as the fluff of snow that gave the child her name. And the baby never seemed to nurse very long, and Chosen began to wonder if something had gone wrong with her milk. She began to think, Poor little Snow Blossom, where are you going?

BEFORE SANCHESS and the elders determined their move to the buffalo ranges, the band of Kiowas came. They were warriors, out early on the war trail. It was Wasp who first came with the news of their arrival. He had been scouting along the canyon's mouth, and there were some in the band who suspected that he had been waiting for them, even though he had never said as much.

They all put on their best clothes and painted their faces. The women took out the last of the pemmican and made mush of bone marrow and mesquite beans. There was much excitement, as though the Kiowa war party heralded the coming spring.

They came along Prairie Dog Town Branch in single file, about twenty of them, all on fine ponies and with a small herd of extra horses coming behind. A few wore the delicate porcupine-quill headdress so favored by the Kiowas. They had shields on their left arms, covers still on, and many carried lances and a few had guns. Their shirts were decorated with fine patterns of tiny trade beads, and some wore breastplates of pipestem bone. They were a very handsome party of fighting men, and the people of Sanchess stood along the ridges of the small canyon hills, waving and shouting welcome.

Wasp rode out to meet them, and everyone watched as he talked with the leader. Then he led them to the wolf-head tipi, where Sanchess and his bodyguards waited, Otter Tongue standing on his left side, Running Wolf on his right. Their faces were painted ocher and blue and Running Wolf held his chief's war lance, out of its case, the scalps of Madoc's Fort blowing out in the soft breeze that came along the canyon floor like the breathing of a spring foal.

As they moved up a small rise through the cedars toward the waiting chief, Chosen and Kwahadi came to the front of their lodge to watch. The Kiowas rode directly past her, only a few feet away. Their faces were haughty and proud and there was vermilion on their high cheeks and Chosen could see otter-fur tassels on their buckskin shirts. They had hatchets hanging from their saddles, some with blades shaped like knives with decorative holes, like the ones she knew came from the Osage and, before that, a long time ago, from the French.

She could feel Kwahadi trembling with excitement under her arm, and there was in her breast a certain thrill at watching these men pass, so arrogant and self-confident.

Then she saw him! She knew at once it was Skull. From the descriptions she had heard of him, she expected to see a strange man. Even so, there was a shock as her eyes found him.

He wore a small fur cap, a ring of black fuzz around the top of his almost hairless head. His ears lay flat against his skull, like mussel shells pressed into white mud. The sun had peeled and blackened his fair skin so often that it was now splotched with liver-colored markings.

She looked at his hands. They were small, almost childlike, gripping reins and hide-covered lance. He was dressed in heavy skins, fur side out, making his body appear gross and fat and his head even smaller than it was. His face was puffy, expressionless, as though no thinking went on behind it. As he passed, his eyes turned to Chosen for a frozen moment and she saw the lifeless glaze of them. It was like looking into the depths of a murky pool of stagnant water where nothing could live.

Then he was past her lodge and she saw the slouch of his body in his heavy robes. A revulsion that made her quiver came like vomit, leaving its sour taste in her mouth. She pulled Kwahadi back into the lodge.

"I want to see," he protested.

"Then go see," she said, almost savagely. "Go to the lodge of Sanchess and see, because I hope it is the last time you will have a chance to see them."

The boy dashed from the lodge, leaving the door flap hanging open. Chosen sank to the floor beside the low fire and in her mind was the image of that round, puffy face with the lusterless eyes, the lips slack. She pulled Snow Blossom's cradle board to her and placed it across her knees and swayed back and forth, crooning a low, choked song.

From somewhere in her mind came the name, and she resisted it with such force that she shuddered again, violently, and felt her throat grow tight. But despite her efforts, the words came, and she said them aloud in the language she had thought long forgotten.

"Dafydd! Dafydd Parry of Madoc's Fort!"

THAT SAME afternoon the Kiowas moved up the canyon to make their own temporary camp. Wasp and his wife and Roadrunner went with them, as well as Cloud and three other young men of the band. And Yam Eater, although they didn't know that until evening, when Stonefoot began to look for her.

"Now he'll have to find a new wife to take care of those two children of his," Sanchess said in his robes that night, Shade beside him.

"Yes," Shade said. "Because she'll not come back this time. She knows that this time Stonefoot will cut off the whole nose!"

"The nose doesn't concern me," he said. "What concerns me is that she and all those young men of ours will be out with those Kiowas this summer when they go to burn the wagons along the road to Santa Fe."

Sanchess determined then that he would move the band to one of the tributaries of the Brazos for the summer hunt, away from the Santa Fe Trail, away from the depredations being committed there, in order to stay as far as possible from any of those bluecoat soldiers patrolling the northern reaches of the southern high plains. He might sympathize with the bold strokes against the whites, but he kept remembering what Iron Shirt had said about retaliation.

What Sanchess did not know was that the Kiowas this summer were not going north to the line of the Cimarron. Raiding on the Santa Fe Trail had become very dangerous; the traders were well armed and coming in large groups, and the threat of bluecoat soldiers was always there. So they had decided to make their forays of the summer in the east. Along the Brazos!

FIVE

My home is with The People.

18

IT WAS THE YEAR THAT GETting the Lodgepoles came to his power. He was anxious to have the medicine of the wolf, because that was very strong power indeed. Besides, his father had it and Wolf's Road had had it and Running Wolf as well, both of these men his uncles through marriage to Chosen, the sister of Sanchess. So he had plenty of advice from within the family and never approached Finds Something for assistance in his search. Finds Something grumbled about this, but only to his wife, Horned Lark, who mostly ignored him.

It was a time of great fun for Chosen because, as Lodgepoles' aunt, she could tease him about things everyone else had to be serious about. And she did, unmercifully, reminding him of how she had cleaned his cradle board many seasons ago, and how she had rubbed his naked bottom with cottonwood-root powder, and how she had been harsh in her punishments when he grew older and misbehaved for his mother, Wapiti Song.

Kwahadi thought it all undignified, this business of his mother making light of someone involved in the serious search for power.

"Don't worry," she said to him, laughing. "When your time comes, your aunts will tease you too. It's one of the things an aunt is good for."

Kwahadi knew what aunts were good for in another respect as well. Any time Chosen was having trouble controlling her son's high spirits, it was Shade who came to apply the discipline. Of course, it didn't happen often, because a boy growing among The People was allowed a lot of freedom so that he might develop initiative and audacity. But there were limits, and when those limits were reached, Shade appeared. There was only one person in the band whom Kwahadi feared, and that person was Shade.

Through all the preparations for Lodgepoles' coming to his medicine, Sanchess tried to conceal his pride. But the women around him could not be fooled, and even when he spoke of it gruffly, as though he were not interested, they snickered and rolled their eyes.

Lodgepoles went to Running Wolf for his instructions, and they spent many nights in Running Wolf's lodge, in quiet conversation and singing. Now and then, when they had been there until late, Chosen would bring them roasted meat, cutting her eyes toward the boy and grinning impishly but saying nothing because this was men's work and not to be made light of with Running Wolf present. She had found that her husband's temper could flash like dry cedar thrown into a hot fire.

When the night came for Lodgepoles to leave for his four-night vigil, Chosen watched from the door of her tipi. To her he was still only a child of fifteen summers, and now he was marching away into the night, taking the bundle of things Running Wolf had told him to take and walking straight, his head up, like a great chief going out to make a treaty with the Cheyenne.

It took longer than anyone had expected. Instead of four nights, Lodgepoles stayed out five. Sanchess had been irritable through it all, and on the fifth night, his son still somewhere out in the dark prairie, he became as dangerous as a buffalo cow with calf. Everyone stayed away from him, but during the night he called for Wapiti Song. Then he sent her away without copulating, and back in the tipi with Shade, Wapiti Song laughed about it.

"That husband! You'd think it was him out there looking for his medicine," she said.

"If this lasts much longer, he'll be out there looking for the boy."

"Don't call Lodgepoles a boy in front of Sanchess," Wapiti Song said, still laughing. "He says Lodgepoles is a man now."

"Not yet. Maybe he won't find any power at all."

That stopped Wapiti Song's laughter, because such a thing was very embarrassing, when a boy went out and had to return without having found anything.

At Running Wolf's tipis there was worry as well. Running Wolf's reputation was at stake here too. Grasshopper's two sons and Kwahadi talked about it, sitting under a brush arbor and chewing on the evening ration of dried meat.

"Five days is too long to find it," said He-Dog.

"He's looking too hard for one thing," Red Fox said wisely, because he was the oldest of this group. "Maybe wolf power doesn't want to come."

"Maybe a wolf has already come," Kwahadi said. "And eaten him!"

That disturbed them and they stopped eating. But then Grasshopper brought out some fresh liver from the day's kill, well sprinkled with gall, and they forgot about Lodgepoles.

On the sixth evening Lodgepoles returned, looking worn but happy, and everyone knew he'd found it when they saw him go directly to Running Wolf's tipi. He stayed there only a short time, then went to his father's lodge, where Sanchess stood waiting impatiently at the door of the wolf-head tipi. They spoke for a few moments before Sanchess began to bellow for his wives to bring food for his son, the new man in the band.

Chosen went as well, taking soup, and Lodgepoles was sitting in the place of honor in the wolf-head tipi, gorging himself on the meat his mother and Shade had brought. His face was smiling, greasy with the meat, and he told them he had seen a vision of the wolf. But he told them no more because it was very secret and powerful and some of the power would go away if he told too much.

Sanchess sat well back in the shadows of the lodge, smoking the pipe he had already offered to his son. Later, after everyone was gone, Sanchess called Wapiti Song back again.

"Tomorrow there will be a tipi for our son," he said. "Now that he is a man, he'll need his own lodge so the girls can slip in and see him at night."

And now Sanchess did not send Wapiti Song away so soon.

In her bed robes, Chosen thought of Lodgepoles' happiness and of her own. Now there would be no more teasing and she would miss that. But seeing Lodgepoles coming to his manhood made a special gladness in her heart, and she remembered that day in the high pines of the Sangre de Cristo Mountains when he was born. It had been the real beginning of her becoming one of The People.

She thought of Kwahadi and He-Dog and Red Fox, and knew that soon they would be going on their quest for power. And she thought of her brother, Skull, but tried to put that from her mind as she always did when she thought of him. But the image of his face was hard to put aside. It kept coming to her just before she slept and it gave her troubled dreams, with a horror so deep and powerful that she was afraid to mention it to anyone.

And how could she mention such a thing anyway, without revealing that Skull was her white brother? She had no notion of how the people in this band would react to such news, and she was afraid to find out. She only knew that anytime Skull was mentioned, Sanchess showed marked distaste, perhaps even hatred. She had a dread of being associated with such thoughts in the mind of Sanchess.

IT WAS a good hunting range, although most of the men grumbled that the herds were no longer as large as they once had been. Still, there were plenty of chances to take meat, and two days after Lodgepoles returned, he was out with the others on a hunter pony Sanchess had given him, with one of old Iron Shirt's horn-reinforced bows and a quiver of arrows on his back.

He wore only loincloth and moccasins, his hair was loose in the wind, and there was fresh ocher paint on his cheeks. Beside him rode Running Wolf, holding a hunting lance butt down on one knee. They came on a small group of buffalo only a short distance from the camp and watched from downwind for a while before riding in. Running Wolf bent close to the boy so he could speak softly, and he saw the light of excitement in Lodgepoles' face.

"You've seen this many times before," Running Wolf said. "You know what to do. If you don't, that horse does."

"I know what to do," Lodgepoles said.

"Good. Pick a good one, now. That little cow there." And Running Wolf pointed with his lance.

"She's not very big!"

"No, but she'll make good meat for your lodge and she hasn't got a calf to protect. So maybe she won't be too angry when you start putting arrows into her."

"I'm ready. I'll take the little cow."

"Good. We'll walk our ponies in as close as we can. Then, when I say it, we run, you on the right side. Get close to her."

"I know. I'm ready." And his voice shook with the excitement.

The other hunters were holding back, waiting for the headman's son to make his run before they disturbed the entire herd. Some were smiling, leaning lazily on the withers of their ponies, remembering their first times.

Running Wolf and Lodgepoles rode forward slowly, the wind in their faces. They could smell the droppings from the herd and it made Lodgepoles' excitement even greater, just the smell of them. The buffalo continued to graze, and they were very close when one of the old bulls on the edge of the herd lifted his head and snorted. The others began to mill, blowing air through their large nostrils like gusts of wind under a tipi wall.

"Now!" Running Wolf shouted, and they kicked their ponies into a dead run.

Lodgepoles could restrain himself no longer and gave a loud whoop of joy. The little cow he was closing on turned in fright and started to run. His pony carried Lodgepoles alongside quickly, and the cow started to veer away, but Running Wolf was there on her far side, and drove her back against Lodgepoles' pony.

Lodgepoles sent his first arrow true, driving it in behind the ribs and up into the vitals, and even as he was fitting the next one to the bowstring, the little cow went down, throwing up a huge cloud of dust. The two hunter ponies turned sharply away, as they had been trained to do, and when Lodgepoles drew rein he was laughing. From behind them came the shouts of the other men, who were now ready to make their own run into the buffalo.

"One arrow!" Running Wolf said. "That's good. Before long I'll teach you how to take them with the lance."

"Give me your lance now," Lodgepoles said.

"Another day," Running Wolf said. "Come on. I'll help you skin out your first kill."

That evening, Otter Tongue went through the camp announcing to all that there would be a celebration in honor of the headman's son, a man who had killed his first buffalo with a single arrow. And whose new name would be Wolf Paw.

When she heard that, Grasshopper laughed.

"There are so many men with wolf medicine in this band, it's hard to keep them straight!"

But when she saw the expression on Chosen's face, she stopped laughing and turned away and was sorry she had said such a thing, because one of those wolf-power men had been Chosen's first husband and was now gone.

Everyone knew it would be the time for Sanchess to make gifts and lay out a feast. So the next day the men hunted for only a little while and then came into camp to bathe themselves and get on fresh paint. The women brushed down smocks and shirts and combed the fringes on leggings, and the drummers looked to the hide covers of their drums.

The small cow that Lodgepoles had killed was butchered especially for the celebration, none of it sliced in thin strips for drying, but cut into roasts and by evening placed on spits over a number of fires near the wolf-head tipi. The hide was stretched on pole racks so that everyone could see the hole where the single arrow had entered.

Some of the older men could remember when Sanchess had first gone out and old Iron Shirt, not so old then, had sponsored a celebration. Of course, that celebration was a little different. When Sanchess had his manhood recognized, it was after a war party against the Utes. The older men recalled how well he had danced, a very young man then but already with those piercing eyes, and they remembered how he had told them of his exploits in his singing.

In the lodge of Stinking Bottom, his first wife was preparing him for the celebration. As she had done for some time, she braided lengths of horsetail hair into the war lock to make it appear longer than it really was.

Stinking Bottom sat cross-legged, staring into his fire, his eyes glazed like a dead man's, his mouth hanging open. For some time now, he had said things that made no sense, when he spoke at all. Often, no one could understand his words, as though they were in a foreign tongue. Sometimes when it rained in summer, his wives would have to bring him into the lodge because he was not even aware that it was raining. Everyone in the band had become a little afraid of him, saying he had become one of the Lost Ones whose thinking had gone crazy.

But his wives stayed with him faithfully, treating him like a child, caring for him as they would one of the sons they never had.

"That boy will be a fine dancer," the woman said and Stinking Bottom rolled his eyes as though the sound of her voice hurt his ears. "His father was a fine dancer, your nephew."

"Young and strong," Stinking Bottom shouted, throwing his head back, a sudden gleam in his eyes, a memory of some past glory. Then he hung his head again, mouth sagging open. "My back hurts. My knees hurt."

"You are still young and strong," she said.

But she knew he was no longer strong, although of an age with Sanchess. When she and the other wives had bathed him that day, she had looked closely for the return of the terrible sores to the private parts of his body, but they were not there. They had not been there for a long time. But she knew that inside him there was some evil medicine.

"Now, you look like a brother to the great Iron Shirt," she said, setting back on her heels. "A beautiful man for the celebration of your nephew's son."

"Young and strong," Stinking Bottom mumbled.

Everyone began to gather with the setting sun, waiting expectantly in the purple shadows that grew across the campsite as the red sky in the west gave way to the blackness creeping from the east. The dogs came as well, smelling the roasting meat, and while the people waited they watched the children chase the dogs with sticks, and everyone laughed because soon there would be much meat.

The bright star was in the west, marking the going of Sun Father and the coming of Moon Mother. They called her Daughter Star because she was always seen most brightly when she was between her parents. It made them sigh with contentment, seeing everything as it should be and no cloud in the sky. They watched Chosen and the women of Sanchess tending the roasting meat and they sighed again, tasting the smell with their tongues as well as their noses.

From far off, a coyote sent up his first call and they thought it was a good sign. Wolf's little brother didn't sound so mournful tonight, they said, as though he knew something nice was about to happen.

The drummers came and sat in a single line facing the east. As they waited, they rubbed their hands across the skin heads of the drums, heating them with friction. Now the children stopped playing with the dogs and came to stand nearby, and old Finds Something came too, and sat at the end of the line of drummers, trying to keep his buffalo-horn headdress in place on his head. His bare belly gleamed with vermilion paint, like a giant red gourd.

Sanchess appeared and everyone shouted, "Hoy, hoy!" He was wearing doeskin finely set with porcupine-quill beads given him by the Kiowas many seasons ago. His hair hung loose except for the scalp lock falling down his back, and from above his left ear an eagle feather stood up, the vane glistening with blue-white color, like new snow under Moon Mother's gaze.

Sanchess turned to Otter Tongue and made his first announcement of the celebration.

"Take meat to Lost It in the pony herd," he said. "He has served my father well, and me, and now he will serve my son."

"Hoy, hoy!" they all shouted.

If Otter Tongue was attending his chief, Running Wolf was not. He was with Lodgepoles, as the sponsor of this new man in the band. Soon after Sanchess seated himself near the drummers, Running Wolf and Lodgepoles came, with straight backs, their faces carefully painted, their hair loose. Lodgepoles was wearing clothing with long fringes, but only from the waist down to his feet. His chest was bare except for a necklace of pipestem bone and a red trade bandanna. Below his right ear hung a feather of the hawk, a good hunter. He had been carefully groomed by his grandmother, Woman Who Runs, and when they saw him, everyone shouted, "Hoy, hoy!"

Sanchess had his pipe brought to him, Shade passing it into his hands already tamped full of tobacco. Before he smoked with his son and Running Wolf, he offered it to the sky, the earth, and the four directions. Then everyone began to eat and the drummers tapped tentatively on their drums with the long sticks and switches. After the eating was well under way, Lodgepoles rose and walked into the center of the circle and the dance began.

Moving with the tempo of the drums, Lodgepoles sang of his vision. On the fifth night a wolf had appeared to him and spoken in the voice of a man who had had that power and was now gone to the land beyond the sun. Everyone knew he meant Wolf's Road, but the name was never mentioned because the names of the dead were taboo. But everyone knew and thought it was good.

Lodgepoles continued to dance, but his singing stopped before he told them anything about what the wolf had said. Then he started to sing again, about little buffalo cows and how beautiful they were and how to hunt them.

"That new man is a fine dancer," Big Wolf said. "He's almost as good as my son Running Wolf."

The drums were insistent, and along the fringes of the crowd there were those who could not resist the rhythm and they began to dance as well. First were the children, and they were soon joined by many of the women and finally the men.

Lodgepoles could dance as long as he desired, but he knew there were other parts to this ceremony, because Running Wolf had explained it all to him. So, after singing about the kindness of the buffalo for coming each year, he stopped and took his place beside Sanchess.

Sanchess had already sent Otter Tongue to the pony herd, and now he and Lost It, holding meat in his hand

and eating as he came, led two fine war stallions into the circle. Sanchess gave one to his son and the other to Running Wolf and everyone shouted, "Hoy, hoy!" knowing there would be more.

"Now I will take some sticks," Sanchess said, and Wapiti Song handed him a number of short mesquite twigs. "I'll throw these sticks into the circle and whoever gets them will have a horse from my herd!"

He tossed a number of the twigs onto the dancing ground and the young women squealed and ran to pick up the sticks and thus win a pony. Sanchess threw a second handful and once again the young women ran to retrieve the sticks. The men watched, making no move toward the prizes because they were too proud to run in with the young women and bend down to pick up a twig.

Altogether, Sanchess gave away ten horses, not counting the ones for his son and Running Wolf.

The dancing began once more, everyone joining in, singing their own songs and shuffling their feet on the hard-packed earth. Lodgepoles sat beside his father and behind him sat his mother. He smiled shyly at the bold girls who had won ponies and now danced before the band's new man with suggestive glances.

It was a fine celebration and the dancing lasted well into the night, well after the moon had come to play her light across the camp in silver ripples. Before it was finished, Chosen returned to her own lodge and there behind the tipi she saw Kwahadi, dancing and singing alone. When he saw her watching him, he stopped abruptly, but as he saw her smile, he began to dance again.

Later, in her bed robes, Chosen felt old in this band, for she had seen three generations. Iron Shirt and Sanchess and now Lodgepoles, each taking his place among The People, not because each of them was the son of a chief, but because each had his own good medicine. And she knew there was more to it than that. She knew they were at an advantage in the quest for leadership because each had seen his father, as hunter, as war leader, as peace headman.

She pictured Lodgepoles grown older, having his own wolf-head tipi, his wives around him. She saw him directing his people on their hunts and campsite locations and routes of march. And she thought of Kwahadi, dancing still behind the tipi, even though the rest of the camp was sleeping, singing silently and hearing the drums only in his heart. Perhaps he was close enough to Sanchess to see how a chief was supposed to act. And she remembered the words of Woman Who Runs.

"He'll be a great chief someday!"

And somehow they left her strangely disturbed.

IT WAS in that year too that they saw the black children.

A small party of Panetekas came to their camp to share meat with them and later pitched camp a short distance away to spend the night. They were going to Red River, they said, to sell their captive children, and it surprised the people of Sanchess because they had never gone there to sell captives, but had dealt only through Comancheros.

Most surprising were the captives themselves. They were all young children, four of them, and they had skin of a very dark color, darker than any Mexicans these people had ever seen. They crowded around the black children to stare at them, but nobody molested them. It gave everybody an uncomfortable feeling, watching these strange children. Afterwards, in a meeting in the wolf-head tipi, the elders gossiped about it.

"I've heard of those black ones," Red Moccasin said. "But I don't think I ever saw one."

"I've seen them before," said Big Wolf. "But those I saw were grown men. There are some in the settlements of the white man in El Paso del Norte, I think."

"These came from the north," Black Mountain said. "Those Panetekas told me all about it. They have many of them there and sometimes they run away."

"Yes," Red Moccasin said. "The Panetekas catch them and take them back across Red River and sell them to the white man or to some of those tribes the white man has moved there, like the Chickasaws or Seminoles."

"The white man keeps these black ones as slaves," said Big Wolf. "Our old chief knew that and told me about it. Some of those new tribes keep them as slaves too. And they run away and the Panetekas catch them and take them back."

"Going from the Red to Mexico is a long way without horses," Red Moccasin said. "The Panetekas say these black ones try to walk. But they say they've been catching them for many seasons."

"They should have told us about it a long time ago," said Black Mountain. "We could do some of that business too."

Everyone laughed.

"Did you see the scars on the arm of that one little girl?" Big Wolf asked. "Like mourning cuts."

"Somebody wanted to see how deep the black went," Sanchess said. "My father told me many things about these black ones. He told me how some of our forefathers saw them first among the Spanish soldiers. And the Panetekas have seen them many times in the towns and settlements of the white men to the east. The Texas white man keeps these black ones to dig in the ground and grow their corn and tend their horses and cattle."

"I wonder how much the white man gives for those black ones?" Red Moccasin asked. "Not as much, surely, as he does for his own children."

"I don't think the Panetekas are too smart," said Black Mountain. "Why do they take back only the children? The grown ones would be more valuable as slaves. Those children can't do much digging in the ground."

They thought about that a long time, passing the pipe and staring into the fire. Finally, Sanchess spoke.

"My father told me the men of these black ones are very strong. He told me that his father said he once saw one the Spaniards claimed could lift a pony in his arms."

"I'd hate to try and pick up one of those heavy white-man horses," Black Mountain said, and they all laughed again.

"Especially with one of those big white-man saddles on him," Big Wolf said and they continued to laugh, thinking about a man trying to lift a big horse in his arms.

"I think those Panetekas make a mistake," Black Mountain said. "Not taking grown men to sell north of Red

River. If they're so strong, those white men and the other people up there would pay pretty good for them."

"Maybe those children are all they can catch," said Red Moccasin. "Or maybe those children are the only ones who try to run away to Mexico."

"The Panetekas say these black ones cross Red River in small parties, maybe three or four families," Sanchess said. "They bring their children with them. But without horses. So they are all easy to catch."

"What happens to the grown ones in those parties?" Red Moccasin asked.

But no one answered. They all knew what happened to the grown ones, even without the Panetekas having told them about that part.

19

THE WHITE MAN CALLED THEM the wild tribes. They were those who lived by the horse and the buffalo, high plains people who made their homes in the temporary but highly effective hide tipis that could weather almost anything except direct attack by a tornado, could be moved quickly, and could provide warmth and shelter from rain and sleet. These were the hunters who moved with the great herds.

And they were warriors too, teaching their male children from the start of their awareness the arts of making war against any enemy. They hunted and fought in bands, following their livelihood and establishing ranges that they then held unto themselves and their allies within a loose but, to them, precise area of dominance: territory that they claimed in the manner of a hunting wolfpack, without marking of trees and stones by urine, but through scouting parties and the will to exclude intruders.

There were many intruders now. The territory was being violated not only by the white man but all those other people the white man had pushed there. Everywhere in Texas, the white settlements and the camps of other foreigners were pressing into the prairie where once there had been only the mesquite and the hornbeam and the buffalo. The lap robe industry in the land of the Great Father in the east was profitable, and the herds were being decimated by hunters of all colors who came not for the meat but for the skins, leaving the rotting carcasses with nothing taken but the hide and tongue. For pickled tongue was a large delicacy in the east, and profitable too.

And so, in the white man's year of 1854, the wild tribes

rose up strongly. The young men were on the blood trail, like wolves protecting their domain—but now against an enemy more powerful and more pervasive than any of the old enemies had ever been.

Yet along the Brazos that year, the band of Sanchess found peace and tranquility, making their summer kills for winter meat. They were peaceful in mind because there were none among them with the foresight of a dead chief who had always tried to look beyond the next rise of life's ground to see what lay beyond!

What they, or even that dead chief, could not have known was that their way of life was at an end. All that remained was the late summer going down to fall. It was a time when they did what they had always done. Earth Mother was good. Sun Father was powerful. Moon Mother was loving. Their young people begat, their children grew. Their arrows flew straight, their blood lances flowed with courage. But they were in their Season of Yellow Leaf!

THEY WERE on the White Fork of the Brazos and ready to move north to Peace River, near the Red, when Cloud and Roadrunner came. And this time Roadrunner brought a scar that would be unlike the other two he so cherished. This one still ran red, the dark blood from his belly staining his loincloth and leggings.

There was no celebration, even though the returning warriors had many white men's horses and three white captive children, all girls. The sight of Roadrunner with his pinched features and greenish skin, the black blood on his clothing, told them that victory celebrations were not in order, but that soon perhaps there would be another kind of ceremony, for Roadrunner's funeral.

They came in daylight but not in the manner of a successful war party. It was as though they were running, a thing Sanchess marked in his thinking. And indeed they were. But Cloud said nothing to anyone about what had happened, nothing about the war party they had been with all summer, striking deep along the Trinity and the lower Brazos, leaving behind them the rising columns of black smoke from burning buildings as they rode away, always pursued now, but each time eluding pursuit by taking routes where there was no water, killing some of their ponies to drink the blood.

He told nothing of the captives they had taken and how many had died. Or of how Wasp and his two women had stayed with the Kiowas when they split off and rode toward the Wichita Mountains north of Red River. Or of Yam Eater's bravery in one fight when she rode beside Wasp with a bow in her hands, protecting the party's rear as they escaped. Or of how Roadrunner had come by his belly wound.

They carried Roadrunner into the lodge of his grandfather, Black Mountain, and Finds Something was summoned. But Black Mountain and Sanchess, seeing the wound, knew there was little their medicine chief could do for a man gut-shot with a white man's heavy lead bullet. Already the women of Black Mountain and Cloud were keening, and before the sun set, most of the lodges in the camp had women mourning.

"That's a bad wound," Finds Something said. "I'll use my most powerful medicine but I don't think it's going to do any good."

"It will be worth many horses if you can make my grandson whole again," Black Mountain said.

"I don't need horses. I've got too many of those already. But I'll do the best I can. Send one of your women for Horned Lark and tell her I need prickly pear."

The camp watched through the night, as the moon came and went across the sky. The wailing of coyotes sounded like death songs. Sanchess sat in his lodge late into the night, watching his fire go down until Shade came and placed mesquite branches on the low flames, then left without speaking. Sanchess waited for Cloud to come, to tell him everything that had happened. But Cloud never came and Sanchess could only imagine. Uppermost in his thinking was the white man's pursuit.

"I don't like it," he said aloud, and his own words recalled his father's face in the firelit lodge, as though old Iron Shirt were there beside him, explaining about the white man.

With the coming sun, Cloud made his distribution of spoils. He gave horses to his grandfather and to some of the warriors who had ridden with his brother, Gizzard. But he gave nothing to Sanchess, as though trying to avoid his chief. The children he kept, and everyone knew why. If Roadrunner died, Cloud would dispose of those children. Traditionally, if a band warrior was killed by an enemy, that enemy's captives in camp fell on evil times.

In the light of the new morning sun, Chosen saw the children for the first time. She looked into the little faces, terror-stricken and drawn, the eyes wild, like those of an animal caught in a trap. None of them were as old as she had been when Sanchess came to Madoc's Fort. The oldest was no more than six summers. They were naked, their backs blistered by the sun. And Cloud's wife, Sharpens Her Knife, treated them with great cruelty, beating them with sticks and giving them no water.

Watching, Chosen saw the dogs snarling and snapping their teeth near the children, and she moved in among them with a stick of her own and beat the dogs away. Sharpens Her Knife ran from Cloud's lodge, furious.

"Stay away from those children," she shouted, but Chosen turned to face this older woman, the stick ready in her hand. "Stay away, Blue Eyes!"

"Those children will be the mothers of our children someday," Chosen said, holding the stick before her. "Give them water or I'll do it myself!"

Sharpens Her Knife started to speak and then stopped, her mouth open, her eyes looking beyond Chosen. When Chosen turned, she saw her husband and Otter Tongue moving toward them, blanket-wrapped and without expression, but saying by their presence that this woman with the stick in her hand was a member of the family of Sanchess.

"If you want them to have water, then give it to them," Sharpens Her Knife snorted, and turned abruptly back into Cloud's tipi.

At that moment Chosen realized for the first time the kind of power she had, not because she was a woman of many horses, but because she came from old Iron Shirt's lodge. And she knew as well that Running Wolf was not here because he was her husband but because he was bodyguard to Sanchess, her brother.

"Bring me water," she said sharply, and watched Running Wolf's eyes widen and then go bleak with anger. And Otter Tongue was holding back a smile. "And meat!"

"If you want such things, woman, get them yourself," he said.

"I will," she said savagely. "And while I get them, you keep the dogs away from those children!"

She marched away, turning her back on the bodyguards of the band's headman as though they were children too. She had no reason to believe that a wife could talk to her husband in such a way, at least not publicly. But somehow, knowing now that she had it, she wanted to test her power.

And when she returned with a parfleche of water and a gut sack stuffed with fresh pemmican, the two men were still there, gazing with apparent lack of interest at the children, yet there just the same, keeping the dogs back with sharp words and kicks.

Later, as they moved through the camp together, Otter Tongue laughed at Running Wolf's continuing anger.

"That wife you've got needs a good switching," he said.

"Yes," said Running Wolf. "But she's the daughter of our old chief and deserves some respect herself."

"A man's wife is a man's wife, no matter who her father might be." Otter Tongue was still laughing because he knew that Running Wolf, the best lancer of buffalo in the band and a highly regarded warrior, was embarrassed to be ordered about by one of his wives. And the younger of them at that.

"Besides," Running Wolf said lamely, "she means much to Sanchess, who's my friend."

But both of them knew there was more to it than friendship. Both of them knew it was not good to provoke a man like Sanchess.

"I'll cut some switches and use them tonight," Running Wolf said. And Otter Tongue laughed again.

Both of them knew no switches would be cut.

*   *   *

ROADRUNNER WAS in great pain but he made no sound. He lay on a bone hammock covered with buffalo hides with the hair left on, in a sitting position because to lie flat made the pain worse. The women of his family passed in and out of the tipi, bathing his face in cool water. They tried to feed him marrow soup but it no sooner went down than it came up again, causing more pain.

His eyes were glazed but in his mind he saw Chosen come into the lodge and heard her speak of the times before he came to his power. Of the times they had played in the pony herd, when they were children and as yet he had no scars to show his courage. But it was only in his thinking, for she never came.

Outside the tipi, old Finds Something was calling on all his gods, burning various secret things not known even to Horned Lark, and dancing with his buffalo-scrotum rattles. He had been there all night and he would stay until this was finished, one way or the other. From time to time he went into the tipi and touched Roadrunner at various places across his naked body. The prickly-pear compress he had applied to the wound was soggy with blood.

At midday, Sanchess came again to Black Mountain's lodge, and his bodyguards were with him as though this might be official. He went into the tipi for what he supposed would be his last look at a living Roadrunner, but Roadrunner did not recognize him. Sanchess placed his hand on the young warrior's head and felt the heat, as from the coals of a mesquite fire.

Cloud and Black Mountain were waiting outside the tipi, and Sanchess thought that now at last Cloud would tell him everything that had happened. But Cloud said nothing and Sanchess thought that a bad sign. He turned to Black Mountain and spoke, softly and with great deference because this had been a member of old Iron Shirt's council of elders.

"We will move the camp with the next sun."

The old man, stooped with age, his eyes red-rimmed and almost sightless now, shook his head and the sparse braids along either side of his face danced out in the wind.

"My grandson cannot travel too well now."

"Father," Sanchess said softly, "Roadrunner will go to the land beyond the sun before the moon comes tonight."

The old man nodded because he knew it was true. He turned his eyes toward the horizon even though he could see only a short distance, only as far as the nearest tipis.

"It's better to die young," he said. "Except that then one cannot watch his children and his grandchildren grow, as I've done."

Black Mountain turned then and walked slowly away through the lodges, the dogs coming to run beside him and smell his friendly old legs. Sanchess watched him go and then turned to Cloud, a new and bitter light in his eyes.

"Wasp?" he asked abruptly, rudely, making his words harsh. "Has he gone to the land beyond the sun as well?"

"No," Cloud said, avoiding Sanchess's eyes.

"It's a mark of small respect to me that you've told me nothing about my brother's son."

"Your brother's son is with the Kiowas still. He and his woman. They were riding to winter camp when we left them."

Sanchess waited for more, but saw that no more would come and his face grew harder still, his eyes glinting with anger.

"Those white captive children," he said. "We may need those children to bargain with the white man. You have not forgotten how to bargain, have you?"

"No."

"Good. If you harm them, I will be greatly displeased. It would be a disservice to The People."

"If Roadrunner dies, as you say—"

Sanchess cut him short. "Roadrunner will die before the moon comes! And he will die because he was in a wrong place, and you took him there. The old days are gone! These are not captives of some Ute or Pawnee enemy, but of the white man. The ones you lead to our camps where the women and children sleep. If harm comes to those captives, I will take it as a great disservice to our people and as a personal wounding of my own honor!"

"We have always—"

"This is not always! This is now! And your own grandfather, who is a man of much wisdom, will tell you that new ways must be found."

Cloud started to speak again, his own face dark with anger now. But, looking into Sanchess's eyes, he clamped his jaw tight shut and turned suddenly and went into his father's lodge, where Roadrunner lay.

It didn't take Sanchess long to catch up with Black Mountain in his slow walk away from the tipi where the young man was dying. As Sanchess drew alongside, Black Mountain stopped but his eyes were still on the horizon he could not see.

"Your son is a brave man," Sanchess said. "Cloud is wise in the old ways of The People. But times have changed now. Tell him I will pay as many horses as he wants for the lives of those captive children."

"He will require no horses," Black Mountain said. "But there is sorrow in me for him. Because he was not a man when I was young, when times were good and The People were not so concerned with changing their ways to accommodate the white man."

And having spoken, the old man moved away toward the river, his shoulders bent forward as though under a weight. Sanchess watched him go and ground his teeth and tears came to his eyes. His two bodyguards, still following close behind, looked away, their faces stolid but their own eyes moist.

Sanchess was wrong about Roadrunner dying by moonrise. He died before sunset and the band went into deep mourning.

They buried him near the camp and marked it in their memory as a place to avoid in the future because it held the spirit of one of their dead. And later, at the lodge of Black Mountain, Cloud restrained the women of his father, and his own wife, who came from their lodges with clubs. After he had driven them away from the three white captive children who were cowering in the dark under a brush arbor, he called to his wife.

"And bring me clothing to put on those children. We may need them for bargaining with the white man. Has your reason left you, woman?"

* * *

SANCHESS LED them to a place on the Peace River not far from its confluence with the Red. It was a wide valley with plenty of grass to fatten the ponies for winter. And there were mesquite and cottonwood along one side of the stream. There was a scattering of jack oak as well, and some persimmon. The leaves on the hardwoods were beginning to take on a yellow tint and in the late day's sunlight they looked golden.

Chosen had her lodge on a rise not far from the wolf-head tipi. Beside her own lodge were those of Grasshopper and Running Wolf. It was a good time of year, the days not so hot and the air growing cool with the coming of purple shadows in the evening. She sat before her lodge with Snow Blossom's cradle board beside her, visiting with Shade and Grasshopper and watching Kwahadi show his skill with the bow a short distance away, competing with other boys, all of them releasing their arrows toward a rolling willow hoop.

"Look at him," Shade said, laughing. "He's better than those other boys already, and some of them are close to the time of finding their medicine."

"Yes, finding power," Chosen said, and laughed too. "He is asking already to go to his uncle Sanchess to help him in his search."

"Only eight summers old," Grasshopper said. "My own sons haven't started that yet. But they soon will. And they are all so young."

"It's been a good summer for power," Shade said. "Wapiti Song's Getting the Lodgepoles going out. It was a great medicine he found. The power of the wolf."

She and Chosen exchanged glances. Wolf power was very good. But of course there were many restrictions that went with it, restrictions on what a man might eat profitably and when he could safely copulate. Some young men turned it down because they didn't want the restrictions.

"It's a fine thing, watching the young men grow to manhood," Grasshopper said. She pointed to Snow Blossom in her cradle board. "And someday they will all be after that one."

"Yes," Chosen said, looking at the baby, whose cheeks

were not as full and healthy as Comanche babies were supposed to be. "It's true."

They sat in the lengthening shadows of their brush arbor, watching the camp. Woman Who Runs was working on a pot of her secret soup at the tripod-hung pot before the wolf-head tipi. Fresh meat and dried prairie onions and wild turnips were in it, and thinking of that, Chosen said, "I wonder where Yam Eater is now?"

"North of the Red," Shade said. "Among those Kiowas. She'll enjoy the next sun dance with them, when all the young men are rutting after her."

"She may be in danger of losing her nose," Grasshopper said, and she and Shade laughed.

No one in the camp was butchering. There had been few buffalo here, and some of them were unhappy with those Wichitas who had reported big herds. But it was a fussing thing, with no anger in it because they had had a good season of hunting along the Brazos and there was much pemmican and dried meat. They knew that this camp was only for a few days of rest before going on north of Red River and into the Quartz Mountains for the winter.

"I would rather go to Palo Duro again," Chosen said, thinking aloud, and Shade looked at her sharply. "I always think of Palo Duro in this season."

Shade laughed explosively. "I think about Palo Duro in all seasons. These Nakonis, always moving. I'd rather be with my own people, whose name your son wears. In all seasons!"

Snow Blossom began to cry weakly, and Chosen lifted the cradle board to her breast and fed the child. They looked across the camp silently, three women who understood one another's thoughts. They could see the other women moving about their tipis, tending their trade pots suspended from tripods over outside fires. There were groups of older men, smoking and talking, and children playing naked, and dogs wandering aimlessly among the lodges, looking for bones.

Before Running Wolf's lodge, Chosen could see his shield in its cover, hanging from a tripod of short poles, taking the strength of the last of the day's sun. She had never been allowed to tend Running Wolf's shield, that being the duty of his first wife. She had never been allowed to attend any of his weapons, as she had those of Wolf's Road. And she missed that. Even though she was a woman of more horses than Grasshopper, even though she was the sister of the band's headman, she missed grooming her husband's shield.

There was the strong, sweet scent of roasting meat and the musty smell of summer's dying grass all around them. The dome of sky seemed to hold in all the good things close to Earth Mother. In the west it was flaming red and orange and streaked with the fleece of clouds turned scarlet. High overhead it was pale blue, turning then to gray and violet in the east. The first coyote started his night's song far toward the place where the sun would rise again, toward the Trinity, toward the white man's country.

The three captive children from Cloud's lodge moved together toward the river, carrying water hides, Sharpens Her Knife following and switching them. They were partially clothed now, but in the late sunlight their skin looked lifeless, like the petals of a dead yucca plant. They went like puppies through the lodges, huddled close together, dragging their parfleches behind them. Chosen thought of her brother Daffyd and shuddered and quickly tried to think of something else.

"They will be the mothers of our children someday," she said, and Shade looked at her for a moment, but said nothing.

In the evening there were mockingbirds singing in the cottonwoods, and always the coyotes, far off. Sometimes in her tipi, lying alone and uncalled by her husband since the incident of the water and the white captive children, Chosen lay listening to the night sounds and watching the glow of firelight, dim along the hide walls of the lodge. Sometimes she heard an owl calling from the trees along the river and sometimes there was the croak of frogs, as though it were a new spring already.

She thought often of those white captive children, going like tiny flags of truce through the camp. And she knew they were still alive because of Sanchess. No one else would have had the power to persuade Cloud and his family to spare those children. And at those times she thought, Yes, I loved my Wolf's Road from the time I saw him. Yes, Running Wolf is good. Their power is with him who crosses the sky each night on his silver path. But Sanchess would have been the best husband of them all!

THERE WERE LOW CLOUDS OVER the Peace River that morning and a wind from the west, blowing gently but with a sharp edge to it, as though warning of winter's approach. With dawn came a flock of redwings, but only a few of them paused in the cottonwoods before rejoining the others flying south. All the color seemed drained from the land so that there were only shades of gray, black at one end of the spectrum, dirty white at the other.

The short grass, dried by summer heat and wind, moved gently, making soft sounds like Earth Mother breathing. Prairie dogs were barking from one of their towns on the far side of the river but then were suddenly still, even though the grass continued to whisper.

In the far west, night was still on the earth, and the roll of the plains there disappeared into the lowering overcast. But in the east the contours of the land were beginning to show sharply, and above that the clouds were moving toward the light of coming sun.

The women had begun to move about the camp, preparing morning fires for the first meat of the day, and a few children appeared among the lodges, collecting their sleepy thoughts for another round of play, even though there was the threat of rain. The dogs were mostly in the lee of the tipis, acting as though it were colder than it really was, standing with tails between their legs and heads down or else lying turned on themselves, noses tucked to tails.

Dead leaves from the brush arbors broke loose and fluttered through the camp like wispy animals running across the ground. Some of the dogs watched them with only a passing interest, knowing these were not animals. In the cottonwoods, the leaves still clung to the branches and fluttered with their fragile murmuring. Below them, the water of the Peace flowed silently between banks where the night's tiny growths of rabbit ice were already melting.

A few of the young girls were going toward the river with empty water bags, walking without the usual banter between them, still numb with sleep. From downstream they could hear a single crow cawing, a bleak, dismal sound muted by the wind.

The men lay in bed still, enjoying the warm robes on this last day on the Peace, the move north already planned for the following day, when there would be no late sleeping. Favorite war ponies were tethered beside many of the lodges, as they usually were, even though there had been no hint here of danger from enemies close by.

At the pony herd, Lost It was the first to see them coming, and he knew at once what was happening. They were Tonkawas, about twenty of them, coming from downwind and riding hard, and he saw them only after some were already close to the first ponies. He kicked his mare toward the camp, shouting a warning, but he had gone only a short distance before two of the Tonkawas bore down on him, firing with white man's guns.

He tried to turn back and then saw the two boys who were helping him tend the ponies, and the Tonks were around them, using clubs. Lost It watched the boys struck down before the first bullet found his back and he collapsed like an old hide, slipping from his mount and hearing the animal yips the Tonkawas were making, and he knew they would drive the herd away from the campsite. As the horses began to mill and then run, their hooves created a gentle tremor in the earth, and as he lay facedown, it was the last sensation he had of anything.

KWAHADI WAS in his mother's lodge when he heard the first faint shouts from the pony herd and then the shots. He ran out into the camp naked, just risen from his robes, wearing only moccasins. He could hear the ponies running, whistling with surprise, and going on a little way he saw the riders on the plain, rushing at the ponies, waving blankets. He ran past the wolf-head tipi and then heard the other horses from the far end of the campsite, a heavy, metal sound of shod hooves.

When he turned he saw them coming, on big horses with heavy leather saddles. They were shooting with the small guns, one in each hand. They wore large hats with wide brims and he saw the flash of badges on the breasts of their coats and although he had never seen a badge before, he knew it marked them as some kind of white-man soldier.

He started running back toward his mother's lodge because he didn't know what else to do, and even though such a route took him directly toward the oncoming horsemen. By then there was screaming and the thunder of the guns. Men were coming from their tipis, half-dressed or still naked from sleep.

Suddenly Shade was beside him, pulling him up short, her face hard and her teeth showing, grinding hard together. She pulled him by his arms, although at first he resisted. Until he saw Sanchess going to meet the coming riders, fitting an arrow to his bow. But there was a new burst of firing and he saw the top of Sanchess's head go up in a fountain of red and black and the great warrior was down before the charging, iron-shod horses.

"Come on!" Shade screamed into his ear. "Run, boy, run!"

They ran for the river, dodging between the lodges. All around them the people were running, some of them quietly, silently frantic, some of them keening. But soon, with Shade pulling him along, the sounds of firing fell behind and they splashed into the stream and on across, never looking back. The water was not deep and they didn't have to swim. On the far bank, Shade kept pushing him on, out into the prairie.

The camp behind them was like a disturbed anthill now, kicked in with the pointed toe of a hard leather boot. Women were running aimlessly, screaming, children were crying, and the men were trying to resist. But they had been roused from sleep and were standing before the rushing horses and the guns half-clothed, half-armed.

Stonefoot had his revolver, the one he had as damages for his wife's first indiscretion, but it misfired and he was struck by the heavy lead balls of the white man.

Black Mountain walked from his tipi, stooped over, staring about with his bad eyes as though this were any other morning. He didn't see them until it was too late to run and they were upon him, riding past with shouts, striking him down with the barrels of their heavy pistols.

Getting the Lodgepoles stood before his mother's tipi, shouting a song to his new medicine, holding a skinning knife up defiantly in one hand, and they shot him as they flashed past.

The attackers charged through the camp and turned their heavy horses and charged back again, then again, and again, shooting in all directions. A few had uncoiled hemp ropes and were throwing loops over the tipi poles above the smoke holes, pulling down the lodges. Some dismounted quickly, expertly, and ran into the tipis, guns up, then dragged children and women out.

Cloud, at the door of his lodge, tried to defend his wife and the three captive white children and was shot four times, twice when he was down. They were inside then, shooting at Sharpens Her Knife but missing as she rolled into a bundle of uncured hides, but taking the captive white children by the hair and dragging them out screaming in terror, throwing them up onto the backs of horses behind other white men, yelling with triumph.

Running Wolf was caught in his collapsed tipi, dragged down by the hemp ropes and running horses, and when he emerged, trying to pull his lance from the debris, he was shot in the face and fell back among the tangle of lodgepoles and hides, the crimsonlike war-party paint running down his naked chest.

And they were shooting the war ponies on their short tethers beside the lodges, concentrating on them as though they knew that the men in this camp were most dangerous when mounted. The squealing and screaming of the wounded horses, dying, sent vibrations shrill and chilling through all of the rest of the bedlam.

Some were setting fire to anything that would burn, using the embers under the tripod-suspended cookpots, using the clear liquid they carried in small cans on their saddlebags, which flamed up with the touch of fire, splashing it on tipi walls and on hides bundled and made ready for the travois for the journey north of Red River.

Old Finds Something stumbled from his lodge, wearing nothing but the knee-length moccasins in which he slept, and his tattered buffalo-horn headdress. When he saw what was happening, he sank to the ground on his back and began to sing, but that didn't save him. Close behind him came Horned Lark, and she stood over him for only a moment with her bow, but that was finished quickly as well and she fell across the great belly of her husband.

They slashed the parfleches and spilled out the fresh pemmican and dumped the new-cut meat onto the burning robes and tipis. They found many arrows in the scattered litter of the camp and threw those onto the fires as well, where the flames consumed the work of countless hours in winter lodges; after a moment, the trade metal points glowed red in the heat. They found scalps and burned those too, and moccasins and smocks and empty cradle boards, saddles and harness for travois, and leggings and shirts with the long Comanche fringes—all burned, quickly, efficiently.

Women carried their small children, running toward the open prairie, away from the camp, their older children running behind, crying, trying to catch a firm hold on their mothers' skirts. And there too was Stinking Bottom, crawling away, unable to stand, the blood running from his mouth and nose and from the wound in his stomach. His wives had dashed on ahead of him, unable to help, leaving him to make his own labored way. But not far.

Some of the people ran for the cover of trees along the Peace, and the white men let them go, sending only a few random shots after them. Otter Tongue ran toward the pony herd and found it gone, almost out of sight across the rolling land, the Tonkawas trailing behind, yelling and waving their blankets. Otter Tongue turned there, where the pony herd had been, his bow ready, and waited for the charge of the white men. But they made no advance toward him, doing their work in the village, charging their horses back and forth. And running beside them were the camp dogs, barking wildly and with hackles raised, snapping at the churning hooves.

All the cookpots had been overturned, all the brush arbors burned, many of the lodges set aflame as well. The odor of burning hide came along the wind to Otter Tongue, still waiting for the white man's charge, and as he stood smelling the destruction of his band, the tears ran down his cheeks.

Soon there were no more moving things in the camp except the white men and their horses and the dogs. In the scattered debris were the awkward forms of those who had fallen. And now the white men were slowing their mounts, more of them going down to search in the last of the lodges that remained.

Chosen sat in her tipi, stunned, still calling weakly for Kwahadi and clinging to the cradle board, bent forward, sheltering Snow Blossom's face with her breasts. She had begun to cry without tears, a low wailing, when two heavily whiskered men burst through the lodge door, revolvers smoking in their hands.

"Nothing here," one of them shouted, and the other threw embers from the fire against the hide walls of the tipi. "Just a squaw!"

They were almost gone again when one of them paused, staring at Chosen, seeing her rigid features, her wide eyes glazed, hypnotized with fear. He came to her quickly and the other shouted.

"Watch yourself, she may have a damned knife under that cradle board!"

The man holstered one of his pistols and took her hair in his hand, yanking her head back, staring into her eyes as the other one came over, ready to shoot.

"Jesus Christ!" the first one said. "This here's a white woman. Look at them eyes!"

"By God, it is!" the second one said. "Hey there, squaw. You a white captive?"

Chosen could feel her heart pounding against her ribs, and the baby began to cry. She could smell the strange odor of them now, this close, of sweat and gunpowder and leather.

"What's your name?" the first one shouted. "Name. How you called?"

Without being willed, the words came, choked but clear enough for them to hear.

"Morfydd Annon," she said. "Morfydd Annon Parry!"

The man released her hair and both white men stood back, astonishment on their faces.

"Parry? Jesus Christ, that was a long time ago," the first one said. "This here's one a' them little girls they took. Jesus Christ!"

"Get her outta here," the second said. "Before this place burns down around our ears!"

ALL OF IT had taken only a little less than thirty minutes. And then they drew away, carrying with them the three white captive children and Morfydd Annon Parry, still clutching the cradle board tightly to her breast. They moved out of the camp as fast as they had moved in, pausing only on the first rise to look back. Then on toward the southwest, with three of them falling behind to act as rear guard.

Far to the east, the Tonkawas circled the pony herd until they came across the route of the retreating white men and joined them. After that, there was the sound of more shots as the horses in the pony herd were killed. But only a few shots, because it was a waste of ammunition. Most of the ponies were left throat-cut and kicking on the prairie.

At the smoldering camp they left behind, Otter Tongue moved cautiously back to the smoking scatter of the lodges still standing. He found the body of Sanchess and he found the scalp lance, somehow intact and left overlooked in the wolf-head tipi that had only partially burned. He took it and started toward the river, running, and there along the bank found his wife, Cactus Wren. A stray bullet had struck her in the neck and he knew she was dead even before he bent and touched her gently. But he didn't cry because he was beyond crying now.

Without knowing what had happened to his children, he crossed the stream and started toward the far high country in the west, walking steadily now with his short waddling strides, the blood lance of Sanchess at his side, the scalps blowing out in the wind.

Farther toward the west, beyond the fringe of mesquite that grew near the river, Shade and Kwahadi looked back. They could see the smoke from the burning camp.

"Palo Duro," Shade said, a savage note in her voice, an acceptance. She slipped off her smock and handed it to him, standing naked except for her moccasins. "Put this on. We've got a long walk, in cold weather or sun, but a long walk."

He stared at her and she slapped him hard across the face.

"Stop looking at my old womanhood!" she screamed. "Time enough for looking at women later, after you've come to your medicine among my people on Llano Estacado!"

Holding the garment, he faced away from her, looking again at the rising smoke that was whipped away by the wind to join the low clouds. Her anger left her then, and she put an arm around his shoulders and turned him toward the west.

"We'll make time for mourning later," she said gently, seeing the wetness in his eyes. "But now we have to run. So come with me. There'll be no meat for five days. But I know where the water is."

"Where are the others?" he asked.

"Scattered," she said simply.

They saw no one from the camp, but Shade knew some of them had escaped, like themselves, and were lying now in the grass, hiding, waiting to be sure the white man was gone before returning to the camp to salvage what they could.

Where were they all now? Grasshopper and her sons? Wapiti Song? Running Wolf? Woman Who Runs, mother of her husband? Maybe when she heard the first sounds of iron-shod horses coming into camp, she had rolled herself into her robes and died. Shade didn't know.

But she had no intention of going back. She had seen her Sanchess fall, and there was nothing else she wanted in that camp, so she pushed the boy along quickly even as he slipped the smock over his head. They moved now into the lower elevations so they could not be seen from a distance.

"Palo Duro," she kept saying, as though speaking of

what lay ahead would make her forget what was behind. "Palo Duro!"

"Without ponies?" Kwahadi asked, bewildered.

"Yes. Without ponies. Your forefathers had no ponies either. Now we have none. So we walk. Five days. Maybe six."

Stumbling through the dried summer grass, Kwahadi moved with the wind against his face and he could not believe there were no horses. He had never known a world without horses. And behind him, Shade seemed to understand and she spoke to him.

"Don't worry. My people still have plenty of horses. In Palo Duro."

And then a cold rain began to fall.

BESIDE THE Peace, in the band's final campsite, the rain came in a slow curtain. The falling water hissed in the fires, slowly extinguishing them but making an even thicker, more pungent smoke. And now, with the rain, the wind had died and the smoke clung to the ground in a gray cloud. Some of the lodges were still intact but standing empty, their door flaps hanging loosely. But mostly there were only the lodgepole frames, naked and blackened, like the skeletons of strange beasts.

The dogs wandered aimlessly through the wreckage. They sniffed the still forms. They tested with their tongues the vermilion pools on the ground where rain and blood ran together.

21

BANGOR OWEN SQUATTED BY the fire, where the flickering light played across the Ranger badge on his coat. He looked hardly older now than he had when the Comanches scalped him and left him for dead at Madoc's Fort. He looked a little harder, but no older. His beard was still black, close-trimmed, and when he took off his wide-brimmed hat, the hair was long enough at sides and back to comb over the bald scar at the top of his head.

Off to the west he could hear coyotes, and he wondered how many were feasting at the village they'd hit along the Peace. They had come almost eighty miles since then, riding without pause and using extra horses all the way, slowing only for graining and watering the horses, chewing their jerked beef without leaving the saddles, putting distance between themselves and their enemies. Bangor had been fighting Comanches since the year after Madoc's Fort, when he'd joined the Rangers, and Captain Josh Burnett, heading this party, had been at it even longer. So they were accomplished at their task.

Now they were on the West Fork of the Trinity and far enough away from possible retaliation to relax a little and build fires for coffee. Even so, there were night guards on the horses. They had learned that too. No matter how safe you felt, you always put guards on the horses.

There had been rain late in the day after they'd made their strike, but now it had cleared and the black sky was studded with stars. The wind had died and it wasn't entirely uncomfortable, but no one was shedding coats.

Around the fire were a number of them, and a little way

back, barely visible in the flickering light, some of the Tonkawa scouts squatted and smoked. At another fire nearby were the recaptured children and the white woman with her baby. Captain Josh sat cross-legged across the fire from Bangor Owen, frowning with the effort as he made notes in a small leatherbound book, notes he would need for filing his report when they reached Fort Worth.

Everyone was quiet. Usually on these forays there was exhilaration at success, but soon that died when everyone began to think of some of the things they'd seen. The only sounds now came from the horse picket, where a Ranger was crooning a soft song, from the snap of burning mesquite, and from one of the men cleaning his huge Walker Colt revolver and spinning the cylinder.

Soon some of them began to move back out of the firelight to bedrolls, but Bangor Owen remained, staring at the flames. The Tonks disappeared silently into the darkness, and the fire where the captives slept died to embers and then there was only Bangor Owen and Captain Josh caught in the little orange world of light, enclosed all around by the night.

"Well, I reckon I've talked to everybody now and got it down," Captain Josh said, slipping the leatherbound notebook into a coat pocket. "It was a pretty good one."

"We caught those people by surprise," Bangor Owen said.

"Yeah, which is the only way to catch 'em. Best I can figure, we killed seventeen men. Four women. Couple of their kids got caught in the line of fire and got hit by random shots."

"Some not so random."

"Well, hell, Bangor, when one of them sprouts comes boilin' outta the tipi, it's hard to sit there and try to figure out his age. They're like rattlesnakes. The little ones are as dangerous as the big ones."

"I know all the reasoning."

"That old woman with the fat man, the fat man with that horn headdress. Now there was a bad one. She give us our only wound. Lucky it wasn't a serious one, but she had to be dealt with in a hurry."

"No argument from me on that one."

"Yeah, and the pony herd. After we give the Tonks what they wanted, we killed three hundred and seventy-five horses. That's my tally."

"Mine as well."

"A lot of those people got away, but they always do. Anyhow, they ain't much danger to nobody without their horses. An' then the best part was those three white kids we got back."

"And the woman."

"Yeah, her too."

Captain Josh took a cigar from his shirt pocket, and after he had it lit with a mesquite stick from the fire, he squinted at Bangor Owen.

"One chance in a million," he said.

"Yes. Everyone thought she was dead long ago. Like a ghost out of the past she is."

"No family, you say?"

"None left that I know of. The Comanches took care of that at Madoc. God, I used to take her on my knee and tell her stories. She was a pretty little thing then."

"Ain't much on looks now. A real squaw."

"That's the kind of life it is," Bangor Owen said, a little of the Welsh way with words still in him. "Wind and sun and hard work, that's what it does for a woman. Not thirty years old yet."

"Hasn't said a word."

"Only her name, to them that found her. Her name! I wonder how long it's been since she said that name."

"Well, that papoose she's got looks more dead than alive to me. I never seen a Comanch' baby, even a half-blood, looked as pale as that. What is it, anyway? Boy or girl?"

"I don't know. She holds that cradle board like somebody clutching a log in the river. I guess we scared her out of her wits. She doesn't even know me, who held her on his knee."

"It was a long time ago."

"Sixteen years! God Almighty! She called me Uncle Bangor, then."

"What'll we do with her? Give her to some church folks, I reckon."

Bangor Owen was silent for a long time. It was a thing he'd been thinking about since they'd first found her. And now he knew it was time to put it into words.

"Me and my Mari, we'll take her in. Children of our own all grown up and out on their own now. We've got room for her. I owe it to Granfer Parry. I owe him that."

"Well, the story I get is that if your man Parry hadn't cheated those Comanch' in some kinda deal, none of it woulda happened."

"I don't claim he was a saint. But I owe him something. I wouldn't be in Texas, likely, if it hadn't been for him. We'll take in his daughter and no complaint with the bargain."

"It won't be easy," Captain Josh said, rising and flipping the stub of his cigar into the fire. "Some people don't take kindly to them as has been among the wild tribes that long. More red stick than white. But I allow you've got first call on her, bein' almost related like you are."

"I owe it to the old man," Bangor Owen said. "And to that little girl I used to hold on my knee."

IT WAS HARD to understand why this was all so familiar. In her confusion and shock, she still groped for some pattern in it all. As she lay with the cradle board beside her, staring into the starry sky, she was only vaguely aware of what had happened back there on the Peace, having seen little of it. But she knew from the sounds that it had been terrible.

The baby was crying again and would not nurse and she sat up in the blanket they had given her and rocked back and forth, holding the child, crooning softly. Earlier, as soon as they camped here, she had cleaned Snow Blossom, using dried grass for a fresh diaper in the cradle board wrapping.

The smells of this camp were so different from those she had come to know. The big horses didn't smell like the ponies in the band's herd. The cured leather of saddles, the sweat on the whiskered faces, the dried beef they had given her, all of it gave off odors strange and foreign and frightening.

She had eaten none of the jerky. Her stomach wouldn't accept it, just as Snow Blossom seemed to be rejecting her milk, vomiting after each feeding and then refusing to feed at all, only crying weakly, softly, like a coyote cub. They had given them water and even that tasted differently, taken as it was from a canvas canteen.

All these men made so much noise when they moved! They wore heavy boots and spurs that rattled, and a few wore chaps to protect their legs in mesquite, and their movements caused the squeak and flutter and flap of leather, like great bats. And the iron-shod horses stamped noisily along the picket line, making what seemed to her a great racket with their metal shoes.

But part of it was something she had seen before, these shadowy figures moving about the fire. Maybe in a dream only. And the face of that one man. She knew him from some distant past, long obscured with the passing of the seasons. She had thought the memory long wiped out. Until they had taken her from the tipi and she had seen his face and the tears welling in his eyes.

She knew she had called him Uncle Bangor once. But she gave him no indication that she knew. He was kind to her, had brought her the blanket and the water and the beef. He had tried to talk with her while all the others stayed clear of her, staring at her with some manner of scorn on their faces.

At first she had thought him to be her father. But then she remembered the white scalp hair on the lance of Sanchess and knew it wasn't true. Now her mind was still too stunned, too muddled for her to take it any further in her thinking.

The camp had quieted and she knew most of them were sleeping. The baby finally stopped crying and she lay on the ground and pulled the blanket over herself and the cradle board. But she didn't sleep and after a little while she saw the dark form approaching and she stiffened under the blanket.

Bangor Owen squatted beside her and she could hear the faint jingle of his spurs and the creak of his leather chaps. He bent close, trying to see her partly hidden face.

"Morfanna?" he said softly. He touched her shoulder

gently but she said nothing, lying rigid under his hand. "Morfanna? Don't you remember me?"

"I remember you!" But she said it in Comanche, and knew at once that he didn't understand.

"My son Kwahadi?" she asked, this time in slow English, and saw the smile on his face in the dark growth of beard.

"Just fine he'll be," Bangor Owen said. He moved his hand to touch her face, but she drew away quickly. "We'll be home by tomorrow night. To your Auntie Mari. Everything will be all right. You'll see."

He was gone then, into the night, his chaps whispering away to final silence as he went.

Suddenly she knew why all of this was like a dream revisited. That dark form bending over her in the night along the Colorado, and she still a child. And the face above hers, not whiskered and smelling of gun oil and whiskey, but the face of Sanchess! And for the first time since they had appeared with their heavy horses and their guns, the tears came, salty and hot, wetting her face.

THE TONKAWAS veered off the next day, herding their captured Comanche ponies before them. Morfydd was glad to see them go, because they frightened her. Even though Bangor Owen rode stirrup-to-stirrup with her all the way, she was afraid they might take her baby. And there was in her mind the sound of words spoken by an old man with a moon face: "They say the Tonkawas eat people. But I've never seen it."

Soon after that, there were ranch buildings. Some were of frame construction but mostly they were soddies. All had extensive pole corrals, and in some of these were the great-horned red cattle. They stopped at one such place to water horses. Half a dozen white men came out, along with two women, and stared at Morfydd and the cradle board hanging from her saddlehorn. They all made a great fuss over the three captive white children, taking them into the house. When the children reappeared, each was wearing an oversized sunbonnet.

Morfydd dismounted but stayed beside the horse, and

Bangor Owen brought her water in a large tin dipper. She could taste the metal of it. He offered her jerked beef once more, but she shook her head. She dipped her fingers into the water and pressed their wetness against Snow Blossom's lips, but the baby made no response.

They moved on downriver until at dusk they came to the outbuildings of Fort Worth. The wooden structures looked cramped and close together and permanent. Already Morfydd was feeling as though air would not come into her lungs, as though she were suffocating. The riders began to move off in their separate directions, waving and calling to one another, until they were all gone except Captain Josh and Bangor Owen, riding on either side of her. She sensed that they believed she might bolt, might turn this big horse back and gallop toward the high plains.

She became aware of the people then, the men driving wagons drawn by large mules, or riding on horseback, each staring at her as they passed, a few speaking to Captain Josh but he saying nothing, only nodding his head sharply and looking grim-lipped. She saw the women dressed in cloth that was thin and flimsy, as thin as gut wrappings for pemmican, but not so tough.

The house was a small frame affair on one of the many roads that led to the center of this thriving new city on the Trinity. As she walked into it, feeling the hard wooden floors through the soles of her moccasins, Morfydd's bewilderment was a mixture of having seen many of these things before, yet now seeming to see them for the first time. It left her in a trancelike numbness. She was unable to resist them as they guided her along, even had she wanted to resist.

She saw the overstuffed chairs in the orange glow of lamplight, smelled the coal-oil stuffiness of the room. They led her through a door and she saw a bed and a side table and a lamp with a large glass globe, translucent, with rose-colored flowers painted on it. Barely hidden beneath the bed was a white enamel chamber pot and she had a flash of recognition, recalling that once she had been required to empty one just like it each morning into a two-hole outdoor privy.

They brought a beef stew, which she couldn't eat, and

water for drinking in a crock pitcher with a cup to match. They brought a large basin of steaming water, and the woman was saying something about bathing the baby. She tried to look closely into the woman's face, to recognize some feature there, but no memory of it came.

Morfydd sat on the edge of the bed, feeling its lack of strength and support. The cradle board was beside her, and then she was aware of the woman taking the baby, still speaking of bathing the child, and Morfydd made no protest as the woman carried Snow Blossom from the room. She sat alone then, staring at the window where the night outside had grown to darkness. She could see the reflection of herself in the pane of glass, her hair unkempt and hanging in tangles to her shoulders, her face hard and brown from the sun.

Then the woman was back, the men beyond the door that was closed now. Morfydd could hear their voices coming from some other room in this strange place, the tones sounding a quiet urgency.

She allowed herself to be undressed, without shame, with no feeling at all. She felt the warm, wet cloth against her body as the woman sponged her, still talking. And the loose-fitting nightgown drawn down over her head, a soft, checkered flannel. It made her feel as though she were still naked, the material lying along her skin like a layer of soft air.

There were no shoes that would fit her, the woman was saying, taking the hide skirt and the moccasins and the basin of water and the towels out of the room, leaving Morfydd alone once more, with the door closed. She lay back on the bed, seeming to sink into the feather tick like a rock sinking in thick water. She closed her eyes, and after a little while the woman was back and Morfydd heard the rush of air as the woman blew out the lamp. Then her soft tread out of the room and the click of the door closing. There were no more voices from nearby, but farther back in the house she could hear them. She felt completely alone.

MARI OWEN had the cradle board on the kitchen table. Her

husband and Captain Josh were sitting in a far corner beyond the cookstove, drinking coffee from white china mugs without handles. They watched her silently as she unlaced the cradle board cover and lifted out the baby.

"I hate to wake this baby," she said, more to herself than to them. "But there's nothing more for it. What a mess. How long's it been since this child was changed?"

She gently unwrapped the deerskin blanket and began to clean the baby, who lay inert on the tabletop.

"A girl," she said. "It's a girl baby."

"I thought it was a boy," Bangor Owen said. "She spoke about a son. Only words I've heard her say."

"Well, this isn't any boy," Mari Owen said. "She must have another one out there somewhere."

Bangor Owen and Captain Josh exchanged a quick glance.

Suddenly, Mari Owen stood upright, looking at the tiny white form, her finger tips pressed to her lips. The child lay with eyes half-open, arms out at either side like limp strips of pale cloth.

Bangor Owen knew his wife well, and even though he couldn't see her face, he knew there was something wrong. He placed his cup on the edge of the stove, rose, and moved to her side.

"What is it, Mari?"

He could hear her heavy breathing, and for a long time she stood silently.

"This baby's dead," she whispered at last.

"Dead? It can't be dead! I heard it crying—"

He stopped because now he remembered that he hadn't heard a sound from the cradle board since the night before, and until then there had been a constant whimpering.

"My God!"

Captain Josh was beside them quickly, feeling the small body, turning it over. His hands looked huge and rough against the pallid skin.

"I don't see no wound!"

"It's not from a wound, Josh," Mari Owen said. "It's from something else. Who knows what?"

"I can't believe it," Bangor said.

But she had seen one of her own infants die without apparent cause, and she knew it was true.

"Sometimes these little ones just go," she said softly, and her eyes were moist.

"My God, what'll we do?" Bangor Owen asked.

"We get that undertaker out here," Captain Josh said. "That's the first thing we do. How long's this baby been dead, Mari?"

"I don't know, but not long. She's not discolored enough to have been gone for long."

"I'll get that undertaker," Captain Josh said. "It won't take long. I'm sure glad there ain't no wound!"

After he was gone, the other two stood looking at the tiny body, somehow unable to cover it yet, somehow unable to look away.

"I reckon we'd better tell Morfanna," Bangor finally said.

"No need to bother her now. I think she likely knows. I expect she's known from the time it happened."

SHE CAME from sleep hearing the voices. Someone new had come into the house. She could hear him speaking loudly, stridently. There was the clumping of heavy boots on the wooden floors and the front door slamming a number of times and outside a team of horses snorting and the rattle of trace chains and then the creak of ungreased wheels.

After a long time the house was quiet again. The seam of lamplight under her door was gone. She lay staring into the dark until she was sure they were all asleep and then she rose slowly, almost painfully, and went to the door and opened it. She moved toward the smell of the kitchen, with great patience, feeling her way, groping in the darkness with her hands out before her. The odors of coffee and white flour were strong to her, and by the time she found the kitchen, her eyes had grown accustomed to the darkness and she could make out the forms of table and chairs. There was still a low red glow of fire from the bottom grate of the cookstove. Her fingers searched until she found what she wanted, hanging from wall pegs behind the kitchen table.

Holding the knife first in one hand, then in the other,

she cut long diagonal slashes along her lower arms. Four cuts on the right arm, four on the left. She placed the knife, sticky now, on the table and slowly retraced her steps through the house to the bedroom door, closed it gently, leaving a thick smear on the knob, and went to the bed. She lay on her back and could feel the soft, warm flow of liquid onto the covers. After a moment she rose and lay on the floor, pulling a blanket down from the bed and rolling into it.

Her wounds ached and she could feel the blood clotting already in the shallow cuts. Tomorrow her arms would cause her great pain as she tried to begin a new life in this wooden house among strangers who were supposed to be her family now. But they were hardly family. So she welcomed the coming hurt because it would be a reminder of how things had been on the day after Iron Shirt died, when she first slashed herself in mourning and thus became in every way woven into the fabric of the wild tribes.

She made a low, almost whispered keening, singing as she had done the day old Iron Shirt went to the place beyond the sun. There were no words, only the sound of mourning, like the slough of a winter wind outside the tipi door flap. After only a few minutes she heard the trace of bare feet across the house to her door, pausing there, uncertainty in each movement. She stopped keening and lay without a sound and then the steps moved away again. She knew it was the man, this Uncle Bangor, because she already recognized his step. But after he was gone, she didn't sing again.

Drifting into a half-sleep, she heard the house creaking like the soft rubbing of bare cottonwood branches in some winter camp, when there was snow on the ground and the limbs of trees were covered with ice, the wind moving them sluggishly. Somewhere a mule brayed in the town, but she heard only the sound of a distant coyote beyond some far ridge, howling with sadness. Some ridge a long way from here, near Palo Duro or along the upper waters of the Brazos or in the foothills of the Sangre de Cristo Mountains.

The raid into Mexico came to her, dreamlike, the vistas long and dry and cruel, heat waves from the earth making the horizons dance like green moss along the banks of a slow-flowing stream. She could hear the sounds of the warriors going out in the darkness, their ponies snorting with anticipation and eagerness, then see them when they returned, the captive Mexican children tied by their feet to the horses' backs, the black-painted faces of Running Wolf and Sanchess and Wolf's Road. She could hear their cries of victory, see them dance at the fire that night after all the stolen horses had been given as gifts.

Iron Shirt's face came into her dream-thinking, pale and round, eyebrows plucked, bright with excitement in the lodge fire as he told the stories of The People's history. How they had once had only dogs to pull the travois and everyone walked and how warfare then was a game because on foot there was no way to break free from an enemy after killing. Then the horse came and was so big that everyone thought him a god. Then they learned that he was not a god at all, like the wolf or the eagle, but a friend to be cherished like a good wife. Then warfare changed because The People's warriors could go deep into an enemy's country and get away quickly. Everything changed after the horse came.

They no longer had to drive the great buffalo off cliffs, she heard Iron Shirt's voice saying. They no longer had to approach the meat of their winters like stalking wolves. Now they could ride among them, faster than the buffalo could run, killing as many as they needed. Yes, she heard Iron Shirt say, everything changed when the horse came.

Trooping across her mind were the Spanish soldiers, none of whom she had ever seen. But now she saw them in sleep, just as Iron Shirt had described them. He had seen only a few himself, in his early boyhood. But the stories of his own grandfather were so vivid that in the telling of them they came to life in the mind's eye, and Iron Shirt told it in the same way, making them come alive even though they had been gone for a long, long time.

There was then the caress of spring's first breezes along the banks of the Washita, and the caress of hands, either those of Running Wolf or of Wolf's Road or of Morning Thunder before he became a pukutsi, or of Sanchess. And the harsh laughter of Shade with the note of cynicism yet joy, and the taste of old Woman Who Runs' bone-marrow soup. And the sweet smell of fresh pony droppings when she went to the herd to groom the little gelding, with Lost It staying close by, watching with his bleak, smoky, slave's eyes.

The gentle winds of Palo Duro moved across her dream's face, cooling the anguish with their odor of cedar and of hump roasts turning brown over low mesquite fires and the sounds of laughter while the children played, chasing the dogs through the long shadows that ran like purple and pink paint across the ridges of pinyon and yucca.

She woke then, not knowing at first what the sound was, but then realizing it was rain, falling cold and hard against the wooden shingles of the house, driven by the wind against the windowpane. But with none of the soothing whisper of security it had made for sixteen years on the buffalo-hide covering of a high plains lodge. And awake, she recalled her dreaming, her dim yet distinct recollection of things gone.

There was a spirit-quality about these images, yet they were as real as flesh and bone. Like looking at the flames of a high celebration fire, knowing they were there, searing bright in the night. But no sooner leaping up than gone, to be replaced by others, each individual, each with a burning existence all its own, never to be repeated again in exactly the same way, but each leaving its imprint etched on the soul forever!

EPILOGUE

WINTER CAME to Palo Duro as it always had, raging on the tableland above, but the wind at the canyon floor hardly strong enough to make loose hair blow out before the face. Only the Antelope Comanches were there, with a few survivors from Peace River who had made it that far on foot and had been taken into the band as lost children might have been.

There were not many because The People had had the horse for so long, they had forgotten how to survive without him.

They were all welcomed and new tipis were put up for them and the families shared their household goods with the newcomers, and returning from winter hunts, the young men shared their kills.

And that year, spring followed closely, the weather turning warm in the Moon of High Wind. Along the banks of Prairie Dog Town Branch, the blooms turned the yellow and gray sandscape red and blue and purple. When the band moved up to the high plain of Llano Estacado, the cottonwoods were already leafing.

There were many hawks in the sky that day, making their high, piercing calls as they hunted. And roadrunners worked the canyon floor, rushing like released arrows through the breaks of mesquite after the mice or sidewinders that had come out for the warm sunlight. There was the smell of cedar and of new life flowing in every green thing.

The band moved up through one of the narrow defiles that sloped sharply toward the high prairie above, the travois ponies pulling hard, the warriors already well out ahead, scouting the flatlands beyond the canyon rim. It was a long snakelike procession, for this was a band that had not yet been decimated by incursions of white men and others, as all the other groups of The People had been.

Shade and Kwahadi were in the van of the march, for

they had few things to move, and all of those things had been given them by Shade's people among the Antelope band: her travois pony, Kwahadi's young stallion, a tipi, the bare necessities of clothing other than what they wore, a small bundle of robe bedding. The sun was only at midday when they came up onto the plain and felt the freshness of the strong wind against their faces.

Kwahadi was leading, like a man, although he was still a boy. And when his pony reached the rim, he turned back along it and rode a little way before he drew rein so that he could look back down into the canyon. In the high sun, the walls of rock glistened with their minerals, and up the gorge where the band's women and children were moving, there were the cedar and pinyon and juniper, like dark green ribbons of felt clinging in long lines to the deep red strata.

Shade drew in her travois pony and dismounted, hobbling the horse with a rein tied to the left foreleg. She walked through the new grass that rippled around her feet like water, going to stand beside her nephew. As she came up, the sunlight struck Kwahadi's high, well-formed cheekbones and she marveled at how much he looked like his father, her brother. Wolf's Road.

She stood at his knee and together they watched the band moving below them. A hawk dipped below the canyon's rim, sailing effortlessly down the course of Prairie Dog Town Branch, wings motionless. They could see the sparkle of sunlight at many places along the canyon floor, where it touched the meandering stream.

"When we came up from the canyon the last time," he said, "she was with us."

Shade knew of whom he spoke. She reached up a hand and laid it gently on his thigh, but she did not look into his face. Only this past winter, in the camps of her own family, she had told him that his mother had been a white woman. "She was not of our blood," Shade had said. "But in every way she was one of us!"

At the time she had been apprehensive about Kwahadi's reaction to such a truth. But he had taken the news without a single change of expression. He had sat, that night in their winter lodge, much as his father had before him, much as Sanchess had, much as old Iron Shirt had, staring into the small mesquite fire.

"She has been taken back by her own people," Shade said now, the words whipped from her mouth by the hard wind.

And Kwahadi replied as he had that night in the winter tipi: "She is Nermernuh. She is of The People."

After a few heartbeats, he added, "Someday I will go and find her and bring her back where she belongs!"

Shade moved away a short distance and squatted in the grass like a man and thought about her dreams. And wondered if she should tell him. But, always a woman of truth and willing to face the things that she knew, she decided to say it.

"I had a dream about her," she said. "In the dream she had gone to the place beyond the sun."

Kwahadi sat on his pony without movement, without expression, staring down into Palo Duro Canyon, his lips firmly set, his eyes shining like chips of gray volcanic rock in the sun. When he spoke, she could hardly hear his words in the wind.

"Then I will bring her back from wherever they have put her. I take that oath. I'll bring her back. And caress each bone!"

She rose then and went to her travois pony, and he turned his horse from the canyon rim and followed closely. She mounted and they rode toward the line of march of The People, the wind in their faces, seeing the flat, far horizon. Flat as the blade of a metal knife. Far as the imagination, and faint and windswept and dancing on its edges in the sun's heat. Riding toward the next camp, toward this new spring. Riding toward the buffalo!